THE FORBIDDEN SPIRE

Matthew E. Yetter

THE INFINITE CONFLICT

BOOK ONE

WONDER WORLD
PRESS

The Forbidden Spire
The Infinite Conflict, Book One

Wonder World Press
First Edition

Softcover ISBN 979-8-9939020-0-5
Hardcover ISBN 979-8-9939020-1-2
eBook ISBN 979-8-9939020-2-9
Audiobook ISBN 979-8-9939020-3-6

Manufactured in Canada.

Book Design | Petya Tsankova
Cover Illustration | Luke Fitzsimons, used under exclusive license
Maps and Chapter Icons | Matthew E. Yetter
Editor | Leonora Stewart
Proofreader | Robert Berg
Publishing Management | TSPA The Self Publishing Agency, Inc.

Acknowledgements

This book would not exist without the quiet persistence of a few extraordinary people.

To my beta readers—thank you for your insights, your honesty, and your willingness to walk through this world with me before anyone else had the chance. Special thanks to my mom, Sam Yetter—always encouraging; Stacy Schwarze LaPrad—the original inspiration for Evan; Kristy Martin Hutchinson—my favorite ding-a-ling. And deep thanks as well to AnnellaJo Perry, Gretchen Morrison, Jody Jeffers, Jordan O'Neill, Natasha Jemejcic, Wyatt Schipman, and Carol Simonsen. You sharpened the edges where they needed it and reminded me where the heart of the story lives.

To Leonora Stewart, your copy edits didn't just polish the prose—they respected its rhythm, deepened its meaning, and honored its soul. Working with you has been one of the great joys of this journey.

To Robert Berg, whose proofreading went beyond catching mistakes and strengthened the clarity and flow of every scene.

To my incredibly talented cover illustrator, Luke Fitzsimons—you captured the essence of my vision and made it more than I imagined.

To Petya Tsankova, whose design sense gave Necsis its shape and presence.

To The Self-Publishing Agency—especially Megan Williams, Ira Vergani, and Kayla Felix—thank you for your guidance, professionalism, and belief in this project from the start. You gave me a path forward, and the confidence to walk it.

To First Presbyterian Church of Dillon, you are a constant source of love and warmth—the family one chooses in life.

To anyone I've forgotten to name, please know your fingerprints are still on these pages. I'm grateful, even if I forgot to say so.

Lastly, to every reader brave enough to enter the world of Necsis: thank you. I hope you find something here worth remembering.

For my father, Jerry,

who never cared much for fantasy— but who encouraged me to explore the world, and all life has to offer. You gave me the freedom to try, and the quiet kind of belief that never needed to be spoken.

A Note About the Map

There is a map included in this book,
but a full-color, high-resolution, zoomable version
is available on my website so you can
follow along with the story.

Necsis.Quest/lore-home

DRAKERATH
The Landrise
Emberhold
IRONSPIRE
Merchant's Rest
SYNDAR
Edron Station
Khorvael
WESTER
ENDARL
REDSTONE
N
THE NINE KINGDOMS

GRYPHON'S ROOST
ERYNDOR
CYPRAEA
LUTHENHOLME
Ravensford
Eastgate
STORMHAVEN
VERDANCE
VELSARIA
FALTHERIS
ZAPHARA
0 30 90 MILES

The past is not gone. It waits in the choices we have yet to make.

Laerith of Athosta, Second Reckoning

Prologue

The Three Sisters stood like sentinels, their conical peaks raking the sky.

Two smoldered, as they had for countless generations, thin trails of smoke unraveling into the cold blue above. Red fissures bled down their flanks—lava, slow and sullen, carving fresh wounds into old scars.

That was expected. It was the third, the Silent Sister, who had kept her peace through all the long centuries.

Until today.

Without warning, the mountain tore herself open.

The sound scoured the wastelands like a scream, a raw cry that shattered the brittle quiet. Ash and fire spewed heavenward, an obsidian plume devouring the sun. Lightning danced in her throat. Boulders—some the size of cottages—hurtled skyward, then rained down across the scorched land like cast dice.

There were few left in this part of Drakerath to bear witness.

The northern wilds beyond the Landrise had long since burned away their welcome, leaving only broken ridges, crumbling stone, and a stubborn few outcasts clinging to the margins. But even the desperate knew better than to dwell too near the Sisters' feet.

Yet far from the blast, balanced precariously on the crumbling lip of the Landrise, a tower shook.

Stone groaned. Books toppled. Ink ran black across the cracked floors. Dust rose in lazy spirals as the tremor passed.

At its heart, an old wizard stood very still.

Sorendir did not move at first. His hand braced him against the desk, the other lifted in a half-finished gesture, as if the eruption had plucked him clean from one thought and left him standing in the bones of another.

The calculations he had been working on—a delicate lace of chalk on the slate beside him—were forgotten.

He turned at last, drawn to the balcony.

Beyond the open doors, the sky was thick with ash. All three peaks burned.

The moment engendered in him not surprise, but recognition, as if some long-dormant note had sounded at last, deep and resonant, stirring marrow and memory alike.

A soft breath escaped him.

"Finally," Sorendir said, and there was no fear in his voice.

He moved with a swiftness that belied his years, crossing the battered tower to a plain desk tucked deep in shadow. A scroll lay there, weighed down by a golden medallion whose surface shimmered faintly in the dimming light.

The medallion was no simple ornament. Its delicate lattice etchings of interwoven arcs and angles caught what little sun remained, reflecting twisted geometry against the scroll's brittle surface.

Sorendir lifted it carefully. Reverently. An eyebrow rose. Did it feel... warmer somehow?

The parchment unfurled beneath his fingers with a softness that defied its age. The script upon it was crisp, untouched by time, as if it had waited, patient and immutable, for this very day.

And the words, once mere prophecy, now rang with the echo of inevitability:

When Sisters three weep tears of flame,
Outlanders four shall stake their claim.
Powers long dormant shall waken anew—
The mind, the craft, the strength all rue.
The fourth shall tread where shadows dwell,
Through fire and strife, the bonds to quell.
What once was riven must be whole,
By heart unbroken and steadfast soul.

Sorendir nodded—a small, decisive motion, the tip of his beard brushing against his chest.

"Gharn!" he called.

But even before the name left his lips, slippered feet could be heard hammering up the spiral stair—quick, panicked, familiar. Sorendir chuckled under his breath, the sound as dry as old parchment.

"Not yet," he murmured, half to himself. "Oh, no. Not just yet."

The door burst inward on a gust of dusty air, and Gharn skidded into the chamber, half-bracing himself on the jamb. His sharp eyes darted from Sorendir's face to the scroll—and froze.

"You didn't," he snapped, the words quick and strident. Fear sharpened his voice, but the loyalty beneath it was older, deeper. "If they think this was you..." Gharn paused, his expression growing taut. "...they'll tear the tower down stone by stone. They'll bury us under it."

He stared past Sorendir, past the crumbling balcony rail, to where the Three Sisters crowned the world with smoke and flame. Understanding dawned.

"By the Three..."

"Not blind yet, I see," Sorendir said mildly, teasing but not unkind.

There was affection there—weathered by years, unshaken by fear.

Gharn scrubbed a trembling hand across the thinning wreath of hair circling his head. His gaze returned to the scroll, to the medallion cradled in Sorendir's palm. His face tightened.

"You're serious."

"It is time," Sorendir said, his eyes returning to the horizon, to the burning peaks.

Gharn scowled. "You've said that before."

Sorendir offered no argument—only truth, wrapped in the quiet certainty of a man who had studied the balance of things longer than most civilizations had stood.

"I have had ample time to study," he said, and in his voice was the finality of the stars themselves.

He rolled the scroll with tender care and set the medallion atop it once more, the two artifacts twining purpose and prophecy.

"Go to the embassy," Sorendir said. "Leave word. If they have not arrived yet..." He smiled—small, secret, inevitable. "...they soon will."

Gharn opened his mouth to object but closed it again. Muttering darkly, he turned and vanished down the stairs.

The tower settled into silence.

Sorendir remained where he stood, scroll tucked beneath his arm, medallion glinting faintly in the half-light.

Outside, the sky darkened with ash.

The Sisters burned.

The world shifted.

And somewhere, far beyond the reach of any spell or prophecy—

Time began, once again, to turn.

I
Crossover

If I can't even propose properly, why would she believe I'm worth marrying?

The thought spiraled, chasing its own tail as Rick repacked the picnic bag for the third time. Or was it the fourth? Each time the zipper made its way around, a new doubt surfaced, fractal and branching: Had he packed the glasses? The napkins? Would the cheese start to sweat, destabilizing the whole aesthetic?

He sealed it again and stared at the backpack. Not a basket. He'd considered a basket—briefly. But Evan wasn't a basket-and-blanket kind of girl. She'd see right through it. The backpack was more discreet. Practical. It made sense.

Besides, a backpack could hold anything. An unknown variable. It felt... appropriate.

He stood, fidgeted, then froze mid-movement, only realizing afterward that his right hand had begun sketching equations in the air, a derivative this time, solving for an unknown.

Except the unknown here wasn't a number. It was a person. And she was anything but abstract.

Rick's gaze lifted, snagged by the full-length mirror across the room. His reflection stared back at him—lean, slightly lanky, caught in the soft tilt of the glass. Jeans, navy shirt. Neat. Always neat. Presentation mattered; structure mattered. Even now, he caught himself judging the angle of his collar, the symmetry of his sleeves.

The mirror showed the rest too. Tousled hair, where fingers had plowed distracted paths. Dark circles he hadn't noticed before, muting the blue irises.

And speaking of the eyes—*Why do I look like I'm bracing for impact?*

He flattened his hair with both palms—one measured swipe, then another. It didn't help. He still looked... off-center, like a diagram smudged just enough to ruin the proof.

Chad would have made it look easy. Chad always made everything look easy. Rick's younger brother coasted through life as if friction didn't apply to him. Girls liked him. Coaches loved him. Professors forgave missed deadlines when he grinned just the right way.

Rick adjusted his cuffs again. Two folds. Even. Precise. A small, stubborn assertion of order.

The velvet ring box on the dresser drew his attention—and something clenched hard in his chest. Two months' savings, transformed into gold filigree petals cupping a single diamond. Perfect, just like he'd known it would be when he had first seen it under the fluorescent lights at the Flagstaff Mall. His hand hovered for a second too long before he picked it up.

"I can't believe I almost forgot this."

"I can," came Chad's voice from the doorway.

Rick turned, and there he was: leaning against the frame, arms crossed, like the universe itself was weightless in his orbit. Twenty-one. Broad-shouldered. Annoyingly perfect physique. Hazel-eyed. A scatter of freckles across sun-darkened skin beneath unruly blond hair. The kind of grin that said *Trust me*—and usually, foolishly, people did.

"You know what today is," Rick said, trying to sound cool and collected.

"Exactly why I'm surprised you didn't notice your sleeves were uneven."

Instinctively Rick's hands jerked up, inspecting the cuffs. They were perfect. *Of course they are.*

Chad's grin widened. "You make it too easy."

Rick exhaled sharply through his nose. "Are you done?"

"Not even close. But I can pace myself." Chad unfolded himself and wandered over, nodding at the bag. "Want me to take this out to the car?"

Rick hesitated. He didn't trust anyone with cargo this delicate—but it was Chad, and trust, Rick reminded himself, was part of the equation too. He handed it over. "*Carefully.*"

"I'll cradle it like a prototype." Chad's tattoo caught the light as he took the strap—circuit lines or schematic diagrams inked onto the bicep that strained his short sleeve, as intricate and inexplicable as the guy himself.

Rick watched him vanish down the hall. His footsteps faded, and with them, the static tension that had filled the room.

The silence left behind was, unexpectedly, centering.

Rick turned back to the mirror.

The man staring back was still braced, still tight—but there was something steadier in the set of his shoulders now too.

Resolve, maybe.

He pocketed the ring box and grabbed his keys from the nightstand tray. His thumb brushed over the key chain—the pi symbol Evan had given him—and a warm pulse answered in his palm. *She believes in you.*

"Okay," he whispered. "You've got this."

He stepped out into the hallway, shutting the door behind him with a soft, deliberate click.

Across the hall, Chad's room was a battlefield of laundry and tangled bedding. But the workbench against the far wall was meticulous—a single half-assembled device waiting atop it like a riddle in mechanical form.

Gravity, kinetics, inertia. It had been electrogravitics last month. Maybe flux dampening now.

Or just another joke. Rick couldn't quite tell.

He tore his eyes away and followed the steady *tick-tick-tick* of the mantel clock down the hall, into the morning that was already starting to skew strangely.

Toward his date with destiny.

Chad bounded down the stairs two at a time, backpack slung loosely over one shoulder, heading for the living room.

A small grin played at the corners of his mouth.

Pushing Rick's buttons never got old—especially when they were so well labeled. Just now had been particularly satisfying: Rick wound up tighter than ever, all stiff edges and anxious eyes, a dog chasing its tail. Chad would have to thank Evan for that later.

He skirted the couch and spotted his father hunched over the mantel clock, glasses perched at the tip of his nose like a warning sign. Albert's finger hovered, accusingly, near the minute hand. "Have you been messing with this again?"

"Nope," Chad said casually, already halfway to the front door. "Learned my lesson." *Twelve years ago.*

The antique clock had been a wedding gift to his grandparents. Sentimental, irreplaceable, and strictly off-limits. Chad had discovered its sacredness early, courtesy of one too many curious screwdrivers and the sharp sting of consequences that followed. He wasn't nine anymore. Give him ten minutes now with his full tool kit, and it would run perfectly —better, even. Not that anyone would notice. Or trust him.

Out front, he stashed the pack in the trunk, alongside the rest of Rick's meticulously organized gear, then headed back inside. Albert was still fussing over the clock, as if the mechanism had offended him personally.

"What's wrong with it?" Chad asked offhandedly, stopping nearby.

Blue-gray eyes—just like Rick's—flicked to Chad with mild accusation. "It's running slow."

Of course. Imperfection topped the list of things their father couldn't tolerate. Chad was suddenly aware of the comforting weight of the Swiss Army knife in his cargo pants pocket. He could fix it—he could fix almost anything. But that wasn't the point.

Rick came downstairs, perfectly composed, exactly as he wanted the world to see him. Chad knew better. That right hand in the jeans pocket would be stroking the pi key chain like a rosary bead. Rick was always one breath away from imploding. But never in front of the parental units. Never where it counted.

Their mother, Alice, emerged from the kitchen, towel in hand, an aroma of ginger trailing in her wake. She adjusted the little wooden cross by the staircase, then smiled warmly at Rick. "All set for your big day?" she asked, kissing him lightly on the cheek.

Rick nodded stiffly.

"She'd be a fool to say no," she said, giving his shoulder a small squeeze.

"And that girl is no fool," Albert added solemnly, nodding as if bestowing a blessing.

Chad bit back the words crowding his tongue. Evan's intelligence was unquestioned—simply because she worked in a bookstore. Never mind that it was filled with tarot decks and incense rather than literary classics. Rick didn't care, and their parents didn't know. For once, Chad kept quiet.

"I've planned it as well as I can," Rick admitted, adjusting his cuffs again. "I just hope I don't mess it up."

"You won't," Alice said firmly, disappearing into the kitchen and returning with a carefully wrapped plate of cookies. She handed it to Rick with a reverence usually reserved for sending knights off to the Crusades. "The Lord's blessed you with that gift."

Chad almost laughed, bitterly. If it were him, he'd have been lucky to get a sandwich and a quick pat on the shoulder.

Alice brushed past him, touching his arm lightly. "And you, Chad—try to stay out of trouble. Follow Rick's lead, for once."

"Sure thing, Mom." Chad's voice was easy, humor covering the ache beneath. "Rick's got perfect plans. I've got comic relief covered."

His parents chuckled, oblivious.

Inside, the dismissal landed heavily. They never saw him. Not really. Rick was the mathematician, the prodigy—he had taken after their father, then outpaced him. Chad was background noise, the guy who fixed things, bulldozed across fields of opponents, or threw balls through hoops. They attended games dutifully, cheering without really understanding what they cheered for. Support without connection.

Some things were just easier to laugh off.

Scooping up his CamelBak before following his brother outside, Chad turned his face into the breeze, the sharp scent of ponderosa pine pulling him out of himself. Above, the San Francisco Peaks loomed like guardians, Agassiz's summit brushing the sky like a snow-dusted pyramid. It helped. Reminded him he was built for days like this.

A shadow flickered briefly across the mountainside and made him look for rain clouds. The sky remained unblemished. Chad's pulse skipped, unease crawling up his spine, but he shook it off. *Probably just my mood,* he thought. *Always being stuck in Rick's shadow.*

At the car, Chad set his backpack in the rear seat, then hesitated, glancing back at Rick. His brother stood tall, composed, ready to conquer the day. Chad envied him that clarity, briefly considered speaking up—sharing any of the thousand small things he'd kept bottled inside. But the moment slid away, disappearing, as always, into the silence between them.

He climbed into the passenger seat and leaned his forehead against the cool window, letting his breath fog the glass. Rick had his perfect plans. Chad had the background.

What made him think today would be any different?

No, he thought, watching his reflection fade against the passing scenery. *This is Rick's big day. Anything else can wait.*

Evan stood by the smudged window of her tiny apartment, eyes tracing the parking lot below, searching for the sleek black sheen of Rick's Mazda. She couldn't explain the unease prickling beneath her skin. It had been there since she'd woken up that morning—quiet, insistent, lingering just beyond her conscious grasp. Maybe it was the dream she'd had, vivid and unsettling. Maybe it was something else, something less tangible. She rarely let dreams linger, especially ones she couldn't unravel. Probably just anticipation, she decided. She knew what Rick was planning.

I'll say yes, she thought. *But he'll have to earn it.*

Her faint reflection in the window grinned impishly back—green eyes bright, watchful, auburn hair pulled loosely into place, stubborn strands curling gently against her cheekbones. She smiled softly. She was easy to read, even to herself.

They made such a strange pairing. Rick was all equations and precision, carefully composed, everything planned in advance. She drifted through life on feelings and instinct. He pressed his shirts and wore neatly ironed jeans. She draped herself in shawls and couldn't care less about makeup. Yet she didn't love him despite their differences; it was *because* of them.

Rick anchored her, quietly but firmly, giving her stability in a world that spun a little too freely beneath her feet.

She glanced back at her shoebox of a space—an efficiency apartment barely big enough to breathe in, let alone live. The kitchenette gleamed, mostly from neglect. Scarves cascaded over the chair. It wasn't much. She hadn't had the opportunity to accumulate more in the few years she could remember. But it was hers. And it mattered.

A flash of polished black caught her eye. She wrapped herself in a shawl and stepped into the crisp morning. Rick's car, immaculate even now, slipped neatly between the lot's lines. Both brothers got out. Chad lingered, leaning against its open door, while Rick moved toward her with earnest purpose.

He always did.

"Need me to carry anything?" Rick asked.

She raised a playful eyebrow. "How could I? Kind of hard to pack when you've kept your plans a secret."

He flushed slightly, sheepish, but then he really saw her. His gaze softened, shedding the calculations that usually shadowed his eyes, leaving only warmth. "You look perfect," he said.

Her heart skipped, just slightly.

She caught the small motion—Rick's thumb caressing the pi symbol in his hand. The irrational number had been a joke when she gave the key chain to him, but he'd cherished it quietly ever since, endearing in his earnestness.

Then Evan turned her gaze toward Chad, who still leaned casually against the passenger door, hair tousled as though by choice rather than neglect. His grin carried easy sarcasm. "I didn't realize we'd need supervision today," she said lightly.

Chad shrugged expansively. "You'd both be lost without me. Rick's hopeless with maps. And GPS—"

"Back seat," Rick said swiftly, silencing Chad with a look that was equal parts brotherly irritation and genuine affection. "My lady gets the front."

Evan laughed softly, letting Rick guide her gently by the hand, a chivalrous and slightly silly gesture that warmed her more than she'd admit.

Birdsong rose around them as if on cue.

Fifteen minutes later, Highway 89 stretched ahead, guiding them northward. The ponderosas thinned, replaced gradually by dark volcanic stone. Sunset Crater loomed—red and black, unchanged by centuries. It stirred something deep in Evan's chest, unsettling yet familiar.

Rick glanced at her, seemingly sensing her shift in mood. "Everything okay?"

"Just a dream," she admitted reluctantly. "A volcano—not this one, but still."

His concern sharpened, eyes narrowing. "Something bad?"

"Not you," she assured him quickly. "Just... vivid. More vivid than usual." She kept back the lingering nausea, the sense of reality slipping just slightly out of sync since waking. Flashes like this weren't uncommon—handy in tarot readings, useless and unnerving in her personal life.

From the back, Chad offered his own insight. "Sunset Crater's small potatoes. Did you know the San Francisco Peaks are actually the remnants of one huge volcano? When it erupted, it flung debris into space."

Evan's lips quirked faintly. *Of course Chad knew that.*

"I did," she answered. "The Hopi say the Peaks are home to the kachinas."

Even this far away, the Peaks dominated the horizon, starkly majestic, white-capped and timeless.

"It feels spiritual somehow, doesn't it?" she murmured.

Chad's shrug was audible. "I guess. I just think it's cool you can ski up there in the morning and water-ski down on Lake Mary in the afternoon."

Classic Chad.

Comfortable silence settled among them as Rick drove, Chad scrolled his phone, and Evan absorbed the changing scenery. Juniper scented the air, dust and dry earth replacing pine. She noticed the sign for Sunset Crater go by, but Rick pulled left, toward the mountains.

She blinked in surprise. "We're going to Lockett Meadow?"

He smiled, gentle triumph in his eyes. "You mentioned once that you wanted to see the Inner Basin."

Months ago. She'd forgotten she'd even said that. But Rick hadn't. Her heart softened.

"Maybe you'll spot one of your kachinas," Chad teased from behind. "As long as the pond's not bubbling."

She ignored him, smiling faintly.

The dirt road twisted upward, threading through pines and aspens. Rick slipped into tour-guide mode, carefully describing routes, viewpoints, and geology. His over-explanation, meticulous and earnest, had once irritated her—and occasionally still did. But it was also reassuring. He wanted everything perfect. For her.

She watched him closely, sunlight softening his profile, and felt her unease ebbing gently.

"I trust you," she said quietly, sincerely.

Rick's fingers brushed the key chain again where it danced next to the steering column, a subtle reassurance. Evan leaned back, breathing easier, gaze drifting contentedly out the window.

The road wound upward through the ponderosa forest, a rugged ribbon of dirt threading around tree trunks and steep slopes, sun dappling the windshield as though through parted fingers. Rick kept both hands steady on the wheel, even as his index finger traced idle circles over the worn leather grip. Behind them, civilization had dropped away—miles of highway replaced by the soft crunch of gravel, jarring potholes, and a sense of solitude.

Then the view unfolded before them.

Lockett Meadow spread wide within the protective curve of the Inner Basin. A green carpet brushed lightly with wildflowers, half a mile across—white, purple, yellow blooms bobbing gently, uncertain as to whether winter had fully surrendered. A glassy pond mirrored the sky, impossibly still, holding its breath.

Rick navigated into the small, primitive campground without hesitation. He'd scouted it weeks before, when the road had finally become passable by anything less capable than a four-wheel drive. He knew the perfect spot: optimal angles, the best proximity to open sky and meadow views, just enough trees to provide shade. There were only two other cars parked there—absolutely ideal.

Evan leaned forward in her seat, her green eyes widening with delight, tiny flecks of gold appearing briefly, as they always did when her emotions ran deepest.

So far, so good. Rick exhaled slowly, willing the butterflies in his stomach to settle.

He found a space beneath an aspen just starting to unfurl its first delicate leaves. Stepping out, he inhaled deeply. The air felt impossibly clean and still, as if almost holding itself back for fear of intruding. No wind stirred, no insects buzzed. Just the gentle metallic clicks of the car cooling.

Don't overthink it, he told himself. *Let her be the poet.*

Evan got out next, her shawl catching gently around her shoulders. She walked a few paces toward the meadow before glancing back, eyebrows arched curiously above sparkling eyes. "So... what's your plan?"

Rick opened the car's hatch, revealing the carefully packed picnic backpack. He paused just long enough to slip the velvet ring box discreetly from his pocket into a side pouch, then reconsidered the campground tables. "Let's head toward the pond," he suggested, hoping it came across as casual. "Too beautiful out for shade."

Her smile was knowing, amused, effortlessly reading him as she always did. Rick hoisted the pack onto one shoulder, offering his hand. Evan's fingers slid comfortably between his, her free hand briefly touching the golden circle of the Möbius strip pendant at her neck—a quiet, habitual reassurance. He'd never learned its origin, and she couldn't recall it either. But she wore it always, a mystery she carried openly.

In the back seat, Chad stretched, pulling out his own battered daypack. "That's my signal," he announced cheerfully. "Trail's calling. Might reach snow level; might not." He flashed a teasing grin. "You two behave—don't do anything I wouldn't appreciate."

Rick shot him a glance that should have wilted him where he stood.

Chad waved once, striding briskly toward the Inner Basin Trailhead, boots crunching over gravel until the sound faded.

Rick and Evan walked slowly across the meadow. Midway, Evan's hand shifted gently from his, sliding comfortably around his waist, drawing them close together. He felt a quiet joy in that simple proximity.

They chose a spot carpeted with wild crocuses and shooting-star blossoms. Rick spread the blanket deliberately, unpacking the backpack with practiced precision: silverware, plates, linen napkins—all selected with care. Evan laughed softly as she examined each thoughtfully selected item, clearly pleased.

Worth every penny, he thought, relaxing slightly.

They ate in companionable silence, savoring smoked gouda, rosemary crackers, fresh strawberries, and chocolate truffles. Rick's pulse quickened each time his fingers brushed the hidden side pocket, unable to find a moment to retrieve the box unnoticed. He forced himself to remain patient.

"You enjoying yourself?" he asked finally, aiming for casual but feeling it miss slightly.

Evan's smile was indulgent, eyes shimmering gently. "Very much."

He passed her another cracker, hesitating before speaking. "You've never been here before, right?"

Immediately he winced inwardly, recalling their earlier conversation. Worse, she wouldn't remember beyond three years ago. But Evan only tilted her head gently, letting the slipup pass without comment.

"I expected more birds," she said instead, her voice contemplative as she glanced around. "It's too quiet."

"The quiet's nice," he responded automatically, though now he heard it too—the unnatural stillness. He cleared his throat, his hand hovering near the hidden pocket, pulse quickening. *Ease into it. No rush.*

Evan watched him, her head tilted slightly in that familiar, expectant way—attentive but patient, gently amused.

"So, uh..." Rick began, then hesitated when her expression changed abruptly.

Evan stiffened slightly, brow furrowing as she scanned the trees, the pond, the meadow.

"What is it?" he asked, instantly alert, worry prickling.

She shook her head faintly. "Something feels... wrong," she murmured. "Like we're... I don't know... inside a painting. A dream I can't quite wake up from."

Rick's heart sank slightly, though outwardly he straightened, attempting reassurance. "It's probably nothing—just nerves," he offered weakly, though his own senses sharpened.

He noticed now what Evan had intuitively grasped. It wasn't just quiet —it was *absolute* stillness. The grass, trees, flowers: everything had frozen in place.

His hand moved toward her instinctively, then paused in midair. "Probably nothing," he repeated, softer this time, eyes scanning the edges of the meadow, counting shadows.

Wishing irrationally that Chad were still nearby.

Chad moved easily through the thinning trees, boots crunching over brittle pine needles and patches of stubborn snow. The trail had disappeared long ago—if it had ever been a trail to begin with—but he didn't mind. Up here, with nothing but sky, stone, and scrub, he felt like he could finally breathe. No coaches barking at him. No professors expecting him to be some slightly dumber version of Rick. No parents waiting quietly for his next wrong word. Just the wind, the rocks, and the open space where expectations couldn't reach.

He tilted his head back and breathed deeply. The wind at this elevation was thin, edged with the last traces of winter. It slid past his face like a secret too small for words.

He grinned. This was his kind of place.

The slope steepened as he climbed, trees thinning to stubborn clusters. He picked his way carefully over a tumble of basalt boulders, stepping from stone to stone, avoiding the dark pockets where ice still lingered, clinging to the mountain's shade like a grudge. Above him, Humphreys and Agassiz loomed, high points along the crater's rim, blanketed in white. Humphreys stood solid and solemn; Agassiz cut upward like a pyramid draped with a white shroud. The sky above them was clear, endless—a perfect day.

He found a perch just below the last line of trees and let his pack drop beside him. The Inner Basin stretched out like an amphitheater beneath him—wide, green, cupped by the silent arms of the Peaks.

After settling onto one of the larger rocks, he pulled out his phone and framed a few shots of the ridgeline—the bright wash of sunlight over the trees, the harsh, beautiful lines of the crater rim. He checked for service. *No bars. Figures.* The towers were all on the far side.

Still, he stayed a while longer, letting the silence stretch out. Letting it settle inside him as the sunlight seeped into his bones.

Until something shifted.

It wasn't a sound. It wasn't a movement. Just... *something.* A ripple at the edge of his awareness. His skin prickled before his brain caught up. He turned.

And froze.

Down beyond where they'd entered the basin, the air shimmered. Not heat. Not fog. Something else. Like static. Like the world's signal had glitched.

Beyond it, Sunset Crater flickered. One moment solid, the next winking like faulty TV reception, the mountain itself blurring in and out, wavering.

"That's not how mountains work," Chad muttered.

He blinked hard. The effect disappeared. Sunset Crater stood firm and immovable, like it always had.

Chad let out a breath, realizing his hand had tightened painfully around the edges of his phone. *Idiot. You should've gotten a picture.*

But he didn't lift the phone again—not yet.

Slowly he rose to his feet, scanning the basin, the ridgelines, the sky. The air felt wrong, heavy... like a thunderstorm was waiting to happen.

He looked at his watch. Two more hours before Rick would expect him back. Plenty of time—except something deep inside him said otherwise.

He turned, retrieving his CamelBak, and started picking his way down the rocks. The descent was harder, steeper. He had to watch his footing, forcing himself to slow even as everything inside him screamed to move faster.

"Let them have their moment," he muttered. "Don't screw it up."

But his legs didn't slow.

When he was almost to the shelter of the trees, something caught his eye—to the east, beyond a shallow rise.

Another shimmer.

But this time it wasn't a ripple, and it wasn't fading.

The landscape beyond was… wrong. Too vivid, like looking at something drawn in ink instead of light. Two versions of reality bleeding together, sharp and too vibrant.

His breath caught. *I wasn't imagining it.*

As his pulse pounded in his ears, he realized that this time, whatever was happening wasn't going away.

"What if it's something dangerous?" he said aloud, and hearing the words made the possibility all too real.

That tore it.

He launched down the last rocks, boots pounding against stone and frozen soil, and leaped recklessly into the trees. Branches clawed at his jacket. The cold wind flattened against his face. He didn't care.

The picnic. Rick. Evan. He ran faster.

He hurdled over fallen branches. Dodged patches of stubborn ice. The ground cover blurred beneath him. He was running on pure reflex.

He glanced once at his watch. Over an hour had passed since he'd left them, walking at a casual pace. It would take fifteen minutes to get back, maybe ten if he pushed.

"For once," he muttered between breaths, "just get this right."

No jokes. No act.

Just run.

The afternoon, already unnervingly still since they had arrived, seemed to seize up around them. Not metaphorically. Not figuratively. Evan blinked, and in the brittle silence that followed, she could hear her own breath—too loud, too uneven. Pressure wrapped around her skin, neither hot nor cold. Just... *weight.* Like the air itself was thickening, pressing inward, squeezing the breath from her lungs.

Her hand flew instinctively to the pendant at her neck, gripping the twisted gold harder than she meant to. When she forced herself to let go, the shape of it was pressed deep into her palm.

No wind. No birdsong. Just the rising thrum of something she couldn't name—something that wasn't sound.

Vertigo hit her hard. She braced one hand against her temple, squeezing her eyes shut for half a heartbeat.

When she opened them again, Rick was staring at her across the blanket—confused.

"I'm sorry," she said, faster than she meant to. Yet her voice sounded steadier than she felt. "I know this was meant to be special. It *is* special. But we need to leave. Now."

Rick's face fractured, warring emotions flickering across it too quickly to catch. His hand clenched the blanket tightly enough that his knuckles paled. His jaw worked, biting back words. He didn't move.

Of course he didn't. He was still trying to fit her fear into a model that made sense. Still trying to solve her panic like it was a math problem. But this wasn't solvable. It wasn't rational.

She saw the shift in his gaze. The moment he realized this wasn't just her being nervous.

But he was still lost.

She reached across the blanket and caught his hand. "Trust me," she said, willing him to hear everything she couldn't explain.

It worked. Rick swallowed hard, set his jaw, and began cramming everything back into the pack. Not his usual meticulous movements. He was harried, shaky. Evan stuffed in whatever she could grab, fingers clumsy with adrenaline.

Something crawled across her skin. She batted at it, expecting ants, but there were none. The tingling stayed.

Rick's voice broke through. "What's happening? Do you know?"

"No!" she cried. "I just know we don't have time."

Images from her dream clawed their way back—earth tearing open, fire bleeding into sky. Her stomach roiled.

As they hurried for the car, she stumbled. Rick's arm shot out, steadying her.

Almost there.

"What about Chad?" he asked.

Panic spiked, but before she could answer, his brother burst from the tree line, sprinting flat out toward them. Rick saw him too, and they broke into a run.

They all reached the Mazda at nearly the same instant. Chad collapsed against the car, gasping for air, hands braced against his knees. His shirt was soaked with sweat, his face pale.

"Did you—" He choked. "See it too?"

Rick blinked. "See what?" Then he wrinkled his nose. "Do you smell that?"

Evan caught it then—a metallic tang in the air. Ozone. And something worse underneath. "Get in the car!" she barked.

Fingers shaking, she fumbled at the handle. Rick was already in the driver's seat, the engine rumbling. Chad half-fell into the back.

No one asked about gear. No one cared about doors.

Rick punched the gas, slamming the car into reverse. Chad yelped—his door still half-open—as Rick braked, twisted the wheel, and shot forward.

Evan braced herself against the dash as they careened down the rutted road. Every jolt hammered up her spine. Her stomach lurched with each bounce.

Sweat slicked her palms but not from fear. This wasn't just wrong—this was *alien.*

"What happened?" Rick barked over the sound of tires slamming against the dirt.

"What do you mean?" Chad coughed out.

"You said, 'See it *too*?' See what?"

"That!" Chad's hand shot between the seats, pointing.

Evan's heart sank.

Ahead, the road stretched—and something shimmered across it.

A wall. A curtain. A... wrongness.

Light writhed where it shouldn't, like an aurora rising *into* the air.

Reality bent, rippling upward from the ground. The air swam like heat off pavement—but wrong. Not just refracted. *Warped.*

And behind it, glimpses of... otherness. Fractured images, shapes that flickered too quickly to understand.

Like a slot machine's tumblers spinning too fast to land.

The closer they got, the harder it became to look. Evan's head pounded. Her stomach twisted. The familiar logic of the world felt fragile, thin.

Heat slammed into her—not from outside but from within. Crawling under her skin, buzzing along her bones.

Her breath caught.

Every nerve screamed a warning she couldn't ignore.

"It's not just a curtain," she whispered. "It's a door."

"Gun it!" Chad shouted.

Rick floored it, and the front of the Mazda punched into the churning light.

Evan's stomach dropped, hard and sudden—not like falling but like being ripped loose from gravity itself.

The car jerked violently. Metal shrieked. Light swallowed everything.

She tried to scream, but the sound stretched and warped until it wasn't even her voice anymore, nor even human.

The taste of burnt metal flooded her mouth—sharp, wrong, suffocating.

Then a snap.

Like the world had tried to swallow them and choked.

Everything inverted.

And then—

Nothing.

II
Necsis

Rick's head throbbed, a relentless, discordant percussion behind his temples, like a grade-school band—all enthusiasm, no skill. Before he even opened his eyes, he felt it: heat pressing against the side of his face, sharp and merciless. Too hot. Too bright. He blinked against the glare.

A bird sat perched on the battered hood of the car, peering at him through the cracked windshield. For a heartbeat, it registered as a crow—sleek black feathers, a curved beak. But as his vision steadied, the wrongness sharpened. Its wings were too long, the tips tapering to bladelike edges that shimmered faintly, like oil on water. And its eyes—not dark but shifting, deep wells flickering with pulsing embers.

The bird cocked its head, studying him with a gaze that felt too focused. Too knowing.

Rick tensed, bracing instinctively for a caw, but when it opened its beak, the sound that emerged was two voices woven together. Soft, layered, unsettling. *Two tones. Simultaneously.* The impossibility played with his still-groggy mind. *How...?*

Before he could blink, the creature bristled—and vanished. No flap of wings. No burst of motion. Just... absence, as if it had slipped between heartbeats.

Rick sucked in a breath, his hand knocking against the steering wheel. The jolt rattled something loose in his mind. *Evan.*

He was alert now, his heart lurching painfully against his ribs.

Twisting toward the passenger seat, he sagged with relief. She was slumped forward, her chestnut hair tumbling like liquid copper over her shoulder, rising and falling with each steady breath. She looked impossibly small against the light from outside.

His hand found hers almost before he could think, his fingers brushing her knuckles. Warm. Alive. A ragged breath escaped him.

Evan jerked awake with a gasp that sharpened into a choked cry, her hands flailing until her gaze locked on his. "Rick?" Her voice was raw, trembling.

"I'm here," he said, his own voice rougher than intended. "You're okay. We're okay."

Not even close to true—but even partial truths mattered in that moment.

She blinked hard, nodding as if trying to will herself to believe it.

A low groan from the back seat dragged Rick's attention away. *Chad.* Relief warred with confusion as Rick turned—and froze.

Beyond the cracked windows, the world was... changed.

Gone were the towering ponderosa pines, the familiar rise of the San Francisco Peaks. In their place stretched a shattered landscape of black igneous rock, jagged outcroppings casting long shadows across a plain of ash and dust. The sky above blazed a shade of gold that belonged to no desert he'd ever seen.

"What the—"

Rick fumbled with the seat belt, shoved the door open, and staggered out. A wave of heat assaulted him, a wall of pressure that coated his skin in sweat almost instantly. His boots crunched against gritty ground as he turned in a slow, disbelieving circle.

No forest. No mountains. No sign of Flagstaff.

Evan came around from behind the car to stand beside him, brushing his arm—a quiet tether he hadn't realized he needed until he felt it. Chad stumbled after her, squinting against the glare, sweat plastering his usually chaotic hair to his forehead.

"Where are we?" Chad rasped.

Rick had no answer.

Chad pulled out his phone reflexively and held it aloft. After a moment, he shook his head. "No signal." He angled it this way and that, as if attempting to coax service bars from thin air.

Rick barely heard him. His gaze snagged on the ground—the trail behind the car. Skid marks. A short stretch of them. Beyond that, the earth lay undisturbed.

He moved closer, crouching despite the protest from his aching skull.

There—a line. Faint but unmistakable. Perfectly straight, slicing across the earth like a surgeon's scalpel.

He brushed his fingers across the boundary. The soil on one side was coarse and volcanic, the other finer and paler. Same hue; subtly different texture. No blending. No transition.

Following the line, he found a boulder split cleanly in half—the cut surface smooth as glass. And a plant—strange and yellow-spined—had been severed so precisely it looked sculpted, its missing half simply... gone.

Something had carved through the landscape with impossible precision.

Rick jerked his hand from the line as if stung and backed away, heart hammering. *Danger.*

"Uh, Rick?" Chad's voice behind him, tight with uncertainty.

Rick turned—and his stomach dropped.

The car... Its entire front end was gone.

Not crushed, not twisted, but sliced clean off at the front tires, exposing the mangled engine like an anatomy display. Fluids dripped steadily onto the cracked ground.

Chad, with that trademark gallows humor that surfaced whenever he was rattled, muttered, "You don't usually get to see the inside of an engine like that."

Rick shot him a glare. His mind reeled, scrambling for something—*anything*—to anchor him, to explain, but this went so far outside logic he felt like he was falling.

"What's that?" Evan asked suddenly, pointing beyond the wreckage.

Rick turned.

A thin plume of smoke curled into the sky beyond a low ridge.

Without thinking, he scrambled up the rough slope, Evan and Chad close behind. The ground burned through the soles of his shoes, but he barely noticed.

At the top, the world opened before them—and Rick staggered.

A shattered plain of volcanic wasteland sprawled as far as he could see, the surface cracked and crumpled like a discarded sheet of aluminum foil. And beyond it, looming like sentinels, rose three volcanoes—alive, their flanks streaked with lava rivers, smoke writhing upward into the molten sky.

Rick stared, throat working uselessly.

Not Arizona.

Not anywhere he had ever heard of.

Beside him, Chad pivoted, his jaw slack as he took in the view. His voice, when it came, was a strained whisper. "Um... guys?" His eyes were fixed upward.

Rick didn't want to look. Some part of him—the desperate, rational part—screamed to keep his gaze forward, to hold onto something familiar.

He turned anyway, and the last shreds of reason shattered.

Two moons hung low in the sky. One was pale but far too large. The other, small and unnaturally bright. Neither bore the patterns he knew by heart.

Chad's soft voice broke the silence, stretched thin with disbelief. "Toto, I don't think we're in Kansas anymore."

Rick closed his eyes for half a second, feeling Evan's hand slip into his without a word. Her fingers tightened, grounding him.

He squeezed back—once, fiercely—then opened his eyes and faced the impossible.

Evan felt like a fifth wheel.

Rick and Chad busied themselves at the car—wrecked though it was—sorting the salvage with grim focus. The ground crackled underfoot, volcanic grit shifting like brittle snow with every step. So far they'd gathered the clever picnic backpack with its half-finished meal, Chad's hardly-touched CamelBak, and the emergency kit from the hatchback. Rick inspected each item with clinical precision, stacking supplies into neat piles on the back seat.

Chad found the emergency radio. His face lit up—the first sign of hope Evan had seen since they had all woken up here—but it flickered and died as quickly as it had come. He scanned the bands twice. Static, and nothing more. With a sharp, frustrated twist, he clicked it off.

"Was worth a shot," he muttered, his shrug stiff around the edges.

Rick didn't even glance up. He was already sorting the protein bars by their expiration dates, his movements efficient to the point of being mechanical.

Evan lingered nearby, trying to help. Every offer ended the same way —a polite deflection, a kiss on the cheek, a touch to her arm. Not unkind. Just methodical. Rick needed to think, to solve, to control. Chad needed to move, to fix. Neither had room right now for anything less tangible. And the cracks were starting to show.

"The number-one rule when you're lost," Rick said tightly, folding a blanket into a square with almost military precision, "is to stay put and conserve resources."

Chad snorted. "Yeah, if anyone's actually looking for you. Which they're not. Unless you think they've extended the search grid to other planets."

Rick's hands stilled—briefly—then resumed their work, even more rigid than before. Evan saw the tells Rick thought he concealed—the tightening of his shoulders, the way his thumb compulsively brushed the bridge of his nose. He wasn't even looking at the volcanoes anymore. Or up at the sky.

Two moons. No matter how many times she looked, it was still true.

They weren't on Earth.

Her mind drifted back to the curtain of light—the impossibility of it— and the certainty that had seized her before they crossed it. *It's a door.*

But to where?

A chill traced down her spine despite the suffocating heat. She pulled her shawl tighter around her shoulders. On the breeze, the faint smell of sulfur twined through the dust. At least the smoke from the volcanoes was blowing away from them. For now.

The argument brewed thicker in the air between the brothers.

"Look," Chad said, pacing in a tight arc behind the car, "we can't know where people are—but we can damn well figure out where they aren't."

Rick didn't lift his head, but his eyebrows rose. "Do tell."

"They won't be by the volcanoes," Chad pressed, ignoring the jab. "Which means heading away from them is our best shot. Find better terrain. Maybe water. Anything."

"And maybe a convenience store is just over the next ridge," Rick said dryly, folding the blanket a little too sharply.

Evan winced inwardly.

Rick's sarcasm wasn't like his brother's. Chad used humor like a shield—an invitation to deflect. Rick used it like a scalpel—precise, cutting, meant to wound.

"Maybe I think it's better than standing around with our thumbs up our—"

"Enough," Evan said, cutting across them before the crash could happen.

Both stopped. Chad flushed, his hands flexing restlessly at his sides. Rick went rigid, like a door slamming shut.

"Chad's right," she added, voice steady even though her stomach twisted to say it.

Rick stared at her, his blue eyes going cold, distant. For a moment, he looked less like her Rick and more like some stranger locked behind glass. His mouth opened, closed. He glanced at Chad, then away.

"Fine," he said finally, voice as jagged as the barren land around them. He didn't argue, just folded inward.

Evan's chest ached. Not for herself—for him. For how hard it was for Rick to surrender even this much.

He glanced toward the invisible line that had cleft this world—the scar across the earth where their reality had torn—and exhaled a breath that sounded more like defeat than agreement. "I didn't want to stay near that thing, anyway."

Neither did she.

The line radiated wrongness, even now. Looking at it twisted her stomach, the same way leaning over the edge of Hoover Dam had the previous summer—that gut-deep scream of gravity, scale, consequence. She hadn't needed Rick to warn her not to step close.

"How much do we have for supplies?" she asked, forcing her voice to be light, practical. Something to pull them back.

Rick rubbed his forehead, the gesture tight with frustration. "Three days, maybe five if we're careful. But without more water, it won't matter."

"Then we'd better make that time count," Evan said, summoning a brightness she didn't feel. "Can I carry something?"

Rick didn't answer right away. His jaw flexed once, hard, before he shoved the last of the gear into Chad's CamelBak.

It was Chad who finally spoke, forcing a grin that was pure armor. "With two strapping lads like us? Nah. You get to be queen for the day." His tone was teasing. His eyes weren't.

Evan saw it—the tautness in his arms and calves, the way he avoided her gaze. Chad was close to breaking, covering it with bravado because somebody had to.

It was sweet. And heartbreaking.

She smiled anyway, because sometimes pretending a little was better than shattering altogether. "Lead on, then," she said.

Rick hoisted the pack in silence. Chad grabbed the emergency radio and tucked it under his arm. Evan fell into step behind them as they moved away from the wrecked car, from the impossible line gouged into the earth.

Anything was better than standing still. Especially when she had the creepy sensation the world itself was watching her.

At least she'd worn her hiking shoes.

They trudged forward, the ground shifting beneath them in tiny betraying slips. The volcanic grit slid under their boots like ground glass. Rick walked two steps ahead, shoulders stiff, focus narrowed so tightly it barely left room for breath. He was retreating into task and motion, hiding from the ache he didn't know how to fight. Chad muttered under his breath, kicking stones from underfoot with sharp, aimless energy—his anger closer to the surface, more raw. More honest.

Frustration knotted under Evan's ribs. They were both trying so hard.

Both too stubborn. Too scared.

Understandable but exhausting. *God, sometimes they make it so hard to hold them together.*

Evan drew a slow breath and let it out, feeling the air scratch its way through lungs that wanted to tighten instead. She let the wind carry it away, as if she could shed the weight along with it.

She loved Rick. That had never been in doubt. She loved him with a fierceness that still startled her sometimes, when she saw all the careful, precise ways he tried to protect what he couldn't name.

And Chad... Chad she loved very differently, but no less. Even if he didn't always know how to ask for it.

They were hers. For better or worse. And no matter how impossible this world had become, no matter how high the odds stacked against them—she wasn't about to let either of them fall apart.

Not if she could help it.

The crunch of volcanic cinders underfoot kept time with their march, the sound almost—*almost*—soothing in its regularity.

Chad didn't know where they were heading. Only that anywhere had to be better than standing by the wreckage and waiting—for what, he had no idea. Besides, the car—its front sheared off like a shop project gone wrong—had grown creepier by the minute.

No machine deserved that.

No fixing it, either—not even if he'd had a full shop and every tool in the catalog. That thought stung more than he cared to admit.

He jammed a hand into his pocket and closed it around the familiar shape of his Swiss Army knife. The metal was warm against his skin, the edges worn smooth by years of handling.

"A good tool can't fix everything," Uncle Jake had said once, pressing it into his hand. "But it's a start."

That was the day Chad had found his calling. Mechanics. Rick had his calculus. Chad had machines. Things that made sense. The knife couldn't fix whatever mess they were in now—but it grounded him.

He patted it once, then cast a final glance over his shoulder. The Mazda sat dirty and broken against the fractured land, like some gutted beast.

When they crested the next rise, it vanished from view. *Good riddance.*

He almost walked into Rick, who'd stopped dead ahead.

"Is that a road?" Rick asked, squinting downslope.

Chad followed his brother's gaze. Calling it a road was generous. It looked like a drunk partier had scribbled a line through the wasteland and someone had decided to call it infrastructure. Rough. Narrow. Crooked as hell. But unmistakably worn by use.

"At least we know there are people," Evan said quietly beside him. Hope, cautious and thin, laced her voice.

Of some kind, Chad thought grimly. *Maybe even the friendly sort. Wouldn't that be nice!*

They picked their way toward it.

The road wasn't rutted in the traditional sense. Ruts needed moisture. Instead, all the loose soil had been knocked aside in places to reveal bare stone. The rest had been baked hard by sun and time. Scattered piles of manure dotted the path, so dried out they didn't even attract flies.

Chad grimaced, giving the nearest one a wide berth anyway. "Those tracks," he said, pointing. "Too thin for tires. Wagon wheels, maybe."

Rick crouched, studying the impressions. "Maybe." His voice was dry as the dust underfoot.

"And those," Chad added, indicating a second set of prints, "definitely aren't from cattle. Unless Flagstaff's gotten a whole lot weirder."

He frowned. The hoofprints didn't look right—too long, too narrow. Not horses. Not anything he recognized.

Rick made a noncommittal grunt and straightened, brushing grit from his jeans. His movements were stiff. Slower than usual.

Chad felt it too—the weariness creeping into his bones, the heat dragging at his limbs. If heat had a smell, it was this—dusty, sharp, heavy enough to coat the inside of his mouth. Every swallow felt like sacrificing one more precious drop of water.

"Look," Evan said, shielding her gaze with one hand as she stared ahead of them.

Chad squinted into the glare. There—a thin smear of movement against the horizon. Dust kicked up by something big. Or a lot of somethings.

"I wonder if we should get off the road," Rick said. His voice stayed level, but Chad caught the tension underneath.

"Good idea," Chad said immediately. No argument for once.

They scrambled up a slope, seeking shelter behind a scatter of jagged rocks. Chad's heart picked up, but it wasn't from the climb. It was the anticipation. And fear.

"What if they're not friendly?" Evan asked quietly.

Chad didn't answer, and neither did Rick. "There," he said instead, pointing to a low outcropping. "We can watch from behind that."

They crouched as the sounds reached them—hoofbeats, the creak of heavy wood, the faint clatter of metal on metal.

Chad peered through a gap between the rocks. A wagon rumbled into view first, trailing plumes of volcanic dust. It looked straight out of a history book—a Conestoga written large, canvas stretched taut over heavy hoops.

But the creature pulling it wasn't a horse or a cow. It was... something else. Broad and hulking, with horns that curled like those on a bighorn sheep.

Flanking the wagon were soldiers. Chain mail glinted dully beneath sun-bleached tabards. Their mounts were sleek and lean as greyhounds, moving with a disquieting smoothness. They sniffed the air as they passed, sharp snouts questing.

Chad huddled lower. *Definitely not Kansas.*

The column slowed.

One of the soldiers—the one closest to their hiding spot—reined up sharply, scanning the hillside with practiced eyes.

Chad's gut twisted. Their tracks. He shrank farther behind the rock, heart pounding against his ribs.

Too late.

"You there!" a voice barked. Strong. Crisp. No-nonsense. "If you're bandits, you've laid a right-sorry ambush. If you're friends, come out before we decide you're not."

Chad shot a look at Rick and then Evan. Rick's jaw was tight, his hand resting protectively on Evan's shoulder. Evan nodded once, her expression steady.

They didn't have a choice.

"Last warning," the soldier called.

Chad stood slowly, hands raised, palms forward. He didn't need Rick to tell him—*Look harmless. Look small.*

"We're not enemies!" he called. His voice cracked on the last syllable—dry mouth—and he grimaced. Hopefully, they'd chalk it up to nerves.

The three moved down the slope toward the soldiers with care.

The soldiers' details sharpened as they approached. Their armor was battered but functional. The tabards bore a strange symbol—a black circle pierced by a thin silver spire.

At least no one fired any weapons.

"You can put your hands down," said the soldier who'd spotted them. He was stocky, square-jawed, with a rough grin that wasn't exactly unfriendly. "You've got the look of Outlanders. That right?"

Chad blinked. *Outlanders?*

Rick beat him to the punch. "You're not speaking English," he said sharply.

The man's grin widened, his expression oddly like Rick's when he'd just solved a puzzle. "Nope. You're speaking yours. We're speaking ours. Necsis handles the rest."

Chad frowned, his brain scrambling to catch up. "Necsis?"

Before the soldier could answer, an older man rode up. His face was weathered leather, his eyes sharp under a tangle of sun-bleached hair. A white braid cord looped over one shoulder. "Necsis," he said, reining in beside them, "is the name of this world."

He reached into a saddlebag and pulled out something that looked like a soccer ball crossed with a porcupine.

"Each bump," he said, gesturing at the spiny fruit, "is a Shift. Pockets where other universes bleed into ours. You came through one. In between are stable zones, like where we now stand. Inlands, we call them."

Chad's brain did a full-system crash. *Universes? Shifts?*

Rick, predictably, objected first. "That's not possible."

The man's expression said he'd heard it before. "You appear thirsty," he said simply, and he tossed the fruit toward them.

Chad caught it reflexively. The spines were surprisingly soft. He looked at it, then at the landscape around them, and decided not to argue. He cracked the fruit open. Inside, it split neatly into juicy sections. He pulled one out and took a cautious bite.

The flavor was bright and tangy—like citrus turned inside out. The juice soothed his parched throat instantly. He broke off another piece and handed it to Evan without a word. She smiled faintly in thanks.

But Chad couldn't shake the officer's words. *Stable zones. Bleeding universes.* He wasn't sure what scared him more—that the man believed it or that he said it so casually.

A low rumble vibrated through the soles of his boots.

Chad stiffened, whipping his head toward the volcanoes. Smoke roiled upward from one of the peaks, thick and dark.

The soldiers didn't even blink.

"Not so silent today," the officer said, his voice cool. He flicked a hand. "Sergeant."

"Captain Gallus?"

"Take Andrus and Kenwick. Get these three to Emberhold." No debate. No elaboration.

The officer wheeled his mount about and rode off without looking back.

Chad, Rick, and Evan were left standing there—three strangers, three extra mounts, and a whole lot of questions.

"Do you know how to ride?" the sergeant asked.

Chad met Evan's glance, then Rick's. His own face must have looked about as poleaxed as theirs. *Ride or walk? Not much of a choice.*

The horses—he was calling them horses, no matter how sharp their teeth were—looked surprisingly cool up close. Alien. Powerful. Real.

Chad patted the knife in his pocket. Solid. Familiar. "When in Rome," he muttered, moving toward the least bitey-looking one.

Whatever came next, he figured he'd better hang on tight.

The patrol disappeared into the shimmering heat, the last clatter of hooves fading into the haze. Rick's head swam. None of this made sense. He dragged in a breath through his nose, but the sulfur-stained air only thickened the dizziness clawing at him. Universes bleeding between worlds. Shifts connecting them. It sounded like the fever dream of a bad science-fiction novel.

Movement at his side was Evan stepping closer and laying a hand on his shoulder. Grounding him.

Rick dropped his own hand over hers for a moment, anchoring himself to her calm. "You okay?" he asked, hearing the raw scraping in his own voice. He brushed a strand of hair back from her temple, fingertips skimming her skin.

Not feverish. Not clammy. Normal.

But she hadn't looked quite right since the soldier had named this world. Her smile was too tight. Her fingers still clutched the pendant at her throat, knuckles pale against the chain.

She gave a small shrug. "I just felt off for a moment, but it passed." Her words said one thing. Her body said another.

Rick filed it away. A problem he didn't have the tools to solve—yet.

Later. For now, she was standing. Breathing. Here.

The sergeant cleared his throat. "Name's Jens. Half-day to Emberhold. We need to move. You ever ridden before?"

Rick turned to him, grateful for the excuse to pull himself together.

"Horses," Chad stated, eyeing the spare mounts. Rick caught the hesitation—not fear but unease.

"These are horses," Jens said easily. His voice was rough but not unfriendly.

Rick watched his mouth move, and the thought clicked: the lip movements didn't match the words perfectly. Like a foreign film dubbed just well enough to fool a viewer if they weren't looking closely. Beyond words, something deeper was being translated. Concepts. Meaning that said a horse was a horse.

Of course.

The thought was dangerously manic, and Rick shivered despite the heat.

Mounting was awkward. It had been years since he'd last been on a horse, but old instincts trickled back. He settled into the saddle, adjusting for the leaner, longer frame of the animal beneath him—faster than any horse he remembered.

His gaze snagged on one of the soldiers—Kenwick, if he remembered the name right. The man's skin had a faint green cast, and small tusks curled from the corners of his mouth. *Orc.* The word surfaced without effort, even though it made no sense.

Kenwick caught him staring and bared his short tusks in something halfway between a grin and a challenge. "Haven't seen an orc before?" the soldier asked, amused—and maybe a little wary.

"Not unless you count when Chad made me play *World of Warcraft*," Rick said before he could stop himself.

Chad barked a short laugh.

Jens tilted his head. "You travel between worlds where you come from?"

"No," Chad said, slowing as he realized how absurd it sounded. "It's a… computer game. Stories. Uh, pictures in a box?"

Kenwick muttered something under his breath.

The air tightened.

"Maybe," Evan said lightly, "instead of trying to explain where we're from, we let them tell us where we are."

Rick shot her a look of gratitude.

Jens chuckled—a rough scrape of sound. "Probably for the best. It's not wise for Outlanders to dwell on their pasts."

He nudged his mount into motion. They fell into line, leaving the ruined road behind.

That statement had carried more finality than Rick liked. His hand started dancing again, and he stilled it. Adjusting his balance, he let the motion of the horse settle into muscle memory. His thighs ached almost immediately—*Great*—but at least they weren't stumbling across volcanic rock anymore.

We'll see what my butt has to say about this tomorrow. He focused outward as they rode.

The landscape drifted past—a cracked wasteland under a sun too large, too bright. Plants dotted the terrain, wrong shades of green, wrong shapes. The air shimmered over the rocks, bending the horizon in uneasy waves.

Now that the first shock was wearing off, the alienness pressed in harder. Tiny details gnawed at the edges of reason. But the worst wasn't the plants nor the sky nor the endless dust—it was the logic problem clawing at the back of his mind.

He needed to understand.

Rick urged his mount a little closer to Jens. "You said that thing we crossed—the Shift—connects to another world?"

Jens nodded without glancing over. "Aye."

"And the terrain matches up?"

"As close to perfect as makes no difference."

"Every time?"

"Every time," Jens said.

Rick swallowed. "But how?"

Jens shrugged. "It's the way of the Shifts. How they are." Not an answer. Worse—an acceptance.

Rick let the horse fall back beside Evan. She glanced over at him, the worry clear in her eyes.

He worked it through, anyway. His mind couldn't help itself. Infinite possibilities. Infinite chances. Somewhere out there, perfect matches had to exist—not by design but by sheer probability. He murmured, "A million monkeys."

Evan's voice was quiet. "What?"

He glanced at her—the furrow in her brow, the faint hope in her gaze. She was holding on.

He squeezed the reins tighter, forcing the words out. "There's a thought experiment. I think it goes something like if you had a million monkeys typing at random, given infinite time, eventually they'd type the complete works of Shakespeare."

Chad snorted from a few paces back. "Sounds messy."

"It is," Rick said. "The point is probability. Something astronomically unlikely becomes inevitable with infinite attempts." He shifted in the saddle again, grimacing. "Like roulette. You know the odds of hitting double-zero ten times in a row?"

Evan shook her head but smiled faintly, as if encouraging him.

"One in over six trillion," Rick said. "Basically impossible. But infinite time means it happens anyway. Over and over again." He turned back to Jens. "The Shifts. Is that what you call the region or what happens when it changes?"

"Both," Jens said.

Rick rubbed the heel of his palm against his forehead. "How many regions are there?"

"Countless," Kenwick answered from behind.

Rick's mouth went dry again. "Infinite worlds," he murmured. "Infinite matches. Infinite chances to find a landscape that fits."

He looked at Chad. Saw confusion giving way to something harder—something that tightened his brother's grip on the reins.

Rick felt it too, like a lead weight sinking into his gut.

Zero chance of finding their way back.

He couldn't say it aloud. Not to Evan.

Instead, he asked, "Jens, can you control them? The Shifts?"

The sergeant's mouth tightened. "No more than you can command the weather."

Rick sat back hard in the saddle and rubbed his forehead again, the pressure doing nothing to ease the throb behind his eyes. *We're trapped.* He didn't say it aloud. Didn't need to.

Chad summed it up for all of them, his voice bleak.

"We're so screwed."

The grind of hooves on cinders softened as they rode south, the ridges thinning around them. The ground shifted underfoot from brittle volcanic grit to dry, cracked earth, sprinkled here and there with stubborn patches of yellowed grass.

Chad sat stiffly in the saddle, the acid ball in his stomach growing heavier with every mile. The realization they had no way back wasn't a slow creep anymore. It was a sucker punch, square in the gut.

Jens and the soldiers rode ahead, talking low. They didn't check behind them much. Didn't need to. Where would they run? Into the wasteland?

Chad glanced at his watch—8:17 p.m. *Has it really only been twelve hours since we left the house?*

The thought of home—*real* home—punched him all over again.

He twisted his wrist absently, the familiar weight of the watch a small comfort. Solid. Anchoring.

Jens must have caught the motion. The sergeant's gaze fixed on Chad's wrist with a sharpness that made Chad's skin crawl.

Chad lifted his arm half-jokingly. "Just a watch. Cool, right?" He tapped the face. Digital numbers blinked in the fading light. "Stopwatch, alarm, messages from my phone—"

"Phone?" Jens cut in, sharp.

Chad blinked at the sudden tension. The other guards were watching too now, hands twitching toward their sides. *Okay. Weird.* But he pushed on, holding up his phone like he was sharing a toy at show-and-tell. "This is a phone. You can call people, send messages—instant letters. No carrier pigeons needed." He grinned, trying to lighten the mood.

No one smiled back, although Kenwick's tusks made it almost look like he did. A bulldog with an overbite.

Jens leaned in slightly. His eyes narrowed, not curious—wary. Like Chad was waving around a loaded gun. "Put it away," he said. The words were soft. The iron beneath them wasn't.

Around them, the soldiers reined back, forming a loose ring. Casual.

Too casual.

Chad swallowed and slid the phone back into his pocket, feeling the atmosphere tighten like stretched wire.

The third guard made a gesture—a spiral drawn in the air, then a pushing motion toward Chad—muttering words Chad couldn't entirely catch.

Fragments floated: "...hand... we thrive... thought... guide..."

Evan's voice brushed his ear. "Maybe we keep the revelations to a minimum from here on out."

Chad nodded stiffly, the prickle at the base of his neck refusing to fade.

They rode on without another word, and the terrain eventually changed again. A river appeared out of the desolation, winding its lazy way southward, carving a gash into the earth—a lifeline where none should exist. Scrubby plants clustered along its banks, growing denser the farther they traveled. The road bent to follow the river's edge as it plunged into a deep cut through the land ahead.

The sun, low and heavy on the horizon, slanted across the landscape in sharp angles, throwing everything into harsh relief, and Chad caught his first glimpse of the town.

Buildings huddled along the riverbanks—ramshackle, smoke-stained, sagging under their own weight. They sprawled outward like a broken jaw, shadows pooling thickly between them.

Nothing about it looked inviting.

"Miner's End," Jens said, waving a hand like he was pointing out a gas station bathroom.

Chad grimaced.

The air here was heavy—smoke and mildew wrestling for dominance, laced with something sweeter that made his stomach turn. Faces peered from cracked windows and doorways as they passed—hollow-eyed, following them with silent suspicion.

One building stood straighter than the rest—two stories, small windows. Guards lounged out front. A checkpoint.

The travelers dismounted. One of the guards sauntered up, voice a slow drawl. "A fresh catch from the Shifts, eh?"

The man's skin was sallow, almost damp-looking. *Bureaucrat,* Chad thought. *Paper pusher with a badge.*

Jens didn't rise to the bait. "Three Outlanders. I'm to take them to the embassy. After we deal with the contraband."

Chad stiffened. *The what?*

Jens turned toward him, his mouth twisting in something that might have been sympathy. "I'm sorry. We have to confiscate your technology before we proceed."

Chad stared at him. "It's just a watch."

"It's the law," Jens said evenly. "You'll understand more later. But for now, it has to go."

Chad glanced sideways. Evan tilted her head—that analytical tilt she had when she was putting things together. Rick's jaw hung slightly open.

Around them, the guards subtly closed ranks.

Suckered. Chad's stomach twisted into a cold knot.

One of the guards produced a sack that looked older than half the buildings here. He held it open expectantly.

Evan moved first, dropping her phone into the bag with a hollow shushing sound. She nodded toward Rick and Chad. Rick followed, his face already sliding into problem-solving mode. His phone landed atop Evan's with a dead sound of finality.

"I also have a radio and flashlight," Rick said tightly.

"What powers them?"

"Batteries."

Apparently, Necsis understood that much. Jens' gaze flicked downward and the devices vanished into the bag.

Then the sack loomed in front of Chad. He stared at it, chest tightening. The phone in his pocket. The watch on his wrist.

Contacts. Pictures. *Memories.*

Pieces of a life suddenly impossibly far away.

Evan's hand brushed his arm—steadying, silent.

I can't.

His fingers fumbled at the watch clasp, every second peeling away another layer of home. He thought of the pictures he hadn't backed up. Texts he'd never read again. Friends he'd never talk to.

The click of the clasp sounded loud in the stale air.

He dropped the watch into the sack. Then the phone.

The bag closed with a jerk of the guard's hand. Chad felt the tether snap—and just like that, his last link to home was gone.

"Anything else?" Jens asked. "Be warned, if you're caught with forbidden tech later, the punishment is exile. Back to the Shifts."

Chad's hand brushed his pocket where the Swiss Army knife rested. He hesitated. The flashlight attachment—small, concealable.

Some things were worth the risk.

He shook his head, matching Jens's gaze with a blank stare.

The sergeant's eyes lingered, then slid away.

"The Ban keeps us safe," Jens said, quieter. "Since the wars. I know it seems strange. But it's for the best."

Chad didn't answer. He let the silence carry the weight for him.

The other soldiers stayed behind with the mounts. Jens led them onward on foot through the crumbling skeletons of Miner's End.

Chad walked in silence, the loss gnawing a hole in his gut. *So, what now?* he wondered. *Build a sundial?*

Evan's hand touched his, just for a moment. "It'll be okay," she said, low and sure.

He wanted to believe her.

God, he wanted to.

The stench of smoke and rot thinned gradually as they descended. The ground sloped downward, the river carving deeper into the land. And with it—change.

The ravine widened first into a gorge, then into a full valley—a deep scar cut by time and water. A bridge spanned it high above, stone streets dropping down on either side with it. The farther they walked, the more the world transformed. Smoke gave way to the smell of baking bread. A breeze teased sweat off his skin. Ahead, faint music floated on the air—strings, voices, laughter. Chad's stomach growled on cue.

Shadows thinned. Color returned. Stone buildings gleamed in the sun's dying light—whitewashed walls catching fire in gold and red, green vines spilling from carved balconies.

Above them, the cracked higher walls still loomed—but here, hidden away, something new grew. Alive. The city reminded him of those old documentaries of medieval Europe, dense and close and breathing.

"It's like London and Petra got into a fight," he muttered, almost to himself. "And nobody won."

Rick barked a short laugh. A real one. Chad swallowed down the tangle in his throat. Rick was holding it together. Meanwhile, Chad felt like he was unraveling at the seams. *Even here, I can't get out of his damn shadow.*

"Emberhold," Jens said, gesturing toward the golden heart of the hidden city.

And Chad, still fighting the ache behind his ribs, couldn't help but wonder—was this salvation?

Or just another prison, dressed up pretty?

III
Sponsorship

Evan felt Chad's anger before she saw it. It bled off him in waves—harsh, raw, the way a forge's heat spills out into open air. Every line of him was drawn so tight she half-expected him to shatter at the smallest provocation. Rick, by contrast, moved hollowly, as if whatever fire he might have had inside had already guttered out. No anger. Just a heavy, resigned calm that scared her more.

The city's slope steered them toward a squat, battered building wedged against the cliffside like an afterthought. Its shallow stone facade was cracked and bleached, worn by too many years of wind and neglect. No sign hung above the door. No welcome was carved in the lintel. The structure sat slightly apart from its neighbors, shunned even in this city of outcasts.

Jens halted in front of it. "The embassy," he said, voice low. "Mari and Fenton'll get you sorted. Good people." He hesitated, his gaze scrutinizing all three of them, lingering on each. A warning lurked behind his words, unspoken but heavy.

"Trust them," he added. "I'd hate to have to come back in ten days to collect you."

With that, he turned and strode uphill, boots tapping a precise, retreating rhythm against the stone.

"Ten days?" Rick asked the air.

Neither he nor Chad moved. Their shadows stretched long on the sun-bleached ground.

Evan squared her shoulders. Someone had to lead. She stepped toward the battered door, every nerve taut. Cracks spidered through layers of peeling paint, colors bleeding into each other—white, green, ochre—like memories too stubborn to be scrubbed away. She lifted her hand to knock, but the door swung open before her knuckles touched wood.

A man stood there—thin, sharp-featured, his hair reduced to a wispy comb-over that clung to the sides of his head. His eyes raked across them with the speed and detachment of someone used to measuring strangers against hidden checklists.

"Three, is it?" he said, voice clipped and economical, like he paid for each word. He stepped back, opening the door wider. "Come in, then."

Evan felt Rick drift up beside her, softly touching her shoulder as they stepped inside.

The embassy's interior surprised her. It was actually carved into the cliff wall rather than built against it. Instead of the cold stone she'd expected, the space was filled with the warm glow of candles tucked into battered sconces and nooks. A long table dominated the common room to the right, its mismatched chairs worn smooth by generations of use, an imposing fireplace against the wall beyond it. The heavy scent of baking bread curled in the air, mixing with the richer, smoky undertone of the fire crackling in a wide hearth.

"You're Fenton?" Rick asked, voice low but steady.

The man nodded briskly. "I manage the embassy. Mari oversees the living quarters." Without ceremony, he moved stork-like toward a desk burdened by a massive ledger and a scattering of papers weighed down by stones. "We'll get you registered first," he said.

Before he could start scratching with his quill, a voice called from deeper within. "Hold a moment, Fenton!"

A woman appeared, bustling into view with a swirl of aprons and flour-dusted skirts. She was plump but not heavy, her cheeks pink from kitchen heat, her brown eyes crinkled at the corners from years of laughter rather than frowns.

She beamed at them all like they were long-lost grandchildren. "Let's sort their rooms first, dear." Her gaze landed on Evan, softening even further. Evan felt her chest unclench, the tension she hadn't realized she was holding easing a fraction.

"How many rooms?" Mari asked gently.

Without hesitation, Evan slid her arm through Rick's. She felt his startled flinch—then, a heartbeat later, the way his hand found hers, squeezing lightly. "Two," Evan said.

Mari's smile deepened, eyes twinkling. "Very good. Second and third doors on the right," she said, waving down a hall that tunneled deeper into the cliffside. "Fenton will give you the keys."

With that, she bustled off again, her absence leaving the room feeling quieter, emptier somehow.

Fenton dipped his quill and gestured to the ledger as if there had been no interruption. "Names. Skills."

Evan answered first, voice steady from years of practice in staying calm when everything felt upside down. Rick spoke next, each syllable clipped and careful.

Chad hesitated, then muttered, "Mechanical work."

The comment drew Fenton's rheumy gaze for an uncomfortably long time. "Labor," he mumbled to the ledger. The scratching of the quill sounded disproportionately loud against the silence of flickering candles.

As Fenton wrote, Evan's gaze wandered. There was a familiarity to the place she couldn't quite name—the smell of bread, the way the chairs didn't match but still belonged. It reminded her of the little bed-and-breakfast Rick had taken her to last winter. Cheap but cozy. Loved, if worn.

Her mind was still turning that over when Chad's voice broke into the stillness. "What's the deal with technology here, anyway?"

The scratch of Fenton's quill halted.

Very slowly the embassy manager looked up. Without a word, he jabbed a bony finger toward a placard hung slightly askew on the wall. Evan's eyes skimmed it instinctively, the unfamiliar characters resolving themselves into words in her mind with unnatural ease:

If gears turn on their own, beware,
Lest they lead to foul despair.
If power sparks without your hand,
It falls beneath the Ban's command.

Tools that help but never replace
Keep balance strong in every space.

Fenton's voice was flat. "Engineers nearly destroyed Necsis. The Ban ensures they will not do so again."

Chad's mouth opened, closed. His fists clenched at his sides. "So what happens to our stuff?" he demanded.

"Confiscated?" Fenton asked.

Chad nodded, and the man continued without a flicker of sympathy. "Most destroyed. A few pieces—if deemed instructive—get sent to Ironspire for determination by the court wizard."

Rick tensed beside her. Evan caught him mouthing a single word: *Wizard?*

Before the knot of anger and confusion in the room could tighten further, Mari reappeared, bearing a tray with a squat teapot and three mugs, each chipped and mismatched. "Tea?" she offered brightly, setting down a tin containing cookies as well.

Evan accepted a mug with gratitude, savoring its rough warmth against her palms. Rick did the same, although she caught the slight tremble he suppressed as he lifted it. Meanwhile, Chad muttered something that might have been "Thanks," staring into his cup like it held answers.

Fenton reached into a drawer and withdrew three small cards, each hand-lettered with neat, precise script. "Carry these at all times," he said. "They mark you as Outlanders. You have ten days to find sponsorship."

Rick's voice, when it came, was almost too calm. "And if we don't?"

"Exile." Fenton might as well have been commenting on last week's weather.

Mari's smile dimmed. "You are returned to the Shifts."

The silence that followed wasn't natural. It was heavy. Alive—but then Mari clapped her hands, the sound brittle in the heavy air. Then she forced a smile, bright and determined, like someone throwing open shutters against a storm. "But that's rare! You'll find something."

With that, she ushered them toward the hearth, where a stew simmered, thick and savory.

Evan let herself be steered, but the weight of those words clung to her like wet clothes.

Ten days.

Ten days to carve out a future—or disappear forever.

Chad woke to a head full of wool and a viciously kinked spine. The mattress—if he could call it that—creaked beneath him as he sat up. He rubbed the back of his skull, rolling his shoulders until something popped. *We really are living in the Dark Ages,* he thought.

He dressed automatically, his limbs moving without real energy, and stumbled out into the embassy's main room. The long table stretched out before him, its scarred surface littered with bowls and mugs. Evan and Rick sat close together near the far end, shoulders brushing lightly, talking in low voices. Across from them, hunched over a bowl of untouched porridge, was a stranger.

Chad slowed.

The man—thin as a rake, glasses perched precariously on a beak-like nose—traced a crumpled scrap of paper with one trembling thumb. His lips moved soundlessly, though Chad caught a whisper as he drew closer. "No. They won't. Not him... maybe tomorrow."

Chad slid into the seat across from Evan. "Who's that?" he asked under his breath.

Rick shrugged without looking up. Evan, though, studied the stranger with a gaze that made Chad's chest tighten—bright-eyed, too knowing. The same look she'd worn in the meadow, just before everything fell apart.

Mari appeared, bustling in with a tray. She set bowls of porridge and mugs of warm milk in front of them, pausing just long enough to rest a gentle hand on the stranger's thin shoulder. "It'll be alright, Korvan."

He flinched but didn't lift his head. She whispered something more —too low to catch—then moved on without fuss.

Chad picked up his mug. Warm milk. Normal enough. The porridge, though... He grimaced as he forced down a spoonful. More glue than grain. At least there were nuts.

He hoped that was what they were.

Fenton swept in next, lurching forward with his arms full of paper. He dropped rough maps in front of each of them. "Emberhold," he said curtly. "Sectors marked for Outlanders. Trade quarter, market quarter, some labor wards." For once, his attention drifted—not toward them but toward the muttering man at the table's edge. His lip curled faintly before he turned away.

Chad barely had time to wonder about it before the door slammed open with a crack loud enough to rattle the dishes.

A diminutive man stormed inside, misshapen felt cap pulled low over wiry gray hair, a tool belt jangling against his hips. He made a beeline for their table, ignoring Fenton entirely.

Stopping a few feet away, he swept off his cap with a theatrical bow. "Sorendir requests your presence at his tower. An honor not given lightly." His voice, low and resonant, seemed too big for his frame. Without waiting for a response, his too-large hands jammed the cap back onto his head, and he spun smartly on his heel before marching straight out the door he'd left hanging open.

Fenton stared after him, mouth opening and closing like that of a fish pulled from the water. "That mad wizard," he muttered, scuttling to slam the door shut.

Rick's brow furrowed. "What was that about?"

Mari reappeared, wiping her hands on her apron. She smiled, but it was stretched tight at the edges. "Sorendir lives up in Miner's End," she said. "Gharn's his assistant. Brusque but loyal. If Sorendir's invited you—" She hesitated, then pressed on. "—it could be a sponsorship offer. You'd do well to hear him out."

She glanced—just once—toward Fenton, who was scribbling furiously in his ledger. "Just keep your heads about you," she added softly. "And trust your instincts. Not every helping hand means well."

Chad exchanged a look with Rick and Evan. Neither looked reassured.

"That's the second wizard mentioned in two days," Rick muttered. "Talk about superstitious—" he cut off mid-thought, eyes tightening.

Evan rubbed at her temple. "Let's not rush," she said. "We've got ten days. Let's see what else is out there first."

Rick nodded a little too quickly. "Maybe split up today? Cover more ground."

Chad forced a grin he didn't feel. "Sure. What's the worst that could happen?"

*

The market quarter hit Chad like a hammer.

Noise. Color. Heat. People everywhere—shouting, bartering, shoving past with bundles and carts and sacks. The map Fenton had given him sat crumpled in his fist, half-forgotten.

He should have felt energized. Challenged. Instead, every breath scraped his throat raw.

He had tried looking for work the first place that Fenton had circled—a quarry loading crew—and had barely made it through the foreman's bored speech. The second was worse: a tannery, the stench rolling out in waves thick enough to taste.

Hard labor didn't scare him, but being treated like a warm body instead of a mind—that he couldn't stomach. He hadn't refused their offers—that would have been foolish—but he'd delayed in responding.

His stomach growled, a traitor to his pride. He ducked into a shadowed nook between buildings, hoping to find somewhere to breathe, and found a dry, cracked well instead. *Figures.*

He scuffed his boot against the stone rim. "Great. Not even water."

"Pump's busted," said a voice nearby.

Chad turned. A gnome—the word came to Chad unbidden—wiped greasy hands on his pants. Not much taller than Chad's waist, the figure squinted up at him from beneath wild, gray eyebrows.

"Been at it all morning," the gnome added, jerking a thumb toward the sad, rusted mechanism.

Something stirred in Chad's gut. Familiar. Solid. "Need a hand?"

The gnome nodded eagerly, introducing himself as Ipsen.

In minutes, Chad was elbow-deep in the pump's innards, feeling more like himself than he had since... well, maybe since forever.

Ipsen chatted nonstop while Chad worked. Gossip. Politics. Random complaints about "shiftless Outlanders"—said with a wink. Drakerath, Ipsen claimed, was "progressive" compared to other kingdoms. Velsaria would enslave you. Eryndor might gut you for the crime of existing.

"And magic?" Chad asked, squinting into the rusted guts.

Ipsen snorted. "One of the Three Powers, same as always. Magic, Mind, Machine."

Chad didn't know what to say to that.

Upon finding the jammed piston, he pulled out his modified Swiss Army knife—flipped the flashlight on without thinking—and used the pliers to free a small blockage it revealed. The pump shuddered, coughed—and roared back to life.

For the first time since they had met, Ipsen went silent.

Chad glanced up—and froze.

Ipsen's face had gone pale, and his eyes locked on the knife like it was a loaded weapon. "Put that away," Ipsen hissed.

Chad snapped the knife closed and shoved it into his pocket, but the damage was done. Ipsen grabbed his sleeve and dragged him toward a shadowed alley.

"You fool," the gnome spat. "Didn't they warn you? About the Ban?"

"What's your problem?" Chad snapped, jerking free.

Ipsen's face twisted. "The Ban's the only reason Necsis isn't a wasteland! Engineers—" He spat the word. "—like you almost tore the world apart."

Chad bristled, fists clenching.

Ipsen backed away, breathing hard. "I was going to offer you sponsorship. Despite..." His gaze flicked to Chad's pocket. "Forget it," he muttered, spinning on his heel and vanishing into the crowd without a backward glance.

Chad stood there, heart hammering. People stared. He ducked his head and shoved his hands deep into his pockets, walking fast without a destination. *You blew it.*

Again.

*

The embassy smelled of stew and fresh bread when Chad stumbled back inside that evening, exhaustion dragging at his every joint.

Evan sat slumped at the long table, eyes closed, as Rick massaged her temples. She cracked one eye open at his approach and smiled wanly.

"She has a headache," Rick uttered without letting go of her.

Chad dropped heavily into the seat across from them. The stew in his bowl smelled better than anything he'd tasted in days, but he barely had an appetite. Dinner passed in fits and starts. Awkward conversations. Near misses. Dead ends.

"We didn't have any luck either," Evan said, squeezing Rick's hand over the table.

Rick nodded grimly. "There were some possibilities this morning, but it got worse the longer we stayed out. Every conversation ended before it started."

Chad stared into his bowl, the food having lost its flavor when he thought of the two offers he'd passed up that morning. *Did I make a mistake?* Then he remembered what Ipsen had started saying just before interrupting himself. Words slipped out before Chad could second-guess them. "Maybe it's not just bad luck."

Evan lifted her head. "What do you mean?"

He toyed with his spoon. "Ipsen—a gnome—almost offered me sponsorship. Then he changed his mind. After..." He trailed off. He didn't want to explain the knife. Not now. Not yet. "It felt like someone was leaning on people. Warning them off."

Evan shivered visibly. "I felt like we were being watched all day."

Rick's frown deepened. "If someone's working against us..."

"It's just a feeling," Evan said quickly, trying to cut the tension. "But maybe we should be more careful."

Chad leaned back, letting his chair tip onto two legs. Nine days.

Nine days to find someone willing to take on three strangers.

The walls of Emberhold seemed a little closer tonight.

Rick sank into a chair near the embassy's hearth, exhaustion grinding against every bone. His feet ached from the day's endless trudge—something Chad seemed to glory in but Rick preferred in far-smaller doses. His shoulders locked into a stiff, unyielding knot, like he was carrying half of Emberhold on his back.

And still, the physical fatigue barely scratched the weight pressing down on his mind. *It's all too much.*

He accepted—grudgingly—that they were no longer on Earth. The evidence had piled too high to deny it. Either that, or he was suffering the most vivid psychotic break in recorded history.

That thought frightened him more than the idea of crossing universes.

No, what gnawed at him wasn't the setting. It was the ticking clock. Ten days, now eight.

The embassy's main room flickered in the low firelight. Across the room, Korvan paced near Fenton's desk, the map clutched tight in one hand. Rick knew that map—the inked streets, the circled names—because his own looked exactly the same. Except Korvan's bore more heavy strikethroughs. More dead ends.

The man muttered as he paced, voice barely audible. "They don't want to risk it. No one does. Not after the wizard showed interest."

Rick caught the quick, fearful glance Korvan shot his way. Not anger—fear. Rick looked away, jaw tightening.

The day had started better.

*

At breakfast, Fenton had doled out fresh leads like rations. Rick's paper listed three countinghouses needing clerks. Evan's had a pair of seamstress shops and a tavern. Chad's included a blacksmith, a steam smith, and another stone quarry.

Chad had scratched the quarry off immediately, muttering something Rick hadn't caught.

Fenton's assurances—"Young people usually find something quickly"—had almost made Rick believe they had a real chance. Almost.

Mistress Flemmit, at the first countinghouse, wore clothes tailored so tightly to her figure that Rick had wondered if she'd simply not wanted to pay one penny more for fabric than absolutely necessary. She had greeted him with a scowl that melted into a businesslike smile the moment he passed her barrage of math problems. Hired on the spot, he was installed at a cramped desk.

Compound interest. Amortization schedules. Profit ratios. Safe. Predictable. Comforting. Numbers made sense. Numbers obeyed.

Hours passed. No offer of lunch. No break. Just page after page of ledgers dumped onto his cramped desk, ink-stained and crooked. Rick flexed his hand, shaking out the ache building in his fingers.

Sponsorship, Fenton had called it. *Opportunity.* Rick grimaced as he scratched out another column of figures. It looked more like indentured servitude with a prettier name.

But success was success, tedious or not. And without sponsorship, there was no future.

He stretched at the desk, rolling his neck—and caught a client's glance flicking toward him. A brief whisper to Mistress Flemmit. Her head jerked around like she'd been slapped.

Rick felt the shift before she'd even approached. By the time she'd reached his desk, the pleasant facade was gone. She peered down at his work, frowning.

"I'm afraid your figures are incorrect," she said tightly.

Rick blinked. "Where?"

She jabbed at a sum—one Rick knew was right. When he tried to walk her through the steps, she cut him off with a brittle laugh. "No matter. I'm afraid..." She cast her eyes about the room as if looking for an escape. "My nephew is getting married. Yes, that's it. I won't have time to train someone new."

Less than five minutes later, he was standing outside with two unfamiliar coins in his palm and a locked door at his back.

The rest of the day unraveled the same way. Silent rejections. Polite brush-offs. Whispers at the edge of his hearing.

By late afternoon he'd stopped trying to count the failures.

*

The embassy's fire crackled weakly, throwing long, distorted shadows across the walls. Rick tapped his fingers against the chair arm, his mind turning over variables. There had to be a pattern. There always was. It was just buried deeper this time.

Every problem has a solution. If you look hard enough.

He traced equations in his mind. Probabilities. Correlations between sponsor age, profession, proximity to trade hubs. The data refused to align.

The front door swung open, letting in a draft of chill air—and two familiar figures. Evan shook her head slightly, the gesture small but heavy. Chad followed, shoulders slumped, map crushed in one hand.

No luck.

Mari bustled in behind them from the kitchen, carrying her customary tray of tea and tin of cookies. She set it down at the table with a soft clink. "No sponsorships today, then," she said gently.

Rick shook his head.

Chad snagged two cookies with the desperation of a man preparing for siege. "By the end, it felt like shops were closing just at the sight of me."

"Same," Evan murmured, settling into a chair with a wince.

Mari's brows knitted. "I'm sorry, dears. Outlanders usually find work quickly. Especially with useful skills. This..." She hesitated. "This is peculiar."

Peculiar. Rick's mind snapped back to Flemmit's sudden turn. The whispered words. The fear in her eyes. He leaned forward, elbows braced on his knees. "Sorendir."

Mari's mouth thinned. "If word's spread that he's shown interest—"

"It has," Rick said flatly.

Fenton spoke sharply from his desk. "It wasn't from us." A little too quickly.

Mari repositioned the teapot with unnecessary care. "Sorendir's never shown interest in Outlanders before. This is highly unusual."

The fire crackled. Korvan's pacing continued, jagged and restless.

Rick's gaze slid to Evan—and stilled. She pressed her fingertips to her temples, wincing. "Headache?" he asked, already half-rising from his seat.

She nodded, eyes squeezed shut. "It's like... everyone's shouting."

Rick hesitated, started to step closer—then froze when she flinched.

"It hurts more than it should," she whispered.

Slowly Rick sank back into his chair, hands curling uselessly in his lap. Evan wasn't prone to dramatics. If she said something was wrong, it was. The embassy walls felt closer now, the fire's light harsher. Every sound—the scratch of Fenton's quill, Korvan's muttering and his footsteps—pressed tighter against him.

Rick closed his eyes briefly. When he opened them, his voice came out low. "I think... we need to hear Sorendir out."

Chad nodded from across the room, expression grim. "It's probably the only real lead we've got."

Rick glanced at Evan, expecting her to agree, but she didn't speak right away. Her hand had dropped from her temple, and her eyes were bright. A small, warm smile lit her face. Then her gaze shifted to Korvan, with his ceaseless pacing. The lines in his forehead were deeper now. Every few strides, he muttered something under his breath.

Evan cleared her throat gently. "You were there when Gharn made the offer," she said. "Maybe he was offering sponsorship for you as well."

Korvan stopped. His eyes found her.

"You could come with us," she added, voice careful but kind. "If you wanted."

Rick's chest tightened—not from worry but from something sharper. Gratitude. She didn't have to offer. It wasn't the obvious play. But of course she did. Of course she saw him. *I should've thought of that,* he admitted silently.

But the man's face was already paling. "No," he said. "Absolutely not."

Rick leaned forward, frowning. "What's wrong with coming with us?"

Korvan's mouth twisted. "I've heard stories. About the madman in the tower—and his pet gnome." Evan flinched at the phrasing. Even Chad stiffened slightly. But Korvan was already shaking his head. "You want to become part of some experiment, be my guest. I want nothing to do with it."

Without waiting for a reply, he turned sharply and left the room.

The bang of a door slamming at the end of the hall made Rick flinch. The fire popped behind them. The embassy had gone quiet again—too quiet.

Rick stared after him, the variables in his mind clashing like bad data—nothing aligned.

Just unease.

Chad stood at the base of the tower, arms crossed, trying not to feel like the thing was judging him. It loomed above—a crooked finger of dark stone jutting up from the cliff's edge, overlooking the cleaner lines of Emberhold's better districts. Cracks spidered across its face, and moss clung stubbornly to the seams, defying gravity. The heavy front door sagged on iron bands so ancient they curled like dead vines.

But the courtyard between the tower wall and the low stone fence was spotless, stone tiles scrubbed until they gleamed. Two planters, each cradling a stubbornly green tree, stood by the door like small sentinels against the crumbling facade.

Gharn leaned against his walking stick beside the entrance, battered cap pulled low over his wild hair. His expression hovered between impatience and amusement, like he was watching a pratfall play out in slow motion. "You came," he rumbled. "Good. Was starting to wonder if you'd grown spines and buried yourselves."

Whatever that means, Chad thought, eyeing the gnome warily.

He opened his mouth to reply, but Rick beat him to it with a muttered, "Let's just get this over with."

Without another word, Gharn shoved the door open.

Inside, the air hit Chad like a physical thing—dense, warm, and thick with the smells of burning oil, parchment, and something sharper that prickled at the back of his throat. Subtle spiral etchings unfurled across the plaster walls, blooming and twisting as they caught shadows that danced as he moved.

Rick slowed immediately, brushing his fingertips near one of the designs without touching. "Fibonacci sequence," he murmured, voice almost reverent.

Chad didn't know what that meant and certainly didn't like the way Rick said it—like it was familiar. Like it made sense.

Footsteps echoed from above.

A man descended the crooked staircase. *Old* didn't seem strong-enough a word for him. Wiry, hunched—but still he moved deliberately, like each step had been calculated in advance. His silver-white beard narrowed to a sharp point, and his robe, once black, was now washed out and patched, stitched through with intricate red diagrams that tugged at the edge of Chad's memory. A gold medallion swung lightly from a fine chain at his chest, catching the low light and scattering it in sharp, deliberate glints.

But it was his eyes that pinned Chad in place—sharp, golden, alive in a face so lined it looked carved from old wood. Those eyes locked on to Rick, and the room seemed to tilt.

"Three," Sorendir said under his breath, a flicker of disappointment crossing his face. "I expected... No matter."

"Korvan stayed back at the embassy," Chad offered, feeling awkward the moment the words left his mouth.

Sorendir barely acknowledged him. He turned away with a distracted wave. "Welcome. Come."

They followed him up the spiraling stairwell. The etched designs crawled alongside them, winding like grooves inside a shell. Chad kept his eyes low. Looking at the patterns too long made his head ache.

At the top, Sorendir led them into a broad parlor crammed with sagging shelves, battered tables, and odd devices that clicked and ticked faintly when they passed. Books leaned precariously in uneven stacks. Scrolls littered chairs and sideboards. Glass orbs flickered intermittently, like dying stars.

In the center of the chaos, six plain chairs had been arranged neatly around a low table. *Six.* Chad's skin prickled.

Gharn shuffled past them and set down a battered tin of cookies with a thump that sounded loud in the closed space.

Rick, predictably, drifted toward a large map pinned to the far wall. Evan stayed close, her shoulder brushing Rick's, her hand ghosting near his arm like she might catch him if he fell.

"The Nine Kingdoms," Sorendir said, joining Rick. "The blank spaces are Shifts. Roughly thirty miles across each. Stable lands weave between them like oil dancing on water."

Chad studied the map with interest as Rick leaned in, eyes hungry—the way he always did when given a puzzle to solve. That old spark was back, small but unmistakable.

Evan spoke first. "Why did you invite us?"

Sorendir's smile was warm. Too warm. It didn't reach the sharp edges of his gaze. "Did I?" he said, tilting his head slightly. "In another time, another place, you might say you invited yourselves."

Chad shifted uneasily, the weight of the tower pressing more heavily on his shoulders.

Rick folded his arms in front of him. "Why are we here?"

"Isn't it obvious?" Sorendir asked, voice maddeningly gentle. "I wish to sponsor you."

Rick's mouth tightened. "Why?"

"Because," Sorendir said, "you, my boy, are a wizard. Or will be."

Rick barked a short, humorless laugh. "What is this, Hogwarts? I don't believe in magic."

"Among infinite realities, infinite laws," Sorendir said smoothly, "magic isn't just possible. It's inevitable. As are other talents." His focus drifted for a moment to Evan.

Rick hesitated—not much, but enough that Chad caught it.

Sorendir lifted his hand and spoke words that curled the air between them. And Rick vanished.

In his place stood a mule—compact, dark-coated, and unmistakably furious, those blue-gray eyes glaring daggers at the world. It brayed at them, baring teeth.

Chad's laugh burst free before he could stop it. "Rick's always been stubborn."

Evan wasn't laughing. She crossed to the mule without hesitation and ran her hands along its flank. "It's him," she said grimly. She turned sharply toward Sorendir. "Change him back."

Sorendir snapped his fingers, and Rick stumbled back into human form, breathing hard, his glare sharp enough to cut stone.

"Fine," he bit out. "Magic exists. Doesn't mean I can use it."

Sorendir gestured to a cluttered shelf. A thick book lifted itself free and floated lazily toward Rick, who caught it reflexively, then turned it around in his hands as if searching for wires. He opened it. Frowned. "This looks like... a mathematical proof."

"In a way," Sorendir said, smiling. "Magic here is mathematics. You think like a magician already."

Chad dropped into the nearest chair, the familiar ache of being left behind blooming in his chest. *All about Rick.*

Again.

He grabbed a cookie from the battered tin and bit into it without thinking. The buttery crumble coated his tongue, bland and dry. His gaze dropped to the tin, and recognition jolted through him like a live wire.

"Mari made these," he said aloud, barely realizing he was speaking.

The pieces clicked together faster than he could stop them. *How could he have these cookies unless he had a connection with the Embassy? Could that mean...* "You're the one," Chad said, standing so abruptly his chair scraped loudly against the stone.

Sorendir didn't deny it. Just watched, maddeningly calm.

"You sabotaged us," Chad said, anger rising hot and fast. "You're why no one will sponsor us." He dropped the half-eaten cookie onto the table with a soft thud.

Rick stiffened, turning toward Sorendir sharply. Evan reached out, catching his sleeve, though her hand trembled slightly.

Chad shook his head. "I'd rather take my chances with exile," he snapped, turning on his heel and stalking toward the stairwell, hiking boots thudding against the stone.

Behind him, Rick's and Evan's voices tangled—low, urgent—but he didn't slow. The spiral walls blurred past, twisting as he descended, the air pressing closer with every step.

Above, Rick's voice echoed faintly down the shaft. "We need to think."

Chad didn't stop.

The tower door shut behind them with a heavy, final-sounding thud. Evan flinched despite the sun on her back.

Chad stalked ahead, fists clenched, radiating heat that had nothing to do with the late afternoon. Rick walked beside her instead—quieter, thoughtful—but the tight line of his jaw betrayed the storm circling behind his eyes.

They left the courtyard in silence and soon threaded into the cracked streets of Miner's End, the path winding toward the broken spine of the city. Evan let her eyes roam the narrow alleys, but it was the pressure in her head she noticed most—shifting currents of thought she couldn't quite grasp, shadows of emotion brushing against her skin.

Here the stones were uneven and dark with old soot. The buildings leaned together like old men huddling for warmth or gossip. Noxious odors of ash and waste mingled in the air. Flies swarmed in every alley mouth, massing on piles that she didn't want to examine too closely. People moved in quick bursts—darting glances, heads down, shoulders hunched. A soot-smeared elf with a pointed cap passed by without meeting her eye. A gnome struggled to lift a basket half his size. Three dwarves argued over the price of rusted scrap in voices pitched just low enough to sound dangerous. Not many humans here, and none of them looked especially safe.

"Progressive toward Outlanders," Fenton had said.

Maybe. But from where Evan stood, "progressive" here just meant you were allowed to be poor instead of dead.

She wrapped her shawl tighter around her shoulders. The buzzing in her head swelled and receded like waves breaking against stone. She tried to block it, but they slid in anyway—dozens of scattered impressions. Hunger. Distrust. Pain masked by anger. She blinked hard and focused on Rick's steps beside her, steady and grounding.

"There's more to it," she said aloud, surprised by her own voice.

Rick looked over. "More to what?"

But she was focused on Chad, who half-turned without slowing. "Your anger," Evan clarified. "It's not just about Sorendir sabotaging us."

Chad gave a brittle laugh. "Isn't that enough?"

Rick's voice was cool. "We don't know it was him."

"Then why didn't he deny it?" Chad stopped in the middle of the street, turning to face them. Arms folded. Defensive. Daring.

Rick lifted both hands. "Circumstantial. No direct proof."

They started walking again. Evan kept her gaze low, tuning out the city's motion. But Rick wasn't looking at the streets. His eyes kept flicking back toward the tower, toward Sorendir. His fingers twitched slightly at his sides.

"You're curious," Evan said softly.

He glanced at her, gave a slight shrug—but didn't deny it. "It's math," he said after a pause. "Magic. If it's structured... if it's applied math... that's... *elegant*."

She slipped her hand into his. His fingers curled around hers almost automatically, grip warm and familiar. Evan didn't respond aloud. But a small smile touched her mouth. This was more like the Rick she knew. The one who never stopped thinking. Never stopped solving. Sorendir's words echoed in her mind... *other talents.*

Had something changed in her? Had this world sharpened something? She thought back to the road with Jens—the subtle dissonance that had risen unbidden when someone lied or masked an intent. At the time, she'd dismissed it as intuition, but now the dissonance had grown into a low-frequency hum she couldn't switch off.

She felt too much. Heard too much. The city was loud even when silent.

I have to find a way to block it, she told herself. *Before it blocks me.*

The streets slowly smoothed beneath their feet. Cracked stones gave way to more orderly paving. The leaning buildings grew straighter. Emberhold's cramped-but-cleaner heart surrounded them.

Chad had cooled enough to match their pace by then, though his jaw was still tight. "Maybe he didn't sabotage us," he muttered grudgingly. "Not directly." He glanced sideways, daring them to contradict him.

Evan didn't.

"Still don't trust him," Chad added.

"Neither do we," she said, calm and quiet. Rick squeezed her hand once in wordless agreement.

The embassy came into view—drab facade, familiar windows. A place that had once felt like a prison now looked like shelter. They climbed the short steps and slipped into the warm common room. Candlelight flickered against battered stone walls.

Mari bustled in almost immediately, apron dusted with flour, cheeks pink from the stove. "Welcome back, dears! I've just set the kettle on. Come, come."

As they settled around the long table, Korvan stood up with a scowl and stalked off down the hall. Evan's throat tightened as she watched him go. *At least he didn't slam the door this time,* she thought, but the defense was half-hearted at best.

Mari returned with a tray—teapot, chipped mugs, and a small plate of shortbread. Her humming didn't stop until she poured for all three.

Chad accepted his tea with a grunt that could have meant anything. He stared into the mug like it might offer answers. After a long pause, he said too casually, "Funny thing. Sorendir served the same cookies."

Mari brightened. "Oh! I'm not surprised. I've known Gharn for years. Such a nice man. It's a shame more people don't give him a chance. Makes him a bit cranky, poor thing." She winked. "Anyway, I gave him the recipe ages ago. I'm so glad he still uses it."

Evan studied her face. The cheer. The pride. Nothing underneath—

Just Mari.

When the woman bustled off again, humming under her breath, Chad let out a slow sigh. "Fine," he muttered. "Maybe she's not working with him."

Evan didn't say anything, and neither did Rick. Some victories weren't worth pushing.

They ate dinner quietly. Korvan didn't leave his room—not even for the smell of fresh cake drifting from the oven. Mari wrapped his portion anyway.

Later, in their shared room, Evan sat on the edge of the bed, slowly tugging off her boots. Rick leaned against the doorframe, arms crossed. "Head any better?" he asked.

She winced. "It's like... background static. Constant. Worse around people."

He crossed the room to crouch in front of her, resting his hands on her knees. "Maybe," he said, a smile flickering at his lips, "you need a mental mute button."

Despite herself, she laughed—low and breathy, but real. "If you get Chad to invent one," she said, brushing her fingers along his jaw, "I'll be your first customer."

Rick leaned into the touch, closing his eyes briefly. "We'll figure it out," he said quietly.

They got ready for bed in comfortable silence. When he climbed in beside her, she curled into him without needing to ask. His arm slid around her back, anchoring her. No speeches, no promises.

Just warmth. Contact. Stillness.

*

The morning dawned gray, as if to echo their low spirits. They rose early and parted at the door—Chad heading in one direction, Rick and Evan in another. Maps in hand, faces set, they tried again.

The market quarter was a blur of motion and noise. They checked taverns, shops, warehouses. Always the same. Polite faces. Quick refusals. Doors closed before they could knock. Each rejection tightened the knot in Evan's chest. The buzz behind her eyes flared and dimmed in strange patterns.

Rick felt it too. She could tell by the way his shoulders tensed, the way his eyes flicked from detail to detail, searching for some invisible pattern he could solve.

Just past midday, Chad rejoined them, looking like he'd walked through a dust storm and lost the argument. "Forget it," he said before they could ask. "The quarries won't even talk to me now. The tannery either. I think I'm banned from the whole labor quarter."

They found a bench tucked behind a shuttered bakery and collapsed onto it. Evan rubbed at the corner of her eye, staring at the creases on her map without really seeing them. She felt it again then. Not the rejection—but something sharper.

A shape on the periphery of her vision. Movement. A flicker of color near the alley mouth beside a nearby inn, where a man stood in fine merchant clothes, his insignia unfamiliar. And standing next to him—

Fenton.

The stranger murmured something. Fenton nodded. Then he looked toward Evan—and their eyes met, just for a heartbeat. He blanched, said something quick, turned, and vanished into the crowd.

"Rick," she said, voice low and steady.

He followed her gaze, but Fenton was already gone. Still, she knew this wasn't coincidence. It wasn't Sorendir, not entirely, nor Mari.

They were being boxed in, step by step, soft walls closing. And even now, she had the sense that someone else was watching.

Her hand found Rick's again.

She didn't let go.

The door of the embassy slammed open with a crack that echoed against the stone walls. Evan pushed through first, her anger a palpable force ahead of her.

Rick followed, a half-step behind Chad, the ache in his chest sharpening with every stride. He couldn't blame Evan for the fury—he felt it too, simmering low and tight. But unlike Evan, who wore it raw and unshielded, Rick shoved it down, sealing it away as he always did when everything started tilting out of his control.

Behind the battered desk, Fenton scrambled to his feet, his expression contorting into a brittle smile that didn't touch his eyes. "Is there—"

"Why?" Evan's voice cut through the room like a blade.

Fenton flinched. "I'm not sure I understand—"

"Why have you been working against us?" she pressed, stepping forward until only the desk separated them.

"I haven't—" Fenton tried, but his body betrayed him. His shoulders hunched inward. His gaze darted toward the door. He wouldn't meet her eyes—or Rick's when Rick moved to Evan's side, heat burning behind his own.

Rick opened his mouth to add pressure—and the door slammed again. Boots on stone.

They all turned.

Sergeant Jens entered, flanked by two guards. Their uniforms were crisp, their movements sharp, efficient. "Korvan?" Jens asked briskly.

Fenton, pale now, pointed down the hallway and handed Jens a key. "Last door on the right. He's been in his room all day."

The guards moved with swift certainty, disappearing down the corridor. Rick barely had time to trade a look with Evan before a cry split the silence. "Please! Just one more day! Someone was going to meet with me, I swear!"

Rick stiffened. Beside him, Evan reached blindly for his hand and clutched it tight. Moments later the guards reappeared, dragging Korvan between them. His body hung limp. His boots scraped uselessly across the floor. No blood, no bruises, but whatever fight he'd once had was gone. Utterly gone.

"Just one," Korvan whispered. "One more day." Then his gaze snapped to them. "This is *their* fault! Nobody will talk to Outlanders now, because of them." His words trailed off into a whimper. "Exile *them*."

Rick couldn't tear his eyes away. It was Korvan's surrender—his total, hollow collapse—that chilled Rick more than any struggle could have.

The guards hauled the miserable man outside without ceremony. Jens paused in the doorway, glancing back at them with something that might have been regret.

Chad said nothing. Evan stood frozen, still gripping Rick's hand so tightly it hurt.

"I'm sorry you had to see that," Jens said. His voice was quieter now. "It's not often. But the law is the law. We don't have room for the unemployable." He tossed the key back to Fenton, who fumbled the catch. It landed on the desktop with a quiet, final clink.

Rick swallowed hard.

"I hope," Jens added after a beat, "that the next time we meet, it'll be under better circumstances."

Evan's breathing had become fast and shallow. Chad stood rigid, fists clenched so hard the knuckles had turned white. Then Jens was gone, and the embassy was too quiet.

"Why didn't he come with us?" Chad growled, his face resembling a tragedy mask.

"Would it have made a difference?" Rick glared at him. "It's not like we really heard Sorendir out, is it?"

The fire in the hearth crackled uselessly against the cold pit growing in Rick's chest. From somewhere behind the kitchen wall, the scent of Mari's stew wafted out, rich and savory, a cruel mockery of what they'd just witnessed.

Mari stormed in a moment later, a rolling pin clutched like a weapon. She didn't spare them a glance. Her eyes were locked on Fenton. "Are they right?" she demanded.

Fenton stammered, backing up until the desk hit the backs of his legs. "I... I only—"

"Answer me!"

He crumpled under her glare. "I didn't know what else to do!" he blurted. "When Sorendir shows interest, you don't get in his way. He's mad. You know it. A human wi—"

Mari didn't let him finish. Her face darkened, and she lifted the rolling pin.

Fenton yelped and bolted for the door, shielding his head with his arms as she chased him into the street, her voice rising into furious threats Rick couldn't quite make out.

When Mari returned, rolling pin still in hand, her face softened the instant she looked at them. "Fenton's a coward," she said tightly. Her lips trembled, and for a moment Rick thought she might cry. "But even so... the law is the law."

Rick nodded stiffly. He already knew. They all did. No sponsorship meant exile—lost to the Shifts. A death sentence disguised as procedure.

Moments stretched long in the silence. Mari set a tray down on the table with mechanical care. Tea. Cups. A plate of bread that none of them touched. She hovered by Evan's side for a moment, then gently patted her shoulder. "You'll be all right, dears," she said, the heaviness in her voice belying the lightness of her words.

She disappeared back into the kitchen, leaving them alone with the fire, the tea, and the weight of what they'd seen.

Chad sank into the nearest chair. He leaned forward, elbows braced on his knees, staring at the steaming tea in his cup. "We don't have a choice, do we?" It wasn't a question.

Rick crossed to the hearth, the fire's heat barely registering through the numbness creeping over him. *Think.*

He could still hear Korvan's broken voice echoing in the hollows of the embassy... *Please. Just one more day.*

There was always a solution.

He flexed his hands, clasping them tightly behind his back to keep from fidgeting. The fire popped. A single ember floated up—and guttered out before it reached the chimney.

Slowly Rick drew a breath. Straightened. When he turned to face them, he forced himself to meet their eyes—first Evan's, then Chad's. "We're going back to Sorendir," he said, his voice steady.

Evan's lips compressed. Her answering nod was nearly imperceptible, but she didn't look away.

Chad just sighed. A hollow, tired sound.

Rick held their gazes a heartbeat longer. Forced himself to believe it was still a choice.

Even if it wasn't.

IV
Allies

"I really wish you'd wait until morning, dears."

Mari's voice drifted from the hall, equal parts concern and resignation. Rick cinched the picnic pack tighter, the strap rough against his palm. It didn't weigh much, but leaving it behind would have felt like severing the last real thread connecting them to who they were. He brushed Evan's cheek with his fingers. She smiled—small, knowing—and some of the tightness binding his chest loosened.

She understood.

"Are you sure?" Chad asked from behind Mari, the strap of his CamelBak slung over his shoulder. The tension in his expression betrayed his worry. Or guilt.

"It doesn't matter," Rick said, hefting the pack higher. "Fenton didn't exactly leave us a choice."

Chad's expression dimmed further.

Mari fretted a step closer. "But must you leave tonight? The upper city's not always friendly after dark."

Rick shook his head, already moving toward the door. "We'll be fine. We know the way."

The heavy embassy door swung shut behind them with a hollow thud, cutting off Mari's protests. Night pressed close, the lamps lining the street burning low—pale islands of light barely holding back the dark. Rick turned right, leading the way uphill. *Onward and upward.*

The stone walls of the ravine loomed higher in the gloom, their rough faces swallowing the sparse light. Emberhold's terraces climbed with them, jutting unevenly into the sky like broken steps. The city, lively by day, now seemed half-abandoned. Shadows clung to sagging doorways and crooked alleys.

Rick kept his mind on the path ahead. Up the ravine, follow the main street, crooked stair on the left. Easy. Logical.

Except it wasn't.

Familiar landmarks dissolved into the dark. Where he expected an open square, a dead end lurked. Where there should have been shops, shuttered windows stared out like sightless eyes.

He stopped at a junction, frowning. A battered street sign swung lazily in the faint breeze. He could read it—still marveling, distantly, that he could—but the name meant nothing. One branch of the street twisted sharply uphill, narrow and close. The other sloped downward into deeper shadow.

Rick's fingers found the key chain in his pocket, the cool, worn metal tracing familiar shapes against his fingertips.

To the left, a stubborn potted plant hung from a crumbling windowsill, a lone splash of green in a world of decay. To the right, a faint metallic scrape. A muttered curse, swallowed almost before it reached them.

The back of Rick's neck prickled.

Left, then.

He led them upward, boot soles rasping against rough stone. The street narrowed further, the walls pressing closer. Every so often, a door or window broke the gloom—more often barred than open. The occasional lantern dripped yellow light that only made the shadows seem deeper.

Rick glanced back. Chad followed a step behind, his usual easy slouch gone stiff. One hand hovered near the strap of his CamelBak, like he was ready to swing it if needed. Evan stayed close to Rick, her hand brushing his now and again, small and steady against the rising tension. They climbed in silence, the only sounds their breathing and the occasional distant clatter from Miner's End above. The air grew colder the higher they went, but not crisp. Heavy. Stale.

Fifteen minutes later, the alley ended against a sheer cliff wall. A door stood embedded there, framed by cracked stone planters gone wild with dead vines. It looked absurdly domestic—like a front porch dropped into the middle of a graveyard.

"Yet another picture-postcard moment," Chad said. His voice was light, but Rick caught the strain beneath it. The way Chad's gaze flicked restlessly from shadow to shadow, never settling.

Rick felt a flash of gratitude—and irritation. Humor didn't fix anything. But sometimes it helped hold things together.

Still, they were at a dead end, so he knew they'd all have to turn back the way they had come. "If you've got a better idea," Rick said, trying for lightness but landing closer to sharpness, "I'm all ears."

"Hey, you're the brains of this outfit," Chad said, shrugging. "I'm just the comic relief. Remember?"

Rick glanced at him, but in the half-light, Chad's face gave nothing away. It was always hard to tell with Chad—where the jokes ended and the armor began.

The alleyways twisted tighter. Rick's gut itched with the certainty they weren't alone. Blurred figures slipped past in the corners of his vision—hunched shoulders, cloaks, hats pulled low. Faces he couldn't quite catch. Could they be seeing the same figure twice? Three times?

Footsteps echoed behind them. Always faint and stopping the moment Rick did, but slightly out of sync. The cliffs and winding streets warped the sound, playing tricks with distance—but his instincts said otherwise. He halted under a crooked lamp, pretending to study another leaning sign.

Evan edged closer, warmth brushing against his side. Not fearful. Not yet. But ready.

"Maybe we should have waited for morning," Rick muttered, mostly to himself.

Evan heard. Her arm slid around his waist, squeezing briefly. "We're fine," she said, but her quick glances toward every shadow said otherwise. Rick curled his arm around her shoulders automatically. She rose slightly on her toes, her breath brushing his ear. "We're being followed," she whispered.

His heartbeat leaped painfully.

Above them, just across the ravine, Sorendir's tower clawed at the stars. It should have been reassuring—a fixed point. A goal. Instead, the crooked spires and flickering cold light from a high window felt more like a warning.

Close. Too close to turn back. Rick squared his shoulders. There was always a way forward. Always a solution.

He just had to find it before the shadows found him first.

Chad's eyes flicked toward the alleys Evan had glanced at, nerves prickling. *Mari was right.* He wasn't the paranoid type—usually. But something about this place in the dark crawled under his skin, set his pulse hammering. A flicker of shadow near an angled doorway caught his attention. He slowed, fingers brushing the worn shape of his multi-tool through the pocket of his jeans. Cold steel. Familiar weight. A small, stupid comfort in a world where comfort felt scarce.

He glanced at Rick, at the way his brother's shoulders hunched, drawn tight. Rick never hunched. He was a wall—solid, stubborn, certain. Chad had spent most of his life leaning against that certainty, even when he'd pretended otherwise. Seeing Rick like this—folding in on himself—made the darkness around them feel even deeper.

The street ahead narrowed, buildings slanting inward. No good escape. No open space. Chad's instincts screamed at him to say something, to break the tension before it broke them, but Rick already looked tight enough to snap. And Evan—Evan had that look again. That quiet, too-knowing calm that made Chad feel like she already knew how this would end.

He forced a grin anyway, an armor he barely believed in. "Almost there," he muttered, too low for either of them to call him on the lie. "Piece of cake."

They rounded a corner.

And walked straight into silence. No lanterns. No windows. No stray cats scuffling through refuse. Just a narrow corridor of deepening shadows pressing in from both sides, like jaws ready to close.

Chad's hand curled tighter around the multi-tool.

Evan stopped dead. "Wait."

A scrape of boot leather against stone, and the first figure stepped out of the darkness, club swinging idly from one hand. Another followed.

And another. The stink of unwashed bodies hit Chad like a fist—sweat, fear, something sharp and metallic riding underneath. They moved with slow, deliberate certainty. Predators who knew their prey was cornered.

The leader was easy to spot: half a head taller than the others, shoulders as broad as a doorway, gut straining the frayed hem of his shirt. His voice, when he spoke, was soft and almost singsong. "Look at this. Three little pigeons. You carrying any eggs for us, pigeons? Or do we need to pluck you first?"

Laughter barked out, harsh and hollow. Four men blocked the path ahead. More chuckles answered from behind, unseen but far too close.

Chad fought the instinct to turn and look. *Don't show fear. Don't give them an excuse.*

A brittle voice rasped from behind, "Yeah, that's right. Best make it easy on yourselves."

Slowly, carefully, Chad slid the knife open inside his pocket. His fingers found the familiar coldness of the blade. He breathed shallowly through his nose. Tried to focus.

Evan stepped forward, chin tilting up. "We're Outlanders," she said, calm and sharp at once. "We haven't been here long enough to have anything worth stealing."

The leader's eyes gleamed. "You have your clothes, don't you?"

Chad's teeth clamped together. His grip tightened until his knuckles ached.

The thug to the leader's left, missing most of his teeth, leered at Evan. "Pretty little thing, ain't she? Be prettier without clothes, I'm thinkin'."

The others laughed, nodding, their eyes stripping her with a lazy malice.

Rick straightened.

Not a gradual thing—no shifting weight or warning. One moment slouched, the next standing tall, towering over the gang leader. Chad blinked. For a second, Rick didn't look like the brother he knew.

"We have an appointment with Sorendir," Rick said, voice carrying a calm authority Chad had only heard once or twice before. "You want to risk getting on his bad side?"

For half a breath, the world seemed to pause.

Two of the thugs shifted. Lowered their weapons slightly. Uneasy murmurs stirred behind them.

Chad dared a breath. *Brilliant. Absolute genius, bro.*

But the leader's eyes narrowed. His smile thinned. "You lie, pigeon. That mad wizard don't see nobody, never."

"Yeah," croaked Toothless. "Ain't nobody ever seen him. Only that runt he sends out. I bet he ain't even real."

Chad tensed, the moment slipping away like sand through his fingers.

Then—movement.

A flutter of cloth from above.

A cloaked figure dropped from a ledge and landed soundlessly beside a leaning building. Chad jerked back instinctively. The figure didn't even glance at them. Just stepped forward—slow, unhurried—to stand between Rick and the gang. Shorter than the leader by a head. Average build. Unremarkable, if Chad hadn't noticed how the thugs flinched from the stillness radiating off him like heat.

The leader tried to bluster. "What are you—"

Steel flashed. The leader stumbled, hands clamping to his throat. Blood sprayed between his fingers as he dropped, twitching.

It happened so fast the air barely had time to stir.

The figure moved again—two steps, two more bodies folding soundlessly to the ground.

Chad staggered back, heart slamming against his ribs. Panic exploded around them—boots scuffing on stone, thugs shouting. The cloak flared—there, then gone—as the stranger blurred past him. No—behind him. Silent as a thought.

A gasp from Evan snapped Chad's gaze forward. One of the thugs, undistracted, rushed Rick and Evan with a cudgel raised high.

Chad didn't think. His hand shot from his pocket.

The knife found flesh with sickening ease, sliding deep into the man's side. Time buckled, and he felt the give of muscle, the sudden hot slickness, the man's breathless grunt.

The cudgel clattered to the ground. The man staggered, clutching his waist, trying to flee—but only made it two stumbling steps before a sword thrust out from his back. He crumpled into a heap.

The last thug tried to bolt—but the stranger was already there. Another blur. Another body falling bonelessly to the dirt.

Silence crushed down. For a long moment, the only sounds were the ragged pull of Chad's breathing and the distant drip of something wet hitting stone.

The stranger knelt, cleaning his swords on the dead leader's shirt without urgency. "You will want to clean yours too," he said, glancing over his shoulder. His voice was mild. Almost amused.

Chad looked down at the knife in his hand. Slick with blood. Real blood. Not a movie prop. Not a nightmare. His stomach twisted. His fingers went numb. *I killed him.* The thought seemed surreal.

Except he hadn't—not really. It was the stranger who had finished him. Still, it didn't feel any less like murder.

Clumsily he wiped the blade on his jeans, fumbled it closed, shoved it deep into his pocket like he could bury it along with everything else. He bent over, hands on his knees, sucking in shallow breaths. The sting at the corners of his eyes surprised him.

Were the tears for the man he'd stabbed? Or for the part of himself he'd just lost?

He straightened slowly. His heart still thundered, but he locked his face down tight.

Rick had stepped in front of Evan without hesitation, shielding her with his body. His stance was pure instinct—protective, solid. A barrier between her and everything that had just happened. "Who are you?" he demanded of the man, voice hard.

The stranger slid his swords into twin sheaths hidden under his cloak. "Your savior, it would seem," he said, without so much as a heavy breath.

Chad stared. The man looked—ordinary. Brown hair. Forgettable face. Average height and build. He could have passed unnoticed anywhere, except for the way he moved. That easy stillness, that sense of a coil half-unwound.

Dangerous.

"That's awfully convenient," Rick said, voice sharpening.

"For you, yes," the man said mildly. "Not so convenient for them."

He glanced at the bodies without remorse. "Matthias," he added after a beat, as if it was an afterthought.

Rick nodded curtly. "Thank you, Matthias. Goodbye." He turned away without waiting for a reply.

"Rick!" Evan's voice snapped after him, sharp with exasperation.

If Matthias took offense, he didn't show it. The barest twitch of a smile tugged at the corner of his mouth.

Chad hesitated only a second before scrambling to catch up. No way was he getting left behind with the... mess.

They'd barely gone twenty paces before Matthias called after them. "Caution is wise," he said. "But the dark is dangerous. Some shadows have teeth."

Rick stopped. Chad saw the tiny tremor that ran through his brother's hand before he clenched it into a fist.

"Are you really going to the wizard's tower?" Matthias asked, voice carrying easily through the dark.

"Yes," Evan said quietly.

Matthias nodded, as if that confirmed something he'd already guessed. "Then you will want someone who knows which shadows to avoid. There will be others. Bandits are drawn to newcomers like flies to meat."

Chad's stomach twisted. Dangerous might be exactly what they needed right now.

Rick hesitated—longer this time. "You're offering to escort us?" he asked finally. "Why? What's in it for you?"

Matthias shrugged—casual, almost careless. The first human gesture Chad had seen from him. "Let us say I have little use for thieves." He said it lightly, almost offhand, but Chad followed his gaze to the bodies cooling on the stones.

He swallowed hard and wondered if this was what survival was going to look like now. As Matthias took the lead, he fell into step behind Rick and Evan, the weight of the bloodied knife pressing against his thigh like a brand.

And didn't look back.

Matthias knew his way around—that much Evan had to admit. The ease with which he guided them toward Miner's End impressed her, though she grew increasingly certain he wasn't choosing the fastest route. Instead he wove a cautious path, steering them through winding side streets, skirting the tightest alleys, avoiding pools of shadow with an instinct that felt less like wariness and more like calculation.

Something about him gnawed at her.

Nothing obvious. If anything, it was how completely unremarkable he appeared. Plain face, free of scars. Hair mousy brown, cut short, and forgettable. Average height. Average build. Eyes a muddy brown. The kind of man she would forget the moment she turned away.

And yet...

The tickle at the back of her mind refused to fade. She was sure she had seen him before. At the market, maybe? Or in passing? A hundred blurred faces filed through her memory without offering answers. Still, something didn't fit.

Until he moved.

There was no wasted motion—no unnecessary step, no casual glance. Every shift of weight was measured, every stride precise. Not in a conscious, trained-soldier way. Something colder. More instinctive.

Predator, her mind supplied before she could stop it.

Evan drifted a little closer to Rick, feeling his unease pressing out ward, subtle but unmissable. He didn't speak, but she caught the way his hand brushed against her back now and then—comforting, steady, protective.

Matthias's armor didn't creak. That struck her next. She remembered the groan of leather when Rick had taken her riding—the way it flexed and shifted with every movement. But Matthias moved in silence. His armor flexed soundlessly—oiled, maybe, or made from some material better cared for than anything she'd seen since arriving here. A faint, sharp smell clung to him—treated hide and something faintly metallic beneath the stink of Miner's End.

"You seem... well prepared," Rick said eventually, his voice neutral. Almost too neutral.

Matthias glanced back, the corners of his mouth twitching into something that might have been a smile. Or not. "Experience teaches quickly. Mistakes do not offer second chances."

The words answered nothing. Evan felt the half-truth of it settle between them like a stone.

Chad—walking so close he nearly clipped Matthias's heels—grinned. If he caught the evasion, he gave no sign. But his hand twitched restlessly toward his pocket, again and again, like he couldn't forget the weight of the knife resting there.

Evan watched him, a knot forming low in her chest. She caught it—the flicker of something raw and vivid behind Chad's easy expression. It wasn't guilt, exactly. Or shame. It was something rougher. Harder to name. *Wait...*

She realized that had been a flash of true empathy.

"So," Chad said brightly, breaking the moment, "what brings you to Emberhold? Doesn't seem like a place people come to for the scenery."

Matthias gave a soft, unremarkable chuckle. "Let us say the people are more interesting than the view."

Does he ever actually smile? Evan wondered.

Chad laughed as if it were the best joke he'd heard all day.

They crested the lip of the ravine.

The air changed. The faint breeze that had funneled through the valley vanished, replaced by the thick weight of stagnant smells—manure, damp wood, smoke, and something sour that had no easy name. The light dimmed as the larger of the two moons set. The light still provided by the smaller moon felt as if it had decided Miner's End wasn't worth the effort. Buildings sagged inward, listing like tired sentinels. Roofs were patched with tarpaulins and scavenged boards. Walls were cracked and mottled with mildew.

Evan wrinkled her nose but said nothing.

"Good thing you came along when you did," Chad said, still grinning.

Matthias tilted his head slightly. "It is."

Rick's jaw twitched—a tight, almost imperceptible movement. "How did you happen to be nearby just then?" he asked, voice pitched just a shade too casual.

Matthias stopped and turned. Even though he stood a full head shorter, the way he looked at Rick shrank the difference between them.

Not aggressive. Just... steady.

"I was returning to my inn," Matthias said. "Saw movement. Suspicious behavior. I chose to observe and wait." Simple. Plausible. Polished.

Evan watched Rick's posture shift and felt his skepticism without needing to see his face. "From a rooftop?" Rick asked, still too casual.

Matthias shrugged with a certain inevitability. "Can you think of a better vantage point?" He turned without waiting for an answer and slipped down a side street with steps so light they barely stirred the dust. Chad followed without hesitation, drawn forward like a moth tracking the faint heat of a flame it couldn't see.

Evan watched him go. It wasn't admiration, not exactly, on Chad's face, nor even hero worship. It was something more dangerous—something nameless.

Rick caught her gaze as they moved after them, and his eyebrows lifted, a silent *What can you do?* It almost made her smile.

Almost.

The slums swallowed them whole, and the shadows grew teeth.

By night, the tower looked even less plausible.

Rick stopped short, frowning, when it came into view. It loomed at the cliff's edge, crooked and jagged, jutting outward as if daring gravity to object. The stone, dark and uneven, seemed to drink up the remaining moon's dim light. Cracks veined its surface like brittle ice, and the walls bowed subtly—too subtly—giving the impression of instability without surrendering to it. No symmetry. No logical axis. As if it had grown out of the earth in open defiance of reason itself.

Around the tower, the slums thinned to nothing. The surrounding ruins—half-collapsed workshops, blackened timber frames—gave way to an uneven wasteland strewn with debris, shattered tools, and the skeletal remains of trees long dead. Rick had noticed it before. But now in the moonlight, they clawed upward like twisted hands, and the air seemed heavier—carrying a faintly unpleasant tang he couldn't place.

He felt Evan press lightly against his arm.

Chad, at least, managed a lopsided grin. "Guess wizards aren't good for property values." Rick's lips twitched despite his mood.

Ahead, Matthias led them along a rough, half-forgotten path toward the gate, its pristine condition standing out against the surrounding decrepitude in unmistakable warning. Rick's gaze climbed higher, toward the tower's upper windows: narrow slits, black and unblinking.

No faces.

No glints of reflection.

Which somehow made it worse.

The courtyard beyond formed a rough semicircle, hemmed against the cliff. In the silver light, Rick noticed something he had missed before. The cobblestones weren't random. They spiraled outward from the tower's base—an elegant curve, precise in its proportions. Fibonacci again. Order, buried inside the chaos. And somehow that small touch of logic made his skin crawl even more.

The tower door loomed ahead—massive, weathered wood banded with iron, a twisted brass knocker dangling at its center. Rick hesitated, and Evan's hand slipped into his without a word. Chad gave a small shrug, eyebrows lifted in a silent *It's why we came,* while Matthias stood silently by, unreadable.

Rick drew a slow breath. Squared his shoulders. Stepping forward, he grasped the knocker. The ring fell against the wood with a heavy, jarring sound that echoed too long in the thick night air, and almost at once the door swung inward.

Golden light spilled out across the cracked stones, warm and strangely inviting. A small figure stood in the doorway—gnarled hand still clutched around the handle, intent green eyes flicking over them all. Rick caught a slight pause as the gnome's gaze touched Matthias.

"About time," Gharn grumbled. "Don't just stand there letting the cold in."

Rick hesitated half a heartbeat longer, then stepped inside.

The space beyond was smaller than he remembered. The ceiling pressed low, and he instinctively ducked before realizing that wasn't needed. Thick curtains draped the doorways to other rooms, muffling faint bubbling sounds. A colorful rug wove tangled geometric shapes across the floor. Darkly stained timbers were carved with similar designs —as if they tied the room's geometry together in the same way that they supported the walls.

Gharn shut the door behind them with a solid thunk.

Silence settled—heavy, expectant.

Movement caught Rick's eye—at the curve of the staircase winding upward. Sorendir descended slowly, hand trailing the rail without truly leaning on it. His black robe, stitched with faded sigils, whispered faintly with every step. His silver-white beard was neatly trimmed. His eyes—sharp, golden. Unsettling.

They found Rick first and did not look away.

Rick felt it in his bones—that sense he sometimes got the moment before a solution revealed itself. A vibrating stillness, an anticipation of answers. Sorendir's gaze held that same quality, like he was studying a problem to be solved.

A variable to be defined.

The old man smiled, slow and deliberate. "Welcome back," he said, voice warm as a hearth fire—and somehow just as dangerous.

Rick swallowed against the dryness rising in his throat. *Practicalities,* he reminded himself. *Focus on what matters.* "Your offer still stands, we hope," he said carefully.

Sorendir's gaze swept over them all—Evan, Chad, and finally, Matthias. Where it paused. The corners of his mouth twitched. "Ah," Sorendir said, almost to himself. "The fourth. What an expected surprise."

Rick stiffened. He remembered Sorendir's words from their first meeting: *I expected...* Even then, the old man had known it wasn't Korvan. But how? Rick pressed his fingers together in a calculating rhythm and forced them still.

Gharn, oblivious—or pretending to be—bustled off through one of the curtained archways, muttering about tea.

Sorendir stepped closer, folding his hands behind his back. His gaze returned to Rick, open and unblinking. "You must have questions," he said.

Rick's mind spun, parsing probabilities. Fenton's sabotage. Matthias's improbable rescue. Their arrival here, desperate and out of options. Too neat. Too many variables collapsing into a straight line.

But they needed what Sorendir offered. Options mattered more than certainties.

"Some," Rick said, voice neutral. "But they'll wait."

Sorendir's smile deepened—not triumphant. Satisfied. "Wise," he said. "Come. You must be tired after your long day." He turned toward the staircase.

Rick caught a flicker from Matthias—a tightening of the jaw, the barest narrowing of the eyes. Gone in an instant, but Rick felt the ripple it left behind. He said nothing.

They followed Sorendir upward, the tower's architecture bending subtly with each turn—as if the angles of the world shifted the higher they climbed. Rick's hand slid along the polished rail. Underneath the wood, the stone vibrated faintly. Not noise. Not motion.

A breath.

The tower felt alive.

He pushed the thought aside. Practicalities first. But the question gnawed at him all the same: Why did Sorendir need them?

And what had they already agreed to simply by crossing that threshold?

V
Magic

The stairs spiraled upward with a lean that made Rick's balance shift just enough to notice. Each step gave a faint groan under their boots, the sound muted by age and use.

Sorendir climbed steadily ahead, his robe brushing the stone like a whisper. Rick followed close, Evan and Chad a few steps behind. Matthias was a shadow at the rear, quiet and a little too still. The air thickened as they climbed, warming slightly, scented with something he couldn't quite place—burnt oil, maybe. Or chalk dust. Leather and old paper.

Rick's fingers skimmed the stone wall as they ascended, letting the cool surface glide beneath his touch. It was pitted and irregular, but beneath the wear, he could still feel the precision. Fractal geometry etched into the very bones of the place—subtle but unmistakable. Not decorative. Designed.

He traced a loop absently, thumb mapping a perfect arc. But the pattern didn't quiet the churn in his stomach.

This wasn't just about magic. Sorendir had shown too much interest—had studied them too closely. All of them. Even Chad and Evan, if subtle comments he'd made on their prior visit were to be believed.

And then there was Matthias, who still hadn't explained how he'd known to find them. The man had shown up too conveniently. Rick's brow furrowed. Korvan hadn't made the cut, but Matthias had? Why?

Rick slowed, falling into step just behind the wizard. "Mind telling me," he said, voice low, just for Sorendir, "why you're so interested in us? We both know I'm the only one with an aptitude for what you practice."

Sorendir chuckled, light and dry. "Astute." The word landed too easily. Preloaded praise. Sleight of tongue, if not hand.

They emerged into the same circular chamber as before, pale moonlight spilling through the tall slits of window to paint shifting stripes across the stone. The air was still, heavy with echoes. But no dust. Artifacts ringed the room—glass orbs, a tangle of copper wire that looked like a frozen explosion, a half-melted astrolabe. Shapes meant to be deciphered. Or to distract.

Rick's eyes caught on a figure carved into the back of one chair—three overlapping circles, a spiral nested within their intersection, connected to each. He didn't know what it meant, but something in it itched within his mind.

Sorendir crossed to the center of the room and turned to face them. His robe whispered over the stone as he moved. "You have questions," he said. "Perhaps you would prefer to hear the offer first."

Rick didn't answer. Arms folded. *Let him talk.*

"Would you like to go home?" Sorendir asked, and the words hit like a lightning strike.

"We don't have a home anymore," Chad muttered, dropping into a chair. It creaked under him.

Rick's gaze flicked around the room. The same six chairs. One for each of them now that Matthias was there. A prickle climbed his spine. It was all too neat.

"I meant your real home," Sorendir said, smiling faintly. "Your universe."

Chad straightened. "Earth?"

Evan's hand drifted to the pendant at her neck, fingers brushing it once before falling away.

Rick hesitated. He wanted it—God, he wanted it—but...

"The Shifts," he said carefully. "They can't be controlled. That's why people avoid them."

"Normally," Sorendir agreed. He turned to a map stretched across one table—aged parchment, parts of it seemingly obscured by clouds, others painted in delicate, impossible lines. His finger traced a curve along its edge, hovering near one of the mystery spaces. "But there is—or *was*—a way."

He turned again. "The Heart of Necsis," he said. "An artifact forged during the Triune Era, when the Three Powers—Magic, Mind, and Machine—still worked in concert."

Rick narrowed his eyes. "You're saying it can control the Shifts."

"Precisely. It is a fusion of all three. A bridge between realities." Sorendir's tone softened, almost coaxing. "With it, you could find the path home."

Behind him, Matthias shifted slightly. Rick glanced back—and caught it. Just a small motion. Not nerves, not surprise.

Recognition.

"And if someone controlled it," Matthias said, voice quiet, each word carefully shaped, "they would control far more than a path."

Sorendir's gaze sharpened. The scholar vanished—for a blink—and something colder stood in his place. "Indeed," he said softly. "Which is why it was hidden."

Rick's pulse jumped.

Sorendir's eyes lingered on Matthias a beat too long before he turned back to the map. "There is a complication, however," he said.

"Of course there is," Rick muttered.

"The Heart has been lost. For three centuries. Together with the Thought Masters and their sanctum... Haven."

Rick cocked his head. "The who?"

"An order of psychics. They championed Mind just as the Engineers had Machine."

"And Haven?" Evan's voice was quiet. Careful.

A faint smile tugged at Sorendir's mouth, though his eyes gave nothing away. "They kept its location secret, even from their own allies. Some whispered another name for it—the Forbidden Spire." He let the words hang a moment, then flicked his hand as if brushing them aside.

Chad exhaled sharply. "So you want us to locate something no one's found in three hundred years?"

"It was never meant to be found," Sorendir said. "Not until the right time."

Rick frowned. "And you think this is the right time."

"I know it is," Sorendir said. As he gestured toward the window, his voice dipped, and Rick felt the words settle like dust in a tomb. "The

Silent Sister erupted five days ago. For the first time since the prophecy was written."

Evan stiffened beside him.

"That," Sorendir said, "was also the day you arrived."

The silence that followed felt brittle. Taut. But Rick's mind was already spinning—threading variables: The eruption. The arrival. Sorendir waiting. None of it random.

"There's more," Evan said, her voice too steady. "Isn't there?"

Sorendir inclined his head toward her. "Yes. A prophecy. Written when the Heart was first forged. It speaks of four Outlanders."

Rick exhaled slowly. "Of course there's a prophecy." But that wasn't what his mind fixated on. *Four.* His eyes moved to Matthias.

Still as a statue, and just as unreadable.

"You think—" Chad began.

"I know," Sorendir said. "It is no accident you were brought here."

"No," Rick said. "Matthias isn't an Outlander."

"Isn't he?" Sorendir asked. His tone remained mild, but his gaze was flint as it tightened on Matthias. "Tell them."

Rick watched them both closely.

The other man paused for a moment. "I am not…" Matthias said at last, "originally from Necsis." That was all. No elaboration. No expression. Just those words.

"How did you know that?" Chad asked Sorendir, his tone suspicious. "Have you two—"

Sorendir's expression was bland as he interrupted. "It is a wizard's prerogative to know things." His eyes bored holes into Chad. "No, I have never met the man before this night. But his skills are required, and that is enough."

Matthias's expression turned even more calculating.

A chill licked down Rick's spine. "So we're the Chosen Ones now? Magic, prophecies, lost artifacts—and we're just supposed to go along with this?" He settled into the chair next to Chad. The wood felt worn beneath the varnish. "It's too much."

Evan touched his shoulder. Her fingers were warm. "And Southwatch?" she asked, nodding toward the map. "That's where your hand lingered."

“The Heart was last used there,” Sorendir said. “I believe the clues to its location still remain. If you choose to seek it, that is where your path must begin.”

Rick clenched his jaw. It was too clean. Too pat. And yet...

“You can stay here,” Sorendir said. “Adapt. Or you can seek the Heart. Forge your own fate.”

Rick heard the words for what they were: a performance. Framed like choice, but not really. He shook his head. “So this is the part where we pretend we have a choice.”

He looked at Evan. Her smile was small but resolute. Then Chad—who just shrugged. Then Matthias, who had reverted to unreadable silence.

Rick turned back to Sorendir. “We’ll go to Southwatch.” But in his mind, the equations were already assembling. This was a trap. Or a test.

And either way, the only way out was through.

Sorendir kept talking—names, places, details—but Rick heard little of it. His mind was already running numbers, searching for a pattern. For a way out.

The door closed behind them with a soft click.

Evan leaned against it for a moment, letting the tower’s hush settle around her. The scent drifting around her was a mix of old stone, beeswax, and something like juniper. Faint warmth clung to the air like memory, not enough to chase the chill in her skin.

Across the small room, Rick sat on the edge of the bed—shoulders slightly hunched, hands steepled, thumbs resting just beneath his nose, as if solving something only he could see. Moonlight slanted through the narrow window above, silvering the chamber and stretching his shadow long across the floor.

Neither spoke.

Evan pushed away from the door and crossed to him. The quiet between them wasn’t strained, but it wasn’t easy either. Not tonight. She sat down beside him, close enough that their knees and shoulders brushed, and stared at the uneven pattern in the stone floor where their shadows merged.

"You don't trust him," she said.

Rick exhaled through his nose. "I don't trust what he's not telling us." His voice was low, calm, but there was an edge underneath. Not anger. Something sharper. Wary calculation.

She nodded slowly. *Fair. But still...* "The idea of going home," she murmured, fingers brushing the fold of her shawl, "it's hard not to want that."

Rick's silence deepened.

"You think he's lying?" she asked.

"Not exactly." He leaned back on his hands, gaze lifting to the dark crossbeams overhead. "Just that he's being... selective with his words. He's setting the board. We're the pieces."

Evan watched him. The way his jaw tightened when he spoke. He wasn't wrong. But it wasn't just the game that bothered him. "And the Thought Masters?" she asked.

He didn't answer right away. His eyes stayed fixed on the ceiling. "They were the last to know where the Heart was." He turned his head and looked at her. "But that's not why you're asking."

Her breath caught—not from surprise but from being seen so clearly. She let it out slowly, her fingers tracing the pendant's circle at her throat. The metal felt warmer than it should have. She didn't know if the sensation was real or in her mind. "Maybe they didn't vanish," she said. "Maybe they hid."

Rick tilted his head toward her. "In that Haven place he mentioned."

"Or what's left of it," she said. "Didn't Sorendir say it's now called the Forbidden Spire? That name alone..." She shivered—not theatrically. The name had weight. Like something in a dream that clung too long after waking.

Rick's mouth twitched, but the expression faded before it could become a smile. "Nothing about this place is welcoming."

No argument there. She let the quiet stretch again. Then, softer, "What if this is happening because of me?"

His brow furrowed. "What do you mean?"

"My intuition." She flexed her hands in her lap, but they didn't stop trembling. "The things I've sensed lately ... they're stronger. Changing. I don't know what that means."

Rick sat up straighter. He reached out and gently took her hands in his. "Maybe," he said. "But if you are part of whatever this is—we're in it together." The words were quiet. Measured. But solid. No embellishment. No qualifiers.

Something eased inside her chest. A knot she hadn't realized was there began to loosen. She leaned against him, tucking herself beneath his arm, feeling the steady beat of his heart through his shirt. His breath was warm against her temple.

"So," she said eventually, voice muffled against his sleeve, "we find Southwatch. Look for clues."

Rick's nod was slow. Deliberate. "Then let them lead us to wherever Haven is hiding in Luthenholme."

"Find the Heart. Go home." She tipped her head back just enough to look at him. "No pressure."

His mouth twitched again. This time the smile stayed, small but real. "A walk in the park," he said.

"Sure," she snorted softly. "Because everything so far has been so easy."

Rick's arm tightened around her shoulders. "One step at a time, Evan. We'll figure it out."

She closed her eyes. Let herself believe him.

Just for tonight.

Outside the tower, the wind stirred the trees. It carried the scent of ash now, faint but unmistakable. Evan felt it without rising, without looking.

The world was already changing.

The wagon creaked as Chad dropped another crate into place, careful not to catch a splinter. Dust curled up around his boots, golden in the morning light slanting across the stable yard. Sweat was already sticking to his back despite the hour. Across the yard, Matthias carried a sack slung over one shoulder like it weighed nothing. Didn't even grunt. Chad wiped his palms on his jeans and looked over the growing pile. Crates of dried goods. Coils of rope. Bundled herbs. A bucket of nails. Packs of grain. Spare tack.

Too much for two people.

Exactly right for six.

Near the gate, six lean not-quite-horses stood loosely tethered. Hooves chipped at the stones, and long, twitchy ears flicked at flies. Chad still hadn't gotten used to them—their creepy smoothness, the way they moved like cats with hooves. But they were clearly built for speed.

As Matthias approached, they danced toward the wall—something they'd done all morning. Chad wondered if the man didn't still have some blood on him from the night before.

He squinted toward the tower. Rick was still inside. Still with Sorendir. Still learning.

He turned back to the wagon, grabbed another crate, and heaved it into place with more force than necessary.

A shadow passed beside him. "You are good at this," Matthias said, looping a rope along the wagon's side. His voice was calm, neutral—not a trace of sarcasm.

"Yeah, well." Chad flexed his fingers, already sore. "Somebody's gotta lift the heavy stuff while the wizard nerds solve the universe."

Matthias didn't respond at first. He finished knotting the rope, tested it once, then straightened. "Brains without hands do not get far," he said. "It is builders who shape what endures."

Chad blinked at him. He'd expected a joke. A shrug. Not... a fortune cookie. Matthias turned away without waiting for a reply. Chad stared after him a second longer, then lifted another crate. "And what about you?" he asked. "What exactly do you do?"

Matthias paused with one foot on the wagon bed. "Whatever is necessary." That should have sounded like a deflection. And maybe it was. But it also sounded true.

Chad watched him hop up and start securing the last of the crates. Matthias was fast. Efficient. Quiet. A flicker of... something itched in the back of Chad's mind—but he pushed it down. He stacked the final bundle into place, then leaned against the wagon, arms crossed. Across the yard, the bizarre horses shifted restlessly, snorting softly. But Chad's eyes drifted back to the tower.

"Wonder what they're doing up there," he muttered.

Matthias, perched on the edge of the wagon bed, said nothing.

Chad's jaw tightened. They were doing something. Learning something. Starting something. Meanwhile, he was still here. Moving boxes. *Again.*

He turned toward the tower door—and nearly ran into Gharn. The gnome appeared with a bag of tools slung over one shoulder and a scowl. "Don't stand there staring. Things don't pack themselves."

"I'm done," Chad said. "Everything's tied down."

"Are you, now?" Gharn grunted. "Just means you had the easy job."

Chad blinked. "I'm sorry. The what, now?"

The gnome dropped the tools with a metallic thud and advanced on Chad. "You want to know the secret to strength, boy?"

Chad stepped back slightly. "Sure. Enlighten me."

Gharn's eyes narrowed. "It's not what you carry when everyone's looking. It's what you still carry when no one is." He turned and stomped off again, muttering about fools and wasted time.

Chad rubbed the back of his neck, watching him go. The horses huffed, and a breeze stirred the dust. He stared at the tower again, where his brother was still holed up with the wizard. With a sigh, he dropped into a squat beside a wagon wheel and rested his forearms on his knees. The ache in his thighs was familiar. So was the one in his chest. "Guess we'll find out soon enough," he murmured.

The tower loomed above.

And the shadows stretched a little longer.

The stairwell ended in a heavy oak door, its varnished surface gleaming despite its age. Sorendir pushed it open without ceremony and stepped inside. Rick followed—and stopped cold.

Chaos. Layered and yet somehow deliberate.

Books spilled from every surface—towers of them leaning at precarious angles, as if in defiance of natural law. Charts and diagrams hung at odd intervals along the walls, curling at the edges where the parchment had grown brittle. Shelves sagged beneath the weight of accumulation. The air smelled of old paper, candle wax, and something acrid—ozone, or maybe scorched copper. Rick's fingers twitched toward a crookedly pinned sheaf of notes. He stopped himself just in time.

"Not quite what you expected?" Sorendir asked over his shoulder, already picking his way through the clutter.

"No, not quite," Rick muttered, stepping carefully between a broken glass alembic and a stack of worn tomes threatening to collapse.

At the far end of the room, a pair of doors opened onto a balcony. Sorendir moved to them without hesitation. Rick followed, drawn by the odd, filtered light slanting across the stone. Outside, the volcanic wastes stretched sharp and silent. The Three Sisters loomed against the horizon. Two still smoked, their dark slopes etched with scars.

The third was still. Watching.

"The Silent Sister has gone quiet again," Sorendir said softly. "For now."

Rick studied the old man's profile. Calm. Controlled. Like a man waiting to see if a crack in the wall would widen. "That means something?" Rick asked.

"It always does," Sorendir replied.

Rick blew out a bit of air in a half-chuckle. *I should have seen that coming*, he reflected.

The man turned, robe whispering as he moved. "You said before that the script looked like an equation."

Rick nodded. "It did."

"That's because it is."

Sorendir picked up a battered candle from a side table, muttered a word too soft to catch, and cupped the base with one hand. A scent—char and wick—hit Rick's nose, and the candle flared to life.

No match. No spark. Just—

"I added heat to the wick," Sorendir said, setting it down. "Basic arithmetic."

Rick stepped closer. The flame flickered, steady. His finger started to write in the air even before he realized it. "If you subtracted heat instead—"

"It would be extinguished. Or burn without warmth. Or light without fire. The effect depends on the terms. And the intent." Sorendir's voice was still calm, but there was an edge now—like a theorem too elegantly phrased to trust.

Rick's thoughts spun. Heat. Light. Mass. Force. Energy was a function of— "But how do you express the terms?" he asked. "How do you speak it?"

Sorendir tapped his temple. "Language. Letters are symbols for sounds, as you know. Those same sounds can represent numbers. This forms the incantation, which sets the structure. Each gesture trims the equation or fills in values where the words would outpace one's tongue. The intent—" He held Rick's gaze. "—determines the solution."

Rick's fingers curled. "So gestures and words are syntax. Objects—"

"Variables," Sorendir confirmed. "Tuned by context. Defined by need."

Rick breathed in slowly. "And lazy math?"

"You'll still get a *result.*"

A pause.

"It just may not be one you survive."

Rick let the silence stretch as he walked slowly to a desk buried in scrolls. A book lay open, pages filled with ink that had faded to sepia. The symbols meant nothing. Then, slowly, the script began to shift—not physically but conceptually. Letters into functions, symbols into values. It was a puzzle. Tightly wound. Deeply structured. And he could solve it.

He *wanted* to solve it.

The air around him shifted. Not temperature. Not pressure. Focus.

He glanced back toward the candle. "So arithmetic is foundational. But algebra distributes. Geometry structures. Trigonometry manipulates perspective."

Sorendir's eyes lit up faintly. "You grasp it faster than most. Yes, these disciplines are what we call Low Magic."

"And High Magic?" Rick asked. He already knew.

"Calculus. Integration. The math of movement. Change. Possibility."

Rick's throat tightened. Whether from fear or excitement, he couldn't be sure. "That's how you turned me into a mule."

The amusement vanished from Sorendir's face. He crossed the room in two strides.

"High Magic," he said quietly, "is not arithmetic with flair. It is power wielded at the edge of comprehension. Beautiful. Precise. And waiting to punish you the moment your ego outruns your caution."

Rick met his gaze. Didn't blink. "You used it on me without asking."

"I did."

"You took the risk."

"I calculated it."

Rick clenched his jaw. "On me."

Sorendir's voice dropped. "And you lived. The question is whether you *learned*."

The room was too quiet. The candle hissed softly.

"You should fear High Magic," Sorendir added. "It carries dangers the uninitiated cannot comprehend. It waits. And it always collects."

Rick turned back to the book. His pulse steadied. He could feel it now—beneath the diagrams, beneath the layers of paper and parchment, beneath the very floor: a current. Tethered not to emotion or will, but to *intention*.

He hovered his fingers over the open page.

He could shape this. Master it. Control it. The thrill of clarity tightened in his chest. He knew he wouldn't look back.

Couldn't.

The hook was already set.

The meal was simple—bread, cheese, a stew that looked delicious and tasted even better—but Evan barely registered the flavors. The dining room radiated an old, lived-in warmth: firelight against dark stone, smoke curling upward into the thick beams overhead, shadows soft at the corners. Between Gharn's excellent cooking and no longer having the threat of exile hanging over them, the mood should have been comforting—but the current around the table was off.

Chad leaned back in his chair, mid-laugh. Whatever Matthias had said had struck the right nerve. Gharn muttered into his cup, but even he seemed a little less jagged. Matthias didn't smile. Didn't laugh. He just nodded slightly, like he was cataloging Chad's amusement as another data point. As if warmth were a language he didn't speak.

Evan watched a moment longer, then turned her attention to Rick. He hadn't touched his stew. He sat with his hands braced lightly on either side of the bowl, eyes unfocused, like he was still trying to solve a problem that wasn't in the room. His fingers tapped an absent rhythm against the rim of his mug—steady, analytical. But there was a slight tremor in the motion.

She nudged his knee under the table. No response. He wasn't withdrawn. Wasn't shut down. He was just... elsewhere.

Something in him had unraveled, even if only by a thread.

"So," Chad said, grinning toward Rick, "how's Intro to Wizardry?"

Rick blinked. His gaze sharpened like a lens refocusing. "Lit a candle," he said flatly. "Also lit a few books. Not on purpose."

Sorendir chuckled. "*Vedorian's Treatise* was largely theoretical nonsense. A mercy, if anything."

Almost everyone around the table laughed—Chad most of all. Even Gharn cracked a smile. Matthias simply looked... interested. Rick managed a crooked grin, but Evan saw through it. His shoulders remained tense. His eyes too bright. It had taken something out of him—more than he was letting on.

"You said we leave tomorrow," Matthias said, placing his cup down with slow precision.

The room shifted. Just slightly. Even the fire seemed to hush. Sorendir's expression didn't change, but Evan felt the difference. A subtle tightening behind the eyes. Cold intent behind a warm gaze. "No reason to delay," he said easily. "Unless there's something you'd like to disclose?"

Matthias met his gaze. "Nothing worth delaying for."

Evan shivered.

The tension passed, dissipating like breath in cold air, but it left an aftertaste.

"Two months to Southwatch," Gharn muttered. "Longer if the gods feel cruel."

Chad groaned. "Two months?"

"Assuming no bandits, landslides, or wagon fires," Gharn added, standing to collect the empty bowls.

"And after that?" Evan asked.

Gharn glanced sideways. "Luthenholme's at least another month. Depends what you find."

"If we find it," Chad said, his cheer fading. "That Haven place. The Forbidden Spire. Or whatever it is now." Evan caught the quiet fear in his voice. The scope of it all—how far, how long, how unknown.

"It's not meant to be easy," Sorendir said gently. "Nothing worthwhile is."

Rick stirred for the first time in minutes. "You could've already gone yourself," he said, voice low. "If you knew where to look. Why us instead?"

Sorendir didn't blink. "Because I'm not in the prophecy."

Rick's mouth twisted, but he didn't reply. Evan laid a hand on his forearm. He didn't pull away. But he didn't relax either.

"Besides," Gharn said, stacking plates, "we were waiting."

"For what?" Evan asked.

"For the Silent Sister to speak again," Sorendir said. "We came here a long time ago. Before Gharn had proper whiskers."

Gharn snorted. "Still had more sense than you."

A ripple of laughter passed around the table, lighter this time. But there was something behind it. A depth beneath Gharn's usual grumble.

"He means a lot to you, doesn't he?" Evan asked softly, smiling.

Gharn stared into his bowl as if it contained the secrets of the universe. "Sorendir gave me a place when Khorvael cast me out," the gnome said. His voice didn't rise or tremble. It just *was*.

Evan looked at him. "Your home."

"A long time ago." He didn't elaborate, but the silence that followed said enough.

Evan rose quietly and began collecting dishes. Rick's was still mostly full, but she took it anyway.

The moment her fingers touched the ceramic, her perceptions expanded, and the world narrowed.

Rick's mind—exhausted and sharp. Chad—bright but flickering. Gharn—rooted. Solid. Wounded. Sorendir—

She gasped. The bowl clattered—not loud, but loud enough.

Rick looked over, brow furrowed. "You okay?"

"Fine," she said too quickly. She forced a smile, but it didn't reach her eyes.

Sorendir was still seated. Still smiling gently. But what she'd touched—it had felt like standing on the edge of a cliff in the dark. Like wind, teeth, and old stars that had long since gone cold.

She turned quickly and escaped into the kitchen. The water helped. The mundane clatter of rinsing dishes steadied her. Only when she began drying the plates did she realize there was someone she hadn't felt at all. She paused, dishcloth half-folded in her hands. Matthias—there had been nothing. No presence. No flicker of him.

The dishcloth twisted in her hands.

It could have been the distraction—the fall of the bowl, the surge from Sorendir. Maybe.

She stood still for several seconds, breathing slowly, then folded the dishcloth and returned to the room. Matthias glanced at her, still expressionless, as if nothing had happened.

She looked away.

Rick was back to staring at the fire. Chad had leaned into the gnome's ramble about wagon wheels. Matthias remained still and silent.

And Evan sat quietly at the edge of the circle, unsure who was still whole.

Or if any of them were.

Gharn lay on his pallet, staring up at the ceiling of his cramped room, the stone rough and unadorned. Every time he shifted, the mattress groaned beneath him. He closed his eyes. Opened them. Closed them again. Sleep stayed stubbornly out of reach. *It's the journey,* he told himself. The first in decades. That alone was enough to stir the dust in his bones. But they would pass near Khorvael. And *that*... that was a different ache entirely. A deeper one.

He didn't need to see the city again. Didn't want to. But the thought of it pressed against the back of his skull like a weight he couldn't quite set down. Stone halls that had once welcomed him. Names he didn't speak anymore. Laughter that had turned to whispers the day they cast him out. He blew out a breath and folded his arms behind his head. But it wasn't just the journey.

It was *Matthias*.

The man was hollow in a way Gharn couldn't name. Not by deed. Not by word—he was too careful for that. But there was a silence in him where something vital should have lived. Gharn didn't trust it. Didn't like how the man moved. Didn't like the way he watched. And he especially didn't like that Sorendir wouldn't explain it.

Scowling, Gharn sat up and swung his legs off the pallet. The floor was cold beneath his feet. He grabbed his cloak from the peg and shrugged it around his shoulders. If he lay here any longer, he'd wind himself too tightly to breathe.

He padded into the hallway, joints stiff. This far into the night, the tower was quiet in the way only old buildings could be—settled deep into itself, every creak and shift a memory. He moved without lighting a lamp. He knew where Sorendir would be. Not in his chambers. Not in the lower rooms.

A soft sound came from the room shared by Rick and Evan, and Gharn paused. It had sounded vaguely like a whimper, but now there was only silence. With a shrug, he continued on and climbed the stairs, avoiding the loose runner near the top by habit. The door to the study stood ajar. He pushed it open and stepped inside.

Sorendir stood at the balcony, his back to the room, robes catching slightly in the cold breeze that swept in from the cliffs. His posture was still but not relaxed.

"You couldn't sleep either," Sorendir said quietly, without turning.

Gharn snorted. "You always do that."

"I don't do it *on purpose*."

"You're still smug about it."

Sorendir said nothing, and Gharn crossed to stand beside him at the railing. It barely reached his shoulders, but tonight he didn't care. The night stretched black and sharp. In the ravine below, Emberhold crouched in the shadows like a tired beast. Above it, Miner's End lay silent, lights guttered out. Beyond that, the horizon shimmered faintly—residue from some distant Shift.

Gharn stared past it. He'd seen that shimmer all his life. Tonight it barely registered. Tonight his focus was narrower. "Why him?" he asked.

Sorendir didn't feign confusion. "You mean Matthias."

"I don't trust him."

"I know."

Gharn ground his teeth. "He's not right. Doesn't move like a soldier. Doesn't sound like a traveler. He knows *things*, and he's too careful about what he doesn't say."

"Agreed."

That stopped him. "Then why?" Gharn asked. "Why is he part of this?"

Sorendir's voice was quiet. "Because he has to be."

Gharn looked up sharply. "The prophecy doesn't say who the fourth is. I've read it. A dozen times. Why couldn't it have been Korvan?"

Sorendir's hand tightened on the railing. There was a long pause, and for the first time, Gharn noticed the parchment clamped in that grip. "You've read… *most* of it," Sorendir said at last.

Gharn turned toward him slowly. "What?"

Sorendir held up a crumpled page—no, two. Gharn recognized one instantly. The other—the other had been hidden.

Until now.

"You lied to me." Gharn couldn't believe how much his voice trembled as he spoke the words.

"I held back what you weren't ready to carry."

Gharn stepped forward, reaching to snatch the pages—and froze.

Movement on the horizon. At first he thought it was a trick of the moonlight, but it wasn't graceful. It flowed, but in jerks.

Shadows. Dozens. Hundreds.

He focused more carefully. Some had too many limbs. Others, none. Slithering, dragging, pulsing shapes. No symmetry. No mercy. "By the Three…" he whispered.

Sorendir dropped the parchments, and they fluttered across the stones like broken feathers. Gharn lunged instinctively, reaching for them—but a hand caught his shoulder. Sorendir's. "It is time," the old wizard said.

"What aren't you telling me?" Gharn demanded, his chest tightening as the wind snatched the papers into the night. His gaze returned to the shapes in the distance. Drawing closer. "That—*those*—they're not in the prophecy."

"Not the part *you* read," Sorendir said.

Then he unfastened the chain around his neck. The medallion swung into view—heavy, old, too bright in the moonlight, as if catching a light source that wasn't there. He pressed it into Gharn's hand.

It was warm. Too warm. Like holding forged steel that hadn't finished cooling. It felt... wrong. Or too *right*.

"No," Gharn said. "No. I *can't*."

Sorendir's smile was gentle. "You must."

He turned and crossed the room. Gharn didn't follow—not at first. Instead he looked down at the medallion, then in the direction the prophecy fragments had blown. Then back at the horizon.

The shapes were nearly to the far side of the slum. Whatever they were, they didn't belong here.

He could stay up here and watch. Or he could follow his friend.

Gharn wrapped the medallion tightly in his fist and turned after Sorendir. The tower door banged open against the stone.

And far below, in the dark belly of Emberhold, the first warning bells began to ring.

VI
Attack

Agony.

Screams burst through the dark, jagged with pain. The air was choked with sulfur and something worse—burnt copper, rot, fear. Captain Gallus's world spun in fits and jolts. Blood covered his vision. His scalp was torn open to bone, and the shard of his own blade glinted in his shattered hand.

But it wasn't the broken blade that hurt. It was what was sticking into him. A spear—black and ridged, curved like it had grown from bone—protruded from his gut. He was impaled.

Above him loomed a creature whose eyes were too large, too many. Each orb mirrored fire and his own death with a terrible kind of joy. The monster wasn't holding *the spear. The spear was a part of the monster.*

Its mouth stretched into something like a smile. Toothsome.

Gallus screamed.

Evan screamed with him.

She bolted upright in bed, knees drawn to her chest beneath the twisted blanket, spine pressed to the cold stone wall. Her breath came in short, shuddering bursts, one hand clutched tight around the twisted ring pendant at her neck. Sweat clung to her skin despite the chill of early dawn.

Beside her, Rick stirred sharply. "Ev?" His voice was thick with sleep but laced with alarm. He was already pushing himself upright, one hand reaching across the narrow bed to steady her shoulder. "You're shaking. Nightmare?"

Evan didn't answer. She was still seeing—still *a part* of it. Her body trembled, every muscle drawn tight, not from cold but from the aftershock of something deeper.

Rick's hand moved to the back of her neck, grounding her. "Hey. You're safe. I'm right here."

She turned to him, eyes wide, and opened her mouth to speak—but the words caught. *It wasn't a dream.* But before she could say this aloud, footsteps echoed in the corridor outside. Quick. Sharp. Deliberate.

The door flew open.

Matthias stood there, already dressed, already armed. His expression was unreadable. "We leave. Now." Evan didn't argue. She was moving before her mind caught up, throwing on her shawl to cover sweat-drenched clothes.

Just then, Chad emerged from his own room, blinking against the lantern light. "What's—" Chad began, voice groggy.

"Outside," Matthias snapped. "Do not ask. Move."

Evan didn't need elaboration. She pushed Rick back into the room and threw his shirt—the first article of clothing her grasping hands found—to him. They dressed quickly.

"What do you think is going on?" Rick asked, his eyes large with worry.

Already sliding her foot into the first of her shoes, she shook her head. How could she explain what she'd seen?

When they returned to the hall, Chad was still there. Evan grabbed both brothers by the arm and pulled. Rick hesitated half a heartbeat—reflex more than resistance—then followed.

They burst into the courtyard. No moons. No stars. Only firelight—distant, flickering, and wrong. The quiet of Emberhold had broken. Now it wailed: a city waking to nightmare. Screams carried on the wind. Wood cracked. Metal clashed. A voice barked orders, strangled by panic.

Evan stumbled to a halt. The horses were *ready*. Saddled. Bridled. One already hitched to the wagon. Five stood in a loose half-circle, jittery but held in place. Matthias strode among them, checking straps, adjusting a girth, barely glancing up when they arrived. "The others?"

"Haven't seen them," Rick said.

"No," Evan murmured, forcing back the surging tide threatening to overwhelm her. "They're still upstairs."

Matthias didn't respond.

Chad stepped forward. "Need help?"

Matthias pointed toward the wagon. "Harness the last horse."

Chad moved without question, hands already finding the buckles. As he did, Evan took a step toward the horses—and stopped. *Five already saddled.* The thought struck her like a dissonant chord. Too perfect. Too prepared. But before she could say anything, the tower door slammed open again.

Sorendir emerged, regal even in haste, his golden eyes scanning the courtyard. Gharn followed hard on his heels, face pale, arms laden with scrolls and a half-stuffed satchel. The wizard didn't speak—just strode toward the lead horse and swung into the saddle with surprising ease.

"Mount up," Sorendir said. "Ride hard. Do not stop." He didn't wait for a response. He simply kicked his heels, and the horse surged forward, shod hooves striking sparks from stone.

Evan turned back to the others. Chad and Matthias had finished the wagon. Gharn clambered up beside the reins with barely a word, casting one look back at the tower as if memorizing it.

When Evan touched her horse to climb into its saddle, there was a connection. It was terrified. Its muscles quivered. Ears twitched. The animal next to it tried to bolt and without thought she reached for them both—not physically but deeper. A wave of calm, not hers, but channeled through her, her own fear braided into the tether, disguised. They responded—just enough.

Then she reached outward—deeper.

Chad: focused, heart thudding too fast, but finding strength in action.

Rick: torn between confusion and calculation, trying to solve this like a problem with a clean answer.

Matthias—

Nothing. Not resistance. Shielding? No, absence. His presence was like staring into polished obsidian: smooth, flawless, *cold.*

A rumble split the air. Deep, resonant. Too long to be thunder. Too close.

The horses spooked. Hers tensed to rear beneath her. Evan grabbed its reins, whispering nonsense syllables—"Calm, calm, calm"—until it stilled. The others followed, herd instinct kicking in. Whatever was coming... it would be here soon.

And there would be no reasoning with it.

Screams tore through Emberhold like jagged glass.

Not just panic—pain. Real, raw. Rick's mind tried to catalog voices: male, female, young. But there were too many. And they kept coming. Some ended mid-scream. Those were the worst.

Ahead, Sorendir had already disappeared into the dark, his horse devouring the distance toward the bridge marking the route down through the Landrise, through the city. Gharn yanked the wagon into motion behind him, reins taut, jaw clenched.

Rick swung onto his horse without thinking. Evan was already up. Chad moved fast, latching the last buckle on the harness as Matthias vaulted onto the saddle of the first remaining horse. Everything blurred—except for the certainty in Rick's chest: they were leaving too late.

They slid between the gateposts, passing through the no-man's-land surrounding the tower like angry shadows. Beyond, Miner's End greeted them not with silence but with howling.

They rode into it anyway.

The sky above Emberhold was fire. Somewhere a building burned, casting wild shapes across the walls of the ravine. Smoke caught in Rick's throat, and his horse tossed its head, ears swiveling wildly. His pulse kept trying to match the hoofbeats, racing too fast, then lurching off beat.

Beside him, Evan's hands were white on the reins, her jaw set. Beyond her, Chad hunched low on his mount, his weight rolling forward like a sprinter about to take off.

They rounded the first corner—packed dirt giving way to cobbled street—and suddenly the ravine opened up on their right. The city spilled downward in a series of crisscrossing lanes and terraces, crowded tight with homes and workshops. Between the streets, footbridges hung like spider silk over drops too deep to see the bottoms.

Clanking chain—sounding like a dozen Slinky toys moving at once—announced the arrival of guards from the city below. They seemed to grow up from the ground ahead, and Rick realized they had reached the way down. A familiar shape was in the lead.

"It's Jens!" Chad's voice was strangled.

The guards spared no attention for Rick's group as they turned away into the deep slum. Rick shook his head as they disappeared between the buildings. No amount of money could have persuaded him to follow.

Moments later a clash of steel came from where the men had gone, followed by mixed shouts, screams—and an unearthly roar like a tree being twisted in half.

The Outlanders fled.

Sorendir led the way into the ravine. At its base lay the lower city—the only way off the Landrise. And their path ran straight through it at an angle that felt too steep in the night.

The wagon clattered ahead, already rattling with dangerous speed. Rick's stomach tightened. The load was too heavy, the angle too severe. Gharn fought the reins, trying to keep the buckboard steady.

Ahead, shadows flickered across the far wall of the ravine—misshapen, loping.

"There!" Chad shouted, pointing to the upper edge. "Look!"

Rick did. Shapes crept along the ridge—twisted silhouettes. Something leaped into the air. A figure—no, a person—falling.

A scream spiraled downward. Then—*crack!* The sound echoed up to them, sharp and final.

Rick jerked his eyes away.

A moment later the wagon jolted. A front wheel struck the stone wall with a loud thunk, skidding sideways. Gharn shouted, his words lost in the chaos.

"It's going to crash!" Rick yelled.

But Matthias was already surging forward, his horse bounding ahead. In a single motion, he was off the saddle and onto the wagon, grabbing Gharn by the collar and throwing him to the empty mount without pause.

Rick reined aside as the horse bolted past, barely avoiding a collision.

Matthias was gone from the wagon again—somehow now atop the horse pulling it. His blade flashed once, severing the harness. "Yah!" he called.

The horse leaped forward. The wagon dragged for a moment more, then listed violently to the side. The axle cracked. Crates pitched, a barrel rolled free and shattered—then the whole thing went over the edge.

Rick's breath caught. He felt it in his legs, his hands, his teeth. The crash hit like a body blow—wood against stone, splinters, silence. If Matthias hadn't acted—

"That was... amazing!" Chad breathed.

"Stop gawking and get *moving*!" Gharn's voice cut through like a whip. He was already urging his horse forward, the gnome too small in the saddle, the stirrups too low for his legs.

Rick turned to glance back—and froze.

Something burst into view from a side alley. It moved on four legs—no, six. Without symmetry. Its shoulders rose higher than its head, giving the impression it had no neck at all. Its mouth opened first vertically and then sideways—double-jawed.

Its eyes locked onto Rick. They were vertical, with slitted pupils deep as oil.

And they *understood*.

The horse jerked, and Rick nearly lost the reins. He didn't think—just kicked forward, grabbing Gharn's horse by the bridle and yanking himself half out of the saddle to keep up. He wasn't even sure if he was steering.

The monster charged behind them, and they fled.

The streets widened as they descended, but it was little help. The city was waking up, its citizens in chaos. People spilled into the streets, eyes wide, voices raised but not in understanding. Confusion reigned. Some stared. Some shouted. Some blocked the road until the horses nearly trampled them.

Rick saw a man carrying a child, turning the wrong way. A woman shrieked and vanished beneath something that leaped from a rooftop. The air reeked of blood, smoke, and spoiled meat—ash mixed with the scent of baking bread. He couldn't reconcile the smells.

They cut through the marketplace. Stalls lay overturned. Fire licked along the awnings. And the creatures were *there*—everywhere. Some crawled across buildings. Others dropped from balconies, limbs distorting mid-fall before they landed on human prey.

Rick couldn't look. Couldn't *not* look. Evan shouted something, and he followed her voice into an alley, Matthias already ahead.

The path narrowed—buildings pressing close. Stone walls were streaked with soot. The horses went single file, their riders crouching low to avoid hanging signs and clotheslines.

A child stood in the alley.

Realization barely registered before Matthias, moving with uncanny speed, reached down, lifted her in passing, and deposited her on a crate without a word. Her eyes were wide and unblinking. She didn't cry. Just stared.

The wall loomed ahead. Guards atop it were sending arrows into the streets below, and a dark shape pounced from a rooftop to the battlements. A scream cut short.

The group turned and raced on. There was a wide service lane behind the outer wall—open, flat. Designed for troop movement. It gave them space. And speed.

Rick's horse surged forward, sweat lathering its sides. The hooves of the others thundered all around him. His teeth chattered from the vibration in his arms.

Ahead, the gate. People fleeing through it. *Still open.*

As they reached the final alley, he saw a dog facing the darkness. It was barking, hackles raised. Just as they passed, a black shape exploded into view. Giant jaws closed around the hound, and Rick saw blood splatter across chitinous features. His horse almost threw him as it leaped to avoid the creature.

And they were through the gates, continuing down the road at a breakneck pace.

Freedom.

Then—

Evan screamed, and Rick turned. She sagged in her saddle, one hand to her head. He reached out, steadied her. "What happened? Are you hurt?"

"Rick..." Her voice broke. "He's not going to make it."

His blood ran cold. *Chad?* He spun, but Chad was there, Gharn behind him.

Then he saw who was missing: *Sorendir.* The wizard was off the road, dismounted. Standing still. Facing the inferno.

Facing the monsters.

The air changed. Rick didn't know how he felt it. Only that he *did.*

And the sky behind them burned.

Evan cried out. Not a startled noise—something deeper. Pained. Desperate.

Chad looked up just in time to see her clutch her head like someone was driving nails through her skull. Rick pulled alongside her fast, catching her before she slipped from the saddle. Whatever she'd said, it had clearly hit him hard. Rick's eyes went wide. He twisted in his own saddle so sharply his horse reared slightly, and for a moment their gazes locked across the road.

And in Rick's face, Chad saw fear. Not for himself. For *Chad.*

It struck like a physical blow. Chad dropped low, his hand searching out his knife—small as it was—before he could stop it. He looked behind him, half-expecting to see a clawed nightmare about to leap.

Nothing. Only Gharn, barely hanging onto a saddle way too large for him. The gnome's feet couldn't hope to reach the stirrups, but he gripped with his knees, bouncing with each stride like a child on a trampoline made of chaos.

How is he still with us? Chad wondered. It had to be sheer will.

Then he saw Sorendir.

The wizard stood on a small rise beside the road, alone, his figure limned by firelight from behind. His horse bolted toward the rest of the group, riderless.

But Sorendir didn't move. He stared back toward Emberhold. Toward the city's ruin. Toward the monsters.

"Why isn't he running?" Chad whispered. "What is he *doing*?"

Then it hit him. *Wizard.* Of course.

Relief surged in his chest like sunlight breaking through black clouds. "He's got this," Chad breathed. "Took him long enough, but now he'll do some big-ass spell and—"

"No!" Gharn's voice cracked, sharp as snapping wood. "No, he's not—"

Chad blinked down at him. The gnome's face was pale, drawn tight with grief, eyes shimmering with unshed tears.

And then Sorendir moved. He hunched—just slightly—as though bracing himself.

And he *grew.*

At first Chad thought he was imagining it. But the wizard's frame expanded rapidly, bones stretching, joints snapping into new shapes. Skin hardened to scale—silver and sharp-edged. His robes tore away as wings unfurled behind him with an audible snap.

The man disappeared. In his place rose a reptilian shape. Thirty feet long. Then forty. Amber eyes blazed like gemstones the size of fists, and it let out a roar so deep it felt like it could have torn the sky open.

Chad's horse screamed and bucked. He hit the ground hard, his shoulder catching the impact, and dust filled his mouth. He rolled, blinked, and saw silver wings sweeping upward into the air, reflecting firelight like mirrors for the gods.

"Holy shit," Chad whispered. It was more magnificent than any special effect in any movie he'd ever seen. And it was *real.*

Gharn was suddenly standing beside him, tugging at his arm. "Get moving, you lummox! He's buying us time!"

"He... he turned into a *dragon*!"

"No, he didn't," Gharn said. Then softer, broken, "He just stopped playing human."

Chad looked at him again. Gharn wasn't even meeting his eyes—he was watching the sky. Tears streamed silently down his face, and his beard trembled.

Another roar, answered by a shriek from the horde. Chad looked back toward the city. Some of the monsters had paused, eyes fixed upward. Black dots were taking to the air, angling to intercept the dragon.

And on the ground, others were moving again. Toward them.

"Oh, crap."

He grabbed Gharn without thinking, lifting the gnome under one arm like a child and running—full sprint—toward his friends. Heat slammed into his back, and he fell forward, rolling and twisting to shield Gharn. When they stopped, a wall of fire stretched across the road behind them—high, hot, crackling.

To the left, the dragon wheeled upward again, his wings beating thunder into the air.

"Way to go, Sorendir," Chad murmured, stunned.

Gharn rolled away from him, coughing and sputtering. "You oversized… idiotic—"

"You're welcome," Chad said, grinning weakly.

Their friends were suddenly there. Matthias rode bareback, leading another horse. "You lost something."

Rick and Evan were close behind, both ashen, eyes locked on the horizon.

"That fire won't last," Rick said. His voice was tight.

Chad nodded. He climbed back into the saddle and extended a hand to Gharn. "You coming?"

"Are you *asking* this time?" the gnome grumbled. But he took the hand and swung up behind him.

Evan's voice was quiet. "It's not enough."

Chad followed her gaze. High above, the dragon fought, but there were so *many*—black shapes darting from every side, trying to drag him down.

"If you want to survive the night, ride," Matthias said.

Chad kicked his heels and didn't argue.

For a few minutes, it seemed like they had a chance. The fire slowed the ground pursuit and the dragon kept the air clear. But the fire began to gutter. The flanking monsters reappeared.

And ahead—the dragon dropped low and landed heavily in the road. When they reached him, Sorendir was a man again. Barely. He was naked. Bloody. Hunched and trembling. Cuts crisscrossed his skin. Some were so deep Chad could see ribs through the blood. *He's dying.* And the weight of this thought settled over him like iron.

But Sorendir looked up, eyes still burning gold. "Keep… going," he rasped. "Don't… stop."

"No!" Gharn's cry behind Chad cracked like a bone snapping. "Sorendir—please!"

"You know what to do, my friend." Sorendir tried to smile. "Now go."

They didn't move.

"GO!"

Matthias turned his horse sharply, and Chad followed. Behind him, Gharn clung on tightly. He could feel the gnome's body trembling. Evan passed beside them, silent tears streaking her cheeks. Rick came last, jaw locked, face like stone.

They could hear the monsters again—closer, louder.

Chad looked back. Sorendir stood tall, as if through will alone. He raised both arms, reaching skyward. His mouth moved, but Chad couldn't hear the words. And then—

The ground rippled.

Not shook. *Rippled.* As though something *deep* beneath had stirred.

An arc of earth erupted before Sorendir, shards rising into the air. Dozens, splitting into hundreds and then, thousands.

The shards floated, turning, changing. They gleamed like steel or crystal—or something in between. Each sharpened to a perfect point and hovered in the air, waiting.

Chad couldn't breathe. The air was too thick, the sky too quiet.

The horses slowed. Even the sound of their hooves seemed muted.

Then—Sorendir dropped his arms.

The air screamed as the blades launched in perfect synchronicity, slicing through the sky. Every one of them hit. Monsters fell mid-step, mid-leap, mid-flight. Screeches were cut short, wings torn, bodies flung backward in tatters.

Then—*nothing*.

No roar. No hoofbeats. Just air and the faint crackle of distant fire. No one spoke.

Sorendir stood alone amid the carnage. He turned, raising one hand in farewell. Then his body cracked, darkened, and faded to gray as he disintegrated. Dust scattered on the wind, glittering in the light of dawn. He was gone.

For a moment, silence. And then Gharn's scream—a long, low sound of something damaged beyond repair.

Evan was trembling—not visibly but, deep inside, every part of her buzzed with a low, relentless vibration, like her bones were trying to shake themselves loose. They'd ridden in near-silence since sunrise, the only sounds the plodding of hooves and Gharn's wracking sobs.

The wizard's sacrifice had come and gone like some mythic wave, and now that it had receded, it felt like something vital had been pulled from the world. Something ancient. Irreplaceable. Her heart ached with the absence.

Even Chad was quiet. She'd grown used to his movement, his energy, his sarcasm. But now he rode with his head down, one hand on the reins, the other holding Gharn's arm tightly where it wrapped around his waist. The gnome clung to him, small and hunched, his grief a raw throb that pressed against Evan's senses like a bruise. *Such a kind soul,* she thought, watching Chad gently mumble something.

Rick rode beside her, and his hand brushed her knee. When she looked over, his eyes were soft, searching.

"I'm fine," she lied. He didn't push.

They crested a low rise, and the trees fell away. The plains of Drakerath opened before them—rolling fields, bright with spring growth, dotted with windmills whose sails turned slowly in the morning breeze. Wildflowers caught the sun. Bees drifted lazily through the air, their hum soft as a lullaby.

It was beautiful.

And it felt obscene.

She inhaled deeply, expecting the air to carry soot or blood—but it didn't. It smelled of flowers. Warmth. Life.

Behind them, the plume of smoke from Emberhold still rose—distant, quiet. A scar on the horizon. She shivered anyway. *How long until it spreads?* The question lodged deep. No answer came.

"Demons," Chad had said. The name stuck.

Matthias called a halt. Evan nearly collapsed dismounting. Her knees locked, and her thighs burned—her whole body felt used up, like she'd been wrung out and left to dry.

Cripes, I feel old. The thought surprised her but felt true. Not physically—emotionally. Like years had slammed into her all at once. She wrapped her shawl tighter around her shoulders, even though the sun was warm.

Something had changed inside her. She could feel it in the way she felt the others—their exhaustion, their pain. The ache in Rick's chest that he hadn't let himself look at yet. Gharn's grief, still sharp. Chad's guilt, quieter but growing.

Her sensitivity had always been there—intuitive, emotional. But now it felt... tuned. Like someone had dialed the world up to a higher frequency and handed her the only receiver.

So why do I feel dread? The thought lingered, but she pushed it aside and joined the others in unsaddling the horses. They were spent, coated in sweat and trembling with fatigue. She found a currycomb and began working gently over each one. The rhythmic scrape of bristles soothed her, and the horses leaned into the touch like it mattered.

They'd carried them through hell. They deserved kindness.

When she finished, she stepped back to stretch her shoulders and saw Gharn approaching Rick. The gnome looked haggard, but his sobs had stopped. He moved with purpose now. Grief hadn't vanished—it had crystallized into something sharper. Into determination. She moved closer without thinking, drawn by the energy in the air.

Gharn stood before Rick and hesitated. Then, with a trembling hand, he reached into his pouch and drew out a small glint of gold. "This is for you," he said, voice rasping.

Rick looked up slowly, as if surfacing from deep water. His gaze dropped to Gharn's hand, then widened. "No," he said, voice hoarse. "I can't."

"You must," Gharn said. His voice wasn't loud, but it carried. Like flint scraping steel. "Sorendir said it was yours. That it's always been yours."

Evan's breath caught. She recognized it now—the medallion. The moment pulsed around them, thick with potential, like a coin tossed in slow motion, spinning, waiting to land.

Rick didn't move.

Gharn stepped closer. "Please," he whispered. "Take it."

Rick extended his hand, and Gharn placed the medallion in his palm. The instant Rick's fingers closed around it—the air shifted like the world had been holding its breath and just now let it out. Evan felt the change ripple across her skin.

And just like that, the moment was over. But something had started. She didn't know what. Not yet.

VII
Changes

How could we have been so wrong? Gharn hunched beside the fire, arms wrapped tightly around his ribs as if they could hold him together by force. The flames barely cracked. It was kindling, not comfort—a pitiful excuse for warmth in a world that had just turned to ash.

He forced himself to look northeast. Smoke still bled from the crack in the Landrise wall, rising thick and oily where Emberhold had once stood.

Had it only been a night?

Ninety years he'd lived in that city. Most of them spent grumbling about the stink, the idiots, the stairs. He'd cursed the place a hundred times—but he'd never imagined it gone. Not like this. Not flattened. Not erased.

And Sorendir—

He squeezed his eyes shut and rocked forward. The tears tried to come again, but he fought them back the only way he knew how: fury.

Stupid, stubborn, brilliant fool of a dragon. Sorendir had been more than a master, more than a friend. He'd been a father in everything but blood—and half the time, Gharn had treated him like a faulty gear shaft. Now he'd never get the chance to say thank you. Or sorry. "Fire and strife," he whispered.

"What was that?" Chad's voice cut through the stillness as the boy shifted another log onto the pile.

Gharn startled. He hadn't meant to speak aloud. "The prophecy," he muttered. "It said there'd be fire and strife. I just..."

"Didn't think it meant demons torching a whole city?" Chad's voice was dry. Not mocking, just tired. Broken in its own way.

Gharn rounded on him anyway. “You think this is funny?”

The kid’s eyes widened. “What? No! I didn’t—”

Gharn turned away before he could finish, the anger already fading to smoke. “What a waste of time,” he muttered. The words felt flat, like embers trying to spark in wet ash. He stood, and his boots crunched frost-bitten needles as he pushed into the trees. Not far. Just enough to put a trunk at his back and the others out of sight. There, in the hush between branches, he let the breath out slowly. It shuddered.

The ache beneath it didn’t.

What was he supposed to do now? Sorendir was gone. Emberhold was gone. The prophecy—the thrice-damned prophecy—had saved no one.

He slid down until he sat in the mulch and moss, head tilted back against bark that pressed cool into his scalp.

I wasn’t meant to lead.

But Sorendir had asked it of him. Not with grand speeches, just with a medallion and a look. That damned dragon always had a way of making impossible things sound inevitable. Gharn rubbed at his eyes, then let his hand fall.

He would move. He would guide them. Because if he didn’t—if he stopped now—he might never start again. And someone still had to see this through.

Even if he didn’t believe in it anymore.

Chad watched Gharn vanish into the trees, the gnome’s back hunched as if bracing against a storm only he could feel. For a moment, Chad debated calling out. He didn’t. “I wasn’t poking fun,” he muttered instead.

The woods didn’t answer.

Rick looked up from the saddlebag he’d been sorting through. “People hear what they expect to hear. If you crack jokes all the time...” He trailed off, the implication hanging there like smoke.

Chad scowled. “I don’t joke all the time.”

Evan didn’t say anything for a moment, merely watching Chad with sad eyes and a half-smile. She sat next to where Gharn had been, placing the currycomb beside her with gentle care, like she didn't want to disturb the space he'd left behind. "He just lost everything," she said softly. "Be patient with him."

"We've all lost everything." Chad kicked a pebble into the fire. "Our entire world's gone."

"But it's not," she said. "We might get back. His is actually... *gone.* Even if we never return, Earth is still there. His people aren't."

Chad let out a breath and shook his head. "You're right." He regarded her with lowered eyes. "I hate it when you make sense." He stared down at his boots. Their tread was packed with soot and dirt. His jeans were stiff with grime, and his shirt itched where it clung to skin dried of sweat. "I don't think I've ever gone this long without changing clothes."

"We're going to need everything," Rick said. "Food first. Gear. Clothes. The wagon took most of what we had."

The mention of food made Chad's stomach tighten. "Matthias'll come back with something." The guy might have been emotionless, but he got things done.

"*If* he comes back," Rick said, frowning.

"He will," Evan said. "He wants the Heart. You saw him—he covered it well, but he wants it."

"Can you blame him?" Rick ran a finger along a stitched seam. "Controlling the Shifts could prevent another Emberhold. Nights like that—no one should have to go through them."

The fire popped, and smoke drifted sideways, catching Chad in the face and drawing up memories he didn't want—red skies, the scream of something with too many limbs, Sorendir's final gesture. He flinched. "I'm still calling them demons," he muttered. "Even if they're not from Hell, they're just as evil."

"Are they?" Evan's voice was gentle, but her eyes searched his. "What they did was horrifying, yes. But so is a swarm of bees. Or locusts. They may not even be sentient."

"And maybe they are." Chad met her gaze. "You want to give them the benefit of the doubt, go ahead. Me, I'll assume hostile until proven otherwise."

Rick looked up from the ground, face pale. "The one I saw... it looked at me. It *knew*. And it hated me."

Chad gave a bitter smile. "So we're agreed. Demons."

Evan didn't argue. "I'm too tired to debate semantics."

Rick wrapped an arm around her. She leaned in, head against his shoulder. It was a small gesture they shared often—familiar. Automatic. Chad looked away. He told himself it wasn't jealousy. Just... something missing. Something he didn't have.

"So, now what?" he asked.

Rick's fingers still rested on Evan's arm. "We need more information. And supplies."

"And new clothes," Chad added.

A voice spoke behind them, soft and dry. "We need to go to Ironspire."

Chad startled. He hadn't heard a single footstep. One moment there had been only firelight and smoke—the next, Gharn was there, standing just beyond the ring of warmth like he'd been conjured from shadow. He looked worse than before, his shoulders slumped, his eyes red-rimmed and dull. Even his mustaches drooped.

Chad took in the sight, drew breath to make a quip—then let it out, suddenly unwilling to meet the small man's gaze.

"What's there?" Rick asked.

"It's the capital," Gharn said. "Closest city with supplies. Wagons. Food. Maybe clothes that don't stink like goat sweat. One or two weeks' ride, depending." There was no sarcasm. No dry wit. Just the facts, spoken like someone reading off a list he no longer cared about.

Chad glanced at Evan. She met his eyes, and he saw it mirrored there—that flicker of concern. Gharn wasn't just grieving. He was unraveling.

"We'll also need to inform the king," Gharn went on. "Sor—" He swallowed hard. "Sorendir knows the elven adviser. *Knew*." The word scraped out of him, barely audible.

"I'd like to meet an elf," Chad offered. He tried to sound casual, not eager. But Evan's eyes narrowed slightly anyway.

I'm being careful, he thought. *Sensitive. Honest.*

Gharn barely turned his head. "Only because you've never met one." The old Gharn would have laced those words with bite. This one sounded like he didn't care either way.

Chad didn't know what to say to that. None of them did.

Then Matthias returned with rabbits strung over one shoulder, moving like nothing was wrong. His eyes swept over the group, calm and unreadable, before he knelt near the fire and began preparing the meat. Chad watched him in silence, then pulled his Swiss Army knife from his pocket. If he couldn't build anything, he could at least help clean a rabbit.

It wasn't what he wanted to do, but it was something.

*

Chad slept better than he had expected. The rabbit had been dry, gamy, and barely seasoned, but after the night they'd survived, it might as well have been a five-star meal. His bed was just a rolled saddle blanket and a half-collapsed saddlebag for a pillow. It didn't matter. His body sank into the hard-packed earth like it had finally been given permission to stop.

He didn't stir until Evan touched his shoulder.

"Your turn," she whispered.

He blinked at her, confused for a second about where he was—then groaned. "Figures."

She offered a tired smile and retreated toward where Rick tossed in his sleep.

The fire had died to a warm core, just a few orange-glowing embers giving shape to the clearing. Chad added a log and settled in. The silence was strange—so total it felt artificial. But no howls rose, no screams, just the occasional pop from the coals and the quiet breathing of those around him. For a little while, it felt like they were just camping.

Until morning came, and the smoke was still rising in the distance.

*

They broke camp without much talk. With so little to carry, it didn't take long. Gharn sat motionless near the fire ring. The others moved around him as if he were just another piece of wreckage. When Evan tried to hand him a strip of leftover rabbit, he didn't even blink.

Matthias spoke up as they saddled their horses. "We do not need to go all the way to Ironspire," he said. "We can find supplies in smaller towns."

Rick raised an eyebrow. "But won't it be harder to find what we need?"

Matthias shrugged. "Fewer people. Fewer chances for complications."

Chad thought that sounded smart, but Gharn looked up at last, his eyes dull. "It's our duty," he said. The words felt hollow, like they were born of momentum rather than conviction. Like he was just parroting something Sorendir might have said.

Chad flinched. He didn't know why, but the sound of that voice—empty and resigned—cut deeper than any argument.

*

The road was a well-beaten path of compressed dirt, flanked by dry grass and the occasional crooked fence. They passed farmland dotted with lazy cows and slow-plodding oxen. Chad tried to make a game of counting them but lost count before the first mile was up.

He wasn't sure how much time had passed. The sun was high by the time hunger started to gnaw again. He caught himself staring at a herd of cattle, his thoughts drifting to burgers, steak, even greasy fast-food sandwiches he'd once turned his nose up at.

Every so often, he saw Rick toying with the medallion again. Fingers turning it over, again and again, like if he stared hard enough, it might tell him what to do.

"Can I see it?" Chad asked at last.

Rick started, as if caught doing something private. His hand moved to put it away, then paused. With a small shrug, he handed it over.

It was heavier than Chad had expected. Dense. Solid. The surface was warm—not from the sun but from something internal, like it remembered being worn. He turned it in his hand.

It was perfectly round, convex on both sides, smooth except for the faintest of lines—lines that didn't feel ornamental. When the light hit them just right, they revealed a pattern.

Not letters. Not art. A network. Flow-like. Measured. *Circuitry?* His breath caught. Just for a moment, he felt something like recognition stir in his chest—then he blinked, and the pattern seemed random again.

Probably just seeing what I want to see.

"What?" Rick asked.

Chad shook his head. "Nothing." He passed it back.

Rick tucked it into his pocket.

"You could wear it," Chad said. "I mean, Sorendir gave it to you."

Rick glanced at Gharn, then looked down. "It just doesn't feel right."

"Why not?"

"I don't know," Rick said quietly. "Because it feels final. Like putting it on makes it all real." He ran his hand through his hair and let it rest behind his neck. "I mean—I know what I saw. What I felt. That spell Sorendir cast..."

"Wow," Chad said, the word low and reverent.

"Yeah. Wow. But seeing it and doing it myself are different things. I managed one spell, and that was with a tutor after hours of trying. What should I do now? Start chanting multiplication tables and hope for lightning?"

A grin tugged at the corner of Chad's mouth. "That sounds like something I'd say."

Rick didn't smile. He just stared ahead down the road.

"Look," Chad said after a while, his voice quieter, "math is your thing. Always has been. And you're amazing at it. If magic really is math, then you're the one who'll figure it out."

"Maybe."

Chad looked down at his hands, resting on the reins. "You know what my thing is? Mechanics. Electronics. Technology. Everything this world treats like garbage." His voice rose before he realized it. "I fix things. I build. That's who I am. And here? That means nothing. I can't even charge a battery, let alone build a system. It's all gone."

Evan turned to look at him. Her mouth opened, but no words came. She closed it again. Her face softened for a breath—then she turned away.

Even Matthias looked over. So did Gharn.

Chad's hands clenched the reins. His throat burned, and he swallowed, but the pressure in his chest kept growing, tight and hot. "At least one of us has a purpose."

But before Rick could answer, before anyone could respond, he kicked his horse into motion and rode ahead—toward the nearest farmhouse.

He still had coin from the embassy, and someone was going to sell him something.

*

They didn't say much over dinner. The mutton was tender, the stewed potatoes better than they had any right to be, but the silence said everything. The way the others moved around him—avoiding eye contact, sitting just a few inches too far away, offering short replies when none were required—spoke louder than words.

Chad told himself he didn't care. It had been justified. He wasn't sorry. Not really. And the food helped. It was warm and rich and grounding, and for the first time in a long time, he felt full. Even the canteen water tasted cleaner than usual—still metallic but not unpleasant. He drank deeply, letting it wash the tension from his throat.

Rick, at least, looked at him. Really looked. And there was something in his brother's eyes that Chad couldn't place. Not pity. Not judgment. Something closer to... respect? It didn't make sense. But he didn't question it—not out loud.

After dinner, he helped clean up. It wasn't because he had to but because pretending everything was fine was easier when his hands were busy. He scrubbed the plates with a handful of green grass, wiped them dry with a corner of his blanket, and stacked them like they were part of a ritual he actually believed in.

Rick stepped away from the group and sat down alone, just outside the circle of firelight. He pulled something from his pocket. Chad paused mid-wipe. *The medallion.*

Rick glanced up and met his gaze. There was a faint smile—quiet, not triumphant.

Then he lifted the chain over his head. Chad exhaled—slow, unsteady.

Rick's fingers brushed the surface of the medallion, and it caught the light—a shimmer rather than a flare. Subtle. Almost a breath.

Then Rick's body jerked. His spine arched like someone had pulled a string tight inside him. His eyes rolled back, the whites showing just for an instant—then his knees gave out.

He collapsed. No cry. No gasp.

Just a soft thud, barely louder than the wind.

Where am I? Rick stood in a boundless black void. Or maybe he was floating. It was impossible to tell. There was a vague sense of ground beneath his feet, but when he crouched to touch it, his fingers met only emptiness. No resistance. No weight.

Vertigo rolled through him, sudden and sharp, and he staggered back, arms flung wide for balance.

He turned carefully in a full circle. Nothing. No stars. No sky. No sound beyond the pulse hammering behind his ears.

Breathe. Just breathe. He closed his eyes and counted down from ten, the numbers giving him something to hold on to.

At six, a voice spoke. "A well-ordered mind. Good."

Rick's eyes snapped open. He spun toward the sound, the motion nearly pitching him into a fall. The vertigo hit harder this time, and he barely managed to stay on his feet. Standing a few paces away was—

Himself.

Despite the absence of light, Rick could see the figure with perfect clarity. It was like looking into a mirror warped by time: the man before him bore the same sharp gray-blue eyes, the same angles to his face—but was older by ten, maybe fifteen years. Weathered, tempered. The lines around his eyes told stories Rick had not yet heard.

The man wore neither tattered shirt nor dust-choked pants. Instead, a black robe trimmed with intricate red embroidery hung from his shoulders, and at his chest gleamed a golden talisman.

The medallion.

Rick's hand shot to his own chest, clutching the amulet still strung around his neck. The Other smiled slightly—no mockery, no warmth. Only the weight of recognition.

"Who are you?" Rick asked.

"Who are *you*?" the Other replied.

The question hit harder than it should have. Rick opened his mouth to answer—*I'm Rick Johnson*—but something in the man's voice made him hesitate.

He wasn't asking for a name. He was asking for something deeper.

"I am me," Rick said at last.

A ghost of amusement touched the Other's lips. "You call that an answer?"

Rick bristled. *This is ridiculous.*

The Other cocked his head, raising an eyebrow. Waiting. When Rick didn't elaborate, the man folded his arms across his chest, his stance relaxed but unyielding. "If you don't know who you are, how can you know *what* you are?"

Rick's jaw clenched. "I'm tired of your games," he snapped.

"That is what you feel," the Other said calmly. "It is not what you *are*."

Rick sucked in a breath through his nose and exhaled through his mouth—long and slow. *Center yourself. Solve it.*

"I am Rick Johnson. Son of Albert and Alice Johnson. Brother to Chad."

The Other's smile widened by a fraction. "That is what you are. It is not *who* you are."

Rick realized his fists had balled tight at his sides. *Testing.*

That's it. He's testing me.

His mind raced. Logic spun through the available variables—and faltered. There was no proof here. No equation to solve. Only questions that circled themselves.

"You're the medallion," Rick said finally. Not a question. A conclusion.

The Other didn't react. He only watched with those piercing eyes, patient as the void itself.

"Who are you?" Rick asked again.

The Other lifted his arms slightly to either side, and the darkness shivered. The void unraveled, the blackness pulling apart into threads of fire, spiraling and coiling and braiding themselves into patterns that pulsed like living veins of light.

Numbers spun around them—pure and cold and beautiful: Bertrand's postulate, Gödel's completeness theorem, the irrationality of *e*, prime spirals... Proofs Rick knew, along with even more he didn't, bloomed and collapsed in an endless dance.

This was a universe made of sense, and Rick's chest ached at the sight of it.

"What is holding you back?" the Other asked. The words rang louder than sound. They pressed against Rick's skull, against his ribs, vibrating through him.

The equations spun faster, coalescing into a luminous figure. Evan. She stood across from him, her face lit from within, eyes wide with the quiet faith that had always terrified and inspired him in equal measure. *I believe in you,* she mouthed—words he remembered from a thousand moments before.

The question cut through the memory. "What is holding you back?"

Rick shook his head, a sharp whip. Evan wasn't the obstacle. She was his anchor. His North Star.

"No," he said aloud. "She's not holding me back."

Evan dissolved into a thousand motes of light, the numbers swallowing her and reweaving themselves into another form. Chad. His brother stood there—mop of tousled hair, hazel eyes wide and questioning.

Rick felt the old ache of guilt stir—how many times had he seen Chad look at him like that? How many times had he failed to live up to it?

But it wasn't Chad who held him back. If anything, Rick was holding back Chad.

The figure blurred again, shifting—family, friends, professors, faces, and possibilities flashing too fast to hold. "What is holding you back?"

The question drove deeper with every iteration and Rick staggered as the void pressed closer.

The numbers spun into fractals, into galaxies, into patterns so intricate they burned into his mind. He felt himself splintering—thoughts unraveling into noise, spinning outward with no center to hold them.

Who are you?

What is holding you back?

Who are you?

What is holding you back?

The pressure built until his skull felt ready to crack. A migraine blossomed behind his eyes, a star collapsing into itself. His breath hitched, and his knees buckled, but still the questions kept hammering him. And then—

Stillness. The numbers froze. The void held its breath.

Rick saw it. Saw *through* it. The two questions were the same. *Who are you? What is holding you back?*

One and the same.

The answer was simple. Not a solution. Not a proof. A truth.

"*I* am," Rick whispered.

The void shivered.

The Other smiled—small, real—and inclined his head.

"Now," he said, "we may begin."

Evan knelt in the dirt, cradling Rick's head in her lap. Her fingers moved instinctively, brushing a stray lock of hair away from his forehead. His skin was warm—too warm—and his lashes fluttered, the frantic movement beneath his lids betraying dreams that wouldn't let go.

He wouldn't wake. She fought down the rising panic, focusing on the rhythm of her hand against his hair. The weight of him. The reality of him. If she could just hold him tightly enough, maybe it would anchor him.

Come back to me. She started to reach for the medallion.

"Don't!" Gharn's voice cut across the firelight like a blade.

She jerked back reflexively, her hand flying to Rick's shoulder instead, gripping hard. His breathing was shallow but steady.

Gharn knelt a few feet away, his face etched with something that wasn't quite fear—but wasn't far from it. "You could kill him," he said.

Evan's mouth tightened. "What do you know about this?" Her voice was too sharp, too cold. She didn't care.

"Only what Sorendir told me," Gharn said, his expression twisted in what could only be anger. "Once he puts it on, only he can safely take it off."

She narrowed her eyes. "That's all?"

Gharn's shoulders sagged, and his gaze dropped to the fire. "That's all he said," he murmured. "I swear it." His voice sounded brittle and cracked. Like everything else around them.

Evan didn't let go of Rick. Her palm pressed against his chest now, feeling the steady drum of his heart through his shirt.

"I'm sorry," Chad said from her left. He crouched close but didn't meet her eyes—or Rick's. "I shouldn't have pushed him."

"Oh, get over it," she snapped without thinking.

Chad recoiled, blinking fast. His jaw clenched, and when he did look at her, the tears in his eyes made her chest ache.

She softened immediately. "I'm sorry. That was too harsh." She tried to smile, but it didn't stick.

Across the fire, Matthias watched them, silent and unreadable. The light caught his eyes—two cold stars, gleaming back at her. He reached for a piece of firewood. Calm. Mechanical.

React, she thought fiercely. *Feel something.*

As if in response, his hand froze above the pile. Only for a second—but she caught it. *Did I do that?* The wood clattered into the fire with a low whoosh, sending a flurry of sparks into the sky. Evan turned away as smoke stung her eyes. When she looked back, Matthias was staring at her—blank-faced but staring. Straight through her.

She dropped her gaze to Rick at once, her heart hammering. *Does he know?* But before she could chase the thought further, Rick gasped—a sharp, tearing breath—and his body jerked against her lap. His eyes snapped open, wide and wild, unfocused.

"Rick," she whispered, her hand tightening on his shoulder.

He blinked rapidly, head turning as if searching for something—and then he found her. His whole body eased, and he slumped into her touch. He was panting, but the desperate edge faded with each breath. Slowly, painfully, he sat up. She helped him, steadying him with a hand against his back.

Gratitude swelled inside her, fierce and overwhelming.

"What happened?" he rasped.

"That's what we want to know," Chad said. No trace of humor in his voice. Only worry.

Rick rubbed at his temples, and his brows knitted together. "I don't know," he said slowly. "It was... some kind of test."

His eyes widened, and he straightened a little.

"And a... lesson," he added, like someone remembering a word just out of reach.

He turned inward for a moment—Evan could see it, the way his gaze clouded—and spoke a few halting syllables. Strange, sharp sounds. Not English. Not anything she knew.

He lifted his hand slightly, twisting his fingers, and above the fire, light bloomed.

It wasn't flame. It wasn't even brightness she could trace to a source. It was as if the very air above them had come to life with pure white light, casting their camp into stark relief.

Chad shielded his eyes with a curse. Evan squinted, blinking away the afterimage already burning into her vision.

Rick closed his hand, and the light snapped out—leaving them gaping in sudden darkness, the fire crackling softly at their feet.

"What the hell was that?" Chad demanded, voice high and pinched.

"Magic," Gharn whispered.

The way he said the word made Evan pause. Not wonder. Not fear. Certainty. And… indifference? As if this was something he'd expected all along—and now that it had come, he no longer had the strength to care.

Rick nodded faintly. His hand brushed the amulet where it rested against his chest. His smile was small. Tentative. "It's like…" He struggled for words, squinting into the firelight. "It's like I received years of education all at once. I understand things I didn't even know existed. And it's…" He shook his head, laughing once under his breath. "It's overwhelming."

He winced suddenly, one hand flying to his temple. His face pinched with pain—sharp and raw before he masked it.

"You okay?" Evan asked, touching his arm again.

Rick squeezed his eyes shut. Exhaled sharply. His whole frame tightened, bracing against something invisible, and then he forced himself to relax. Loosened his hands. Lowered his shoulders. "What a headache," he muttered.

But Evan saw it—what the others didn't. It wasn't just tiredness or exertion. Something had cracked.

And sitting there, with his hand over the medallion and the fire flickering shadows across his face, he looked somehow—heavier.

Not in weight but in spirit.

VIII
Ironspire

Chad tugged at the saddle's straps, testing the tension with a practiced hand. The morning had long since lost its chill, but the air still carried a faint, dewy coolness that clung stubbornly to the ground. Across the smoldering remnants of the campfire, he caught sight of Rick and Gharn standing together, their figures drawn against the flat light. Gharn murmured something low, almost conspiratorial.

At first Chad thought nothing of it—until Rick stilled, shoulders locking tight as if against a blow. Gharn kept speaking, his voice quiet but insistent. Rick finally nodded, a small, rigid movement. Then he turned away, his face closed off.

Chad shifted, a half-formed call caught behind his teeth. Something in Rick's posture—the way he seemed to be holding himself together through sheer force—made Chad hesitate. Whatever Gharn had said, it wasn't something Rick was ready to talk about. Chad rubbed the back of his neck, unsettled without knowing why. A breeze lifted a swirl of dust around his boots, gritty against his skin, and for a moment the world felt just slightly... thinner.

Matthias swung into his saddle without a word and started down the road, not bothering to check if anyone was following. Chad gave a small, resigned grunt, pulled himself up into the saddle, and fell in line.

It was going to be a long week.

*

Eight days later, the city came into view near midday, first just a smear against the horizon, then a jagged collection of towers that sharpened as they approached. Six, maybe seven spires—most gleaming white in the sun, but one—taller, starker—stood out, black as char. Chad figured that must be where Ironspire got its name.

Rick stayed withdrawn for most of the journey, riding in silence even when Evan tried to draw him out. Chad noticed her studying Rick more than once, her brows pulling together in that way that said she sensed more than she let on. *We're not imagining it,* Chad thought. Rick was rattled. Badly.

Gharn offered no help either. He rode with a closed-off air, staring straight ahead like he was already miles away. Whatever emotional black hole he'd crawled into after Emberhold, he showed no sign of climbing out.

As the day wore on, the road slowly grew crowded. Wagons laden with produce creaked toward the city, drivers shouting to one another over the racket of iron-rimmed wheels and braying animals. Others headed out, hauling crates, textiles, casks. Trade life, going on without a hitch. Without a care. Chad envied them a little.

They reached the gates as the sun began to slide toward the western rim of the world, and he let out a low whistle. The city walls rose sixty feet if they were an inch, thick enough that even a siege would have to think twice. Squat towers punctuated the ramparts at regular intervals, and heavy doors—each at least a foot thick—stood open, folded inward along the walls.

Guards loitered in the archway, tabards dulled by dust and heat. Their armor gleamed dully beneath, but their expressions spoke only of boredom. They barely glanced at the travelers filing past, waving most through without a second look. Beyond the gate, a broad boulevard stretched straight as an arrow toward the city's heart. Mature trees lined either side, casting blessed shade over the road. In the distance, the black spire of the palace loomed like an angry finger thrust into the sky.

The farther they rode, the thicker the press of humanity became. Noise battered at Chad's ears—shouts, clattering carts, the clang of distant forges. Smells layered atop each other in thick, confusing waves: roasting meat, sweat, horse dung, spices, something acrid and pungent he couldn't place. The city *felt* heavy—pressing in from all sides. The buildings seemed to lean, reflecting noise and heat until it all tangled in Chad's skull.

He wasn't the only one feeling it. Evan rode hunched and small in her saddle, occasionally pressing a hand to her temple. Rick's slumped shoulders hadn't straightened since morning. Even Gharn looked diminished, his gaze fixed straight ahead, unseeing. Only Matthias seemed untouched, though trying to guess what *he* felt was a fool's game.

The normality of it all gnawed at Chad. After what they'd seen in Emberhold, how could life just *go on* like this? *No TV. No radio. No news,* he reminded himself. No way for word to spread. Still, it grated.

He scanned the shops they passed—a weaver's, a carpenter's, a tanner's—but saw no glimmer of tech. No hints of anything more advanced than simple foundries and gear workings. He'd been hoping, he realized with a dull pang. Hoping a city this size would have cracked the Ban somehow. That someone, somewhere, had said "Screw it" and wired up a generator in a basement.

Nothing. Chad clenched his jaw, frustration knotting in his gut. How was it that Rick, whose skills should have been worthless here, was a *wizard*—while he, who could actually *build* something useful, had to hide what he knew like a criminal?

It's just not fair. Before he could sink deeper into the thought, the boulevard spilled into a great open square. Massive buildings flanked the area, proud and angular. At the far end rose a clock tower, its face a marvel of engineering.

Chad reined in instinctively, staring.

Figures marched in mechanical parade across the clock's facade, music playing in time. It was beautiful. Precise. But simple—basic gears, cams, ratchets. Probably weights or a pendulum regulating it behind the scenes.

He swallowed, a heavy taste rising in his mouth. It reminded him of Munich's famous Glockenspiel but stripped of all the elegance and innovation he knew was possible. Like a museum exhibit instead of a living craft. Even here, surrounded by throngs of people, it was the Middle Ages with a fresh coat of paint.

The scent of raw meat baking in the sun wafted from a butcher's stall nearby, and Chad wrinkled his nose. No refrigeration. No preservation but salt and smoke. Just then, Evan waved suddenly from up ahead, jolting him from his thoughts, and he followed her off the boulevard, down a quieter side street, where the others were already dismounting beneath a painted wooden sign swinging on chains. A crowned horse in elaborate barding grinned down at them, its carved tongue sticking out in a playful gesture that Chad found surprisingly comforting. At least humor was universal.

Two boys ran up as they dismounted, taking their horses' reins without a word. They led the animals away through a narrow gate between buildings, their footsteps muffled by the dust. Chad swung his pack over one shoulder and followed the others inside. The heavy wooden door creaked shut behind him, sealing out the city's clamor.

The sweet smell of pipe tobacco hit him immediately, rich and curling in the dim air. He blinked, letting his eyes adjust to the lower light. For a heartbeat, the drifting smoke conjured the wrong memory—the charred sky over Emberhold, the screams. He clenched his jaw and shook it off. Not here. Not now.

The common room was simple but well cared for, with polished wooden tables catching the gleam of scattered lamps. A portly man in a mostly clean white apron bustled toward them, wiping his hands. His mustache was a dense, bushy thing—clearly compensating for the absence of any hair atop his head.

"Welcome to The Noble Nag," he said, voice roughened by years of shouting across crowded rooms. His gaze flicked across them, quick and dismissive—until it landed on Matthias, who gave a slight tilt of his head toward Gharn, a silent nudge. The innkeeper pivoted smoothly, as if that had been his intention all along, and beamed down at the gnome.

"Is your suite available?" Gharn asked, sounding about as enthusiastic as someone ordering cold stew. Chad almost smiled. Even worn thin, Gharn didn't waste syllables.

They were led up a narrow stair to the second floor and found themselves in a spacious parlor. Comfortable chairs and couches framed a low table at the center. Four doors branched off: two bedrooms, a large closet, and—when Chad swung one open—something better than gold. An oversized porcelain tub dominated the last room, gleaming faintly in the lamplight.

"Pardon, my lord?"

Chad turned, startled, to find a young woman balancing a steaming bucket in each hand. *Lord? Yeah, that'll be the day.* He stepped aside, letting her pass. She poured the water into the tub, curtsied without waiting for thanks, and disappeared. A second girl arrived moments later, bearing more hot water.

Chad's aches from the saddle screamed louder at the sight. A hot bath. No locker room Whirlpool ever looked sweeter. Maybe this medieval thing had its moments after all.

*

They ate in the parlor that evening, lounging in chairs, grazing from platters of meat, cheese, and fresh bread while each waited their turn in the bath. At one point, Gharn pulled aside Matthias, who left immediately after. When Matthias returned, he carried bundles of folded clothing under one arm.

"It's time to get rid of your Outlandish clothing," Gharn muttered as Matthias set the bundles down with a thump. "Even if we were not going to the palace tomorrow, you stick out too much as you are."

Chad snagged his bundle and sniffed theatrically. "And reek," he added, casting a sideways look at Rick. No one laughed. Either the joke had missed, or it hit a little too close. Maybe both.

Gharn retreated into one of the bedrooms without another word. Sulking, maybe. Chad understood. Words weren't going to fix what they'd lost in Emberhold. He glanced at Rick and Evan, then opted for the second bedroom with them, leaving Gharn his solitude. He wondered briefly whether Matthias would bunk with Gharn or just claim a couch in the parlor—probably whichever option annoyed Gharn least.

After his turn in the bath, Chad dressed in the new clothes, feeling awkwardly self-aware. The black trousers were tight through the hips and thighs, buttoned high at the waist with no belt loops. Logical design, given the lack of belts. Still felt weird. The white linen shirt was cut loose, the fabric rough against his skin compared to the blends he was used to. He fiddled with the collar, trying to decide whether to button it fully or leave it casual. Leaving it loose felt more natural.

The calf-high boots, though, were another story. Stiff. Flat-soled. No arch support to speak of. He grimaced as he tugged them on.

He glanced toward the corner where his old clothes lay crumpled. A pang of homesickness knifed through him. *I could swap the soles from my hiking shoes onto these boots,* he thought. If he had time. If he had tools.

He didn't.

Shaking his head, he patted his thigh, feeling the reassuring weight of his knife tucked against him. At least *something* familiar remained.

In front of the mirror above the washbasin, Rick stood, inspecting himself with a grim expression.

"Looking for gray hairs?" Chad quipped.

Rick jerked as if stung, shooting him a sour look—irritated but... guilty too? That made no sense.

"I just—" Rick looked away, shoulders tense. "I just feel out of place, I guess."

Chad nodded, the levity slipping away. "Yeah. I hear that. I feel like I'm wearing somebody else's clothes." He let out a sigh he hadn't meant to. "Somebody else's life, for that matter."

They drifted back to the parlor, where Evan curled up with Rick in an oversized chair, her shawl draped around both of them.

Chad went to the window. Night had swallowed the city. Pools of orange gaslight puddled here and there along the street, but most windows had already gone dark. Even the vendor carts had vanished, leaving the square hollow and strange. Across the way, the clock tower loomed, its mechanical figures frozen mid-parade. Chad stared at it, mind turning. Water pressure? Steam? Weights? Horses yoked to turn massive gears?

It made him think of the old mantel clock back home. He hadn't meant to break anything. He just wanted to understand it. They wouldn't want him poking at their clock here either. He could almost hear his father's voice: *Leave well enough alone, son.*

Chad blinked hard, willing the sudden wetness from his eyes. Everything was close enough to familiar to hurt—and different enough to keep hurting. Which, come to think of it, pretty much summed up how he felt about himself these days. It was like he was shedding layers, piece by piece. And he wasn't sure what was left underneath.

The sensation wasn't exactly welcome. But it wasn't enough to drown out the faint pulse of anticipation building in his chest. Tomorrow.

He looked at Rick and Evan—tired, worn thin, but together—and found himself smiling back when Evan caught his eye. Tomorrow might actually change things.

We get to meet a king.

Evan's skin crawled the moment they stepped outside. The morning light should have felt clean, fresh. Instead, the air pressed against her like a warning.

They left The Noble Nag early, urgency humming in every step. Her instincts screamed that time was short—and a sharp pang of guilt twisted her stomach. Maybe Matthias had been right not to want to come here at all. But the people deserved a chance. A chance Emberhold never had. Maybe they could give it to them.

They hurried through the waking streets. Vendors were already setting up—carts crammed with flowers, sweet rolls, bright scarves, hand-carved baubles. Smiling faces called out as they passed.

"A posy for your hair, love? Would match those green eyes perfectly!"

"A fine scarf, deary—soft as a kitten!"

"Fresh rolls! Still warm from the oven!"

The flowers smelled rich and golden, thick with dew. The scarf brushed her fingers as they passed—cool and impossibly soft. The rolls gleamed, their sticky glaze catching the dawning sun like jewels, but Evan barely noticed. The sweetness turned sour on her tongue. All she could taste was ash.

These people were all so normal.

So unprepared. Where were the guards? The soldiers?

Even this city's towering walls wouldn't stop what she had seen in Emberhold if it came here. Not on their own. She tightened her grip on Rick's hand, clutching his arm through the coarse linen of his new shirt. His presence steadied her but only just.

The palace rose ahead of them, gilded and radiant. Unlike the fortress castle Evan had half-expected, it looked... delicate, almost like a pile of rose-gold pillows stacked atop each other. Filigreed towers curled toward the sky, light catching on their golden accents.

Only the black tower broke the illusion.

It jutted from the far end of the compound like a needle forged from shadow, stark and grim against the morning light.

Their path ended at the palace gates—massive, ornate things of twisted gold. Elegant. Fragile-looking. Closed. Two guards flanked them, standing stiff as statues, faces blank beneath crested helmets. Their armor was polished, but Evan could feel the tension bleeding from them like heat from stone.

Gharn stepped forward, fidgeting in his green robe, which fell in straight lines around his wiry frame. His hair was pulled back severely, making him seem even smaller, more brittle. "What time does King Arlos hold court today?" he asked, voice brisk, almost too sharp.

Nervousness. Evan felt it in him—like a live wire beneath the words.

The guard didn't so much as blink. His gaze stayed fixed on the boulevard. "No court," he said flatly. "Not for a month now."

Gharn blinked rapidly, visibly thrown. Evan felt the jolt ripple through him—shock, confusion, a surge of something like fear. Still, he pushed on. "I am Gharn of Emberhold," he said, summoning a steadiness Evan admired. "I come on behalf of Sorendir the Wise, with an urgent warning for the king."

For a heartbeat, the morning seemed to hold its breath. The guard's expression didn't change. His gaze never shifted. "I said," the man repeated, "no court. Go home."

Gharn's lower lip trembled. His right hand clenched into a white-knuckled fist. He opened his mouth, and—

Rick stepped forward. "He can't." His voice was low but carrying. "Emberhold is gone."

This time, the guard's eyes flicked sideways. Met Rick's. "What do you mean, gone?"

"Destroyed," Rick said. "Attacked. Burned."

"You haven't heard anything?" Chad added, his voice sharp.

One of the other guards shifted. "Rumors of more smoke than usual to the north. But volcanos erupt. It's what they do."

"Nothing of the attack?" Gharn snapped. His voice cracked on the word. A dangerous glint sparked in his eyes—the first real fire Evan had seen from him since Sorendir's death. "Never mind. Where's Ithindar?"

The name landed like a stone in a pond.

The guards exchanged brief, uneasy glances. Finally the second guard stepped to the side, reaching for a cleverly hidden lever embedded in the golden gate's intricate design.

"Ithindar?" Rick asked, low enough that Evan barely caught the query.

Gharn didn't look at him. "The king's chamberlain," he said. "And a wizard."

Chad made a face. "Oh, great. More wizards. Why not?" The sarcasm was light—but underneath, Evan caught the weariness. The frayed edge of hope thinning just a little more.

Minutes later a man emerged through the gate. He wore a black uniform embroidered with gold thread, the intricate designs catching the sun as he moved. He looked to be in his early thirties, though there was a hardness to him that made him seem older. Black hair was slicked back over a strong brow, a faint scar tracing its way down toward sharp jade-green eyes. A short-cropped beard accentuated the harsh lines of his jaw rather than softening them.

Evan tensed as his hand casually came to rest on the pommel of his sword. This was not a man accustomed to being questioned. His voice, when it came, was soft—but carried an edge that brooked no disobedience. "Yes?"

The guards straightened immediately. "Captain Thorne," one said. "These people request audience with Ithindar."

The second added, "They claim Emberhold has fallen."

Thorne's only reaction was a slight lift of one eyebrow. His gaze swept over them, weighing and measuring with a soldier's efficiency.

Then he nodded. "Admit them. I will escort them myself."

"Yes, Captain."

A smaller door opened within the main gate. Thorne was already striding away, and they had to hurry to keep up. Gharn all but jogged, his green robes billowing. Evan and Rick matched pace behind him, with Chad and Matthias bringing up the rear. The paved courtyard flashed past in a blur of stone and gilded fixtures. Page boys in black and gold opened the massive palace doors without a word.

Inside, the air grew heavier.

The entrance hall blazed with wealth: towering paintings, their frames so thick with gold leaf it looked like they might collapse under their own weight; walls tiled in patterns of rose and ivory; a vaulted ceiling painted like the sky itself, clouds curling luminous and soft across an endless blue. Sunlight from high windows made the gold shimmer and seem to move.

Chad let out a low whistle under his breath. Evan understood the reaction. The place was beautiful—impossibly so. But something about it made her skin itch. Like a trap baited too sweetly.

Thorne led them quickly into a smaller chamber off the main hall—a sitting room, furnished with carved chairs and a low table laden with untouched crystal decanters. "Wait here," he said curtly. "Speak to no one."

He vanished through a side door before they could ask anything more. The silence thickened.

"What was that all about?" Rick asked, low.

Gharn shook his head, his face drawn. "This is wrong. Where are the nobles? The courtiers? The palace should be full by now."

Before Evan could voice the same unease tightening in her gut, Thorne returned—with another man in tow. She blinked. *Beautiful* didn't even begin to describe him. Tall, commanding, with skin so smooth it seemed to drink the light. Long hair the color of honey flowed back from pointed ears. An elf. His black-and-gold robes marked him as a man of power, but the green vines embroidered down the sleeves spoke of something older, deeper. Tradition or magic—maybe both. Power radiated from him as naturally as breath. Authority clung to him like a second skin.

"Ithindar!" Gharn exclaimed, rising from his seat, raw relief and anger warring in his voice. "What in the Three's name is going on here?"

The elf's expression softened fractionally, a ghost of a smile tugging at his mouth. "You never did learn patience, Gharn," he said, voice low and warm. He lifted a hand, forestalling Gharn's rising outrage. "I jest. And poorly timed, it seems. I see the grief in your eyes."

The words, delivered gently, did something Evan hadn't expected—they steadied Gharn, just a little.

"Sit," Ithindar said. "Tell me what has transpired. Captain, stand guard."

"Yes, my lord." Thorne drew the heavy curtains closed with a soft whoomph, sealing them into a pocket of dim, gilded silence.

Gharn told the tale, voice cracking only once—when he spoke Sorendir's name at the end. At that, Ithindar lowered his gaze. A brief flicker of sorrow crossed the elf's regal features.

"Two terrible losses," he said quietly when Gharn finished. He placed a hand on Gharn's thin shoulder, the gesture one of genuine mourning. "Sorendir was already a legend when I was young," Ithindar said. "It hardly seems possible that he is gone."

Gharn choked back a sob, folding into himself again. Evan could feel him receding, the fragile anger that had kept him afloat crumbling away.

Ithindar straightened abruptly, robes whispering against the floor. "We must not speak further here," he said, voice sharpening. "Return to your inn. Prepare to leave with haste. I will come before sunset."

Evan opened her mouth to protest—to demand answers—but stopped herself. The set of Ithindar's jaw left no room for argument. Without another word, he turned and slipped through the curtains.

A moment later Thorne reappeared, the heavy drapes parting around him. "I will escort you back to the gates." The finality in his voice brooked no refusal.

As they trailed back through the gleaming palace, Chad muttered, "What the heck is going on here?" The raw frustration in his voice made Evan's heart squeeze.

Thorne said nothing for a moment, his expression carved from stone. At last he spoke, low. "This is not the place for answers. Trust Ithindar. He will find you when the time is right."

Within minutes they were outside again, blinking in the harsher sunlight. The smaller gate clanged shut behind them—a hollow, echoing sound that made Evan flinch. It felt less like being let out and more like being shut away.

"We should leave immediately," Matthias said grimly. "This city is not safe."

Gharn, his face pale and slack with grief, shook his head. "We wait." Evan caught the undertow in his voice—defeat, not conviction.

"We can't leave, anyway," Rick said. "We still need supplies."

Matthias hesitated. For one moment, Evan thought he might turn and walk away without another word. Instead, he nodded once. "Very well." But the detachment in his voice was colder than ever.

The gates loomed behind them, silent and unmoving. The festive bustle of the market continued—but Evan no longer heard it the same way. A flower vendor called out, voice lilting and bright, but it grated against her nerves. The city's cheer had curdled. Every smiling face, every hawker's cry felt sharp now—like the glittering edge of a blade held just a breath from cutting.

Evan pulled Rick's arm closer before realizing it, the market's false cheer rattling against her bones.

Rick paid the vendor, trying not to let uncertainty show on his face. The coins felt wrong in his hand—too heavy, too soft at the edges—and he had no real idea if he was overpaying. But Matthias, looming quietly at his side, hadn't intervened. Rick took that as a good sign. Although he kept the thought to himself, he had to admit—having Matthias around made things easier.

Still unsettling, though.

It was like shopping with a house cat the size of a mastiff: useful for keeping trouble at bay, but Rick never quite forgot he was a mouse by comparison. He mentally crossed flour off their list, hoisting one heavy sack while Matthias, without visible effort, gathered two more. They merged back into the market's thinning currents, angling toward The Noble Nag. Rick hoped Chad would have managed to find a replacement wagon by the time they got there.

But his mind kept drifting backward, snagging on something he couldn't quite name. The vendor's demeanor had been nervous. Guarded. And not just his. Across the square, a shopkeeper hurriedly shuttered his stall—far too early for any normal closing. Shoppers darted between booths with their heads down, and conversations clustered low and tight, like students in an overzealously monitored library.

Even the air felt wrong.

Why does it feel like everyone is holding their breath? Outwardly everything looked normal—or close enough to fool most strangers. But the cadence was off. Movements sharper. Exchanges brisker.

Rick frowned, scanning the square more critically. "I don't get it," he said aloud.

Matthias shot him a sidelong look, unreadable as ever.

Rick pressed anyway. "Does it seem like everyone's on edge, or is that just me?"

A beat of hesitation. Then, "Too few guards."

Rick's stomach tightened. He hadn't noticed. Not consciously. But now that Matthias had pointed this out, he realized it was true. Emberhold's smaller market had always had a visible guard presence—half a dozen soldiers at minimum, even on slow days. Here, in a square ten times the size, he spotted only three—and they weren't patrolling. They stood grouped together, talking quietly, weapons sheathed.

He was still watching when a new voice called out. "Maddocks, you dog. It *is* you!"

Beside Rick, Matthias's step hitched—almost imperceptibly, but Rick caught it.

A man limped toward them, leaning heavily on a crutch. His face was a map of old scars, the worst cutting down one side into a twisted half-smile. Despite it, his expression radiated pure joy. "Been a long time," the man said, stopping a few paces away. "I know I look a sight since Bleaker's Ridge, but I can't have changed so much you don't recognize me... Argus, remember?"

Matthias faced him fully. Expressionless. Not guarded. Not cautious.

Blank.

Rick felt the temperature of the moment drop.

"You do not know me," Matthias said, voice low and iron flat.

Argus blinked, visibly reeling. His hand trembled on the crutch. He opened his mouth—closed it. Swallowed. Tried again.

"Have it your way, then," Argus muttered. His shoulders sagged. He adjusted his coat with fumbling fingers and limped away, disappearing into the crowd without looking back. Rick thought he caught a fragment of muttering—"Too high and mighty for us grunts"—but it was quickly swallowed by the market's fraying noise. Rick's grip tightened on the sack of flour. Old comrades didn't usually pretend not to know each other. Not without a reason.

Ahead of him, Matthias resumed walking, his pace steady, almost lazy despite the weight he carried. The crowd parted around him without a word.

Not out of deference but out of instinct.

*

"I'm telling you, there's something off about that man." Rick hunched forward in the parlor, elbows braced on his knees. The door to the stairs stood open behind him, so they could hear if Gharn or Matthias returned. He'd just finished recounting the incident with Argus. The nervous energy hadn't left him—it clung to his skin like static.

"Maybe he's a spy," Chad offered, fiddling with the edge of his belt. "Or whatever passes for special forces around here."

Rick considered it. "But why would a spy fall in with us?"

"Or special forces," Chad said stubbornly.

"Or special forces," Rick echoed with a tired smile.

Evan curled a strand of hair absently around one finger, her brows drawn. "It could be as simple as him being in the right place at the right time. He saved us from those bandits. Maybe he saw a bigger opportunity when he learned what we were after."

Rick drummed his fingers lightly against his thigh. "Sorendir knew something," he said. "But he didn't share it."

Chad snorted. "Like anything about that wizard made sense."

Rick nodded slowly. "He wanted Matthias with us, but it felt like he didn't entirely trust him either." He turned to Evan. "Do you get anything off him?"

Evan's finger froze mid-spiral. She looked down, biting her lip. "Nothing," she admitted. "Everyone else... I can usually sense something now, but not with him. It's like he's blank."

Rick frowned. And why did she sound almost guilty about that?

Before he could push further, footsteps thudded up the stairs. Rick tensed, gesturing sharply for silence. Moments later Gharn entered the parlor, no longer in the ridiculous robe. He was followed by Ithindar—and, unexpectedly, by the palace captain. Thorne, if Rick remembered right. Gharn beckoned them forward.

They gathered near the center of the parlor. Rick noticed that Matthias lingered against the far wall, arms folded, half in shadow. Watching. Not joining. *Typical.*

Thorne closed the suite door behind them and planted himself in front of it, hands clasped loosely behind his back. Guard stance. At the palace, Thorne's composure had been unshakable. Now Rick caught flickers of tension—the subtle roll of his shoulders, the slight shift of weight from foot to foot. *He's worried,* he realized. *But hiding it well.*

Ithindar remained standing, robes pooling like ink around his boots. "I apologize for the—unusual circumstances of this meeting," he said. "You have likely noticed not all is well in Ironspire—or the palace."

"Matthias pointed out the missing guards," Rick said carefully.

Thorne's jaw tensed, a small but telling tic.

"Your friend is perceptive," Ithindar said. "King Arlos has made a series of troubling decisions. Our garrison has been sent west on indefinite maneuvers, the court dismissed, audiences canceled. Even I can barely gain his ear—and I have been Lord Wizard to Ironspire since his grandfather's reign."

Gharn clenched his hands, his voice rising. "Recall the soldiers!"

"I cannot," Ithindar said quietly. "The king's authority is absolute within his own kingdom. And he no longer listens."

Gharn sat back, trembling slightly. "The High King must be warned."

"High King?" Chad asked. "Just how many kings do you people need?"

"Outlanders?" Ithindar asked mildly.

Gharn nodded, favoring Chad with a dark look.

"Drakerath is one of the Nine Kingdoms," Ithindar explained. "Each is ruled independently but bound by a federal compact under Syndar."

Rick muttered under his breath, "Sounds like the United States."

"And about as effective," Chad added dryly.

Gharn pressed on, ignoring them. "Can you reach Valirion?"

The elf's gaze dropped. "No. I have been unable to make contact for two months. That is why Captain Thorne is here."

Gharn looked ready to explode from frustration. Rick could feel the tremors beneath the surface.

Thorne stepped forward. "I will accompany you partway. I carry a message for the High King. I will deliver it myself."

"And what of our quest?" Gharn snapped.

Ithindar lifted a calming hand. "Peace, my friend. Though I never fully shared Sorendir's faith in prophecy, I respected it. And I respect your mission."

The elf smiled faintly. "Thorne is one of the few I trust implicitly. He knows the kingdom's roads—and dangers—better than any. He will travel with you as far as your paths align. His rank may smooth your passage where words fail."

Rick listened, weighing every word.

If Ithindar truly trusted Thorne, it made sense. Travel would be faster. Safer. And if he was being honest, Rick wouldn't mind another set of watchful eyes on Matthias.

Thorne stood silently, letting the weight of Ithindar's endorsement settle. But Rick caught something else too: the way Thorne's eyes flicked briefly to Matthias, then Chad, then dismissed the others. Measuring them. Assessing. Rick could practically hear the mental calculus—

Matthias: dangerous but useful.

Chad: solid, fit, maybe unreliable.

Rick and Evan: civilians, question marks.

In Thorne's view, traveling with this group wasn't charity. It was tactical. He was betting he could reach the High King faster with them—at least until he needed to peel away.

Rick sat back, exhaling slowly. It made sense. He still didn't like it.

"A military escort," Chad said, grinning. "Why not? We're practically diplomatic envoys now."

Rick added w*arn the High King* and t*rust no one completely* to his ever-growing list of priorities. He suppressed a groan.

Across the room, Thorne caught his gaze—a silent, assessing stare that made Rick sit up straighter without meaning to. *Marine,* Rick thought grimly. Maybe not in name but in soul.

A glance sideways showed Chad eyeing the captain with open mischief. Rick winced internally. This was going to go great.

And Matthias, as always, simply watched. Expressionless. Unfathomable.

Rick shoved down a sigh and set his mind to the task ahead. *Loads of fun,* he thought sourly. *Loads.*

Is he hitting every hole on purpose? Evan's teeth chattered within her skull as the wagon lurched and bounced with every cobblestone. Gharn sat beside her on the seat, driving the rig, while Captain Thorne rode ahead, his uniformed presence causing people to give way. The rest of the group rode as they could, most finding it easier to stay in the wagon's immediate wake. She had to admit Thorne was already smoothing their progress by his mere presence.

Unfortunately, it seemed unlikely to last. The man was an unknown factor in an already tenuous situation. She laughed at herself when she realized she was now mirroring Rick's way of thinking. *Sometimes empathy sucks.*

The basic idea was sound, though. She sized up her traveling companions.

Rick, abruptly gifted with a power he'd never even dreamed existed. Something had been bothering him ever since the incident with the amulet, but he refused to talk about it, and she pretended not to notice when he changed the subject.

Chad, a wizard in the mechanical sense, cast adrift in a world that couldn't even accept steam power. He wanted desperately to get out of his brother's shadow, yet now that shadow seemed to stretch longer than ever. No wonder he reeked of frustration.

Gharn, a man who seemed to have devoted his life to serving a master who had little more than a week ago sacrificed himself. He'd spent years—decades, even—being looked down upon by people who had judged him based on his association with what they'd believed to be an old fool. And had they known the truth, it would most likely have been worse. The gnome's mood fluctuated between deep anger and hopeless despondency, for which Evan couldn't blame him. She only hoped he would find a new purpose before he allowed the old to pull him under—and the rest of them along with him.

And then Matthias, that frustrating man who never answered questions without spawning a half-dozen more. Maddening. Which was also all she could say about him, because somehow she just couldn't read him the way she could the others.

Finally, Calladorn Thorne. Wary. Watchful. Disillusioned. Determined. She had felt the complex ball of emotions with which he'd looked upon the palace as they passed on their way to the city's south gate. The more she observed him, the more she got a sense of him—the more she came to understand duty and honor were his defining traits. She didn't need to be psychic to see Rick didn't trust the soldier, but she felt otherwise. They could trust him completely. *So long as we don't impede his mission.*

A particularly strong jolt brought her out of her reverie, and she glared at Gharn despite her intention to be sympathetic to his situation. Following so close behind a horse wasn't helping her mood either. She idly wondered if the stable boys at the inn had been feeding the animals beans rather than hay.

"The seat has good springs, I swear." Chad, riding beside the wagon, must have seen her sour expression and misunderstood its source.

"So you said," she answered without unclenching her jaw. On the plus side, she wouldn't be walking bowlegged whenever they stopped for the night. No guarantee her bottom would escape bruises, though.

Beyond Chad, the city continued about its daily business. She found it ironic how they'd come to this place of shelter, only to find it wasn't as safe as it seemed and they had to abandon it the very next day.

The people knew something was wrong, even if they couldn't put a name to it.

No, she was ready to leave this place behind. At least on the road, they could see the dangers surrounding them. Here—it felt like the people were more trapped than protected by the tall walls. *I'll miss that bed, though.* No point in lying to herself. She wondered how many more nights it would be before she got to enjoy that kind of comfort again.

A cold shadow fell across her, causing her skin to prickle. As they passed through the gate, the sound of the wagon wheels clattering over the paving echoed within the confined space. Peering up, she saw the gash hiding a portcullis. Beyond that were a variety of holes staring down at her with sightless eyes. Murder holes. And then, sky again. The sun, slipping toward the horizon, bathed her with warmth.

Now that they had cleared the city walls, the cobbled road finally gave way to packed earth. The difference was immediate—and blessed. The wagon continued to jostle and bounce, but without the punishing clatter of stone beneath the wheels. Evan shifted, grimacing as sore muscles and bruised bones lodged their protests. Her backside, in particular, had developed a very articulate sense of betrayal.

I wonder...

Closing her eyes, Evan reached inward—not to fight the pain but to face it. She let the discomfort rise. Let it crash through her without resistance. Pain was real. Pretending otherwise only gave it teeth. But by embracing it—

It dulled. Flattened. No longer an enemy clawing at her thoughts. Simply another part of the landscape she moved through.

When she opened her eyes, she realized the city walls had already fallen far behind them—a gray line softening against the last light of day. It must have taken longer than it seemed to find that fragile balance.

Ahead, the sunset bathed the left side of the walls in a rich orange glow, warm and almost welcoming. To the right, shadows swallowed the stone, cloaking it in darkness. Evan studied the split and wondered which path lay before them: the road lit by fire or the one swallowed by shade.

Rick rode just behind the wagon, his horse moving with far more confidence than it had that first grim day after Emberhold. When he caught her watching, he straightened automatically, offering a crooked smile that warmed her chest despite everything. She smiled back—small, real. His free hand brushed lightly against the wagon's side, a casual, grounding touch he probably didn't even realize he gave.

But it was the slump in his shoulders, the way the smile faded too quickly, that betrayed him.

"It's strange to be traveling again, isn't it?" he asked. His voice was light—but Evan heard the weariness beneath it.

She nodded. "At least we're not leaving a fallen city this time."

The words had barely left her lips when a low horn sounded behind them. The note carried across the fields like a living thing, vibrating in her chest. Evan's spine stiffened, and she turned sharply, scanning the distant skyline. Farther back, Matthias reined his horse around, scanning as well.

Another horn joined the first.

Then another. And another—a grim chorus rising from the city they'd just abandoned.

The wagon didn't slow. If anything, it picked up speed.

Gharn hunched forward in the driver's seat, urging the horses faster without a word. Chad pulled his horse to a stop, wheeling around to face the distant walls. His hands clenched at his sides, fists tight with helpless rage.

There's no fixing this, Evan thought. The certainty of it rooted in her like a stone. She shivered—and it had nothing to do with the sun slipping below the horizon.

The city's calm had shattered. She could hear it in the overlapping horns, their voices grinding against each other like broken gears.

And worse—she could feel it. A low, thrumming knot at the base of her skull, vibrating with the sudden, collective fear of thousands.

"Keep going!" Thorne shouted from up ahead, his voice carrying over the growing din.

But Evan saw the truth in his posture. He wanted to turn back. Burned to do it. His body leaned toward the city, toward duty—but his mind knew better.

The moment he accepted that he could do nothing—that they could do nothing—hit Evan like a blow. She recognized it because she felt it too.

Chad kicked his horse back into motion, catching up to Thorne with a grim set to his jaw.

Rick urged his mount closer to the wagon, riding tight alongside her. "They're better defended than Emberhold was," he said. But the words fell flat between them, hollow and half-hearted.

They both knew the truth.

From her other side came a broken sound. Gharn. The gnome sat rigid in the driver's seat, his head bowed, his shoulders trembling. Soft, muffled sobs barely rose above the creak of the wagon wheels and the city's distant cries.

Evan's heart twisted. She reached toward him instinctively—then let her hand fall, helpless. What could she say to him when she felt the city's death in her own bones?

The wagon rolled on, the wheels grinding against dirt that was already cooling under the dying light, carrying them away from Ironspire—

And whatever fate was falling behind them.

IX
Breaking

Duty had never settled more heavily on Calladorn's shoulders than it did that first night away from Ironspire. Each time a horn sounded behind them, it lanced through him like a blade. The blasts came quickly at first, urgent and insistent, as though sheer noise could pull him back. As the night deepened, they thinned—fewer, fainter—until a final solitary cry rose against the wind, low and keening, before it was swallowed by the dark. He rode with his eyes fixed ahead, but the silence that followed rooted itself inside him.

The kingdom had been lost well before these strangers appeared at the palace gates. But how? How had it unraveled so completely?

He sifted through the memories as they traveled, seeking the moment where it had slipped beyond saving—but there was no clear break. No battle, no rebellion. Just a slow, insidious decay. By the time he had recognized the rot for what it was, the kingdom had already become a pile of leaves awaiting a stiff wind.

The old commanders—men like his father—had been retired or reassigned to meaningless posts. The king himself, once wise and deliberate, had grown capricious. And when Ithindar had finally approached him in private, the king had seemed to listen.

Until the next day at court, when he had publicly and viciously humiliated his adviser. It was the last court King Arlos had held. Threatening Ithindar—his own adviser—with exile had told Calladorn everything he needed to know: *Protect what you can.*

And so Calladorn found himself here—riding away from the city he had once sworn to defend, tasked instead with shepherding a fragile, bewildered group of strangers into the unknown.

When they had first appeared at the palace that morning, part of him had dared to hope. If their warning had sparked even a fragment of the king's old resolve, perhaps it might have turned the tide. But Arlos had not even deigned to hear them, much less act. Even if the strangers' story had been a lie, Drakerath had already fallen. All he could do now was carry word to Syndar and pray that it would not be too late for others.

Two hours into the flight, the road narrowed and slipped beneath the cover of forest. The air changed—cooler, heavier with the scents of damp earth, mossy bark, and leaf rot. Shadows tangled between the trees, and even the wagon's clattering rattle seemed muffled by the hush. No breeze stirred. The moons—both fat and nearly full tonight—poured white gold over their path, making travel possible where otherwise they would have been forced to halt.

It was poor comfort.

"Demons," the boy Chad had muttered, one of his few words since they had fled.

The memory prickled. Calladorn adjusted his grip on the reins, letting the rhythmic sway of the horse beneath him bleed some of the restless energy from his muscles. His shirt clung damply to his skin. Dew. Morning would not be far behind.

A soft hoot broke the quiet. An owl, somewhere off to the right. *Normal,* he told himself. Familiar. Yet the sound fell strangely against the stillness, like a word spoken too loudly in a sanctuary. Behind him the wagon creaked and groaned over a rut.

"Captain Thorne?" Evan's voice called softly.

He slowed, steering his mount to the side to let the wagon pull alongside. The woman sat high on the seat, cloaked in a shawl, Gharn slumped beside her in exhausted silence.

"Calladorn," he corrected gently. "We are not an army."

She smiled—a small, weary curve of the lips that nonetheless carried warmth. "Calladorn, then. Will we be stopping soon?"

He touched the place over his heart where the folded letters rested, a habitual check he scarcely noticed. His first instinct was to say no—to press on, cover more ground, put as much distance between them and the city as possible. Every hour counted. But Ithindar's last charge to him had not been merely to deliver warnings. He was to watch over these travelers, protect them. Their safety mattered too. And weary horses would carry them nowhere.

Calladorn inclined his head. "There is a clearing ahead. We will make camp until dawn." He nudged his horse back into the lead. Rick rode up beside him a moment later, his mount uneasy but manageable under his rigid grip.

"You know this road well?" Rick asked, voice low enough not to carry.

"I do."

Rick hesitated. "How far have we come?"

How far have we escaped? Calladorn thought, the bitterness sharp in his mouth. "About eighteen miles," he said aloud.

It wasn't far enough—not if their enemy had wings. But for tonight it would have to be.

The clearing revealed itself like a bowl of shadow pooled between the trees—bare earth, scattered stones, the brittle skeletons of old firepits.

"No fire," Calladorn said as he dismounted.

Chad, who had been leading the second horse tied to the wagon, gave a soft protest. "It's cold."

"It will grow colder before dawn," Calladorn agreed, loosening the cinch on his saddle. "But a fire would draw eyes. And if these... demons can fly, as you said..."

Chad swallowed visibly and said nothing more.

They made camp with quiet efficiency. Canvas was stretched from one side of the wagon to the ground, creating a rough lean-to. Stones weighted the edges. Blankets were unrolled beneath the makeshift shelter, while the horses were tethered along a line strung between two trees.

Calladorn watched, marking small details. Rick and Chad moved among the horses with an ease that surprised him—brushing down the animals, checking hooves and girths. They weren't soldiers. But they weren't helpless either. And it appeared Rick had been the one to determine what supplies were needed for the journey. He had the makings of a good quartermaster.

After a meager meal of dried fruit and hard bread, the group crawled beneath the wagon's shelter to rest. Calladorn lingered, pulling his cloak tighter against the growing damp, and moved toward the boulder he had marked earlier as a vantage point.

It shifted.

He froze instinctively, hand darting to the hilt of his sword—only to find Matthias already seated there, turning calmly to face him.

"I will keep watch," the man said.

Calladorn studied him. The fireless dark sharpened every line of Matthias's frame—armor well cared for, sword easily at hand, posture at once relaxed and alert.

"Where did you serve?" Calladorn asked quietly.

"Mercenary."

Not an answer he liked. Mercenaries fought for coin, not cause. Their loyalties could turn with the wind. Still, the man had traveled willingly with this group—had fought alongside them.

Calladorn hesitated a moment longer, then nodded once. "Wake me in two hours."

He turned back toward the shelter, feeling the weight of Matthias's gaze track his every step.

*

Two hours later the sky had paled from coal to ash, the first uncertain strokes of dawn brushing the tree line.

Calladorn rose awkwardly from where he had lain. Sleep had never truly come, only fragments of rest slipping between long stretches of listening—to the owl's last calls, to the rustle of creatures unseen, to the steady silence of Matthias keeping watch. The man stood motionless near the perimeter—an unbroken silhouette against the lightening east, his posture neither strained nor relaxed. A statue carved from twilight and discipline. Calladorn watched him a moment longer. Matthias had kept faithful vigil. But whether he'd been watching for enemies or studying the group itself, Calladorn couldn't be certain.

A bird's musical call split the air. Beneath the wagon's lean-to, a ragged snore rattled. At least someone had found sleep.

He rose, shaking the lingering chill from his limbs, and set about breaking camp. Matthias joined him without a word, shaking the dew from the canvas, folding blankets, packing gear. Their movements were efficient, practiced. Calladorn wondered—had Matthias learned such habits in true campaigns or in darker kinds of service?

By the time the others roused, bleary and groaning, everything was ready but the bedrolls. Calladorn allowed himself a brief grin as Chad stumbled off into the woods in desperate search of a bush. Some men just weren't made for mornings.

The wagon rolled again before the sun fully cleared the trees. They chewed dried meat and fruit as they traveled, the conversation sparse and muted. Calladorn took the lead once more, with Rick and Chad riding close beside him. Evan drove the wagon steadily, and Matthias—unsurprisingly—fell into the rear guard without instruction, as if it were the only place he belonged.

Chad yawned, his voice still rough from sleep. "How far until the next town?"

Calladorn shrugged. "This road's less traveled than the King's Highway. Safer, under the circumstances. Villages lie scattered every five to ten miles. Only one has an inn—and we'll reach it in a few hours, if that's what you're wondering."

"What? No. I was thinking... the people. Should we warn them?"

Calladorn glanced sidelong at the boy, reassessing. There was a depth there he hadn't expected. A thread of duty, frayed but present. The same question had gnawed at Calladorn through the night. They hadn't been able to save Ironspire. They might save others—but at what cost? Every stop delayed their greater mission. The kingdom's salvation depended on Syndar now, not a handful of scattered farms.

Yet...

"Yes," Calladorn said at last. "We'll warn them, but we won't stop. After that, their fates are their own."

Chad nodded, a tight motion. His lips pressed into a thin line.

Rick spoke next, his gray-blue gaze sharp with calculation. "What else should we expect on the way?"

Calladorn guided his horse around a fallen branch before answering. "In another week, we'll reach the edge of Drakerath. The Shifts crowd the border there, leaving only a thin passage up into the mountains. We'll have to rejoin the King's Highway at that point, but it sees little travel—mostly caravans moving goods between kingdoms."

He adjusted the reins absently, scanning the road ahead. "A week beyond that lies Merchant's Rest. From there, three weeks to Wester. Another four weeks to the city of Syndar..." He let the words trail off into invitation.

"If you are with me that long," he added.

Rick's scowl deepened, a flicker of frustration crossing his face before he smoothed it away. "We're headed for Southwatch. Gharn knows the way. I don't."

Calladorn noted the distaste coloring the words. This one didn't like having his course set by others. He recognized the trait all too well.

*

The next days passed beneath leaden skies, pregnant with rain but holding back on delivery.

Villages went by. Each time, Calladorn rode ahead with one of the others to find the mayor and deliver their warning while the wagon caught up. Each time, they left behind them a town bustling with activity like a kicked anthill.

He hoped it was enough.

Then they rejoined the main road and left the forest behind. The sun climbed higher, but the air grew cooler as the road ascended. The trees grew scraggly, thinner, battered by altitude and wind. Somewhere ahead, Calladorn knew, the land would bare its throat—and show him what he dreaded.

He recognized the rock formation when it appeared: a jagged thrust of black stone split like a broken spearhead. His chest tightened.

He forced his breathing to slow as they crested the rise.

The foothills fell away before them, revealing a sweeping view of the forested plain—and beyond it, Ironspire.

Or what remained of it.

The proud towers were gone. In their place, a monstrous pillar of black smoke coiled skyward, a wound torn open against the horizon. The black cloud clawed eastward, an obscene tendril reaching for the eastern border, staining the blue heavens with its filth. Calladorn had known what he would see. Had prepared himself for it.

It didn't matter.

The breath shuddered from his lungs unbidden. His fingers locked around the reins until the leather bit into his gloves, until his knuckles paled. His jaw trembled, clenched hard enough to ache. *It's a necessary retreat,* he told himself. *Duty, not failure.*

The words rang hollow.

He had left them. Left them to burn.

A hand touched his shoulder. He flinched—almost—then stilled. It was Chad, mounted beside him, face drawn in sober sympathy. "I'm sorry," the boy said, voice roughened by genuine feeling.

Calladorn stiffened reflexively, every instinct urging him to reject the comfort. Sentiment weakened. Sentiment distracted.

But he didn't pull away. Nor did he speak. He couldn't trust his voice. Instead, he drew a breath—sharp, burning—then another. The cold air tore at his throat, but he welcomed it. Each inhalation anchored him, braced him against the hollow ache in his chest.

At last he turned his mount, nudging it forward.

Ahead, the road bent deeper into the mountains. Above, storm clouds gathered—a dark pall against the fading blue. The world mourned with him.

He didn't look back.

Wind whipped at Rick's cloak, snapping it like a sail and threatening to tear him from the saddle. Hunched low, he gripped the clasp tighter against his throat, trying to keep the hood pinned down. Icy rain lashed his face, each droplet a needle against his skin. In weather like this, he'd discovered it was smarter to let the horse pick its own way. Four legs were steadier than two, and he was grateful to be riding. Walking in this churning mess would have made him even more miserable than he already was.

Squinting into the downpour, he lifted his head enough to check on Evan. There wasn't much to see. The wagon moved at a crawl, its passengers huddled under sodden cloaks, dark shapes against the graying world. He could tell who was driving now only by Gharn's smaller size.

Rick's heart swelled. *I hope she's doing all right.* He wished he could be the one riding next to her, but Gharn's size forced him to be always on the wagon.

Beyond them, Calladorn rode point, his figure stoic against the sheeting rain, though no guidance was needed—the road allowed only one direction: forward. To their right, a cliff loomed, water streaming down its face in gleaming torrents. Most of it crossed the road, carving new ruts with every rill, sending the wagon lurching as its wheels dipped and bucked. Some runoff raced alongside them, bubbling underfoot, but most of it went over the edge to their left, vanishing into mist.

Rick risked a glance that way but saw only the pale, thrashing veil of rain. Somewhere across the valley stood another range of mountains, but the world beyond the ledge had disappeared behind a shifting white curtain. Even the valley floor was hidden—he only knew a river wound below them by the faint, angry rush of unseen rapids.

"Travel without a car sucks," Chad said from Rick's right. His cloak, gripped close around his body, left only his face exposed. Wet hair plastered his forehead, water trickling down his nose and chin in steady rivulets. Rick didn't answer, but he agreed.

Without warning, his horse skittered sideways. Startled, Rick yanked the reins and reached to pat its soaked withers. "Whoa! Easy!" The horse huffed sharply, ears pinned flat against the wind.

Then everything happened at once.

A dark shape barreled past between him and Chad, bumping hard against Rick's leg. *Matthias.* Rick's horse reared, panic jolting through its body. He had no chance to recover—the next thing he knew, he was tumbling backward, slamming into the mud with a jarring thud. He rolled instinctively, avoiding the lashing hooves, and scrambled clear just as the horse fled down the road behind them.

A low, grinding rumble pulled his head up. The rear wheel of the wagon was sinking. The road's edge, destabilized by the runoff, sheared away with a sudden, sickening crack, and the wagon tipped, listing sharply toward the edge.

"Evan!"

He caught a glimpse of her face, white and stricken beneath her hood. Gharn leaped from the seat, landing hard against the cliff wall, and

Evan tried to follow, clambering after him. The wagon bucked again, the horse straining wildly against its traces. Calladorn appeared at its head, seizing the bridle.

Leaping from his saddle, Matthias threw himself against the wagon's rear corner, boots digging into the treacherous muck. His muscles bunched, arms corded with effort as he fought to haul it back from the brink. In a surreal flash of clarity, Rick registered the man's face: not straining, not grimacing—calm, almost serene, as if pulling a wagon from disaster were nothing out of the ordinary. Chad was there a moment later, throwing his own weight into it.

The wagon stuttered, teetered—and kept sliding.

Rick struggled to his feet, slipped, crashed down again. Mud slicked his palms, chilled through his drenched clothes. He looked up, and for an instant, Evan's gaze locked onto his—raw terror written plain across the distance.

No. No, no, no. This wasn't happening.

His heart slammed against his ribs. His breath caught, too thick, too shallow—and then the fear broke apart. It splintered, fell away, leaving something else behind.

Clarity.

The world became vectors. Arcs. Forces. The wagon's weight pulling it over the cliff's edge, the frictionless slide, Chad and Matthias straining against physics they had no hope of defeating.

As his hand stretched forward, Rick's mind overlaid the scene with lines of motion, like chalk sketches on a board—angles, velocities, fulcrums. Every variable, a thread he could trace.

The wagon's back end was lifting, its center of gravity shifting higher with each jolt, inertia pulling it toward destruction.

His hands moved instinctively, carving symbols into the stormy air. Sharp, clean gestures, as natural to him as breathing.

Force equals mass times acceleration. Adjust for friction—no, for water, slope, unstable gravel. Correct for shifting load, for torque, for center-of-gravity displacement.

His mind raced, the calculations assembling themselves faster than conscious thought, and he exhaled sharply. The equation locked.

Rick spoke—not shouting, not panicking. All precision. "*F* equals *ma*, directed by theta, dampened by mu kappa, transfer energy—redistribute—stabilize."

The words cut through the storm, each syllable weighted, sure. The air twisted. Reality buckled, subtle and sharp. And he felt it yield. Felt the forces he had named shift under his hand.

And he knew, deep in his core, that it would obey.

For a fraction of a second, Rick stayed frozen, watching the impossible outcome unfold exactly as he had calculated. Warmth infused him. Suffused him.

Then it went wrong.

Too much.

He knew it even as it happened, the certainty lancing through him as sharply as the storm's cold. The wagon didn't just slide to safety. It jolted as if struck by an unseen hammer, the rear wheels slamming onto the fractured roadbed with a sickening crunch. The whole structure shuddered under the impact, teetered—and held. Just enough. The tipping inertia broke. The wagon's path jerked violently away from the cliff's edge. Chad and Matthias were flung like rag dolls and crashed into the cliff wall on the opposite side of the road. There was a crack—wood, maybe something more—but Rick didn't have time to sort it out.

Pain knifed through him, sudden and raw. He gasped, staggering a half-step backward. It wasn't just his muscles or his bones—it was deeper than that, a pull against the very core of him. His skin prickled cold. The rain felt heavier. A deadweight dragged at his limbs.

Something had been taken, he could feel it. And yet—the wagon was safe. He locked onto that fact like a drowning man to driftwood. The wagon was safe.

Evan was safe.

His knees buckled. His vision shrank at the edges into a gray haze. He forced air into his lungs—sharp, ragged breaths scraping against the tightness in his chest. Somehow, through sheer stubbornness, he lurched upright before anyone could see the tremor that ran through him.

"Rick?" Evan's voice—sharp, alarmed—cut across the rain.

He turned his head toward her, the motion slow and heavier than it should have been. She wasn't looking at him, not exactly. She was staring at the road where the wagon should have gone over.

She had seen.

"That—" She swallowed, rain streaking her face. "That wasn't—" She tried again, voice shaking. "You didn't just do that, did you?"

He dragged the corners of his mouth into a smirk. It felt brittle, hollow. "Just... physics," he said, the words scraping past the rawness in his throat.

For a heartbeat, she looked like she might believe him. But deep inside, where he couldn't lie to himself, another truth thrummed. This wasn't just physics. It was something else. Something that still hummed in his blood, dangerous and exhilarating.

But Evan, clinging to the wagon's side, was safe. He pulled her into his embrace, squeezing hard. Her head pressed back against his chest and his still-thudding heart.

Gharn hauled himself out from under the wagon, mud slicked across his face and tunic. Rick's heart lurched when he realized just how narrowly the little gnome must have escaped being crushed. Their eyes met—brief, sharp—and Rick saw it there.

Gharn *knew*. He knew exactly what had happened.

Rick's stomach twisted. "Oh no," he muttered under his breath. He turned away quickly, scanning the scene, needing something—anything—to focus on.

Chad crouched by the wagon's rear, pale beneath the rain, hands pressed to the undercarriage.

"What?" Rick said aloud, voice still rough-edged.

"The axle," Chad answered grimly. "Whatever you just did—it couldn't take the stress. It's bent."

Rick's mind stuttered, flinched toward rational calculations—stress factors, torque, material tolerances—but found nothing comforting there. "Can we still travel?" he asked, steadying his voice.

Chad hesitated, squinting through the downpour, then gave a slight nod. "Maybe. If we take it slow. But the wheels are gonna weave like a drunk on roller skates."

Rick nodded once, feeling the cold dig deeper under his skin. He turned toward Calladorn, who had finally soothed the trembling draft horse. "Is there anywhere safe ahead?"

Calladorn gave a grim nod. "There is a cave. Travelers use it sometimes. I haven't been this far, but I have heard of it."

"How far?" Rick pressed.

Calladorn shook his head. "I don't know. Close, I think. I had hoped to reach it before... this happened."

Rick ground the heel of his hand against his forehead, forcing rain from his eyes. "Will you be able to fix it when we get there?" he asked Chad, the question heavier than it should have been.

Chad shrugged helplessly. "Beats me. Depends how much more beating it takes before we get there."

Rick nodded again, more by reflex than thought, and a flicker of movement caught his eye. Matthias appeared out of the storm, leading three loose horses by their reins. His armor was streaked with mud, but he moved easily, almost lazily.

He handed the reins to Rick without ceremony. "You people need to stop losing things," Matthias said blandly.

Rick blinked at him, rain dripping from his eyelashes, the absurdity of the moment crashing into him like a wave. Had Matthias just made a joke? Rick stood there, stupidly holding the reins, soaked to the bone, knees shaking harder than he wanted to admit. The only thing that kept him upright was the lingering, treacherous echo of what he'd felt in the instant the magic had answered him—the impossible clarity, the certainty that for one heartbeat, the universe had *listened.*

And part of him wanted to feel it again. Badly.

He pushed the thought away, tightening his grip on the reins until the leather bit into his palms. *Later.* He'd deal with it later.

Right now they had to move.

The fire grew, crackling and snapping softly, casting long, quivering shadows across the uneven stone walls. Smoke threaded upward, drawn by drafts that slipped between the crevices overhead, barely visible against the dark.

Evan lingered by the horses a while, her hand stroking damp coats with a currycomb in slow, soothing arcs. The animals shifted uneasily, heads tossing, muscles bunching with nervous energy each time a thunderclap rolled through the tempestuous sky outside. She whispered nonsense words to them—comforts without meaning, but the tone seemed to help.

She also projected calm in mental waves, gathering it in her heart—an imagined warm glow that she then pushed through her arm. It was fumbling at first, but each new attempt brought greater proficiency, and the animals relaxed visibly.

When their trembling lessened, she allowed herself to step back, wiping her hands absently on the sides of her cloak. The fire's warmth beckoned across the cold stone floor. She hesitated for a moment, glancing toward Rick, still seated motionlessly near the flames.

If only I could do the same for him, she thought, hiding her grimace. He hadn't stirred since the moment they'd gotten the fire going. His body was rigid, his hands loose but slack against his knees, as if letting go of anything would cost more energy than he had left to spend.

She crossed the distance slowly, her boots making soft scuffs against the driest patches of rock.

Rick sat hunched, his damp clothes steaming faintly in the fire's glow. The skin beneath his eyes had gone darker, bruised-looking, and there was a drawn tightness around his mouth that hadn't been there before. His lips were slightly parted, as if even breathing had become an effort.

Evan knelt beside him, letting the fire's warmth catch her too—soak into the chill that had dug itself deep under her skin. She didn't speak at first. Just shared the space with him, lacing her fingers into his. The ghost of a smile touched his lips, and he squeezed back but didn't look up.

Across the fire, Gharn sat cross-legged, feeding small sticks methodically into the flames. His movements were careful, precise, as if each action had to be remembered and enacted from some distant place. His salt-and-pepper beard was plastered to his chest, still dripping, and the sleeves of his tunic were streaked with grime.

Chad rummaged through one of the wagon's chests, muttering darkly under his breath about "ancient tools" and "dungeon crafts class rejects," while Calladorn crouched nearby, sharpening a blade with slow, even strokes. The rhythmic rasp of stone-on-metal threaded through the crackle of the fire and the muffled roar of rain outside. Only Matthias remained apart, standing near the mouth of the cave, arms folded, his gaze trained on the storm with the patience of a fisherman on a placid lake.

Evan focused her attention back on Rick. “You scared me today,” she said quietly.

He didn’t flinch, but his eyes, when they lifted to hers, were shadowed and raw. The firelight caught the lines of exhaustion etched into his face, making him look suddenly older. “I scared myself,” he admitted, the words rough.

Evan tucked her legs beneath her, leaning closer to his side. She could feel the tension vibrating through him, a current barely contained beneath the surface.

“You’re not okay,” she said gently. Not a question. Just truth.

Rick gave a soft huff that might have been a laugh if it hadn’t been so hollow. “Tired,” he said. “More than I thought I’d be.”

She reached up to brush a rain-matted lock of hair from his forehead. His skin was damp but not from the rain now—a cold sweat, his pulse fluttering just under the surface. Rick closed his eyes at the touch, a faint shudder running through him. When he opened them again, there was something terribly vulnerable there—and something he was trying, desperately, to hide.

“You don’t have to pretend,” she whispered.

His throat worked as he swallowed. “I know.” But he didn’t lean into her. Not the way he usually did.

Evan hesitated—then shifted closer anyway, pressing her side lightly against his. After a moment’s frozen breath, Rick finally allowed himself to lean in, his weight slumping ever so slightly against her shoulder. She closed her eyes, resting her temple lightly against his damp hair, letting the moment stretch.

Chad cursed under his breath somewhere beyond them as a tool slipped from his grasp and clattered loudly onto the stone. Calladorn said something low in response—something about patience—but Evan scarcely heard it. Her world had narrowed to the warmth of Rick against her, the steady but ragged rise and fall of his breathing, and the cold sense that he was slipping somewhere she couldn't follow.

Not yet. Maybe not ever, if she could find a way to hold him here.

The fire cracked loudly, spitting embers, and Rick flinched before catching himself. Evan pulled back slightly, searching his face. "You're freezing."

"I'll be fine," he said automatically.

Liar. But she didn't call him on it. Instead, she took one of the spare blankets Gharn had found among the wagon's supplies and wrapped it around Rick's shoulders, tucking him in as if anchoring him back into their world. Rick's hands remained limp for a moment—then he gathered the blanket tighter around him with a small, grateful motion.

The silence between them wasn't empty. It was full—of fear, and trust, and unspoken things that loomed larger than any storm outside.

The rain hammered the world beyond the cave mouth. The fire guttered. And in the middle of it all, Evan stayed pressed close to him, offering everything she could, even though she was starting to understand that it might not be enough.

Her lips compressed into a thin line, wishing she knew what it was about using magic that had affected him so strongly. But then, Rick was so very self-controlled. Magic had to be shaking his worldview to its core. And worse, he'd almost killed Gharn trying to save her.

She hoped that was all it was.

*

The stew simmered in the blackened pot, the rich scents of herbs, root vegetables, and meat thickening the air around the fire. It was almost absurd, Evan thought—how something so simple could feel like salvation.

Gharn ladled generous helpings into mismatched bowls, handing them out with a gruff efficiency that belied the care in the portions. The biscuits, somehow browned to near perfection despite the primitive conditions, steamed invitingly where they soaked up the broth.

Evan's mouth watered before the food even reached her hands. She accepted her bowl with a quiet "Thank you" and folded her legs beneath her, finding a relatively dry spot close to Rick. He shifted slightly to make more room, brushing against her arm as he moved. The contact was brief, but she felt the warmth of it all the way to her bones.

Around the fire, the others dug in with the same unspoken gratitude. Even Calladorn, who still carried the rigid tension of a soldier at rest, let himself relax a fraction, his sword set carefully within reach but his posture easing as he accepted a bowl from Gharn with a nod.

Rick managed a tired smile when he caught her watching him. His hand trembled faintly as he lifted the spoon, and Evan pretended not to notice.

"This tastes amazing," she said aloud, savoring the first rich mouthful.

Gharn grunted, not quite looking at her. "Well," he muttered, staring into his bowl, which he cradled more than ate from. The others mumbled agreement between bites—Chad, Rick, even Calladorn offering variations of the same sentiment. Evan caught the way Gharn's shoulders hunched in tighter, the stew forgotten in his hands.

She glanced across the fire, meeting Rick's eyes. He lifted his eyebrows slightly, the unspoken request clear: *Say something.*

Chad spoke first. "Hey, Gharn," he said, clearing his throat. He wiped his mouth on his sleeve before continuing, "Why don't you tell us something about your people?"

Gharn prodded at a piece of biscuit floating in his bowl. "Like what?" he asked, his voice neutral.

"I don't know," Chad said, a little more hesitant now. "Are you from Drakerath? Somewhere else?"

The firelight caught in Gharn's sharp green eyes as he lifted them and considered Chad for a long moment. "You really want to know?" he asked, his tone oddly flat.

Chad nodded. "Yeah. I do."

Rick murmured his agreement, setting down his own bowl carefully. Calladorn said nothing but watched Gharn with the stillness of a man who knew the weight of old memories.

Gharn placed his bowl on the ground beside him, the metal spoon rattling against the rim. His gaze shifted from Chad to Rick, then to Calladorn, then Matthias—who offered no response at all—and finally to

Evan, who met his eyes squarely, letting him see the sincerity there. No pity. No demand. Just openness.

Gharn sighed through his nose and tugged absently at his beard. "I'm from Khorvael," he said at last, his voice rougher than usual. "A city in Wester. Perched right at an entrance to the Deeps."

The way he said this made the hair on the back of Evan's neck prickle. She remembered what Gharn had said before, but now his use of the name carried an ominous tone.

"Khorvael was... one of the last," he continued. "Built into the cliff faces. We thought maybe if we stayed close enough to the old ways, the stone might welcome us back one day."

The fire popped loudly, and several of the horses tethered at the wagon shifted nervously. Evan reached out absently, her thoughts brushing the mind of the nearest, feeling it settle beneath her mental touch.

"Gnomes and dwarves," Gharn said, picking up a crumb of biscuit and rolling it between his fingers. "Not always friendly. Spent more time fighting each other than living together, back in the Deep Days. Wars over veins of ore, water sources—stupid things that felt important at the time." He gave a rough chuckle, devoid of humor. "Funny how fast a grudge dies when the holders are both running for their lives." The firelight painted hollows under his eyes, the lines of age and loss etched deeper.

No one rushed him. Chad only nodded, his bowl forgotten in his lap. Rick leaned forward slightly, his eyes sharpening with the analytical focus Evan had come to recognize—the one he used when facing a complex system he couldn't yet solve.

"What were you running from?" Rick asked quietly.

Gharn's lips compressed into a thin line. "But Khorvael wasn't home," he said instead. "Not really. It was... survival. Nothing more. My grandparents used to sit near the Deeps' entrance, staring at the door like they were waiting to be called back. Part of me thinks they were." He shook his head slowly. "They knew better. We all did."

Evan spoke softly, reluctant to break the spell but needing to understand. "The Deeps... what are they?"

Gharn's gaze turned toward her, and for the first time, she caught a flicker of something old and wary behind it.

"The underground," he said. "The Deeps don't Shift. Unlike the surface. What's there... stays there. Always has. But the laws of distance don't work right. A step in the Deeps might cross miles. A day's walk might carry you only across a courtyard."

Calladorn stirred at that, his posture sharpening slightly, but he said nothing.

"We built our lifeblood there," Gharn said. "Trade routes no surface traveler could match. Networks no army could control. A secret world beneath your feet." He paused, the fire reflecting in his eyes. "And then one day, it was gone."

The fire crackled, the sound suddenly too loud.

"What happened?" Evan whispered.

Gharn raked a hand through his damp hair, the motion more weary than angry. "It came," he said. "Velgô-pahz." The words in his native tongue twisted strangely in the air, as though the fire itself recoiled. "A hunger without shape. Without sound. Our strongest warriors, our cleverest minds—they tried to stop it. Failed." His voice dropped lower. "The Dark Horror."

A ripple passed through the group, so small it might have gone unnoticed if Evan hadn't been watching them so closely.

"We collapsed tunnels," Gharn continued, his voice scraping raw. "We sealed gates, abandoned cities. It wasn't enough. Nothing was." He looked directly at Evan. "You don't kill the dark," he said. "You just close your eyes—and hope it doesn't notice you."

The fire popped, sending a brief spatter of sparks up into the darkness overhead.

Matthias shifted near the cave mouth. The movement drew Evan's eye—and for an instant, she thought she saw something flash in his expression, something almost like... recognition.

"And those who remain?" Matthias asked quietly, his tone unreadable.

"Exiles, all." Gharn's mouth twisted. "The young ones? They pretend it's a myth. The old ones? They pretend it never happened." He picked up his spoon again, studying the battered curve of it. "We do not speak of it. We endure."

The fire crackled. The storm howled beyond the narrow shelter of stone. And for a long moment, no one moved.

Finally Chad cleared his throat, his voice rough. "Thank you," he said simply.

Gharn grunted, waving a hand in dismissal. "Hmph. Don't thank me. Just eat your damn food before it gets cold."

A chuckle broke through the tension—not loud, not forced, but enough. The small sound echoed around the cave, more defiant than joyous. Evan sat back, wrapping her arms around her knees. Rick shifted closer unconsciously, the side of his leg pressing lightly against hers.

The firelight danced across their faces. Rain hammered the stone beyond their fragile haven.

And for a little while, huddled there together, they almost felt like a family. A broken one. A forged one. But a family nonetheless.

The wagon was a wreck. They'd propped it up on two barrels scavenged from the supplies, the wheels stripped off and stacked nearby, and Chad now lay under it. He was thankful that the wide cave mouth provided dry ground rather than mud.

He was not happy about what he saw.

He glared up at the twisted axle, rainwater still dripping off the frame from the previous night's storm. The damage looked even worse now that he had a clean view.

The priority was obvious: straighten the iron axle. If the rear wheels stayed cockeyed like this, the wagon wouldn't roll properly. The rims would grind against the ground at angles they weren't built for, forcing one wheel or the other to drag at every rut, rock, and slight unevenness in the road. Just as it had getting it here in the first place.

It wouldn't be like a car, where speed would make a bad axle vibrate so badly a passenger would think their teeth might rattle out of their head. No, wagons didn't move fast enough for that.

But it would still kill their progress by inches. One wheel would catch. The other would drag. Then swap. Over and over, stressing the whole frame until something finally gave. Best-case, they'd limp forward at a snail's pace, turning what Calladorn had called a one-day journey into three. Worst-case, a wheel would snap, and they'd be stuck. Helpless.

The left wheel wasn't too bad, just scraped and battered. But the right one had slammed into the cliff when Rick's magic had wrenched the wagon back from the abyss, throwing Chad and Matthias aside like they weighed nothing.

Chad's side still ached from where he'd hit the wall, and he had a deep, spreading bruise he could feel every time he moved.

He still wasn't sure he believed what had happened. One second, he and Matthias had been losing the fight to keep the wagon from sliding over. The next, it had ripped out of their hands and snapped back like a slingshot.

Because Rick had said a few words. *Magic* words.

Chad blew out a sharp breath, forcing his mind back to the task. *Focus.*

Two of the spokes on the right wheel had snapped clean through. Three more were cracked. He could splint those—ugly but functional. Maybe. But the axle had to be straightened first, or it wouldn't matter. He tightened his grip on the mallet—a heavy iron-headed brute he'd scavenged from the tool chest—and took aim.

Clang!

The sound echoed off the cave walls like a shot, setting the horses to dancing. The axle shivered, but only barely. He gritted his teeth and hit harder.

Clang!

Harder still.

Clang!

If he were back home, this would have been simple. He'd have had access to real tools. Cut the axle at the worst point, heat the metal, bend it straight in a jig, weld it closed again. Precision work. Machine work. Not this. Here he only had a hammer and a prayer.

Clang!

The technology had been here once. Better tech than anything Earth had ever dreamed of.

Clang!

And when a Shift dropped new tech into their laps—

Clang!

—they had wrecked it. Because they were terrified of progress.

Clang! Clang!

Probably smashed it with a rock like cavemen, thinking they were saving themselves.

CLANG!

The axle barely moved. Chad's breath was coming hard now, his arms tight with useless anger.

He swung again. Nothing.

Again. Still nothing.

A low, frustrated growl rumbled in his throat. He hurled the mallet down beside him, the impact jolting up his arms and setting a sharp ache in his wrists.

For a second, he just lay there under the wagon, chest heaving, the cold stone pressing against his back through the wool blanket they'd laid down. His hands flexed unconsciously, clenching and unclenching around nothing. All the rage boiled behind his eyes. It wasn't just the axle.

It was *everything*.

The Ban. The Shifts.

The loss of his workshop. His tools.

His *world*.

He couldn't fix anything. Not with what he had. Not with what this backward world gave him. He couldn't even fix a damned wagon axle.

And Rick—Rick just spoke a few words, waved a hand—and a fully loaded wagon moved like a toy. Rick could do the impossible. Rick had power now. And what did Chad have? A mallet that might as well have been made of clay, pounding on a world that refused to change.

Chad let out a shuddering breath and rolled out from under the wagon. He sat up stiffly, wiping mud and straw from his tunic without really seeing what he was doing. It honestly felt like they *wanted* to live in the Dark Ages. And maybe they did.

The thought hit him harder than he had expected. For all the people he'd seen since arriving here—merchants, smiths, even an elven adviser to kings—not one of them had wanted to move forward. Not really. They clung to the way things were, even if it killed them.

Even if it killed people like Rick. Or Evan. Or him.

He stared at the axle again, feeling that mix of pride and bitterness rise thick in his throat. Pride that Rick had done something no one else could have. Bitterness that his brother's shadow now loomed even larger. Darker and deeper.

Both feelings were true. Both of them burned.

Chad closed his eyes, pressing the heels of his hands into them until stars burst behind his lids. He couldn't keep doing this. Couldn't keep being dragged by forces he couldn't fight. There had to be another way.

The wagon creaked faintly in the stillness, the sound hollow in the cavernous silence, and Chad let out a long breath, forcing himself to steady. His hands still shook faintly as he reached for the mallet again, but this time, he only held it loosely in his lap. No more pointless swinging. He needed to think.

There had to be a *better* way.

Wiping sweat from his brow, Chad caught a sound outside the cave—the steady, rhythmic scuff of boots against stone, paired with deep, measured breaths. Curious, he stood and slipped around the wagon. Calladorn stood in the middle of the rain-washed road, shirtless in the faint sun, his sword extended. The blade caught what little light filtered through the stormy sky, glinting silver.

Chad froze, half-forgotten mallet still dangling from one hand as Calladorn moved through a series of forms—no, not just forms. They were *art*. Each transition flowed into the next with impossible precision, the blade an extension of his will. Every turn of his wrist, every pivot of his foot was deliberate. Clean.

The man's body moved like the sword was a part of him. No hesitation. No uncertainty.

Muscle defined Calladorn's frame, but it wasn't the heavy, gym-forged muscle Chad had always associated with strength. This was lean. Functional. A whipcord tension that moved as easily as breathing.

And the chest hair—there was something oddly real about it, a stark contrast to the gym bunnies of home. Unpolished. Unselfconscious. He didn't look like someone trying to impress anyone.

He just... *was.*

Chad found himself mesmerized, the frustration boiling inside him ebbing into something quieter. Centered.

Calladorn pivoted through a tight turn, blade flashing in a low arc just above the ground, before coming upright again—facing Chad directly. For a brief moment, their eyes locked, one on either side of the raised sword. Before Chad could quite register the moment, Calladorn turned away smoothly, continuing the sequence without pause. The last few movements were a blur of steel and sinew, and then Calladorn slowed, bringing the sword upright before bowing his head slightly toward the blade. He held the pose for long seconds before walking toward the wagon, breathing deeply but evenly, sweat beading across his chest.

He grabbed his shirt and coat from the seat rail and shrugged into them without rushing.

"You do that often?" Chad asked, his voice rougher than he had expected.

"It helps me stay centered," Calladorn said simply, pulling the coat closed with an economy of motion that matched everything else about him.

Chad nodded, glancing down at the damaged wheel by his feet. *Centering.* Maybe he could use a little of that himself. Calladorn had years of training with a sword, but Chad—he had years of training too. Just... a different kind.

He stared at the battered axle and the broken wheel, and suddenly the answer hit him square between the eyes. *You idiot...* Heat. *Of course.* His brain flooded with plans even before he could speak. "Rick!" he hollered, waving his brother over.

Rick, seated beside Evan at the fire, startled upright and strolled over, his cloak rippling behind him. "Did you get it fixed?" he asked, raising a brow, wary but curious.

"No. But I will. And you're going to help."

Rick narrowed his eyes, suspicion creasing his forehead. "I know that look. You're cooking up something dangerous."

Chad grinned, feeling a rare rush of pure excitement.

"To fix the axle," he explained, pointing, "I need either a jack or a way to heat the bend. We don't have a jack. But we *do* have a heat source."

Rick's face went pale. He stepped back instinctively. "No."

Chad planted his feet. "Listen—"

"No, Chad," Rick snapped, his voice taut. "You can't ask this of me."

And there it was—the fear. Raw and unvarnished. Chad reached out to grip Rick by both shoulders. They were rigid under his hands.

"I know you overdid it last night," Chad said, steady, "but that was different. You acted on instinct. You didn't have time to think."

Rick swallowed hard, his Adam's apple bobbing.

Chad squeezed his shoulders, grounding both of them. "This is different. Controlled conditions. No panic. You'll have time to focus, to do it *right.*"

Rick's mouth worked soundlessly for a second. Then he turned away, raking a hand through his wet hair.

Chad leaned in, lowering his voice. "Rick, we need that heat. Otherwise, the wagon's deadweight."

A stray breeze gusted through the cave mouth, carrying the scent of rain and wet stone. Neither of them moved for a long moment.

Finally Rick exhaled a breath that shook a little at the edges. He scrubbed both hands over his face. When he looked up, his expression was taut—but resigned. "Show me where you need it."

Relief punched through Chad's chest so hard he almost sagged.

They rounded the back of the wagon together. As Chad knelt to point out the worst bend, he caught movement out of the corner of his eye. Calladorn stood by the fire, drying his sword now—but his gaze wasn't on his weapon. It was on Chad. And the expression gave the impression the man was seeing him for the first time.

Their eyes met again across the space between them, and Chad's stomach gave another little twist—sharp, bright. He tore his eyes away, focusing back on the axle, ignoring the heat rising under his collar.

One thing at a time. First, fix the wagon. Then figure out the rest.

X
Tensions

For the first time in his life, Rick felt powerful.

Not clever. Not competent. *Powerful.*

He wasn't used to the feeling. Growing up, he'd been the one picked last, the one fumbling passes in gym class and tripping over hurdles set too low to excuse him. Physicality had never come naturally to him—especially not the way it had to Chad.

What Rick had was his mind. Books, numbers, problems he could solve while the rest of the world ran faster than he ever could. Over time, he had built a wall of achievement around himself—neat, unassailable. Impregnable.

Until Evan.

The memory crept up on him as the trail curved along the ridgeline, pine needles crunching softly beneath his horse's hooves. That day he'd wandered into the Crystal Magic bookstore—he hadn't meant to stay. It was the crystals in the window that had drawn him in: perfect geometry caught in stone, ordered and serene.

But she had stolen his breath first. A young woman with copper-threaded hair, green eyes alive with something he couldn't yet name, and a voice low enough to resonate deeper than his ribs. "Try a reading," she'd said, smiling.

He hadn't believed in that sort of thing. Still didn't. But he'd sat. Plunked down a crumpled twenty without knowing why.

The first card she turned over: the Magician. He hadn't thought of it since. Until now.

Until the memory rose sharp and electric, and for one strange moment, he could almost smell the faint incense curling through the bookstore again, mixing with the resin scent of the forest around him.

Back then the card had felt like encouragement. Now—it felt different. Colder. A warning he hadn't recognized.

The sun beat down, making the battered trail shimmer where ruts dried to dust. Rick shifted in the saddle, muscles protesting faintly—still sore from the wagon ordeal, but manageable now.

Saving the wagon had been instinct. Raw. Immediate. One second, Evan had been slipping toward the cliff's edge, and the next, the equations had surged up inside him like a tidal wave, faster than thought.

And it had worked. It had felt *good.* Exhilarating, but also terrifying—something bigger than logic could contain. Even the collapse afterward, the hours of tremors in his hands, the splitting headache pounding behind his eyes—the way he'd unbuckled his bedroll later with hands he could barely keep steady—none of it had mattered in that first burning flush.

Was this how Chad felt all the time? Strong? Sure of his body, sure that if he moved, the world would move with him?

Or—Rick's mouth twisted in a tight grimace—maybe strength came with its own chains.

Later, heating the axle had been different. *Deliberate. Controlled.* He'd mapped the variables, calculated the heat flow, adjusted for impurities in the iron. No wild surge. No aftermath of dizziness. Hands that held still. That had felt even better.

A crow called harshly from a stand of twisted pines, and Rick's horse flicked its ears. He steadied the reins automatically, forcing his fingers to relax. Up ahead, the valley opened wide: a patchwork of green fields and distant rooftops glinting like scattered coins under the sun. Merchant's Rest, still hours away. And beyond that... the rest of this broken, beautiful world.

A breeze stirred the scent of warm earth and pine sap. In the distance, the river murmured over stone, a faint, persistent whisper threading through the hills. It should have been perfect.

Instead, it scraped against Rick's nerves like sandpaper.

Magecurse. The word Gharn had used hovered at the edges of his thoughts, a sour taste he couldn't spit out. Magic had a price.

Low Magic, Gharn had said, wasn't bad. Spells based on simple math—arithmetic, geometry—cost little. But the higher the spell, the greater the toll. The exact nature of that toll... Rick rubbed his temples with his free hand.

He didn't want to dwell on it.

He'd told himself he would be careful. Precise. Sparing. He wouldn't need to use magic again unless it was an emergency. He could outthink the need. Outsmart the danger.

But of course, the axle had bent. And Chad had asked for his help. And Rick had decided a small use of magic—that wouldn't be so bad. Not as dangerous.

The saddle creaked beneath him as he shifted his weight, the leather warm and pliant beneath him. His fingers brushed the edge of his medallion beneath his shirt, feeling the faint pulse of its presence—a heartbeat that wasn't quite his own.

He should have told them, right after Gharn had explained the truth. Instead, he had lied—first to himself and then to them. He'd told himself that silence was safer. That if he just didn't use it, no harm would come. No price would be paid.

But emergencies didn't wait for careful decisions. Emergencies demanded action. And Rick—God help him—had discovered that action felt good.

The wagon bumped along the uneven track ahead. Rick's gaze snagged on the wheels—the way they shuddered slightly over stones and ruts. His hands itched with the knowledge of how easily he could fix it. How easily he could make anything better—if he let himself.

He looked away.

Chad rode beside Calladorn, laughing at something Rick couldn't hear. Carefree. Unburdened. Rick clenched his jaw. If he confessed now—if he told them about the cost—Chad would blame himself for asking Rick to intervene. Evan would worry. They would start treating him like glass, fragile and breakable.

Or worse—with looks of mixed pity and disdain.

He couldn't let that happen. Not when they needed focus. Not when the road ahead demanded more from them than any of them had yet realized.

And I'm not an addict. The thought came too strongly, but it was true. He had control.

The pine-scented air gusted again, fluttering Evan's shawl where she sat on the wagon bench. She turned slightly, glancing back over her shoulder, and her green eyes found him. Calm. Searching. Seeing more than he wanted her to.

Rick's horse stumbled slightly over a loose patch of gravel, and he tightened the reins automatically, covering the lurch in his gut. He thought about riding up beside her. Telling her everything.

Instead, he smiled—a little too quickly, a little too tightly—and gave a small, casual nod. Evan studied him a moment longer, and then she smiled back, the kind of smile that said she didn't believe him, not entirely—but would let it pass for now.

The moment slipped away like water through cupped hands. The river's whisper carried up from below, steady and indifferent.

Rick adjusted his seat, forcing his breathing into a measured rhythm, feeling the easy sway of his horse's gait beneath him. The medallion pressed against his chest, light and heavy at once.

He had power now. So what if it had a cost? He would carry it alone.

Because that was what Rick Johnson did: solve the problem.

No matter the price.

Merchant's Rest squatted before them, a sprawling confusion of stone and timber where three mountain valleys converged like the branches of an ungainly tree.

Matthias had always despised the place.

His companions, however, looked ready to weep for joy at the sight of it.

"Are those shrines?" Chad asked, pointing ahead where slender towers flanked the road. Two more stood at the outlets of each remaining road, forming an uneven ring about the plain.

Gharn, perched on the wagon bench, shook his head. The wagon clattered beneath him as they continued forward. "Signal beacons," he said. "Fires are lit when the road beyond becomes impassable. It warns the caravans not to waste their time."

"Does that happen often?" Rick asked. It was the first time he had spoken in hours.

"Toward Drakerath, not often. That pass doesn't climb high enough. The way to our right, to Wester, is even lower—you can tell by how the river flows down that way. But when the snows melt in the higher mountains, flooding can wash the road out."

Rick nodded, his posture slightly loosening. "That's the way we are going, correct?"

"Yes."

"And the other road?" Chad asked, craning his neck to look across the eastern rise.

Gharn gestured. "Leads over the high pass to Syrillia, and from there, Eryndor."

"Elves," Calladorn said grimly.

Gharn nodded, his sharp gaze flicking to Rick. "The only folk likely to be wizards anymore."

Matthias noted how the gnome's words landed—a pointed glance that Rick missed but should not have. Curiously, Evan—so often perceptive of tensions—also missed the deeper meaning. Her instincts, usually so keen, seemed dulled this day.

Merchant's Rest bore neither wall nor gate. It had long been an unspoken agreement among the Nine Kingdoms that the place must remain neutral. Commerce demanded it. Were any kingdom foolish enough to claim the settlement, the others would retaliate with a vengeance swifter and more destructive than any army: an economic embargo. The cost of conquest would never be worth the loss.

Instead, the trade guilds held sway, puffing themselves up with the notion they ruled a tenth kingdom of their own design. It was not something they spoke of openly, but every merchant here understood that coin carried a power sharper than any sword.

Matthias knew another truth as well. Where coins flowed thick, rot festered unseen. Commerce bred desperation as much as wealth, and where desperate men walked, thieves always followed. It was a cycle as old as cities, as detestable as it was inevitable.

The wagon rumbled over the polished stones of the main thoroughfare, the damaged axle protesting but holding for now. The road, like the caravanserai itself, had been kept in immaculate repair—nothing could be allowed to hinder the passage of goods. Yet the side alleys, Matthias observed, slumped in neglect. Mud and refuse pooled there, shadows gathering thick and dangerous. The stink of ambition masked the rot well enough for fools.

Overhead, catcalls broke the murmur of trade. Three women leaned from a battered balcony, laughing and beckoning. Their postures were artful: bent at the waist, arms emphasizing what little their blouses pretended to conceal. Scents of perfume and smoke drifted down to the travelers, faint but unmistakable.

Calladorn's head locked forward with soldierly rigidity. Rick flushed scarlet, dropping his gaze. Evan caught the exchange and offered a faint, almost imperceptible smile before leveling a glare sharp enough to skin the women where they stood. Chad, recipient of the loudest enticements, stared fixedly at his saddle, as though the cracked leather held profound mysteries.

The women gave Matthias no notice at all. Just as he preferred.

Ahead, the road terminated against the walls of the caravanserai—a monstrous fortress-palace of commerce, more imposing than most castles Matthias had ever seen. Gilded in places, fortified in others, it embodied the philosophy of the settlement with brutal clarity: only trade deserved defense.

The encircling street—colorfully called "the Bracelet"—held the city's shops.

Three gates broke the caravanserai wall, leading to the internal court, where caravans gathered and dispersed. The roads from the three connected kingdoms all met here before spidering outward again. People flooded the space between—merchants, drovers, guards, laborers—swarming like insects about their nest.

Yet something was wrong.

Matthias narrowed his eyes, cataloging the subtle cues. The hasty glances. The way conversations died mid-word. The tightened grips on reins and satchels. The undercurrent of unease seeping through the crowd.

Evan rubbed her arms, as if chilled. Matthias felt the tension radiating from her like heat off sunbaked stone. "What is our plan from here?" she asked.

"We repair the wagon, then continue to Wester," Calladorn said at once.

Gharn grunted. "Won't work. We were lucky getting here—"

"You call that luck?" Rick snapped. His right hand twitched at his side, fingers moving like they were sketching invisible patterns.

Gharn ignored the comment. "Leave without a caravan, you're dead. Bandits don't care about papers."

Calladorn argued, predictably, that duty demanded haste, not caution.

"Better slow and alive than dead by the road," Gharn growled, his bushy brows knitting tightly.

Matthias tuned them out. Gharn was correct, of course. Bandits were not the real danger, anyway—not here. The worst threats wore legitimate colors and smiled as they slit your throat.

His attention sharpened as firelight flared atop the eastern beacons. One, then another—bright against the midafternoon sky. The square around them hushed, a communal breath held too long.

Snow in this season was impossible. Something else had happened.

Calladorn stiffened, instincts taking over. Gharn swore under his breath.

Matthias, keeping his voice level, said, "Where will we be staying the night?"

"What?" Gharn sounded distracted.

"Inn. Which one?"

"The, um, Wayfarer's Refuge."

Matthias nodded once, a curt finality in the motion. "Go there. Now." Without waiting for agreement, he wheeled his horse around and galloped eastward, leaving the others to scramble however they chose.

The crowd churned at his passing, unsettled and restless.

It took several minutes to locate the mark. Matthias threaded through the press of bodies with practiced ease, his senses tuned to every flicker of movement. His eyes parsed the clutter of signs, carvings, and graffiti until he found it—a small symbol, no larger than a thumbprint, etched into the corner post of a leaning structure just beyond the caravanserai's reach. At a careless glance, it could have been dismissed as another scratch in Merchant's Rest's battered skin, but Matthias knew better.

A sideways eye with a heavy lid—the mark of the local network.

He dismounted without slowing and tied his horse to a rusted hitching post in one fluid motion. He crossed the street without urgency and vanished into the mouth of a narrow alley where the city's facade gave way to truth.

Here the stones wept moisture, the stench of decay pressed against the skin, and the noise of the Bracelet dulled into a muffled, wary hush. Matthias moved like smoke through it, unseen and unremarked upon.

He found Mouse near the crumbling mouth of a side passage, huddled beneath a sagging awning, his back turned. For once fortune favored Matthias: the man was alone. "What news?" Matthias said quietly.

Mouse jerked upright with a yelp, spinning on his heel. He was typical of his breed—scrawny, stooped, and jittery, with a face that seemed half-formed from bad habits and worse ancestry. His patched coat hung off his wiry frame like an abandoned banner, and his oversized ears twitched at every distant footfall. Seeing who addressed him, Mouse flinched, then composed himself with a forced grin that exposed a ruin of teeth. "Mattis! By the Three, you gave me a fright, you did." He tried for outrage, but the effect was pitiful.

Matthias waited. "I asked you a question," he said at last.

Mouse's fingers worried at a raw patch on his forearm—nervous habit or genuine rash, it made no difference. His hand, however, was swift enough when Matthias withdrew a small pouch from his belt and tossed it lightly toward him. The coin made a hollow jingle as he snatched it from the air and clutched it to his chest as though expecting it to vanish.

Matthias said nothing.

Mouse bobbed his head, voice dropping to a conspiratorial whisper. "Word just come in not a half hour ago. Syrillia's been attacked, it has. Monsters, they say. The gryphons've pulled back, leavin' caravanners stuck behind the pass, none coming through."

Matthias narrowed his gaze. That, at least, would explain the signals.

Mouse mistook the look for disapproval. He leaned closer, his breath sour and damp, the stench of rotting teeth nearly tangible. "But I got more. Word from Drakerath. They say there are impostors at the palace in Ironspire. Some say the king himself."

Matthias stiffened, though only slightly. That rumor was dangerous. The wrong ears catching it could lead to questions no one should be asking—questions with answers far too costly.

Mouse, emboldened, chuckled—a dry, scraping sound—and his expression slid into a leer. "You don't want that word gettin' about, do you? For the right price, I can see it—"

The rest of the sentence never came. Mouse's eyes went wide, more with surprise than fear. His mouth sagged open. A thin thread of blood welled from the corner of his lips. His knees buckled, and he crumpled soundlessly to the muddy ground.

Matthias knelt without haste, cleaning his knife against the man's filthy coat before returning it to its hidden sheath. He plucked the coin purse from Mouse's slack grip and weighed it once in his palm before stowing it back beneath his cloak. Regret stirred in him—a faint ripple above a surface long since hardened.

Mouse had been reliable. Discreet, for the most part. Matthias would have preferred to let him live. Killing valuable assets was messy work, wasteful and shortsighted, but loose ends frayed if left unattended.

He rose, brushing the dirt from his knees, and stared down at the crumpled body. In death, Mouse looked smaller still, a tangle of rags and wasted flesh. Better this way. Parasites left to fester could only cause rot. It was cleaner—more efficient—to excise them before the infection spread.

Matthias composed his features into the familiar, impassive mask and turned back toward the square. Business awaited.

And business, like the river of gold that fed Merchant's Rest, tolerated no distractions.

The Wayfarer's Refuge buzzed like a hive about to swarm.

Half the voices around her made no sense—jumbled talk about trade routes and border patrols, names she barely recognized. The other half made too much sense, setting her nerves on edge. Evan sat near the hearth, its crackling fire sounding harsher than it should have, as if the logs shared the agitation rippling through the crowd. She leaned into Rick, letting his arm curl protectively around her waist. His warmth helped. A little.

The smells of the place layered thickly in the air—spiced potatoes from the kitchen, smoke from candles, the headiness of ale, perfumed travelers trying to mask the odor of sweat from the road. Across the room, a woman sat on a crooked stool atop a makeshift stage, coaxing a mournful tune from a battered lute. Her voice wavered above the din, fragile as a cobweb, the tune sounding vaguely Irish.

Evan stared at her tankard, untouched on the table in front of her. She still had not acquired the taste for ale, and probably never would. It seemed symbolic somehow—being in the middle of everything but apart from it too. She shifted slightly against Rick. He tightened his arm automatically, almost too fast, like he was reassuring both of them. Evan frowned faintly but let the matter go.

They were stuck here. Gharn and Calladorn had dropped them off before vanishing into the heart of the city—the massive central structure Gharn called the caravanserai—to arrange their next move. As for Matthias... Evan made a face without meaning to.

"Maybe he left," Rick said, low and sudden.

She blinked at him, startled. It was as if he had plucked the thought straight from her mind. "What was that?" she asked, masking her surprise.

"Oh, nothing." Rick shrugged, trying for casual. "Just wondering where Matthias disappeared to."

Across the table, Chad paused mid-bite, a wedge of roasted potato frozen halfway to his mouth. He shook his head. "He wants the Heart too badly to just bail."

Rick leaned forward. "You think so? Did he say something?"

"Yeah. That night back at Sorendir's tower." Chad raised the potato the rest of the way into his mouth.

Evan smiled faintly to herself. Chad wore the dumb-jock mask well, but he caught more than anyone gave him credit for. Always had.

Rick nodded thoughtfully, scanning the restless crowd. "I keep hearing gryphon riders mentioned," he said after a moment.

"Same here." Chad shrugged, chewing. "Patrols out of Syrillia, I think."

Syrillia. The name lodged uneasily in Evan's mind—east of Drakerath, if she remembered right.

"It sounds like one got here about the same time we did," Chad continued. "The guy said something about a destroyed caravan."

Evan's fingers curled lightly against Rick's side. "That doesn't necessarily mean demons," she said, hoping the words could anchor the possibility into fact.

Rick's mouth tightened. "I have heard monsters mentioned," he admitted, voice low.

Chad nodded grimly, pushing food around his plate. "This sucks. Listening to rumors. No way to know what's true until it's way too late."

"Word by horseback," Evan muttered, her frustration simmering just below the surface. "Feels like we're blind."

Rick sat rigid beside her. He had folded his hands, thumbs worrying each other, knuckles whitening. Evan had never seen him quite like this—usually he leaned into tension, picking it apart until it made sense. Now he looked like he was trying to hold something broken together with sheer will.

"It can't be demons," Rick said finally, almost to himself. "The Shifts are random. You can't coordinate through them."

"But..." Chad started, glancing between them.

Evan picked up the thread, thinking aloud. "What if Syrillia and Drakerath are close enough to share opposite sides of a single Shift? Like a bridge."

Rick tensed. She saw it—the instinctive urge to argue, to reject anything he had not thought of first. He struggled with it for a heartbeat. Two.

"She is right," Matthias said, his voice smooth and sudden.

Evan jumped slightly. She had not even heard him approach. She bit back a curse. *Damn that man.*

"Where did you go?" Chad demanded, giving voice to what Evan wanted to ask.

"Gathering information," Matthias said, his gaze sweeping the room instead of meeting theirs. His stance was loose—casual, even—but Evan caught the fine tension in his jaw, the slight coiling of his shoulders. A snake lying still, waiting for the right moment.

Matthias's eyes flicked down, catching hers. He held the gaze deliberately, a slow and measured thing. One corner of his mouth lifted—a smile or a smirk, she could not tell. The fire cracked louder beside him, and the flickering light danced across his face, giving his bland features a sharpness. *He knows,* she thought, her stomach tightening.

The night around the campfire, when she had tried—accidentally—to push into him... it hadn't been her imagination. It hadn't been her being tired or overwhelmed. He *had* felt it.

And he'd understood.

Evan refused to look away, though everything in her screamed at her to do exactly that. She locked her gaze with his, refusing to yield.

After a moment, Matthias let it go. His eyes shifted toward the door just as it opened. Relieved, Evan turned to see Calladorn duck inside, holding the door for someone shorter. *Gharn.*

Evan waved them over, grateful for the distraction. Gharn veered toward the bar without hesitation, but Calladorn cut a straight path toward them through the crowded tables. He looked different. For the first time since fleeing Ironspire, some small glint of fire appeared in his eyes. Gone was the uniform; instead, he wore a workman's shirt and vest, simple brown trousers, a wide-brimmed leather hat shading his face.

His sword still hung at his hip, though.

"We leave tomorrow," he said, wasting no time.

"The wagon got repaired already?" Chad asked.

Calladorn shook his head. "No. We have a new one. Better suited to long travel. Our supplies—"

"Such as they are," Gharn interrupted, dropping into a chair with a tankard in each hand.

"Such as they are," Calladorn repeated dryly, shooting the gnome a glare. "They are being loaded now. We depart at first light."

Rick leaned in closer, voice low enough that only their table could hear. "What about Merchant's Rest?"

Calladorn arched a brow. "What about it?"

"Should we warn them?" Rick asked.

Gharn shrugged even as his shoulders slumped, taking a deep pull from his ale. Foam clung to his mustache as he wiped it away with the back of his hand. "And what good would that do?" His voice was as bitter as the ale.

"If people go to Drakerath, they'll die," Rick said, anger crackling just under his careful words.

"Word reached here before we did," Calladorn said. His voice had lost any hint of warmth now, his face closing like a gate. "The beacons were lit a half-hour ago."

Gharn slammed down his empty mug with a thud. "Nobody's blind. Nobody here is stupid. Those who stay will stay. Those who run..." He shrugged again, a heavy, tired motion. "That's the way of things."

Evan leaned into Rick, feeling the tension vibrating through him. Tomorrow they would move west, leaving this broken place behind, but she had the gnawing feeling that the rot would not stay behind them for long.

Sleep refused to come.

Chad lay staring at the ceiling, his mind resisting peace, running endless loops like a stuck track. Signal fires. News traveling by horseback. Word of mouth like something out of a storybook. This whole world felt like it had unplugged itself.

When he was younger, he had loved *A Connecticut Yankee in King Arthur's Court,* had dreamed of being Hank Morgan—taking future knowledge and making life better for everyone stuck in the mud of history. Electricity, telegraphs, gunpowder. Even knights riding bicycles. It had seemed like such a romantic idea.

Now, actually trapped inside that reality, it felt more like a bad joke.

The square of moonlight creeping across the rough wall caught his eye. Tiny dust motes swirled and glittered in it, slow and aimless.

He imagined anyway.

Lines stretched across Necsis—wires strung between towns, messages flying instead of plodding on horseback. One network. One innovation.

A telegraph.

He could build one. It wouldn't even be a challenge.

And just like that, the fantasy unraveled. In his mind's eye, he saw soldiers storming in, faces hard, voices chanting: *Ban the man!* Not dismantling things carefully—no. Smashing wires, wrecking machines, hurling rocks like cavemen. Not just destroying the work. Destroying *him.*

Chad sighed, a long, low breath that seemed to pull straight from the pit of his stomach. *I hate this world,* he thought bitterly.

Restlessness gnawed at him. He sat up, running a hand through his hair.

Across the small room, Rick and Evan shared the other bed, tangled together in sleep. Rick's feet dangled past the end of the mattress. Evan shifted slightly, murmuring something too soft to catch.

Chad smiled in spite of himself. Odd couple or not—control-freak Rick and free-spirited Evan—they fit. Somehow they balanced each other in ways he would never have guessed. Still, he worried. Rick had been off since Emberhold. Withdrawn. Like he was sitting back, letting life happen instead of charging into it. The old Rick—the one Chad looked up to—had always grabbed problems by the throat. But lately...

The wagon had changed something. First saving it, then helping repair it afterward with magic. Chad had seen the difference. The spark back in Rick's eyes, even if he tried to hide it. *My own personal Merlin,* Chad thought, raising an eyebrow.

The grin faded. That hadn't ended well for Hank Morgan either.

He rose and padded across the creaky floorboards to the window, the cold glass numbing his fingers as he leaned into it.

Outside, the mountains loomed, silver peaks rising above a low layer of mist. The cloud bank obscured their bases, making the mountains look like they were floating, untethered.

Motion below caught his eye. At first it was only shadows stirring—but as his eyes adjusted, he saw a figure in the courtyard, moving with precise, measured grace. Calladorn.

The soldier stepped and turned, his sword flashing silver under the moonlight. His movements flowed together like water, forming a pattern Chad could not quite follow but could sense all the same.

Balance. Discipline. Not fighting an enemy—fighting himself. Keeping himself anchored when the ground kept shifting underneath.

Chad pressed his forehead lightly to the cold pane. Calladorn always looked so confident, so sure of himself. Even after watching his home burn. Even after losing everything. And yet here he was—repeating the same patterns, day after day. Not because he thought he was invincible, but because he knew he wasn't.

Chad swallowed against the tightness in his throat. He understood, suddenly, why Calladorn moved the way he did. Why the ritual mattered. It wasn't about power. It was about survival. Because the world didn't care if he sank or swam.

Chad turned away, silent on bare feet.

He crawled back under the rough blanket, staring up at the dark ceiling while Rick's steady breathing and the crackle of the banked fire filled the silence. He understood Calladorn better now, but as he closed his eyes, a heavier question pressed into him, stubborn and unyielding.

What is my own place in all of this?

XI
Caravan

The caravanserai courtyard seethed with motion.

Anxious to be off, Calladorn reined in his instinct to scowl as he took it all in. The sheer scale of it—the ordered chaos—impressed him. Workers moved with a precision that spoke of long practice, shouting to one another over the clatter of hooves and the sharp ring of hammers. From the outside, the place had looked like a single massive structure, but inside, it opened into a vast circular courtyard, enclosed by thick walls and pierced by three great gates: Drakerath to the north, Syrillia to the east, and Wester straight ahead.

Wide doors punctuated the inner ring wall at regular intervals, leading to stables, storage houses, blacksmiths already hammering their trade into the morning air, and more besides. The air was thick with the scent of leather, horse sweat, hot iron, and sawdust—a living tapestry of movement and industry.

Calladorn's gaze swept the massive space, noting the arrangement of the wagons—thirty at least, perhaps more. Landschooners. Great beasts of burden themselves, their canvas-draped frames and arched roofs giving them the look of resting animals, heads bowed to drink from the stone-paved earth. Most were already hitched to their teams, draft horses the size of small bulls, all muscle and restless stamping. Stable hands rushed among them, finalizing preparations, or brought out still more animals for the landschooners that still waited.

Their own wagon—if it could even be called that—slouched nearby. Half again as large as the battered relic they'd limped into Miner's End with, it was built for endurance across the often-treacherous paths between kingdoms. A guild standard—and guild-mandated—landschooner. Expensive even to rent, but ownership was beyond their reach. Only the wealthiest merchants bothered to invest in their own, and the Caravan Guild was careful to keep it so.

Another layer of control, Calladorn thought grimly. He shifted the missive in his inner pocket—safe against Eryck's medal—and fought down the renewed twist of impatience. A month, trapped on the slow crawl to Syndar with merchants and gossipmongers. Twice as long as it would take for him to make the journey alone. But necessity allowed no room for pride.

His survey drifted to his companions. Gharn climbed the short ladder to the driver's bench—his movement a trifle unsteady, too deliberate by a hair—and sat heavily, the reins coiled and forgotten beside him. He stared toward the Wester gate, not really seeing. Calladorn recognized the posture well enough. Gharn's grief, sharp and recent, gnawed at him more than the gnome would ever admit aloud.

Nearby, Evan moved with restless energy. She admired the horses, murmured a greeting to a passing stable hand, and offered a friendly smile to the neighboring wagon's driver—small, harmless interactions that nevertheless left ripples in her wake. She accepted Rick's hand up to the seat with a laughing ease that Calladorn both envied and pitied. Rick followed, climbing up after her, eyes wide with the hunger of someone cataloging everything he saw, weighing the efficiency.

Chad, though, moved differently.

The youth circled the landschooner at an easy pace, ducking down to inspect the axles, trailing his hand along the stretched canvas as if testing its tension. He opened side compartments, examined the yoke fittings with a clear interest in the mechanics that made Calladorn pause. This wasn't just dutiful curiosity. Nor was it the cursory glance of a soldier looking for weaknesses. It was the scrutiny of a craftsman.

That realization caught him off-guard—as did the subtle acknowledgment that Chad had begun to change. The boy who had stumbled through Ironspire behind his brother now moved with a quiet ownership of space. He didn't blend in, exactly, but he no longer wore the world of Necsis like an ill-fitting cloak.

He's finding his feet, Calladorn thought. *So like Eryck.* The thought stirred something bittersweet.

As if sensing the weight of his gaze, Chad glanced up. Their eyes met—briefly, sharply—and Calladorn saw it then: the instant stiffening of Chad's spine, the flash of red creeping up from his collar. A sudden, awkward averting of eyes. It hit like a faint jolt, unexpected and oddly personal.

Calladorn looked away, feigning interest in the landschooner's front fittings, but his mind stayed snagged on the image of Chad's flushed face, the way he had looked—almost guilty. Almost... exposed.

Eryck had been self-conscious too. Even in the pursuit of his interests. The resemblance struck hard enough to leave a bruise.

I failed you, brother. The thought surfaced unbidden, and he clenched his jaw against it. Ten years gone, and the guilt still cut as deep as ever, a wound that refused to scar.

A loud voice, heated with argument, broke the moment.

Calladorn turned toward the noise. Three men stood near the neighboring wagon: two traders, judging by their finer cut of clothing, and one guard, whose easy hand on the hilt of his sword marked him more than any uniform could.

"I'm telling you, they were monsters," one of the traders insisted, voice rising.

The other merchant snorted, dismissive. "You believe every tavern tale. Might as well fear your own shadow."

"Then explain the east roads closing!" the first snapped. "Explain the gryphon riders abandoning their patrols! Something's wrong."

The guard raised a hand, placating. "Does it matter? We're bound for Wester. Not Drakerath. Not Syrillia. The trouble's behind us."

"That's what you think," the merchant muttered darkly. His gaze swept the courtyard, and for a moment it snagged on Calladorn. The distrust was plain enough—and understandable.

Calladorn held his stare without flinching until the man looked away, dragging his companions with him.

You're right to be afraid, Calladorn thought grimly. *But you're not afraid enough.*

Not yet.

He turned back to his own preparations but made a silent note: before they left, he would speak with the caravan's guards. Learn their names, their strengths, their habits. If trouble came, he needed to know who he could count on. And who he could not.

"All officers gamble with men's lives," Gallus had told them once. "But the good ones hedge their bets."

Words to live by.

Upon reaching the rear of the landschooner, Calladorn unlatched its heavy door and swung it outward. The interior was surprisingly efficient. A narrow aisle ran between barrels and crates packed tight at the back, before widening halfway along the wagon's length. From there forward, a padded bench stretched along one side, while built-in cabinets rose opposite, their brass latches glinting dully in the morning light. Toward the front, a half-door led to the driver's bench beyond. Above, the canvas roof bowed outward over an attic space crammed with spare supplies—rope, tarps, tools lashed in bundles against the frame.

No wasted space. A merchant's design—pragmatic, thorough, profit-minded.

The air inside already smelled musty, thick with the faint tang of oiled canvas and damp wood, souring slightly under the rising heat. Calladorn wrinkled his nose and closed the door with a solid thunk. By midday, it would be a miserable place.

As he turned, he found Matthias standing a few paces away. The man said nothing, only watched, arms folded loosely across his chest. His expression, as ever, hovered on the line between impassive and amused, as if quietly entertained by a joke no one else could hear.

Calladorn felt his jaw tighten. There was something about Matthias that set every instinct he had on edge. The way he appeared without sound, the way his gaze weighed and measured, without ever quite committing to hostility—or allegiance.

Like a spider in a web, waiting.

Before he could snap something regrettable, salvation came in the form of a call from the courtyard center, punctuated by three sharp raps of metal on wood. "Your attention, everyone!"

Calladorn stepped forward, moving to stand beside the driver's seat for a clearer view. At the center of the caravanserai, a man stood atop a low wooden platform. Even with the added height, he barely cleared the shoulders of the two men flanking the stand—both thickly muscled, bare-armed, and alert. And the man himself was no less imposing. His bald crown gleamed with sweat, and his stocky frame spoke more of solid muscle than indulgence. A thick crimson braid looped over his left shoulder, its bright dye unmistakable: high rank within the Caravan Guild. In one hand he carried a quarterstaff banded at both ends with polished metal, which he now tapped twice more against the platform, silencing the restless murmur of the crowd.

"I am Caravan Master Nardo Thargrip," he announced, turning in place so that all assembled could see him. His voice carried easily across the courtyard, clear and firm. "It falls to me to see you safely to Edron Station."

Calladorn noted the practiced ease of his delivery—no hint of self-doubt, no overcompensation. Authority earned, not blustered.

"For the next six weeks," Nardo continued, "my word is law. Obey my team's instructions, and you'll find me fair. Disobey—and you'll be left to fend for yourselves. No refund. No appeal." He let the words hang, the staff rapping once more with a hollow boom.

Six weeks. The thought was galling. Alone, Calladorn could have covered the distance in half the time. But with his duty to escort the Outlanders, they were forced to use the caravan.

The merchants continued whispering among each other in small groups with the bored indifference of people who'd heard the speech many times before. Others, however, hung on every word—especially those traveling with children—families in search of a new home. A few travelers exchanged uneasy glances.

Nardo waited until the tension settled before adding, almost conversationally, "Believe me when I tell you, it's a mercy compared to what awaits those who stray. The land we'll cross, and some who dwell in it, are less forgiving than I am."

Another boom of the staff.

Calladorn allowed himself a small, private smile. The man might not wear a uniform, but he could have held his own among Drakerath's training masters. There was discipline here, and clarity.

But there was something else too, which made his amusement wither. Subtle, almost buried—the way the guards flanking Nardo shifted their weight, the way their hands strayed toward their belts without drawing attention to them. A glance exchanged too quickly between them. *They're uneasy,* Calladorn realized. *Even here, even now.*

It was a flicker—gone before most would notice—but it sharpened his focus more than any of Nardo's warnings.

The caravan master pressed on, lifting his staff to indicate the broad Wester gate behind him. "In a few minutes, we open the gate. My wagon will lead. Then each of you will follow in single file, beginning with—" He pointed with the staff to the wagon immediately to the right of the gate, then swept it in a slow arc encompassing the full circle of gathered landschooners. "This order."

When he stopped, his staff pointing to the wagon nearest the gate's left, Calladorn realized with a grimace it would be some time before their own wagon reached the threshold.

"You," Nardo said, addressing the last wagon's owner with a wry grin, "will be bringing up the rear. I hope you don't mind the taste of dust."

A ripple of uncertain laughter traveled through the gathered crowd —merchants, families, hired guards. Most chuckled more out of obligation than amusement. Nardo's white teeth shone in a brief smile, the expression flashing like lightning and vanishing just as fast. Then he hopped down from the platform with a grace that belied his bulk. One of his men lifted the platform and slung it over a shoulder, moving briskly to the head wagon.

There would be more such speeches, Calladorn suspected.

"I guess we're off, then," Chad said, coming to stand beside him.

The first wagon creaked into motion, iron-banded wheels grinding out the slow cadence of inevitability.

Calladorn exhaled through his nose, estimating quickly. Their turn would not come for some time—no more than a third of the circle had even bothered to take up reins yet. A half hour just to get clear of the gate.

He forced himself to be patient, though the low rumble of dissatisfaction stirred in his chest. The slow crawl of progress grated against every instinct honed in Drakerath's fast-paced campaigns.

Every day they delayed was another day Drakerath suffered. Another day the north bled. Another day of slow progress, choking on dust.

How am I still hungry after eating all that dust? Chad wiped his forehead with the back of his hand, then glanced down at the towel he'd just used.

Filthy. Again.

The dust on the road to Wester didn't cling so much as invade—fine, gritty, and determined to become part of you. But even after a full day of riding, walking, and riding again, it somehow managed to taste fresher than the trail food.

At least the wagons had stopped. Now they stood circled up beside the road, a bonfire crackling cheerfully in their center like a tavern hearth for the open wilds. Chad snorted under his breath, thinking back on the end of the day. The way the guards had tried—and mostly failed—to guide the procession into a proper ring while Nardo barked from his little platform like a rooster trying to organize a stampede. It was about as effective as herding cats.

At least today had gone better than the day before. They'd probably have it figured out by Edron Station. Maybe.

Gharn, in his typical way, had already claimed the title of camp cook. He stood beside the built-in galley tucked along the wagon's outer wall, stirring something in a heavy-lidded pot while muttering at it like it might talk back. Chad had admired the design earlier—pull-down surfaces, fold-out compartments, hidden drawers that clicked satisfyingly into place. Nothing wasted. Everything tight.

It made him think—grudgingly—about himself. No fold-out compartments. No tidy edges. Just raw bulk and nowhere to stow it. Even here, in a world this alien, he still didn't seem to fit. *Talk about wasted space.*

Movement at the edge of the firelight caught his attention. Calladorn. The captain moved like a blade in wind—fluid, unhurried, but deliberate.

His sword whispered through the air in precise arcs, feet gliding across packed earth as if the ground bent to meet him. Chad folded his arms and watched, eyes narrowing, the noise of the camp fading beneath the rhythm of steel and breath. It wasn't just skill. It was *control.*

Chad had spent years turning muscle into impact—on the field, in the gym, in that one bar where some guy thought "college kid" meant "easy target." But none of that mattered here. Not really. Not in a place where monsters didn't care about touchdowns or weight class. Here strength without purpose wasn't just useless. It was dangerous.

Calladorn pivoted into a low stance, blade lifted in a defensive guard, before holding it still, eyes closed. Then he exhaled, slow and even, lowering the sword with a shake of his arms. "You going to keep watching," he said without looking over, "or did you have something to say?"

Chad blinked. He hadn't expected the man to acknowledge him—not yet.

"I, uh..." He rubbed the back of his neck, cheeks warming. "I wanna learn."

Calladorn turned at that. One brow lifted. Sweat clung to it, but his expression was unreadable. "Learn what, exactly?"

Chad gestured vaguely toward the sword, suddenly conscious of how out of place his hands felt. "That. How to fight. Properly, I mean."

A faint smirk tugged at one corner of Calladorn's mouth. "It seems you've held your own well enough so far, or you wouldn't be here."

Chad snorted. "Are you kidding? I've done nothing but run. We're only alive by luck." His throat tightened as a memory surfaced—sharp and ugly. That night in Emberhold. Matthias appearing from nowhere. The knife in his hand, the way it slid in. How it stuck.

"I know how to throw a punch. Tackle a guy. Maybe get in a lucky hit. But that's not going to cut it out here. Not for long." He realized he was glaring and tried to make his expression earnest instead. "I need skill."

Before Calladorn could answer, two figures broke from the shadows just beyond the fire's edge—caravan guards, their red-trimmed tabards smudged with dust.

"Captain," one of them called, breath a little short.

Calladorn turned, brow lowering slightly.

"Forgive the interruption," the taller of the two said. "We were wondering if you'd seen Kazrik. He wasn't there when Seln went to relieve him overnight."

The second cleared his throat. "Last anyone saw, he was talking with you before his shift."

Calladorn frowned. "Aye. We crossed paths by the mess tent just before dusk. He had a bad blister on his heel. Said he'd rewrap it before watch duty. Didn't mention anything else."

The two guards exchanged a look.

The second man's voice was edged with hostility. "Seems you've been chatting to everyone—"

"He left his things." The first interrupted him. "Bedroll, pack—even his belt dagger. And no one's seen him since. Not even a trail out."

Calladorn's expression darkened, though his voice remained measured. "You think he deserted?"

The second man hesitated. "That's the thing. If he had, he wouldn't have left behind rations. Or his coin."

Calladorn nodded once. "I'll keep an ear open. Let me know if anything turns up."

The guards murmured thanks and retreated into the shadows, voices low. The second glanced back darkly just before they left the circle of firelight.

Chad watched Calladorn watching them. Something in the captain's stance had changed—more guarded now. Not fearful, exactly. But alert. Like when Rick was adding up variables that didn't want to sum cleanly.

Then he turned back. "Show me," Calladorn said, eyes narrowing slightly.

Chad blinked. "What?"

"Show me what you know." Calladorn motioned to the space where he'd been practicing. "No weapons. Just you."

Chad hesitated at the edge of the practice space, rolling his shoulders to shake out the tension knotting there.

No point in backing down now.

He set his feet—shoulder-width apart, knees bent just enough to feel stable—and tried to mimic what he'd seen from Calladorn. It felt... awkward. Like speaking a language he'd never learned, the words thick and clumsy in his mouth. Only now it was his whole body struggling to speak.

Calladorn faced him, silent, unreadable. Waiting.

Chad threw a testing jab, shifting his weight forward as he moved. Calladorn stepped aside with casual ease, not even raising a hand—just a tilt of the head, as if watching an overeager child miss a mark.

"Again," Calladorn said.

Chad set his jaw and lunged harder this time, aiming squarely for the center of Calladorn's chest. He barely registered movement—just a blur—and then Calladorn's hand caught his wrist and twisted.

The ground hit Chad's back a heartbeat later, the impact driving a grunt out of him. Dirt puffed up around him in a dusty halo. Flat on his back, blinking up at the fading sky, he managed, "Okay. So that's what it feels like from this side. Ow."

A hand appeared in his line of sight. Calladorn offered no words, only waited. Grimacing, Chad grabbed it. The captain hauled him up with an effortless pull that made Chad feel even heavier and clumsier by comparison. His face burned with humiliation. He kept his gaze low, stopping somewhere near Calladorn's collar rather than risking his eyes.

But when Calladorn spoke, there was no laughter in his voice. "You're strong. Quick. But you throw yourself into a fight like a man who's never had to finish one."

Chad brushed dust from his sleeves, trying to pretend his pride didn't sting. "What do you mean?"

Calladorn shifted his sword back to his right hand, the blade gleaming dully in the firelight. He lifted it lazily, pointing toward Chad as he stepped back into the firelit circle. "Because against a real opponent, you won't get another chance." His tone softened a notch—not pitying, just plain.

"You have potential," Calladorn continued. "And you're right. You need more than strength or luck. But if you want to survive here, you need to be willing to start from the beginning."

Chad felt something leap in his chest, sudden and buoyant. *Does that mean...?* He straightened unconsciously, the bruised embarrassment forgotten. "So you'll teach me?"

Calladorn studied him for a long moment, the fire casting sharp edges across his face. Then, slowly, he nodded. "I will. And you'll listen. No shortcuts. No excuses."

Relief and excitement surged through Chad so quickly he almost missed his own grin. "Sounds fair."

For the first time, Calladorn smiled too—brief but real. "Then let's begin." He moved to adjust his stance again, then paused, a flicker of shadow passing across his face.

"What is it?" Chad asked, frowning.

Calladorn shook his head once, curt. "Nothing. Just something Gallus used to say—'Strength alone is enough to get you killed. It doesn't—'"

Chad blinked. "Captain Gallus?" The name shot out of him before he could think better of it.

Calladorn froze. It was like flipping a switch—one second open, the next locked down. His shoulders stiffened, his hand tightening fractionally on the sword hilt. When he turned toward Chad, his eyes were hard, the warmth extinguished.

"How do you know that name?" Calladorn's voice was flint-sharp, cold enough to bite.

Chad stumbled over his answer. "He—he was the one who found us. When we first got here. Led the patrol that... I guess rescued us."

The silence between them stretched taut.

Calladorn's jaw clenched and unclenched once, and his free hand lifted briefly to his chest, fingers brushing lightly over whatever he kept hidden there. Without another word, he sheathed his sword in a sharp, practiced snap and turned on his heel to stride away from the firelight without looking back.

Chad stood frozen, watching him disappear into the dark. *What the hell was that about?*

*

Later, as the camp settled and the night deepened, Chad sat with the others by their wagon, the fire burning lower but still warm against the cool air. The crunch of boots on the gravel made him look up. Calladorn approached from the shadows, his posture taut. As he neared, he hesitated—just for a breath—his hands shifting as if to tug at a cloak or jacket that wasn't there. Then he squared himself and crossed the remaining distance.

He stopped beside Chad, his hands closing into loose fists. "I owe you an apology," Calladorn said, voice low and deliberate. "We'll begin your training tomorrow. If you still wish to learn."

For a second, Chad couldn't find his voice. He only nodded—quick and emphatic.

The captain returned the nod, just once, a small but solid thing. "Good."

Without another word, Calladorn turned and headed toward the wagon's back door, his boots whispering over the packed earth. Chad watched him go, heart still thudding—not from fear this time, but something almost like hope.

Matthias rode along the caravan's outer perimeter, keeping to the ridgelines when possible, his horse's hooves crunching softly against sun-baked gravel. He circled the wagons in long, deliberate arcs—far enough for space, never far enough to seem detached.

Above him, a hawk cried out, sharp and cold against the thinning sky. The stink of manure clung to the wind, sharp enough to cut through the dry heat. A week on this road had done little to soothe the travelers' nerves. If anything, the tension had only thickened—drawn tight as a bowstring, then tightened further.

What fascinated him was how quickly that tension bled away once the fires were lit. During the day, they spoke in guarded tones, shoulders hunched, eyes scanning the tree lines and the narrowing mountain passes. But at night, something softened, as if firelight alone could ward off what haunted them. As if danger required darkness and would honor the unspoken boundary drawn by flame.

They had seen no signs of attack. No tracks. No screams. No blood. And yet something had changed.

The conversations had shifted. Idle speculations had given way to quiet warnings. Rumors no longer sprang from boredom but from fear. He heard them as he passed between wagons, gathering facts the way others gathered wood—without ceremony, without pause.

"...camp found empty, not even bodies left..."

"...no sign of struggle. Just gone."

"The gryphon riders aren't patrolling like they used to. They've pulled back to protect their own."

Each tale distorted in the retelling, yet behind the variations, the core remained intact. The roads were no longer safe—not in the usual sense. And the assumption that the Nine Kingdoms were protected by the Shifts—that no danger could cross the unstable zones—was beginning to crack.

It was a dangerous crack. Not because it revealed something new but because it revealed the truth: The Nine Kingdoms functioned on illusion. On the belief that as long as the bridges were guarded and the roads maintained, the world would hold. That safety could be mapped and named.

But the truth was simpler. And older. Nothing in this world was fixed. Not land. Not safety. Not power. And now, that understanding had begun to seep into those who depended on it most.

He watched them break into pairs—merchants sharing whispered dread, wagon guards walking closer than usual. The camp was becoming its own rumor engine. Whispers repeated during the day grew louder at night, only to have evolved again by morning. By the third time around, even the ones who had started the story looked uneasy hearing it told.

Still, he knew how to listen. Some voices were more telling than others.

"...I heard it from a Syrillian runner, before the mountain pass closed. Whole squads vanished—no bodies, no word. The towers on their eastern border never even lit the beacons."

"They say the elves know something," another guard murmured. "But Eryndor's court won't talk. Nothing. Not even a formal complaint."

Matthias cataloged each thread. Sorted by reliability. Weighted by tone. It was the elves' silence that struck him most. The Eryndori rarely involved themselves in human matters. But they always signaled when they intended to withdraw completely. Silence, for them, was not passive. It was preparation.

Across the clearing, Calladorn barked a short laugh—sharp, surprised. Chad must have said something amusing. The sound grated. Not because it was loud but because it was familiar.

He had spent years cultivating distance. Mastering detachment. But lately—without permission, without plan—he had begun to feel the shape of connection pressing at the edge of his solitude. These people, with their shared glances and quiet loyalties, made something he had carefully erased start to reassemble itself. Piece by piece.

It was not welcome. And it was not safe.

He nudged his horse sideways as a pair of guards approached from the rear column. They walked together, not casually. Not anymore. Voices low, hands near weapons.

"I told him not to go alone," the taller one muttered. "But he insisted. Said it would just be a minute."

"And then he was gone. No noise. Nothing."

"I know. I turned away for a second. That's all it took."

Matthias let them pass, eyes following without turning his head.

They were not speaking hypothetically. A man had vanished the previous night, and another had disappeared two nights before that. Kazrik, the first, had left his belongings behind. Seln, the second, had vanished during his watch shift. Matthias had heard the stories. Not secondhand—directly, quietly, from the guards… and from Nardo himself. The caravan master had stopped rotating the guards. Ordered them doubled up. No single watches. No wandering.

It had not helped. The third had gone to relieve himself and never returned. The fourth had been standing less than six feet from his partner when he disappeared. No sound. No warning. When the man turned back, there had been nothing but dewy grass and empty air.

Now the guards walked as if the shadows themselves might reach out and snatch them.

Because they might. Something was hunting them.

And it was clever.

It knew how to wait. How to observe. How to disappear without a trace.

Matthias was not ready to say what he suspected. Not aloud. Not until he had confirmation. But the signs were there. And none of the others—Calladorn, Chad, Rick, Evan, not even Gharn—had put the pieces together. Not yet.

The other travelers knew even less, trusting the guild escorts they had hired. Escorts who now lied to them and pretended everything was fine.

As the road descended into a shallow valley, Matthias rose slightly in his stirrups. The caravan was stretched out behind him, a slow-moving coil of wagons and horses, ringed by anxious eyes. Above, the western sky had begun to darken. Clouds had gathered at the rim of the northern peaks, boiling low and heavy. The wind had shifted. The smell of rain carried with it the memory of Drakerath. The storms they had outrun felt as though they were returning. He turned in the saddle, studying the high ridges to the east.

If the river swelled too quickly, they could be cut off. Boxed in. Even nature seemed to be closing the net.

Matthias exhaled slowly. The pieces were moving, the game was well underway.

And the others had no idea they had already been placed on the board.

The days were beginning to blur.

Every morning they broke camp at sunrise until the ritual unfolded with practiced weariness: fires doused, gear stowed, horses hitched. Nardo's voice barked across the circle like a crow on the warpath, directing crews to fetch water, check wheels, tighten straps. The guards, bleary-eyed and brittle, moved like men on borrowed time.

Evan tied a scarf across her nose and mouth before climbing up to the reins. The dust was relentless—clinging, choking, embedding itself in every fold of her garments. Gharn, seated beside her, tugged his own scarf higher but said little. He took his turn with the reins, but increasingly she found herself driving longer stretches alone.

He always seemed to have a flask within arm's reach. When he did speak, it was even odds whether the comment would be bitter or maudlin, and she was growing tired of bracing herself against the weight of his moods. Tired of being the counterbalance. She had considered pushing him, the way she had accidentally tried with Matthias, but held back. That attempt had accomplished little beyond confirming how unpredictable her gift could be.

Still, it was becoming harder not to reflect him. If Gharn didn't pull out of this spiral soon, she might have to take the gamble.

By evening, the wagons would draw into a circle again. The bonfire would be lit. People would cook, eat, murmur about the weather, the roads, the smell of rain on the air. Yet beneath the surface, something had changed. Even without Calladorn's private updates—delivered low over dinner, like storm warnings too quiet to rouse the children—Evan could feel it.

The guards were spooked. Jumping at shadows. Eyeing the brush. Eyeing each other.

And now the travelers were beginning to feel it too.

A guard had vanished every night since they'd left Merchant's Rest. Ten of the twenty they'd set out with, now gone without a trace. Until last night, when a traveler had vanished, leaving Nardo unable to maintain the illusion of normality. A father, traveling with his wife and two children, gone without a sound.

They had all heard the quiet commotion this morning. The stammered explanations. The hollow assurances that he might have wandered off, gotten turned around. But everyone knew. It was the same pattern.

The same silence.

Now, with dusk settling and the evening fire just beginning to crackle, Nardo stood at the center of the circle once more, this time without his usual gruff command. His voice, when it came, was steady—but not strong.

"No one goes out alone," he said, his words carrying across the ring of travelers. "Not for a moment. Not to relieve yourself. Not to fetch a tool. Not even within sight of the fire. No exceptions." He looked tired. Not just in body but in spirit. "We do not know what is happening. Only that it is happening. If you feel uneasy, trust it. If you hear something, tell someone. If you see something—do not investigate alone."

The mother stood a few paces behind him, her face blank. Her hands twisted the edge of her shawl as though it were a lifeline.

Evan's gaze drifted to the children. A boy and a girl, sitting close together on a low stump near the wagons. The boy stared at the fire, unmoving. The girl's arms were wrapped around her knees, chin tucked low. They looked like they had been drained of color.

Without speaking, Evan crossed the circle and crouched beside them. "Hey there," she said gently. "Rough day?"

The girl looked up, wary. The boy barely blinked.

"I used to have a toy like that," Evan said, pointing to the wooden horse the boy held limply in his lap. "Mine was smaller. Probably would have fallen apart just looking at it."

He glanced down at it as if seeing it for the first time. Still didn't speak.

Evan reached into the dirt beside her and palmed a small stone, letting it roll between her fingers. Then she flicked it into view, letting it seem to appear in her palm as if from nowhere. The girl's head rose slightly.

"Magic," Evan whispered, winking. "But only the good kind."

The boy's brow furrowed. "Magic isn't real," he muttered.

"Isn't it?" she said, and with another flick, she made the stone vanish.

The girl blinked. "Where did it go?"

"That," Evan said with a grin, "is a secret." She made the stone dance between her fingers, catching the firelight, then tucked it behind the girl's ear and brought it back again. The girl gasped. The boy blinked once. Then again.

"Do it again," he said, not quite smiling. But not scowling either.

Evan nodded. "Once more. But only if you promise to share secrets too, someday."

He shrugged, but she took it for a yes. With one last flourish, she let the stone drop from her closed fist as if it had fallen from the sky, then nudged the toy horse gently into the girl's arms. The boy didn't protest. A moment later the girl reached out and touched his shoulder. He smiled —faintly, but that was enough.

Evan stood and stepped back. Sometimes magic didn't have to be real to work.

*

Later, back at their wagon, the fire low and the wind picking up, Rick sat beside her while the others settled in. She leaned into him, grateful for his warmth, but her mind kept circling.

They were being hunted.

The guards knew it. The travelers did not—not really. And every day, the gap between those two truths grew thinner.

Calladorn and Matthias returned, cloaks dusted with grit. Calladorn looked drawn. Matthias, as always, unreadable.

"We will be rotating into the watch schedule starting tonight," Calladorn said, his voice low.

Rick nodded, unsurprised. "Makes sense."

Chad looked up sharply. "What about me?"

"You are not ready," Matthias said flatly.

Chad's mouth opened. Closed.

Evan reached over and put a hand lightly on his arm. "Not yet," she said softly. "But you will be."

Chad swallowed hard and looked away, while Rick offered a glance that spoke quiet relief. Evan caught it and matched it.

*

Later, curled beneath a blanket with Rick's steady breath warming the nape of her neck, Evan found herself staring into the dark, mind spinning through everything they had seen—and everything they had not.

She thought of the children—their loss, their resilience. She thought of Gharn and his slow decline. She thought of Chad, how badly he wanted to matter. And she thought of Rick.

Of the day they had met.

She had never told him, but she remembered that tarot reading. Remembered the card she had drawn for him. Not the one she had shown. That had been the Magician.

The real card—the one that had come up first, the one she had palmed and slid to the bottom of the deck—had been the Tower. She had drawn it, seen its lightning-cracked spire and plummeting figures, and thought, *No.* He did not need ruin. He needed hope. So she had drawn the next card instead. The one she thought he deserved. Only now she wondered... had the Magician been his all along?

Or hers?

She curled tighter against him, eyes shut, heart aching with questions she could not ask and would not understand if she could. Sleep came slowly.

And when it did, it brought no answers.

Five weeks out from Merchant's Rest, Gharn hit his limit. It didn't come with a great moment of revelation, burst of anger, or tearful confession. It came the way most real endings did: slow, dull, inevitable.

He sat atop the wagon bench, scarf pulled up against the dust, the reins loose in one hand and a flask in the other. Every jolt of the wheels rattled up through the seat into his spine, but he barely felt it anymore.

He felt buried.

Not under dirt or stone, but under a mountain of expectation he had never wanted. Get them to Southwatch. Uphold the prophecy. Save the world.

Step by plodding, miserable step.

Sorendir was gone—sacrificed on that hellish night in Emberhold—and still, still, the thought of him could bring tears, blurring Gharn's vision until the road became a smear of brown and gray. *You were supposed to be the one leading us,* he thought for the thousandth time, the words as bitter as the drink that burned its way down his throat. *Not me. It was never supposed to be me.* He drank again.

Out of the corner of his eye, he caught Evan watching him, her lips pressed together in a line, her eyes narrowing slightly before she turned her gaze back to the dusty horizon. He ignored it.

Let her judge. Let them all judge. They weren't the ones carrying the wreckage of a broken plan, half a prophecy, and the death of a friend who had been… who had been… Gharn swallowed hard.

His mind returned, as it always did, to that night in the tower. To the moment the scrap of prophecy had torn free, fluttering away into the darkness like a dying moth. Gone before he could catch it.

Had it been an accident? Or had Sorendir let it go on purpose? The question gnawed at him, an open wound he could not stop picking at.

He gripped the flask tighter, the leather creaking beneath his fingers.

What had been written there? What had Sorendir known that he had chosen not to say?

What had he decided Gharn should not know?

And now here he was—dragging an oversized wagon full of half-prepared Outlanders toward a relic of history, chased by enemies they could barely comprehend.

Southwatch. Another month and a half if they stuck to the main roads and pushed their animals hard, swinging northeast toward Syndar before descending through Endarl's borderlands.

Assuming the weather held. Assuming no more disappearances.

Assuming the demons didn't find them first.

Gharn took another swallow, feeling the fire hit the bottom of his stomach and spread outward in a false, fleeting warmth.

It was all assumptions. All hope.

And even if they reached Southwatch—what then? Find Haven, if it still stood. Find the Heart, if it could be found. Unlock some ancient power buried beneath a dying world and hope the strangers from Earth cared enough to help save it.

Hope, he thought savagely. *Hope is for fools.* He cursed Sorendir under his breath. Cursed him for leaving. Cursed him for believing. Cursed himself for still caring.

All he wanted was for it to be over. For the journey, the burden, the endless suffocating responsibility to end. And if he had to gamble to make that happen sooner… well, maybe that wasn't such a bad idea after all.

He leaned forward slightly, the reins slack between his fingers, and narrowed his eyes against the horizon's dusty glare. The road to Southwatch curled southward like a cautious animal, skirting the Shifts. But there were other ways. Shortcuts.

Dangerous, untested, foolish.

Still, they existed.

Gharn spat over the side of the wagon and took another drink. *What's one more risk,* he thought grimly, *when everything else is already broken?*

*

That evening, Gharn called a council.

After dinner, while the rest of the travelers huddled close to the bonfire—some laughing too loudly at nothing—he led their group to a smaller fire just outside the ring. The blaze there was quieter, its smoke thinner, its light more honest. Sparks drifted upward, vanishing into the black where stars waited. From here, the noises of the main camp were just a murmur. And they could keep an eye out for ears that did not belong.

Rick was the first to sit, dropping onto a cut log with his usual efficiency. "You said it's important?"

Gharn waited until they were all seated—even Matthias. Five sets of eyes, all looking at him. He had rehearsed the words, over and over. Still, they jammed in his throat like grit in a gear. "This journey is taking too long," he said finally.

Calladorn gave a tight nod. "Agreed. No one wants to reach Syndar more than I do. But we're stuck with the caravan until Edron Station."

"I don't care about Syndar," Gharn said flatly.

The effect was immediate, like dropping a firecracker into a council of elders. Voices overlapped.

"We have to warn—"

"The demons—"

"The High King—"

"Is your problem," Gharn snapped, loud enough to cut through them all. He fixed his gaze on Calladorn. "Not mine. And not this group's. Our goal is Southwatch. Fast. As fast as possible. And unless I'm mistaken, your orders were to join us only until we needed to part ways."

"Which was supposed to be just before Syndar," Chad said roughly. His eyes pinged between Gharn and Calladorn like a ball bouncing between paddles.

Whose side is he on now? Gharn wondered as he leaned forward slightly, letting his voice become quiet. Measured. "What if I told you we could be in Southwatch in two weeks?"

That got them. Silence rolled in like a held breath.

"How?" Rick asked, his tone already sharpening with possibility.

Gharn inhaled slowly. "We go through the Deeps."

This time, silence didn't just settle—it *landed*. Rick tilted his head, already calculating. Chad's mouth had gone slack. Calladorn looked like Gharn had just suggested jumping off a cliff and hoping the ground moved. Only Matthias showed no visible reaction—just leaned back and crossed his arms, like he was watching a game unfold two turns ahead.

Evan leaned forward instead. "Didn't you say the Deeps were deadly?"

"They're dangerous," Gharn said. "Yes. I'm not sugarcoating it. But every day we're out here is a risk too."

"It's too dangerous," Calladorn said. His tone was clipped. Final.

"You've got your mission. You won't be going," Gharn answered, trying to keep the edge out of his voice. He mostly failed. Calladorn's glare could have cut through metal armor.

Turning to the others, Gharn continued, "Khorvael's four days from Edron Station. One of the old entrances. I know of another, not far from Southwatch. Less than half a day. Between them—remember how I told you distance works different down there?"

Rick and Evan both nodded.

"We could be through in a day. Maybe two."

"I also remember you saying your people were driven out of the Deeps," Chad said. "The Dark... something?"

"Dark Horror," Evan murmured.

Gharn nodded. He didn't let his expression crack. "It's a risk. But we'd stay on the fringes. No cities. No magic to draw its attention. My parents had a map, and I used to study it for hours. I remember the routes."

"This isn't risk," Calladorn said. "It's suicide. If we go to Syndar, the High King can send escorts for the road south. Even if he doesn't, I could go with you myself. We'd move faster than the caravan. It would be safer."

Chad nodded. "He's got a point."

Then Matthias spoke. "We cannot know the High King will help. He may try to stop us." He bent his neck, eyes shadowed by firelight. "And if that happens, we will have wasted months."

That made them pause.

Rick traced idle shapes in the dirt, his fingers moving like he was solving an equation no one else could see. "The sooner we get the Heart, the sooner we go home," he said at last.

Exactly what Gharn had hoped for. Getting home *would* be Rick's priority. Getting away from magic. From the medallion. From whatever he feared was growing in him. A part of Gharn felt slimy for playing that card, but he shoved the sensation down.

"Evan?" Rick asked.

She frowned, lips pressing together. "Syndar feels dangerous," she said after a beat. "I don't know why. The Deeps... I don't feel anything. Which might be worse."

"Your intuitions aren't always right," Chad offered.

"They've been getting stronger," she countered. Then she sighed. "We're still a week out from Edron Station. Let's table this for now. We've got time to decide. Right?"

Gharn tried to keep his disappointment hidden. He nodded. "We do."

But even as the firelight crackled and the others began to rise, stretching and dusting off their hands, a shape moved toward them from the direction of the main fire. Nardo. His face looked like granite softened by rain. "You shouldn't be out here by yourselves," he said. The words carried, sharp-edged and hard.

Then his eyes found Calladorn and Matthias. "A word," he said quietly.

They stood without question and followed him a few paces off. Gharn watched them go.

When Calladorn returned, his jaw was set. Matthias followed behind, unreadable as ever.

"Another one's gone," Calladorn said.

Everyone stilled.

"This time, though..." He glanced at Evan, then Rick. "...someone saw it happen."

XII
Splintered

The silence following Calladorn's words wasn't immediate. It sank.

Gharn froze mid-motion. Evan stopped breathing. Chad's mug tipped into the fire with a soft hiss—but no one moved to retrieve it. The campfire crackled, now too loud.

Calladorn met no one's eyes. "It was one of the travelers. A woman." He waited and let them sit with it.

"A witness?" Rick asked, his voice low, clipped.

Calladorn nodded once. "Her husband."

The circle began to stir—just slightly. Rick and Evan reached toward each other as one, their hands clasping. She glanced toward Chad, whose jaw had clenched so tight the muscles stood out beneath his cheekbones.

"Return to the bonfire. Now," Matthias ordered.

For once Calladorn found himself in full agreement with the man. He nodded. "We've been asked to meet with Nardo and the witness. I'll share what we learn." He ushered them back between the wagons, then turned to look at Matthias. As usual, the mercenary's face was unreadable.

Suppressing a sigh, Calladorn headed toward where Nardo had said they would be waiting.

*

"I opened the door for her," the man said, voice thin and shaking. "Was helping her up. She had one foot on the step when—" His hand hovered in midair, as if still reaching. "It was just there, behind her. Big. Lopsided. I thought it was a wagon shadow at first—then I saw the eyes.

Too many. All blinking at once. And the mouth..." He trailed off, throat bobbing.

"Gods. It just—" He pressed both palms against his face. "It opened wide and... took her. Head and shoulders in one bite. Hauled her away. I didn't even hear her scream."

No one spoke. The torchlight flickered against the wagons, throwing his features into angular shadow.

"They were only ten paces from the main fire," Matthias said, voice low. "It waited until she was perfectly positioned—between light and dark."

"She was right there," the man whispered. "I had her hand."

Nardo gave a slow nod, expression unreadable, then he turned to one of the younger guards. "Stay within the ring, but take him to my landschooner. Give him a drink. Let him sit—not with the others."

The guard hesitated only a moment before moving. The man went quietly, as if the last of him had left with his wife.

When they were out of earshot, Nardo let out a breath and turned back to the cluster of those who mattered now—Matthias, Calladorn, and three of the caravan's senior guards. "That makes twelve," he said. "Always at night. Always quick."

"No tracks?" Calladorn asked.

"None. No blood either. Just a scarf. Taken same as the others."

"There is a pattern, even in the nights it skips," Matthias said. "Deliberate. It watches us. Knows how we move. Knows when we are weakest."

One of the guards—Kerrick, grizzled and broad-shouldered—shifted uncomfortably. "If it's hunting us, shouldn't we hunt it back? Go now, sweep the rocks. Flush it out before it hits again."

"No," Calladorn said. "That's what it wants. To separate us. Draw us out. The moment we scatter, we lose."

Nardo rubbed a hand over his face. "We can't keep this quiet. People will know by morning."

"They already suspect," Matthias said. "Rumors have been spreading since the second night. Containing it now will not help. Controlling the response might."

Nardo met his eyes. "Then tell me how."

"Change the light," Matthias said. "No more central fire. Spread the illumination. Use torches—ring the outer line of wagons. Push back the dark at every angle."

"And the wagons?"

"End to end," Matthias said. "Close the gaps. One entrance only, inside the circle."

Calladorn nodded slowly. "It's what we did in Hallowfield before the siege. We forced them to fight on our terms. This isn't so different."

"Except it's not afraid of light," Kerrick muttered.

"No," Matthias said. "But it hides from it."

"And if it stops hiding?"

Calladorn's jaw tightened. "Then we'll know what we're dealing with."

A long silence followed. Nardo broke it with a nod. "I'll give the orders. No one walks alone. Fires lit and wagons locked before sundown." He looked toward the dark edge of the camp, where the husband had vanished into the night. "We're already bleeding. We can't afford panic on top of it."

No one argued. They just started moving.

When they were out of earshot, Calladorn spoke for Matthias's ears alone. "We already know what it is."

Matthias answered with a single sharp nod.

*

The camp looked different now.

At the end of the next day's travels, the wagon ring had been reformed. Their original loose semicircle was gone—replaced by a wall of wood and wheel, all backs pressed inward. Small fires ringed the outside like sentries, flickering in uneven rhythms, lit fully two hours before dark would descend. The central fire ring had been left cold.

Calladorn stood there, arms crossed, watching the sunset's shadows stutter across canvas and skin. The camp's tone had changed. The chatter was hushed and movement deliberate. The illusion of safety—shattered. He turned back toward their own land schooner. Chad sat beside it, fiddling with something at his feet. When he looked up, the light caught the circles under his eyes.

Calladorn approached slowly. "You should rest. We may not get another quiet night."

"I'm not tired." Chad's voice was even, but the lie sat poorly on his tongue.

"You've been through enough today."

"I know," Chad said. Then, after a pause, "That's why I need it."

He stood. The wooden practice sword rested in his hands—polished smooth from use, the grain darkened with sweat. "Please."

Calladorn hesitated. It wasn't just need in the boy's voice—it was fear of stillness. Of doing nothing. And something deeper. He gave a single nod. "All right. But I won't go easy on you."

Chad's smile was tight but real. "I'd be insulted if you did."

Calladorn unbuckled his belt and set aside the blade. He picked up the second training sword, heavier than it looked. He rolled his shoulders, stepping onto the flattest patch of ground within their ring of wagons.

Chad mirrored him, his stance already second nature—knees bent, elbows soft... Centered.

Calladorn lifted the sword. "Begin."

Wood cracked against wood. Chad lunged, feinted, twisted back. Calladorn countered easily—but had to adjust. Again. And again. The boy's movements had sharpened. He wasn't just reacting now—he was adapting. Testing. Noticing.

They moved through a short series of exchanges, sweat beading along Calladorn's temples despite the cold. Chad pressed harder on the next one, and Calladorn had to pivot wide to keep the tempo.

Another strike. Parried.

Another. Glancing blow to the side.

He stepped back, ignoring the crowd that had begun to gather. "Again." Chad didn't hesitate.

They fell into rhythm—faster now, swords clashing with increasing intensity. Around them, a few heads turned. Gharn was watching from the wagon steps, eyes narrowed. Evan leaned forward, arms wrapped around her knees, lips pressed together.

Calladorn lost track of time. The training became motion and breath.

Just enough discipline to hold the form. Just enough fire to matter. He blocked Chad's last strike with a twist that left their blades crossed. Locked. Their faces a foot apart.

"You're holding back," Chad said, breathless.

"I'm not."

"You are."

Calladorn didn't answer. Just disengaged with a sharp snap and lowered the sword.

Chad stepped back, chest heaving. "I need to be ready."

"You're not a soldier."

"I don't care."

Calladorn watched him carefully. The lines in Chad's face weren't from the fight. Lowering the practice sword, he reached out and gripped Chad's shoulder. He spoke quietly. "You blame yourself."

The muscles tensed further under his grasp. "I do." The words were a whisper.

Calladorn let that hang in the air. He thought of Eryck—of the way grief settled into the joints and made everything heavier.

Gesturing to the onlookers to disperse, he led Chad out of the ring. Quietly he said, "We all carry someone we couldn't save."

Chad looked away.

Calladorn reached into his pocket and pulled out the medal. Not the one still pinned to his uniform, folded in a chest in the wagon. The other medal. The one that had never known ceremony.

"What's that?" Chad asked.

Calladorn turned the medal over once, twice, weighing it, then closed his fist around it. "A story for another day." He let it fall back into his pocket. When he looked up, Chad was still watching him. Not pushing, just present.

"I'm still going to Syndar," Calladorn said. "But I don't have to go alone."

Chad blinked. "Wait—what?"

"If you want to come."

The torchlight behind Chad shifted, making the edges of his hair glow. The boy's eyes lit up for a moment, but it passed. "I... can't."

Calladorn masked disappointment. "I understand." He looked to the west, where the sun was a sliver above the ridgeline. The danger was almost here.

They returned to the fragile safety of the wagon ring.

The darkness crouched just beyond the reach of the firelight. Watching. Waiting.

The night passed without anyone being taken. Just the slow return of morning—golden light slipping over the ridgeline, catching the smoke of spent torches still trailing thin fingers into the sky. After an uneasy roll call, the relief was palpable. Even the horses sensed it. They moved with less tension, as if the whole camp had exhaled at once.

Chad wasn't sure he trusted the sense of security. The thing had skipped other nights before, like it was toying with them. It would take many more before he felt confident that they had stymied their pursuer. He sat at the reins beside Evan, spelling Gharn for a while so the gnome could rest off what was clearly a brutal hangover. The gnome had emerged this morning looking like he'd aged ten years overnight—grumbling, snapping at Rick, and then climbing back into the wagon without another word.

Chad glanced skyward. The sun was already climbing, hard and bright in a sky scrubbed completely clear of clouds. The road shimmered ahead. Dust kicked up from the wheels clung to his neck and hair, and the wooden seat beneath him radiated heat through the back of his thighs. "How does he not roast alive in there?" he muttered.

Evan followed his gaze toward the wagon. "Gnomes are stubborn, I think. They'll survive just to spite you." She leaned back, arms folded loosely across her lap. "Honestly, it's a miracle he rolled out of bed."

Chad hesitated. "Do you think he'll be okay?"

Her shoulders rose, then fell in a small shrug that said more than words. "That depends on him. He's not happy we haven't made up our minds yet, but..." She looked back toward the wagon's rear door, as if trying to see through it. "...it feels like more than that. It's been building."

"Since Ironspire."

Evan shook her head. "Since Emberhold, I think."

That tracked. Something had shifted after Sorendir's death and had only deepened in the days that followed. Chad let the quiet stretch for a while, the road passing beneath them in rhythmic pulses. The hoof-beats and wagon creaks became a kind of lull—a backdrop against the thoughts circling in his mind.

He kept thinking about the night before.

Calladorn's offer. The way his voice had softened when he'd said it. *I don't have to go alone.* And then Chad, swallowing the one thing he'd wanted most, saying he couldn't go.

He hadn't slept much afterward. Not because of the tension in the camp as everyone dreaded the next attack. Not because he doubted the choice—though maybe part of him did—but because the words had kept playing back. Over and over. The way Calladorn had looked at him. The way he hadn't pushed. The man's eyes had merely lingered, steady, in a way that still made Chad's chest tighten when he thought about it.

What if that had been a door opening, and Chad had closed it? He shifted on the bench, uncomfortable. Not just from the heat. Something deeper.

The decision Gharn had posed two nights ago still weighed heavily. Two priorities—both real, both urgent. Southwatch or Syndar. The Heart or the High King. One meant home. The other meant hope for a world that wasn't theirs. And yet... They'd seen what the demons could do.

They'd seen the bodies.

The people of Drakerath hadn't really welcomed them, although some had helped. Chad couldn't forget that, even if part of him still hated this place for how backward it was. The Ban. The fear. The blind hostility to anything different. But the people? The people were real. Were good. Most of them. And they were dying. Jens, for sure. Fenton and Mari. Ipsen. Probably all of Emberhold. Maybe even Ironspire. The weight of it pressed against his ribs.

He couldn't pretend the Heart was more important than all that. Not when it was only for the three of them. Not when others were already bleeding.

But still... the Heart meant Rick. It meant Evan. It meant going home. It meant safety.

It also meant being the unseen son again.

He sighed and rubbed his palm against the side of his thigh, grounding himself in the pressure. "The Forbidden Spire is in Luthenholme, right?" he asked, trying to keep his voice casual.

Evan nodded. "That's what Sorendir said. We just don't know where, which is why we need to go to Southwatch."

He closed his eyes a moment, picturing the map from Sorendir's study. Southwatch—far south. Luthenholme, due east of Syndar. Meaning... after Southwatch, they'd have to backtrack. Toward Calladorn's path.

An idea began forming—half instinct, half logic. It wasn't fully formed yet, but it had bones. Routes. Timelines. Contingencies.

In his peripheral vision, he caught Evan watching him, eyes narrowed in quiet suspicion. He didn't look at her—just kept staring down the road as it unfolded before them, dust rising and falling like breath.

*

Chad hurried through his dinner at the steps of their wagon, barely tasting it. The stew was bland—uncharacteristically so. Gharn must have forgotten the spice blend again, or maybe just hadn't bothered. It sat heavy in Chad's stomach, but that wasn't what drove him to finish. He was restless. Eager.

He'd figured it out. The perfect solution. Both missions—Calladorn's and theirs—could succeed. All it took was trusting what they'd already been told.

Across the fire, Calladorn sat ramrod straight, eating mechanically. He hadn't spoken much all evening, and his usual air of composed restraint had tightened into something sharper, more brittle, like a drawn bow. The waiting was wearing on him—Chad could feel it. Saw it in the slight clench of his jaw with every bite. The way he kept glancing east, toward the road ahead.

Time to do something about that. Chad cleared his throat. "I've been thinking about the prophecy."

The conversation stilled. Heads turned. Gharn froze mid-chew, brow furrowing.

"What of it?" the gnome asked, guarded.

"You and Sorendir said we four were destined to find the Heart, right?" Chad gestured broadly, including Rick, Evan, Matthias—and himself.

Gharn's eyes dropped to his plate. "We… Sorendir was certain, yes." His voice was leaden. "He sacrificed himself for that belief." He stabbed at his food like it had insulted him.

Chad's grin widened. "Well, that solves everything, doesn't it?"

No one replied. Evan raised an eyebrow. Rick squinted. Matthias sat completely still.

Chad pressed on. "Don't you see? We can make both missions work. We don't have to choose. The prophecy already chose for us."

Rick looked at him like he'd started speaking in tongues. "No, I don't see. What the hell are you talking about?"

Chad's grin turned triumphant. "Let me break it down." He raised one hand and began counting off fingers with the other. "One, the prophecy says all four of us find the Heart. Not one, not two—all four. That's locked in."

Rick opened his mouth, but Chad steamrollered on. "Two, that means we can go through the Deeps. We have to succeed—because if we didn't, the prophecy couldn't come true."

Now Gharn was staring at him, a strange, unreadable look tightening the corners of his eyes. Chad nodded at him, undeterred. "Three, if we all end up at the Heart together, that means if we were to split up for any reason, then we must still come back together at some point before it's found. Which means—"

He turned to Calladorn. "I can go with you. To Syndar. Help deliver the warning. We buy time, you recruit support, then I—or maybe even we—swing east to Luthenholme and meet the others there. After they've been to Southwatch."

Calladorn's eyes hadn't left him since he'd started talking—not judging, just watching like he was trying to decide what Chad actually was.

"It all works," Chad finished, breath short with excitement. "It's perfect."

The silence that followed felt like a held breath.

Rick's expression hovered somewhere between baffled and scandalized. His mouth opened, closed, opened again. Like his brain had skipped gears.

Evan blinked. Slowly. "You're... really serious about this?"

Chad nodded. "Completely."

Matthias was the first to speak. "I do not like either option," he said. His voice was neutral, but his jaw had tightened. "The longer route is safer. The more controllable it remains, the less likely it is to fracture."

Evan frowned. "It's a clever theory, Chad. But you're putting a lot of faith in fate." She looked away, then back. "That's not something I believe in. Even if I did... what if splitting up changes the outcome? What if we're meant to reach the Heart together because we stayed together?"

Chad shook his head. "Don't you understand? We fought the prophecy before we even knew it existed. We turned Sorendir down. Not only did everything force us back, it brought the fourth into play." He looked at Matthias for support, but the man remained impassive.

He continued anyway. "The only reason we're even alive is because the prophecy predicted it." His voice sharpened. "You were there. You saw what happened. If we hadn't left that night, we'd be dead. That's not just coincidence." He glanced around the fire. "You think it was luck? It was because of the prophecy. Gharn even said Sorendir had been waiting for this."

Gharn's lips compressed into a thin, unreadable line.

"Look," Chad said, tone growing gentler, "I know it sounds crazy. But it's the only thing that explains how we keep making it through. Why we survived the crossing. Why Sorendir knew we were coming. How we all came together. It all fits." He turned back to Calladorn. "And it means I can accept your offer. Without feeling like I'm abandoning the rest of them. I can do both. Help make sure your mission succeeds—and still be there when they need me."

Calladorn didn't answer right away, but something in his face changed, just a flicker. The barest softening of his eyes. Chad wasn't sure if it was approval or something else entirely and didn't know if he wanted to know.

Gharn scowled from beneath heavy brows. "You're mighty keen on marching off with the stiff-necked soldier. Are you trying to be useful? Or just trying to be different from your brother?"

The accusation stung.

Across the fire, Rick looked deeply uncomfortable. Was it because Gharn was right, or was there another reason? Yet Chad could tell Rick hadn't found a flaw in the logic, either, or he would have said so. And Rick didn't like not being the one to figure things out first. Evan folded her arms, brow furrowed. She didn't argue again, but she didn't agree either. Matthias, as always, gave away nothing.

Chad sat back and let the silence stretch, his pulse still high. If he was wrong, everything broke. But if he was right—

Then this was the first step toward setting everything right.

Evan climbed into the wagon and immediately regretted it. The heat hit like a wall—thick, unmoving, suffocating. Even with the vents propped open and the flap pinned wide, it felt like crawling into a forge. The interior was bathed in the faded scent of dust, sweat, and sunbaked wood. Her skin was already damp by the time she lay down beside Rick, and the coarse blanket beneath her scratched her skin like burlap.

They'd drawn the short straw tonight. It was her and Rick's turn to sleep inside. The others were out in the middle of the circle with their fellow travelers. Probably clustered together, half keeping watch for the demon, half trying to get some sleep.

In the cool air. *The bastards.*

But someone needed to stay in the wagon and safeguard their meager belongings… and tonight that someone was them.

Even without the heat, she likely wouldn't have slept, though. Not with the pent-up fear radiating off everyone to the point it felt like she was being buried under a lead blanket.

Not after Chad's bombshell.

She lay rigid, one arm between them, the other thrown across her eyes as if it could block out the weight pressing in on her thoughts. Too hot to cuddle, too restless to lie still, she reached for Rick's hand. Their fingers laced loosely, but it didn't help much. She could still see the look on Chad's face. That maddening certainty. That crooked grin like he'd just solved the puzzle the rest of them hadn't even realized was there yet.

"How can he be so reckless?" she whispered, each word crisp and bitten off, like they hurt her to say.

Beside her, Rick shifted—his skin slick against hers for half a second. She couldn't tell if it was the heat or the tension making him squirm.

"It's crazy," he said eventually, voice low. "But the logic's... sound. Assuming the prophecy is valid."

She pulled her hand away, disguising the gesture by running it across her forehead. The headache wasn't feigned. Her temples throbbed, a dull pulse matching her frustration. She felt Rick hesitate beside her. "I'm sorry," she muttered. "It's just..." She let out a shaky breath. "I knew he was stewing on something all day. I could feel it. I just didn't think it would be this."

Rick rolled onto his side to face her, one arm tucked under his head. He looked as worn out as she felt, but his expression was soft. "Have you gotten anything, about either path?"

Evan stared at the dark canvas above them, jaw tight. "Nothing about the Deeps," she admitted. "Which might be a good thing. But Syndar..." She swallowed. "It still feels wrong, like a game of Russian roulette—dread, but with nowhere to aim it. It scares me, Rick. And I don't even know why."

She looked at him then, her voice quieter. "Going to Syndar is a terrible idea."

His eyes didn't leave hers. But his mouth did that thing—parting like he was about to speak, then flattening. He blinked.

"You're holding something back," she said. "Don't. Just say it."

Rick exhaled slowly, then raised his eyebrows a fraction. "It just struck me... we're debating prophecy by consulting your intuition. That's all." Something in her expression must have shifted, because his hands went up immediately in mock surrender. "Sorry. You asked."

She rolled over onto her side, back to him. He was right, and she hated it. But just because he was right didn't mean she was wrong.

The air inside the wagon thickened with silence. Outside she could hear the faint sounds of shifting guards and distant murmurs from the ring of firelight. The camp had held last night, but that didn't mean they weren't still waiting. Expecting. Evan closed her eyes and tried to center herself. The last thing she needed was to start mirroring that paranoia.

She felt Rick's presence behind her—warm, steady, familiar. Safe. That helped. But her mind was already spinning back to Chad. To what he'd said. The confidence in his voice. The way he believed so deeply that this plan—*his* plan—was the answer.

She thought of Calladorn too. And what Chad must have seen in his eyes to make him want that path so badly.

A quiet ache pulsed in her chest. Not jealousy—not exactly. More like grief for what Chad was about to walk into. She remembered what had happened when Rick put on the medallion—how she'd reached for Matthias in desperation. How she'd tried to will him into action.

And maybe... maybe he had moved.

Maybe she hadn't believed it enough or hadn't pushed hard enough. Or maybe she'd been afraid—of what it would mean if she could.

But maybe she'd been thinking about it all wrong.

Evan pictured Chad now. That smirk. That conviction. *Going to Syndar is a terrible idea,* she thought.

Not quite realizing what she was doing, she bundled the thought tightly in her mind. Felt the shape of it. The certainty. The warning. Not a wish. Not a plea. A command.

She *pushed.*

Morning brought no rain. Only heavier clouds, dust, and the taste of consequence.

Matthias stood at the edge of the encampment, a dented tin cup in one hand, steam curling listlessly from its surface. The air was dry and metallic—wind shifting just enough to drag the fires' smoke sideways through the half-dismantled wagon circle. Another day's journey loomed. Edron Station by tomorrow nightfall, if Thargrip was to be believed. And with it, a choice.

He watched the Outlanders emerge from their landschooner. Rick came first, helping Evan down with careful hands. They kissed. A performance, perhaps, but not a hollow one. They moved like people who had built something together—something real enough to hurt when it cracked. They joined the others for breakfast: oats, boiled flat and flavorless. Gharn's cooking was deteriorating by the day, but no one commented.

Matthias took his time eating. His expression did not change when Chad came bounding from the other side of the ring like a dog too eager for a game. He grinned at Rick, then stooped to start rolling up the canvas awnings—now converted to a rude tent—with the exuberance of someone who knew he had made an impression—and believed it had been a good one.

"Morning, bro!" Chad called.

Rick tensed in a way few would notice, but Matthias did. A half-beat delay before returning the smile. A subtle squaring of the shoulders, like a man bracing for impact.

"So, you're still determined to go to Syndar?" Rick asked.

Matthias's eyes narrowed.

Chad froze, the canvas slipping through his hands. His brow creased, and his eyes went distant. "Are you kidding? Going to Syndar is a terrible idea."

The phrase was flat. Mechanical, as if recited. His hands flexed once against the canvas edge. Then again.

"Going to Syndar is a terrible idea," he repeated, softer.

A sudden motion caught Matthias's eye. He turned his head just enough to see Evan, who stood behind the wagon, hands rising to cover her mouth. She looked as if something vital had snapped inside her.

And then she ran, a gust of wind kicking dust into the gap she left behind.

Matthias took a slow sip from his cup. Outwardly calm, his mind raced. *So, she does have the talent.* It was crude. Untrained. But clearly, it was growing.

Rick stared after her. Then at Chad. Then at nothing.

They packed in silence. What little needed saying was said without force, the day's preparations moving forward with practiced momentum, but Matthias continued to watch.

Rick interrogated his brother during the loading. The words themselves were harmless, but what emerged was clear. Every mention of Syndar summoned the same phrase, in the same tone, with the same vacant cadence, as though something had been overwritten. And then Chad would move on as if it had been utterly normal.

Rick's expression grew tighter with each repetition, his body more rigid. It was not coincidence. Not pattern or trauma. It was design.

When Evan returned, she came with the stiffness of someone who expected a magistrate's sentence to be read aloud—*guilty*.

Rick was waiting. He did not yell, not at first, but the sharpness in his voice was clean—precise. It struck deeper than volume ever could. "What the hell was that?"

Evan flinched. "I was just trying to—"

"To what?" Rick's voice cracked. "Manipulate him into staying?"

Matthias stood with the others now, close enough to observe, not near enough to intrude. Calladorn had gone rigid, arms crossed, his eyes fixed on Evan as if her shape had changed. He stepped back, just slightly, not out of fear per se. Caution. For once Matthias found himself in agreement with the man. *She is dangerous.*

Gharn, perched on the bench above, took a slow pull from his flask. Said nothing.

"I'm sorry!" Evan said. Her voice frayed at the edges. "I had no idea it would be like this. I only wanted to discourage him, not—"

"Brainwash him?" Rick's voice had risen to a shout—hands clenched so tightly the knuckles stood out like bone. His eyes blazed.

Evan took a step back. Her mouth opened, but for a long moment, no words emerged. "I'm sorry," she finally whispered.

Matthias tilted his head. She meant it. That was not what interested him, though. What did was how Rick looked at her then—like something in him had fractured.

The silence stretched. Rick spoke again, his voice low—controlled only by exhaustion.

"Fix. It."

Evan stared at him for a long moment. Then slowly, she nodded, closed her eyes, and drew a breath so deep it seemed to hollow her out.

At the wagon, Chad had just climbed to the top step beside Gharn. He stopped, every muscle tense. Exhaled hard, as though being squeezed.

Then sagged.

He looked down, confused at first, then turned—not to Rick or Gharn but to Evan. His eyes shone, confusion giving way to hurt and betrayal. "You didn't have to do that," he said.

He stepped off the wagon, boots landing harder than they needed to, and walked away. No one followed.

The horn sounded a few heartbeats later—one long, mournful blast. It was time to go.

Matthias drank the last of his tea, the bitterness remaining on his tongue, and he let his gaze linger on Evan, who had not moved, then Rick, who looked ready to shatter, and finally Chad, who no longer seemed like a boy.

A crack had formed. Not a break—not yet—but he could feel it now, the first real fault line. And he felt something else as well—

The need to put distance between himself and Evan.

They didn't speak for the rest of the day, not even when they lay down for the night.

Rick had kept himself busy—packing, tightening canvas, inventorying supplies with a focus that bordered on obsessive—anything to keep from thinking too hard. But thoughts didn't need invitations. They returned anyway. In quiet moments. In the shadows behind every task.

He loved her. That hadn't changed, but now, beneath that love, something else stirred. Something new. Something colder.

He feared her.

And he hated that. Hated that he could even feel that. Evan was the one who made things make sense when this insane world didn't. She was the anchor he clung to when magic and death and prophecy swirled too high to breathe.

And yet last night, she'd reached into Chad's mind and twisted something. She claimed it had been instinctive; unintentional... yet it had happened. If she could do that without meaning to—what else could she do?

Could she do it to him? Would he know if she had?

That question had chased him all day like a shadow under his skin. And no matter how he tried to shake it, it always ended in the same place: he wasn't sure. He wanted to believe it had been an accident. That her guilt was real. That she wouldn't cross that line again.

But even love couldn't outrun fear forever.

And so, when night fell and the fire dimmed and it was time to find space among the others beneath the makeshift tent, Rick didn't join her. He found a spot near the edge instead. Far from Gharn, who'd claimed the landschooner with a snort and a swig. Emotionally far from Evan, who curled beneath her blanket a few paces away.

She didn't try to close the distance, and he didn't offer. He knew she was hurt, and right now he didn't care.

The night air was cooler than the day's had been but not enough. It clung to his skin like damp linen, thick with the scent of old smoke, sweat, and canvas. The caravan murmured with uneasy stillness—breathing it in, waiting for what came next. The fires burned low. The stars were occluded, especially to the north, toward Drakerath.

He closed his eyes. Sleep came slow and grudging.

*

It was Evan who shook him awake.

"Rick," she whispered, urgent. Her fingers gripped his shoulder. "A girl's gone. She walked out through the gap."

He blinked at her, heart pounding. Her face hovered close, half-shadowed, sharp with alarm.

"Wha—?" His brain was still in a fog. "How do you know?"

Evan's eyes were earnest. "I feel her."

Then she pointed. There—the only exit from the tight ring of wagons. And the guard was asleep.

Rick was upright in an instant. His boots lay beside him, and he shoved them on with fingers that felt clumsy. Chad slept nearby, curled up beneath a blanket. Rick grabbed him by the shoulder. "Wake the others. Someone's outside the ring."

Chad sat up, blinking, then nodded and scrambled to his feet.

Rick turned back to Evan, who was already slipping from under the canvas and past the useless guard. He followed, and the night greeted him with a chill that raised goose bumps across his arms and chest. The fires surrounding the wagons had mostly burned down, now casting flickering pools of orange that only made the dark seem deeper. Beyond them, the void yawned.

Lightning flared to the north. For an instant, the mountains reared up, jagged and black against the sky. Thunder rumbled long after, low and distant—the storms had returned.

"Where?" he asked.

Evan turned, squinting into the dark. "That way," she said, already walking. Her voice was steady but tight, and he didn't question her.

Another figure emerged from the circle of wagons, boots silent on the ground even as he hurried to catch up. Calladorn. He fell into step beside them without a word, sword bare in one hand, the other ready near the hilt. They stepped into the dark.

The land sloped down toward the river, the footing uneven. Rick could hear the water before he saw it—a low, steady rush that grew louder with every step. He nearly stumbled on a half-buried root, catching himself on Evan's arm.

"There," she whispered, pointing ahead and to the left.

A faint sound—crying.

They hurried forward. The moonlight was faint—only the smaller moon was visible through the haze—and the trees thinned as they neared the embankment. The river cut a jagged path below them, the trail downward slippery and half washed away.

"Water's higher," Calladorn muttered. "Storm's upstream."

Rick swore under his breath. The current had been ankle-deep that evening. Now it snarled hungrily at the base of the slope.

They reached the drop-off. Below, barely visible in the gloom, a small figure clung to a rock jutting from the water. Long hair hung in wet clumps around her face.

“She’s there!” Evan exclaimed, crouching.

“She’s going to lose her grip,” Calladorn added, his voice taut. “The water’s still rising.”

Rick’s breath hitched. The current had swallowed half the gravel bar since sunset.

They needed light. He shaped the equation in his mind, fast and instinctive, whispering under his breath as he moved through the syllables. The air around them glowed faintly at first, then with more certainty—a cool silver-blue light that didn’t sear the eyes but pushed the darkness back.

And in that light—they saw *it*.

Beyond the girl.

On a narrow island, half-submerged, something crouched. It rose as the light touched it. Long limbs bent in too many places. Skin like river silt, slick and sagging. Dozens of eyes clustered where a face should be, each one reflecting the light back in a glimmering, wet stare. It stepped forward.

“By the gods,” Calladorn breathed.

“Back,” Rick said. “Evan, get back.”

“But—”

“Now!”

She hesitated—but obeyed.

The creature moved closer. The water reached for the girl, for the stone, for the bank. The current was no longer passive.

Steeling himself against what would come next, Rick closed his eyes. Found the flow upstream. The tension. And altered it.

The river shifted.

A surge redirected outward from the southern bend, back upon itself, the pressure slackening near the bank. Water drained away from the girl’s feet, and a path began to form—muddy, slick, but passable.

Evan moved, Calladorn following behind her, sword ready.

The waters piled upon themselves, mounting higher even as they drained away from around his allies. The girl slipped—then caught herself. Her eyes were wide, mouth open in a soundless scream.

The creature advanced—three-legged now, or maybe dragging something behind it. It stepped into the river, and the current resisted it.

Rick focused—and struck, adjusting the angles, diverting the flow. The current spun sideways and swept in around the island like a closing hand. Water climbed, surged, *roared,* and the creature howled—but the sound was thin. Half-liquid.

The demon flailed.

Rick held the equation steady, his lips moving in a whisper, his pulse pounding in his ears.

A sphere of water swallowed the thing whole. The creature vanished within a waterspout that rose snakelike into the air.

"Go!" Rick shouted, voice hoarse.

Evan reached the girl first. She scooped her up, Calladorn guarding her flank. Together they scrambled back across the makeshift channel. The moment they were safe, Rick released the vectors, allowing the river to return to its course. The spout collapsed upon itself with a thunderous crash. The surge rolled over the edge of the bank and licked at his boots.

Nothing rose from the waters.

At the slope, figures appeared—guards, caravanners, Gharn among them. Hands reached down. Pulled them up.

No one reached for Rick.

He let the light go, and the darkness returned. His knees buckled.

Calladorn was there, a hand on his arm, a firm grip, pulling him up.

"You can't let them see you do that," Gharn said, voice low—not angry but not kind either.

Rick barely managed a nod. The cost hit him then—not as pain but as a sudden, hollow fatigue, like something essential had been poured out of him.

Around him, people whispered. Guards exchanged glances. The girl, pale and soaked, clung to Evan. Her eyes were locked on Rick.

Not grateful—afraid. She backed away, then ran.

Rick swayed. Chad caught him from the other side, easing him away from the edge.

"Easy," Chad murmured. "We've got you."

Rick could feel eyes on him. Could hear the word, "Wizard," drifting through the crowd like smoke.

"Wizard." He couldn't tell if it was reverence—or fear.

He let Chad and Evan guide him back toward the fire. His legs moved without input; his head felt full of water and ash. Somewhere someone pressed a blanket over his aching shoulders, but he couldn't get warm. The river roared behind him, and the word continued to follow.

"Wizard."

Reverence or fear. Not unlike how he'd felt about Evan. He sighed as sleep claimed him.

Edron Station took shape over the course of hours, slowly heaving itself up from the yellowed grass plains like guilt that refused to be ignored. The sun was bright and cloudless, shining down with cheer it hadn't earned. It should have been a relief—this milestone, this stop, this civilized checkpoint between everything they'd fled and everything still to come—but after last night, nothing felt clean.

Gharn should have been ecstatic to be seeing the end of the caravan, but he felt numb instead. He sat on the wagon bench beside Evan, who hadn't said a word since they'd hitched up the horses. She hadn't touched her food that morning or looked anyone in the eye. She wasn't even casting aspersions on him when he pulled out his flask again—an act that normally earned at least a sigh. But not today. Instead she was hollow. Withdrawn.

And she wasn't the only one. The rest of the caravan had grown quiet too. In a few cases, it was quiet reverence, but for most, it was the quiet of distance. It had started before dawn, with the whispers. "Wizard."

At first Gharn had thought the remaining guards were just being their usual self-righteous selves, but then he overheard two of the traders near the supply wagons as they passed the landschooner.

"A human wizard. He *must* be insane."

"Wouldn't have let him near us if we'd known."

The tone wasn't panic—it was something worse. Cold. Casual.

By the time the sun was fully up, it was obvious they weren't just talking about Rick anymore. People had started giving the whole group a wide berth. No one came to refill their water jugs or waved when they passed. One woman actually pulled her child behind her skirt, as if Gharn himself might breathe fire and devour the boy whole. Which was funny, in a bitter sort of way.

He remembered when people had looked at Sorendir like that. Same distance. Same hush. Same Powers-forsaken suspicion. It wasn't even magic that scared them. Not really. It was what it meant to use it. What it cost. They didn't understand it, so they invented stories. They knew the histories—and decided Sorendir must be mad. The same conclusion lingered in the way these people were looking at Rick now. Maybe even Evan too. Guilt by association. Maybe one of *them* was insane. Wouldn't be the first time, would it?

Gharn took a long pull from the flask and let it burn all the way down. Again, he wondered why Sorendir hadn't chosen to masquerade as an elf instead, but it was all a distraction to keep from thinking about the real problem—the party was going to split, and it was his fault. He could see it in the dynamics within the group.

It had started with that thrice-damned idea to go through the Deeps, born out of desperation and too many nights of staring into too much silence. And then Evan's psychic blunder had made everything worse, pushing Chad so hard he had snapped in the other direction. And now Rick had gone and revealed himself in front of half a caravan, and nobody had reached to pull him out of the river afterward. Not one, save Calladorn.

No one really spoke to another all day beyond the minimum. Rick, Chad, and Evan hadn't even made eye contact. Gharn couldn't decide if it felt like a powder keg or a grave.

He shifted the reins and let the wagon jostle over a rut, the motion bouncing his spine just hard enough to remind him he was still here—still in this mess, still failing.

Could he stop it? He didn't think so. He couldn't exactly walk the Deeps idea back. Not without looking like a drunk who'd made it all up. Trying would only rob him of what little credibility he had left, and maybe that was for the best. He didn't deserve to lead. The world kept turning forward while he felt frozen in place.

Maybe the best decision he could make at this point was to do nothing at all.

He took another swig and didn't flinch at the taste.

*

They arrived in the early afternoon.

Edron Station was much like Merchant's Rest. Familiar layout. Friendly signposts. The neat geometry of a caravanserai designed to accommodate three directions of travel. Khorvael and the home of his birth were to the south, Syndar to the east, Merchant's Rest to the north. Yet there were no rumors of invasion or war. It ought to have been a welcome reminder that not everything in the Nine Kingdoms had gone mad.

No one said it aloud, but the tension twisted tighter as they passed under the stone arch. Choices hung in the air like smoke—where to go, who to follow, what to risk—and for a while, no one addressed any of it.

Calladorn went to secure horses, as the ones they'd used for the last two months were guild property. Matthias helped Chad and Rick unload the last of their supplies. Much of that would need to be quickly sold, since they wouldn't be taking a wagon for the next leg of their journey. Evan wandered aimlessly for a bit before disappearing into the landschooner, reemerging later with a broom, a rag, and a quiet look that said *Leave me alone.*

Gharn, for his part, went to the accounts office, where he waited in line, eventually signing the papers and reclaiming the surety. The numbers didn't matter. Sorendir had left them flush in every kingdom west of Faltheris. But the math still mattered to him. It always had. Clean ledgers were easier to control than feelings.

By late afternoon they'd reconvened at The Randy Rooster—a name Chad found hilarious, especially once he saw the painted sign out front. Gharn should have rolled his eyes. Instead, he stared at a wood knot.

They gathered in a private room for dinner. Roast pig. Spiced greens. Flatbread and sweet wine. Someone, maybe Evan, had insisted on a table with a door they could close. The scent of pipe tobacco drifted in from the common room through the cracks in the wall, faint and lingering. It almost reminded Gharn of Emberhold. Almost.

Matthias took the seat farthest from the door, eyes always on the corners and the exit. Calladorn chose the one closest to it—back to the wall, angle to the exit. The watcher and the protector—both paranoid, both practical.

Chad sat near Calladorn. Rick and Evan positioned themselves on opposite sides of the table, as if even geometry could no longer be neutral. Gharn sat last.

It felt like a wake.

He cleared his throat, eyes roving over the group. "So..." he said. "The time has come. Decisions?"

Matthias spoke immediately, voice cool. "The original plan is the best plan. Continue to Southwatch by road."

"I just want all of this to be over with. The sooner the better." Rick didn't look at Evan as he spoke, but then he turned to Gharn. "Are you certain you can get us through the Deeps safely?"

Gharn sighed. No small talk. Rick had gone straight for the knife. He should have been ready for that.

He stared at the scratched wood of the tabletop, fingers drumming once, twice.

"Truthfully? I'm not certain I can get us anywhere safely. Not anymore. You've seen what happened in Emberhold. In Ironspire. The caravan should have been safe, and—"

"That is not an answer," Matthias interrupted.

Of course it wasn't.

No, I'm not certain. That was what Gharn wanted desperately to say. *What I am is desperate. What I am is out of plans.* But he swallowed it all down.

"Fine," he said instead. "Velgô-pahz is a force we don't understand. If it catches us, it'll kill us. But it's not everywhere. The Deeps are massive, and it sticks to the ruins for the most part. We know where those are. We can avoid them, keep our heads down. No magic—" His eyes locked on Rick. "—and we'll be in and out before it even knows we're there."

Rick leaned back in his chair, arms folded. "That's good enough for me. I'm in."

Gharn nodded, unsurprised.

Evan's lips trembled. Her voice was barely a whisper. "I agree."

They all turned to Chad, who brushed his fingers across the tabletop, the steady rhythm almost masking the way one leg bounced beneath it. Gharn watched his face. There was a flicker there—something held too still, too carefully. His mind was already made up. The only question was how much he'd let them see.

Evan shifted slightly in her chair, tension winding through her frame like a spring being pressed too tight.

After a long minute, Chad exhaled through his nose and shook his head. "Two nights ago, after I suggested splitting up, I went to bed second-guessing myself."

Evan made a soft sound—too quiet to be called a sob, but close enough. Chad turned to her. His expression wasn't angry. His eyes were calm, and the muscles in his face relaxed in a way Gharn hadn't seen in days.

"If you'd done nothing," Chad said, "I'd probably be joining you. But whatever you did, I can't get over it. Not yet." Each word landed like a nail. "I need to be my own person. And as long as I'm with you, I'm going to be second-guessing everything."

He paused just long enough for the silence to sting.

"So, no. I'm going to Syndar. And we can all meet up again in Luthenholme." He looked at Rick then. Pressed his lips together. Shrugged.

Rick swallowed, and a small, uneven smile tugged at the corner of his mouth. "I understand."

A single tear traced down Evan's cheek. It hit the table with a sound Gharn hadn't expected to hear—but there it was. A soft, liquid tap. The kind that made him feel things whether he wanted to or not.

"I'm sorry," she whispered. The words didn't fix anything, but they hung in the air anyway—fragile and honest.

Gharn's heart ached. He wanted to say something—offer a balm—but what good was another apology from someone who'd already failed them all? He turned instead to the only one who hadn't spoken. "Three of us for the Deeps," he said. "And two for Syndar. What say you?"

Matthias didn't answer right away, instead resting his elbows on the table, fingers laced beneath his chin. "Syndar is a mistake," he said finally. "What reason do we have to believe the situation there is any different from Ironspire?"

For a fraction of a second, Gharn thought he saw something shift in Matthias's eyes. A crack in the armor. Reluctance, maybe. Or disappointment.

"We don't," Calladorn said flatly. "But it doesn't matter. I have a duty."

"Even if that duty may get you killed?"

"Especially then." Calladorn's jaw clenched. He met Matthias's stare unflinchingly, and something unspoken passed between them.

Matthias nodded once, then turned to Evan. "Where you are going, my skills matter little. It is Syndar for me."

Gharn blinked. Relief warred with surprise. Of all of them, Matthias had been the hardest to read. Sorendir had insisted he be part of this mission—but Gharn still didn't fully trust the man.

No. It was better this way. Gharn would sleep easier knowing Matthias was far away.

He rolled out a map of the Nine Kingdoms in his mind, tracing the mountain passes east of Syndar. "Ravensford," he said. "When we've each completed our missions, we meet again in Ravensford. Can you remember that, boy?"

Chad nodded. "I can."

"Good," Gharn said. "It'll likely be you, but whoever gets there first takes a room at the largest inn and waits for the rest. Simple."

A quiet chorus of assent moved around the table—nods, mutters, but no one looked excited. It felt like a contract being signed at a funeral.

Gharn reached into one of his belt pouches and pulled out the bag with the refunded deposit—plus a little more he'd added earlier in case this was the outcome. Inside was a letter of deposit with a counting-house in Syndar. He slid the pouch across to Calladorn. "Use that to get to Syndar," he said. "If you stay there, or go back to Drakerath, send the rest with Chad and Matthias when they head for Ravensford."

Calladorn nodded once and tucked the pouch into his shirt. And that was that.

Gharn forced himself to sit straight and look composed. It was an act. Behind the mask, he could feel the fear still chewing at his gut. Despite everything he'd said, the Deeps terrified him.

He should have walked it back. Sided with Matthias, sat them down and told them straight that the long way was safer, smarter, but too much damage had already been done. Even if Rick and Evan changed their minds, Chad would still go to Syndar, and what kind of leader backpedaled just because the numbers didn't break his way?

He took a long drink from his cup, swallowing the heat and the guilt all at once. Maybe the council in Khorvael would refuse to open the Deeps. Most likely would, actually. And if they did—then they'd return to the long road, and Gharn wouldn't have to lose more face than he already had.

He drained the last of his wine and stared at the empty cup.

One more chance, he thought. *That's all I need.*

The mare pawed the ground, her exhaled breath curling into soft white ghosts in the predawn air as Chad tightened the saddle's cinch strap.

The streets around Edron Station were already alive—quietly, insistently. A woman pushed a cart piled high with produce toward the market, its wooden wheels clattering across damp cobblestones. The night's light rain still lingered in the air, giving everything a faint sweetness. Other travelers emerged from The Randy Rooster's wide doors, shrugging on packs, murmuring farewells.

Chad's companions had said nothing yet instinctively split into two camps, one on either side of the courtyard, fifteen feet of wet stone between them.

It might as well have been a continent.

We're split now, he realized with a twinge like ice on the back of the neck. *Us and them.*

He glanced across the mare's back at Rick, Evan, and Gharn as they finished their own preparations. It felt surreal. Back home, this kind of distance meant little—Flagstaff to Chicago—maybe two days by highway. But here, on horseback, skirting Shifts or taking mysterious dark roads... it could be months. Several.

Still, his heart felt strangely light. Not free of sorrow—but clearer—like this was a choice that had needed to be made for a while. He caught a glimpse of Calladorn checking the saddle on his own mount and smiled to himself. Training every day had sharpened his sword work faster than he'd expected. And the captain might even be a friend now. That thought warmed him more than the inn's breakfast fire had.

Calladorn looked up, as if sensing Chad's eyes on him. He gave a small, measured nod.

"We're almost ready to go," Rick said, stepping into the silence. Chad hadn't heard him approach.

Matthias already sat astride his horse by the edge of the courtyard, an unmoving silhouette.

Calladorn's hand came down on Chad's shoulder. "We'll wait around the corner. Take your time." With that he led the horses away without ceremony, boots quiet on the stone, leaving the two brothers alone.

For a moment, neither moved. Neither spoke.

Chad had a thousand things he wanted to say—jokes, reassurances, thank-yous, apologies—but they all tangled together into a knot too tight to pull loose. The silence swelled, heavy with everything unspoken.

Rick solved it the old-fashioned way. He opened his arms, and Chad stepped into the hug, awkward but real. It felt—strange. Like a goodbye that shouldn't be, as if one of them knew something the other didn't. Rick held on a second too long, his breath hitching slightly near Chad's ear. "Take care of yourself, okay?" he said.

Chad nodded as he stepped back. "You too, bro." His eyes flicked toward Evan. She stood beside her horse, head bowed, arms crossed. Shoulders drawn up like she was holding herself together. "Keep an eye on her," he said. The words came out harsher than he had meant.

Rick's lips pressed into a thin line. "Are you sure you won't come with us?" There it was—just the faintest edge of pleading in his voice.

Chad thought of Calladorn waiting just out of sight. Of Matthias, silent and unreadable. Of what it felt like to finally make his own decision, without Rick, without Evan, without anyone else tugging the leash. "I have to do this."

Rick didn't argue, but his eyes narrowed, as if measuring Chad up, trying to solve a puzzle without all the pieces. Chad's stomach twisted—but he didn't flinch.

Rick nodded. "Just don't get in over your head, all right?"

And that did it. Chad flushed. "For once I don't need you telling me what to do." The words shot out, hot and sharp. The second they cleared his lips, he felt the sting—but he didn't take them back.

He couldn't.

Rick looked stunned. The silence after that wasn't long, but it felt like it lasted a year. Chad turned on his heel and walked away.

Around the corner, he stopped. Pressed one palm to the wall, breath coming a little too fast. The stone was rough under his fingers. Honest. Like the anger still buzzing in his chest.

He almost turned back. Almost.

Instead, Chad squared his shoulders and walked back toward his companions. *It's only a short split,* he told himself. *He needs to know I'm serious.*

So do I.

XIII
Council

Evan enjoyed being on horseback again, a comfortable saddle beneath her rather than a wagon's semi-padded seat. It was the only comfort she felt about the journey.

Rick stood rigidly after Chad's outburst and departure, staring after his brother. His shoulders sagged, his head drooping under invisible weight as he crossed back to his horse and mounted—all without so much as a glance in her direction. "Let's go," he said, guiding his horse in a circle far wider than necessary, posture stiff and withdrawn.

Gharn opened his mouth as if to speak but seemed to reconsider upon noting Rick's tension and sighed instead, shaking his head. He followed astride a small, shaggy piebald mount, meeting Evan's eyes with shared sadness.

Drawing her shawl close—her taste in clothing had oddly required the least change here—she tapped her horse into motion and followed.

They departed Edron Station as the sun crested the mountains to their left, bathing her skin in a warmth that failed to touch her heart. To the left, mountains formed a rugged wall stretching parallel to their southward course, then curving westward. To the right lay vast plains dotted with animals she initially mistook for bison, until closer inspection revealed double-eyed creatures with plow-shaped snouts, steadily burrowing.

"For grubs," Gharn explained softly.

She nodded absently, gaze fixed ahead. "You said Khorvael is a day away?"

Gharn pointed to distant peaks. "Tucked into that corner. Beyond lies nothing but Shifts until another range rises. Endarl is past that."

Endarl... and Southwatch.

Evan turned in her saddle to glance toward the green valley at the range's northern end, guilt stabbing sharper as she imagined Chad traveling toward danger because of her choices. Calladorn and Matthias were with Chad, but did that reassure her or simply deepen her unease? Matthias always unsettled her; now his absence felt less comforting than she wished.

She had misstepped badly with Chad, yet her intentions had been protective. Every thought of Syndar tightened her stomach with dread she couldn't ignore.

All she'd wanted was to steer him gently toward safety, but that subtle guidance had become interference. Maybe it was because he'd already been reconsidering, turning her push into a shove. *Overconfident,* whispered a voice within.

Evan nudged her horse forward, closing the distance to Rick. She yearned to repair the hurt between them but waited for him to speak first, grateful he didn't move away.

They rode silently for over an hour, hoofbeats punctuating the quiet. A gentle, earthy scent hung pleasantly, yet strangely, in the air.

Rick finally broke the silence. "What did you do?" His voice was quiet, but it carried a vulnerability she hadn't anticipated. The question cut deeper for its calm simplicity.

"I wish I knew," she answered truthfully, voice low. "I've never directly influenced someone like that before, and what happened was... too much." The admission frightened her even now.

Rick sighed deeply, the tension in his shoulders relaxing only slightly. "I know you meant to protect him. Protect us." He hesitated, staring into the distance, wrestling internally with something unseen. When he met her eyes again, she read hurt and also confusion. "But now... now I don't know how much I can trust you."

Evan blinked rapidly, feeling the sting of tears. *I'm sorry,* she pleaded silently.

"I can't just let this go yet," Rick continued softly, voice weary and vulnerable. "But I do understand." He looked away, focusing on the road. "Please... just don't do it again."

The silence that followed was heavier than shouting could ever have been. Evan watched Rick ride ahead, battling the urge to reach out psychically. She wouldn't make that mistake again.

A rustle in nearby grass drew her attention, and she saw a bird of prey rising, clutching a small, struggling creature. She shivered at the symbolism, feeling trapped by her own choices.

*

Khorvael was stunning.

Buildings stacked intricately, tunnel-like streets sheltered by patchwork canopies of colorful cloth. Sunlight filtered softly through openings, illuminating carved pillars, stained glass, and murals depicting lost grandeur. Earthy spices scented the air.

Despite its beauty, Evan felt alienated, detached, as though she'd entered a dream meant for someone else. Her discomfort stemmed not from clothing or appearance but subtle cultural nuances: gestures she didn't recognize, murmurs she couldn't interpret, expectations she couldn't fathom.

"Why is it so quiet?" she asked Gharn gently.

"Noise echoes here," he replied absently, eyes haunted by memories. He'd been gone for decades, and Evan sensed that his thoughts lingered painfully on Sorendir.

Gharn suddenly stumbled, eyes fixed ahead. A gnome woman stood in the street, townsfolk respectfully moving around her like a river parted by a strong boulder. Her severe bun and trailing left sleeve lent her a regal air. Behind her stood an older gnome man, goggles atop his balding head, looking remarkably like Gharn.

Gharn stepped forward, bowing deeply, hands clasped behind his back, fingers subtly trembling.

The woman's eyes flickered briefly over Rick and Evan, sharp and measuring, before returning skeptically to Gharn. A swift storm of emotion crossed her features, unreadable yet powerful. Then her expression softened, eyes twinkling. Her voice—with oddly slurred vowels—held a lyrical warmth. "Oh, get over yourself and give your mother a kiss."

Evan watched Gharn's tension dissolve into embarrassed relief. She felt a quiet envy watching their relationship mend so easily.

If only her own mistakes could be so easily forgiven.

Gharn's mother—Durnya—led the small group deeper into the city. Her sleeve trailed two feet behind her on the paving stones, which were set with a smooth perfection shaming anything done with human hands.

When Gharn had last seen his family, his mother's sleeve had scarcely reached her knee. Clearly, her status had significantly grown in the intervening years. It was yet another reminder of all he'd missed in his decades away. No wonder both gnomes and dwarves gave room for them to pass, nodding respectfully as they did.

Torvik walked silently at her side, positioned respectfully to her left. Gharn took his place to his father's left, glancing uneasily at Rick and Evan, who trailed quietly behind. After so many years in Drakerath, Gharn felt an uneasy sense of claustrophobia. He had grown used to being able to see for miles rather than one or two blocks. Used to having sky and sun overhead. The weight of the city pressed in on him, a stone ceiling lowering inch by inch. He flexed his fingers, resisting the urge to fiddle with the tools at his belt.

"I was astounded to hear of your return," Durnya said.

"News travels quickly if you—"

"But not half as astounded as by your long absence," Durnya talked over her son, sweeping his words aside. Her tone was firm.

"I didn't think I'd be welcomed back," Gharn replied, sensing his father's amusement at his predicament. Torvik's slightly raised brows clearly said, *You're on your own, son.*

Without breaking stride, Durnya glanced back imperiously. "You may speak."

"The city is very organized," Rick said.

"Of course it is," Durnya replied without turning fully. Her voice carried the subtle pride of one used to such compliments. "This isn't some human warren. We have high standards here."

Gharn hesitated before daring to break the silence again. "Mother, you know why I couldn't come back. Not after..."

"A minor mishap. No one died. Nothing irreparable."

"An entire district flooded," Gharn protested, face heating. His eagerness to prove himself had backfired in the worst way. When the pump malfunctioned—no, when it exploded—he hadn't been the only one covered in sewage and shame.

Torvik snorted softly, a sound too small to be real laughter but too deliberate to be anything else.

Durnya stopped suddenly, pivoting to face him fully. "An unfortunate inconvenience. But you ran rather than face it."

Gharn clenched his jaw. Her words stung because they were true. He'd carried the guilt of that day for decades, but to hear it voiced so bluntly made his chest tighten. He had been young, reckless, and he'd fled rather than face shame head-on. Now he saw clearly how it must have appeared to his family.

The moment stretched awkwardly.

"What's that?" Evan asked at last. Her gaze focused on the city's back wall, heavily fortified and built out from the face of the mountain itself. Steps led down from the city proper to a semicircular courtyard devoid of people, except for burly dwarven guards spaced at regular intervals around its perimeter, all facing inward. They focused their attention on a set of massive stone doors built into the wall, reinforced with metal. Unlike the rest of the city, this was utilitarian in the extreme, utterly without ornamentation. Although it was impossible, Gharn felt like a cold draft emanated from the door, bringing a scent of mildew.

Durnya's sternness faded into a visible wince of deep-seated unease, the kind associated with old wounds never fully healed. "The Deepingate," she said softly.

"Has it ever been opened?" Rick asked quietly, his eyes narrowing thoughtfully.

"Not since we built it," Torvik answered, speaking for the first time.

"And if fortune holds, it never will be," Durnya said firmly, turning away. "We have happier matters to discuss—such as Gharn's return home."

Gharn followed numbly, his earlier embarrassment now mixing with dread. He'd forgotten how swiftly his mother could shift conversations, setting traps he never saw coming.

*

The family home appeared unchanged from his childhood memories. The ceilings were tall but the doors short, forcing Rick to duck awkwardly as he passed between rooms. Gnomish decorating tended toward clutter, with every available surface—be it wall or tabletop—crowded with pictures, knickknacks, gadgets and other bric-a-brac. There could never be too much of a good thing.

When Rick sat in a dwarven guest chair, he looked ridiculous with his knees protruding at sharp angles. Evan accepted Torvik's offer of cookies, their aroma sweet, as she gracefully sank onto a floor cushion.

Gharn sat across from his mother, clasping his hands tightly to keep them from shaking. Safely away from scrutinous passersby, he prepared to state their case and decided to run with the hardest part first. "We need to enter the Deeps," he said, carefully keeping his voice level.

Durnya stared at her son and his companions with open-mouthed shock. Gharn didn't think he'd ever seen her so out of sorts.

"We need to reach Southwatch," Gharn said.

"Then take the road," Durnya snapped.

"We can't. There's no time." Gharn spoke clearly now, refusing to let his mother's sharp tone silence him. He explained the prophecy, the arrival of the Outlanders, the looming demon invasion—everything leading them to their current desperate plea. With each word, he watched his mother's face carefully, hoping she understood. Rick and Evan occasionally interjected comments, especially when Gharn was too choked up by emotion to continue.

"These demons," Durnya said when the tale was finished. Her fingers drummed on the arm of her carved wooden chair. "Are they truly so unstoppable?"

Gharn nodded soberly. "And we don't know how long their Shift will remain open. Some have lasted years."

"And others mere moments," Durnya interjected sharply. Gharn nearly protested but bit back the words, seeing her eyes narrow in warning. "Everything you say indicates this is likely to be one of the longer ones. And while I rarely hold prophecy in very high regard, it's clear Sorendir did." As she gazed at her son, her smile was knowing. "Oh, don't look so surprised. Did you really think I wouldn't keep current regarding my own son's dealings?"

Gharn blushed, then realized he was making a habit of it this day. He discovered he was holding his breath, awaiting his mother's decision.

Trying not to fidget, he wondered which of the possible outcomes he truly hoped for.

Durnya's fingers stilled on the armrest, then curled into a fist. A breath, slow and controlled. When she spoke, her voice carried none of the earlier dismissal. "Torvik, fetch your grandfather's map."

As the man hurried off, Rick asked, "Does this mean you'll help?"

She gazed back at him with fire in her eyes. "Our people have already lost one home. I don't intend to lose another."

Torvik returned with a large piece of parchment that Gharn knew well. After removing the leather strap that held it shut, he unrolled it on the table while everyone helped move trinkets and curiosities to make space.

Rick, tracing the map's lines with his finger, let out a low whistle. "This is complex," he said. His eyes devoured the page.

Torvik grinned. He was a mapmaker, like his own father and his father before him. "The Deeps are a challenge." He spoke with quick animation, his hands gesturing with nearly every word. "They cover multiple levels, you see. Not at all like the lands above. Twisting and turning over and under each other." As he spoke, he lifted portions of the map that were cleverly stitched along one edge, to reveal layers underneath. "In addition... my son told you how distances work down there, yes? Well, the map needs to show not only passage length but speed. That's what the colors are for. Red lines indicate slow passages, and blue are fast."

"The brighter the color, the greater the effect," Rick finished for him.

"Yes, yes! You understand." Torvik's head bobbed furiously. "Now, let me see... You need to reach the exit near Southwatch, over here. But you need to keep to the fastest ways while avoiding the cities. That won't be easy..."

Durnya tapped Gharn on the shoulder and led him and Evan into the adjoining room while Rick and Torvik planned. "That is a very intelligent young man you have there," she said to Evan. "You love him?"

"Very much." Evan's chin jutted forward determinedly.

"Good. Men like him aren't easy to manage. You'll have your hands full."

"Human relationships are more like dwarves', Mother," Gharn commented.

"And look how well that worked out for them," Durnya shot back. "Years of war before we were all forced out of our homes and into working together." Then she laughed, a musical warble. "Never mind. Weightier matters and all that. And speaking of dwarven men..." Durnya's mirth faded, and she looked intently at the two of them. "You've convinced me, but I can't order the Deepingate opened for you. Tomorrow the council must be convened."

The three travelers followed Durnya into the council chamber. Rick's boots clicked against the polished stone floor, the sound echoing off the walls. Every step felt heavier. The exhaustion clung to him—weight behind his eyes, pressure in his ribs. His thoughts pulled in too many directions, fraying at the edges, but he couldn't afford to falter. Not now.

The room was an impressive blend of gnomish and dwarven sensibilities, split down the middle as if by a fissure. One side was a seamless tapestry of intricate metalwork, all graceful lines hinting of change—the flow of water or the growth of vines. The other was a monument to permanence, solid stone carved with geometric precision. The chamber itself was circular, a balance of light and shadow from high-set lanterns that flickered against the smooth, darkened ceiling embedded with stones that sparkled like a sky of stars.

It felt ancient, yet alive.

Six council members sat at a crescent-shaped stone table, three dwarves and three gnomes. Rick took them in at a glance. The dwarves, all men, sat like statues of authority, their thick beards adorned with simple metal rings, their eyes keen and measuring. The gnomes, all women, were more animated, their sharp eyes darting between each of them, weighing, calculating. Four empty seats stood in the open part of the floor, facing the council. Guided by a middle-aged dwarf, Rick sat in one of the chairs, followed by Evan and Gharn in the others.

Six silver lines ran from the seats at the table to a circle in the center of the room—the focal point of the crescent. Ignoring the order to sit, Durnya confidently walked to the circle, perhaps expecting her presence alone to sway the decision. Her voice cut through the room, firm and commanding. She sketched the group's needs in broad yet clear strokes, emphasizing the danger the demons posed. "The journey through the Deeps to Southgate is not a choice, Councillors," she concluded. "It is a necessity. We seek your permission as a formality."

"You forget yourself, Durnya," one of the gnomes said, her voice hard. "You may have beaten me at *kinstet* when we were children, but that was decades ago, and this council will not be bullied." All five of the others nodded, muttering among themselves.

Rick winced inwardly, feeling his heart twist as hope slipped away.

Durnya sniffed, turned, and glided to her seat. As she folded her arms, a shadow of irritation flickered across her face, gone as quickly as it had come.

Rick exhaled, squared his shoulders, and stepped forward. He tried not to show his exhaustion. He couldn't afford that now—only this moment mattered. Coughing behind his hand, he cleared his throat. "We do not seek to bully or demand," he began, his voice steady despite the weight in his chest. "We're desperate. We've seen firsthand the devastation brought by the demons. They are a plague, as bad as that of Velgôpahz." He used the name deliberately and was gratified to see eyes widen. "The Heart must be found. We once sought it so we could return to our home. But..." He paused, taking time to make eye contact with each member of the council. "...we see now that it's the key to saving Necsis. We *must* reach Southgate, and the fastest way is through your tunnels."

A councillor—Durnya's coaching that morning identified him as Rhest—leaned forward. The eldest of the ruling dwarves, his beard was streaked with silver and gleaming with golden beads. "If you misstep and attract the creature's attention..." His voice was slow and weighted, like stone grinding against stone. "Knowing its name will not save you."

Evan came forward, taking Rick's hand as she joined him in the circle, distracting him. She smelled of lilacs. "Do you understand the price we will all pay if the demons aren't stopped? As we traveled from Merchant's

Rest, we heard rumors, and so I'm sure they've reached you as well. The demons have reached Wester. How long until they are on your doorstep? We wish there were time to take the road. We wish the Deeps were not our best option. But we could also wish the demons had never come, for all the good that would do."

She spoke with such conviction. A calm inner strength filled her words, and Rick looked at her, keeping his expression carefully neutral. *Is she using her power on them?* he wondered. With a sinking feeling, he realized he wouldn't blame her if she was. And how was that any different from what she'd done to Chad?

The realization made his stomach turn inside out.

One of the gnomes, her hair a mass of wiry gray curls held in place by a jeweled silver comb, tapped her fingers against the table. "There is good reason the doors have remained shut since the Exile."

Gharn stepped forward, drawing their attention. "I know the history of the Deeps. It's as personal for me as it is for you. I know what we lost when we left, and this—" He gestured contemptuously at the grand chamber. "—is a pale reflection. But if the demons remain unchecked, we lose everything—above and below." His voice was firm but not pleading. He was speaking as one of their own, not as an outsider. "If there's even a chance this can help, isn't it worth considering? The Dark Horror has never left the Deeps, and not because of a stone gate. The risk is ours, alone."

Rick felt the weight of their scrutiny pressing down on him. He squared his stance. "Entering the Deeps is dangerous for the three of us. Refusing us passage is a danger for all of Necsis."

Silence followed. Then the eldest dwarf's gaze dropped to Rick's chest. His expression changed, his brow furrowing. "That trinket..."

Rick hesitated, then touched the cool metal where it had slipped out from the folds of his shirt. He withdrew it, letting the firelight catch the delicate etchings.

"May we see it?" the dwarf asked, extending a trembling hand.

Rick hesitated, but an encouraging squeeze from Evan convinced him. He handed it over. All six council members clustered together, peering at it, turning the thing over in their hands.

"There's a mechanical quality," one of the dwarves said as he traced the lines with a crooked finger.

A gnome nodded. "Feel the warmth? There's almost an... echo in my mind when I hold it."

"Magic, also," said another gnome.

Six heads bobbed in excitement. The dwarf who had recognized the amulet looked at Rick appraisingly from beneath his bushy eyebrows. "When last I saw this medallion, it was worn by Sorendir. How did you come by it?"

Rick exhaled, knowing there was no avoiding it. He extended his hand, palm up, and traced a symbol into the air. A simple one, a small spell—just a figment of light that coalesced into an image: Sorendir, casting his final spell and then turning toward them, his face lined with exhaustion. Looking straight at Rick as he waved. As he died.

The light faded, and the chamber was silent.

The elder dwarf let out a slow breath. "If he trusted you, a human, with this..." He turned to the others, his voice measured. "We have spent centuries in balance. Magic, Mind, Machine. All with their places." He looked at the medallion again. "And this was forged in the Triune Era. All Three Powers woven together."

A ripple passed through the council—unspoken but unmistakable. The shift in their posture, the flicker of something akin to reverence in their eyes. This was no mere relic. It was proof of something older than any of them. Something undeniable. The dwarf handed the medallion back to Rick as if it were the most precious of jewels.

The eldest gnome—the one who had rebuffed Durnya—nodded. "Very well." Her tone held finality. "You have our permission. The Deeps will open for you."

Rick let out a breath he hadn't realized he was holding. The decision had been made. He looked at his companions. Evan beamed back at him. Gharn—his eyes remained focused on Durnya, where she still sat. Her expression remained unchanged, but her fingers clasped each other just a little too tightly in her lap, the only crack in her composed veneer.

But there was no further debate. The council's tone had shifted. The conversation moved from resistance to begrudging respect. The path was open. There was no turning back now.

Gharn sat in his old room, not even bothering to try sleeping. The room had surprised him the night before. It had remained exactly the same as when he'd left—*no, fled*—Khorvael a half-century before. Fifty years, and his mother still hadn't taken the room over to repurpose it into something more practical.

For Gharn, the dream of returning had faded long ago. At first the pain had been too fresh, the memory of Durnya's accusing eyes too daunting. Sorendir had given him new purpose away from gnomish society. In the end, staying away had become a habit. He told himself it was because he was too busy. To be back now, and under these circumstances—

The Deeps! The mere thought made him feel like he was about to vomit. It would be the same for any gnome or dwarf. All dreamed of returning to their homeland yet knew the impossibility of it in their bones. Yet here he was, not only leading Rick and Evan into the place but doing so as his own plan.

After a while, he gave up and padded softly into the main room. To his surprise, his mother stood there, staring at the map where it still lay open on the table. Her white hair rested loose upon her shoulders, and her back was to him—not rigidly straight, as he had always known it to be, but slumped. *Tired... or defeated?* He couldn't be sure.

It didn't matter. The sight of his mother in this state brought up a flood of emotion. Fifty years of walled-away feelings shattered in an instant. He had braced for her coldness, her sharp words—anything but this. The sight of his mother bent under unseen weight cracked something deep within him, and his knees nearly gave way. Clutching the doorframe, he fought to steady himself.

Durnya turned at his sob, and Gharn was amazed to see tears in her own eyes. Overcome, he slumped to the floor. She crossed to him in an instant, knelt in front of him, and took his head in her hands. As she searched his eyes, he sobbed again and leaned into her gentle touch.

One eyebrow rose into a graceful arch, and her head tilted to the side. "When was the last time you trimmed these whiskers?" she asked.

Gharn felt his eyes widen. A tremor of confused emotion began deep within, rolling through his body until it escaped—as a single barking laugh. She laughed with him, helping him back to his feet and leading him to the couch. Sitting, she patted the seat beside her—an invitation to join her on her throne. "It's good to have you home," she said after he sat.

"You know I can't stay."

"Gharn, look at me. No mother wants her son to stay. Our greatest dreams are for our children to go out and become more than we are."

His nose curled, twisting his lip into a sneer, not at her words but at himself. "Then I must be your greatest disappointment."

She slapped him. Not hard—there was no sting in his cheek—but startling enough to make him stare at her. To truly see her. There was nothing hard in those barley eyes, only love. "Listen to me, boy. What do you think happened in that council chamber? I *failed*. That old bat put me in my place when I'd hardly begun. *You* changed their minds. Not Rick with his logic, or Evan with her plea. It was you."

"But Rick's magic—"

"Gave them the excuse they needed. Didn't you see their expressions when you spoke? They listened. You did what I could not." She patted his knee. "I've never been prouder."

Gharn stared, wanting to reject what he was hearing. "I've made such a mess of things. Sorendir, dead. Ironspire, fallen. Our group, fractured. Now I'm leading us into the Deeps. The Deeps!"

"Pish. Stop feeling sorry for yourself. No one could have stopped most of what you're describing. As for the Deeps..." She fixed him with her gaze, suddenly stern. "You're doing something no gnome or dwarf has dared for eight hundred years. You're about to walk our ancestral halls. No one has been brave enough. Until you."

"Stupid, you mean."

"One and the same. Bravery is knowing the stupidity of something yet doing it anyway. Not because it's foolhardy but because it's necessary."

Gharn felt peace sweep through him. His stomach unclenched, and he smiled at last.

They talked long into the night, catching up, sharing their greatest triumphs and deepest failures. The knowledge this might be the last time they would ever get to speak threatened to overwhelm him again. And somehow he knew—she already understood.

One quick strike with hammer and steel—a sharp, crisp crack—and the seal fell away to clatter on the ground.

The councilman stepped away, handing his tools to an aid. Evan looked curiously to see an oversized keyhole now revealed behind where the seal had been. The eldest councilwoman now stepped forward, producing an ornate key with three winglike bits at the end, flaring out from the shaft. Each appeared to be crafted from a different gemstone. Sliding it into the keyhole, she hesitated, looking to the rest of the council.

Evan's breath caught.

The councillors nodded solemnly. The woman whispered something under her breath, sounding suspiciously like a prayer, as she turned the key in one full circle before removing it and stepping away to join her fellow leaders. The assembled crowd seemed transfixed, staring at the gate in profound silence. Evan took Rick's hand, and he squeezed back. *What if it's broken?* she wondered. They would have to take the long way by road, and with the days lost coming to Khorvael, they would be even worse off than before.

Gharn spoke. "I think—"

A low boom echoed, and the stones beneath their feet trembled. Several onlookers cried out; whether in fear or excitement, even they might not have known. Somewhere among them, a child wailed.

The gate... changed. What looked like metal reinforcement moved forward, rotated with a clanking sound like a massive clock ticking, then moved back into the grooves within the stone. A star within a star within a star. The parts now spun past each other, and the gate pulled back into itself before rolling ponderously open with a rumble that set Evan's teeth on edge. It disappeared into a pocket within the mountain's face.

"Chad would love this," Rick murmured, his jaw slack. Evan could only nod in mute agreement.

The entire process took less than a minute before an explosive hiss of released steam brought new gasps from the crowd and, after that, silence. A damp breeze blew out, carrying a pungent scent like mildew mixed with decaying leaves.

The Deeps stood open.

Gharn stared into the blackness beyond, his shoulder shaking almost imperceptibly. He walked to his parents and hugged them both. Evan smiled at the way Durnya returned the embrace, clearly striving to maintain a dignified air. It warmed her to know at least some good had come from this visit. Gharn radiated a sense of purpose he'd lacked since Emberhold. Evan sensed fear—both from Gharn and Rick—but now woven with determination. The pocket where he carried his flask was flat. Empty.

Their friend stared them down, the corners of his eyes crinkling. "Are you just going to stand there gaping?" he asked.

With a final quick squeeze, Evan released Rick's hand and stooped to shoulder her backpack. They had enough travel rations to last two weeks, which should be plenty of time to reach Southgate, find their answers, and reach the closest town.

But when have things gone according to plan? Evan asked herself. Projecting a confidence she did not feel, Evan followed Gharn through the gate, with Rick a few feet behind her.

The stonework changed the moment they crossed the threshold: geometric patterns with missing pieces that had seemingly crumbled away over the years. Some kind of fungus crept onto the road in places. Ahead lay blackness, deeper than any night.

Holding his lantern near his waist, Gharn turned back to the opening, raising his hand in a farewell eerily similar to Sorendir's.

Already the gate was rolling back into place, its layered stars shifting in reverse, grinding into position with a deep, resonant groan—like a tomb sealing itself shut. A single deep bass note echoed into the Deeps, leaving silence punctuated by their breathing and an occasional faint drip of water.

"Only one way forward," Rick whispered, his face deeply shadowed in the meager light, blue eyes gleaming.

Evan nodded, unease settling around her heart. She understood his quiet.

Although unseen, the truth settled around her like the damp air—they stood within a mass grave.

XIV
Intrigues

The stars were sharp tonight. Chad lay on his bedroll, arms folded behind his head, staring up at the vast expanse above. He, Calladorn, and Matthias formed the sides of a triangle surrounding the fire. He could still taste the roast rabbit from dinner—not as good as Gharn's cooking, but with that smoky flavor that only came from a campfire-cooked meal.

It should have been peaceful, the way the sky stretched endlessly, each pinpoint of light distant and unwavering. It reminded him of home—the high-altitude clarity of Flagstaff's night sky—but it wasn't the same. Those weren't his constellations. He could trace the patterns all he wanted, but none of them would lead him home.

His fingers twitched against the coarse fabric beneath him, itching for something to fix, a wire to untangle, a circuit to align—anything to keep his hands busy. Instead, all he had were his thoughts, circling in an endless loop. He replayed the last conversation with Rick for what had to be the hundredth time, picking apart every word, every reaction. The way his brother's jaw had set, how his voice had dropped to that cold, clipped precision he used when he was trying not to yell.

Just don't get in over your head, all right?

And Chad, stubborn as ever, had shot back. *For once I don't need you telling me what to do.*

Even now, his stomach knotted at the memory. He'd stood his ground, yes, but had he done it right? He rubbed a hand over his face, exhaling hard. *You're overthinking it.* But the thoughts wouldn't settle.

Rick was always so sure of things. Even when they had butted heads, there had been an unspoken certainty between them—Rick the planner, Chad the improviser. Rick might have rolled his eyes, might have sighed dramatically when Chad took things in stride, but he had *trusted* Chad. This time, though, it felt... different. The way Rick had looked at him before he turned away, like his brother wasn't sure if they'd be standing on the same side when they met again.

Chad turned over, scowling at the nothingness beyond the camp. He told himself Rick would cool off. They'd meet up in Luthenholme, sort it out, move forward. That was the plan. But what if Rick was still angry? What if that moment—their last words before parting—had broken something between them? *What if we can't fix this?* The thought sank into his chest, solid and immovable.

He tried to shake it off, but instead, another memory surfaced. Rick when they were kids, scribbling equations in the margins of his notebooks, oblivious to everything else. The way he'd ruffled Chad's hair absentmindedly whenever presented with Chad's latest model, like some part of him was *proud*, even if he'd never said so outright.

Chad squeezed his eyes shut.

"Damn it," he whispered. Sleep wouldn't come, so he just lay there, listening to the silence. Eventually exhaustion won, pulling him under into restless dreams—fragmented echoes of his past.

*

Chad's sword slid across the dirt.

Flat on his back, staring up at a very smug-looking Calladorn, he let out a long breath. "All right. That one was on me."

Calladorn reached down, offering a hand. Chad clasped it, letting the older man haul him to his feet and brush away the dirt clinging to his skin. He winced when those fingers found a scrape. The morning sun's warmth was already breaking through the last chill of the night. Matthias packed up the camp, the smell of smoldering embers lingering in the air.

Calladorn bounced agilely on the balls of his feet, flexing his grip on his sword before giving Chad's shoulder a light slap. "You're slower today. Sloppy."

Chad flexed his fingers around the grip of his sword, stretching his neck with a pop as he picked the weapon up. "Yeah, well. Maybe I let you win."

Calladorn raised an eyebrow, unimpressed. "A troubled mind dulls the blade more than a thousand strikes ever could." His expression shifted, the teasing edge fading into something more serious. "Whatever weighs on you, carry it wisely—don't let it carry you."

Chad wiped sweat from his brow, nodding like the words hadn't scored a hit every bit as sound as those from the side of his blade. "Right. Good talk," he muttered, stabbing his sword into the dirt for balance.

Calladorn huffed a restrained laugh. "You could just say thank you instead of pretending not to listen."

"Yeah, yeah," Chad grumbled, but he was already filing the words away in the back of his mind.

The sword came flying at him. Chad nearly flubbed the catch and felt a stab of pain in his thumb as punishment.

"And never stick your blade in the ground," Calladorn said, his eyes no longer joking.

Chad put his lips around the webbing between thumb and forefinger to stop the bleeding, swallowing the retort that almost came. But as he buckled the weapon at his side and they helped Matthias finish packing to continue their journey, Chad realized he was treating the sword with greater care.

Calladorn's words had been meant for now—for the fight, for the journey ahead—but all Chad could think about was Luthenholme, and whether Rick would be there waiting for him, or if the rift between them was already too wide to cross.

*

The next few weeks followed the same pattern.

Thoughts of Rick and Evan gradually grew less consuming the farther they traveled east, and sleep came more easily. He never forgot his friends, but he worried about them less. Whatever would happen would happen.

Besides, I'm great at fixing things.

Each morning brought a new lesson from Calladorn while Matthias watched with barely concealed amusement, always appearing as though he knew a secret the others weren't in on yet. Occasionally he would offer advice, invariably earning a scowl from Calladorn, even though Chad always found the observations to be accurate.

The day would then become another marathon of riding as far as they could without pushing the horses to breaking point.

"Without spares, horses don't let you travel farther in a day," Calladorn told him. "They merely let you cover the same distance faster, with less effort and more supplies."

In the evenings, they shared stories—Chad and Calladorn did, anyway. Chad would talk about Earth, even though thinking of home aggravated his sense of loss and made him second-guess even more how things had played out with Rick. But it was fun to watch Calladorn's reactions when he described things like airplanes, television, or the internet.

Calladorn returned the favor with tales of the gryphon riders of Syrillia, soaring between cities built atop buttes in their canyon kingdom. Or Faltheris, a desert kingdom with oasis cities and intricate irrigation systems. The seafaring kingdom, Velsaria, especially captured Chad's imagination. He couldn't tell if it sounded more like pirates in the Caribbean or Vikings come back to life.

One night, he felt especially brave and showed his knife to them. He'd used its blades before, of course, as well as the striker for making fire, so they thought little of it until he opened the flashlight attachment he'd created.

Matthias seemed disinterested, merely tilting his head and squinting slightly.

Calladorn's jaw tightened, and his eyes glittered as they reflected the light. "Put it away, Chad," he said at last.

"But it's just light. It doesn't do anything else. It won't try to… I don't know… eat babies or something."

"I know. Put it away." He didn't look afraid, and his voice was gentle. But firm.

Chad hesitated. He'd expected curiosity—maybe even admiration. Not this. He clicked the light off, abruptly aware of how small it felt in his hands. "I need to be conservative with it, anyway," he said as he slid it back into his belt pouch. "It's not like I have any way to recharge the battery." Which led to another round of explanations. How did one explain batteries to someone who didn't even know about electricity?

Matthias—when he spoke at all—preferred to try dissuading them from going to Syndar. His arguments were always short and to the point, completely reasonable, and totally infuriating to Calladorn. Each time, the experience left Chad feeling uncomfortable. He liked Calladorn and respected Matthias. Seeing them argue felt wrong, like watching one's parents go at it.

Eventually Chad asked about the Wars of Power, partly in an effort to stop yet another bickering session from erupting and partly because he was determined to understand just what could have been so bad the Ban would persist thousands of years later.

"I'm no historian," Calladorn told him. "My knowledge is mostly bits from my father's library growing up. Eryck liked to read more than I did, but he'd share the stories with me after we'd gone to bed."

Calladorn smiled into the dark, and Chad sensed sadness behind the expression. "You don't have to talk about it," he said.

Snapped back to the moment, Calladorn shook his head. "It's all right. I'm sure you already know how all three of the Powers used to be much stronger than they are now."

Chad nodded.

"The thing to understand is that each has its limits. Magic is limited by the intellect of its user and their ability to focus intent through their spells."

"Equations," Chad said, nodding.

Calladorn shrugged. "Psychic powers were said to be tied to willpower and inherent gifts. Few people had the ability to begin with, and fewer still could hone that skill to accomplish anything of significance. But those few who had the gift were able to control their own bodies to the point where they could stop aging. So even though Thought Masters appeared infrequently, the sect continued to grow and exert greater influence. They kept mostly to themselves, though, because people feared what they could do."

"You mean reading minds?"

"That was part of it, yes. Or bending people to their will."

Chad felt an involuntary shudder, and now had a sour taste in his mouth. "I can understand that," he muttered.

Calladorn's lips thinned, his eyes sympathetic. "Finally, the Engineers. They specialized in adapting technology that came through the Shifts. Some, they kept running—like charging those batteries you spoke of, I imagine. And some devices, they even reproduced. As I understand it, that's where the problem came from."

He drew his sword and balanced it on his outstretched finger. "I don't know how a blacksmith makes steel or forges it into a blade. That doesn't keep me from using it. Or from entire armies being similarly equipped and trained." With a dramatic flourish, he returned the weapon to its scabbard, sliding it into place with a snicking sound. "Now, imagine if my sword were a deadlier weapon."

Chad thought of guns, missiles, and bombs. He understood where this was going. "The Engineers decided technology was the most powerful of the three, didn't they?"

"They tried to rule. The wizards and Thought Masters eventually stopped them, but it was a near thing. Necsis was almost destroyed."

"But why ban all technology? Why not just weapons?"

Calladorn shrugged. "How do you know when a weapon is a weapon?"

The question lingered in Chad's mind until he fell asleep, then haunted him into the next day.

*

With each mile they traveled, Chad became increasingly aware of wealth disparity between the parts of the Nine Kingdoms he'd seen so far and the kingdom of Syndar. The roads became smoother and the villages more affluent, with finely dressed merchants, opulent inns, and decorative banners flying from buildings. Yet it was clear that Syndar's riches didn't reach all its people—poorer farming communities often crouched in the shadows of extravagant estates.

A few days from Syndar, they passed a field where a farmhand was being flogged by a foreman while the other workers crouched and did their best to pick faster. Chad couldn't keep silent any longer. "It's like all the wealth in this kingdom is hoarded in one place. How do people put up with it?"

Matthias sneered in the direction of the field. Chad wondered which figure had earned that pitiless stare—the worker or the boss.

Calladorn shook his head. "They don't put up with it. They survive in spite of it." He gestured to the workers' quarters, then at the mansion up on the hill in the distance. "You think any of this was built for them? No, Chad. It was built to remind them of their place."

He considered that, the thought turning the sweet scent of ripe grain bitter in his nostrils. "There's nothing noble about nobility, is there?" he murmured.

Calladorn must have overheard, because his eyes focused on Chad with an intensity normally reserved for their sparring lessons. It made Chad feel uncomfortably like he was riding naked and exposed, before Calladorn returned his gaze to the road ahead.

"Some nobles live up to the title," the captain said after a while, his voice sounding heavy to Chad's ears. "But no. In most cases, you'd be right."

Power corrupts, Chad thought. It led him to consider how they were taking a message to the most powerful man in Nine Kingdoms. His mind flashed back to the flogged worker, and his knuckles turned white as they gripped the reins tighter.

The city of Syndar made Ironspire look like a slum.

Built on a tall hill, it rose like a many-tiered festival cake, each level more spectacular than the one below. Due to the landscape, the city's main street didn't run straight. Instead it formed a slow spiral, wrapping its way three times around the city, making Calladorn think uneasily of a coiled serpent. Any street seeking a more direct route was forced to employ stairs, making it impassable for carriages or even horses.

This city demanded to be *seen* rather than simply observed.

Calladorn's military mind appreciated the design. Any assault on the city would be repeatedly challenged. Sending an army up the main street would expose it to endless attacks—infantry units could spring ambushes from one building after another while archers picked enemies off from the flat rooftops. It would be a war of attrition. Any attempt to pierce the city more directly would be met with guerrilla tactics as the aggressor tried to navigate the short side avenues, constantly relegated to low-ground disadvantage thanks to the endless stairs.

As much as he wanted to reach the palace—the gilded cake topper with its mountain of onion domes, each shining with a different color in the midday sun—Calladorn decided it would be most efficient to take the long spiral.

"It smells like a perfumery," Chad commented, his eyes drinking in every detail.

Indeed, the scents bordered on overwhelming. It seemed as if everyone wore a fragrance, heavily applied, which then mingled or battled with those of their neighbors. He stifled a sneeze. Sights, sounds, and smells warred for attention, all under an oppressive heat as the tall buildings guarded against any stray breezes that might cool the air.

By the time they reached the palace, Calladorn's temper was already fraying. Upon encountering the lines waiting to pass through the gates, it stretched tighter.

"We're going to be here a while," Chad said, his usually buoyant expression flagging.

Matthias nodded. "The horses can go no farther. I will find lodgings and meet you when you come back out." He dismounted and gathered their reins.

Calladorn didn't like splitting up, but it made sense. He nodded, then looked at Chad. "And you?"

"Staying with you. I..." He seemed to hesitate. "...am curious about this High King everyone keeps going on about."

The line crawled forward as the guards scrutinized every person passing through the gates. They were resplendent in half-body plate armor over leather jerkins, so heavily covered with ornamentation it was difficult to see the underlying metal. Their helmets sported towering red plumes, as if they feared no one would take them seriously without an extra two feet of height. The feathers hung limp in the dead air, drooping like wilted flowers.

Calladorn found the uniforms completely absurd. All that metalwork only served to weaken the steel, rendering it virtually useless as armor—unless its purpose was to roast the wearer alive. The guards' faces were slick with sweat, their rigid postures betraying a desperate attempt to keep from swaying.

Luxurious carriages passed in and out unimpeded, but extra guards at that gate made it clear anyone else attempting to pass would regret it.

As they waited their turn, Calladorn ignored the disdainful way in which other people in line were looking at them—or more accurately, avoiding looking at them—often with their noses turned up as if smelling something foul. One overdressed fop went so far as to pointedly hold a lace handkerchief to his nose.

The guard, when they finally reached him, had a large drop of sweat hanging from his bulbous nose, ready to drop at any moment. Calladorn found it difficult to pay attention to anything else. Despite his sorry state, the man regarded them with a raised eyebrow, making no attempt to hide the way his eyes took the two of them in from head to toe. "And you are...?" It sounded more like an accusation than a question.

Calladorn fought the urge to grind his teeth. "Captain Calladorn Thorne of the Ironspire Guard. I've come with an urgent missive from the palace."

The man's other eyebrow joined the first. "Am I to assume you've misplaced your ambassadorial carriage, my lord?" He seemed to look through Calladorn as if at empty air. "And your companion? The crown prince, no doubt?"

Sniggers came from behind them in line.

Feeling his face flush with anger, Calladorn reached into his shirt and withdrew Ithindar's message. He thrust it into the guard's face. "Do you recognize the royal seal of Drakerath?" he growled.

The guard blinked before turning his banal gaze back to Calladorn. "Should I? This is Syndar. I hardly have the time to know every backwater—"

A bead of moisture traced down the back of Calladorn's own neck. The perfume-choked air was stagnant, the line behind them pressing in despite their pathetic displays of superiority.

"Enough!" Calladorn had reached his limit. "You will admit us. *Now,* Sergeant."

With a dramatic sigh, the guard stepped aside.

Unfortunately, things only went downhill from there. Upon entry to the palace, they were met by a royal page dressed in embroidered livery above hose—one leg red and the other white. That young man escorted them to a functionary with a massive frilled ruff above his collar, who seemed even less impressed than the guard had been. They were informed in no uncertain terms that an audience was out of the question, and they were lucky to have made it even that far, given their inappropriate state. "High King Elrath has no interest in sooty travelers bearing 'dire' news," he intoned, peering at them over spectacles that pinched his too-thin nose.

"Rick would have a field day with this nonsense," Chad whispered in between interviews. "He'd insist on arguing every single point of logic until they let him through just to be rid of him."

Calladorn grunted—the closest thing to an expression of amusement he could muster at the moment.

The fifth courtier to see them was no more impressed with the seal than the four before her. She clasped her hands and managed to give the impression she was looking down at Calladorn despite her eyes being half a foot lower than his—her hair, on the other hand, swept up from all sides and was brought together at the top in a way that made her look like she wore an overgrown thistle blossom. "How urgent can it be, really?" she wanted to know. "If matters were as serious as you claim, word would have been sent to Valirion directly. A foot messenger? Ridiculous."

"Ithindar tried contacting Lord Wizard Valirion but was unable."

"I'm hardly surprised. High King Elrath dismissed him. Three months ago."

Chad looked at her as if she'd suddenly grown whiskers. "So you're saying we can't deliver our message because it wasn't sent to someone who wasn't even here to receive it?"

The woman made a show of sighing and rolling her eyes dramatically. "Oh, very well. Give me your letter, and I assure you it will be delivered to the High King." Putting one hand on her enormously padded hip, she held the other out imperiously, rings glittering on every finger.

Calladorn would as soon have handed her a horse apple.

In the end, they were turned back out onto the street, letter still in hand, with instructions to come back when they looked "more worthily presentable to the court." The gate guard smirked as they passed. Calladorn realized he was stalking around like an offended cat and forced himself to relax.

Chad put a hand on his shoulder. "Don't let it carry you," he said in a conspiratorial whisper.

Startled to hear his own words thrown back at him, Calladorn blinked. For a moment, the absurdity of the situation struck him all at once. The guards, the court, the perfume, the ridiculous plumes—his own temper. He barked a laugh. "Point taken."

Looking for Matthias, he added, "Let's get to that inn. I need to wash this place off me." He felt dirty, and it had nothing to do with having been riding for weeks.

Time was limited. Matthias knew Calladorn and Chad would be occupied at the palace for at least a few hours, but this still left him with little time in which to act. He mounted his horse and led the other two back down the curving street through the city.

The Royal Arms Inn stood just off the main spiral road, below the Great Library. A respectable establishment, it catered to merchants and minor nobles looking for discretion. Calladorn would be unlikely to balk at such a place. It was clean, well kept, and—most importantly—it had a stable large enough to house their horses. The innkeeper, a wiry man with a sharp gaze, nodded as Matthias approached, recognizing him for what he was: an individual who preferred private dealings.

"A room and stabling for three, with a street view," Matthias said, sliding a few coins onto the counter. "Have the saddlebags brought up to our room. And no questions."

The innkeeper's ferret-like eyes appraised him for half a breath before taking the money and pocketing it without counting. "You're paid through the week. Stables are in the back. Room's at the top of the stairs."

Matthias gave a polite nod before sliding an additional gold mark across the counter. "For your silence," he said, resting his other hand on the hilt of his sword.

Licking his lips, the innkeeper made that coin disappear as well, nodding quickly in understanding. Matthias turned away without another word. He had learned long ago that threats were more effective when laced with honey. The bribe had been enough to buy casual silence without being so high as to lead the man to believe gossip was likely to fetch an even higher price elsewhere.

The moment Matthias stepped outside, the mask of the weary traveler slipped away, replaced by a sharper expression. He had work to do.

*

The city breathed in layers, its wealthy, gilded heart a stark contrast to the underbelly festering in the dark. Matthias moved through both with the ease of a ghost. Syndar's streets twisted in labyrinthine fashion, side streets curving away from the primary avenue like so many veins or capillaries, each ending in a hub-like square. The routes up and down the hillside formed narrow alleys of precipitous stairs and blind turns. Most outsiders became lost soon after leaving the main way—targets for those who would prey upon the unwary. Matthias, however, had been here before. It had been years, but some things never changed.

The spiraling King's Way was the city's pride, lined with high-end shops and noble estates. But the farther one strayed from it, the uglier Syndar became. Here power was not just hoarded by the wealthy—it was wielded as a cudgel. Nobles crushed the common folk beneath taxes and harsh laws while businesses exploited both workers and customers, growing fat on their greed.

And there was another force at play in these streets, one that slithered through the cracks in Syndar's polished veneer. Thieves, who operated in gangs, each autonomous—to a point. All answered to the Shadow Council. Matthias had once dealt with them, briefly but long enough to know they were not the kind of people most could afford to cross.

Matthias did not need to ask direct questions. That was the mistake of amateurs. Instead he listened. He lingered at a cloth merchant's stall where an old woman rambled about the latest rumors from the palace, in between asking if particular bolts of fabric complemented her eyes. He loitered near a group of drunk mercenaries in an alley, catching snippets of conversation as they argued with equal conviction over contracts and the best ales. After buying a cheap drink at a warehouse district tavern, he let the barmaid's muttered complaints about disappearing officials—while she made coins disappear into her apron when the owner's back was turned—fill in the gaps in his knowledge.

At a familiar gambling den—a place where debts were both made and collected with crippling interest—he did not play. He watched.

"Are you going to place a wager?" the dealer asked idly between games, toying with the ring in her ear—cheap brass—before she shuffled the deck.

I already have, and for higher stakes than you will ever comprehend, Matthias thought. Besides, he had seen the flash of color from within her voluminous sleeves. The house would always win here. He let the silence stretch, offering only a faint smile.

She shrugged and dealt the next hand. That was the key to Syndar—one did not have to answer, so long as one looked like one belonged.

*

Patterns formed.

The palace was more than a seat of government—it was a wound festering with secrets. On the surface, everything was business as usual, but the tension in the court was palpable even in the streets. The nobles and courtiers cultivated an air of ease, with lavish parties and ostentatious court appearances, but an undercurrent of tension rippled out from the city's center.

The official line was that the Lord Wizard had been dismissed, but the whispers told a different story. Some claimed he had simply left—but why, then, did his chambers still hold his belongings? Others insisted he had been executed behind closed doors. And the most paranoid claimed he had never left the palace at all.

"No one's seen him in months," a merchant's wife muttered as she haggled over silk. "But my niece works in the kitchens and tells me the steward still orders meals for his chamber. Fresh ones, every day."

That last rumor, Matthias thought, was closer to the truth than they realized.

The city's backstreets were a fertile field, and he planted his seeds with expert precision. A few casual remarks, a nudged conversation or two, and new whispers began to spread in his wake. Small, insignificant rumors fed to the right people—subtle shifts in the city's undercurrents. A noble's wife had been seen visiting the palace at odd hours. In one version, she was a secret envoy from Velsaria. In another, she enjoyed secret trysts with the palace steward. A merchant's shipment had been held at the gates for longer than expected—the guards must be worried about plague. Or was it smuggled weapons? Nothing of true consequence, but enough to send ripples through the fragile balance of Syndar's political landscape.

He did not need to overthrow a kingdom to change its course. Only to push.

*

His work done, Matthias made his way back to the palace, gliding smoothly through the streets. If he had gauged it properly, he would not have to wait more than an hour before his companions emerged. It was unlikely they had managed to get through to the High King, but he could deal with matters either way.

Upon arriving at the courtyard outside the palace gates, he surveyed the scene. The crowds had thinned, and now only the least important nobles remained, but even these were dressed so elegantly that the two he sought would stand out had they been present. He smiled to himself. He had been right—they were not here yet.

Unless they have already left. A moment of doubt, quickly suppressed. If they had, they would return here to find him. They needed the supplies he had taken with the horses.

As he moved to a suitable vantage point where he would be able to observe the area while keeping his back to a shadowed wall, he was already crafting the version of events he would share with Chad and Calladorn.

Not lies. Not quite. Just the right truths, arranged in the right order.

And the game continued.

"Over there."

Calladorn looked where Chad pointed, seeing Matthias standing half in shadow by a hat shop. He had half-expected the man to not be there—and if he was honest with himself, he half-wished to have been right.

Seeing he'd been noticed, Matthias approached. "Is the message delivered, then? Can we be on our way?"

The questions were too smooth, and Calladorn suspected he'd read the answers in their expressions as they'd left the palace grounds. "Where are we staying?"

If Matthias was disappointed to not have his bait taken, he showed no sign. "The Royal Arms. It's a full circle down." He paused, his drab brown eyes seeming to size up Calladorn. "We can cut through the alleys." There was a subtle challenge in his tone.

The sky had begun to dim, and Calladorn saw more guards on the street now than when they'd arrived. If this city was like Ironspire, back alleys were unwise after dark, and their experience in the palace this afternoon had convinced him it was *worse* than Ironspire—by far. "The main street is fine," he said, stepping forward. Chad and Matthias followed.

Syndar changed as the sun set. Lamplighters came forth, igniting massive streetlamps with five flames, spaced every fifty feet. Shops closed, their owners going upstairs to their apartments, lighting additional lamps. Revelers spilled out of opulent taverns that clearly catered to the nobility, often in costume and wearing masks in uncountable designs, each more beautiful—or grotesque—than the last. As musicians took up stations on platforms or balconies, the street-goers' capers turned to dance.

"It's like Mardi Gras," Chad commented, dodging to avoid whirling clothes, grinning all the time.

Calladorn felt his neck prickle with a sense of being watched. He watched a line of dancers pass in the other direction, their clothing a riot of color, and used that as an excuse to check behind them. Nothing. Yet between the lighting and flurry of motion everywhere, there was no way to be sure—and the sensation had been following him since they'd left the palace.

"Hold on to your purses," Matthias advised. "This is ripe for thieves."

He observed the alleys and side streets as they passed. While the streets were well lit, the alleys cut jagged gashes between the bright building fronts. Calladorn occasionally spotted shadowed movement within and imagined hungry eyes looking back.

Syndar was a city of many faces.

"Over here." Matthias led them off the main thoroughfare and onto one of the other streets. Spaced farther apart, the lamps left pools of shadow between them. The largest building had three floors and a hanging sign depicting two arms in a wrestling match, a crown perched precariously over their fists. Light spilled from its open doorway, along with music much softer than that flooding the main street. Calladorn nodded his approval.

At the top of the stairs, a bathroom served the entire floor, next to a washroom with a large tub. Eight guest rooms opened off the central stairwell, and the innkeeper led them to one of the front ones, where their belongings already waited. Four beds, a washbasin, and a tall wardrobe filled three of the walls. Opposite the door, a large window overlooked the street below, with a small table and two chairs in front of it to complete the decor. It would do.

They began by sharing a bath. The tub was large enough for four, its water kept heated by a basket of large stones, replaced every half hour by a scullion maid. When she came in during the bath, Chad blushed furiously and looked like he was trying to hide in the water. Even when it was just the three of them, the young man seemed to take a peculiar interest in the walls or ceiling. Calladorn found his modesty both amusing and mystifying. *Outlanders*, he thought.

When they returned downstairs to the common room, Calladorn—dressed once again in his uniform—felt whole for the first time since leaving Drakerath. It was impossible not to stand a little taller.

"Black looks good on you," Chad told him.

Calladorn gave a slight nod, adjusting the cuffs of his sleeves. The uniform was a second skin—one that anchored him in the purpose that brought them to this city. For his part, Chad still wore the same clothes as on the day they'd met. Washed several times since Ironspire, of course, but clearly not suitable for court. Not this court, anyway.

"We'll have to find something appropriate for you in the morning," Calladorn said.

"You still intend to go through with this, then?" Matthias asked, one eyebrow slightly arched.

Calladorn ignored the question, raising a hand to call over the server as they took a corner table.

Soon they had plates of roast meat with vegetables, steaming enticingly and tempting them with the scent of subtle spices. It tasted even better than it looked, a welcome change after a month of trail rations and small game.

"I am to deliver the warning into the High King's hands," Calladorn finally stated. "Ithindar felt—and I agree—this mission is too critical to trust to a functionary."

"Perhaps your caution is deserved," Matthias said. "Rumors abound concerning the Lord Wizard—"

"We know. He was dismissed," Chad interrupted, his expression sour.

"Was he?" The way Matthias asked the question made it pregnant with unspoken meaning.

"Out with it," Calladorn said, in no mood for the man's games—not after their humiliating experiences this afternoon.

If Matthias was irritated, he hid it well. "While it is agreed the Lord Wizard has not been seen in months, no one appears to have seen him leave the city."

"Your point?"

Matthias steepled his fingers in front of him. "Was he dismissed—or was he removed?"

Removed. The word hung heavily in the air, and the minstrel's efforts seemed to fade away. There were many possible meanings in these circumstances, none of them good.

"Do you know something?" Calladorn asked.

Matthias let the question hang. He tilted his head slightly, as if debating how much to reveal. Then with the most minuscule of shrugs, he said, "I know many things and suspect even more. But in this matter? No."

Calladorn felt tension building in his neck again, pulling his scalp tight until it was focused into a single point of pressure between his eyes. Closing his eyes, he clasped the bridge of his nose between his fingers and sighed. "I grow tired of your games, Matthias."

"Then I shall speak plainly. Returning to the palace tomorrow will be a mistake. This city is dangerous, and even if you get through to the High King, I very much doubt you will be pleased with the outcome." Brown eyes glittered at Calladorn. "But since you refuse to heed my council, I am going to retire to our room." He stood, slipped between the inn's other patrons like a whisper, and was gone, leaving Chad and Calladorn to stare at each other over the half-eaten meals.

"We're still going tomorrow, aren't we?" Chad asked, although he nodded as he spoke. It wasn't really a question.

Pressing his lips together, Calladorn sighed again. "I have a duty." He would see this through, no matter how much he suspected Matthias was right. Taking another bite of the mutton, he found it now tasted like sand. Pushing the plate away, he forced the mouthful down with a swig of ale, which had also lost its flavor.

They sat for quite a while following Matthias's departure as the noises of the inn settled around them. Mugs clinking, forks scraping across plates, laughter of all kinds—from deep rumbles to loud cackles. It felt somehow out of place to Chad.

Matthias's statements reminded him of when they'd been walking to the palace in Ironspire. Chad had been so exuberant that morning, knowing he was on the way to meet a king. *And look how that turned out*, he thought, his meal turning to lead in his stomach.

Calladorn sat across the table from him, rubbing thumb and forefinger slowly together as he stared at the floor. When Rick got in this sort of mood, it was best to let him think it through, and so that was what Chad did now. He considered returning upstairs but decided it was more important to stay where he was, supporting Calladorn with his presence if not his words.

After some time, Calladorn looked at him, the corners of his mouth pulling into a half-smile that didn't quite reach his eyes, despite the kindness they held. "You remind me of Eryck at times."

Chad's brows twitched closer together. The words sat there, heavier than they should have been. He fidgeted in his chair, not really liking being thought of as a kid brother—he'd had enough of that with Rick. He cracked his trademark grin, though. "Is that a good thing or a bad thing?"

"You don't have to come tomorrow," Calladorn said, leaning forward. "Don't tell Matthias I admitted this, but he's right about the risk. You should stay here."

Is he serious? Chad thought. After following Calladorn halfway across the kingdom, the man wanted to leave him here now? Why? To protect him? "I'm not backing out because it *might* be dangerous. Hell, this whole planet has been dangerous since I got here."

"But—"

"But nothing. I still think I'm right about the prophecy. So if it is dangerous tomorrow, by your side is exactly where I should be. I can't very well fulfill the prophecy if I'm not around to do it, which means as long as I'm with you, you're protected."

Calladorn blinked at him, a dozen micro-expressions warring on his face. His fingers flexed slightly against the table—then, with a quiet exhalation, he chuckled. "Doesn't your world have sayings about tempting fate?"

Chad sensed the argument had been won and shrugged. "Maybe. I'm a slow learner. Just ask my teachers."

The smile grew wider. "Then we will need to get you suitably attired first thing. I'm thinking lots of lace. Maybe ruffles. Definitely tights."

Picturing himself in such an outfit, Chad snorted through his nose. "Not a freaking chance."

Calladorn gradually raised an eyebrow, utterly expressionless.

Chad felt a blush creeping up his neck. "You're joking, right? Please tell me you're joking."

*

When Chad returned to their room—Calladorn had made a detour to the jakes—he found Matthias standing by the window, his eyes fixed on the street below. The way the man's head turned fractionally suggested that he was aware of Chad's entrance, but his attention remained focused on the outside. Following his gaze, Chad spotted someone too still, lurking across the street in the lamplight's shadow. "Who's that?" he asked, frowning.

"Just a drunk wandering too close to the wrong part of town."

Chad looked back, but the figure was gone. A shiver ran through him, and the room felt suddenly cold despite the evening's heat. Rubbing the back of his neck, he searched the street, nearly deserted now that the evening had grown long. Nothing seemed out of the ordinary.

As he crossed to his bed, he heard Matthias mutter something under his breath. It was faint, almost unintelligible, but Chad didn't understand it. Pulling off his boots, he massaged his feet. Even after months in them, he still wasn't used to the lack of arch support. And after spending so much time today standing on flagstones—

He blinked. *Why didn't I understand?* Necsis somehow made everyone speak the same language, but whatever Matthias had just said, it hadn't translated. Why not? Chad glanced at Matthias again, but he had turned away. The question haunted Chad into his dreams.

XV
Deeps

Three motes of light drifted through the darkness.

The blackness was so absolute it felt like the cavern itself was swallowing them whole. It pressed in from all sides, weighty and oppressive, gnawing at the edges of sanity. It was not merely the absence of light—it was a presence unto itself, a thing that watched, that waited.

Rick kept his eyes forward, but the shadows played on his periphery, shifting and flickering like phantoms just beyond reach. His mind twisted images from the darkness—faceless figures lurking just outside the lanterns' glow, the suggestion of movement in the heavy black. Every so often, he would snap his lantern toward a perceived motion, but the light only revealed empty stone. The trickery of deep places, the mind conjuring images like a fading afterglow because a lifetime's experience told it there had to be *something* visible—somewhere.

The lanterns they carried were unlike any he had used before. They were tall, slender devices, each containing a fat candle whose light funneled through a complex series of lenses. A gnomish design, Gharn had explained, the focused beams allowed them to illuminate their surroundings without blinding each other. A simple solution to a fundamental problem in a world of perpetual night. *Flashlights without the batteries,* Rick thought.

He told himself it was just like hiking Lava River Cave back home—a narrow, winding lava tube near Flagstaff, silent and unlit. Except Lava River Cave had never stretched into an endless labyrinth beneath an ever-changing world. And it had never been home to a nightmare that had driven entire civilizations to flee to the surface, never to return. And it *certainly* hadn't had a ponderous vault door locking him inside.

The air here was thick, unmoving. It smelled of old stone and something subtler, something metallic, as if the air itself remembered the forge work of those who had once shaped this place. The silence was worse. Even the scuff of boots against rock felt muted, swallowed by the enormity of the void. There was no drip of water, no distant skitter of life, no breath of wind to stir the dust of centuries.

The architecture—what remained of it—was proof that the Deeps had not always been a place of desolation. They moved along a tunnel unlike anything Rick had ever seen. The floor beneath them was paved in interlocking stone tiles, set in intricate geometric patterns that shimmered in the lantern light. The walls bore columns carved with designs that twisted and looped in ways that defied normal symmetry—some standing straight, others tilted at strange, unsettling angles. Time and collapse had left the once-pristine carvings fractured, but the artistry still pulsed beneath the ruin. The ceiling arched overhead in a way that made the tunnel feel oddly organic, like the petrified remains of some colossal, long-dead creature. The sheer scale of it dwarfed them.

"How far does this go?" Evan asked in a whisper, her voice barely more than breath.

By unspoken agreement, it seemed they were all loath to speak louder. Whether that was because it simply felt wrong somehow or because they were afraid of attracting the attention of the Dark Horror, Rick couldn't say.

"You've seen the map," Gharn muttered. "Well, that was only a small part of the whole." He cast a wary glance at the walls, as though expecting them to shift at the mere mention. "We follow the old roads. As long as they last."

That was hardly reassuring.

As they walked, the tunnel widened, the walls pulling away into a cavern so vast that their lanterns could not find the ceiling. Something loomed above, catching the faint light—a stalactite, massive and gnarled, like the twisted root of a tree hanging down. Rick had no way of knowing how far it stretched into the inky shadow above. A hundred feet? A thousand? There was no scale here, only blackness.

Around them, the ground erupted into pillars of stone—some jagged, others smooth and curiously sculpted—forming what could almost have been a cityscape of dark towers with hollow windows peering sightlessly at them, like the remnants of a world long abandoned. These were natural, however, the apparent caverns within a trick of the light.

"Is that water?" Evan asked suddenly. She tilted her head, listening.

Rick held still. A sound, distant yet pervasive, filled the cavern—not a drip, not a trickle, but something deeper, fuller. A whisper of motion through stillness, it seemed to come from everywhere and nowhere.

Gharn gave a faint nod, his expression unreadable in the half-light. "There are rivers and lakes. Even forests."

Rick turned to him. "Forests?"

"Ghost trees." Gharn's voice was almost reverent. "They don't grow like surface trees. Their trunks are white, bone-colored, and instead of leaves, they have long strands—translucent, like spider silk. They catch moisture from the air, as well as insects. The oldest of them glow."

Rick tried to picture it, but his mind failed. A silent, luminescent forest deep beneath the world, feeding on darkness. The thought sent a ripple of unease through him.

The tunnel led onward, the old road guiding them through the cavern, past the towers of broken stone. At times, the path seemed impossibly smooth, untouched by ruin, as though the centuries had never reached it. Other times, it was fractured—broken in places as though the very ground had rebelled against its makers.

Eventually the road met a bridge. It was a slender thing, arcing across a ravine that plunged into absolute black. It looked impossibly delicate, too fine to have survived the weight of time. Yet it stood whole.

Rick peered over the edge, his stomach tightening. The bottom was lost to darkness, depth beyond depth, a chasm without end. The lantern's glow found nothing but air. The river below was nothing more than a whisper—a slow breath through the veins of the earth.

Gharn ran a hand over the stonework, almost caressing it. "I don't think we even know how to build its like anymore," he said, his voice a soft sigh that blended into the water's sound.

Rick experienced a moment of vertigo and stepped back, accidentally disturbing a bit of rock that tumbled away in silence, never seeming to hit bottom. He exhaled slowly. "If we die down here, no one will ever know."

Gharn's expression became grim. "If we die down here, we won't be the first."

The bridge waited, silent and patient. They stepped forward.

*

After a timeless time, they came to a crossroads where four ways came together in a circle, from the center of which rose an eight-sided column of carved stone. It wasn't a true octagon but rather a square column with its corners sheared off, so that wide faces alternated with narrow. The thinner faces were carved in geometric designs that flowed one into the next, while the wider surfaces each faced one of the roads and had letters carved in flowing script.

Rick's mind translated the words automatically, and with them, their meanings: *Veilglass Abyss, Zekkivar* (City of Sparks), *Echofang Gorge, Mornzadur* (Forge of the First Flame). He shook his head, amazed again by how Necsis made languages work like that.

According to the signpost, they had just come from the first one. The chasm they'd crossed certainly made it easy to understand the name. From his time examining the map, he remembered Zekkivar and Mornzadur as being cities, automatically ruling them out as destinations. That left only Echofang Gorge as an option.

"Do you know how it got its name?" he asked.

Gharn shook his head, his shoulders sagging. "So much has been lost. I don't..." His voice trailed off as he looked at the column, and his beard trembled—whether from sadness or some deeper emotion, only Evan would know. "The world keeps forgetting."

Evan stood facing Mornzadur, her index finger tracing the circle of her pendant over and over.

"What is it?" Rick asked, walking over to stand beside her, shining his lantern down the glittering roadway.

Still staring into the distance, she cocked her head, her eyes tightening. "Something just feels... *off*. I can't really describe it, but it's like the air feels... I don't know... like something's watching?" She shuddered for a moment.

Rick opened his mouth to argue, to tell her it was just nerves, but—the silence seemed heavier than before. As if something had leaned in to listen. *A trick of the air, nothing more.* His hand twitched. About to put a comforting hand on her shoulder, he hesitated. The conflicts he'd been struggling with flooded back, seemingly amplified by the oppressiveness of the Deeps. He still hadn't really forgiven her for what she'd done to Chad. And the Magecurse—that changed everything.

Questions raced through his mind as he examined his hand in the dim lantern light, looking for signs. Nothing now, but how long would it be? Would they even be able to make it home before the magic killed him? And if they did, would he be too changed for her to still want him? Without knowing those answers, the only way he could really protect her was to push her away. Better a small pain now than a larger one later.

His hand stayed where it was.

For a moment, she hoped. Out of the corner of her eye, Evan saw Rick's hand move toward her, and she held her breath. Since her misstep with Chad, every moment of contact between Rick and her had been at her initiation. Fleeting. They weren't even sleeping together anymore. She was giving him the time he needed, certain this distance wouldn't last forever. But how she missed him.

The hand paused for a moment. Trembled, then returned to its position by his side.

Closing her eyes, she sighed. Emotions warred within him—she couldn't read his thoughts and wasn't sure if she wanted to even if she could, but empathy could still cut like a knife. Putting on a smile she didn't feel, she put her shields up as best she could and turned toward Echofang Gorge.

*

Sometime later the forest of stalagmites gave way, and they found themselves in another tunneled passage, different from the first. The entrance was shaped like a pentagon, with one side forming the path on which they walked. As the passage continued, the edges turned around them, making a slow rotation that caused it to feel like it was they who were spinning. The walls dropped away from the sides of the road.

Rick got down on hands and knees next to the verge and held his lantern so that he could peek underneath, his head turning to look both ahead and behind. "Well, I'll be..."

"What is it?" she asked.

"We're on a bridge. It connects when a side of the pentagon is parallel, but otherwise—" Climbing back to his feet, he did that thing with his fingers, thinking. "I have no idea why they'd build it like this."

Gharn's eyes sparkled. "Sometimes beauty *is* the purpose."

Rick didn't disagree, but his brows pulled together. "Could this be one of the fast passages?" His brows rose as they pinched even tighter. "Or slow?"

"Wouldn't we feel something?" Evan asked. She hoped so. The idea they could be affected without being aware of it made her skin itch.

The gnome shrugged, and they continued on.

Ahead, the tunnel continued to twist, and she fought down a feeling of nausea. The warped tunnel gave her vertigo unless she focused intently on the path directly in front of her—a lesson she had learned after nearly falling over. Their footsteps echoed ominously as they walked, thrown back at them by the close walls and changed in a way she couldn't describe but was deeply unsettled by. It almost sounded like—

She spun and focused her lantern back the way they'd come. Nothing.

"What is it?" Gharn asked, his voice constricted.

She tried to laugh it off. Tried to convince them—and herself—that this place was just getting to her.

"Am I imagining things, or is it light up ahead?" Rick asked.

He was right. Many tunnel revolutions ahead, there was a faint yet distinct glow. It proved much farther away than it had seemed, constantly teasing them with an illusion of being almost there, and the illumination ebbed and flowed like breathing light. As they continued toward that shifting glow, the tunnel opened wider, even as it continued to spin around them, the road widening along with it. *An optical illusion from hell,* Evan thought sourly.

When the tunnel ended, they stood atop a wide, curved stair that descended to the cavern floor below. And there was light. High overhead, crystals protruded from the ceiling, faintly shimmering in all the colors of the rainbow. The room was filled with subtle music, rising and falling as the glow of the crystals slowly pulsed—not all at once but in groups.

"Glowstone," Gharn whispered, smiling open-mouthed as he stared upward. "I've never heard of them as crystals."

"What makes them light up?" Rick wondered.

More interested in the how than the what, Evan thought, fondness welling up within her.

Gharn gave a small shrug. "Energy from the Shifts, high above us. They respond to it somehow."

The crystals sang to each other, the sound moving around the massive chamber like—

"Echoes," Rick said, his mouth hanging open as he surveyed the room. His expression transformed into a delighted grin. "The crystals look like fangs. Which must mean..." He pointed down the stairs ahead of them. "There!"

Evan looked. Sure enough, at the bottom of the steps, a number of paths meandered across the ground, which had more crystals and plants —the first they'd seen on this journey—sticking up in clusters. But then the floor dropped away at the edge of a gorge. Directly ahead of them was a bridge.

Blowing out the candles in their lanterns, they made their way forward. Fifty stairs, each three feet deep, took them to the main level, which was like a park, with graceful walkways running between the crystal formations and what Evan guessed were trees. Their bark may have once been white, but it bled red sap through what looked like a thousand gaping wounds. The branches clawed at the sky like twisted fingers, some kind of fabric hanging from them like tattered bits of cloth.

One of the scraps shifted, just slightly. No wind stirred the cavern air. Evan swallowed hard.

Gharn moaned, the pain in his expression mirroring the vegetation itself. "Ghost trees! But..." He reached out with a trembling hand to touch a drop of red sap but immediately jerked his hand back like he'd been bitten. He pulled a rag from one of his belt pouches and wiped his finger on it, then with a gasp dropped the cloth to the ground. It had a hole in it, and wisps of smoke rose into the air as the rag twisted and charred.

"Give me your hand!" Evan said, alarmed.

The skin where he'd touched the tree was burned and blistering. Seeing it, Gharn blanched despite his tan skin.

Without thinking, Evan clasped her hand around the injured finger and closed her eyes. Reaching within herself, through her arm and hand, she connected with Gharn, feeling his pain as her own. Steeling herself, she drew it into herself. Going deeper, she imagined she could see his tissues and even his cells. She coaxed them, commanded them. And they responded. Gharn's breathing calmed, and his hand steadied in her grip.

With a smile, she opened her eyes and released her hold.

"By the Three!" Gharn breathed. As he turned his hand around in front of him, his expression was one of pure awe.

"You healed him," Rick said, his face matching Gharn's. "How did you know you could do that?"

"I didn't," Evan admitted, just as astonished as they were. "It just felt… right." She felt pain in her index finger but didn't look. Not wanting the others to be aware, she casually put her hands behind her back, concentrating on repairing the damage that was now her own.

Gharn stepped carefully around the still-smoldering fabric, now almost completely blackened. "These are—were—ghost trees. But what happened to them?"

It was a mystery Evan didn't think she wanted to solve. This whole park had turned from beauty to horror in the space of a few short minutes, and she couldn't wait to be away from it. Her companions seemed just as anxious to leave as she was.

They didn't bother with the other paths, and when they reached the bridge, they saw their instincts had been correct. The edge of the gorge was lined by a short stone wall, two feet tall—ideal for gnomes or dwarves but uncomfortably short for humans. Next to that was a wide walkway that ran all the way to the cavern wall at either side, where the chasm continued as if cut through with a giant axe.

The canyon itself must have been three hundred feet wide at its narrowest, where the bridge sloped out over it, and twice that at the far ends. There was obviously no other way forward. Smelling rotten eggs, Evan looked down. Far below, a ribbon of glowing red ran slowly through the bottom of the fissure. No wonder the air was stifling.

"Oh no." Rick sounded devastated. He was looking at the bridge itself, at a crack that grew out from the foot of the span toward its center, growing thinner as it reached the apex of the arch but also spreading out in branches like a bolt of lightning frozen in time.

Evan's stomach churned. There was no way it could be safe, and if not—

"What are our options?" Rick asked, but his eyes seemed to focus inward. Evan knew he was rebuilding the map in his mind.

"The only other routes are to cities," Gharn said hollowly.

"No," Rick said, his voice firmly flat. "You warned against those, and even without the threat of the Dark Horror, there are no viable routes to Southwatch. We'd end up miles out of our way or have to go through slow passages that would leave us worse off than if we'd never taken the Deeps at all."

"Well, we can't go back." Evan pointed out the obvious. "The Deepingate is closed and I'm sure locked again."

Rick examined the bridge again, walking first to one side, then the other. "It doesn't look like the crack goes all the way through," he said finally. "I think it may only be the surface that's cracked."

"There's no way to be sure," Gharn warned. "We can't risk it."

"Every problem has a solution," Rick muttered, seemingly more to himself than to them. Evan wondered who he was trying to convince. "We all have rope in our packs, right?" he continued.

Gharn snorted through his whiskers. "Only fifty feet. We'd need twice that at least."

Rick eyed him appraisingly. "You're strong; I've seen it. We'll tie the ropes together and loop one end around me. You take the other one. Let me lead as far out as the rope will allow. If the bridge cracks further, hold fast and back up."

"You're mad. And if the bridge actually breaks?"

Rick regarded him with half a smile. "Run like hell?"

They had no other choice, though. It was either continue forward or give up.

Several minutes later they were ready, and Rick inched his way out onto the span. Evan held her breath, gripping the low wall until she thought her fingers might dig into the stone. The only sounds were their ragged breathing and Rick's shuffling steps, one tentative move after another. Evan prayed it would stay that way. *Why doesn't he use magic?* she thought. It would be easy, and the bridge could be stabilized. Certainly easier than diverting a river. *Why didn't I think of that sooner?* He was some distance out by that point, though, and she was afraid to yell. Her heart raced; she could hear her pulse in her ears, running way too fast.

And then, a faint crackle, almost too soft to hear. She stared at the crack. Was it wider? She couldn't be sure. Very subtly she reached out to Rick with her mind. She didn't push like she had with Chad. This was a gentle nudge, no more. Reinforcing confidence. Encouraging him.

As if in response, Rick gestured, his hands moving esoterically. A shimmer moved away from him, following the crack, causing a faint glow. He ran. Gharn hurried to keep up, his boot leather slapping on the stone. Knowing it would now be safe for her to do so, Evan followed.

A few minutes later, all three were on the other side of the chasm, panting from the sudden sprint. As soon as Evan was across, Rick gestured again.

He looks so tired! she thought, but she smiled proudly at him. "We made it!"

Rick nodded and opened his mouth—

A loud snap sounded behind them, followed by rumbling. All three turned, and Evan's hand came to her mouth. They watched in horror as the bridge twisted, buckled, then came apart. Starting at the center, great chunks broke off, falling into the depths of the gorge until only short lengths remained standing at either end.

Silence.

Evan realized her entire body was trembling. If they'd still been on that… if Rick hadn't used magic…

Gharn rounded on Rick, raising a clenched fist. "Stupid boy!"

"He just saved our lives," Evan snapped. She couldn't understand it.

The little man quivered, but it wasn't with anger. It was fear. "I warned you," he hissed. "When I first suggested this route, I warned you."

Suddenly Evan clasped both her hands over her mouth, and she knew—she'd made a mistake. Worse, she could sense it. Something had changed in the air, like the way one could feel a change in air pressure before a major storm, or the clouds would shift toward yellow—something was different.

The Deeps had noticed them.

If Gharn had been worried before, he was terrified now. The air had a pressure to it, seeming to breathe around them despite its absolute stillness. The foul scent of decay filled it, stifling him. With the bridge collapsed behind, their options shriveled to one. An old nightmare, long buried, pushed itself to the forefront of his mind—the Deeps opening like a giant mouth beneath home and swallowing him whole. Too late, Gharn understood exactly what the Deeps were: a trap. And triggered by Rick's idiotic use of magic, it had just snapped shut around them.

Feeling like a bucket of icy water had just been dumped over him, he clamped his hands into fists and waited for the end. He wanted to squeeze his eyes shut, like a child hiding from imagined monsters, but whatever was coming, he was determined to face it with them open.

An endless moment passed. The pressure lifted.

Evan's hand clasped tightly around her necklace; her eyelids twitched as she stared into the darkness. "It's gone," she whispered. She had no need to say what "it" was.

Maybe it only knows we're down here but not where, Gharn thought, latching on to the idea like a drowning person clutching a rope from shore. But that only meant—

"It's hunting us," he said, surprised by how calm his words sounded. "Move."

The road ahead entered a new tunnel, this one lit by veins of glowstone embedded in its cylindrical walls. As they made their way down the tube, a figure became visible ahead, leaning with one hand pressed against the wall. They stopped. Watched. It didn't move. Cautiously they approached. A dwarf woman, ash-gray hair running in an intricate braid down her back and archaic clothing enveloping her, faced away.

"I don't think she's breathing," Rick whispered.

He was right. The woman was dead. The hand against the wall appeared desiccated, shriveled across her bones like ruined leather. Her pose was that of someone who'd stopped for a moment to catch her breath. As they carefully walked around her, the face became visible, mummified in the same way as the hand. Gharn's breath caught, and even Rick looked pale, for unlike the rest of her body, her eyes remained just as they had been the moment she'd died. They even appeared moist, although that was impossible. They stared eternally ahead, round with tangible terror.

Bile rose in Gharn's throat, and he swallowed, hard.

"There are more," Rick said so softly Gharn almost didn't hear him.

As his little group made their way through the tunnel, their rapid breathing loud in his ears, they passed dozens of the figures. Most were dwarves, but an occasional gnome was mixed in as well. Even a human. Some had run; some had stumbled and fallen, an occasional kind soul seeming to have been trying to help them get back on their feet. All were in the same state of frozen decay, and the eyes of every last one shared the same frozen scream.

Evan rubbed one of her temples, her eyes tightening to slits. "It's like I can hear whispers."

Gharn didn't ask. He was only too happy when they left the figures behind.

Evan's condition didn't improve, though. She stumbled, and Rick caught her, pulling her close and helping her continue walking. "So many... I can't... I..." Evan's eyes flew open. "Estariel!"

Gharn lurched to a stop, even as she seemed to improve—like saying the word had released all the pressure building inside her.

"What?" she asked, staring at him as he gaped at her.

Gharn forced his expression back to normal. "Nothing. Just... strange is all."

Evan blinked, eyes darting randomly as if she was looking for something, though they remained unfocused. "I… don't know. It just… came out."

Gharn exhaled slowly, returning to the journey at hand.

"Does someone want to clue me in?" Rick asked, letting go of Evan, who was now walking normally again.

Not slowing, Gharn answered. "Estariel. According to history, she was the leader of the Thought Masters during the War of Ascension."

Evan pursed her lips and shrugged. "The name doesn't mean anything to me," she said, her voice firm, both certain and frustrated.

They came upon more figures in the tunnel. These, however, had… melted. It was as if their flesh had turned to wax, sloughing off their frames to drip in oozy shapes from outstretched arms, soaking through their clothing before solidifying again. Small pools like eternal puddles trailed behind each, marking their last footsteps before collapsing, and one left a smear behind where they'd clearly struggled forward even after legs had given out. Another three feet of life. The figure's right arm stretched forward, as if trying to pull forward just a bit more.

Looking closer, Gharn realized their skin actually *was* wax, faintly crackled across the surface. He forced his eyes forward, tearing them away from the ruined people. Forced himself to continue walking.

"I think we know how the Dark Horror got its name," Rick breathed, his voice empty.

Gharn felt his sanity stretching. He didn't know how much more he could bear to see before it snapped.

The tunnel turned a corner and opened to wonder—and nightmare.

Evan stopped short, her eyes gliding across what had to be a gnome village. It was a midsized cave, a few hundred feet across, the walls artfully carved to create facades for homes and perhaps businesses. This wasn't the geometric designs of the dwarves, with straight lines and sharp edges. Here everything had a grace, with curved lines that reminded her of the gnomish side of Khorvael's council chamber.

But where that had suggested life, this shouted it. Walls were covered with vines so realistically carved she expected to hear their leaves rustling. Even the doors curved at the sides, usually asymmetrically. Everything had been tinted with color, making the place come alive. At the cave's center, a large design of glowstone had been worked into the ceiling—Evan suddenly understood the colored glass designs she'd observed while they walked the streets of Khorvael. The gnomes couldn't recreate the beauty of the Deeps, but they remembered.

The light flickered faintly, just enough to make the shadows seem to come alive as they entered the room.

Below the design, in the center of the chamber, curved ramps flowed up to a pavilion with a swept roof that reminded her of an ice-cream cone. Carved vines dripped from its eaves.

Yet the beauty was tarnished. Faded. Crumbling. Here a portion of a carved wall had fallen away in ruin. There the colors became brittle and flaked. In places, the patterns of decay took on a sinister tone, resembling shadowed faces staring out from the walls. Evan blinked. There actually *were* faces, twisted in agony, blending into the stone itself. When she saw bits of frayed cloth sticking out of the walls as well, she understood and shivered, her stomach clenching.

Rick's expression matched the feelings she sensed swirling within him. A mix of awe and revulsion. She'd been keeping mental tabs on him since the incident at the bridge and—aside from being bone-tired—he thankfully seemed fine. Unaware she'd nudged him into action.

Tears dripped from Gharn's eyelashes, his own emotions raw and more primal than what he'd felt after the death of Sorendir. That had been the loss of a beloved friend. This—the gnome was mourning the death of his entire culture.

She reached out mentally to soothe him, a mental balm to help manage his grief so he could find his equilibrium again. When he looked at her, his eyes were sharp. Determined. The transformation that night after their meeting with the council remained, and she gave an internal sigh of relief. But then his focus turned to something behind her, and his eyes widened. Feeling an icy finger slide down her spine, she turned to see.

In the central gazebo, something moved.

A small boy. Human, perhaps six years old, with pale skin, blond hair, and gray eyes. Even his lips were pale, as if there wasn't enough blood circulating through his body. Every instinct screamed at Evan that something was wrong, but the boy appeared real. Vulnerable.

"Impossible," Rick breathed.

He was right. There was no way a child could survive in this place. Nothing lived here except fungus and those horrible ghost trees. But the boy was there just the same, walking slowly toward them, his head pushed slightly forward, and his eyes held fear. The child seemed to be studying them as much as they him.

His eyes fixed on Evan, and his lips parted with a slight tremble. "Mommy?"

Evan's heart skipped. The poor thing looked so lost, so alone. "No, I'm not your mother," she said, gently. "Who are you?"

"Where are they?" the child asked, looking around. "Why won't they play with me anymore?"

"Who?" Evan asked. In the back of her mind, a voice screamed a warning at her, pounding furiously. *This is wrong!*

Something pushed it down to a whisper that was brushed away, like a bit of cobweb.

As he pointed to the houses, the child's expression darkened. "Them. They ran away and left me alone. All alone."

She realized he wasn't pointing at the houses. He was pointing at the walls. At the figures in the walls. *Poor thing.* "You're lonely?"

He nodded solemnly, his shadow following suit soon after. Her mind recognized the timing was off, even as she ignored the detail.

Why aren't Rick and Gharn moving? The nearly silent scream tickled her mind, and she brushed her forehead with a trembling finger. *Why am I sweating?* Evan's breath caught. Something about the child's motions—there was no weight to them. His clothes didn't shift as he moved, as if they were just part of the surrounding air.

"Will you play with me?" the boy asked. His eyes looked at her with a sharpness far too old for his years. And with hunger.

Something swelled within her chest, pressing up through her throat and out of her mouth. A soft wail that grew in volume, turning into a scream. With it came the realization that this little boy was pushing her, bending her mind to his will. Somehow he was manipulating all three of them.

God, he's strong!

Her mind struggled within his grasp like a fly caught in a spider's web. Her hand trembled uncontrollably at her side, and she focused on that. Forced it to lift, raising shaking fingers in a warding gesture. It was enough. Shields slammed into place, protecting her from this... *creature's* control.

The boy's eyes turned into black voids that filled the sockets, reflecting nothing. His expression twisted in anger. "Why won't you play with me?" As he spoke, the child's voice warped and became guttural—a roar that spurred her to action.

Evan grabbed Rick and Gharn by their arms, throwing up shields for them as well. It took every ounce of strength she possessed, but she felt them each jerk, released from the child's mental grip.

As she threw up her shields, the boy staggered. The voids of his eyes flickered, for just an instant, with something else—something desperate. Then, with a snarl, he changed. Skin bubbled, boiled, and flowed beneath clothes that became gauze before melting into a roiling shadow that swirled around him like smoke. A child no longer, the features stretched, warped; the limbs elongated—growing larger as they twisted and darkened. For an instant, his hands reached out, fingers clawing at the air—as if something inside him still fought. Then the flesh melted away, leaving only smoke and shadow. A deep, booming laugh echoed through the hall, shaking stone and causing pebbles to fall from the ceiling.

As they fled, Evan glanced back. Where the boy had been, there was now a massive black cloud that enveloped the pavilion and everything around it. Amorphous black tentacles spread out from it, shattering stone wherever they brushed a surface. And in the center of it all was the boy's face, now several feet tall...

Velgô-pahz grinned a rictus snarl.

The weight of the unspoken name rang through the cavern, vibrating through the stones. As if the Deeps themselves remembered it. The force squeezed Evan's skull. She gasped, pressing a hand to her temple as the air itself seemed to tighten around her.

Rick surfaced as if from a bottomless pool. The paralysis that had held him shattered. Evan gripped his arm painfully, her fingers digging to the bone, but he scarcely noticed. Broken free from the creature's hold that had suppressed all will—to think, to move, almost even to breathe—he lurched into motion. Limbs churned sluggishly, but a surge of adrenaline pushed him forward, Evan and Gharn at his side.

Aside from the path they'd entered by, there were two other ways out of this death trap. With no time to second-guess himself, he picked one, hoping against hope he'd remembered the map correctly. If he was wrong—he didn't even want to consider the possibility.

Whatever he'd thought the Dark Horror to be, his imaginings were as far short of the mark as if he'd tried to fire a rifle at the moon. This entity—this *thing*—used its victims. Toyed with them. And if there was one scrap of knowledge he'd gleaned while under its power, it was that the creature was bored beyond comprehension.

He ran, his breath coming in gasps that seared his lungs.

"*Stay with me.*" The voice echoed balefully behind them at the same time it slipped into his mind, casual in its malevolence. "*I... love... you.*"

Rick blanched. Beside him, Evan bore an expression set in stone. Her jaw clenched tightly as she ran as well, nostrils flaring with each labored breath.

Gharn started to slow. "Keep going!" he panted. "Don't wait."

Silent communication passed between Rick and Evan as they caught each other's eyes. Slowing as one, they grabbed the gnome under the armpits and hauled him—yelping—forward.

Behind them, the dark mass continued to roll, billowing down the corridor, filling it with darkness somehow even deeper than what they'd walked through at the Deepingate. That had been the absence of light. This... this swallowed the light whole.

Yet for all its roiling ferocity, it didn't gain on them. Tasting bile, Rick knew why. The creature was deliberate. Ponderous. It never rushed, because it didn't need to. It would catch them eventually, and until then, it would savor their fear. Even if they were on the right route, Rick somehow knew the monstrous entity would wait until they were nearly out. It would allow them to see the exit and feel a moment of hope—which it would delight in dashing at the last moment.

There was only one chance, and he'd decided weeks ago that he wouldn't hesitate when this moment came.

Letting loose Gharn, he stopped in the middle of the corridor and turned to face their nemesis.

"What are—" Evan almost screamed at him.

"Go!" he interrupted, turning his will toward the problem at hand.

Equations leaped into his mind, their mathematical perfection dancing in precisely orchestrated control, his hands moving to supplement the numbers and fill in gaps where words weren't enough. In front of him, he compressed the air, forcing the molecules together into a lattice. Wind whipped past him from behind, blowing his hair and pulling at his clothes, filling in the vacuum he'd just created. It was foul and dusty from years of not being disturbed, but he used it anyway, pressing it into the layers he'd already constructed.

As he worked his magic, the Dark Horror *paused*. Just for a moment. A ripple passed through its form, not hesitation but... recognition. And then it struck.

Rick's body trembled as his energy was leached away; the air snapped into place, everything beyond his spell rippling as if viewed through a Fresnel lens. For a moment, the Dark Horror looked nearly beautiful as it approached, slamming into the wall Rick had constructed and spreading out from the initial point of contact to fill the entire space beyond with the darkest night. As it smashed into the barrier over and over, the tunnel walls rattled, and he almost lost his footing. *So powerful!* he thought as he turned to run again, praying the shield would last. And a part of his mind wondered—was he referring to the enemy or to himself?

He soon caught up with Evan and Gharn, helping her once again.

"Did you stop it?" Evan asked.

Gharn shook his head. "You bought us time, lad."

Rick hoped it was enough.

An explosion behind nearly shattered his eardrums, and he knew it had broken through.

"It's *pissed,*" Evan croaked, still running as hard as she could while the two of them helped Gharn forward. Her face was a mask of pain.

She was right—the monster was moving faster now. It had grown tired of playing with its food.

Light appeared ahead of them. Not the shimmer of glowstone but actual sunlight. *Escape!* But Rick didn't dare to hope. This was what he'd been fearing, and he could feel the Dark Horror looming closer. With cold certainty, he knew—it had timed its approach. Not done playing with them, after all.

In desperation, he worked more magic, this time strategically weakening the tunnel's structure. Gravel and then chunks of stone began raining down on them, but he didn't stop. Gathering the last strength he possessed, he practically pulled his companions with him as he brought the tunnel down in their wake with a cataclysmic roar. A cloud of dust billowed past them, blotting out the sunlight and choking their lungs.

They kept running anyway.

They crossed into sunlight.

Evan first, she slowed and put her hands on her knees, gasping painfully for air. Having spent so long underground—she couldn't know how long—the warmth almost burned. Gharn came up next to her, his breath escaping in wheezes, covered in dust. They were in a cave opening of some sort, light streaming in and making the shadows preternaturally dark where it didn't reach.

Where's Rick?

She turned back to the tunnel, still choked with billowing dust. Sounds of falling stone ground out of sight. "Rick?" she called out, feeling panic rise.

A shape moved, resolving into a man, his tall form slumped at the shoulders, one hand pressing against the wall as he stumbled forward.

"Oh, thank God." Relief flooding through her, Evan ran to help him and put his free arm over her shoulders. He sagged against her, feeling almost too light to be real.

As the dust continued to settle, Gharn watched them come, his eyes squinting at Rick. "No," he breathed, his face growing pale.

Confused, Evan turned her head to look at Rick, his blue eyes a mere foot from hers, crow's-feet crinkling as he squinted into the sun. He held up his other hand to shield himself from the light. Her breath caught, and she became aware of a ringing in her ears.

Rick had never had crow's-feet. Now his skin had lost some of its smoothness. His forehead sported strong lines running parallel with the brows and hairline, and two short vertical creases jutted up from the inside corners of his eyebrows. They gave him an even more thoughtful presence. His features were leaner, the bone structure more defined. Even his nose was slightly larger.

It was Rick—but it wasn't. Evan realized she was looking at a man in his thirties. "What... how?"

Rick smiled wanly. Moving slowly, deliberately, he crossed the cave opening and sat in the sunlight, leaning back against the wall. Tilting his head back, he closed his eyes and sighed, the sun revealing every detail of that unfamiliar face.

He felt so calm in her mind. So at peace. Gharn, however, was a tight bundle of anger and grief.

She rounded on the gnome. "Out with it!" Her mind held him like a cat with a captured mouse.

Gharn gulped, his eyes bulging.

It was Rick who spoke. "It's the Magecurse." Still with that calm, knowing half-smile, his piercing eyes held her fast. She forgot about Gharn. "I pay the price for my... *gift*."

How can he be so calm? she wondered. Fury and confusion stormed within her in equal measure as she put the pieces together. "You mean... when you cast a spell—"

"He ages," Gharn said, his voice cracking.

She whirled on the gnome. "You knew about this?"

"He's the one who told me," Rick said. "The morning after I put the medallion on."

Her mouth worked silently, chewing on what she was hearing.

His eyes pleaded with her, betraying a hint of fear as well. "I... thought it would be better this way."

"For who? You? Because it sure isn't for me." With the confusion gone, all that remained was white-hot anger. Her voice turned venomous as she glared at Gharn. "And you're just as bad."

She stalked out of the cave, feeling her heart pounding against her chest. One hand shook as it clasped the pendant hanging there. Feeling sick, she hardly saw the pines or noticed their fragrance. Her thoughts ran in circles, recognizing that she wasn't truly angry at either of *them*.

It was her fault.

She had pushed Rick to use magic at the bridge. She was why the Dark Horror had found them. And she was why he'd had to use magic to defend against the creature.

Rick had given up ten years of his life, and she was to blame.

Tears welled in her eyes. The sun held no warmth.

XVI
Audience

Chad woke to an argument in full swing. In whispered tones—obviously trying not to wake him—Calladorn and Matthias debated the day's plans. A glance out the window proved the sky had only just begun to lighten toward dawn. Chad tried to pull the blanket over his head and get a little more sleep, but now that he was aware of the conflict, he couldn't block it out.

"The gaze of this city is turned inward," Matthias said. "And the kingdom's along with it. Even if they take your warning seriously, they will never take action."

"It's the duty of the High King to protect the allied nations," Calladorn answered, his voice firm.

"Duty," Matthias scoffed. "The only duty this court knows is to its ledger books."

"Once Elrath gives the command—"

"The nobility will dither," Matthias interrupted him. "They will find a thousand reasons to delay action."

"While kingdoms fall?" Calladorn sounded exasperated.

"Distant kingdoms. They will not care until these so-called demons are on their doorsteps. Why should they? No invasion has ever come through the Shifts. Why inconvenience themselves to put an end to something that in all likelihood has already been ended by the Shifts themselves? Why drain their coffers?" Chad didn't think he'd ever heard Matthias speak so many words at once.

Calladorn growled. "I've heard what our Outlander friends have said about the prophecy. This is no ordinary invasion."

"Have you read it?"

"No, but—"

"And where is the one who spent the longest time studying it? Where is this Sorendir?" Matthias was relentless as he hammered Calladorn with questions.

Chad couldn't contain himself. He threw back the covers and sat up. "You know full well he's dead! You were there."

Matthias's smile didn't reach his eyes. "But Calladorn was not. As I recall, he has never even seen one of these creatures. He did not read the prophecy. His words to the court will mean less than nothing."

"And that's why I'm going," Chad shot back.

Matthias sat back in his chair, regarding Chad with a steady gaze. "So, after everything, you are still determined to go? I admire your dedication to futility."

"Why don't you come as well?" Chad asked. "You've seen the demons too. Two eyewitnesses will be better than one."

"Because I have no interest in being laughed at by fools."

Calladorn's right eye twitched. "And yet here you are, wasting breath on them." His expression was scornful, every muscle in his face taut.

If Matthias felt that heat, he gave no sign. "Indeed. But not at court."

Chad couldn't understand the man's stubbornness. So what if they got laughed out of the court? At least they would have tried. It felt to him like this was a case where doing nothing was worse than doing the wrong thing. Why couldn't Matthias see that?

He pulled on his trousers and then his boots, studying Matthias as he did so. The man's posture was so relaxed, his expression so calm. So sure of himself. And the way his eyes searched Chad—and Calladorn as well—made him think of a hawk watching a field for mice. "What will you be doing while we're at court?" Chad asked, his words somewhat muffled by the shirt as he pulled it over his head.

"Perhaps I shall visit the Great Library."

Chad froze mid-movement to stare at the man. *Reading? Is he kidding me?* "Yeah, 'cause dusty books have been real effective so far," he muttered.

As he stared back at him, Matthias's eyebrows crept upward. "Those dusty pages may contain something to affirm the prophecy." The brows shot up the rest of the way. "Or deny it."

Chad sighed. "Fine. Be that way. But when we come back with something useful, I'm throwing it in your face."

Matthias remained still, watching them both with that same unreadable calm. Finally he rose and glided from the room without a word, leaving the door—like their mouths—hanging open.

The morning was a flurry of activity.

After Matthias left, Calladorn and Chad shared a quick meal of sweetened porridge in the common room. They then headed into the city, starting with a visit to a countinghouse to redeem one of the letters of credit Gharn had sent with them. Calladorn hated the necessity, but he knew their plans would be expensive under normal circumstances and made worse by urgency.

From there, they found their way to the garment district—a curved street running off the King's Way, where shop windows featured a rainbow of men's and women's fashions, from the gaudy to the excessive. They initially found only dress shops, with designs that made Calladorn's brows rise as necklines plunged. If this was what ladies wore in Syndar, it was no wonder the city didn't really come to life until after dark. Anyone outdoors during the daytime heat in such attire would be fainting before she'd walked ten feet.

"How long does it take to put something like that on?" Chad asked as they walked past one of the more elaborate displays.

"It depends on how many servants assist," Calladorn answered, chuckling to himself over the way the young man's head tried to turn in every direction at once.

Even Calladorn—jaded as he was from growing up a noble, followed by a decade at the palace in Drakerath—found himself daunted by the sheer excesses on display here. Ribbons and lace were one thing, and to be expected. Even feathers. But insects? Glass fragments? Wood? *Syndar's nobility must be running out of ways to impress one another.*

From the ladies' level, a wide stair led up to the establishments that catered to gentlemen. These stores featured far fewer flowers and considerably darker wood. The clothes, however, were just as elaborate—what they lacked in lace, they made up for in embroidery. He chose the largest store, for the simple reason their visit would likely be the most successful. Holding the door open, he waved Chad inside. The boy rolled his eyes at Calladorn's gently mocking half-bow.

They were immediately accosted by the proprietress, an elderly woman with sharp eyes and sharper pins. Her nose wrinkled subtly at the sight of Chad, but Calladorn's uniform seemed to garner some respect.

"We're due in court this afternoon," he informed her.

She paled. "I beg my lord's forgiveness, but it's simply not possible. Appropriate attire takes weeks to prepare. Why, the embroidery alone—"

"This morning," Calladorn insisted, interrupting.

"But there must be three sittings, and my seamstresses need time to work. Even if you select fabrics we have in abundance, it will require time. No. A morning is not possible. I'm sorry, my lord."

"What about one of these you have on display?" Chad asked.

Calladorn didn't think she could have been more scandalized if he'd stripped naked. Her eyes bulged, and her mouth opened and closed like that of a landed fish.

"But they are displays," she protested. "They've been *seen*."

"But it can be done," Calladorn pressed.

"Well, yes, if we can find one that fits. The young lord has very broad shoulders, after all. Adjustments will need to be made—"

"We will wait," Calladorn said, giving a nod of finality.

She understood. At a clap of her hands, staff swept in from back rooms, surrounding them in a flurry of activity. The woman introduced herself as Madam Laurant and directed her team with the brisk commands of a seasoned soldier. Soon nearly every display stand in the establishment was stripped down while Chad and Calladorn were ushered into an adjoining chamber, its curtains drawn behind them.

Chad was directed to stand on a riser, and one coat after another was paraded past them. Most were dismissed by Madam Laurant as being too small, but three seemed suitable. After trying them on, it came down to one of sapphire blue with sleeves that were white from the middle of the biceps down to the cuffs, where they became blue once again. The collar and front were trimmed with silver embroidery, as were the chest panels. On the outside of each sleeve, blue from the main coat flowed into the white in a daggerlike design. This was also embroidered in silver, with the design's hilt continuing up to the top of the shoulder.

Throughout the process, other assistants took Chad's measurements and scurried off to retrieve trousers and shirts. In the end, they settled on a white shirt to complement the coat, with a discreet fall of ruffles at the neck. Trousers a slightly darker shade of blue than the jacket completed the ensemble.

As they chalked lines for the tailoring that would be required to fit the clothing properly, Chad's expression was pained. "This is ridiculous. It's a jacket, not a suit of armor—ow!" He jumped.

"Pardon, my lord. A pin slipped." Madam Laurant sounded apologetic, but her mouth twitched.

Calladorn smirked. "You want to play the court game?" he asked Chad. "You wear the uniform."

Once the initial fitting was done, they waited on a couch at one side of the room, snacking from a tray of berries and cheeses.

"I'm going to feel like a peacock wearing that," Chad muttered. At Calladorn's laugh, he frowned. "You have peacocks here?"

Shaking his head, Calladorn smiled. "Not as such, I'm sure. But at the word, I pictured a ryna bird. It has gaudy orange plumage that it fans when it seeks a mate."

"Not a peacock, then, but close enough. It's interesting how the translation gave you something close enough that you understood my meaning."

"That's how Necsis works. When you speak, you want to be understood, and so you are."

Chad's eyes widened. "And what if I didn't want to be understood?"

Calladorn was confused. "Then... why speak?"

"Last night Matthias said something," Chad said, rubbing his forehead. "I thought I just hadn't heard him clearly. But what if...?" His words trailed off.

Calladorn studied him, noting the way his brow furrowed. The boy was a puzzle—brash one moment, contemplative the next.

They were interrupted by the return of Madam Laurant and her team. The tailors had done their work well, and everything fit perfectly. For a small fee, they would deliver the clothes to the Royal Arms so the outfit would stay clean while Calladorn and Chad completed the morning's errands.

The next stop was several streets away, at a cobbler. As they walked, Calladorn felt a tickle between his shoulder blades and had the distinct feeling of being watched. He turned quickly—too quickly—but there was no one close enough to be watching. Just nobles in idle conversation, a merchant inspecting bolts of fabric, a servant hurrying down the steps. He shook it off, but the feeling lingered.

Chad's eyes followed him, his expression tight. "I swear someone's been staring at us since we left the inn," he confided, his voice pitched for Calladorn's ears alone.

Both of us, then. It was not a cheerful thought.

The cobbler was a bespectacled fellow with his chestnut hair pulled back in a severe ponytail, making his already-slim frame appear gaunt.

"Do you have anything with arch support?" Chad asked, his voice sounding resigned.

"Arch... support, my lord?"

Chad sighed. "Never mind. No... wait. You know the bottoms of a person's feet aren't flat, right?"

"Of course." The man's posture was rigid.

"So why do you make shoes with flat soles?"

The cobbler hesitated, his head tipping to one side as he thought. "That is simply how it is done." But to Calladorn's surprise, he didn't sound convinced.

Chad grinned. "Try reinforcing your soles to fit the foot. It'll be all the rage. Trust me."

When they left a short time later, Chad had a pair of boots that rose above the knee. The man's severe expression had been transformed, and it wouldn't surprise Calladorn if he spent the rest of the day considering Chad's unusual idea.

As they walked in search of a place to hire a carriage for the afternoon—one befitting someone of station—Calladorn became aware of the hard soles of his own boots. He had never thought about it before. But now he considered how sore his feet often were after a day on duty. Could Chad's suggestion change that? He pondered his companion. The boy... no, the young man might act brash, and even like a buffoon at times, but he was perceptive and intelligent. If he'd enlisted in the military, Chad would have either risen far or been drummed out.

It would have been interesting to find out which.

Chad squirmed. The shirt's fabric was soft. Luxurious. But it had been starched to within a hair of its life and made his shoulder blades itch. The only thing that helped was rubbing against the coach's padded leather seat. The ruffles at his throat would have been a distraction if they hadn't felt so much like he was wearing a bib.

"You need to stop that," Calladorn said, his expression serious. His eyes twinkled, though.

"You going to give me a back scratch?" Chad shot back, then froze mid-contortion.

The man smiled grimly. "I'm serious. If this is going to work, you need to appear bred to that fabric. Own your identity as a noble."

With a sigh, Chad composed himself and stared out the window as the Great Library rolled past. *Matthias was right,* he thought. *Was it just three or four days ago I was complaining about nobles? Now here I am, pretending to be one.* It felt ridiculous. Worse, he was certain the palace staff would see through the act and toss them out on their ears.

"I keep forgetting, you *are* a noble, aren't you? Calladorn Thorne. Or is it Your Grace?"

The smile faded. Calladorn's gaze focused on something near the carriage's roof over Chad's shoulder. "His Grace is my father. I never had much use for titles."

Unsure how to respond, Chad let the silence stretch on. If the demons had flooded Drakerath enough to spill out into the far corner of

Wester, there was little hope anyone remained alive in the kingdom. *What do you say to that?* he wondered.

The carriage slowed. They were approaching the main gate, with a line of people streaming along the left side. With some amusement, Chad saw it was the same guard standing out there. If anything, his plume drooped worse than yesterday.

"Now for the first test," Chad said.

Calladorn nodded fractionally, his posture somehow at full parade attention despite his sitting down. He looked resplendent in his uniform, each button burnished, and the boots polished nearly to black mirrors —every inch the officer.

When the coach reached the gate, it stopped. A guard stepped forward, and Chad tensed. Calladorn casually held up the missive from Ithindar—presenting it so the seal was clearly visible.

"Sir!" The guard saluted smartly, stepped back, and waved them through. Chad exhaled a breath he hadn't realized he was holding.

The carriage entered a circular drive, with an elaborate fountain in the center to their right and steps to the left, leading up to grand doors. Nobles who must have been in the vehicle in front of them were halfway up by the time Chad felt theirs come to a stop. A liveried footman stepped forward and opened the door to allow them to exit. A slight gesture from Calladorn indicated that Chad should lead, and—with a *here goes nothing* look—he obliged, stepping down from their carriage and onto carpeting. The rug was nearly spotless. Either servants scrubbed them like crazy each night, or these nobles never allowed their feet to touch dirt.

"What happens when it rains?" Chad asked quietly, trying to maintain proper decorum as they ascended the staircase side by side.

"I doubt the weather would dare," Calladorn murmured from the corner of his mouth. Chad nearly stubbed his toe on the next step up.

A flash of movement caught his attention. He glanced past the soldiers smartly lined up next to the steps and saw a figure just vanishing behind a column. He frowned, trying to place why it bothered him—something about how smoothly the person moved.

But then they were at the top, heading for the great doors, and he had no time to think about anything other than the task at hand.

*

Stepping into the palace was a very different experience from the day before. It seemed that if someone arrived with sufficient pomp, everyone assumed they belonged. Yet the more Chad advanced inside, the more he felt like an impostor. As he'd gotten dressed earlier at the inn, Calladorn had informed him the suit had cost as much as an average house in Ironspire, a fact Chad had difficulty believing. How could it be, then, that standing here, he was suddenly feeling underdressed?

All the men he saw—other than the uniformed staff—wore elaborate coats or robes of nearly every possible color and cut. In several cases, their sleeves were long enough to touch the floor, and the only reason they could use their hands was thanks to slits in the fronts of the sleeves through which they stuck their arms. Embroidery was everywhere, in elaborate designs from floral to birds in flight. And for all the frilliness of his own shirt, Chad realized it was downright modest. Many carried fancy canes as well. As they were all walking without limping, it was obvious the sticks were for show.

The ladies were worse. Where men's colors were bold, theirs were invariably intensely bright or ostentatiously pastel. Enormous skirts seemed to be competing with each other in an effort to be the widest and most impractical. There was no conceivable way anyone could sit in one of those outfits, and Chad imagined they'd need a shoehorn to even get through double doors. Not all skirts were round, however. Some were flat in the front and back while stretching out to either side in virtually straight lines above the hips before dropping to the floor two-to-three feet later. These could at least get through doors, at least—if they turned sideways.

One woman actually seemed to have her dress on upside down. The skirt was tight around her hips and legs, with a top like an inverted dress—complete with petticoats in differently colored layers—ballooning out all around her torso. Chad wasn't sure how the whole thing stayed upright, or how she wasn't constantly falling over, she looked so top-heavy. She resembled nothing so much as a walking dust mop.

And their hair! Many were styled to look like birds, complete with feather accents, and their owners glared at one another like a pecking fight would break out at any moment. Tall hairdos with artfully curled ringlets practically glued onto the face vied with styles that flared out like bizarre halos. Then there was the woman with a braided cage in her hair containing an actual bird. Chad didn't even want to imagine the state of the woman's scalp by the end of the day. Assuming she even fed the bird before getting dressed—which he thought less and less likely as he came to understand these people.

"Thorne!" A man with hair the color of cherrywood, except where it was graying at the temples, waddled toward them. His crimson coat was embroidered in orange and gold flames, and the lines of his face were asymmetrical in the manner of someone for whom sneering was a state of rest. That the coat actually managed to be buttoned at the front despite the man's enormous girth was a testament to the skills of his tailor.

Calladorn stiffened almost imperceptibly, his eyes going flat. "Oakmont," he said, his voice devoid of inflection.

The man stopped in front of them, blocking the way forward unless they stepped around him. "I heard a rumor yesterday about a scraggly beggar from Drakerath and his boy—" His gaze flicked for a moment to Chad. "—demanding an audience. Of course, I didn't believe them for a moment when they mentioned the Thorne name."

Somehow the way he spoke managed to turn the meaning of the words on their heads. Chad ground his teeth as he realized this man was reveling in the moment and trying to bait Calladorn. They were drawing an audience as well—several lords and ladies were paying attention with hungry expressions. *They live for moments like this,* Chad realized.

Oakmont continued. "Now here you are. How peculiar. Finally climbed down from your high horse, have you? Or are you here to beg for scraps?" He smiled wickedly.

Calladorn's return smile appeared genuine, but his shoulders were squared severely. "If I *were* to beg for scraps, it would certainly not be at your table. You always did enjoy your feasts, but... really?"

Oakmont's smile slipped for a moment before he turned his glittering eyes on Chad, who realized too late he was smirking slightly after

Calladorn's comment. "And what is your problem, boy?" he asked, his voice unctuous.

"Me? Nothing. I was just feeling sorry for you is all."

"Whatever for?"

Chad grinned. "You must be in constant pain, with that stick shoved so far up your ass."

Ladies tittered, and more than one man guffawed. Oakmont's already florid face began turning purple. Before he could recover, Calladorn nodded politely and stepped around him, Chad following.

"That was... original," Calladorn murmured as they continued toward the audience hall. His tone carried an air of approval. Chad grinned wider.

Calladorn steeled himself.

Stepping into the opulent audience hall, he gave a cursory glance to the preening nobles arrayed along its length. Summer sun shone through stained glass along the room's length, casting lurid colors upon those gathered. A floral incense scented the air—not enough to be an irritation but still strong.

A herald stepped forward, and Calladorn whispered in the man's ear. He nodded and strode to his station beside the door, where a page waited with his heavy metal staff. As he did, Calladorn removed the missive from its chest pocket, gesturing for Chad to take up a position just behind him and to the right. At the same time, another page stepped up with a cord, and Calladorn raised his hand to allow the lad to bind his sword into its sheath.

"Peace binding," he whispered to Chad.

They waited, and Calladorn calmed his thoughts, concentrating on keeping a steady breath and slowing his racing heart. *He must listen!* he thought, trying to convince himself that Matthias had been wrong. The idea they might have made this trip for nothing—that he'd abandoned his home for naught—was too impossible to consider. It was the High King's responsibility to serve all the kingdoms. His duty to—

Clang! One sharp rap of metal on stone cut through the sounds of conversing nobles like a knife. Heads turned, and the herald's staff struck twice more. "Calladorn Thorne, the Marquess of Eagle's Reach, son of Gladden Thorne, the Duke of Drakerath." His sonorous voice resonated down the hall. One more clang of the staff completed the introduction. Silence reigned in the chamber.

They want a show; let's give them one. Calladorn marched forward, trusting Chad to follow, as he'd been coached to in the carriage. He took his time, the only sounds being those of their boots hitting the marble floor and his scabbard slapping against his thigh.

At the far end, seated on a massive throne, was High King Elrath. Carved from a single chunk of black onyx, the throne featured nine golden rays on its back—one for each of the kingdoms he ruled—fanning out from above his head. A wide beam of light shone from somewhere behind and high above, angled to serve as a backlight. It bathed the High King in an almost-unearthly glow, causing his shadow to stretch across the floor directly in front of him. The symbolism could not have been clearer. The High King cast a long shadow, and to speak with him, one either had to step into that shadow or be blinded by his radiance.

Elrath was a lean yet powerfully built man in his late thirties or early forties. His high cheeks made his face appear almost gaunt, and he had flowing golden hair without a trace of gray in it. A gold circlet set with nine rubies rested upon his brow. He lounged nonchalantly on the throne, one leg thrown carelessly over its arm, his elbow resting on the other to support the hand that toyed with his chin.

Calladorn forced his jaw not to clench.

"Friend Calladorn," Elrath said, his tone matching his posture. "What news from our happy kingdom of miners?" His voice was high and reedy, not at all what Calladorn expected from someone of his physique.

Inwardly bristling from the insult to his people, Calladorn stopped at a point where only his body was within the spotlight. "It is a happy kingdom no longer, Your Supreme Majesty. In the time it has taken us to reach you, Drakerath has likely fallen."

Low mutters came from the assembly.

Elrath languidly raised an eyebrow over emotionless eyes. "Oh? Have the volcanoes finally blasted it from existence? Buried it under lava?"

The mutters turned to chuckles.

Matthias was right, Calladorn thought, his heart breaking even as it sank. Swallowing his anger, he lifted the letter. "Lord Wizard Ithindar requests the aid of the Nine Kingdoms."

The man raised an index finger slightly, and a page stepped forward to relieve Calladorn of the missive and take it to the throne. Only then did the High King sit up, barely glancing at the seal before breaking it. He began to read.

Calladorn prayed, hoping his fears were unfounded and action would be taken at last. He glanced at Chad, standing a few feet away. The young man raised his eyebrows.

The sound of crumpling paper snapped his attention back to the throne. Elrath's dark stare fixed on Calladorn as he cupped the paper ball and languidly extended his hand. With deliberate slowness, he turned his arm and allowed the paper to drop to the floor, where it rolled down the steps. Calladorn watched it fall, his last hopes going with it. His shoulders slumped.

"Does Ithindar jest with us?" Elrath asked, his querulous voice low yet carrying through the hall's silence.

"Majesty?" Calladorn didn't understand.

"An invasion from the Shifts? Monsters?" The High King leaned forward, his eyes turning wild. "We ask again... Is this a jest? Or do you simply take us for fools?"

His mind reeling, Calladorn heard a shuffle from Chad and an intake of breath. Without withdrawing his eyes from the High King, he gestured to prevent the boy from saying something rash.

Elrath didn't miss the interplay. Looking at Chad, he leaned back again on his throne. "Is this one of the Outlanders that crackpot mentioned? Or one of the monsters? We confess, it doesn't appear to be very frightening, Thorne."

"The demons are real," Chad said, his voice hot as he took a step forward.

The High King's eyes narrowed dangerously.

"Majesty," Calladorn hissed from the corner of his mouth.

"The demons are real, Your Majesty," Chad amended. "I was there the night they slaughtered Emberhold."

"It speaks!" The High King laughed, clapping his hands in apparent delight, but Calladorn saw no trace of a smile on his face. The assembly joined in uncertainly. "Valirion? Advise us." There was nothing but silence in response. "Oh yes. How silly of us to forget. We gave him the sack."

He's mad, Calladorn thought. But the eyes staring down at him from the throne weren't demented. They were cold. Calculating. They looked at Calladorn as if he were prey, and for an agonizing minute, he was sure their executions were about to be ordered.

Then the High King laughed again, echoed by the gathered nobility.

No, Calladorn thought. *Not nobles. Sycophants.*

"We have decided it's a jest. And a good one at that. We applaud you and your pet monster." Elrath clapped slowly and silently, and finally certain of the desired response, the audience joined in with thunderous applause and feigned laughter.

Calladorn felt his face burning. Squaring his shoulders, he waited.

Once the sound had died away, the High King glared at them once more. "But our humor is not boundless. We would suggest, Marquess, that you take yourselves from our presence forthwith."

Calladorn's jaw—his whole body—trembled, but he refused to be cowed by this useless man. Coming to attention, he raised his hand in salute, executed an about-face, and began to march back the way they'd come. Chad turned to follow as he passed.

"Oh, and, Thorne?" Elrath's indolent call caused Calladorn to stop, although he did not turn. "Do not return. We have no desire to learn how... creative we might become if you did."

Calladorn and Chad left the chamber in the same silence with which they had entered. Only this time the nobles looked frightened rather than amused.

Chad's mind reeled. Witnessing the exchange between the High King and Calladorn had twisted his stomach into knots. It was one thing to know the nobles to be petty and even cruel, quite another to witness it firsthand. And the nation's ruler? As he turned to follow Calladorn out of the hall, Chad risked one last surreptitious look at Elrath. The man's eyes locked with his, pinning him like a moth on a display board. There was no cruelty in those eyes. No emotion at all that Chad could detect. The man's expression was a mask. His eyes were not.

An involuntary shiver ran up Chad's spine, lodging between his shoulder blades. Following Calladorn, his back itched worse than it had in the carriage, and not from the starchy fabric. Calladorn, for his part, marched through the chamber with tremendous dignity. The nobles might as well have been standing naked in his presence. It was like he wore his honor as a suit of armor, and no sly smiles, no pitying stares could touch him.

Chad felt his throat constrict. *Calladorn's more like a king than Elrath on his best day.*

A page must have been dispatched the moment they left the audience hall, because by the time they reached the bottom of the staircase, their coach was already being brought back around. The sky was bright azure, without a cloud to be seen. Looking back at the palace and its many-colored domed spires, Chad couldn't understand how the place could seem so bright and beautiful when such malignancy lurked within.

Calladorn climbed into the carriage first. Following, Chad spied something on the ground in his peripheral vision and stepped over it—a short length of dual-colored cord. The peace binding from Calladorn's sword, removed and dropped in the few moments they'd been waiting. Within, Calladorn sat with the sword across his lap in its scabbard, his grip tightening and loosening rhythmically.

The carriage lurched into motion, and they were on their way back down-city, the low roar of countless voices washing over them, but not able to remove the emotional stain left by the High King's vicious laughter.

Calladorn stared at the coach's floor, his mouth occasionally twitching for a moment as he thought. Chad watched him, wondering what all of this meant for them. They had expected Calladorn to return to his kingdom with reinforcements while Chad and Matthias continued to Luthenholme. Chad still had to make that trip to meet the others after Southwatch. But what would Calladorn do?

The thought of Rick hit like a gut punch. Chad had been so determined to get away from Evan—the memory of what it had felt like to be trapped within her will still made him tremble—as well as to get out of Rick's shadow. But had that shadow really been so bad? Surely not compared to the High King's. And now, as he thought back on their parting and how he'd behaved, his cheek twitched in shame. Had he acted any differently from the nobles? *I hope they're having more success than we are,* he thought as his eyes began to sting.

It was a silent trip back to the inn.

XVII
Echoes

Escaping the Deeps should have been triumphant.

A half hour after exiting the caverns, Gharn still shook with mixed excitement and relief. They had done something no one else had accomplished in hundreds of years—no gnome, no dwarf—none had entered their ancestral home and lived. Yet here they were. Not only had they seen the Deeps for themselves, but they had also come face-to-face with the Dark Horror. Gharn couldn't think about the malevolent entity without perspiration beading on his forehead.

It was incredible they had survived. They should be celebrating. But the price was so high. They had explained it to Evan: magic was paid for with life. The more powerful the spell, the more it took from the person casting it. A simple spell might cost mere minutes, but a powerful one—

His eyes kept wandering back to Rick—to his transformed body. It wasn't just the lines on his forehead—those were stronger now but had always been there. It was the way he carried himself. The set of his jaw. The slight lack of coordination in his movements, like a teenager still trying to figure his body out after a growth spurt, but without the energy of youth.

Gharn had warned the young man of the price magic demanded, but to see that price written in lines like this was heartbreaking. At least ten years gone in a matter of minutes. With their short lives, humans were simply not meant for magic. Even Sorendir, with the near-immortality of a dragon, had been conservative in his craft. And had ultimately fallen to it, despite that.

Evan clung to Rick like a drowning person to a timber, touching his face and murmuring "I'm sorry" over and over. Rick flinched every time she said it. Otherwise, he merely sat there with his back against the stone. Evan held him, but he did not hold her back.

"Enough of that now, girl," Gharn said, trying to sound firm without being unkind. "It's no one's fault. He acted to save us."

"But I..." She hesitated for the briefest of moments. Her expression hardened, and her voice matched it as her grip tightened around his arm. "Why didn't you tell me?"

Rick's lip twisted, and he slowly pried her fingers loose. As he looked at her for the first time in a while, his jaw set firmly. "This is why," he replied, his low voice almost a monotone.

Evan's breath caught, and she stared at him. "I don't understand."

"I'm not a cripple, Evan. I don't want to be fawned over. I don't want your pity." His voice grew harsher with each sentence. As he finished, he climbed somewhat unsteadily to his feet, as if his legs were stiff. The motion was wrong—not the easy grace of before, but slower, deliberate. Not old but... tired. Bone-deep tired.

Gharn expected him to wince, to groan, to stretch out the stiffness. He didn't. Just shouldered his pack like nothing had changed, like he wasn't feeling every second magic had stolen from him. Setting his jaw, Rick strode out of the cave. "We should get going."

Evan's lip trembled. "I should have known..." Her voice broke, but then she turned on Gharn, fists clenched. "And you! What's your excuse?"

Gharn's mouth went dry. "It was his choice to make."

Retrieving her own pack, she started to go, then stopped. "I'll never forgive you." And she was gone, leaving Gharn to suffer in silence.

I hope Southwatch is worth it, he thought miserably.

*

The cave opened into a narrow defile filled with evergreen trees, the mountains at their backs. After their long time underground, the fragrance was deliciously alive. A half an hour later, they emerged from the forest into a wide valley. To their left, the land gradually descended into the deeper forests for which Endarl was famous. Somewhere that way, far to the northeast, would be Greenwood Hold, capital of the kingdom. To the right, the land sloped up into a mountain valley.

Somewhere up there would be Southwatch. That they couldn't see it confused Gharn. As its name implied, it was first and foremost a watchtower. For it to be able to overlook the surrounding lands, it would also need to be visible from miles away. He had started to worry they'd taken a wrong turn in the Deeps—who knew where they might now be if that had happened?—when Rick noticed something odd about a section of the ground. It was rocky, but all the stones were flat on one side.

"Paving stones," Gharn realized. Now mostly buried and overgrown with grass that had pushed relentlessly up between the pavers, this had once been a road.

"I don't think anyone's come this way in a long time," Rick observed. Even his voice had shifted. Deeper and steadier, it carried a resonance it hadn't held that morning.

Gharn considered. "This route existed to connect Endarl with the Arathian Empire. When it was cut off, I suppose nobody had reason to come this way anymore."

"I think we should know more about this place's history," Evan said, her voice as sharp as chipped glass. "Or is that another secret you want to keep hidden?"

"Stop blaming Gharn," Rick said with calm authority. "I asked him not to tell anyone."

Evan recoiled as if she'd been slapped, then turned her back on him to face Gharn again. "Southwatch."

With a sigh that felt like it came from his toes, Gharn started walking again. He gestured to the mountain ranges on either side. "This corridor is like the way to and from Merchant's Rest. Those are Shifts to either side, and this is the only way through. Or it was. The Nine Kingdoms lived in the shadow of the Arathian Empire, ruled by an elven wizard."

"Emperor Arathian," Rick said.

Gharn nodded. "He was always power-hungry, so Southwatch was built to defend against him should he ever seek to expand north. It worked for a time. Until he found the Heart."

"How did he get it?" Evan demanded.

Gharn shrugged. "We don't know. What matters is what he did once he had it, which was to wage war against his neighbors. It was called the War of Ascension. The Heart changed everything. How do you fight an enemy that can move armies by sending them into a Shift and then forcing it to align somewhere else? Who can remove an opposing city by turning the land underneath it into a Shift?"

"That kind of power would be unstoppable," Rick said, toying with the token he usually carried in his pocket.

"But he *was* stopped," Evan said. "How?"

"Again, we don't know. Not exactly. There aren't many records, and Sorendir was elsewhere at the time. We know Estariel—leader of the Thought Masters—laid a trap at Southwatch and lured Arathian here. Somehow they were able to get the Heart away from him. He died or was killed—we don't know. After that, the Heart was used one more time to create a Shift just beyond Southwatch, blocking access between the empire and the Nine Kingdoms. Then the records go silent."

Evan snorted. "That's a lot of unknowns."

Somewhere a bird sang mournfully.

"It's all I have to go on." Gharn ran a hand through his thinning hair in frustration. "Sorendir insisted answers would be found here. He never told me why, but—" An image of the paper fluttering away from Sorendir's grasp haunted him. *Do I tell them?* he wondered. He was supposed to guide them. How could he do that once they knew he had even less knowledge than he seemed to? Looking at his companions—seeing the distance between them—he decided secrets came at too high a price. "The night we fled Emberhold, I learned there was more to the prophecy than I'd known."

"So you understand what it's like to have secrets kept from you," Evan said, too sweetly, from above crossed arms. "Interesting."

Rick slipped the trinket back into his pocket and rolled his eyes. "Give it a rest, Evan. Sniping won't..."

His words trailed off as they rounded a corner and Southwatch came into view. Or rather, what was left of it. Ruins sat where a fortress had once been built against the mountain's face, with a tremendous pile of fallen stone splayed into the valley, short sections of wall jutting up randomly within it. It was too much. A wail escaped from his chest, and Gharn fell to his knees as Rick and Evan stared mutely at the ruins of Southwatch.

*

From a vantage point on one of the tallest piles of rubble, Gharn surveyed the scene in disgust as a cool breeze teased his hair. Except for a section of the northern wall, the entire tower had collapsed. The courtyard was buried under debris, and decay had spread through any exposed timbers.

With no strategic value and no nearby resources, the fortress must have been abandoned. Even bandits had no use for it. Whether supporting timbers had rotted away or an earthquake had struck, the result was the same. The tower had broken free from the mountainside, toppling outward. Now its only inhabitants were wildlife. Rodents made their homes within its remains. They chittered angrily at the intruders, then ran and hid when anyone looked in their direction. Above, innumerable birds nested in cracks or outcroppings on the cliff face, or in larger sections of the standing walls. Their cawing cries were raucous.

Scrub growing over the lower portions of the rubble heralded the stronghold's future fate. In another hundred years or so, all that remained would be an irregular hill.

Rick held one of the smaller stones, turning it over and over in his hand. "So much for ancient secrets." Exhaling sharply, he tossed the rock and watched it clatter until it finally came to rest at the bottom of the slope.

It made no sense to Gharn. Why would they have been sent here if there was nothing to find? Sorendir had been so sure. "This is where the path will be revealed," he had said long ago. Had he been wrong? *Was the entire prophecy a sham?* He didn't know if he could bear it, if everything they'd been through was for nothing. The thought left him emotionally numb.

"Where's Evan?" Rick abruptly asked.

This snapped Gharn out of his despair, if only temporarily. After several minutes of searching, they found where she'd wandered out of sight around one of the few remaining sections of wall. She stood staring at the sheer wall carved from the side of the mountain.

"What is it?" Rick asked as they got close.

She didn't respond, and Gharn realized her gaze was unfocused.

Rick reached out uncertainly to touch her shoulder. "Evan?"

The ruins had gone silent. Even the rodents had disappeared, as if they had given up scolding and were now hiding instead. The only sounds were Rick's ragged breathing and Gharn's pulse thudding in his ears.

Moving without a word, slowly and deliberately, Evan crossed toward the wall. She walked as if she were sleepwalking, yet with eerie certainty. The way she moved—it wasn't right. Too sure. Too knowing. Gharn's fingers twitched toward his belt. But for what? What weapon did you draw against a thing like this?

Gharn and Rick exchanged a confused look. "Should we wake her?" Gharn asked.

"I'm not even sure she's asleep," Rick replied. "It's more like she's in some kind of trance."

Gharn realized he was rubbing his hand where Evan had healed it. His breath hitched. "Let her be."

Evan continued unerringly toward a specific place along the wall. Reaching up, she pressed her palm against a weathered stone, then stepped back. A deep grinding sound filled the air as the rock shifted, revealing a darkened stairwell leading downward.

Gharn stared, his pulse quickening. A dead place should not open its doors. And yet—the stones obeyed as if the motion had been set in place long ago, waiting for the right hand. The medallion had responded specifically to Rick's putting it on. Was this similar? Had the stones been prepared to recognize a Thought Master's touch? Either way, Southwatch had invited them in.

Why did it feel so much like the Deepingate?

Evan floated back to consciousness. A moment of confusion gripped her, and she wondered where she was—how she'd come to be standing in front of a looming stairwell descending into the mountain. Cold air flowed from it, wrapping around her limbs. It was too much like returning to the Deeps, and her body shuddered, snapping her the rest of the way awake.

Rick and Gharn stood to one side, their expressions troubled. Gharn's betrayed a hint of awe, while Rick... weighed. Whatever else might have changed, those were still his eyes.

"What happened?" she asked, and her voice seemed to her as if it came from the depths of the stairwell itself.

Rick cocked his head—one half of a shake. "You tell us."

"I don't know. I just—" She stared into the blackness, trying to convince herself it wasn't staring back at her. There was an uncanny sense that the place was waiting for something, and she didn't want it to be her, even though her instincts screamed it was. She sensed a presence, similar to how it had been immediately after Rick had strengthened the bridge in the Deeps. Right after she'd... *No!* she thought, suppressing the anger she felt at herself. She wasn't going to think about that just now. Especially since that anger seemed to resonate with whatever lay below.

"I don't want to go down there," she finished.

Gharn had set his pack on the ground and rummaged through it, producing his lantern. "What choice have we?" His voice had an edge to it. Evan wondered if he was regaining his fire, or—like her—was this place putting him on edge?

Rick whispered something. At his gesture, a glow left his finger and drifted to hover a few inches above his right ear. Gharn huffed, but Rick smiled at him with sad eyes. "What are a few minutes?" he asked.

No, Evan thought, feeling her skin crawl. *Not sad. Resigned.*

She realized she couldn't sense anything right now. Her emotions were too raw to discern where her feelings left off and her imaginings began. Gathering her shawl tighter around her shoulders, she imagined it was a suit of armor. Her fingers brushed her pendant, and she gripped it tightly along with the fabric. A deep breath, and she crossed the threshold.

Nothing happened. Well-preserved stairs descended with a gradual curve that blocked from sight anything that might be more than thirty feet ahead. The walls had curved lines carved into them, but the style differed completely from that of gnomes or dwarves. This place had been constructed by humans. *Not the Deeps, after all,* she thought with relief.

That didn't change how oppressive the atmosphere felt, though, like the mountain pressed down upon them. The air smelled musty and dry, like old leather. Rather than echoing, their footsteps sounded muffled.

After several minutes, the stairs ended in a large chamber, its vaulted ceiling nearly lost in shadow. Forty feet across, it was round, with multiple alcoves opening off its walls and a surrounding gallery higher up.

Directly opposite where they entered, another stair ascended for half a flight before splitting to the left and right—most likely going to that gallery.

A circle of waist-high bookcases rose midway into the room. Full-height shelves stood between each alcove, as well as covering the entire back wall of the gallery. These were filled with thousands of tomes of all sizes. But the covers were faded and washed out, and some seemed to sag hollowly. A couple of shelves had collapsed, spilling their contents to the floor, where aged brown pages crumbled like so many old oak leaves.

"No..." Gharn went to one of the shelves and, with trembling hands, reached out to lift a book gently. It collapsed in his grasp, the leather fragmenting and pages disintegrating to dust before they even reached the floor. Whatever knowledge they'd once held was now lost forever. He moved from shelf to shelf, his agitation increasing with each. "I don't understand," he said, a desperate edge in his voice. "How are we supposed to learn if there's nothing left?"

Despite how loudly he spoke, the words didn't fill the room like they should. The ceiling echoed nothing back. It was eerie.

Which made the fatalism in Rick's words all the worse: "Time always wins," he whispered.

The comment cut her to the heart. She regretted having vented her anger on the two of them. It hadn't been fair, and she knew it. Her true anger was directed at herself, because if she was honest, she had to admit she manipulated people as easily as breathing. This had always been true. It was subtle, using her intuition and empathy to influence those around her. Finding the right words to say was easy when she knew what was going on in the other person's head. She told herself it had usually been for good, such as with the children in the caravan. Yet there were times—like when first meeting Rick—that she'd done it selfishly.

But that was before she'd had real power. Now she didn't simply read people; she was able to directly influence them. Matthias, across the campfire. Chad, to keep him from going to Syndar. Now Rick, at the bridge. She was making a habit of using her powers like this. She'd even promised herself after Chad that she wouldn't do it again. Promised and meant it—only for her to fail at the very first test of that resolve.

Now Rick was paying the price. Her pushing him to use magic at the bridge—being directly responsible for the encounter with the Dark Horror—had forced him to use so much magic... And now he was... not old, exactly, but older. She had robbed him of a decade of his life.

It was a bitter pill to swallow.

And to see him here, acting as if he'd given up hope, only made things worse. She tried to tell herself that the bridge had been necessary. If he hadn't reinforced it, it would almost certainly have fallen with them on it. *Almost* wasn't *definitely,* though. It had been his choice to make, and she'd robbed him of that.

Would she have done the same thing if she'd known about the Mage-curse? She wanted to think not, but she couldn't know for sure. *Never again!* She swore it to herself and tried to ignore that she'd made that same promise before.

She knew it was unfair to both Rick and Gharn to be taking her anger out on them in this way. It was also hypocritical to rail against them for their secrets when she carried her own. She should own up to the fact that she'd pushed Rick at the bridge, but she couldn't shake how justifiably angry he'd been about Chad. How would Rick react to the truth? In his current state, she wasn't able to fool herself into thinking it would be positive.

So she hated herself in silence, and something about this place only made it worse. The air felt thick, and she tried to shake the sense that they were not alone. Standing here, Evan felt like a fly trapped in amber. She wanted nothing more than to run.

But why? The room was empty. There were no other exits. Yet the feeling persisted.

Gharn was on the upper level. She was able to track his progress by the string of muttered imprecations, which also eliminated any need to ask how his search was going.

"Any idea what we're looking for?" she called out, and she was struck again by the way it didn't carry right down here. Her words shouldn't have sounded so... dead.

His head appeared above the railing, bushy brows drooping. "A clue to the location of the Heart, or the Forbidden Spire," he said. "As for what form that might take..."

"Maybe we're looking in the wrong place," Rick said.

"You mean a secret room within the secret room?" Evan asked, trying not to sound sarcastic.

Rick's only reaction was an eyebrow raised in her direction. "I mean, we're paying attention to the books. That's not all this room holds." At his gesture, the light hovering over his shoulder grew brighter and split into a dozen fragments that glided across the chamber. Evan thought they were heading for the alcoves, but instead, they went for the walls in between. Everywhere they touched, the light spread out like water rippling across a pond, casting shadows that lingered. Carvings, previously lost in the shadows, seemed to spring to life.

"Stop doing that," she snapped, more harshly than she'd intended.

Rick turned toward her, his expression unreadable. A long pause stretched between them, as brittle as glass. "It's my life," he said at last, his voice soft. Gentle, even. "My choice."

The comment stopped Evan short. *Does he know?* she thought, feeling a chill tickle her spine. But he was already examining the carvings. She rubbed her forehead, feeling a headache starting behind her eyeballs. The pressure in this place—whatever it was—was getting to her.

Rick's light continued to work its way across the room. Having filled the walls, it moved down across the floor, passing under her feet and merging toward the center of the room. Intrigued, she watched it cross through the ring of bookcases and highlight the carved design in the middle of the floor.

A whisper in her mind drew her to it, even as another part of her wanted to go somewhere else. Anywhere else. The pattern was of two circles, one inside the other to create a ring, with six smaller circles evenly spaced around it. Other curves connected them with each other, weaving them all together, with one in the center. As she approached, she realized each of the smaller circles was the right size for a person to stand within. And from the center circle, more lines twisted like vines across the floor, up the walls in between the alcoves, and all the way to the ceiling, where they spiraled together until meeting at the very top of the dome. Experimentally Evan stepped into one of the circles.

She suddenly felt disconnected. Stretched, and pulled toward the center circle. It was as if she was being focused into it. Gasping from the surprise, she stepped away again.

"What is it?" Rick asked quickly, his voice concerned.

A suspicion was forming in her mind. She waved him away and moved to the center circle, stepping into it. Again the sensation of disconnection struck, but this time she was prepared for it. It was different too, because now she felt incomplete. She waited for something—from the other six circles. At the same time, she was being drawn through the lines radiating out across the room, up the walls and spinning dizzyingly around the ceiling before being flung upward.

The world opened to her.

You can't! The scream came from within her, throwing open eyes she hadn't realized she'd closed. Something inside her slammed shut. A wall. A door she hadn't even known was there. The force of it threw her back into her body, her breath escaping in a sharp, ragged gasp. Her vision blurred, her sense of balance gone—was she still standing? Was she still here?

The world snapped back all at once. The shock was as effective as if she'd been slapped, and she staggered out of the circle. Bracing her hands on her knees, she gasped for breath. Her entire body felt charged—her nerves were so sensitive, the brush of fabric across her skin burning so much like fire, she wanted to tear her clothes off. She could hear Gharn's breathing from the gallery. The scents of moldering leather, wood, and paper hit her so strongly she nearly emptied her stomach. She could even taste paper dust in the air.

Rick was by her side in an instant, supporting her. The pressure of his hands made her bite her tongue to keep from crying out in pain. Whatever he said was a roar that washed over her until she thought her eardrums would shatter. She collapsed under the assault, covering her ears and clamping her eyes tight against the impossible brightness.

As abruptly as it had come, the flood was gone, and she could think again. The only unnaturally loud sound was her pulse pounding in her ears, and even that soon slowed to normal. Rick and Gharn both knelt next to her, fear written large in their eyes.

"I'm okay, I think," she told them, her voice sounding strangled.

"What happened?"

"Are you all right?"

The two of them spoke together, and Evan wasn't sure who had asked each question.

She smiled thinly. "Help me up."

When she was back on her feet, they helped her over to the stairs, where she sat down next to her pack to finish catching her breath. "This whole place is a trap." Seeing them tense, she hurried to reassure them. "No, not for us. For Arathian. I think this was how they lured him here." She unclipped her canteen and took a long drink from it to wash down the taste of blood. Realizing how stiff her fingers had become, she pulled her shawl tighter. She wondered if it had been this cold when they arrived, or was she still feeling lingering sensitivity on her skin?

"How?" Rick asked.

"Those designs. I think if six Thought Masters stand in the outside circles, whoever stands in the center can draw from their power, channeling it into the world above." She shivered. "That thing is dangerous."

"Can it be used to locate the Heart? Or the Forbidden Spire?" Rick asked.

"I—" Evan shuddered again. "—I don't think so. It needs seven people to work right. That much..." Her voice trailed off as she realized her breath was fogging into puffs that hung in the air as she spoke. She clamped her mouth shut as her teeth began to chatter. Not from fear or adrenaline but from cold. The room felt like it was turning into a freezer.

And in the middle, hovering above the design, a shape began to form. Evan couldn't tell if it was becoming visible or reaching in from... someplace else.

With her eyes fixed on something over Rick's shoulder, the blood drained from Evan's face.

He spun about, hands rising as a half-dozen spells came to mind to handle whatever could affect her so strongly. He expected a demon. What he saw—

The words died on his lips, unspoken. *How do you fight a ghost?* he thought. In the middle of the chamber, a figure hovered directly above the center circle. Diaphanous with flickering edges, it was approximately the same size and shape as a human, but below its waist, it simply faded from existence. The face was indistinct—it could have been any race, any gender—but two burning pinpricks of white burned where its eyes should have been.

Those unblinking stars focused on Evan. "Set your magics aside, Wizard. She is the one I seek." The voice sounded like empty branches rubbing together in a winter wind. It was as faint as a distant whisper, but Rick heard every word with crystal clarity because it came from within his own mind.

"Thought Master," Gharn breathed, hugging himself tight against the cold radiating from the apparition.

"What remains of us," it agreed.

Evan rose unsteadily to her feet, supporting herself against the wall of the stairwell. Her chin lifted defiantly. "You came for me?" she asked.

"You dare return?" The voice became cracked stone, brittle with fury. "You dare summon me?"

Rick's mind raced. Summoning he could understand. She might have done that by accident when she stood where it now hovered. But return? That made no sense.

Evan shook her head. "You're wrong. I've never been here before."

"Liar!"

Rick's skull felt like it was splitting open from the inside. His vision pulsed, bending and twisting like the entire room had warped around him. He doubled over, hands clamping against his temples as if that could hold his mind together. Evan did the same, and Gharn collapsed with a gurgling gasp.

Rick's vision swam, and beyond it—images played. He couldn't tell if they were in his mind or figments of the very light he had conjured. Whatever their nature, they raced through his consciousness in rapid succession...

A woman stood in the chamber, her back turned to him, long auburn hair flaring out from her head in a surreal halo, her white robes flapping in an unseen wind. One hand lifted toward a tall elf who stood proudly before her, his lips twisted into a snarl...

The same elf, haughty no longer. His body contorted and bent unnaturally. His limbs seemed about to snap at any moment...

A tower hugged the face of a mountain. Beyond it lay a valley, every available foot filled with rank upon rank of an army. Between them and the tower stood the elf, with the woman floating above and behind him. She gestured, and the elf mirrored the movement...

Air shimmered in a curtain of light. Through it, the army could barely be made out. And then it was gone, replaced by a rugged mountain. Tremors racked the surrounding land, toppling the tower...

Estariel. *The word hissed through Rick's mind, and he fought to stay conscious under its pressure. At his feet, a gnome twitched on the floor. Gharn. Evan lay on the steps, her hands raised defensively, her eyes rolled back in her head until they were nearly all white...*

White-robed figures stood in an assembly. Before them was the woman from the other visions. No one moved, but the air crackled with energy. A figure screamed and collapsed to the ground. Then another...

All the figures were now dead except for the woman and one other—a dignified man with blond hair and black eyes. His jaw was set in determination, his posture proud. He knew his moment had come, but he remained unbroken. A flare of light struck him, so bright the scene became an afterimage...

As the light faded, Rick understood. He was looking at a negative. The specter in the center of the room was the man from the final vision, inverted. With that realization, Rick's perception changed, and he saw the figure for what it was: the ghost of that last Thought Master.

"You broke the law. You murdered us," the specter said.

Rick gritted his teeth against the mental onslaught. He understood now that when Evan had accidentally awakened the circle, she'd awakened this ghost as well. The shade, still trapped in the moment of his death, had fixated on her because of her psychic power. "She's not who you think she is!" Rick shouted.

Black eyes snapped to focus on Rick, and a pulse of unseen force slammed into him, sending him sprawling. He landed hard enough the air was forced explosively from his lungs, leaving him dazed and wheezing.

But it was enough. Evan struggled back to her feet. She stepped forward, but unlike the woman in the visions, her posture wasn't defiant. Her arms were spread in a gesture of openness.

The ghost hesitated.

Still gasping, unable to stand, Rick pushed himself up on one arm. "You died three hundred years ago."

Black eyes swiveled to study Rick, and the ghost's expression softened by a hair. The terrible pressure on his mind eased slightly, and Gharn seemed to relax.

Rick knew he had to make his next words count. "She's an Outlander. She *can't* be Estariel."

A sigh swept through the chamber—deep, weary, a breath stolen from the past itself. Papers fluttered, dust rising in swirling tendrils. Rick's chest loosened, as if the weight of history had exhaled with it. The figure rippled and began fading from view.

"Wait!" Evan stepped toward the ghost. "Please... Where is the Heart?"

The ghost continued to fade, and Rick hung his head, feeling defeated. *So close.*

Another thought drifted across his mind. Not harsh as before, but a caress. "*South. Y—Estariel took it south, but you cannot follow.*"

Rick felt the hairs on his arms stand on end, and a moment later, a crackle of energy flooded the room. Books, furniture, carvings—everything trembled and blurred for an instant. Then it shattered with a sound of breaking crystal. He dropped back to the floor, shielding his head and neck with his hands. Dust settled around him.

His ears still ringing, eyes watering from the dust, Rick looked up at an empty chamber.

"*Your path lies north...*" It was the faintest whisper on his mind.

Then silence, punctuated only by a moan from Gharn as he stirred back toward wakefulness.

"Are you okay?" Rick's voice, ragged and strained.

Gharn was not okay by any measure. He felt like he'd been put through a meat grinder, then reshaped into something resembling a gnome, except parts had been lost along the way. Every fiber of him ached, a memory of being flayed from the inside out by that... thing. He groaned, raising a shaking hand to his forehead, not yet daring to open his eyes. Smooth hands enclosed his, and suddenly warmth flooded through him, washing the pain—but not its memory—away. Evan smiled down at him.

"By the Thr—" The words stuck in his throat. All his life, the phrase had been an expression of wonder. Now it felt like a curse. "I knew the Thought Masters were powerful, but that..."

Aided by Rick, he sat up, studying Rick's face to see if there were any further signs of aging. Thankfully, there were none. He looked haggard, with dark circles under his eyes, but there were no new lines.

Then Gharn saw the chamber. "No," he croaked. "No, no. It can't be." His legs nearly gave out as he took a stumbling step forward. He'd expected answers, but he'd found nothing. The alcoves were empty, the floor buried under sand and dust. All the furniture was gone, all carvings. The walls gleamed in Rick's dim light, reflecting back on themselves endlessly.

Gharn stared slack-jawed at the transformed room. Southwatch was supposed to hold answers. Now it held nothing. Hope fled his body in a long, soft sigh, and a sense of failure settled into its place. Sorendir had trusted him to find the path, and instead, he had led them here. *To ruin.*

Turning his back on the empty room, he studied his companions. Their bodies sagged, and their expressions were grim. "What did the ghost tell you?" he asked, not daring to hope they'd learned something useful.

"The Heart is somewhere south of here," Evan said, her expression pinched.

"South?" That made no sense. "That's impossible."

"Why?" Rick asked.

Gharn shook his head. "There are no routes. No way to get there. If that's where the Heart is, it could be a day's march from here, and we'd never retrieve it."

Rick's finger tapped a pattern in the air by his side as he squinted in thought. "The Heart was used to defeat Arathian. So there has to be a way through." His expression fell. "No. That doesn't necessarily follow. Estariel could have opened a way, then closed the path behind her. Who says she returned again?"

Gharn searched his memories, trying to remember everything he'd read or Sorendir had said about the history of the Thought Masters. The records dried up soon after the War of Ascension. It was believed they had cloistered themselves in the Forbidden Spire, closing themselves off from the world. Was there anything about Estariel, though?

He couldn't remember. "What next, then?" he said, exhaling loudly.

Rick shrugged. "We know more than before, which is a step in the right direction. Before he left, the ghost said our path lies north, which is what we had already planned."

"But *where* is the problem," Evan said.

"She's right." Gharn felt his lower lip tremble as he looked at her. They were still running rudderless through a fog. Without a destination, "north" covered too much territory to be of help. He reached absently for the flask that was no longer there and felt a moment of frustration at being denied.

But is that what I really want? To drown myself in spirits again? His fists tightened in determination. *No. Not this time.* He would not let this be the end. Not yet.

Ignoring the unsteadiness he still felt, Gharn climbed to his feet and ascended three of the steps, so he stood at eye level with Rick. "Broken gears won't mend themselves. We already knew to head for Luthenholme from here, and that hasn't changed. We'll find the Forbidden Spire some..."

His voice trailed off as he noticed something odd about the layer of dust and sand covering the floor, which he only spotted now that he was higher. It wasn't as smooth. Lines ran through it—irregular yet not random. Gharn felt his pulse quicken. They were drawn.

"Follow me!" he exclaimed. Feeling suddenly giddy and not caring how he must look, he bounded down the stairs again, his pain forgotten. "Stay close to the edge—don't go in the center. Well, come on."

The three of them skirted the room until they came to the gallery staircase.

"What is it?" Rick asked.

Rather than answering, Gharn laughed. Then laughed again when the two of them exchanged a look. "You'll see." He hurried around the gallery, checking occasionally until he was sure he'd found the right spot, where he then led them to the railing. "There! Shine that light of yours on the floor."

Their expressions changed from confusion to surprise. Evan's eyes widened, and Rick's mouth twitched into a tentative smile. "It's a map," Rick breathed, all exhaustion gone from his voice. He leaned forward, nearly losing his balance as he scanned the pattern with a sudden intensity. "A path."

Gharn nodded enthusiastically. When the shade destroyed the room, it hadn't been out of pique. He had used the created sand and dust to turn the floor into a canvas. Pointing at the lower left, as they stood in relation to it. "That's Southwatch, there. Endarl forms a big arch, with Greenwood Hold at the top. Above it to the right is Luthenholme. And above that..."

"It looks like a spur of land sticking up," Evan said. "Do you think...?"

Gharn didn't think. He was certain. On every map he'd ever seen, the northern end of Luthenholme was nothing but an impassable void of Shifts. No roads, no land—just chaos. But this map said otherwise.

"It has to be," he confirmed. "The Forbidden Spire."

Spirits soared. The trio spoke excitedly with one another as they ascended the steps back out of the hidden chamber. At Rick's suggestion, they had drawn three copies of the map—one for each of them—which were now tucked safely into their packs. The trials of the past few days already felt like a distant memory.

It amazed Rick how profound an effect a little good news could have on them. That the Heart was seemingly out of their reach didn't matter at the moment. They had a path forward, however tenuous, and that meant the journey through the Deeps had not been in vain.

His sacrifice hadn't been meaningless. Hope bloomed anew.

Stepping back into daylight felt like crossing a threshold, and Rick indulged in the beauty of clouds set on fire by the sinking sun. Some phenomena were universal, regardless of the universe. Evan's eyes sparkled as she looked upward, seeming to bask in the warmth against her face.

Rick stepped to one side, deliberately placing some distance between himself and her, feeling guilty as he did so. Evan's eyes flicked toward him, tight with hurt, and he realized he hadn't been as discreet in his movements as he'd thought. Clamping down on a swell of remorse, he told himself—once again—that this was necessary. He had to be cold for her sake.

They could figure their relationship out again when they were back home, in a universe where magic didn't exist. Where the Magecurse could no longer hurt them both.

Pretending he hadn't noticed Evan's reaction, he looked at Gharn. "How long is the trip from here?"

"Two or three months, I think. It depends on how long until we reach civilization and can buy horses. Southern Endarl is thinly populated, if I remember right."

"Well, I don't know about you, but I'm exhausted," Evan said. She heaved a yawn as if to prove her point. "How long has it been since we last slept?"

"A day and a half," Gharn answered.

Rick covered his mouth to stifle his own sympathetic yawn. "Was it really only yesterday we left Khorvael? It feels so much longer."

They set about making camp in a small bowl within the ruins, sheltered in the *L* of a bit of still-standing wall. Scavenged pieces of timber burned well enough to make a cozy fire. The local wildlife complained indignantly about their presence, but the noises soon faded into Rick's subconscious. By the time the first stars appeared, the group was warm and had full bellies—or as satisfied as they could be with trail rations, anyway.

Rick volunteered to take the first watch, waking Gharn after a few hours. Evan would take the final shift before dawn. As the other two bedded down, he found a spot a little away from the fire, where he could sit with his back to it and benefit from the light without being blinded.

To keep himself awake, he fiddled with the pi key chain that he still carried, running his finger along its hard edges. He'd long since memorized the lines, but the memento still served as a tangible reminder of his relationship with Evan. The keys themselves were more problematic as they clinked softly together in his hands. The car key was certainly useless. Even if they got home, the car would never drive again. The others... he wasn't sure. If they could, by some miracle, return home tomorrow, how would that work? Would people recognize him? Would his parents accept him? How could he even explain the physical change he'd undergone? The house keys would still work, but could he still use them? It felt like an impossible question.

Three troubled hours later, he woke Gharn and took his turn by the fire. As tired as he was, sleep came almost immediately, but the worries followed him into his dreams.

*

A scuffling sound woke him, and he groggily realized Gharn was kicking sand into what remained of the fire. Sitting up, he started to ask what was going on—only to have the gnome clamp a rough hand over his mouth. In the faint moonlight, Gharn raised a finger to his lips, his eyes huge.

The meaning was clear, even if the reason was not. Feeling a stab of fear, Rick nodded stiffly, and Gharn moved to wake Evan. "Quickly," he whispered, barely loud enough to hear over the night's breeze. "Pack your things and follow me." He started to roll up his blanket, moving with deliberate care.

Exchanging a glance with Evan, Rick did the same, tying his blanket to the bottom of his pack. They then followed Gharn from the campsite, stepping with care.

Gharn didn't lead them back to what remained of the road. Instead, they climbed stealthily up the slope that blocked the view of the valley beyond. As they approached the ridge, Gharn signaled with one hand for them to duck, and they inched the rest of the way forward, staying low. By the time they reached the top, they were on their stomachs.

Evan's sudden intake of breath came a moment before Rick could make out the source of their concern for himself. In the valley below, shadows moved against the ground. They seemed to be arrayed in units—

squares of fifty or so individuals each. There was no way to count, because their shapes were wrong—misbegotten and twisted. A tremor born of remembered horror crept down Rick's spine, and he clenched his jaw tightly. The cool night breeze was suddenly bitter against his skin, and it took him a moment to realize a thin sheen of sweat covered him, and a drop of moisture trickled beneath his shirt.

Meanwhile, his mind struggled with the ramifications. He had seen those figures once before. Seen what they did. In Emberhold.

More of the figures were coming from the trees to the west, apparently down from the mountain. Out of the Shift that lay there.

It makes no sense, he thought. There was simply no way beings from another universe could enter across multiple Shifts. Not if they were random. Yet here the monsters were. So either everyone's understanding of the Shifts was wrong, or something else was going on.

Could the demons somehow control them? The possibility shook him to his core.

"How did they find us?" Evan asked, ducking her head back below the edge to keep her whisper from carrying. Rick applauded the move—they were quite a way away, but who knew what those things' hearing was like?

"I don't think they did," Gharn answered with equal softness. "There are more of them than when I went to wake you and put the fire out, but they're not facing us."

Rick turned to peek over again. Gharn was right. As the creatures came out of the forest, they formed into units and faced north. It was an army, but it had no interest in them.

"Greenwood Hold," Evan said, her eyes widening as understanding dawned. "This is an invasion force."

A crushing realization settled over Rick, gripping his heart like a vise. They were trapped. Shifts on three sides of them—one with demons pouring out of it—and the only way forward was directly through that army.

As Rick watched, a small group broke off and started moving to the south. Toward the ruined tower, and toward them. His mouth went dry as he ran through options in his mind.

Hiding? Risky.

Running? Impossible.

Fighting? Not an option.

His old mantra came to mind. *There's always a solution, if you look hard enough.* But even as he pulled Evan into the shadows, Gharn following, he had absolutely no idea what it might be.

XVIII
Betrayal

After midnight, the palace was silent as a tomb.

Matthias moved through the darkened halls like a ghost. The stone beneath his boots was cool, polished to mirror-smoothness, yet damping all but the loudest noises. And Matthias was adept at passing in silence. Even the flickering torches lining the corridor seemed subdued, their flames whispering rather than crackling, casting long, uncertain shadows.

There should have been staff. Maids to clean. Servants to run errands at their lord's every whim. Soldiers to guard the royal personage. Even at night, they should have been going about their duties, ensuring the palace was ready to greet the next day. Instead, the hallways were deserted, as if the inhabitants were afraid to go above the third floor. Frightened of what might lurk in the shadows. Perhaps terrified of the shadows themselves.

His lip twisted grimly. *So like Ironspire in its final days.* Matthias did not like making this visit. There was too much at risk, and too many ways in which Elrath was likely to complicate matters. But his... companions had forced his hand. In ignoring his warnings, they had attracted the attention of the High King—boldly revealing themselves in ways that should have been avoided. Now it was necessary to redirect that interest in order to keep them from being crushed like insects, all while ensuring his own interests remained unimpeded. Games within games, and for the highest stakes imaginable.

He reached the doors to the High King's private chambers. Unguarded. Elrath was nothing if not sure of himself. Placing his hand upon a heavy wooden door, its finely polished surface smooth beneath his fingers, carved in a fanciful scene with a dragon—nothing like the real thing,

Matthias noted with minor amusement—he hesitated. Self-doubt was not an emotion he knew often, but it flickered in his mind now. Brushing it aside, he pushed the door open and stepped inside as if he had always belonged there.

The room was lavish—but wrong. The scent of incense was too thick. Cloying rather than pleasant. Tapestries of impossible craftsmanship adorned the walls, their woven figures twisting when the eye lingered too long, as if the images refused to remain static. Jewels and gold lined the shelves, not as trophies but as if discarded—forgotten baubles strewn among relics of greater importance.

Some of those relics attracted a second glance. What he had at first assumed were jewels were, in fact, the flashing lights of technology. Of course Elrath would consider himself to be above the Ban. Matthias imagined how excited Chad would be to see this room. Or perhaps frustrated. The boy had already guessed that the Necsis elite hoarded technology. To have that belief confirmed... He dismissed the thought. It was irrelevant.

At the far end of the chamber stood a massive, curved writing desk with a game board set upon it, and beyond, an open balcony that overlooked the moonlit city. From this angle, the brightly lit King's Way looked like a coiled serpent.

The High King stood there, his silhouette tall against the pale light, hands clasped behind his back, facing away. His voice came, deep and resonant. "I saw you today."

Matthias did not answer immediately. He had suspected as much. It was part of why he had taken this risk tonight. Behind him, the door drifted shut of its own accord. Remaining silent, he stepped forward, slow, deliberate, past the glinting artifacts. Past the weight of so much power compressed into a single room. He halted just short of the desk.

Elrath finally turned, his expression unreadable in the half-light. "A curious thing, that you would take an interest in an Outlander and some insignificant noble from a scarcely more significant kingdom."

Matthias inclined his head. "I take interest where it is warranted."

Elrath's lips curled—not a smile, not quite. "Warranted." He stepped toward the desk, trailing fingers along the edge of the board as though it were an afterthought. "You don't waste your efforts?"

It was a minor feint, designed to draw him out. Careful to keep his expression neutral, he answered, "I do not."

Eyes gleamed at him with something darker than curiosity. "Then tell me, why were they worth your attention?"

Matthias measured his response carefully. "The Outlander is not alone. There are two others. They seek something—a relic." He deliberately allowed his eyes to flick to the cases scattered around the room. *Let Elrath believe it is a bauble such as these,* he thought. *Or one of them, in fact.*

The High King's fingers stilled atop a tower piece. "A relic?" His voice turned sharp, interest quickening like a blade unsheathed. "And what, exactly, do they believe they will find?"

Matthias exhaled evenly, feigning surrender. The truth, but not all of it. "They call it the Heart of Necsis."

Silence stretched between them, heavy and expectant.

"Its purpose?" Heavily lidded eyes held Matthias trapped. There was no room for lies under that gaze. But misdirection might be possible.

"It is said to command the Shifts."

The eyes narrowed dangerously. "And you did not think this was worth mentioning sooner?"

Matthias held his ground. "I did not have opportunity before this."

Elrath exhaled slowly. He stepped toward the balcony, his robe whispering against the floor. "A powerful name," he mused. "The Heart." He glanced back at Matthias. "Do you believe it exists?"

Matthias kept his expression neutral. "I believe they believe it does."

"You are very careful with your words," the High King said with a low chuckle.

Matthias did not answer. He knew better than to play at modesty.

"And they seek to use it to stop these"—the corners of his mouth twitched—"demons they warned of today?"

"They seek only to return to their home reality."

The High King studied him for a moment longer, then turned his gaze outward to the city at his feet. "Whatever their goals are is of no consequence. I will see to it they never find it."

Matthias felt something cold coil in his chest. He had expected this, but the speed of the decision unsettled him. He had come here tonight to prevent exactly this outcome, to ensure the Outlanders were not crushed before they could serve their purpose. But now the path ahead was narrowing.

"They are being watched," he said carefully. It was even true, as he was the one doing the watching. "If they are thwarted too soon, we lose the opportunity to uncover who else might be looking for the Heart."

The High King studied him. Something calculating flickered behind his gaze. "You think they will lead us to others."

"I think the ripples they create will draw out those who know more than they do."

For a long moment, Elrath said nothing. Then, slowly, he turned fully to face Matthias. "I care nothing for ripples. But if this Heart can do what they claim... ah, *that* would be a prize." His hand clenched into a fist, as if he imagined himself squeezing the Heart.

Matthias allowed himself a thin smile as he inclined his head in affirmation. "Then I will continue to follow them to that prize."

"I had no doubt you would." The eyes twitched, and Elrath's return smile was predatory. "A pity, then, that I've already taken action of my own."

He opened his fist, and Matthias froze, registering the shattered councillor piece revealed in the High King's grasp. His calm vanished as he realized he had been played. Moves and countermoves. The entire time they had been talking—perhaps even before—Elrath had been delaying him.

Frustration surged. For all his guile, Elrath was a fool in his wastefulness.

Without another word, Matthias sped around the desk to the balcony, rope uncoiling in his hands. Ignoring the height, he leaped, vanishing into the night. Laughter trailed after him.

After returning them to the inn, the carriage was dismissed.

Calladorn followed Chad into the Royal Arms, fragrances of fresh bread and hearty stew enveloping him in a wholesome embrace even before he crossed the threshold. His stomach grumbled in reply; the day's stresses had taken a toll, even if they had been entirely emotional.

The few patrons seated around the common room at this early hour watched them pass through on the way to the inn's main stairs at the far end. Their eyes were calculating. Commoners may have been overlooked the night before, but two lords attracted both attention and speculation. He wondered how long it would be before word spread through the city about their audience today. In a city so full of political scheming as Syndar, the only thing that moved quickly was gossip.

Instead of following Chad upstairs, he first found the innkeeper to let the man know they would take their meals in their room tonight. He'd had enough of being on display for one day and suspected Chad felt the same. Anger continued to seethe just below the surface, a flame burning hot even if his appearance was one of calm.

Having enlisted at sixteen summers, Calladorn had been a soldier half his life. He had forgone the commission entitled to him by birth, choosing instead to earn his way through the ranks. It was useless pretending his rapid rise wasn't due in part to his name, but the knowledge hadn't fostered complacency. It had constantly prodded him to work harder, to prove to both himself and those around him that he deserved his rank.

Calladorn believed in what the system stood for—that the nobility had an obligation to serve the people under their care. He wasn't so naive as to fool himself into believing his views were common, but there was a fundamental dynamic. Lords and ladies could only flourish if the commoners thrived or at least did well. The kingdom could only thrive if its nobles did.

What did it mean if that enlightened self-interest broke down? If the ideal he had dedicated his adult life to served only a city of elite snobs... it was repugnant on a level that made Calladorn's stomach twist into knots. Eryck had died for it.

Calladorn walked into their shared room to find Chad wearing the Ironspire shirt again—now freshly laundered. The new shirt, with its ruffles, was tossed over the back of a chair. The young man eyed him with a concerned expression as he came in.

Calladorn gave him a tight smile. "Don't worry. I won't bite."

Chad's chuckle sounded slightly forced. "Are you doing okay?"

Calladorn shrugged. "No, but I'll live. No Matthias?"

"I didn't see him downstairs either." Seated on his bed, Chad draped the courtly coat across his legs and ran a finger across its embroidery. His brow furrowed in thought. "So, um... Marquess?"

Feeling a twinge of embarrassment, Calladorn rolled his eyes. *I should have known he'd catch that.* "I'm the oldest son to the queen's brother," he explained.

"Oh... royalty. Should I bow?" Chad's eyes were wide, his expression earnest.

"Nobility," Calladorn corrected. "And only if you want me to stop going easy on you during practice." He tried for a growl, but it broke into a chuckle. He knew Chad was deflecting his dark mood with humor. The pain of the day's events ran too deep for that to truly help, but he appreciated the effort.

Looking at the coat again, Chad shrugged. "Screw it." He slid the garment on, tugging his shirtsleeves free. When his gaze returned to Calladorn, his eyes were twinkling. "What? It's a nice coat. Besides, if I'm going to hang out with royalty, I've gotta look the part."

Almost reflexively, Calladorn started to protest, but the mischief in the young man's eyes cut the comment short. He snorted despite himself.

*

After dinner arrived, they sat at the table next to the window and discussed what their next steps should be. Calladorn entertained the possibility of staying in Syndar and trying to garner support from influential nobles. "If we can get the right ones on board, they can put pressure on the court until the High King is forced to take action."

"Would that work?" Chad asked, picking at his meat.

Turning the idea over in his mind, Calladorn sighed. "I doubt it. To have any chance, we'd need the support of peerage from Drakerath. If that kingdom's own nobles aren't concerned enough, then why would anyone else be? And the highest ranked among them is—"

"Let me guess," Chad interrupted, his expression souring. "Oakmont."

"Quillian's family, anyway," Calladorn said with a nod. Chad's eyes clouded. "I refuse to call him by his given name to his face. It doesn't matter, though—his parents may hold the power, but they're in Drakerath and he's the one we have to deal with."

"I'm sorry. The way he was going after you, I couldn't—"

It was Calladorn's turn to interrupt. "Don't be. The man's always been an ass. His own parents couldn't even abide him, which was how he got sent here." He smiled reassuringly. "The only thing worse than Quillian's enmity is his friendship. If anything, your comment gained appreciation from other houses. Unfortunately, that's unlikely to be enough to aid our cause."

Chad pushed a potato around on his plate. "All of this would be easier with a proper news network. It's hard to ignore a threat when pictures are plastered across the TV."

Although the last term didn't translate, Calladorn understood the gist of Chad's meaning. "That's part of why we have the Lord Wizards. They can send messages between one another, and since each court has one, it allows the kingdoms to coordinate."

"But Elrath got rid of the one here. Is that common?"

Calladorn shook his head. "It's unprecedented."

Frowning, Chad focused on him. "Doesn't that strike you as awfully convenient? What if the High King knew this was coming and wanted to create chaos?"

The thought took Calladorn aback. It would explain so much. If the High King was in league with—or at least threatened by—the demons... But then he shook his head. "He'd need to have known about the invasion before it happened, and it's impossible for organized threats to come through the Shifts. Their randomness prevents it."

"Prophecy," Chad answered.

"What?"

"I'm on this quest to find the Heart because of a prophecy. Thousands of years ago, it predicted Rick, Evan, and I would arrive where and when we did. Sorendir and Gharn were waiting for us because they'd studied it. Who's to say there aren't other prophecies beyond the one I've heard of?" His eyes widened. "For that matter, the prophecy of the Heart also talks about some sort of big threat it would help end."

"It's an interesting notion," Calladorn conceded. His rational mind discounted the idea of foretelling the future, and what prophecies he had seen were always couched in such vague terms they were useless until after the fact. But he couldn't dismiss the idea entirely. Chad's suggestion would explain a lot. *If the High King is a traitor.*

Calladorn pushed his plate away in frustration. "None of this helps us plan."

"What do you *want* to do?" Chad asked after a moment, his voice unusually timid.

He exhaled sharply in frustration. "There aren't any good options. My mission here has failed. That much is obvious. I should return home. Assuming..." He let his words trail off. *Assuming there's any home to return to.* The idea of saying it out loud came too close to making it real.

"You could come with me," Chad suggested, his voice soft. "If the Heart can help end the threat, then helping us also helps your home. Maybe you're even supposed to use it after we've—" He suddenly stopped speaking and fidgeted in his chair as if he were seated on something sharp.

"After you've returned to your home," Calladorn said for him. He smiled. "Chad, it's good that one of us at least knows his home still exists."

There wasn't much to say after that. They went to bed soon after. Calladorn was too tired to bother undressing but had difficulty falling asleep even so. There were no good options that he could see. He admitted Chad's idea had merit, assuming prophecy could be trusted. Yet it seemed irresponsible to hang the fate of his nation on something so ephemeral.

As he drifted off, he found himself wondering why Matthias hadn't returned. The man might be insufferable, but he was also insightful. When he cared to share.

*

A scratching sound from the door brought him awake, and he rolled over to look. *Must be Matthias,* he thought through his sleep haze. A shadow moved in the crack of light under the door.

Several shadows.

A sense of wrongness settled around him, bringing Calladorn fully alert in an instant. He was already starting to move when the door burst open in an explosion of sound. Light streamed through the ruined door, silhouetting armed men. Soldiers. By instinct, Calladorn's sword was in hand, almost as if it had materialized there. He surged to his feet, the rough wool of the blanket sliding from beneath him. The room was already alive with chaos—shouting voices, the heavy stomp of boots. Chad stirred in the other bed, his movements sluggish with sleep, blinking blearily at the figures storming in.

Calladorn didn't hesitate. He struck. The nearest soldier barely had time to raise his arm before Calladorn's sword slammed against his bracer, the force sending the man staggering back. Another lunged from the left. Calladorn pivoted, parrying cleanly, the clash of steel ringing through the room. He was outnumbered, but he had trained for this. He stepped forward, keeping his movements tight, efficient—

Something hit him hard from the side. The force sent him crashing into the bedside table, wooden splinters digging into his arms. He barely had time to right himself before rough hands seized him, yanking him back. He twisted, slamming an elbow into a soldier's gut, earning a pained grunt, but another blow struck his knee, forcing him down. The sword was wrenched from his grip and clattered to the wooden floor.

He growled, struggling against the weight pressing down on him. A gauntleted fist drove into his ribs, knocking the breath from his lungs. Another pressed his face into the floor, pinning him. He heard Chad shout something—a protest, a curse—but Calladorn couldn't see him through the tangle of bodies and flickering torchlight.

Then the dull scrape of steel drawn across boards. A rush of movement.

Chad.

Calladorn twisted his head just enough to see him. Bare-chested, feet naked on the cold floor, his muscled body taut with tension. He held Calladorn's sword in both hands, his knuckles white around the hilt. His stance was wrong—too stiff, too eager—but there was no hesitation in his eyes.

A soldier lunged. Chad swung. The blade met steel, knocking the attacker's sword aside. The movement lacked the finesse of training but had both strength and the raw force of desperation. Another soldier stepped forward, blade raised. Chad pivoted too slowly, barely deflecting the strike, but he adjusted, shifting his grip, minding his footing—

For a moment, Calladorn almost believed he might hold them off. Then, from behind, a shadow moved.

"Behind you!" Calladorn shouted the warning, earning a painful blow to his kidney.

A sickening crack rang out. Chad's breath hitched—a sharp, strangled sound that made Calladorn's stomach lurch—then his body jolted forward before crumpling to the floor. The sword slipped from his hands as he collapsed onto the rough wood, breath escaping in a sharp exhalation.

Calladorn roared, his body jerking against his captors. A hand gripped his hair, slamming his face down again, and the taste of blood flooded his mouth. Boots shifted around him. Voices murmured, one issuing orders. The world tilted as he was hauled upright, arms wrenched behind his back. Chad's limp form remained sprawled on the floor, his chest rising and falling shallowly—still breathing. That was something, at least.

A sack was shoved over Calladorn's head, the rough fabric cutting off his vision. A sharp tug on his bindings forced him forward, and he stumbled as the soldiers began dragging him from the room.

"This one's heavy," someone said, grunting. "I say we gut him and be done with it."

"Orders were to bring them both," another voice said, harsh like gravel ground underfoot. "Do you really want to tell him you botched the job?"

Calladorn heard more straining. Then his vision exploded, and pain shot through his temple as something hard struck him from outside the hood.

He slipped into darkness.

Cold and shivering. *Why am I so cold?* This was followed a moment later by the realization that something reeked. Chad's eyes flickered open as he became aware of a pressure around his forehead, accompanied by a horrible throbbing on the back of his head. He moved to sit up, gasping as a stab of pain lanced down his neck. A shiver racked his body.

"Easy." Calladorn's voice. Gentle yet strained tightly. "You took a nasty blow."

His eyes flew open as the attack on the inn flooded back—Calladorn overpowered, his own attempt to take up the fight... *I guess that didn't go so well,* he thought, reaching gingerly to touch where he'd been struck from behind. His fingers came away wet.

"You were bleeding pretty badly when I bandaged you," Calladorn said, helping him sit up.

Chad's back brushed cold, rough stone, and he flinched.

"Here." Calladorn took off his uniform coat—already unbuttoned—and set it over Chad's bare shoulders. The man's white shirt was too short and was frayed at the waist rather than hemmed. Torn. An ugly-looking cut was visible on his side. It had bled a fair bit before scabbing.

"You used your shirt to bandage my head?" A confused mix of embarrassment and deep appreciation made him smile awkwardly.

Calladorn shrugged. "I didn't have many other options."

Chad realized he was right. They were in a small cell, maybe five feet by eight feet, with rough-hewn stone walls and a stone floor sparsely covered in dirty straw that clung to his bare feet. He sat on a wooden bench or cot that wobbled as he moved. No blanket. Two of the walls were iron bars. One looked into a similar, unoccupied cell. The other—

A somewhat larger room, about twenty feet by thirty feet, lit by three guttering candles in a free-standing candelabrum in the far corner, next to a wooden door reinforced with iron. A table stood in the center of the room, with brown stains and strange contraptions on it, and odd-looking cabinets lined the walls. Other than the sounds Chad and Calladorn made, the chamber was silent as the grave.

His nose wrinkled in disgust as he became aware again of the stink of the place. Piss, shit, and... *Blood?* He suddenly realized those stains on the table weren't water or mildew. His mouth went dry, and he swallowed hard. Paying closer attention to the other furniture, his heart sank as he came to understand what those items were for. Torture.

"Oh... crap," he croaked.

The cot wobbled again as Calladorn sat next to him. "I think we should have heeded Matthias's warnings."

"Do you know where we are? How long we've been here?" Chad's mind raced, struggling to make sense of their sudden change of fortunes.

Calladorn shook his head. "I don't think we're in the palace. We were both hooded when they wheeled us in here on some sort of cart, so I couldn't see anything. But I heard water, and it smelled noxious, like a sewer. My best guess is it's a secret prison. There's no light, but I'm guessing we've been here for a few hours now." He looked at Chad, his green eyes filled with compassion. "I was beginning to worry you might not wake."

Feeling awkward under the weight of that concern, Chad changed the subject. "Has anyone come in?"

"No."

"So we don't know who captured us, or why."

"They were palace guards."

Chad understood what that meant. "The High King," he said, his voice sounding hollow in his ears.

"The High King," Calladorn agreed.

But why? Chad wondered. They sure weren't a threat to him, whatever his goals were—not after the way he'd seen to it that they were laughed out of court. As he continued to look around the room, morbidly deciphering the purposes of the various instruments on display, he came to the sick certainty that anyone who had a private torture chamber had serious issues. Whatever game Elrath might be playing, it didn't necessarily have to have logical reasons.

Flies buzzed lazily in the far corner. Something lay beyond the table, just out of sight. Chad wondered if he even wanted to know what it was.

Another spasm racked him—this one having nothing to do with physical cold. A deep-seated fear began gnawing at his backbone. "Where the hell is Matthias, anyway?" Chad asked suddenly.

Calladorn's lips pressed tightly together. "I wish I knew."

He was too late. As the High King had known he would be.

Shadows flickered in the street outside the Royal Arms, and Matthias formed a darker shadow within them. Across the way, the innkeeper argued with a captain of the Syndaran guard, his mustache quivering.

"...furniture's in shambles. The door needs to be replaced. Its hinges are broken. Who's going to pay for the damages?"

The captain was a half-foot shorter, but his bearing made him seem the taller of the two. "You've been harboring traitors to the Crown. You're fortunate not to be in prison with them."

"Harboring?" Even in the lamplight, the man's skin paled. "I hardly knew them! That is to say... they rented a room for a few days. Nothing more."

The guard continued to stare, his expression stone.

The innkeeper melted further. "I'm sure you're just doing your duty. Don't mind me. It's been a long night, you understand?"

Matthias had heard enough. Tramping feet announced more soldiers coming from the King's Way. He moved silently back into the alley and considered. The High King would not kill them immediately; he would want to interrogate them—especially now that he knew about the Heart. The question was, where would they be held? Elrath would want something private, where he could come and go unobserved as well as avoid any complications from unwanted ears overhearing what he learned. That ruled out the palace dungeons. No, he would have a special place set up for this sort of thing.

Matthias had no doubt he could find it eventually, but time was a luxury he did not have. The High King would toy with his prey, playing mind games—he had always been sadistic. Eventually they would cease to be diverting and be disposed of, but only after he had learned everything they knew about the Heart of Necsis and the prophecy surrounding it. Calladorn was strong. His honor would prevent him from breaking. But the boy...

Time was limited. Matthias curled his lip in distaste. He would need to enlist outside help. But the Shadow Council would not be easily used.

He would need to move carefully, or they would hinder his plans as much as they helped. Perhaps even sell him out to the High King. That would be ironic. And inconvenient.

Matthias glided through shadowed alleys, at one point watching with amusement when a cat spied him and bolted into the narrow space between two buildings, its body low to the ground. It knew when a more dangerous predator was about.

He planned to return to the Royal Arms shortly before dawn, when the city was at its least wary, to see what belongings might be salvaged. The guards had most likely taken everything, but Matthias did not like to make assumptions. Until then, there were thieves he needed to contact, and a food chain to climb.

Why do I bother? he briefly wondered. It was going to require considerable effort to save those two. Was it worth it?

An insidious thought struck him unexpectedly. *Have I actually come to like them?* He dismissed the notion immediately. He was doing this because Chad was essential to the prophecy and, therefore, to his mission.

But the voice refused to be silenced completely. Instead, it whispered. *Can it not be both?*

Ignoring the matter—ignoring what it implied—he slid into the city's lower districts. Time was too short for... morality.

XIX
Gambit

They were trapped.

Evan crouched next to Rick and Gharn near the foot of the cliff, among the largest remaining chunks of the ruined tower. Its foundation stones had been massive and were now piled haphazardly against the cliff face, forming numerous hollows and small caves, which lay in deep shadow under the large moon's pale light. It would be perhaps another hour before the small, brighter moon rose, increasing the chances they would be discovered.

From their hiding place, they had views of both the tower grounds—buried under rubble though they may be—and the long, sloping valley to the north where the demon army massed. It had been an hour now, and still they came from the western forest like locusts swarming a field—an hour of cowering while a scouting party milled around what remained of the tower.

That they hadn't been noticed yet was blind luck. The entrance to the hidden chamber hadn't closed behind them, and the scouts spotted its dark opening almost immediately. They had focused their attention on it, investigating with obvious interest. Would they see the map in the sand? Evan realized they had done nothing to erase it before leaving. Would the demons recognize its importance if they found it? There was no way to know.

After exiting the chamber, they had fanned out to explore the rest of the ruin. The creatures were lean, primarily walking on muscular hind legs, but dropping onto all fours to clamber over rubble. Their movements were deliberate, economical. But also agile, possessing a feline grace. Evan suspected the monsters could move extremely fast when they wished to. Their limbs had barb-like protrusions, and their hands were wicked with long, thin fingers and sharp claws. Their heads were relatively small, each having two large and two small horns that seemed to be shaped uniquely for each individual. As for skin, it was dark brown or black and seemed chitinous, like an insect's exoskeleton. Hair grew like manes coming off their heads and down their backs in a variety of earthy colors. They were the definition of monstrous, even in the way they seemed to communicate with each other—low whistles and clicks.

Watching them, Evan chewed her lip. They were rapidly getting closer to the campsite. Would the demons be able to tell people had been there recently? That the coals of the fire were fresh?

"I don't think they can track by smell," Gharn whispered.

Evan looked at him. Unwilling to speak more than necessary, she questioned him with her eyes.

"They're searching blind."

She realized he was right. They would have gone directly from the secret entrance to the campsite. *Lucky*, she thought.

Rick wasn't even paying attention to the scouts. He was focused on the main army blocking their escape to the north, his finger moving in that absentminded way of his. Something in his expression shifted as he studied the battlefield, and he suddenly froze. Evan felt his mood change to resolution. He'd found something.

"Why are they avoiding the hills to the east?" he mumbled.

Gharn turned from the scouts, following Rick's gaze. He snorted—more like a puff of air past his mustache than actual sound. "Because that's a Shift." The gnome's eyes suddenly widened, and his face drained of color. "No," he said, his voice harsh despite his whisper. "We can't. There's no way to know how long until it changes."

"If we stay here, we'll be caught." Rick's voice was certain.

Evan licked her lips in thought. "We can't know that for sure."

He didn't bother to argue, merely raising his eyebrows at her before looking back at Gharn. "Is there an average duration? No, it wouldn't matter, since we don't know how long it has been since it last changed. But there are indicators before a change, right? Shimmering lights?"

"A Shift takes as much as two days to cross, but the warning lasts only an hour. If it changes while we're in the middle, we wouldn't have enough warning to get out in time. That's why nobody risks entering them unless exiled. It's madness."

Remembering Korvan—the Outlander in the Emberhold embassy—Evan felt her stomach clench. His fear at being banished to a Shift had been heartbreaking. She knew she should be backing Gharn up, but she also knew Rick would already have thought through every possible argument. He could be infuriating that way. The knowledge didn't stop her from trying to come up with something, but what options were there? The longer they stayed here, the higher the chances they would be found. They had to move, and there was no other route available. "I would rather be stranded somewhere else, alive, than caught," she said at last.

"We don't have to cross it," Rick said. "We only have to get far enough inside that they won't see us."

She hated it. Everything in her screamed not to trust a Shift. But Rick was right—and the risk of staying was worse. Swallowing hard, Evan nodded. Gharn's expression twisted, but his shoulders sagged. Murmuring a string of inventive curses under his breath, he nodded as well.

The decision was made.

Sneaking toward the Shift felt like creeping toward the edge of a blade. Gharn's nerves were taut as he kept his steps light, his breathing controlled. They slipped from one hollow in the rocks to the next, keeping in the shadows as much as possible. He wished he didn't feel like they were trading one disaster for another. A warbling, whistling cry came from over the rise behind them—from the ruin—and his breath caught. He didn't need to see to know...

They've found the campsite. "Faster," he hissed.

In the lead, Rick sprinted down the slope to another large debris pile, ducking into a dark opening. Gharn followed as fast as his bandy legs would allow, pumping his arms furiously. His foot slipped, and he went down with a grunt, only to feel a hand under his arm, pulling him back up and forward. Evan.

The opening between stones led through the pile. Rick had to crouch low, but they were able to get another twenty feet without risking exposure. Gharn's breath sounded like a gale in his ears. He wasn't sure if he was panting from the exertion or from fear. *Probably both,* he thought grimly.

Rick stopped so abruptly Gharn almost ran into him.

"Oh no."

They had reached the last of the rubble from the tower. Ahead, some boulders had fallen from the cliffs and tumbled down into the valley, but they were too few. Too far between. Worse, Intari—the small moon—was cresting the hills. The path ahead lay exposed, and they'd be dark silhouettes against its glow. Impossible to miss. Gharn felt the weight of defeat. He'd gone along with this mad plan, only to see it collapse before it even got started.

More fluting cries, somehow hauntingly beautiful despite the horror of their makers, came from behind. The sounds were clear now, rather than muffled.

"They're on the ridge," Evan whispered, pressing back against the stone she crouched under.

As he looked past her, Gharn's jaw clenched. Intari's light already shone brightly on the ridge, and six misbegotten shapes moved within it. They leaned first one way, then another, as if they were on the precipice of leaping into motion but unsure in which direction to go. One of them stepped forward, crouching low, examining the ground at its feet. Gharn closed his eyes, knowing what it was seeing. Footprints.

A sudden shriek split the air, making the hairs on the back of his neck stand up. His eyes snapped open again. But instead of demons leaping down the slope toward them, as he expected to see, the creatures were jerking in place. Snapping at something in the air. *A bird?* he thought, wonderingly. It was harrying the monsters.

Then came another. And another. Swooping down from above.

Then dozens. Then hundreds. They swarmed out of their nests in the ruins and the cliff walls. Their feathers reflecting the moonlight, they looked like a cloud of silvery blades slicing at the demons. Pecking and clawing, they struck with unnatural unity.

The night was filled with angry cries from both birds and monsters alike. The sound made Gharn tremble, even as he stood slack-jawed. He turned to the others, expecting to see their faces twisted in the same stunned confusion he felt. Instead, he saw Evan. Her eyes were closed, and a sparkle of perspiration shone on her forehead.

By the Three, Gharn thought. She was doing this. Not domination. Not fear. Just fierce, impossible defiance. Maybe that was what made a Thought Master. Her will gave them a miracle. Gharn's despair began turning to hope. But then he saw the way her jaw trembled. Her breathing was turning ragged. Alarm replaced awe. She wasn't going to last. This was a reprieve—nothing more.

Evan's eyes snapped open. "We need to hurry," she said, her voice rasping.

Rick's eyes met Gharn's. Sharing a nod, they moved together. Rick took Evan by one arm, and Gharn slipped underneath the other. They ran—toward the Shift. Toward the unknown.

Nearly imperceptible in the landscape, yet looming as if it were a wall, a line appeared.

Even in their panicked rush to escape the demons before Evan's trick ran out, Rick couldn't help analyzing the details as they entered the Shift. When they'd arrived in Drakerath, it was a volcanic region with little vegetation. As a result, the signs had been geological, such as sheared stones. Here the difference was in the vegetation. Colors were difficult to distinguish in the moonlight, but the grass of Endarl was a darker shade of gray, while that in the Shift was almost silvery. The blades themselves were finer as well, more delicate. There were also shrubs that reminded Rick of sagebrush, coming up to waist height. The group ducked down behind some and watched to see what would happen.

Rick was surprised to see how far they had actually come. The ridge with the demons was about a quarter-mile away. From this distance, the demons were indistinct black shapes in the silver moonlight, surrounded by what looked like an obscuring fog that boiled like a starling murmuration. *The birds.* It wasn't magic, but it was a powerful distraction and an impressive display of Evan's power. To control that many birds—there must have been hundreds—was an incredible feat. He couldn't imagine what it must take to do something like that.

The smile died from his lips as he realized the toll this was taking on her. Evan's hair was plastered to her forehead by sweat, and the corners of her eyes were pulled tight. Now that they had stopped, he could feel her arm trembling in his grasp.

"Are you all right?" he asked, suddenly worried.

Her lips pressed together tightly, and she nodded—two quick jerks. Then, with a long sigh, she relaxed. Her shoulders slumped.

On the ridge, the cloud of birds scattered. Silence hung for a split second before the demon scouts howled. The sound was primal and full of gleeful malice.

Rick scarcely dared to breathe as he waited to see what would happen. Several of the shapes disappeared back the way they had come, down into the tower ruins beyond the ridge. Three did not. Dropping down to all fours, those few slowly began moving down the base of the cliff. *They're tracking us,* Rick realized, his fist closing tightly around the key chain in his pocket, the metal digging into his palm. "Move. Now!"

Staying as low to the ground as they could in order to make use of the cover provided by the brush, they continued deeper into the Shift. The air was different here. More humid, it felt thicker and had a pungent scent that made Rick think of oregano and mint. He hoped it would help mask their scent, just in case the demons could track by smell.

Stealing a look at Evan as they ran, he was relieved to see she didn't look strained anymore. He hoped it had just been the act of concentration that had taken such a toll on her, rather than something more debilitating, like the Magecurse. One case of the walking wounded was enough.

The ground suddenly gave out underneath his foot, and he found himself rolling down a slope. Moments later he rolled to a stop—dirty but unaware of any pain beyond a scraped elbow.

"Rick! Are you okay?" Evan's call was low but urgent.

"Hush, girl!" Gharn cut her off with a hiss. Even in the moonlight, Rick could see the terror in his expression. He wondered which factored more strongly—the demons or the fact they were in a Shift.

"I'm fine." Rick realized he had fallen into a narrow channel where the ground dipped down about eight feet. Only a dozen feet across, it had been invisible in the brush until he'd stepped into it. The sides were steep but sloped, and the channel ran in a gradually curving line in either direction. He realized immediately that if they followed it, they wouldn't need to duck down to avoid being seen by the demons. They could move faster.

"Are they still following?" he whispered up at his companions.

Evan turned, poking her head up a bit, then dropped back down immediately. Grabbing Gharn, she pulled him down into the gully with her—and with much more grace than how Rick had done it. "They're at the edge of the Shift," she said. "But I don't think they're going to stay there."

"How far?"

"Not far enough," she replied, her eyes large.

I knew it was too much to hope for, Rick thought.

Turning left, away from the mountains, he led them at a jog down the trough. He hoped it had been created by geological means, because he definitely didn't want to meet a creature capable of digging this kind of channel.

The distinctive howls of demons carried on the warm air, and he decided such a creature was probably preferable to what followed. And he was absolutely certain that they were being followed. The hunt was on.

Evan's lungs burned.

The small moon's bright light lit the track through the low, rolling hills, making it easy to follow. They didn't run—that was something they wouldn't have been able to keep up for long, even without Gharn's shorter strides—but still, they maintained a punishing jog. The gully or trench they moved along twisted and turned in gradual curves, winding through the terrain. Every quarter-mile or so, it merged into or was joined by another just like it, until there was no keeping track of their route.

"It's a good thing," Rick commented at one such intersection while they caught their breath, and he chose the next route to take. "If it was just one, we'd be easy to follow. Now they have to guess."

"So do we," Gharn muttered, panting heavily.

Rick shook his head. "I'm using the moon's position to keep us moving generally north." He sounded certain, but there was something in the way his eyes darted between ground and sky that made Evan suspect it was an act.

She was grateful for the distraction of the flight, despite its dire circumstances. She felt frayed around the edges. Her burgeoning powers were developing so rapidly, and she wondered where this was all going.

She caught both Rick and Gharn looking at her oddly during their flight, sometimes while they traveled and other times as they took brief breaks. Each time, their expressions seemed to weigh the situation. Calculating. And each time, they looked away again as soon as they realized she'd noticed.

Rick, the man who had to know everything, seemed to avoid any mention of what had happened with the birds. He was probably afraid of what she'd done. Perhaps even more afraid of how she had done it. *Or is it me they are afraid of?* she wondered—not of her powers but of the person using those gifts.

Despite her worry, she avoided reaching out to feel what they might be thinking. She told herself doing that would be unethical—a line she was ever less willing to cross. But if she was honest with herself, she was just as afraid of what she might find out.

More than anything, she wished for guidance from the Thought Masters themselves. Things Gharn had said made it clear they operated under strict rules or laws. The more she discovered that she was capable of doing, the more she appreciated the necessity of strictures concerning what was allowed and what crossed into the forbidden. She hoped the Forbidden Spire would hold those kinds of answers.

But first they had to get there—an outcome that remained uncertain.

Alien howls still carried through the night, their distance and even direction impossible to determine while they remained within the deep rills.

*

The land changed around them, so gradually it was almost imperceptible. The grooves they followed no longer ran through a plain but rather cut between rock formations—hoodoo spires that pointed at the moon, like grasping fingers pushing up from the ground. Each was capped by a flat stone as if the elements had somehow eroded away everything except what was below it. The channels now turned at abrupt angles, zigzagging between the stony shapes. A gentle breeze slipped between them, sounding like the world itself was exhaling—a single never-ending sigh.

Rick stopped. Coming up beside him, Evan realized why. The gulch they were in came to an end just ahead, with formations rising on all three sides.

"We need to try a different route," he said, turning back.

Gharn muttered something under his breath, his eyes darting from point to point along the rim.

The farther they went, the more dead ends they encountered. Rick's jaw became tighter, and he took longer at each spot where they had to choose a direction, his fingers moving like he was drawing a map in his mind. Evan realized his confidence was eroding, just like the terrain around them.

"Do you think we're still following the edge of the Shift?" she asked him during one such stop.

He looked toward where they'd last been able to see the moon, which had been increasingly hidden behind stone spires. "I hope so. It's hard to tell with all these twists and turns."

"We're deeper than you think, boy," Gharn said. His eyes carried a wildness that became worse with each wrong turn, and when some sort of bird called, he nearly jumped out of his skin. Evan didn't need empathy to know he was terrified.

Worse than the concern they'd become turned around was the fact that they could no longer be sure where the horizon itself lay. If the Shift started preparing to change, would they even be able to see the light show? And if they could, were they close enough to make it out in time?

The worry piled higher as the night wore on, and with each time they had to double back to choose a new course. Not wanting to reinforce Gharn's fears, Evan kept her concerns to herself.

With each new corner they came around, she found herself searching for a point of reference that never came—while also fearing they would come face-to-face with their pursuers. She hoped it was just frayed nerves. But the sense of menace pressing at the edge of her thoughts wasn't going away. It wasn't loud—it was insistent. They no longer heard sounds of pursuit, yet the danger pushed at her consciousness with ever-increasing urgency.

*

A low rumble echoed between the spires, punctuated by loud clatters. All three of them froze, Evan grabbing Rick's shoulder to steady herself as her heart threatened to jump out of her throat.

"Is it the Shift?" she asked.

Taking measured breaths, Gharn shook his head. "They don't sound like that. That was something else."

A horrific cry split the air, like nails on a blackboard. It sounded like the demons but far worse. Gharn gasped, and Rick tensed in her grip, which she realized had clenched to white-knuckled tightness.

"Sorry," she croaked, releasing her grasp.

"It's okay. I think I about crapped myself there. What *was* that?"

The cry came again, softer this time—more distant, or maybe just weaker. The way it echoed off the formations made the direction difficult to figure out, but Evan thought it was from somewhere ahead. She tried to reach out with her perceptions, to see if she sensed anything, but all she got was the fear radiating off her companions. It was so overpowering she slammed her shields back into place immediately.

Rick looked at her questioningly, and she shook her head in reply. Something unreadable crossed his face. *Is that relief?* she wondered.

"We either continue forward or turn back," he whispered, and he took a tentative step in the direction they'd been traveling in.

They crept ahead to the next turn, where Rick peeked around the corner before waving for them to continue. The next corner was the same. On the third, he jerked his head back almost immediately.

"Something's there." He swallowed hard.

Evan looked for herself, leaning out an inch at a time until she could see. There was a rockfall from the right side of the gully, looking as if some of the spires had collapsed. At the edge of the debris, something was partly covered by stones and earth. Something black.

It moved.

Evan suppressed a cry of alarm and ducked back. "It's a demon," she breathed.

As if in answer, the fluting cry came again, both harsh and musical. It sounded quieter, despite them now being almost at its source.

"I think it's trapped," she said.

With the surprise behind her, she dared another look. Sure enough, the monster was almost entirely buried under the landslide. Only its head and neck were exposed, along with what may have been a leg. Its movements seemed lethargic.

Not quite believing how much strength of will it required, Evan stepped forward.

"Are you crazy?" Rick hissed, but she waved his protests away.

If it was able to get free, she reasoned, *it would have already.* Even so, she crossed the fifty yards between them with one cautious step at a time. She knew it was foolish. They had no plan for if she was wrong.

"Why are we doing this?" Rick asked from just behind. His voice trembled, but he was with her.

"This is our best chance to learn more about them," she answered.

"And if the others are nearby?"

"I think they would have come already." Then again, she realized they could have been far away and hadn't gotten here yet. "Keep an eye out, just in case."

Rick favored her with a dark expression that warned they would be having words later, but he scanned the nearby spires.

"This is foolish, girl," Gharn muttered.

Evan shrugged, her eyes focused on the creature. A horrid stench like rotting meat assaulted her nose as she got close. The sound of its rapid breathing reminded her of air blown through a straw. It gurgled too. The triangular head lifted as she approached, turning to regard her balefully from four eyes that seemed to burn with hatred. There were spiracles along its neck—the source of the noise—which rotated like a chameleon's eyes. Its jaws held interlocking pincers.

"They do have an exoskeleton," Rick said, sounding intrigued.

Evan nodded, pointing to where part of it had snapped open under the pressure of collapsing rocks. Meat and—organs?—could be seen within. Wrinkling her nose, she realized that was the source of the awful smell.

The creature chittered alien sounds, and its mandibles snapped. She shuddered, remembering her vision on the night they'd fled Emberhold. As much as she wanted to feel sympathy for any living thing in pain—as this creature obviously was—she knew it wouldn't hesitate to slaughter any of them if their positions had been reversed.

"How did it get like this?" Gharn asked, studying the top of the collapse. "Do you think it was trying to climb over from the other side? Jumping from spire to spire?"

Evan was more concerned with the demon itself. Maintaining a safe distance, she braced herself mentally and then opened her mind, reaching out to the monster. She found silence. There wasn't even a sense of presence. Instead, it was like a hole existed in the landscape in front of her, swallowing her senses and returning nothing.

"Damn," she muttered. Seeing Rick watching her with one eyebrow raised, she shrugged. "Either they're so alien I can't read them, or they have the world's best shields." Closing her eyes, she sighed. "This was a waste."

"Not if it teaches us something," Rick answered, his voice hard. He mumbled indistinct words.

Evan opened her eyes in time to witness the demon shudder in a massive spasm that shook the stones it was crushed under. It went rigid, and steam suddenly burst out of its spiracles with an awful hiss, then from every joint in its exoskeleton. The black eyes turned white before shriveling in their sockets. With several popping sounds, the creature collapsed and went still.

"We just learned they're not invincible," Rick said, his expression blank.

Gharn ran a hand through his thinning hair. "Can we go now?" He was right. They still had to get out of the Shift. And there were still at least two more demons hunting them.

As if answering her thoughts, a demon's call rose faintly through the air—pushing them into motion.

*

Night was nearly over by the time they emerged from the spired formations. Sounds of demon pursuit had faded as the night continued, and now the glow of dawn arriving far to the east brought a rueful chuckle to Evan's lips.

Rick looked at her questioningly, and she smiled. "Nothing," she said. "I just... We have a habit of spending nights running from demons." He rolled his eyes.

As soon as they could climb without risking bringing a landslide down on top of them, they scrambled up to where they could get a view of the surrounding landscape.

Gharn immediately groaned. "I was right. We've come too far in."

Evan's heart sank when she looked to the west, where mountaintops were just catching the sun's first rays. That range—the western edge of Endarl—was at least forty miles away. Instead of following the peaks north, the group had been forced considerably farther east.

Exhaustion sank into her bones, and she dropped to the ground in disgust. "How bad is it?" she asked, knowing only that it would be worse than what she wanted to hear.

Rick looked back behind them, at the miles of rugged terrain and the mountains in the far distance that marked the location of Southwatch. He rubbed his nostrils as if he had an itch. "About fifteen miles altogether—twelve north, maybe eight east."

"Might as well be in the middle of the Shift," Gharn growled.

"At least it is still the Shift," Rick said with surprising calm.

Gharn seemed about to say something but instead slid his pack off and rummaged in it, bringing out trail rations. After giving a handful of the mixed fruit and nuts to each of them, he sat on the ground, leaning against the pack. "What now?"

Rick stared into the distance as he chewed. "The smartest move is to go west. It's the shortest route back to safe land."

Evan knew that tone. "But?" she asked.

"The demon army has probably been marching north. We could be walking right back into them."

"So... what?" She eyed the way he crouched—a mix of resolve and exhaustion. "You want to go east?"

He shrugged. "Or northeast. The problem is, it's twice as far, and we're already exhausted."

"What about farther north?" she asked.

"It's hundreds of miles of Shifts that way." Gharn thumped one fist on the ground in a slow, steady rhythm, his expression tense but determined. "We're already committed to this foolishness. But that's an insane risk."

"So is heading back toward where we know the demons are going," Rick answered.

Gharn glowered at him but stayed silent.

"Evan?" Rick asked.

An interesting idea came to her mind, and she wrestled with the question of whether to suggest it. "I might be able to help us move faster," she said at last.

Rick's eyes narrowed.

She almost changed her mind but chose instead to press on. "You remember how I healed Gharn's injury with the ghost trees? I might be able to do the same thing for exhaustion."

"Why didn't you suggest this sooner?" he asked, his voice low.

"I saw how you looked at me after the bird distraction," she said, knowing her tone sounded defensive.

His eyebrows shot up. "What? Looked at you? I... Evan, I was impressed. You saved our asses with that."

Gharn was nodding his head vigorously.

Evan stared at them in mute shock. Of all the things she had thought Rick might say, this wasn't one of them. *How did I misread him that badly?* she wondered. But it was also a breakthrough. For the first time in a very long time, Evan felt *seen*. It felt good.

They had been running for hours. Gharn's lungs heaved, and his throat felt raw, his breath coming in gasps. Rick and Evan ran a few strides behind, letting him set the pace. He hated it. The idea he was slowing them down was infuriating, despite the reality that he had to take two steps for every one of Evan's. But his desperation to escape the Shift gave him determination, even as Evan's ministrations gave him the strength to continue.

It was amazing. Every time he thought he'd reached his limit and could go no farther, they stopped. She would put her hands to his temples, close her eyes, and he could feel the exhaustion drain away, along with the aches in his chest and feet, and the cramps in his legs. A minute later he would feel as fresh as if he'd just woken up from a full night's sleep.

The transformation was more than physical. It was also mental—his alertness heightening, his fortitude strengthening. Colors seemed more distinct and purer, the silvery sheen to the leaves on the plants surrounding them glittering in the sunlight. Sounds were more pronounced, from the rustling of their clothes to the buzzing of alien insects. He could smell the iron in the dust carried by the air, taste it on his tongue, and feel the breeze moving past his face while he ran as if he stood in a gale.

Watching her do the same thing with Rick was incredible. Slumped on the ground in front of her, he would look ready to collapse. His entire body would sag as he took in air with huge gasps. But under Evan's touch, the haggard lines of his face faded, his breathing became measured, and his slouch disappeared. One moment, his eyes were dull and listless. Then, in a single blink, they would be bright and alert.

And on they would run. Miles were eaten up at a pace he would never have believed possible, scrub growth giving way to low trees that grew out rather than up. Their leaves were a drab green that flashed silver when the light struck them just right, causing each plant to shimmer in the breeze.

Far ahead the deeper emerald of Endarl's forests broke the horizon—no shimmer to their leaves, only shadowed promise. They drew steadily closer, but far too slowly for Gharn's nerves. Now that they seemed to have left the demons behind, he should have felt safe. Instead, he felt as if they were being stalked by another predator, only this one was invisible and far more merciless. Time slipped away from them.

Gharn was living a childhood nightmare come to life. Every child of Necsis knew the Shifts were to be avoided at all costs. Each town had stories of children who'd lost track of where they were while playing or had thought to prove their bravery by entering a Shift, only to vanish forever, lost to another world. Even villages days away from the nearest Shift shared this dread. Parents taught their children to never do what Gharn and his companions were now attempting. The Shifts were an enemy that could never be defeated. Now, running through one, Gharn felt like he was inside a massive trap that could spring shut at the slightest misstep.

As the morning sun climbed halfway to its zenith, their situation became more desperate. Gharn realized they were having to make more frequent stops so that Evan could ease their exhaustion. There was apparently only so much a Thought Master could do to push the body beyond its normal limits. And Evan herself looked increasingly run down. Twice now she had collapsed and had to be hauled back to her feet by Rick and Gharn.

"It works differently for me," she said when asked about it during one of their brief breaks. "I can't take away my own exhaustion. I have to push my body harder instead."

Listening to her explanation, Gharn frowned. It didn't make sense. But then, very little about her seemed to anymore. He had the uneasy feeling she wasn't telling them something.

"How much farther?" he asked as the sun approached its apex.

"About five miles, I think," Rick croaked, his voice hoarse despite having just been treated by Evan fifteen minutes earlier.

Gharn sat in stunned disbelief. "How can that be? We've been running for hours."

"I... may have been wrong when I estimated our initial position."

When you guessed, you mean, Gharn thought grimly. An insidious thought crept in. *Are you guessing now?* It didn't matter. They were committed to this course. All they could do was press on.

A ripple in the air from somewhere ahead caught his attention. A surge of panic struck him like a fist to the chest, but when nothing more happened, he started to relax, dismissing it as a heat shimmer. But then another came, and his stomach dropped. Ahead, easily five miles away, the edge of the Shift was visible—the air could be seen. Which meant the Shift was activating.

Evan saw it too. "How long?" she asked.

"It usually takes an hour," Gharn answered, trying to run faster, forcing his arms into a quicker cadence in the hope his legs would move to keep up. Hoping he wouldn't throw himself off-balance by the attempt.

Usually. There was so much uncertainty in that word. Sometimes a Shift activated within minutes of the first signs.

"We're not going to make it," Gharn whispered to himself, his throat tightening.

Rick's boots skidded on loose grit as he caught Gharn and Evan, their combined weight nearly toppling him. Gharn had been trying to help carry Evan, but the gnome's legs had finally given out. Evan's eyes were half-lidded, her body limp, and sweat clung to her brow like morning dew. Her breath came in shallow, rattling gasps.

He was appalled by the sudden decline in her condition. It was too dramatic for simply having pushed her body beyond its normal limits. Almost like... He froze, studying her heart-shaped face and the dark circles under her eyes. She had said she couldn't take away her own fatigue like she could theirs, and now he understood why. She had been taking it into herself, and who, then, could take it from her? It had nowhere to go. She wasn't just burning her strength—she was burning her life. *How could I have been so stupid?* Rick's brain screamed the truth, and he wished he could take his exhaustion back from her. Time was running short—he could see it in the way the air shimmered and rippled ahead of them, a curtain of light rising like wispy tendrils from the ground ahead. Higher up, it was like a curtain of shattered glass, flickering and bending in on itself.

They were still at least three miles away, and the light show was growing more frenetic. And now Evan was spent, with nothing left for herself. A glance at Gharn revealed he was in little better shape, with bluish lips and feet that dragged with each step.

We're not going to make it. The entire world felt like it was collapsing into equations he couldn't balance.

No. He *would* balance them. He had to. He dropped to one knee and skimmed the terrain with his fingers, clearing dust in circular sweeps. He began drawing without thinking—angles, arcs, radii.

"Are you sure?" Gharn asked, his voice managing to sound both desperate and hopeful.

Rick raised a preemptive hand. "It's Low Magic..." The price would be mere days—a month at most. Returning to his calculations, he muttered his thought process with a voice that rasped, dry and raw. "Sine theta over time... Velocity normalized to shared center of mass... Compensate for drag..." He reached into the magic like it was a problem he'd rehearsed a thousand times, building a structure of intent in his mind.

The air cracked.

With a deep thrum, a circular plane of force erupted from the ground beneath him, translucent and glowing faintly blue around the edges, latticed with luminous vectors and curve annotations that shifted as the platform adjusted its balance. It halted a half-foot above the ground, some dirt and even an uprooted plant on its surface.

"On. Now," Rick snapped.

He leaped off the platform and helped Gharn haul Evan onto it. He was pleased to see that it didn't so much as wobble under their shifting weight as he moved them into position with Evan at the center. She lay propped up on one elbow, with Gharn holding her other hand in his. Rick stood just behind them, his feet spaced widely in order to help maintain balance for what came next. His eyes already scanned the way ahead, recalculating.

"Lift plus forward momentum. Start with one G; modulate over trajectory... Keep her steady... Rise fifteen feet to clear any vegetation..."

The disk began to rise, not just lifting but accelerating. A thrill surged through him as wind whipped past his face, dry and biting, and the terrain below blurred. His hands moved in precise patterns, trailing glowing mathematical sigils in the air. Every gesture etched another instruction into the spell's framework.

The disk surged forward. The forest edge—real trees, real safety—beckoned in the distance, beyond the Shift's edge. Each passing second brought it closer. The light display that was the hallmark of a Shift getting ready to trigger pulsed and swirled with increased activity, but it approached quickly now.

Rick let out a laugh—sharp, breathless, disbelieving. "It's working," he muttered. "It's actually working." *If Chad could see me now...* Rick pictured the cluttered workbench in his brother's room and the diagrams centered around his antigravity obsession. But Rick had done it. He had made it real.

He felt giddy. For once there was no fumbling, no hesitation, no social awkwardness. Just numbers, vectors, and force distributions. A world obeying his will. This was what he had always craved—not just understanding the rules but writing them. He imagined he could actually feel the equations humming beneath the surface of reality, responding to him. *Gravity? Velocity? Arbitrary!* With the right inputs, the right calculations, the world bent. He could carry them to safety. He could carry anyone. He could—

The wave hit.

It wasn't physical but temporal. A jolt through his spine, like every nerve ending had just snapped taut. His breath hitched. The air no longer tasted dry—it was metallic. His arms ached and knees trembled. Rick staggered for a moment on the platform, catching himself just before it dipped.

Time. He felt it as a weight behind his eyes. This was a Low Magic spell, little more than a precise application of trigonometry and vectors. Even the disk on which they floated was a simple product of precisely applied forces. He had known the cost needed to be paid. But that time washed over him all at once, flowing through his body and taking vitality away. His breath came in ragged bursts. The magic burned in his veins like wildfire, surging hot, then cold. The thrill began to decay into horror. Not just at the cost, which he'd willingly chosen to pay. Not just at the pain, which he'd expected. But this...

It felt good.

Even now—cells screaming, hands trembling with borrowed years—there was a hunger in his chest.

He could do anything. He could reshape the world. Why stop there? With enough time, enough study, enough control, they wouldn't even need the Heart. He could return them home himself.

A sharp gust staggered the platform. Gharn yelped, trying to shield Evan. The terrain below twisted sharply, and Rick saw it again—the boundary. The air sheared. Just like the car, its image burned into his memory, the impossibility of a missing front half.

The Shift would be a perfect cut across space. If they reached it even a second too late...

His stomach churned, imagining Evan cut in half, Gharn erased mid-step, **and himself flayed open by physics**. The thrill curdled into dread.

He needed to end this. Now. *We don't need motion,* he realized. *We need to not be here.*

His hands formed new gestures, fingers twitching like they were possessed. He stopped seeing the terrain. He saw the curve—their current position, a plotted point upon it. Their destination, another. He needed to remove the space between.

"Invert the plane," he whispered. "Minimize the distance. Let delta x approach zero. Let epsilon shrink."

Light coalesced at the disk's edge. A sharp shimmer like crackle glaze on a glass jar held at the moment before shattering. Evan moaned. Gharn gasped. Rick's heart raced.

"Integral dx over f(x)," he breathed, his fingers sketching gestures that stood in for what the tongue couldn't pronounce. Intent shaping connection. "Collapse the curve. Close the line."

The world ripped as they fell forward into a blinding light.

And as the Shift collapsed around them, time collapsed *through* him.

XX
Interrogation

Misery ruled the day.

The stone beneath Calladorn was cold, but he scarcely felt it. He sat on the floor with his back against the wall, arms resting on his knees, eyes fixed on the flickering torchlight dancing across the opposite wall. In this place, time had no meaning. There were no windows, no shifts in light, only the torch that never seemed to burn down, the fortresslike door, and the waiting. The stink hadn't faded—he'd just stopped noticing it. That bothered him more than the stench itself.

He didn't speak—not to Chad, seated on the rickety cot, not to himself. His mind cycled through the same useless circles. Who had captured them? Why? And where besides the palace would there be a dungeon, much less one with no guards posted, no food delivered, no sounds but their own breathing and the occasional scrabble of a rodent in the shadows? The lack of guards was especially ominous in its implication—whoever had put them here knew they weren't getting out.

He didn't want to believe it was the High King, but that made the most sense. Oakmont might be petty, but he was also habitually lazy. He wouldn't bother with this much effort or be this methodical. But there were others—more powerful lords in Syndar's court, with longer memories and sharper ambitions. Perhaps one of them had seen an opportunity to embarrass Oakmont by striking at a visiting envoy from Drakerath or to rattle the balance of power with an "incident."

A grim thought twisted in his mind: *Either way, it was a waste.* After the encounter in the palace's entry hall, the entire nobility would know that Calladorn and Oakmont were the furthest thing from allies. The only reason another party would remove Calladorn or Chad from the scene would be to curry favor with Oakmont, and the reality was he wasn't remotely important enough as a noble for that to be worthwhile. Calladorn had delivered his warning, been laughed out of court, and was now obsolete. As for Chad, as an Outlander, he had even less value. Which left the High King.

He also couldn't stop wondering what had happened to Matthias. The man had never returned to the inn after their audience—vanished, without a word. Had he fled? Been taken? Or was he playing his own game, waiting for the right moment to resurface? With Matthias, it was hard to tell.

Chad stirred in his huddle, picking a dirty straw into pieces and flinging them one by one through the bars that made up the cell's far wall. The young man didn't say much, but when he did, the words carried too much weight. Worry. Confusion. And a flicker of defiance that cut through both, like a blade refusing to dull. Calladorn had seen the same look before, in Eryck's eyes the day he'd stood in their father's study and declared he was joining the border companies. Afraid of the expected wrath but unyielding. Determined to go, even if it cost him everything.

It had.

If Calladorn had stepped in... if he'd said something... He shoved the thought aside. Now wasn't the time. The past couldn't help them, and the present needed to be survived.

The sound of wood sliding across metal came from the direction of the door, which then opened with a low groan. Calladorn hadn't heard anyone approach but was on his feet in the span of a breath. His rigid posture wasn't a matter of pride—not here in this place—but a reflex, a soldier's instinct. Beside him, Chad scrambled upright, dropping what remained of the straw.

The man who entered the chamber was alone. High King Elrath. Calladorn groaned inwardly at having his suspicions confirmed. Despite everything, he had hoped.

As the man entered, his eyes didn't search the room. They focused directly on the prisoners, a faint half-smile twitching the corner of his mouth. Moving with a slowness that could only be deliberate, he closed the door behind him with a clanging thud. The torchlight reacted to his presence, flaring in the disturbed air.

Despite his deflated spirits, Calladorn saw a chance. The High King was alone, without even a weapon at his side. If an opportunity could be created...

Calladorn put a hand on Chad's shoulder, trying to make it look like a simple gesture, but with pressure to hold him back from stepping forward. The boy chose to sit down, leaning forward with his hands clasped in front of him, elbows on his knees. *Good lad,* Calladorn thought, keeping his expression neutral. He took a half-step toward the front of the cell and to one side, putting more space between Chad and him while also staying a yard back from the front of the cell. Trying to ignore the sudden pounding of his heart, he asked, "Why are we here?"

The High King didn't answer. Folding his hands behind his back, he approached slowly, head tilted to one side like a predator bird eyeing a hare. He stopped a few feet away from the cell, then turned in a languid circle, seemingly making a point of examining the torture devices one by one until he finally came back around to study Calladorn with cold gray eyes.

Calladorn tried again, louder. "There are demons in the kingdoms. This young man watched Emberhold burn. I was there when Ironspire fell. Syrillia faces threats as well, and the enemy is moving into Wester through the wetlands. The Nine Kingdoms stand on a precipice."

"Do they?" the man said at last, his voice thin and reedy. "How tragic." His tone wasn't merely indifferent—it was laced with disdain.

Balling his hands into fists to stop his fingers from trembling with suppressed fury, Calladorn stared at Elrath. "You have no idea what's coming," he said through clenched jaws.

"But I do," the High King murmured. "I always have."

Something about the way he said this took Calladorn aback. The answer was too smooth. Too certain. Chad's intake of breath said he'd noticed too.

"Then why ignore the warnings?" Calladorn demanded. "Why imprison us?"

Chad's question came at nearly the same moment: "What game are you playing?"

Producing a key, the High King fit it into the cell door's lock. "Because," he said, "I'm not ready for Syndar to know."

There was a click. The cell door creaked open.

Calladorn didn't wait—he surged forward. The High King didn't flinch. Neither did Chad. The younger man was only half a heartbeat behind him, fury and confusion burning in his eyes. Together they tackled the High King, forcing him back into the chamber, slamming him into the central stone table with a bone-jarring thud.

They had him. Calladorn's forearm pressed against Elrath's throat, his other hand pinning the High King's right hand to the table. Chad pinned his other arm, throwing his full weight into it. Elrath stared into Calladorn's eyes, still betraying not a wisp of emotion. He might have been sitting in his own throne room rather than splayed helplessly against a stone table. His body felt loose. Calladorn's hackles rose. The High King's body was too relaxed. Too still. Something was very wrong.

And then the High King laughed. Low. Mocking. Too deep.

Calladorn felt it before he saw it—a ripple beneath his grip as the man's muscles swelled unnaturally. The smirk widened, and the flesh began to twist. The features of his face melted, and his eyes lost what little color they had, shifting to inky black pools. The neck beneath Calladorn's arm thickened into exaggerated musculature, and his skin toughened into dark leather like a well-cured hide. There was the sound of tearing fabric. And a gasp—Calladorn wasn't sure if it was Chad's or his own. He struggled to maintain his hold, but the High King was gone. In his place was *something else*.

Moving as if it wasn't hampered in the least by its two strong opponents, the figure rose to full height, towering so that Calladorn's head barely reached its chest. Its face was no longer human, with a mouth split too wide and vertical slits where the nose should have been. There were no ears, and the eyes were lidless orbs.

"You're a demon," Chad whispered.

"An amusing name," the monster said with a voice that rumbled like distant thunder. Despite Calladorn's best efforts to keep the hand pinned, it reached up and grabbed him by the throat, squeezing painfully. The arm was massive, with a wrist so thick Calladorn could barely get both hands around it as he struggled. Out of the corner of his eye, he saw Chad similarly held.

The creature lifted them like dolls, one in each hand, and flung them bodily back into the cell. The door slammed shut with a clang that echoed in the silence that followed. Calladorn lay stunned, unable to move. He could barely breathe. One of Chad's legs was sprawled across his own, and Calladorn felt it jerk as he fought for breath as well.

The demon approached the bars again, the smirk somehow still that of the High King. "You were always going to fail," it said softly. "Syndar fell long before your arrival. Its nobles squabble like crows over carrion, each more eager than the last to grasp at influence I have promised. I play them against each other while my armies hamstring them from their borders."

Calladorn stared up at him, horror and rage burning in equal measure.

"Your warning was an inconvenience, nothing more," it continued. "As long as it remains ignored."

Sitting up slowly, Calladorn's breath returned in ragged pulls as he massaged his tortured throat. The reality of the situation settled over him like a weight. Not just defeat. Something deeper. Something insidious.

He swallowed. "You've been toying with us... since the audience."

The demon's smile broadened. Its shoulders rippled as the monstrous form began to twist once more, shrinking and folding back into the form of the High King. Except for the fur-trimmed cape across his shoulders, his once-fine clothes hung in tatters from a sexless body.

Calladorn's blood ran cold.

"You never had a chance," Elrath stated, his voice still deep and ominous. "You were chasing a ghost through a kingdom already lost." Settling the cloak more regally across his shoulders, he began walking toward the door. "When I return, we'll talk again. I'll have questions. And you will answer—I promise you."

The door groaned open.

Calladorn forced himself upright, using the bars for support. "Elrath!" he shouted.

The figure paused, then turned. His expression settled back into that indolent smirk he had worn in the audience hall. "Elrath? That pathetic creature lies over there." He gestured with a lazy flick toward the darkened corner of the room. "I am Maltharok." And then he was gone, the door closing behind him.

Calladorn stared at the corner beyond the table, where flies buzzed lazily. A cold sweat clung to his neck.

Maltharok. Calladorn pressed his forehead into the bars, their cold hardness pushing back painfully as he closed his eyes. He hadn't failed the mission after all. It was worse than that.

The mission had never mattered in the first place.

Chad's head swam. First, the revelation that the High King was a shapeshifting demon, then almost getting brained on the rough stone floor when the monster had thrown him like a roided-out defensive tackle. Groaning, he reached up to gingerly touch the back of his head, still wrapped in the bandage fashioned from Calladorn's shirt. It was painful to the touch, and he winced, but his hand fortunately came away dry. No fresh blood.

How did he even do that? he wondered. Could all demons change form?

A fly's buzz brought his eyes flying open. "Ironspire!"

Calladorn reached down to help him up. "What?"

The movement brought a stab of blinding pain, and Chad collapsed back onto the cot with a grunt. "Let's not do that again," he said, blinking until the two Calladorns blurred back into one.

"Are you all right?" Calladorn examined him like a doctor, slipping the borrowed coat down to check his back for scrapes. Chad flinched involuntarily at the touch, and he jerked his hand away. "I'm sorry."

Chad wanted to laugh but was afraid it would set his head to swimming again. "Your fingers are cold is all. What's the damage?"

Helping lift the jacket back into place, Calladorn smiled. "You'll live. For now." The smile faded again.

"If we get out of this, I'll have to add 'survived a medieval torture dungeon' right at the top of my résumé."

Calladorn didn't laugh. As he joined him on the cot, his expression was serious. "You don't have to be strong all the time," he murmured.

Silence stretched between them as Chad searched his face, reading the kindness in those eyes. The compassion. He could almost forget the torture racks waiting just outside their cell. Almost. "I'm afraid," he admitted to both of them. Barely more than a whisper, the words still felt more real than he wished.

The ghost of a smile touched Calladorn's expression, and he nodded once. "Me too." He leaned back against the wall, tilting his head back and closing his eyes. For a moment, Chad thought he was falling asleep, but then he spoke again. "What was that about Ironspire?"

Chad had almost forgotten—but now the lazy sounds drifting from the far corner of the room were all he could hear. "Oh yeah! Remember how your king, um..."

"Arlos?"

"Yeah. King Arlos. He was acting weird, right? What if he's a demon too?"

Calladorn's face grew very still as he digested the idea. "I think you're right," he finally said. "But what it means is... unthinkable."

"You think the other rulers are impostors too?"

"Likely. Even if they're not plants, this threat is on a scale we've never imagined. It's not an attack from a random Shift. Somehow it's a true invasion, with a level of planning and coordination that shouldn't be possible." Calladorn's voice trembled. "It goes against everything we know about the Shifts." He looked pale as he tightly clung to the tattered edge of his uniform shirt.

Chad abruptly realized he was trembling. They both were.

*

The silence was worse than Calladorn's screams.

It had weight now, like wet wool pulled tight over the mouth and nose—smothering. It pressed into his ears and filled the hollow in his chest, scraping raw against the places where anger wanted to live but couldn't find air.

Calladorn hadn't moved since Maltharok had left this second time. He lay curled on his side on the cot, one arm tucked awkwardly beneath him, his breathing shallow and uneven. The streak of blood along his temple had started to dry but not the smear at his collarbone. That still glistened, dark and fresh, soaking through the already-tattered uniform shirt.

Chad knelt beside him, unsure what to touch. Everything looked like it would hurt. It was Chad's fault. If he'd just—*No,* he thought. *Don't go there.* The torchlight flickered as if it, too, wanted to look away.

"You're okay," Chad said softly. His voice cracked. "You're okay, Cal."

The man didn't answer, any more than he had spoken to Maltharok.

Chad had heard every word. Every question. Every scream. Each time, Maltharok had looked at Chad, smiling. Those were the only occasions when Chad had ever seen emotion in the man's eyes. No, not the man's. *The creature's.* The screams made his eyes come alive. Maltharok wanted Chad to know what would happen if he didn't talk.

And Calladorn hadn't talked—not yet.

But now Calladorn lay broken and bloody and *silent,* and all Chad could think was how calm he'd been when Maltharok had dragged him from the cell—how he'd walked with his head high and his shoulders squared like some half-dead paladin still clinging to honor because it was the only thing that couldn't be taken from him. Until it *was.*

"Damn it," Chad whispered, voice quavering. He reached out, lightly brushing the sweat-plastered hair from Calladorn's forehead. "Why didn't you just let me go first?"

He wanted to laugh, and maybe cry. His fingers were trembling. There was dried blood under his fingernails—he wasn't sure if it was his or Calladorn's. His own collar and neck were bruised beneath Calladorn's uniform coat where Maltharok had grabbed him earlier, just before choosing which of them to take.

Just before looking at Chad and *smiling.*

If fear had a scent, it was what now assaulted Chad's senses.

He looked again at the table in the middle of the room, its top glistening in the torchlight, yet another drop of blood running slowly down the edge, hanging, ready to drop at any moment and join the pool on the floor. He swallowed hard, despite his mouth being dry as bone.

The instruments strewn around the room hadn't even been used. Chad decided they were for show, meant to serve as a constant reminder of what lay in store. Maltharok's own hands had served as his tools, changing shape, hardening, sharpening... He seemed to enjoy sliding a finger just beneath the skin and—

No. Chad refused to think about it.

Somehow the fact that Maltharok had only transformed his hands and arms in those moments was even more terrifying. The rest of his body had remained human. The face had continued to smile. And he'd asked the same two questions. Over and over, like it was a riddle they just hadn't solved yet.

"Where are the other Outlanders?"

"Who do they travel with?"

Chad noticed what he had never asked. Nothing about why the other Outlanders weren't with them, or what they were doing—which meant he already knew somehow. It chilled Chad worse than the dungeon floor. Whatever the demon pretending to be the High King was, he was *intelligent.* Strategic. He wasn't interrogating for general information—he was seeking specific facts. Narrowing the variables, as Rick would have put it.

He knew about the Heart. How? Who could have told him?

Chad sighed. It didn't matter. Not as long as they remained trapped here. Life had narrowed his focus until the only thing with any real importance was survival. And Chad knew their survival would end the moment Maltharok learned what he wanted to know. But he had no idea how much longer they could keep resisting. At what point would the agony become so bad that death would be preferable?

Calladorn stirred.

Chad jerked upright. "Hey—hey, I've got you." He reached gently for the man's arm. "Don't move too fast, okay?"

A low groan answered him. Calladorn tried to sit up, then stopped, wincing. One of his wrists was starting to swell, turning a dark, mottled red-purple.

Chad's chest tightened. "You shouldn't have to—God, you didn't have to do that. I could've—"

"No," Calladorn rasped. His voice was barely audible, but it was fierce. One eye was swollen shut, but the other opened slowly, bloodshot and unfocused. "You couldn't."

They looked at each other in the flickering half-light, both of them shattered in different ways. Chad swallowed hard. For a second, he forgot about the pain. Forgot about the blood and the smell of burnt something that clung to Calladorn's clothes. All he saw was the man who'd kept his mouth shut through hours of pain. The man who had looked Maltharok in the eye and not begged. Chad understood Calladorn hadn't gone first to save them—but because it might save *Chad*. Not for long, but for a little longer.

He realized his hands were still on Calladorn's shoulders. He didn't feel like it would be right to pull away. "I don't... I... I think if I stay near you long enough, I might... learn how to be as brave as you."

He'd meant to say something else, but those were the only words he could muster.

*

Calladorn fell asleep after a while, and the hours dragged on, the only sounds being his groans every time he moved in his sleep and the growling of Chad's stomach. How long had it been? His mouth was so parched, and his lips had begun to crack painfully. Further proof that their lives only continued until Maltharok learned their secrets.

He felt weak from the lack of food, even a bit dizzy. Undoubtedly another part of the torture. Another way to wear them down so they'd talk.

Eventually the exhaustion became too much, and Chad drifted to sleep as well—still sitting upright, next to his friend.

Calladorn knew he was dreaming, because the pain was distant. Not gone—never gone—but softened by fog and darkness. The cold radiating from the stone walls. The rough wood of the cot on which he lay. A salty tang of blood in his mouth. The incongruity of a pillow beneath his head. Chad's voice, whispering something he couldn't make out, like a prayer mumbled behind a door; the sound of breathing that wasn't his.

Then the door groaned open, and the dream fled.

His eyes opened—the left one now only slightly swollen—in time to see Maltharok striding into the room like a shadow pretending to be a man. The torch beside the door flared in his presence, as it always did, like even the fire knew to fear him.

Mentally bracing himself to face more torture, Calladorn pictured himself going through his sword exercises. Centering himself. In his mind, he and Chad practiced them together. He felt his pulse slow from pounding to a steady thrum. As the demon opened the cell door, Calladorn tried to sit up but didn't make it far. His body refused the command to go more than up onto one elbow, and even that brought wheezing gasps of pain.

Abruptly Chad stood before the not-man, his bare torso grimed with dirt, pieces of straw clinging to the skin. He stood tall. Defiant. "Take me."

Maltharok paused, his head tilting faintly. He studied the young man as though deciding which part to break first.

Calladorn realized the pillow he'd slept on was his coat. Chad must have taken it off and placed it under his head as he slept.

"No." Calladorn tried to protest, but all that came out was a croak. The sound was ignored by both of them.

"How noble," Maltharok said. "Delicious."

He didn't *take* Chad. He stepped to the side and gestured as if inviting the young man into his chambers. A hand tremor was all that betrayed Chad's fear as he stepped forward. The cell door clanged shut, ringing like a death knell, and Calladorn's fist curled into the jacket's embroidered fabric. No one should have to be that brave.

The sounds began quickly. No screams—not at first. Instead, thuds. Grunts. The hiss of breath forced through clenched teeth. Even with eyes squeezed shut, Calladorn could see every motion played out for him in his mind. Every blow. Every choice not to cry out. He knew it would change. How could it be otherwise?

He turned his face to the wall. Not out of shame or because he looked down on Chad for what he knew must come. It was from respect—a way to protect Chad from the indignity of having his suffering witnessed.

Eventually, screams tore free, making Calladorn flinch and grit his teeth. Somehow this one was worse than the others. It wasn't the volume that got to him but the sound, like something ripping that wasn't meant to be torn. And then silence. Horrible, absolute silence. The kind that left too much room for the imagination.

He tried to stand. Failed. The world tilted, spinning until he almost believed he had fallen. Then—Chad's voice. Low. Hoarse. A name. "Evan."

Calladorn froze, a breath caught in his throat.

The silence from outside the cell deepened. When Maltharok's voice came again, it sounded slick and triumphant. "Evan. At last."

No, Calladorn thought impotently. *No, lad. Don't—*

But then Chad said something else. A quickly muttered string of nonsense.

Maltharok interrupted. "What?"

More words. Strange syllables. No rhythm or structure that made sense to Calladorn's ears.

Maltharok's tone shifted. Low. Dangerous. "What are you saying?"

Calladorn pushed himself up slightly, squinting through the bars. Chad was talking. A flood of speech now, fast and forceful—but in a tongue Calladorn had never heard before. It was rough, clipped, and utterly incomprehensible, like the warbled mutterings of a madman, or a prayer uttered backward.

"Speak sense!" Maltharok roared.

Chad didn't stop.

An image of a tailor's shop intruded on Calladorn's mind—and talk of birds. Suddenly he realized what Chad was doing. He was resisting—by telling the demon everything it wanted to know. Speaking with his own language—his real speech—rendering every answer meaningless. It was a verbal shield the demon couldn't pierce.

Calladorn couldn't help it. He laughed. It was a dry, rasping sound that tore his throat on the way out, but it was genuine. *Gods!* The lad was brilliant. Smart, stubborn, and brave in a way that didn't require swords.

Chad turned slightly as if hearing him—and in that second, Calladorn saw in the intensity of those eyes what he hadn't before. The young man wasn't just protecting Rick and Evan. He wasn't just protecting Calladorn. He was protecting all of Necsis.

Maltharok followed the lad's gaze. His expression didn't change, but the air in the room seemed to take on weight, closing around them like a vise.

"So. This is what it comes to," the demon said. He crossed the room in a smooth glide, and wrenched the cell door open, the metal groaning under his pull. Before Calladorn could react, Maltharok's hand—suddenly massive and clawed—closed around his throat and lifted him from the cot. Calladorn grabbed futilely at a wrist that felt like a tree trunk. His legs kicked uselessly, feet trying to find the floor.

"You've made him bold," Maltharok whispered. "Let's see how long that lasts without you."

The monstrous hand flexed, sharp nails sinking into the soft skin of Calladorn's neck. Pain exploded through his ribs. He struggled, but there was no air. No leverage. Even as he felt his eyes bulging in their sockets, his vision began to contract as if he were retreating down an endless black tunnel.

Through the haze, he saw Chad move. "No!" Chad's voice was raw, like the words were being ripped from his throat. "Don't—please!"

Maltharok paused.

Calladorn tried to protest. Wanted desperately to tell him it was a mistake. But his throat was compressed too tightly to make a sound.

"Tell me," Maltharok murmured.

Chad's mouth opened. Closed. Then, "They're going to Haven." Calladorn heard it—the careful wording. Not everything. Just enough to keep Calladorn alive.

A heartbeat passed. Calladorn hit the floor in a heap, gasping, his hands instinctively going protectively to his throat.

Maltharok turned slowly, his shadow dragging behind him like a second body. "Where is it?"

Chad's face contorted. For a fleeting moment, Calladorn thought he might defy the demon again. But the fight had left him. "I don't know," Chad rasped. "I only know where I'm supposed to meet them."

A long silence, in which the only sound was a small splash—a tear striking the table on which Chad lay.

"Where?"

Chad's eyes were closed. His head drooped low. "Ravensford," he whispered.

Maltharok folded his hands—again those of a normal human—in front of himself. He smiled. "You've been very helpful."

He walked across the chamber, sparing the defeated Chad barely a glance on the way out. He didn't even bother to lock them in their cell again. Pausing at the room's reinforced door, he looked back. "Rest now. You'll need your strength for what comes next."

As the door closed behind him, its groan was echoed by Chad. Calladorn lay on the stone floor, coughing weakly, straw poking into his cheek, and not caring how uncomfortable it was. His vision was still blurred, but he saw Chad roll off the table and climb unsteadily to his feet, then stagger back into the cell, where he sank down onto the floor. His back was against the wall—every cut, every bruise garish in the torchlight.

The strength was gone from him, as if his muscles had collapsed in on themselves. Just a boy again. No shields. No cleverness. Broken. But still alive. And still here.

Calladorn reached for him. "It's all right," he whispered.

Chad didn't answer.

Calladorn's hand found a bare foot. Enfolding the arch, he gave a gentle squeeze. And passed out.

*

The pain came in waves now.

Not from the bruises or the clawed neck—not even from the aches of the tortures he had endured. No, this pain was different. He could feel it in the air between them.

Chad still sat slumped against the wall, arms resting limply over his knees, face hidden behind a curtain of tousled hair now as dirty as the scattered straw. His nearly hairless chest rose and fell, but each breath looked like it cost him something. He hadn't moved in what felt like hours.

Maybe it has been hours. The lack of any light other than what the torch provided was getting to him. Calladorn shifted, grimacing at the spike of pain in his side, and eased himself upright. "You did well," he said softly, trying to emphasize each word as he spoke it.

Chad flinched. Nothing more.

"I mean it." Calladorn let silence settle a moment, giving the words space to breathe. "There's no shame in what happened."

"You don't have to say that," Chad mumbled without looking up. "I gave him what he wanted."

"Chad, listen to me. Physical torture... it doesn't work. Your mind walls it off. You pass out or you die. But when it's someone you care about who's being threatened—no one can withstand that."

Chad's breathing slowed some, becoming steadier. But still, he didn't look up. "You're—" He swallowed. "You're not the one who broke," he whispered. His chin quivered.

Calladorn took a deep breath, considering his next words carefully. "I would have. If you had been the one about to die."

Every muscle in Chad's body seemed to tense, then slowly relaxed. His head lifted, revealing a tear-stained face and searching eyes.

Calladorn smiled thinly. "You endured far more than any man should have to. You even outwitted him for a bit. And in the end, you bought us time."

He climbed to his feet, doing his best to ignore the pain, then extended his hand. "I'm surprised it took him so long to try that tactic."

"I think he was enjoying the torture too much," Chad said through clenched teeth. He took Calladorn's proffered hand, though, clasping him by the wrist and allowing himself to be helped to his feet. They hobbled together to the cot and sat down, both moving as awkwardly as newborn calves. Neither spoke for a time.

"How do you stay strong?" Chad asked at last.

Calladorn looked at him, one eyebrow rising, both pinching tighter together. He searched for an answer. "Remember me mentioning Eryck?"

Chad tensed. "Your *kid* brother. Yeah."

"He, Gallus, and I were inseparable as children. Gallus was four years older than me and a natural leader. Eryck idolized him. He taught us both how to swing a sword. The same discipline I've been teaching you."

"I get it. You see me as your little brother." Chad's voice was bitter.

"I did," Calladorn answered honestly. "Now let me finish. When he was old enough, Gallus enlisted, then rose through the ranks quickly and was given a command in the blasted lands above the Landrise. When Eryck turned fourteen, he decided to enlist as well. Father was furious. I was the one who was supposed to follow the family military tradition. Not Eryck, who he saw as being too soft. I... wasn't brave enough to face him and stayed out of it."

Now Chad was watching him, his expression searching. "What happened?"

"Eryck flourished. Got himself assigned to Gallus's command. They waged quite the campaign against bandits. Even Father was eventually proud of him. Until—"

Calladorn exhaled and reached into the tattered remnants of his coat. After a moment, he pulled something small from the inner pocket—a battered medal on a faded red ribbon, its edges worn smooth from repeated handling. He turned it over in his hand, struggling with the raw emotions welling up inside, heightened by the trauma they'd experienced in the place where they now sat.

"They eventually took on a stronghold too big for them to crack. Eryck died saving Gallus's life. This was what they gave us—my brother's worth, memorialized in a hunk of metal." He faced Chad. "Eryck died because I hadn't been the brave one. I enlisted the next day and have paid for my cowardice ever since, and I carry this medal with me to make sure I never make that mistake again."

"What about Gallus?" Chad asked.

Calladorn grunted. "His career dead-ended. After that action, he was never given a bigger command than Shift patrols. That's where you said you met him."

"He's dead now." Chad's voice was quiet. Expressionless.

"What?"

"The night the demons attacked Emberhold, Evan had a vision. She told me about it later." His mouth twisted. "It didn't sound pleasant."

Calladorn didn't know what to think. He'd hated Gallus even more than he'd hated himself, but Gallus had also been the one to find Chad after they'd come out of the Shift. *Life can be strange,* he decided, but the sentiment felt hollow.

"So, is that justice, then?" Chad asked.

Putting the medal back into its pocket, Calladorn shrugged and leaned back against the rough stone. "The universe doesn't balance its scales. We just tell ourselves it does."

Chad propped himself up against the wall beside him. They sat shoulder to shoulder, two broken men holding each other up with the only thing they had left: the fact they were still breathing.

Chad stirred awake, blinking against the ever-flickering torchlight. His head had fallen sideways during sleep, now resting in Calladorn's lap. The older man was still unconscious, his breaths shallow but steady, his face pale and drawn with exhaustion.

Embarrassed, Chad carefully sat up, mindful not to jostle him. His muscles protested the movement, every joint aching as if rusted. He shifted Calladorn gently down onto the cot, easing him flat with as much tenderness as he could manage.

Reaching for the coat they'd been trading back and forth, Chad hesitated. He started to refold it, intending to tuck it back beneath Calladorn's head like before. But then he paused. Calladorn was finally resting, he told himself, and disturbing him might wake him. So instead he slid his arms into the sleeves and pulled the jacket close. It smelled of old sweat and dried blood, but it was warm.

Maltharok hadn't even locked them back in the cell. They could move freely now. Not that it helped. The cell was open, but the dungeon was still a cage.

He circled the small room's central table, ignoring the blood caked on it and the crumpled heap of flesh in the far corner. Instead, he focused on the heavy wooden door barring their exit. No hinges on this side, no latch, just a thick slab of heavily reinforced timber braced—he knew—by a bar on the other side. He'd heard it each time Maltharok came and went—wood on metal, grinding and final.

Pressing his ear to the door, he hoped for a hint of what might lie beyond. Nothing. Peeking through the keyhole revealed only darkness.

Calladorn was still asleep on the cot, chest rising and falling in a shallow, uneven rhythm. Bruised. Beaten. But alive. He hadn't stirred. *He doesn't look like a soldier,* Chad thought. *Right now, he looks... human.*

Everything Calladorn had told him—the story of Gallus, of Eryck, of the guilt he carried—it hadn't made Chad think less of him. Totally the opposite. It made the man real. And for reasons Chad didn't quite understand, that made the admiration sink deeper. Sharper.

Bracing himself, Chad cast a look around the chamber, forcing himself to take in every detail. There had to be something they could use. Somehow. *Every problem has a solution,* he thought, even as he wondered what Rick would think if he could see them now.

Elrath—what was left of him—lay in the far corner.

Chad hadn't dared look earlier, not when it had still felt like hope might shatter if he did. But now...

The stench of the corpse had settled over the room like a second skin. What had once been regal was now ruined: bones cracked at odd angles, flesh not always attached to muscle. The head lolled sideways, mouth open in a soundless scream, eyes missing. Chad's body tried to retch at the sight, but there was nothing to bring up. He was suddenly, oddly, grateful to have been starved while they'd been here. Even so, a hint of bile lingered after his stomach stopped heaving.

Considering the state of the corpse, Maltharok hadn't kept them alive out of mercy. He was like the grade-school bully who liked to pull wings off flies. Only, for Maltharok, the flies walked on two legs. Chad felt a chill settle under the coat. It wasn't fear this time. It was something colder. Harder. *You should've killed us, you bastard,* he thought. *Leaving us alive was your first mistake.*

He limped toward the torture rack. Some of the scattered implements were little more than twisted tools—pincers, hooks, things he didn't want to name. But others could be weapons: a rusted poker, a splintered haft with a weighted head. Even broken, they had heft.

Still, what would it matter? The thing that wore a man's face had already shown them what he was. Claws like iron. Flesh that hardened at will. A monster that could smile while they screamed.

They wouldn't win. Not in a fight.

But maybe they didn't need to. Not if they could get out. If they could run. Maybe there was something here that could break out the lock. And from there, they might be able to reach through to slide the bar...

His hand closed around the poker.

Behind him, a soft sound—wood sliding over metal. Chad froze, his pulse quickening.

Calladorn stirred, and Chad padded quickly on bare feet to wake him up. They had to be ready. The man's eyes snapped wide at Chad's prodding. Groaning quietly, he pushed himself upright.

"He's back," Chad said, voice tight. He handed the poker to Calladorn, knowing he was the better fighter, then looked desperately for something he could use. *The knife!* Remembering it was still in his pocket—Maltharok had never bothered to take it, another example of his confidence—Chad chided himself for being an idiot. The last time Chad had used it against another living being had been in a street in Emberhold, and the experience had left him devastated. This time, Chad knew he would have no regrets.

What's taking so long? he wondered. It was strange that the door hadn't opened yet. Instead, there were scratching sounds.

Acting as one, the two of them moved into position, flanking the doorway. If they were going to die, it wouldn't be sitting down.

The sound stopped. Then, at last, the door creaked open. Chad felt his breath lodge in his throat. Waiting. Tension coiling in every muscle as he drew his hand back to strike.

But it wasn't Maltharok who stood there. It was Matthias.

He looked unruffled. Smug, even. A sword hung loosely in his hand, the tip resting on the stones. Beside him crouched a lean woman Chad had never seen before, her sharp eyes points of brightness beneath a heavy cowl.

Matthias took them in—blood, bruises, makeshift weapons—and smiled like a wolf. "Well?" he drawled. "Do you intend to escape? Or stand there gaping like mooncalves?"

XXI
Freedom

The stink of Syndar's underbelly was a living thing, tangy with piss, rotting citrus, and sweat baked into cracks in the stone. On the night following his companions' arrest, Matthias did not flinch from it. As much as he despised them, he knew these streets too well for that. He walked them like a man visiting old haunts, though he noted what had changed—the faulty oil lamp at the corner of Hasp's Alley, the soot stains that spread across the side of the tannery, the thready red sigils painted fresh above the door of the broken-toothed apothecary. Other men might have missed these details, but for Matthias they might as well have been signs. These territory markers told him someone new had laid claim to this block. He filed the information away.

The streets narrowed as he moved deeper into the city's bowels, into the warrens where light came only in trickles. Here the buildings were close together, and the walls huddled like conspirators, the upper levels of some coming close to touching. Shouts echoed above him from wooden balconies strung with drying laundry and watching eyes. The deeper he went, the more the city pressed in.

He passed beggars without seeing them. When a young boy with darting eyes brushed too close, Matthias turned his head just slightly—enough for the boy to see his face. The child's hand froze halfway toward Matthias's pocket. Although they had never before laid eyes on one another, each recognized the other for what he was.

The boy vanished. Word would spread now.

It was not long before he arrived at the gambling hall serving as a front for the Shadow Council. Tucked beneath the ruins of the old glassworks, its lanterns casting a sickly amber hue through the iron grate that served as a door. The guards outside tensed as he approached but did not move. One narrowed his eyes, while the other spat.

Matthias stepped inside, and the scent of sweat, pipe smoke, and old ale hit him like a wall. The room pulsed with noise—dice clattered; coins sang against stone; curses and laughter collided in the air. Around a central pit, a group of men cheered as a knife fight drew blood. The house did not care who won—it always took ten percent. He moved without hurry, cutting through the crowd. Some glanced up, then quickly looked away. One man stared too long. When Matthias met his eyes, the man blanched and turned his gaze to his drink.

Eventually he reached the back table, where four men had gathered —three seated around a pile of cards and chips, and one standing. They wore the mismatched armor of those too poor to buy a set and too dangerous for that to matter. Cutthroats. One had a faded tattoo that marked him as Syndar-born. Another wore an earring shaped like a wolf's fang—a sign of Brotherhood blood.

"You looking for someone?" the standing one asked, hand drifting near the blade at his hip, its talon-cast pommel marking him as a Raven.

"Yes," Matthias said, and he let that single syllable hang. He did not blink. Did not smile. "Your boss."

Tension settled over the table like a stained cloth. Matthias noted with amusement the way it spread to adjacent tables as well. The man seated to the left reached under his threadbare coat. The one on the right —older, and with a milky eye—shook his head. Slowly.

"You don't want that meeting, friend," the old one said in the distinctive cant of a Velsarian raider. "Last man to demand it lost an ear and a finger just for knocking."

Matthias turned his right hand so the palm faced toward them. His middle two fingers curled to touch the thumb while the two outer ones remained relaxed. "I am not knocking," Matthias replied.

A pause. Then, grudgingly, the man jerked his head toward the curtained stairway at the back. "Your funeral."

Matthias gave a short nod and turned toward it, the four men already dismissed from his mind. But not forgotten.

The stairway was narrow and steep, the kind meant to encourage second thoughts. Lanterns burned low in wall sconces, their oil thick and bitter-smelling. Matthias descended without hesitation. The air grew cooler, damp and musty, and the noise from the hall above faded behind him until all that remained was the creak of his boots and the occasional complaint of an indignant rat.

The passage opened into a small chamber lined with crates and mold-streaked kegs. A side door opened as he stepped forward, revealing a hunched man with a lamp in one hand and a short, broad-bladed axe in the other. His face was wrapped in a stained scarf, only his eyes—keen as the blade's edge—visible.

"This way," the man said, his voice muffled and rough.

Matthias followed without a word. They passed through a series of low tunnels, some shored with beams, others crumbling into damp earth. The stink of mildew and old blood clung to every surface. Twice, they stepped over broken bones. Once, they passed a chained door that rattled as something behind it dragged its nails across the metal.

Eventually they reached a rusted iron door. The guide knocked three times, waited, then twice more before the door opened inward with a groan. It revealed a room lit by hanging cages filled with glowstones—a nearly priceless commodity that would have been markedly out of place in the hall above. But not here.

Half a dozen armed men stood at attention. At their center sat a man on a wide-backed chair that had once been a merchant's throne. Behind him hung luxurious tapestries, the rest of the room garishly decorated with spoils liberated from Syndar's wealthiest. The seated man had the bulk of a brawler gone to seed, his gut straining against lacquered leather. Scars crisscrossed his exposed arms. His knuckles were swollen and tattooed.

As his gaze fixed on Matthias, his jaw set. "You?" the man said. "I thought you'd be taller."

Matthias studied him—the golden hoop earring, the scar running under his left cheek, the triple chins. "I thought you would be... more."

A chuckle rippled through the guards, quickly silenced. The Councillor—the name by which the leader of Syndar's thieving guild was known—tapped a ringed finger against the armrest. "You must want something very badly to walk in here alone."

"Information," Matthias said.

"Ask at any corner in Syndar," the Councillor said. "Information is traded like fleas between mutts."

"And so I come to the chief dog."

The finger froze in its tapping. More silence. "You are lucky I respect gall. Speak."

Matthias did. He laid out what he needed: access to any rumors, records, or whispers regarding a secret prison, vault, or dungeon beneath Syndar, followed by discreet passage to the east out of the city. He did not elaborate on why.

When Matthias finished, the Councillor leaned forward, elbows on knees. "That kind of knowledge is not cheap. And it takes time."

"You have two nights."

The guildmaster's mouth twitched, eventually forming into a smile devoid of warmth. "Arrogant."

"Efficient."

The man studied him for a long moment. Then he nodded. "Come back in two nights. We will have your information. And then we will learn if you have the means to pay for it."

Matthias was already turning before the man finished. He felt the weight of many eyes as he left—some curious, some hostile, a few wary. He did not care. They would do what he asked. He had seen it in the guildmaster's eyes—fear carefully buried beneath bluster. *Someone will pay, indeed,* he thought with a private smile. *And dearly.*

*

The Royal Arms had emptied by the time Matthias returned. Its taproom was quiet, the hearth low. Only the barkeep remained, wiping down glasses with an air of dull suspicion. The man looked up sharply as Matthias entered. Recognition flickered.

"You're the one who took out the front room," the innkeeper said, "with the two the guards dragged out."

Matthias did not answer. He simply extended his hand.

The man hesitated, then reached under the counter and produced a brass key. "Guards kicked the door in," he muttered. "Said your friends were traitors. Room's not cleared yet. Thought it best to wait, since you were the one who paid. Still have the coin for the week."

Matthias took the key. "Good."

The man leaned forward across the counter. "I expect compensation for the damages."

"You expected it from the guard captain as well." Matthias let the words hang and watched the man wilt. *Let him wonder how I know.* He turned before the barkeep could find his voice again.

Upstairs the door hung slightly ajar on a splintered frame. Inside, the room was dim, the curtains drawn. Broken wood from a shattered chair littered the floor. The other chair was overturned. The beds had been ransacked, blankets thrown aside but not removed. All three packs had been upended and left on the floor, their contents spilled and half-trampled.

Matthias stepped over the debris, his eyes already adjusting to the gloom, and began to work methodically, checking the floorboards first. The coin stash was still there. So was the hidden pouch at the bottom of Chad's pack, stitched into the lining with enough care to suggest the boy had expected trouble.

Clever, Matthias thought. *More than I gave him credit for.*

The boy's fine coat hung from the wall hook by the window, its silver embroidery catching the dim light seeping around the curtains. His boots slouched on the floor beneath it. Both went into his pack. Then he collected Calladorn's spare uniform from the floor, refolded it, and slid it into that man's rucksack, along with the rest of his belongings. Knowing the High King as he did, both of them would be in need of this clothing once they were rescued. Assuming there was anything left to rescue.

Matthias's eye twitched in irritation. He told himself this was all a matter of being practical. The boy was the key to the Heart and his plans. That was all that mattered. Calladorn, too, had value: a stabilizing influence, loyal to a fault. It would make him predictable and easy to manipulate—now that he had fallen on his honor, at least.

Elrath's interference was a complication. Nothing more.

Matthias did not sit. He finished his work and opened the curtains, then stood in shadow as he stared down at the street below. He did not light a candle. They would not be escaping without his help, and so there was no need of a beacon to guide them.

Distant voices called in the early dark as Syndar prepared for another night of revelry. They did not concern him.

*

Two nights later, his other preparations made, he returned.

The gambling hall pulsed with the same animal energy. New blood in the knife pit, new players at the tables, but the same guards watching him too closely from the back table, above the same pile of coins. Matthias ignored them all and descended the narrow stair again, his steps unhurried.

The guide from before was gone, but Matthias needed neither him nor the knock. They were waiting. This time, four new figures stood inside the Shadow Council's chamber, while the Councillor remained seated on his throne, ringed fingers laced before him. Matthias found it amusing—and irrelevant—that he had doubled his guards.

"You weren't followed," the Councillor said. It was not a question.

Matthias cocked his head. "What have you learned?"

The man grinned. "Old sewer line, near the Drywell Arch. Long collapsed, but there is a way through. It has served the guild well as a highway under the city—until a year ago. No one who enters returns. Not even rats."

Matthias did not care. "I require a guide. Someone who can pick locks."

The Councillor gestured. One of the figures stepped forward—a girl barely past twenty, wiry and watchful, with a knotted braid of dark hair and a knife tattoo under one eye.

"This is Lyn," the Councillor said. "Thief, climber, lockpick, occasional assassin. She knows the way."

Matthias studied her. Her stance was cocky, but her eyes flicked like a cutpurse's—marking exits, weighing risks. She would do.

He nodded, and the Councillor leaned back again. "Then all that remains is our payment."

Matthias turned to him fully. "I pay you with your life."

Silence fell like a dropped blade, and the guards stirred, their hands twitching toward weapons. One stepped forward. Meanwhile Matthias held the Councillor's stare. Men with far stronger backbones than this man had been cowed by the danger they read in Matthias's eyes when he wished it. And now Matthias did indeed wish it.

The Councillor's face curdled like week-old milk. He raised a trembling hand, and the guard halted. No one else moved.

Matthias nodded once to Lyn. "Now." They turned and left without another word. But he thought with some amusement that the Shadow Council might well "elect" a new master after this. They would certainly be better off.

*

They entered the sewer an hour before dawn. Drawing her cowl over her head, Lyn led the way, torch in one hand, a short blade in the other. Her movements were confident but quiet, her boots barely making a sound on the slick stone. Matthias followed with even less presence.

The entrance had been carved into an old drainage culvert, its bars rusted through. Inside, the air was thick and cloying, every breath a taste of rot. Water dripped from above, and mold crusted the walls.

Lyn did not speak until they were a dozen paces in. "If you want my services from here, you'll pay me. And I won't be bought by pretty eyes."

Matthias produced an emerald the size of a pea and placed it in her hand.

She stared. "Is it real?"

He nodded. *If she survives the night,* he thought, *she may even buy influence within the Shadow Council.*

The gem disappeared into a pouch as she snorted. "You're charming."

Matthias said nothing.

They descended deeper. The stone gave way to worked brick, then to carved tunnel. At each junction, Lyn paused, checked her bearings, and chose a path. Her confidence did not waver, but her voice fell away.

When they reached the archway with the sigil carved in bone, she stopped entirely. "This is it." Lyn's voice was hoarse. "Beyond this, we are in the old city. Nothing lives there. Not anymore."

Matthias stepped past her and into the dark. "Stay close."

She hesitated, then followed, and the tunnel swallowed them both.

Pain. And the faint rustle of movement. Calladorn woke to ribs that protested as he sat up, the scent of blood and wet straw clinging to the air. Instincts flared before memory, driving his hand to brace him against the cot.

Chad stood over him, a heroic silhouette against the flickering torchlight. The young man wore Calladorn's coat again, his broad shoulders keeping it from being buttoned, leaving his chest bare. As Calladorn's wits returned, he saw the poker gripped in Chad's hand.

"He's back," Chad whispered. He glanced at the poker, hesitating for a fraction of a moment before handing it to Calladorn, as if understanding who could wield it best.

Calladorn heard it—a scratching sound from the door. Metal on metal, deliberate and sharp. Something precise. Urgency surged through him, quickening his pulse. They moved in tandem, no words exchanged, one to either side of the door. He knew they had little chance of defeating the creature, but anything was better than rolling over and dying. Calladorn's heart thudded once more, then silence.

The door creaked, and he braced himself. Across from him, Chad's grip tightened around his knife—holding it the wrong way, with the blade pointed up from his thumb rather than down toward the ground.

As the door swung open, Calladorn froze. It wasn't Maltharok—it was Matthias, sword in hand, a smug curl to his lip as if he had orchestrated every moment. Beside him, a young woman crouched with the balance of a predator. Her eyes gleamed beneath a cowl, sharp and unreadable, as she tucked delicate tools into her belt—lockpicks.

Matthias scanned them—bloodied, bruised, makeshift weapons in hand—and smiled like a man laughing at a joke he didn't understand. "Well?" he said, his tone mocking. "Do you intend to escape? Or stand there gaping like mooncalves?"

Calladorn's mind raced to catch up as he lowered the poker slowly, his grip still tight. Relief didn't come. Matthias's appearance had not erased the fear—it had only changed its shape. "Maltharok could return at any time," he said, watching the other man's reaction carefully.

"Your... captor? A noble?" Matthias's expression remained unchanged.

"A demon," Calladorn replied.

The bland brown eyes widened slightly. "Here? Under Syndar? That could explain these tunnels' reputation."

"It's the High King," Chad blurted. "He's an impostor."

The woman gasped, reminding Calladorn of her presence.

Matthias regarded her for an extended moment. "Explanations can come later. As you said, we should not tarry."

They followed without a word.

The halls outside were empty. Not abandoned—cleared. The silence of purpose rather than neglect. The kind of silence that came when rodents were aware of the hawk circling overhead. Calladorn felt his hair prickle, every instinct warning him not to speak. It appeared to be a long-abandoned basement or cellar, without a trace of furnishings. Chad helped him walk, supporting him despite the lad's own injuries. Calladorn appreciated it, the pain in his chest forcing him to keep his breathing shallow even as he gripped the poker like a drawn sword.

The woman led the way, a torch held in one hand and a short sword ready in the other. The dungeon gave way to rougher corridors, then to stairs. One set led upward, but she led them downward into tunnels, then even more stairs down to a ruined old metal gate and beyond it—sewer channels. They were in a cistern. Dry and ancient, five tunnels led out from it, although two had collapsed long ago—if the dust covering the fallen stones was any indication. The other three ran into darkness like veins carved through the bones of the city.

The stink here was different. Not just rot but something older. Wrong. Sweet in a way that turned the stomach, like spoiled meat drenched in perfume. Calladorn knew that odor—the scent of a days-old battlefield.

The woman led them to one of the passages, its brick walls crumbling. Cobwebs drifted lazily in a faint draft that tickled Calladorn's face.

Calladorn saw the first corpse a few turns in. A man, face frozen in a scream, his limbs bent in impossible directions and at the wrong places. Too similar to what remained of Elrath. The woman didn't stop, and neither did Matthias.

That, too, unsettled Calladorn.

Another body. This one crushed against a rusted pipe, her head turned to face behind her back. Calladorn slowed, but Chad tugged gently on his sleeve. "Don't," he whispered. So they pressed on.

Fungal growths clung to the walls here, pulsing faintly. The stone beneath their feet grew damp. Once, their guide stopped to test the air at a junction, then veered left without explanation. Matthias didn't question it.

Calladorn kept watching the man. Grateful to have been rescued, he was still wary. It was too convenient. And Matthias never hesitated, never looked uncertain, never showed the tension that ran like a current through Calladorn's spine. Even the woman cast the occasional glance over her shoulder—but not Matthias. *Why is he so calm, even here?* Calladorn wondered. That worried him more than the bodies. *Have they already encountered other corpses like this? Or does he simply not care?*

Chad noticed too. He said nothing, but more than once Calladorn caught him watching Matthias with a frown.

They reached an archway of worked stone where the air changed. Fresher. Still faintly fouled, but with natural odors rather than the heavy oppressiveness that had weighed on them since the cell. Calladorn had never imagined he would be happy to smell excrement.

After a time, their guide halted at a gate set into a wide culvert. It appeared to be rusted shut, but the woman handed her torch to Matthias and pressed a nearby brick. The entire metal construction rolled aside into the wall.

"A smuggling tunnel," she told them, the ghost of a smile playing upon her lips. "Beyond this, the path leads out. Straight for a mile, then down a collapsed spillway. Another grate is there, opened the same way. You'll be outside the city walls."

Calladorn turned to thank her, but she had already vanished into shadow. Matthias led them on, followed by the sound of the gate moving back into place in their wake.

Half an hour later, they stepped into the open, stars winking down through high clouds. Night air touched Calladorn's face, and he nearly wept at the simple feeling of it. They were free.

He had a thousand questions, but as he looked at Matthias, striding ahead with his usual composure, Calladorn knew this was not the time. The questions could wait. But not forever.

The last of the tunnel's breath clung to his skin, damp and sour.

Chad stumbled as they exited from a narrow, brush-clogged runnel that hid the sewer drain behind them. If they hadn't emerged from it, he'd never have realized the opening was there. If the woman had been right about it being used by smugglers, either they were very good or the route was abandoned. Climbing up what appeared to be a game trail, Chad picked his footing carefully, wincing and grunting with nearly every step. His bare feet were killing him. *I bet they stink to high heaven too.*

"How long has it been?" he called to Matthias's back.

The man barely turned. "Three days."

Chad stumbled. It had felt like so much longer.

"We can't travel like this," Calladorn grunted, his voice rough.

Matthias disappeared over the slope's lip, but his voice trailed behind him. "I have prepared."

That's it? No explanation? Chad shook his head, immediately regretting the motion when it triggered a wave of vertigo that almost made him slip and fall. Stopping to let the dizziness pass, he exchanged a look with Calladorn, who walked as if he was about to collapse under a great weight.

Behind Calladorn, a half-mile distant, rose the city wall. Lights were lit along its length, and beyond that the city slumped beneath the palace, which pointed accusingly at the night sky with many towers. Chad's lips thinned at the sight. *How did I ever think that place was beautiful?* He shivered and turned his back on Syndar, choosing his steps with care as he climbed the remaining feet to a field. The grass felt better underfoot than the stony path. It felt like life, and the dew clinging to it tickled even as it helped wash his feet.

Breathing deeply, the air sweet with flowers, Chad closed his eyes and luxuriated in the moment. They were free.

Now they only needed to stay that way.

"We do not have long until sunrise," Matthias said, breaking the moment. He turned and headed toward where the field ended in an old forest, its trees widely spaced and with massive trunks that twisted as they rose from the ground. There was little undergrowth other than ferns and a lot of moss. It felt even better than the grass had.

Chad's whole body hurt as Matthias led them onward, his chest feeling tight and raw, his legs moving more from memory than strength. Exhaustion was a dull roar under everything else, held at bay only by force of will. But then he saw the firelight. It flickered through the trees, guarded, careful. Chad instinctively wanted to duck as soon as he saw it, but Matthias veered directly toward the light. A clearing opened before them, where three horses stood tethered to a moss-slicked log. Saddlebags, packs, and two rough-looking men sat near a modest fire, weapons close at hand.

They stood when they saw Matthias. Both wore patchwork armor under their forest-green cloaks. The older one sported a bushy beard shot through with gray, and the other had an eyepatch. They hefted cudgels, the gesture promising violence.

Chad immediately felt exposed. Calladorn's coat clung to him with dried sweat and old blood. He tried to square his shoulders, but even that made his ribs complain.

Eyepatch's one good eye slid slowly over the three of them as if he was measuring what he saw. "'Bout time," he said, his voice nasal. "Who's these sorry souls?"

"They look half-dead," said Big Beard.

Matthias didn't answer. Instead, he tossed a pouch. It jingled when caught. Eyepatch grunted, and the two turned to pack their things.

As they disappeared on foot through the trees, Chad approached the gear, recognizing his pack. Within he found his old traveling clothes from Ironspire and even the fancy coat. Chad's fingers brushed the embroidery, and he smiled. At the top of the other pack, Calladorn's spare uniform peeked from under the flap. Chad turned to Matthias. "You knew where we'd come out?"

Matthias threw him a rough towel and gestured toward a canteen that hung from a tree branch. "Clean up, then change," he said. When Chad didn't move, the corner of his mouth twisted. "An educated guess.

I did not know where we would come out of the city but knew you would want to travel east. This seemed the best place to keep our belongings out of sight until we could claim them."

Calladorn—having already stripped down and begun washing himself off—gave a grunt that might have been reluctant approval before asking, "How did you find us?"

Matthias explained. "I did not. I… hired the Thieves' Guild to do so."

Sounds plausible, as far as it goes, Chad thought as he followed Calladorn's example, for once not caring about modesty. The water was cold, but its sting reminded him that he was alive. The towel was soon filthy, but he was relatively clean. Trying not to shiver but feeling almost human again, he dressed in silence, his back turned to Matthias. Travel clothes, the boots from Syndar, and the blue coat with its silver stitching. It made a somewhat unconventional ensemble but felt… right.

Feeling eyes watching, Chad caught Calladorn looking at him—not with disapproval but something gentler. A silent acknowledgment. The man was donning his own travel clothes and winced as the fabric brushed his wounds, but he smiled.

As for their old clothes—what was left of them—those went on the fire, along with the now-rank towels. It hissed and guttered, giving off a foul-smelling smoke. They mounted without ceremony and rode by moonlight, heading toward the dawn.

*

The days blurred.

They traveled by back roads and narrow tracks, avoiding the highway in case of pursuit. By night, they slept beneath trees or in shallow caves, wrapping themselves in cloaks and curling up near small fires just bright enough to cook on. The food was dry meat, hard bread, and once, a rabbit Chad managed to trap.

It felt very much like the early days after leaving Edron Station—at least as far as the routine went. Their dynamics, however, had changed. Calladorn resumed their morning lessons, though they were different from before—less formal. Sometimes more stories than instruction. Chad asked questions without prompting now, not to impress but to understand, and Calladorn answered with a quiet pride that he no longer tried to hide.

One morning, Chad fumbled a term for sword technique. He cursed softly, frustrated.

"Don't apologize for not knowing what you were never taught," Calladorn said, crouching beside the fire with a stick in hand. He drew the movement in the dirt. "You learn quickly. That is what matters."

Chad blinked. The compliment surprised him more than it should have. "Thanks," he mumbled, then added, "You should sit. You're still healing."

Calladorn smirked. "Do not think me fragile just because you pulled me through a sewer."

"I thought you were the one pulling me," Chad said, flashing a quick grin.

They were quiet a moment, then Calladorn said, "You're not the same boy I met in Ironspire."

Chad looked away. "You're not the same stuffy soldier either."

That made them both laugh, though softly. It didn't last long, but it felt real.

They passed a ruined watchtower on the fourth day, its upper level collapsed into itself, wildflowers curling around broken stone. Chad paused beneath it, letting the horses drink from a trickling stream nearby. Calladorn stood beside him, silent.

"I used to think you were all rules," Chad said quietly. "Discipline. Orders. Honor."

"I was," Calladorn replied after several moments. "And I still believe in those things. But now..." He hesitated. "Now I see where they fail. Where they must bend."

Chad nodded slowly. "And I used to think you looked down on me."

Calladorn regarded him for some time in silence. "I did," he admitted at last. "I believed you didn't take things seriously. That you lacked discipline."

Chad smiled faintly. "I still might."

"Might?" Calladorn answered, raising his eyebrows in a mock question. "But you have heart... and courage." He paused, and his eyes seemed to look inward. "Those matter more," he said at last, his voice soft.

Chad swallowed, his throat feeling tight. "Thanks," he said again, feeling like it wasn't enough, but not knowing what else to offer.

The next morning, Chad was sitting beside the fire sharpening his knife when Matthias returned from patrol. His boots were dry, his cloak free of twigs and burrs. If Chad hadn't known better, he'd think the man had never even left.

"Anything?" Chad asked.

Matthias knelt near the fire, checking the simmering pot. "One rider. Westward bound. Did not see us." And that was all he said.

Chad looked down at the whetstone. "You always this calm?"

Matthias didn't look up. "It serves no purpose to be otherwise."

That answer bothered Chad, but he wasn't sure why.

Later, as they rode, Chad kept watching Matthias ahead of him. The man's back was straight. Unflinching, like nothing had changed. But it had. Chad felt it in the lingering bruises, in the nightmares that jolted him awake, in the quiet between him and Calladorn—the comfortable silence of two people who had nothing to prove to one another.

That night, when Calladorn fell asleep mid-sentence, Chad sat alone under the stars. He looked at the flames and then past them. He still had no idea what any of it meant—what they had endured or what awaited them when they met up with Rick and Evan in Ravensford. *What will Rick think?*

But he was still alive, and he supposed that counted for something. And tomorrow they would keep moving.

The morning mist came heavily on the seventh day. Dew clung to their cloaks as they packed camp, silence their only companion. Chad helped Calladorn cinch his saddle as the older man's hand was trembling slightly. Chad didn't comment but just gave a nod.

Calladorn held his gaze a moment longer than usual. "I'm glad you're here," he said quietly.

Chad blinked. "You mean alive, or just pestering you annoyingly?"

Calladorn smirked. "Both."

They mounted, and Matthias led them eastward toward their reunion with their friends.

Toward whatever came next.

Something was wrong. Luthenholme was famous for its hospitality, and Ravensford should have been a town of music and clinking glasses, the scent of fresh bread and sweet wine drifting from tavern doors and bakery windows, but as Calladorn rode down its cobbled main road beside Chad and Matthias, a hush lingered where joy should have reigned.

The townspeople moved warily, their heads bowed even as they studied the newcomers. Guards stood in pairs outside shops, not patrolling but watching—speaking in hushed tones, their faces pale. A merchant pulled a child inside by the collar as they passed, casting a wary look in their direction. No one smiled.

Worse, there were far more men than there should have been—especially around the blacksmith, where a half-dozen townsfolk had gathered. Calladorn's trained eye caught the signs instantly. The blacksmith was fitting iron heads to spears, and several rough-looking men in uniform were sorting through what appeared to be scavenged armor, forcing it into the hands of the people assembled there. A militia—hastily armed and, worse, fearful.

Calladorn shifted in his saddle and felt Chad glance over, uncertain. Matthias said nothing, as usual.

A massive inn came into view on the left, where the main road intersected with another heading to the south. Taking up the entire northern end of the square, it was the largest in town, with timbered walls and a broad porch strung with paper lanterns. This had to be the place Gharn had told them of: The Hearth and Vine. By rights, it should have been brimming with laughter and music, but no chatter spilled from the open doors, and no minstrel played in either yard or hall. Only the smell of roasting meat drifted out—strong and heady, like a mask for something bad. As they tied up their horses at the hitching post out front, no stable boy ran up to aid them.

Something is very wrong indeed, Calladorn thought as he surveyed the town square. There were too few carts, and none at all that he could see was selling produce or meat, which only reinforced the conclusion that a militia had been organized. Those goods had been redirected somewhere, as supplies.

Inside, the warmth washed over them. Candlelight glowed on polished beams, the hearth crackled, and the scent of spiced wine and buttered bread filled the air. It was nearly overwhelming after their rough time on the trail, and Chad smiled as he inhaled deeply. Yet the dozen tables sat empty but one, where a tired man hunched over a bowl, not eating.

The innkeeper looked up as they entered. He was short, round-bellied, and wore an apron stained with grease. His eyes widened slightly, but he offered a quick bow. "Afternoon, travelers. If you're seeking shelter, we've plenty of space."

Calladorn stepped forward. "We are looking for friends. A gangly gnome, a petite young woman with dark brown hair, and an unusually tall, lean young man. They may have arrived ahead of us."

The innkeeper shook his head slowly. "No such folk have been through here that I've seen, I'm sorry."

Chad raised an eyebrow, his lip twisting. "Well... it was always a toss-up who'd get here first. I just hope they ran into fewer problems than we did."

Calladorn said nothing.

"Well, we have rooms to spare while you wait for them," the innkeeper said with a smile. Then his gaze dropped. "You'll have to attend to your own animals, though. I'm afraid the hospitality's not what it should be. None of us have been sleeping well since the news, and we're short-staffed, what with the conscription and all."

Calladorn narrowed his eyes at the confirmation. "Is there trouble?"

The man sighed. "Eastgate is under siege."

Calladorn froze. "Who is attacking?" he asked, hoping for an answer different from his fears.

The innkeeper hesitated. "No one knows. The first riders said it was beasts. Others said monsters. But those who saw them and lived..." He shook his head. "...they don't speak of it."

Chad's eyes locked on Calladorn's. "Demons."

It was a whisper, but the innkeeper's ears were sharp. His face paled. "I don't know about that, good sirs. Only that every able-bodied man has been called to the defense, including my own son, and a good many women have joined them."

"So, what is Eastgate?" Chad asked.

The innkeeper raised his eyebrows but showed no other sign of surprise. Calladorn lifted a hand to indicate they'd continue the discussion later in private. "We'll take a large room for the night, and meals," he told the man.

"We have enough vacancy. You can each have your own room if you wish it."

The way Chad's eyes widened even as he seemed to shrink into himself made Calladorn shake his head. "One room is fine, thank you."

A soft sigh from Chad told him he'd made the right choice, and if Calladorn was honest with himself, he didn't relish the idea of being alone in an empty room either.

*

After settling into their shared room—larger and better-appointed than the one at the Royal Arms, despite being significantly less expensive—Chad rounded on Calladorn. "Eastgate. Spill."

Calladorn exhaled slowly, as though the weight of history itself had settled on his shoulders. "Three days' travel from here, Eastgate is the eastern bastion of Luthenholme—a fortress older than most nations, its foundations laid in the days of the First Accord. There are those who say it was built using the Three Powers themselves."

Chad blinked. "How would that even work?"

Calladorn shrugged. "That kind of knowledge was lost long ago. But for three thousand years, the fortress has never fallen. It guards the narrowly passable corridor between the eastern and central kingdoms. If Eastgate falls, it will not just be a blow to Luthenholme. It will unravel the spine of the Nine Kingdoms."

Calladorn's mind struggled to make sense of it all. Tactics had been drilled into him from a young age. The scope of this assault screamed of an incomprehensible level of organization, as well as numbers. "They are attacking on yet another front," he muttered. "Despite every law of strategy. Despite what should be possible."

"But if we hold Eastgate—" Chad began.

"Then we cripple them," Calladorn finished, feeling a flare of determination. "We force them to regroup. We prove they can be stopped."

Chad's face hardened. "Then let's stop them." He stared out the window toward the road south, the way their companions would come—if they still could.

But when?

"We need to decide what to do," Calladorn said softly.

Matthias stepped away from the wall. "We wait. Action without strategy is folly. We wait here, as planned. Your companions will find you, if they still can."

Calladorn turned on him. "*If.* You're right. We have no guarantees when they will get here. No promises Eastgate will hold until they do. You expect us to sit idle with so much at stake?"

"I expect you to act with wisdom. Two swords and a half-trained boy will not turn the tide of a siege."

Chad bristled. "I'm right here, you know."

"And for all we know," Calladorn added, "the path to the Forbidden Spire lies through Eastgate. If so, helping its defense serves the greater purpose."

Matthias gave no answer, only a faint narrowing of the eyes, like a man calculating the weight of a blade.

"We can leave word," Calladorn said. "Whenever the others arrive, they will know where we have gone." Matthias did not look pleased, but Calladorn no longer cared. He had followed duty in Drakerath. He had followed it to Syndar. And still he had failed. He now stood at another crossroads. "I will not turn my back on what's right," he said. "Not again."

Chad looked at him, then nodded. "I'm tired of running."

Calladorn felt a surge of gratitude at that, mixed with pride. "We leave at first light," he said.

And this time, no one argued.

XXII
Horse

The world fell away. Evan felt as if her stomach were trying to stay on the ground, even as Rick's magical floating disk lifted them skyward. It surged beneath her, so smooth she might not have known they were moving—if not for the wind clawing at her hair. Glowing lines rippled above the disk and below, trailing behind them like a wake of smoke. She gripped Gharn's hand with one of hers, the other braced beneath her. Rick stood just behind them, feet planted wide, his face angled into the wind, eyes blazing with manic clarity.

We're flying. The realization settled in her bones like a tremor. Below them, the landscape of the Shift blurred past, and from this elevation, she could see the way its channels curved and intersected in an almost kaleidoscopic pattern. There was beauty here that hadn't been visible from the ground. Ahead, she could feel the Shift's boundary nearing—its unstable geometry crackling in the air like ozone before a lightning strike. It shimmered, a smear of prismatic distortion masking the forest beyond, hiding safety.

Rick was laughing just under his breath, incredulous, breathless. And she could feel it—his joy. His *rightness.* It filled the disk like a second heartbeat, humming under her skin. For a moment, despite everything, she felt wonder. He was doing it. He was saving them.

But then the air changed.

The light became sharp, too sharp, like crystal about to shatter. The tingling in her skin turned to pins and needles, and Rick's breath caught. She twisted to look up at him, and in his eyes, she saw alarm. A surge of fear, followed by the terrible, calculating panic of a mind moving too fast.

He's changing something, she realized. Her breath caught, she reached for him—

And the world vanished.

Blinding white. Not the kind from an explosion that seared the eyes. This was... *absence.* The disk beneath them was simply gone. Everything was gone. They were weightless. Then not. Her stomach dropped and her knees buckled. They slammed into solid ground, but not from the great height the disk had been at.

Evan gasped, disoriented. They weren't in the Shift anymore.

A dry wind brushed her cheek, and the taste of burnt metal lingered in her mouth. The forest was no longer distant. No longer blurred behind the curtain of the Shift. Its massive trunks rose mere feet from where she lay. And behind them—

She rolled over, already knowing what she would see. The Shift's boundary convulsed like a heartbeat. With a thunder crack of light, it collapsed in on itself. A wave of distortion shot up and down, as if the landscape, with its silvery plants and distant hoodoos, were being stretched into millions of vertical lines. It was falling away, even as it rose into the sky. And then, soft as a gossamer breeze, the curtain of light folded in on itself, replaced by a landscape of barren red stone peeking above drifting dunes.

They had escaped by seconds. Less. Her eyes burned as she turned to Rick. He lay sprawled on his back, legs and arms akimbo, staring up into the sky.

"Rick!" She scrambled to him. Gharn was already there, cursing with shocking force.

Rick looked up at her, lips parted in a faint smile. "Worth it."

Liar! She thought the word with vehemence, her heart writhing like a caged animal.

He was older.

His face—deeply lined, the hair at his temples now threaded with gray. The short beard he had been growing since Edron Station was fully white. As he sat up, his posture, slumped and trembling, spoke of a weariness deeper than exhaustion. He looked sixty years old. At least. It was as if years had been ripped from him—more than twice what he'd lost when fighting the Dark Horror.

Evan fought to keep her expression from betraying the dismay she felt, as if part of her had died.

"He used High Magic," Gharn muttered, horror in his voice. "Gods below."

Evan couldn't move, couldn't speak. Her hand hovered near Rick's face, unsure if touching him would shatter something. She looked down at her own hands—unchanged, unhurt. What had happened to him wasn't a side effect of the... what? The teleportation? It was unique to him. The price of his magic.

The price he'd paid to save them. Again.

Gharn exhaled, sharp and bitter, then looked around. He stood, squinting at the terrain and the massive forest. "I recognize this from my reading. East Endarl."

Evan blinked, struggling to focus on anything other than Rick.

Gharn continued, distracted. "If we'd followed the original path, we'd have had to skirt three hundred miles of Shifts and the marshes above. Would've taken a couple of months—more, maybe—but he cut straight through it. We should be only a few weeks from Luthenholme now, I think. Ravensford's probably a month away." His voice rose slightly, trying to frame it as a win, even though she could feel the pain in his soul.

Evan barely glanced at him. "A month if everything was normal," she snapped. "But is it?" She stared down at Rick, and the world narrowed.

The teleport had saved them. Without it, they would have been trapped when the Shift moved to another universe, taking them with it. Exactly the outcome Gharn had warned them about. And yet—

She couldn't stop shaking, because the price had been *him*.

Even now, she could feel him pulling inward and away. The magic had drained more than years from him—it had taken something emotional. A wall was going up, she could already feel it. His eyes flicked toward her, only for a second, and then elsewhere.

He was sealing himself off. Withdrawing into that razor-sharp mind of his, the same way he always had when hurt—as if protecting her meant hiding the damage. But she *saw* him. She always had. Except now she didn't know how to reach him.

She looked toward the horizon, where they had come through the Shift. The landscape was quiet, unnervingly so. Gone were the spires and hoodoos, replaced by a barren desert with shapes that hinted tantalizingly of buried ruins. Nobody in Necsis would ever plunder them for treasure. The risks outweighed any potential rewards—she understood that now.

They were safe.

They were together.

And she had never felt so helpless.

Children played, but Rick found no joy in watching.

The town was barely more than a cluster of buildings, a cluttered clearing in the forest, built around a flattened tree stump. Fifty feet across, it had steps and even a ramp leading up onto the wood surface, polished smooth over time by untold boots. This was the market square, and it was busy, filled with voices and the scents of sweat, leather, and ripe fruit. Farmers bartered; wives browsed; children darted between stalls. Life moved on here, oblivious to the fact that Rick Johnson had aged twenty-five years in the span of a few minutes.

Rick lingered near the stump's outer railing—near but not leaning against it—his arms crossed so tightly across his chest it felt like he was holding himself in. His right ankle throbbed dully, but he refused to shift his weight off it again. Not while anyone was watching. The beard itched, but he declined to scratch it. He avoided admitting it was because he didn't want to accidentally see the gnarled fingers or feel the wrinkles on his face. Didn't want to be reminded that this body that wasn't his... now was.

The children made Rick's heart ache. He'd never wanted children. Hadn't actually thought about it one way or the other. All he'd wanted was a life with Evan, whatever that might bring. But now the dream tasted bitter and did nothing to nourish his mood.

Permanent structures were built against the stump's edges, including a stable where Evan and Gharn argued with a gesticulating stable master next to a corral. Within it stood exactly one horse—a plain brown beast with a white star on its forehead, munching at a hanging tuft of hay with a suspiciously patient expression. It was becoming easier to overlook how different the horses of Necsis really were.

Leaving the horseman and his corral, they climbed the steps to join Rick. "There's only one horse for sale," Gharn said, stroking his chin as he squinted at the animal. "Sturdy enough. Price is high, but it'll make the trip easier."

"Why only one?" Rick asked, trying to make it sound like he actually cared.

The two exchanged a glance, galling Rick.

"Word is, there's a muster," Gharn answered. "The king's called for defenders, and they've left with all the horses."

"And wagons," Evan added, her eyes boring into Gharn. "So much for a month."

Rick exhaled through his nose. "We can walk. Save the money for something we actually need."

Evan turned toward him, expression unreadable. "Rick—"

"No." He didn't raise his voice, but the word snapped like a closing gate. He turned away before she could say more, before he had to see the look he knew was forming—the one she and Gharn had been giving him for two weeks as they traveled through the forest, winding between its unbelievably massive trees. Pitying. Cautious, like he might break. Insisting on frequent rests with the most thinly veiled of excuses.

They were walking on eggshells, and it made his skin crawl. He wasn't some frail invalid. Yes, he was older. His joints ached when he woke, and sometimes his fingers trembled when he wasn't thinking. But he could still move, still think… still fight, damn it.

It wasn't the ache in his joints or the gray at his temples that twisted in his gut—it was the way Gharn paused every time Rick stood too slowly. The way Evan's smile faltered just before she looked away. He caught glimpses of it constantly. Evan biting back comments, Gharn offering help he didn't need. Every word they spoke came with a carefulness that grated on him like sand in a wound. *And she wonders why I hid the Mage-curse from her in the first place?* he thought, staring at nothing—not realizing he was looking through a passing woman until she turned to glare at him.

A few minutes later, he heard the jingle of coins. He turned just in time to see Gharn handing over a small leather pouch to the stable master. The man grinned, tipped his hat, and led the horse out from the corral. Gharn took the reins and walked toward him, stopping at the bottom of the steps.

"You're the one who needs it," the gnome said simply, extending the reins.

Rick stared at him. Then at Evan, standing to one side, her lips pressed together. "I said no."

"And we ignored you," Evan said. Her voice was sharper than usual, but her eyes weren't cruel. They were tired. Frustrated. "Take the damn horse, Rick. If you won't do it for yourself, do it for us."

The anger surged like a flash of fire. He opened his mouth, ready to push back. Ready to snap, but something in the way her lip trembled stopped him. It wasn't the irritation—it was the *fear* behind it. They were afraid for him.

He clenched his jaw, the heat of humiliation rising to his face. He wanted to scream. To tell them that he was fine. That every time they coddled him, it chipped away at what little pride he had left. But what would it matter?

He said nothing. Just walked down from the stump and took the reins. He mounted the horse in one smooth motion, spitefully proving to them that he still could. The gelding shifted beneath him, calm and steady.

It felt like a defeat.

The animal's warmth seeped into his legs. His back ached already, but he kept his posture straight, refusing to slouch. Refusing to look like what they saw: an old man.

The others said nothing as they left the town and continued down the road into the forest, where the canopy loomed so high it made him dizzy to look up. Rick said nothing either.

But inside, the silence roared.

The forests of Endarl had fallen away behind them. Gone were the cathedral-sized trunks, the shadowed paths, the filtered light that had once seemed to breathe with ancient life but eventually just made Evan feel small and insignificant. In their place, a countryside too perfect stretched in every direction. The vineyards rolled out like a painter's dream—neatly terraced hills lined with tidy rows of green, dotted with white-walled farmhouses whose red-tiled roofs glinted in the sun. This was Luthenholme. It should have felt peaceful.

It didn't.

Evan walked beside Gharn, their pace steady and quiet. The gravel road curved ahead of them, rising and falling with the hills like the swell of a calm sea. Rick rode a short distance in front of them, his back straight, his shoulders rigid. The horse moved with lazy precision, hooves clopping rhythmically along the road, but Rick didn't move at all, except to wave away the occasional overly inquisitive bee. He stared directly ahead, the scenery seeming to be as interesting to him as it would have been to a blind man. Less—they would at least have turned their face to the sun's warmth or breathed in the heady aroma of grapes.

"You think he'll come around?" Gharn asked quietly, watching Rick with narrowed eyes.

Evan hesitated. She wanted to lie, to offer some comforting platitude. Instead she exhaled slowly. "I don't know."

The silence that followed was heavier than before. She could feel it settling over them like a second sky. Walking behind Rick like this made her feel like the distance wasn't just physical, but walking beside Gharn at least brought some conversation.

With Rick, there was nothing.

She studied his posture. The rigid set of his spine, the way his hands curled around the reins. A dozen tiny tells. He was bracing himself against something.

Against her, maybe.

He hadn't shaved since the split with Chad at Edron Station. That had been an infuriating eight weeks ago now, and his beard was no longer stubbled or patchy—it had grown in fully, short but thick and neat and completely gray. Not a salt-and-pepper transition. Not streaked with color. Just silver-gray. And he hadn't cut it or even used magic to change it—though he still conjured light each night. That contrast made her chest tighten. He wasn't rejecting what had happened to him. He was *wearing* it.

She felt a shiver rise beneath her ribs. Acceptance, not resistance—like he'd already made peace with vanishing.

"He's doing it on purpose," she said suddenly.

Gharn glanced at her. "What?"

"The beard. The silence. All of it. He's not hiding from what the magic is doing to him. He's... embracing it."

Gharn frowned but said nothing.

Evan looked down at her hands as she walked. Flexed her fingers once, slowly. The power inside her wasn't dormant anymore. It hadn't been since Southwatch, when the ghost had mistaken her for Estariel. No—that wasn't right. It had begun long before that, when they'd first arrived in Necsis. It had only grown stronger since. Every moment of crisis peeled back another layer. Every time she let herself reach, there was more.

Now it felt closer to the surface than ever—like standing on the edge of a lake that looked shallow, only to find there was no bottom. She could *feel* people now. Not just their moods but their intentions. Their fears. With Rick, the shape of his pain hung just out of reach, like a door barely cracked open.

She could open it. Just a nudge, a whisper of psychic pressure, and she could reach him. But she didn't. She wouldn't. She had sworn it.

Never again.

Not after what she had done to Chad. That single moment—trying to push him away from Syndar because of her premonitions of the danger there—had instead broken something deep and vital. The party had split because of her. And Rick—

She still hadn't told him about what she'd done to *him* at the bridge in the Deeps either. The gentle nudge that had been just enough to tilt the scales and use magic. It had probably saved them. It had also drawn the Dark Horror. *Will I ever have the courage to tell him?* she wondered. The answer refused to come.

A breeze stirred her hair, carrying the scents of grapes and dust. She lifted her eyes to the horizon. The road curved again up ahead, skirting the edge of a vineyard, then disappearing behind another low hill.

An image came to her unbidden. A tower. But it wasn't that of the tarot card. Not anymore. No symbol, this was real—the *Forbidden Spire.* She had never seen it, but she *knew* it now. As if it had always been there, waiting. Lightning raked across its white stone, the sky behind it boiling with smoke and storm. She could almost hear the crack of thunder, feel the charged air on her skin. It loomed in her mind's eye, terrible and unmoving. The symbol of catastrophe.

She looked up at the sky. It was bright, cloudless. The sun rode high, its heat gentle against her skin. The storm wasn't literal, but she had the feeling it was already here.

"He won't let us help," she murmured, more to herself than to Gharn.

"No," the gnome replied. "He won't. Not yet."

She looked again at Rick. He sat perfectly upright, as if the posture itself could ward off weakness. As if he could pretend away the tremble in his hands. He had always hidden behind control. Behind logic. Now he was retreating into silence because it was the last shield he had.

"I want to reach out," she said, her voice barely above a whisper. "I want to pull him back. But if I even try..."

"He'll shut you out completely," Gharn finished.

She nodded. "And I can't lose him."

She wanted to call out—to tell him he didn't need to carry it alone. That she saw him, even now... that she could soothe his pain. *I've learned my lesson.* This time, she'd wait. If he didn't ask, she wouldn't act. But she also knew better than to offer, not in his current state. He wouldn't just refuse—he'd resent her for offering. So she let the silence stretch instead.

The horse crested the next hill, and Rick disappeared from view for a moment. She didn't run to close the gap, though her legs itched to. The road would bring them back together eventually.

She just hoped it wouldn't be too late.

Ravensford had been stripped bare.

Gharn had known it was coming. For days now, they'd passed empty fields—grapes withering on the vine—and shuttered homes. A village square with only elders and children. A roadside tavern where the barkeep had closed early to join the levy. Everywhere they went, they'd heard the same rumor: King Almarion had issued a conscription order to muster forces at Eastgate. The king who'd supposedly spent his reign unable to see beyond his own vineyards had suddenly found steel in his spine, and the kingdom had followed. Nobody they asked could answer why the levy had been ordered or what enemy was being defended against. Half the people they spoke to thought that the warlords of Velsaria had decided to leave their longboats and raid inland. Others whispered that the people of Faltheris had finally had their brains fully baked by the desert sun and started a war.

But Gharn knew the answer in his bones. Somehow, the demons had expanded to yet another front. Drakerath, Syrillia, Endarl, and now Luthenholme. Half the Nine Kingdoms were now at war. Maybe more. He adjusted his collar, trying not to imagine time as a noose tightening around them. They needed to reunite with the others—soon.

So when the rooftops of Ravensford came into view—orderly and sunlit, nestled in the vines like a painting—Gharn already knew. It wasn't the buildings that were wrong. It was the people. No soldiers. No merchants or travelers heavy with gear. No one hale, hearty, or battle-worn. The square was occupied only by the very old, the very young, or those too injured or sick to fight—farmers with canes, children carrying baskets, men with hollow cheeks and limps from injuries that hadn't healed right.

The strong were gone.

Evan said something behind him, but he didn't catch it. His mind had already turned toward Eastgate, a dam that was somehow holding back the monstrous flood.

The Hearth and Vine was easy enough to find—a handsome inn, two stories tall with climbing ivy across its sun-facing side. With wide windows at the front, it looked like a place where someone might drink and laugh and dance. Just then, it looked like a lie.

Inside, the innkeeper was polite but wary, his smile too tired to reach his eyes. He glanced at Gharn's axe more than once. "Three travelers, yes," he said. "Arrived a few days ago, maybe a little less. Took the corner room upstairs."

Gharn felt his jaw tighten. "And now? They're still there?"

"Why, no. Left two days back. Eastgate, like my best wine and provisions… and everyone else." The last part was said as an afterthought.

Gharn barely heard the rest. Something about how they'd traveled light, seemed in good spirits, had left a note. The innkeeper fished it out from behind the bar and handed it over. Gharn took the paper with hands that were already curling into fists. He unfolded it slowly, reading the words aloud:

Rick, Evan, Gharn,

Sorry, but we couldn't wait. Eastgate needs help, and Calladorn is going. I can't let him go alone. You don't need me for the spire. You need Rick. You need Evan. You need the ones who can make a difference. I'm just a pair of hands. And right now, those hands are better off holding a sword than sitting in an inn. I'll be back in Ravensford when it's done. Promise.

Chad

Idiot boy, Gharn thought, and he exhaled sharply. The note crinkled in his grip. He looked up. Rick stood by the window, unmoving. His shoulders were stooped, and Gharn wondered if he was staring outside or at his reflection in the glass. The lad—no, the *man* didn't ask to read the message for himself. Didn't even turn. Evan stood nearby, arms folded, her face unreadable.

Gharn read the letter again, as if the words might change. They didn't.

He crossed the room to the nearest table and sat down hard enough to make the bench slide with a groan. "Two days ago. They'll be at Eastgate soon, if they're not there already." *How can they be so stupid? The boy I understand. But Matthias! I thought he had more sense.*

Evan crossed to him and took the seat opposite. Her fingers curled loosely on the edge of the table. "Then we go after them."

Gharn rubbed his forehead with both hands. The Spire was to the north. They couldn't afford a detour. But the boy—and Matthias, for whatever reason—were essential to the prophecy. "No," he growled at last.

She blinked. "What?"

Gharn leaned forward, knowing what was necessary but still feeling it was wrong. "*We* don't go anywhere. Not all of us." He tried to measure her resolve with his eyes. "You and Rick are going to the Spire. I'll go after the others."

She stared at him. "You can't go alone."

"I can. And I will."

Rick turned from the window. His voice was quiet. "Gharn—"

"No. Don't try to talk me out of it. That fool brother of yours is going to get himself killed trying to play hero." Evan flinched, but Gharn pushed forward. "Calladorn's too proud to drag him back, and who knows what Matthias is thinking? That leaves me."

Evan opened her mouth, then closed it. Gharn gestured around the room. "This town's emptied itself. Every able-bodied soul is either gone to fight or dead already. You saw the streets. If Eastgate hasn't fallen, it's going to. And if it has..." He didn't finish.

"It hasn't," Rick said. "Not yet."

Gharn raised an eyebrow.

Rick shrugged one shoulder. "If it had, we'd know."

Evan looked between them, then gave a single slow nod. "All right. We leave tomorrow."

"I'll need supplies," Gharn said. "Food. Something faster than my feet, if they've got it."

"Take the nag," Rick said, his expression bland behind the wrinkles. It made Gharn's eye twitch. He didn't know that face well enough to guess whether Rick was serious or joking, but either way, the comment just felt wrong.

Gharn stood, brushing crumbs from the table that weren't even his. "You two get to your prophecy. I'll get our strays back. Gods willing, we'll meet back here."

He climbed back to his feet with a sigh. Pausing at the threshold of the taproom, he glanced back.

Rick had turned again to the window.

But this time, his eyes were closed.

Their room at The Hearth and Vine was well appointed—it even had an en suite toilet, which they hadn't yet seen in Necsis. Everything was clean, quiet, and spacious.

Clean, Rick thought. *Too perfect for a world falling apart.* The linens were crisp, the floors swept, the heavy shutters oiled to silence. The bed was soft, the view pleasant. According to Gharn, this was the kind of hospitality Luthenholme was known for. But in a town so hollowed out it echoed, how did a place like this stay pristine? Who was left to clean the rooms, much less rent them? He wondered, absently, if the innkeeper had polished the floors himself. Maybe they'd been given the best room in the place out of gratitude for the business.

He sat on the edge of the bed, hands clasped loosely between his knees, staring at a knot in the wood grain beneath his feet. He hadn't taken off his boots or even his travel cloak. Just sat down and stayed there, as if moving too much might make something else crack.

Evan unpacked quietly across the room, reorganizing their shared belongings to make sure everyone would have what they needed after this latest party split. Gharn was tightening the straps on his pack by the door. It was too early for sleep, too late to do anything useful. The air was thick with unspoken things.

"You're sure you'll be able to catch them?" Evan asked without turning.

"It's not a matter of catching them. If they didn't dawdle, they're already in Eastgate. I'm more worried about what happens after..." Gharn stopped, shooting a furtive glance at Rick. He took a breath. "They've got Calladorn with them. He's experienced and cautious. And Matthias doesn't trust anything that moves. I'll bring them back."

"You'd better," Rick said. His voice was low but steady.

Gharn looked up, caught the edge in it. "I will."

Rick nodded once, then leaned back slightly, as if the weight on his spine had changed. He didn't meet anyone's eyes. "He shouldn't have gone," he said. "Not like that."

Gharn set his pack down with a thump. "He made a choice, Rick. You can't protect him from that."

"I wasn't trying to." Rick looked up, his expression unreadable. "I just… I didn't think he'd leave again. Not after—" He stopped. The memory of Edron Station hovered just behind his eyes. Chad's wounded anger. The way he'd turned his back without another word. Rick exhaled. "He didn't even say goodbye."

"He left a note," Gharn said with a shrug.

The words snapped Rick back to the present. "Not the same." He stared again at the floor. "Maybe he's better off. He doesn't have to see this. Doesn't have to watch me fall apart."

Gharn gave him a look. "You haven't fallen apart."

"No?"

Evan put a hand on Rick's knee, but it hovered there just a second too long before touching.

He looked at her, then at Gharn. "Don't say you haven't noticed. The looks. The half-offers of help. Or the way you pause when I stand up too slow."

"We're not—"

"You are. Both of you. And I'm sick of it." He rounded on them. "You say he made his choice. Well, so did I. *I* made the choice to use magic. Not you." Evan flinched like she'd been slapped, but Rick was too frustrated to care. He kept going. "And I'd do it again without a second thought, because it's kept us safe. So stop treating me like I'm about to die."

The silence sharpened. Gharn hoisted his pack with a grunt. "I'm going to get a second room."

"Will you be downstairs for dinner?" Evan asked, as softly as Rick had just been loud.

Gharn hesitated, then gave a single nod. "Aye." He glanced at Rick, who hadn't moved. "You going to be all right?"

Rick lifted one brow. "That depends. You planning to ask again every few hours?"

Gharn snorted and turned away. "Gods help me, I might." He crossed the room, then paused with one hand on the door. "He's not a child anymore, Rick. And in case you haven't looked in a mirror lately, you aren't either. Try acting like it."

Rick didn't answer. Just stared at the floor again until Gharn left.

Evan stood, brushing imaginary dust from her trousers. She placed the satchel on the bed and began setting out provisions for the morning. There was none of her usual grace in her movements—they spoke of angry efficiency. And then...

The smallest thing. A sigh, a shift of movement, her hand brushing his shoulder as she passed. Too light. Too gentle.

Or too careful.

"Stop," Rick said. His voice was low, flat. But it cut through the air like a blade. Evan froze, hand still halfway back. He looked up at her, eyes sharp. "Stop acting like I'm broken."

She blinked. "Rick..."

"Don't," he snapped. "Don't talk to me like I'm already dead."

"We're just trying to help," she said, and though her voice was calm, there was tension at the corners of her mouth.

"Well, stop."

She drew back, hands folding at her waist. "Is that what you want?" she asked. "For us to just... stop caring?"

Gharn's voice echoed in his memory, stinging. Rick's jaw clenched.

"You want us to stop caring," Evan repeated, quieter this time. "Fine. But don't expect us to sit around and watch you kill yourself."

She stalked out of the room. The door slammed behind her, and Rick jumped at the sound.

He regretted what he'd said.

But he wouldn't take it back. This was what he'd asked for.

If they stopped caring now, it wouldn't hurt so much later.

The morning mist was already burning off the cobblestones when Evan led the gelding around from the stable.

It wasn't much of a horse—a plain brown creature with the most placid disposition imaginable, besides a habit of flicking its tail exactly once every five seconds. More than once, she could have sworn it had actually fallen asleep while Rick rode it. But it was steady on uneven ground, didn't spook easily, and Gharn had already checked the hooves himself. Twice.

Now he stood beside the animal, tightening the final strap on his saddlebag while Evan adjusted the cinch. The quiet between them felt less like silence and more like space deliberately left unfilled. Neither of them had slept well.

She could see Rick from here. He sat alone at the table just outside the inn's front entrance, hunched slightly, facing the market and the two of them—facing but paying no attention. A cup of tea sat cooling in front of him, untouched. He wasn't reading. Wasn't writing. Wasn't doing anything but staring at the cup as if willing it to change shape.

Gharn followed her gaze. "Is he talking to you yet?"

"Some," Evan said. "Enough."

The gnome snorted. "Could have fooled me."

Evan shrugged.

Gharn came around to her side and tightened the strap for that saddlebag with unnecessary force. "You still worried about Chad?"

Her answer was immediate. "Yes."

The gnome tilted his head, eyeing her sideways. "Even after that premonition you had? The one about Syndar? Whatever it was supposed to mean, they made it to Luthenholme. All three of them. Safe."

Evan kept her hands busy adjusting the stirrups for Gharn's short legs, but her fingers trembled slightly. "Maybe it wasn't wrong. It was about what would happen if Chad went to Syndar, which then led to Eastgate. They wouldn't have gone if we'd all stayed together, but now... they're right where the..."

Gharn went still as her voice trailed off. The breeze shifted, smelling of rain, tugging a strand of her hair across her cheek. She didn't brush it away.

"I'll bring them back," he said at last. "Whatever's waiting there, I'll bring them back."

She gave a soft nod, still staring at the saddle. "Thank you."

He fidgeted, then cleared his throat. “And Rick? You still see the Spire?”

Evan hesitated. “Since the day we met. It used to be the Tower card. But now it’s more than that. White stone and lightning. And the ground... like it’s on fire.”

Gharn shifted his weight. “Does he really need to go with you?”

She leaned against the horse, which had fallen asleep again. Ignoring the way the saddle’s edges poked at her, she found calm in his slow breathing. “I wish I knew.”

“You could stop him,” Gharn said. “I’ve seen how much stronger you are now. Those birds...” He shook his head. “You could push him just a little. Make him want to wait here.”

She froze. *Please don’t tempt me,* she thought. *You don’t know what you’re asking.*

Gharn must have felt it, because he backpedaled immediately. “I’m not saying you should. I’m just—hells, Evan, you’ve got more sense than me. But if you think something awful’s going to happen—”

“No,” she said. The word came too fast, too loud. She stepped back from the horse and crossed her arms tightly. “No. I’m not doing that again. I don’t care what I see. I don’t care what it costs. I swore I would never use my powers on the people I love. Not like that.” *Not again.*

Gharn studied her. “Even if it means losing him?”

“Even then.” Her voice cracked. The words hung there between them, brittle as glass.

Gharn looked toward Rick again. Still unmoving. Still silent. “Chad had one thing right,” he said gently. “The prophecy. It identifies all four of you. Rick. Evan. Chad. Matthias. Whatever’s waiting at that tower... Rick survives it. You both do.”

Evan closed her eyes. Allowed the prophecy to wrap itself around her like a threadbare cloak. Not warm or clean enough, but still something. Still comfort. Maybe it held a way to undo the Magecurse.

When she opened her eyes again, she knelt down and wrapped her arms around Gharn. He made a surprised grunt but returned the hug without hesitation, one oversized hand patting her back twice.

“Don’t get yourself killed,” she said.

"You first," he muttered.

They pulled apart. Evan wiped her eyes, trying to pretend it was some dust. They both looked toward Rick. He still sat at the table, still staring into the full cup of tea.

The horse flicked its tail again. Gharn mounted up without another word, Evan boosting him into the saddle. He turned the animal east, and she watched him ride off, willing him to be safe.

The hoofbeats reached him first. A slow, steady rhythm against the cobblestones, echoing through the square with a deliberate finality. Rick didn't look up right away. He waited until the sound had nearly faded before he lifted his gaze.

Gharn, already at the far end of the square, gave no glance back. He rode upright, his small frame perched sturdily in the saddle, the gelding plodding eastward without complaint. In moments, they vanished around the bend. Rick watched the empty space for a time, before following the cobblestones back to his cup.

He hoped Gharn would be successful. Hoped he'd bring Chad back safely. Hoped, irrationally, that Chad wouldn't do something reckless in the meantime–though, of course, he would. He always did. That was the problem with having a brother who believed the world could be fixed if he just tried hard enough.

And then he'd come here, expecting to find Rick. But Rick would be the one who didn't come back. He gnawed the inside of his cheek. *Because not every problem has a solution, no matter how hard you look.*

He shifted in his seat. The tea in front of him had stopped steaming long ago, but he hadn't touched it. The cup sat cooling on the table, its surface catching the morning light like a sheet of dull glass. A film had begun to form.

He thought about the prophecy. Gharn believed in it. Chad had too—maybe more than any of them. And Evan? Of course she would. Prophecies and visions and unseen threads had wrapped around her from the start. That sort of thing was her world.

But Rick had never believed. Not really. Even now, after all of it—after Emberhold and Southwatch, after the Deeps and the Shift—he still didn't.

In fact, he believed even less now. This damned curse that had decided to take up residence in his skin made sure of that. The prophecy said four would find the Heart. Four travelers, bound together. But there were only three of them left.

Or will be soon enough. He let the weight of that truth settle as he leaned against the backrest, closing his eyes for a moment. He was too tired to keep pretending, too tired to lie to himself about what his body was becoming.

He'd get Evan to the Spire. They'd find the path forward, maybe even learn where the Heart was hidden.

But Rick wouldn't be among its finders.

He exhaled slowly, opened his eyes, and reached for the cup. Lifted it to his lips. Cold. Bitter. It felt right that he drank it anyway.

At least he wouldn't have to ride that damned horse anymore.

XXIII
Haven

They'd passed the last vineyard hours ago. The earth beneath their boots had shifted from well-worn track to uneven meadow, and though the late-afternoon light still lingered on the high grass behind them, it couldn't penetrate the murk that hid the feet of the cliffs in the distance.

Somewhere beyond those cliffs was the Forbidden Spire. The map in Southwatch had said it would be here, but Rick couldn't see how. There was no pass that he could make out—no gap in the cliff's face. Now only the soft roll of hills and the looming trees lay between them and that massive stone wall. Even from here, the forest's trees looked sinister, their gnarled limbs overlapping in tangled layers that made it feel like they'd stepped into a cavern even before the forest line.

When they reached it, the air changed with a coolness that clung to his skin. To his surprise, it didn't smell of rot and decay but rather like when an old cedar chest opens to reveal its secrets.

Rick frowned down at the compass in his hand. It had been useful getting them to the forest, but no more. He turned slightly, trying to make sense of the path they'd taken—only to find the same cluster of gray-leafed shrubs standing to their left. Again.

"That's impossible," he muttered.

Evan didn't answer. She was scanning the forest floor, which was pretty enough with its moss over a spider's web of roots. Her shoulders were stiff beneath her shawl, her mouth a thin, unreadable line. Now and then, her gaze twitched up toward a hole in the canopy, seeking signs of the cliffs that were their goal. Too often those cliffs were to one side rather than ahead. Sometimes they were even behind them.

Rick tried to tamp down the irritation rising in his chest. This place was a maze without walls. The canopies were wide, and the trees spaced far enough apart they didn't interfere with vision or require constant course corrections. So why couldn't they get through? *I'm getting too old for this,* he thought with bitter irony.

It didn't help his mood any that a pain had started shooting down his left leg with each step. Sciatica. His energy was flagging as well, too soon in the day, and too sharply for the walking they'd done. Granted, they had come far these past three days since Ravensford, but it was easy going.

"Gharn should be at Eastgate now," he blurted, just realizing.

Evan searched his face, and he smiled in reply. She nodded. "I'm sure he's found Chad, then," she said.

He checked the compass again. The needle spun lazily before settling on north, and the west it showed didn't match the sun. He tapped it, then shook it for good measure. Still wrong. Rick exhaled, pushing a hand through his hair, and realized his fingers had unconsciously traced a looped equation on his palm. Something about vectors and inertial drift. Nonsense here.

"This doesn't make sense," he said, more to himself than to her. "We've kept the cliffs ahead of us for two hours. That should have brought us due north. But now they're behind us again."

Evan stopped. At first he thought it was frustration—she didn't handle circular logic well, and this felt like being trapped inside a Möbius strip. But then she slowly turned her head. Her eyes weren't angry but... curious. Distant. Focused inwardly.

"We're being guided away," she murmured.

Rick's brows drew together. "What?"

"Something's pushing us off course." Her voice was too calm—not panicked, not speculative. Certain.

He studied her carefully. "You think it's magic?" The question felt ridiculous even now, after everything they'd seen. After the wonders he'd done.

"No. This is something different... Subtle." She turned to face him, the wind catching the edge of her shawl and pulling it behind her. "But it's not the land. It's... not me. I'm not pulling us. But something is... I don't know... altering our perceptions just enough to turn us around."

He almost replied with some kind of rational explanation—something about geomagnetic anomalies, perhaps. But even as the thought formed, he knew how flimsy it sounded. And she was looking at him in that way she did when she already knew what he was going to say. Patient. A little sad.

The compass went into his belt pouch, for all the good it was doing.

"You trust me, right?" she asked.

The question caught him off guard. "Of course."

"Then follow my lead."

Before he could respond, she stepped forward and placed her fingers gently on his arm. "I'm going to close my eyes. And I need you to keep me from walking into trees or falling off a cliff. But don't guide me. Don't correct our course. No matter what."

He blinked. "Evan—"

"Just trust me." Her eyes were already closing.

Her hand slid into the crook of his elbow, and she nodded once, as if sealing something inside herself. Rick hesitated for only a second longer before nodding back. He adjusted his grip around her hand so he could gently steer if he needed to. She walked forward with quiet purpose, her movements deliberate. Not drifting or guessing. She was following something he couldn't see.

The wind changed.

It was subtle at first, but as they moved deeper into the trees, Rick felt a shift in the air—like walking into one of the transepts in a cathedral, rather than toward the altar. The light through the canopy was diffuse, eerie. And everything around them felt... too still. Not just silent. Waiting.

He glanced through another hole in the canopy. The cliffs were closer. But it felt like they were walking in the wrong direction. Yet it also felt like the land was unfolding for them. He stopped looking.

Minutes passed—maybe longer. He lost track. All that mattered was her breathing beside him, and the sense of pressure in the air, like a lid slowly being pulled off a sealed jar. And then—

The cliffs loomed so tall it felt like they were curving overhead. They emerged from the trees all at once, sharp and sudden. Rick drew in a breath as the rock wall rose before them in steep, broken ledges. And directly in front of them was a gap. It angled to the northeast, barely wide enough for a splashing creek and the distinct path that picked its way upward.

Evan opened her eyes. They stood at the base of the final barrier, a place carved by time and hidden by perspective. Rick understood why they hadn't been able to see the passage from a distance. Unless the observer was right in this spot, viewing it from this specific angle, the cliffs simply blended into each other, creating the illusion of a featureless wall. *Amazing.*

Evan said nothing at first. Just stared up at the peaks with a strange, unreadable expression. Not awe. Not fear. Something closer to... resignation.

Rick turned to her slowly. He was about to speak when he realized something else. Her grip on his arm had changed. Firmer now. More confident. And she hadn't once tried to shield him. Hadn't even offered to slow their pace. *She's not treating me like I'm made of glass anymore,* he realized. It should have felt like a victory.

Instead, it rattled him.

He studied her face—the creased brow, the faint tremble in her lips, the way her jaw tensed like she was bracing for something. For a moment, the wind pulled her hair across her cheek, and she didn't brush it away.

"You should be happy," he said, gently. "We're close."

Evan nodded. But the motion lacked conviction.

"Then why do you look like we just lost something?" he asked.

Her eyes flicked toward him, startled. Then down again. "You need to be here," she said.

He blinked. "I'm glad you finally noticed."

That earned the ghost of a smile, but it faded too fast. She looked away again, back toward the cliffs. "I had to stop treating you like I was afraid you'd break. It was hurting both of us."

Rick waited. He could feel that there was more. But she didn't say it. "Is that all it was?"

Her expression flickered, then steadied. "Of course."

He didn't believe her, not entirely. Something in her posture indicated she was holding back a truth, like she was carrying a burden she wasn't ready to name. But he didn't push—not yet. Instead, he reached for her hand and held it, gently. "We'll face it," he said.

She looked up at him. "Will we?"

Although they no longer needed to guide each other, he didn't let go.

The crevasse through which the stream rushed was barely wide enough for the water, much less a trail. Stone pressed close on either side, jagged and damp, beaded with water that glistened in the fading light. The sound of tumbling water bounced between the narrow cliffs, making Evan's ears ring. The air smelled fresh and pure, filled with moss and other living things. She moved carefully, one hand skimming the rock wall for balance, the other clutching the folds of her shawl tighter across her chest. Rick followed behind her, breathing hard, his jaw set in determination and a light in his sharp blue eyes. They didn't need to speak, and she forced herself not to glance back and check on him every few seconds.

Above, the cliffs soared—impossibly high, slate-gray against a sliver of sky that was still bright blue. Darkness might be closing in around them here in the depths, but there were still two or three hours before sunset.

They crossed the rushing stream on the remnants of old bridges, some no more than collapsed timbers. Most times, they were able to get through by clambering down to the stream level and wading through—the water was barely a foot deep in most places, for all its rushing energy—then climbing carefully back up to the trail to continue on. The only concern was losing their footing.

A few times, that wasn't possible. In these places, the path was cut into the side of the cliff, too high above the stream, the bank too steep and wet to descend in safety. In those cases, Rick would take her into his embrace and float them across to the other side. Each time, her stomach twisted at the memories it summoned—the bridge in the Deeps, the flight across the Shift. She released him a little too quickly after they touched down on the other side, trying not to look for signs of new wrinkles or more white in his hair.

The farther they went, the harder it was to hear anything but waterfalls. Evan hadn't realized how much she'd come to depend on the little sounds of Necsis—the distant calls of strange birds, the wind combing through trees, even the insect songs at night. Here it was all drowned by the stream. The stone drank everything else.

When Rick walked ahead, he kept his eyes forward. His movements were efficient, economical. He placed each step with care, shoulders hunched against the growing cold.

The weight in Evan's chest hadn't gone away since they had entered the cleft in the cliffs. It had settled within her like she'd swallowed lead—vast amounts of it. She didn't know what waited beyond this pass, but she could feel it waiting. That was the worst part. Not danger, not even fear. Inevitability.

A dozen stone-wrought steps climbed to an opening in front of them, next to a twenty-foot waterfall that squeezed from a narrow slot in the rock above. It was a tunnel, with more steps leading higher yet and a circle of blue at the far end. When they stepped in, the water sounds quickly fell silent, replaced with echoing footsteps.

She swallowed, then spoke without quite meaning to. "I think we should stop for the night." Her voice barely carried in the muffled space, and for a moment, she wasn't sure he'd heard her.

Then Rick halted. He looked back, his face shadowed in the tunnel's darkness. His silhouette nodded once. No argument. No protest. Just a quiet, resigned sort of agreement. "At the first place that looks safe."

It proved to be very close by.

When they emerged from the tunnel, they gaped in astonishment at a mirror-smooth lake that filled much of the valley in front of them. A wide bowl surrounded by rugged peaks, it still enjoyed a bit of direct light from the setting sun. On the side where they walked, the trail faded into a carpet of lush grass that reached to the water's edge on the left and, to the right, scrub trees, struggling to grow in the rockfalls that had spilled down the mountainside.

"It's like the Inner Basin," Rick breathed.

"Prettier," Evan agreed.

He shrugged off his pack and lowered it with stiff care to a large, flat stone some thirty feet from the water's edge. Evan stood still, watching him rub his hands together. His breath curled faintly in the air, despite the sun.

He was thinner than he had been. The endless travel, the sleepless nights, the hunger, the magic—it had all worn him down. His clothes hung a little looser than before, and the way he moved now reminded her of something brittle. On the surface, he looked like he could be his own grandfather, aged and gaunt, his hair threaded with silver that hadn't been there just weeks ago.

But the eyes—those were still her Rick. And so was the man behind them. Still methodical, still focused. Full of that quiet intensity, that relentless drive that had first drawn her to him. And he cared—maybe too much. It showed in every gesture, in every expression.

She closed her eyes for a breath, trying to steady herself. The ache in her chest flared hotter.

Part of her wanted to beg him to turn back. But she wouldn't. And she couldn't press him. Not after the Deeps—not after the bridge.

Evan sat down next to him, not out of a desire to take care of him—although that was there as well—but for the simple closeness. She pulled the shawl tighter around her shoulders and leaned into him. A barely audible splash drew her gaze to the water, where rings rippled out from a spot near the middle of the lake. A fish had jumped for its meal. Above, the sun had set, and the sky was giving way to stars.

The two of them stayed like that for several minutes, in quiet ease.

"Let's get a fire going before it's dark," Rick said at last, moving carefully as he returned to his feet. Suitable wood was easily gathered from where a couple of the more-stunted trees had died. Stones from the lake's edge were formed into a ring near their seat of stone, which Evan figured would also work well as a table. Rick set up the wood within the impromptu firepit, his fingers trembling slightly as he worked. Then he muttered something and gestured. A red glow formed beneath the sticks, which burst into flame. It grew quickly, soon bathing them in light and warmth.

Evan didn't offer to help. She just watched him, her hands folded in her lap, and thought, *This is somehow better than the picnic was.*

Back on Earth. Another life entirely.

The fire had burned low.

Rick sat cross-legged on the flattest stone he could find, close enough to feel the warmth against his shins but not so close as to let the heat make him drowsy. His dinner of dried fruit and nuts settled comfortably in his stomach—he didn't eat much anymore, but today he'd earned it.

The mountain air had turned sharper with the night, cold enough to sting his lungs when he breathed too deeply. He didn't mind. The sky above them stretched cloudless and infinite, the moons casting their pale light down in overlapping halos that shimmered on the surface of the lake.

Beside him, Evan sat with her arms wrapped around her knees, chin resting just above them. Her green eyes tracked the slow ripple of the water, the flicker of the flames, the breeze moving through the sparse scrub trees nearby and making it sound like they were whispering to each other. She hadn't spoken in a while. He hadn't either.

He didn't want to break the peace of this moment—the illusion of stillness and safety—but he could feel the words building in his throat, pushing upward like steam beneath a sealed valve. He glanced at her again and saw the fire dancing in her eyes. It felt almost like it used to between them. He opened his mouth, then stopped. Closed it again. The words weren't ready. He stared into the fire for a long breath.

Then he said, quietly, "I'm scared."

Evan turned to him, her eyes round and moister than smoke from the fire could account for. "I know," she said. Her voice was soft but steady.

She didn't offer comfort. Didn't deny it or try to pull him out of it. She just... acknowledged it. Let it be.

Rick nodded slowly. Rubbing his hands together, he tried to coax back the warmth the fire couldn't quite provide. He could still feel the ache in his joints, the fatigue that had settled deep into his bones. He was running out of time, and they both knew it.

He looked at her again. "What do you think we'll find?" He didn't have to name where.

Her shrug was so small he would have missed it if not for her back brushing his leg. "Answers. Maybe even a cure for you."

His answering snort was tiny but filled with meaning. She looked at him sharply, and he smiled as best he could. "It doesn't track, Evan. The Magecurse first appeared well before the War of Ascension. Before the Thought Masters disappeared. If they'd found a cure—"

"We'd know about it. I know." She reached up to rest her hand on his thigh. "I have to hope, though."

"Hope," Rick murmured, tasting the word as he said it. "I think I lost hope in the Deeps."

Her eyes didn't move. But her body stiffened just slightly.

"Rick... there's something I should tell you..."

Silence again. He placed his hand on hers. Her fingers trembled beneath his. "Whatever it is, it's okay. It doesn't matter."

She pulled her hand away, slowly, as if afraid to lose contact despite it being her own movement. "It's not okay," she said finally. Her voice was a little thinner now, like the cold had seeped into it. "I nudged you. At the bridge. I didn't mean to push. Not hard. I just... I was afraid you wouldn't act in time."

Her chin sank, falling to her breast, her hair tumbling forward to hide her face from him. Her shoulders shook.

Rick's eyes closed—not from pain. Not even from surprise. Just weariness.

"I know."

Her breath caught mid-sob. She looked at him sharply now. "You—"

"Not then," he clarified. "Not consciously. But later. The more I replayed it, the more I realized it wasn't just me deciding. Something... guided my hand. And I've felt it before. Around you."

Evan's face crumpled for a moment, then smoothed again. She looked down at her hands, clasping them around her knees and pulling herself into a tight ball. "I'm sorry." A tear glistened on her cheek, burning hot in the firelight.

He considered her for a long moment. The fire's glow played across her cheekbones, and for a moment, she could have been any age. She could have been the girl from the picnic or the woman who'd grown old beside him after becoming his entire world.

"I was angry with you for a while," he said at last. "But then I realized it was the world I was truly mad at." Feeling the ache in his bones as he moved, he got off the rock and settled down on the ground behind her, reaching around to pull her tight. "You might've saved us... or just me. I don't know. Maybe it was wrong, maybe it wasn't. But I'm too tired to carry that weight anymore."

His fingers laced through hers. They were cold. "You made a call. And we've made it here. That's what matters."

Evan swallowed hard, pulled their clasped hands up to her face, and kissed the back of his. Then she leaned back into him, resting her head lightly against his shoulder.

"Thank you," she whispered.

They sat like that, listening to the lake breathe, the fire crackle, and the stars move above them. For once Rick didn't try to solve anything. He just let himself be there with her.

And it was enough.

The trail was easy to miss.

They'd nearly passed it—just a sharp bend in the rock that became a ledge, a faint line of flattened moss and dirt edging upward into the heights. Rick spotted it first, his hand catching Evan's sleeve with quiet insistence. She followed his gaze and saw it then: the way the stone had worn underfoot, the occasional stack of loose cairns pressed against the cliffside like forgotten waypoints.

They climbed.

At first the trail clung to the wall, switching back over narrow rises and around jagged outcrops. Above, the sky brightened with gold-edged light, the day still feeling young and gentle in the morning air. The wind stirred Evan's hair as she pressed upward, her breath steady despite the altitude. The air here was thin, crisp enough to bite her throat, but clean in a way she hadn't felt before—certainly not on Earth.

This world is so pristine, she thought. *So pure.* For a moment, she felt as if she were one of the Old West explorers—a pilot leading the way into a new frontier. Then her eyes fell on Rick, and the moment of whimsy passed. He was puffing heavily as he climbed, his face ashen. He had fallen behind but kept plodding forward with grim determination written in the lines of his features. She instinctively moved to go back and help him but caught herself just as the motion began. Instead, she waited, taking in the view and forcing herself to be interested in it.

Below them, the valley they'd camped in had softened to memory. The lake was still visible, a blue-green gem in its reflected light, set within the mountain's clasp. The trees had become green smudges, and there was no sign of the fire ring where they'd spent the night wrapped in one another's embrace under a shared blanket.

Rick arrived, pausing beside her to catch his breath.

"Would you like me to help?" she asked at last.

He hesitated. She knew he'd figured out the secret of how her power worked in this regard—that she took his exhaustion into herself—but he nodded anyway.

She put her hands to his temples and concentrated. Felt the two of them become one, pushing his fatigue aside and replacing it with vigor. Her eyes flew open when she discovered just how much his body ached. Yet he relaxed beneath her hands, and his breathing steadied.

"Thank you," he said when she finished, his blue eyes holding her, as mesmerizing as the lake in the valley below.

Reluctantly she let him go, locking the pain and fatigue into a compartment in her mind where it wouldn't affect her. *I'll deal with it later,* she told herself. *Feel it later.*

Only the path ahead mattered now, and the sense that each step brought them closer to something vast.

A final curve brought them to a natural platform carved between two leaning peaks. The trail widened here, opening into a shelf of stone with enough space to stand side by side. It had been paved long ago, and the stones remained smooth even after centuries. A wind swept across it, colder now, and sharp with altitude. Evan stepped to the edge—and froze.

The world opened. Not just a valley but a whole hidden land stretched out before them, cradled in stone and sky—a place untouched by war or ruin. Golden grass rippled in the wind below, untouched for ages by any foot save animal. The valley floor was carpeted in trees—a few evergreens but the majority wearing their proudest fall foliage of oranges and golds. The effect was as if the basin burned with fire. A winding river flowed like a ribbon through it all, tracing glittering arcs that shimmered in the light.

And there, rising from the very center of it, was the Forbidden Spire. Evan's breath caught, and Rick gave a low whistle that echoed faintly off the surrounding mountainside. It was taller than she'd imagined. A single vertical shaft that competed for height with the mountains themselves, with what appeared to be a crown of interlaced stone at the top, ringing a fluted spire around which great birds flew. The bottom of the tower didn't touch the ground. Instead, it was entirely supported on great sweeping buttresses that arched up from the land, coming together in a single spiral that swept around the tower in three graceful arcs, each narrower than the one below. They reminded Evan of a helix—organic and purposeful, like a strand of DNA.

It had clearly been built, yet it carried the grace of something *grown.* Its surface was white, as the snowcapped mountains beyond, but the word didn't do justice, for the color changed with the light—pale gold where the sun struck it directly, soft violet in the shadows. Shifting hues whispered across it, like the sky was painting its reflection onto the stone. There were no visible doors, no windows, no banners or markings.

And yet Evan felt it. Not just its presence but its *origin.* It was not of one Power but all three. Magic. Mind. Machine. Blended, balanced, woven. A synthesis so complete that it defied dissection. A miracle of creation.

Beside her, Rick's posture, always so tight of late, slackened just slightly. His eyes stayed locked on the structure, jaw loosening, not from weariness but from wonder. He let out a small, breathy sound—just shy of a laugh.

"That's it?" he murmured, voice rough with cold and something older.

She didn't answer. She couldn't.

He shook his head, the edge of disbelief in his breath. "Now I get it," he said softly. "Why its real name was *Haven*." A name half-remembered, barely spoken.

And in that moment, she felt it rise in him—a flicker, a fragile spark: hope. Not a solution. Not certainty. But something deeper. The idea that maybe, just maybe, all the sacrifices had led somewhere. That this place —this myth made manifest—might hold an answer.

And then it was gone.

She watched the change in him as clearly as if someone had pulled a veil over his face. His jaw tightened, his shoulders squared, and the wonder faded from his eyes, replaced with calculation. Anticipation. Dread.

He said nothing more. He didn't have to.

Something prickled at the edge of Evan's consciousness, and she turned her gaze back to the tower. Her heart drummed in her chest, not from the climb but from the sense that they were no longer alone.

Something was watching them.

Not the tower itself, though that was how it felt. Not a consciousness, exactly, but a *presence*. Dormant. Coiled. Waiting. It reminded her of Southwatch, and she realized her hand was clasped around her pendant. She stepped back from the edge. Rick followed without a word.

The trail continued from the overlook, descending in gentle arcs that wound down toward the valley. Grass overtook the rock, thick and vibrant, springy underfoot. The wind changed as they dropped in elevation, warmer now, and filled with the scent of water and wildflowers. The soft drone of insects drifted lazily on the breeze. Even here, the world felt untouched. Preserved, but not empty.

The closer they came, the more details emerged. There were no seams, no cracks. Its surface was unbroken, as though it had been formed whole from some impossible material. The buttresses that supported it shone in places, as if they had been polished in patterns—veins of light embedded in the stone. There was something familiar, although she couldn't put her finger on what it was.

As they neared, Evan could hear something new. A hum—faint, constant. Not mechanical, not magical, but something stranger. A resonance she felt rather than heard. She slowed, placing a hand over her heart.

Rick looked at her, questioning.

"It's... alive," she whispered. Her eyes fell on the medallion, which had slipped out from the folds of his shirt, and she gasped. *The patterns!* The veins of reflected light on the tower's surface, so subtle they seemed imagined, were a match for what covered his pendant.

He looked down, taking the amulet in his hand, turning it over so it reflected the sun's light. He didn't question it—just turned back to face the tower, his expression unreadable—but Evan felt an ember of hope kindle within him.

They reached the valley floor just as the sun cleared the ridge above. Light spilled down in sheets, turning the golden grass almost white, setting the river ablaze with color. The tower loomed before them now, impossibly tall, its crown vanishing into the blue.

Evan paused, her breath catching in her throat.

There was a path now. A true one. Carved into the earth, lined with silver stone, and leading directly to the tower. Rick stepped onto it first.

The hum deepened.

Somewhere inside, something responded.

Ravensford trembled in its sleep. The firelight of The Hearth and Vine spilled across the road in broken ribbons, flickering against the rising mist that coiled through the village's narrow streets. Maltharok stood just beyond the inn's threshold, his cloak still damp from the rain earlier that day, the hood drawn low over the face he now wore—one crafted to set people at ease when they saw it. Not at all like the haughty imperiousness of his Elrath guise.

Maltharok waited, eyes closed, testing the air. Bread. Stew. Ale and wine. Sweat and fear. Underneath it all, Chad and Calladorn lingered. A low sound escaped him—almost a laugh. The man calling himself Matthias had thought he was rescuing them. Their scents were easy to pick out having savored their blood. Even after five days and a storm, the trail lingered, bringing him directly to this door. Patience came easily when the scent was this fresh.

He stepped inside.

The innkeeper was a round-shouldered man with flushed cheeks and the overconfidence of someone who thought himself clever. He leaned on the counter with a lazy grin, polishing a mug more for show than cleanliness. "You're not the first to come looking, you know," he said in response to Maltharok's questions. "Those three... they passed through here not long ago."

"Others?" Maltharok asked casually, sliding gold across the counter. With so few patrons, the innkeeper would be hungry for any income he could scrounge.

The coins disappeared into the man's apron, and he smiled. "Strange thing, really," he went on, warming to his tale. "One group goes east—toward Eastgate—and two days later the other shows up. But only one of them follows the first. The other two? They head north." He chuckled, a short, incredulous bark. "North! Can you believe it? There's nothing up there but cliffs and cursed trees. Everyone knows better. You don't last long in those woods—not with the things that roam them, or so they say."

Maltharok inclined his head slightly, as if amused. "And the ones who went north—what did they look like?"

The innkeeper shrugged. "A young woman and her greatfather, I think. Pale fellow, white beard. She wore a pretty gold pendant."

Maltharok's lips curled beneath the hood, though the innkeeper didn't seem to notice. Too taken with the sound of his own voice.

"Told them they'd lose the trail by midday, but they just nodded and thanked me. Very polite, very determined. Although what could interest them up north, I've no idea. Naught but cliffs and trees."

"Did they stay here?"

"Aye, they did."

Maltharok considered. The boy and the captain would have their hands full in Eastgate. Let them struggle. Let them continue thinking themselves free. That scent could be picked up again later if need be. But the other two... they intrigued him. They hadn't rejoined their friends—which meant they had found something worth the split. Something they couldn't afford to delay.

"I think I'll stay the night," he told the innkeeper, producing more coins. "Maybe the same room my friends used, if it's available."

With the common room this empty, he doubted it had been claimed, but he had other options if necessary.

But they weren't needed. The man handed him a key and sent him upstairs.

Upon reaching the room, Maltharok stepped inside and closed the door behind him. Then he closed his eyes and drank the room in. *There they are.* He had their scents now, faint and layered, but unmistakable. Tangled together like threads of smoke. One hale and one broken.

He left the room and then the building, ignoring the innkeeper's wide-eyed stare. The fool had already served his purpose.

Outside, the air was cooler, touched with spruce and rain and something else. He inhaled deeply. There it was again, faint and layered but unmistakable—his quarry. The two who had gone north, just as the innkeeper had said.

He stepped farther into the night, and Maltharok's skin began to peel away. The illusion loosened like old cloth. The pale flesh sagged and shriveled, melting from his limbs as new shapes unfolded beneath. Taller. Broader. The false eyes dimmed, and his real ones burned bright—pits of molten hunger. Fingers lengthened, sharpening to claws. Bone realigned beneath stretching sinew. There was no need for masks now.

The Heart. If they had it, he would tear it from their corpses. If they had merely learned where it was, well, he would take that instead, and perhaps enjoy the experience all the more.

The man calling himself Matthias had claimed the Heart's power was enough to shake the balance. Maltharok's wide maw twisted into a grin. *That kind of power could challenge even the Dominarch.*

He stepped into the night, the last vestiges of his disguise sloughing away. The scent was clear. The prey trapped. They would be tired—worn thin. All the better. He looked forward to tasting what their hope felt like as it died.

And these two would not be allowed to escape.

XXIV
Siege

The mountains narrowed without warning. Paved with stones, the road from Ravensford had been well maintained—a sure sign to Chad that it normally received a lot of use. But from the time they'd set out the day before, a distinct trend had appeared among the travelers they encountered. All were heading east, on their way to report for duty. Some rode, but most were on foot. Each moved slowly, their heads down and shoulders slumped, as if they were headed for the gallows. A trickle of stragglers at first, they swelled to a stream as Chad's group drew closer to Eastgate.

When they camped for the night, Chad caught snippets of conversation. Some were loud, the speakers declaring how they looked forward to proving themselves in a good fight. But those voices were too high, too tightly strained to be genuine, and always faded away after a few sentences. The rest were mutters and whispers in small groups, mixed with furtive glances to the east. None seemed inclined to speak with people they didn't know.

Chad shared a small fire with Calladorn and Matthias. When he realized he'd shifted positions next to it for the fifth time in as many minutes, he knew the mood was getting to him.

"You're better trained than any of them," Calladorn said softly, his expression carrying the hint of a smile.

Chad looked away, feeling a flush creep up his neck, as he stared into the flames. "That obvious, huh?"

"I remember my first battle." Calladorn leaned close, his voice dropping even lower. "And you know the enemy better than any of us."

Picking up a stick, Chad poked at the logs, trying to coax the flames to burn brighter, but when he closed his eyes, he saw the fires of Emberhold. He leaned back with a shiver, throwing the stick back to the ground.

"Eastgate had better be strong," he muttered.

*

For the last hour, their path had wound steadily upward, the road flanked by slumping hills, giving way to limestone ridges. The route narrowed into a canyon, with high, jagged cliffs rising like jaws on either side. Chad had just enough time to feel the weight of that confinement before they turned a bend.

And the fortress was there.

"Whoa," Matthias muttered beside him.

Even Calladorn reined in, posture stiff, studying the fortification before them. His expression didn't change, but Chad felt the slight tremor in his breath. "I'd heard the legends..."

A long silence passed.

Eastgate didn't rise so much as *loom*. It filled the gap between the cliffs with such geometric precision, it was as if it had been slotted into place by the mountain itself. The first wall stretched between the cliffs, rising from the foundations to fluted blind arcades below crenellated battlements. A bastion rose at either end, flush against the cliffs, and rather than being straight, the wall angled back to a gate with a barbican on either side, each with another bastion at the top of the wall. Even from this distance, Chad could make out the massive blocks used in the construction, their edges given away by nearly black lines in the dark gray structure.

The gate itself yawned open, an arched corridor matching the road's fifteen-foot width. From that, Chad was able to estimate the gate's height at eighty feet, making the wall at least 120 feet tall at the battlements.

"The angle of the walls funnels attackers trying to approach the gates," Calladorn said, nodding. "It's a killing field."

Chad nodded. It was awe-inspiring.

But it was nothing compared to the main wall. Located perhaps two hundred feet behind the outer wall, it could have been a part of the cliffs themselves. It soared to the height of the cliffs, curved and seamless.

Additional towers were built into it near either end, rising just as far above the main wall as the outer wall rose above the canyon floor. There were no windows or other openings to be seen—just a single monolithic formation that could have been carved from the cliff's face, except that it was of some marble-like material, shining white where it wasn't shot through with dark gray or black waves that grew from the ground level like moss.

The entire structure reminded Chad of nothing so much as standing at the base of Hoover Dam, looking up, only this was far taller. It was... unnerving. Taking it in, Chad was reduced to a single thought: *Nothing can get over that.*

Hope flickered to life.

Then Calladorn clicked his tongue. "Come on." They crossed the final stretch at a trot.

The gates were already open. A half-dozen soldiers in dust-caked white tabards stood guard outside. More manned the walls above—the outer wall. There was no way to see who might be on the big one, which only looked larger the closer he got.

Isn't this place supposed to be thousands of years old? Chad thought, studying it. He might have believed it of the main wall—but not the outer one. The design was too different, as were the materials used.

There was something about the main wall that made his skin crawl.

As they approached, Chad saw it more clearly: the outer wall's stones showed signs of aging, with small plants clinging to life within nooks and crannies. It was ancient. But the big wall—that looked *new*. Not repaired. Not recently scrubbed or restored. Just... new. Not a single crack ran through it. No discoloration beyond that of the material itself, no pockmarks, no signs of reinforcement. Everything gleamed like it had been carved yesterday from a single slab of stone.

Then he saw the people. Unlike the fortress itself, they were falling apart. One of the guards swayed where he stood, and others milled about uncertainly. The woman leaning on a pike at the gate had a gaze that didn't quite focus.

As they passed into the shadow of the gate, Chad looked up. The portcullis high above had rusted teeth, but the wall was thick, and the hall they walked through was as long as it was tall, like a tunnel through a building.

The courtyard spreading between the forewall and the true wall only underscored the schism. Tents and pavilions were scattered around, some with merchant stalls and others with impromptu smithies with portable forges. A stable stood to the left, built against the cliff. People were milling around everywhere. But that was the problem—there seemed to be no order. No sense of purpose. No discipline. These weren't soldiers ready for a fight—even Chad could tell that. They were a militia on the edge of collapse.

"Name and business?" barked a soldier just inside the courtyard, making Chad lean away. His breath reeked of liquor.

Calladorn dismounted before he finished. "I am Captain Thorne of Drakerath. My companions and I are here to aid in the defense, and we have urgent news for your commander."

A woman approached, wearing actual armor rather than the ratty tabards over standard work clothes that nearly everyone else had on. She was short, barely coming up to Chad's chest, but every bit as wide at the shoulders, with a thick neck and powerful build. Her face was weathered with age and scars that would have spoken of experience, even without her sharp eyes that seemed to take in everything. Her reddish-brown hair was shaved around the sides, halfway up the scalp, but left long on top and pulled severely back into a short braid. Her eyes flicked to Chad and Matthias, then back again.

"You're not staring at my tattoos, are you, soldier?" she snapped.

That was exactly what he'd been doing. On her neck, as well as the right side of her face and scalp, like vines. Chad gulped. She had a presence about her... Dangerous. Unapologetic. He wondered if she chewed nails for breakfast.

Her gaze lingered on Calladorn's sigil, then drifted to the sword at his belt. "Captain, you said?"

Calladorn nodded.

"Just what we need," she huffed. "More officers. Follow me. Sir." Her tone sounded respectful, by a hair. Her expression was also—until her back was turned, when the mask came off. Calladorn wouldn't have been able to see the way her eyes rolled as she set off across the courtyard, obviously expecting them to follow. "Andrus! Get their horses to the stable."

"Yes, Sergeant!" A scrawny kid ran up to take the reins from them.

Calladorn spoke as he fell in beside her. "I would have expected more discipline, even from conscripts."

The sergeant laughed—a single bark. "You've obviously never met Vail."

Calladorn's gait slipped slightly. "The commander?"

"His Royal Highness himself."

Uh-oh, Chad thought. *Arlos. Elrath. Now Vail?*

"A prince?" Calladorn asked.

"In his dreams." She glanced back over her shoulder, opened her mouth as if to say something, then looked back ahead with a shake of her head. "You'll see."

The door to the main wall was like nothing Chad had ever seen. At first it looked like it was just a tall, wide hall cut into the stone, but it had a ten-foot-long wooden floor that seemed to be freestanding, like it was built to be temporary, over a foot-deep gap in the floor. To the right was all solid wall, but to the left was an empty room, ten feet deep. Overhead the ceiling was an extra foot higher than the rest of the tunnel, but only in the area where the wooden bridge stood.

Then it hit Chad. The wall to his right... wasn't a wall. It was a massive block of stone designed to slide across, completely sealing the entrance. Once in place, there would be no way to get past it, no way to push it aside. The ultimate door. He couldn't imagine what it would take to move the thing. He longed to get a look at the mechanisms that allowed it to work.

But then they were past it, and he had other things to occupy him.

Inside, the signs he'd noticed before were even clearer. The fortress walls gleamed under torchlight. Marble? No—too matte. Some kind of limestone, maybe, but with a sheen like glass. The halls were all right angles, perfectly measured, the geometry so exact it made his head ache. He couldn't help it—his fingers drifted to his pocket, to the worn curve of his Swiss Army knife. Something about this place prickled at the part of his brain that counted gears and measured tolerances.

It was *engineered*. That was the word that stuck. Too perfect. Too clean. And someone had tried to hide that.

The torches were hung in soot-streaked stands spaced along the floor. Impromptu walls had been constructed of wood and stood in place. There were racks against the walls, holding weapons. Cupboards and other furniture. Tapestries, mounted on frames rather than hung from the walls. It had the feel of someone deliberately trying to clutter the place. Deface it, even. But nothing was attached to a wall anywhere that he could see—not so much as a single spike driven into the stone.

Was it because they didn't want to? Or because they couldn't? He touched the wall in wonder, and his breath caught. It was warm.

Chad slowed. Matthias noticed, giving him a sidelong glance.

"You see it too?"

Chad nodded slowly. "It's not just ancient. It's untouched—not breaking down at all." No one else seemed to notice. Not Calladorn, who marched beside the sergeant like he belonged there. Not the soldiers who passed with glassy eyes and dragging feet. Not the boy scrubbing dirt off the floor with a brush too small for the job. Everyone was too busy surviving.

Chad looked again at the clean-cut walls, at the seamless joints and spotless lintels. This place wasn't built. It was *formed*.

And he had the strangest sense it was waiting.

The way up was longer than expected. Wide stone ramps switchbacked through the inner wall, climbing steadily. They passed guard stations and fortified galleries, multiple layers of defense that made it clear just how deadly this fortress could be to any who dared breach it.

Following the sergeant in silence, Calladorn tracked every detail, seeing not only what was there but what should have been. At the top of each ramp was a rampart of obviously newer construction, using a different stone from the surrounding wall. Spouts—he counted six each time—angled down from the tops of the battlements. It was ingenious. Oil could be released, making the ramps impossible to ascend. If boiling, it would be brutal. If burning... His nose curled at the thought, and he shuddered.

A small number of properly supplied troops could hold each ramp against vastly larger forces.

The first few landings also had loopholes in the walls to the left and right, with rooms beyond. Slits for concealed archers. A deadly crossfire. It was a sound strategy but strange, because these were also different constructions from the rest of the fortress wall. It was as if someone had walled up corridors, converting them to defensive stations.

Once they reached the third landing, he became certain. The walls facing in on either side were flat only because of the newer construction. Halls had been sealed off. Why? Even his untrained eye could tell that it had been done long ago—the mortar had yellowed with age.

There was also a channel in the walls on either side of the ramps, chest height. At the top of the ramp, the outer one continued to the far wall, where it disappeared into a hole. Those confused Calladorn at first, until he spotted a slight difference in appearance between the top third and bottom two-thirds of the endcap walls. They were cantilevered, allowing the wall to tilt open. He would have bet anything a mechanism lurked behind those false walls. Something that would roll down the ramps, guided by the tracks in either wall. It might be a heavy roller to crush anyone unfortunate enough to be on the ramp. Or it might be more creative, such as scything blades.

Whoever had built Eastgate had known war. Intimately. Then, for unknown reasons, someone had come back through and mucked it up. Even so, he concluded that if the garrison were even half as disciplined as the stonework, the fortress would be unassailable.

But the footsteps behind him were weary, the voices echoing through the halls were ragged, and the air smelled not of iron and oil but of unwashed bodies and overcooked rations.

And why were there no lifts? By the time they reached the upper ramparts, his thighs burned. The final ramp emptied onto a vast platform—not a parapet but a proper yard, surrounded by four imposing towers. The massive main wall bowed inward on each side here, forming an hourglass shape between the cliffs. With stone tiling underfoot, grooved for traction, the space was wide enough to train five companies side by side. It was arrayed with racks of weapons, pallets of quarrels, buckets of sand.

And siege engines—gods, there were so many. Ballistae with arms like tree trunks, catapults strung with thick cables, even a pair of trebuchets that looked as if they'd been dragged from some ruined castle and retrofitted. Some were weathered and misshapen, patched with iron bands and spare timber. Others gleamed as if fresh-forged. Calladorn frowned. They seemed out of place. Too inelegant for the design perfection of this fortress.

He turned toward the eastern vista. And froze.

The canyon on this side was wider—a long, arcing bowl stretching away from the fortress like the hollow of a cupped hand. Far beneath them, the canyon floor boiled with motion. It took a moment for his mind to parse the scale, and then the shapes resolved.

Demons.

Too many to count. Worse than Chad's description of Emberhold. Worse than anything he'd imagined at Ironspire. They swarmed across the lowlands in clusters, some large as wagons, others small and quick, bounding like insects. Even at this distance, he could see claws, spines, and rippling flesh. A great hulk with a pair of curving tusks bellowed, the sound faint but still audible.

He realized his hands were clenched, and he forced them to open. There would be no escape. If Eastgate fell, there would be nowhere to run.

A squat tower stood in the center of the wall-top yard, long, with rounded ends. Two stories, with wide yet short windows wrapping the upper level. Unlike the rest of the fortress, this looked lived-in—sandbags, crates, signal flags.

The sergeant stopped at the doors leading into the nearest end. "This is the command tower. I'll wait here."

Calladorn raised a brow. "You're not joining us?"

"Not on a bet," she said. Then, more quietly, "You'll see." She leaned with her back against the stone and closed her eyes as if she planned to nap while an army of monsters filled the valley below.

Inside, the air was stuffy and redolent with pipe smoke. A curved stair led up to the second floor, where a long table dominated the space. Maps sprawled across it, anchored by metal markers, and seven men stood around it.

One among them drew the eye. He was tall, with immaculately combed gray hair. A blue sash across a spotless uniform. Medals lining both sides of his chest in rows that strained the fabric, and epaulets heavy enough to double as pauldrons. When he turned, his jaw was square, his nose sharp, his posture impeccable.

Commander Vail. He looked every inch the soldier, but unlike the sergeant, he had no scars. The weapon at his side was a rapier rather than a sword—good for dueling or personal defense but useless for real fighting.

The man's pale blue eyes spared them only a disinterested glance as they entered. "Over there," he said, waving vaguely toward a small table on one side of the room, piled high with dirty plates and uneaten food.

"Sir?" Calladorn said, coming to attention.

Vail looked at him at last, eyes narrowing when he saw the black uniform with its golden embroidery and stopping on the captain's insignia at Calladorn's collar. His eye twitched, and he looked at his aides, who shrugged.

"You are...?" he asked at last.

"Captain Calladorn Thorne of Drakerath." He felt a muscle in his neck begin to twitch and tried to ignore it.

Vail blinked—an owl in the sunlight. "A bit far from home, aren't you?"

Someone chuckled—a towheaded sycophant with poor posture.

Calladorn bristled. "We heard about the conscription order in Luthenholme and came to lend aid."

"Ah. Yes." Vail's perfectly trimmed mustache quivered as the man's mouth worked silently. "Our good king has quite the sense of humor, doesn't he?"

If there was a joke, Calladorn couldn't see it. "Your pardon?" he asked. *I will not beg. Not of this... fop.*

Vail made a small dismissive gesture. "Turning the kingdom upside down over some... wild animals. On the other side of the wall, no less."

The officers beside him shifted, but none spoke. None met Calladorn's eye.

Vail continued. "You are far from home, Thorne, so perhaps you don't know. Eastgate has stood for three thousand years. Once sealed, it cannot be breached. We will wait this inconvenience out. The beasts will eventually go away, or they'll eat one another. Either way, Almarion will look even more the fool than he already does."

Chad cleared his throat. "We have information—about the High King. About what he's planning. You need to hear it."

Vail turned his gaze on Chad as if he'd found mud on his boots. "Oh, you're not the porter either?" He blinked again. "Pity. The only plan I need to hear about is how *Captain* Thorne intends to organize the rabble camped in my courtyard."

Calladorn stepped in. "Commander, if you'll allow us a moment—"

"No. I won't."

Silence fell.

Vail turned back to the table. "These walls will not fall."

His aides nodded in near unison. One patted his powdered forehead with a kerchief. Calladorn studied their faces. Waxen, nervous, too eager to agree. Not one bore a single scar. Not one had dirt beneath his nails. They were officers the way a bard was a king.

Chad drew breath to speak again. Calladorn touched his arm—a warning. If they pushed further, Vail would have them locked up. That was obvious now. And if that happened, no one would be left to lead.

He took a breath and let it out slowly. "Very well. We'll see what we can do."

Vail waved a hand. "You want to waste your time organizing conscripts, fine. Just don't waste mine."

Dismissed.

Back in the sunlight, the sergeant raised an eyebrow. "You see." Her tone was steady. It wasn't a question.

Calladorn looked again at the siege engines. At the canyon beyond. This fortress didn't need a traitor to fall. It only needed its defenders to trust the stone more than their own eyes. He turned back to the courtyard, jaw tight, spine straight. "What's your name?" he asked the sergeant.

"Halvard. Bram."

"How long have you been posted here?"

"Three years." She studied him.

"Then I assume you know how the ramps work." A statement, but the question was there all the same. If Halvard was half the sergeant he thought...

She scowled. "They're a trap of some sort but were walled off centuries ago. Hells, half the original construction is closed off."

"Care to change that?"

A wicked grin split her face, full of missing teeth. "Yes, *sir*!"

Calladorn nodded. If Vail wouldn't lead, then he would.

Matthias stood at the edge of the upper yard, hands behind his back, watching the canyon below with a narrowed gaze.

Five hundred feet below, the demons milled in clusters. They snarled and roared, their cries numerous and loud enough to carry even to this height. They shifted their weight from one clawed foot to the other. But they did not act.

Directly below, they swarmed within the courtyard and boiled over the foregate. The entire area, lost. Beside him, Halvard was telling Calladorn how the monsters had mounted a surprise attack in the night, the foregate falling within minutes, but not before the wall's eastern door was sealed.

Like Emberhold, a sudden, crushing attack, Matthias thought. *Numbers over finesse. Whoever their commander is, they lack subtlety. And now they have stopped?* They waited. Matthias did not like it.

Beside him, Calladorn paced. Not like a soldier. Like a man trying to bleed off rage through motion. The captain's eyes scanned the yard with increasing dismay.

"How many soldiers do we have?" Calladorn asked.

Halvard shifted her balance. "Soldiers? Twenty-seven. We had a skeleton contingent of forty before this, but..." Her voice trailed off, her gaze drifting to the foregate below before snapping back to Calladorn. "At last count, we had two thousand militia. They've been billeted in the first-floor barracks within the wall."

"And no one is training them?" Calladorn asked.

"No, sir." Her lip twisted as she spoke.

Calladorn swore. It was the first time Matthias had ever heard him do so. "No sparring. No drills. No posted rotations. Not even a blasted roll call."

They left the ramparts and walked the ramps back down to ground level. Calladorn continued to study the structure and ask questions.

Matthias followed the line of Calladorn's gaze as they walked. Slumped figures clustered against walls, rusted helms rested on crates, spears lay in bundles as if forgotten. No readiness, no urgency—only fear and fatigue.

Halvard spat to the side as they walked. "This place hasn't been used for defense in over a thousand years," she said. "Back then, they could man it proper. Now? Not enough weapons, not enough officers. And even if there were, no one even remembers what half the fortress does."

Calladorn turned sharply to her without breaking his stride. "How many levels are there?"

Halvard shrugged. "We don't know. Sealed long before my time. Not enough personnel to patrol them, they said. Not enough reason to try. And with no proper garrison, it was safer to lock them away."

Calladorn's expression sharpened. It was not anger, precisely. It was clarity. He moved fast after that, issuing orders in clipped succession. "*Master* Sergeant," he said. She blinked, and he smiled. "Vail may not realize it, but he ordered me to organize conscripts. I can't commission officers, but I also can't execute those orders without a command staff. I'm promoting you. Do you have a problem with that?"

Her eyes sparkled. "None at all, sir."

"Good. You know who has experience, who can lead. Find them. Make them sergeants. Organize these conscripts into squads. I want drills running before midday."

Halvard straightened, the corners of her mouth twitching upward as her hand started to rise.

"And open the sealed levels," Calladorn continued before the salute could continue. "We need every inch of this place, every resource, and we have the bodies for it. As long as the demons remain stymied by the wall, I intend to make use of the time. I want those levels explored and documented. Anything useful gets brought to my attention and put to use." He turned. "Chad, that job is yours."

Matthias glanced at the younger man. Chad's posture stiffened, and for a moment, he hesitated. The weight of expectation settled visibly on his shoulders. His fingers flexed at his sides. But then—something shifted. His gaze flicked to the walls. The ramps. Not with panic but with precision. Matthias saw the change. It was like watching a child drop a mask. Chad was no longer waiting. He was calculating.

Most boys in his position would have asked for guidance. They would have searched the faces around them, hoping for reassurance. They would have puffed their chests, put on a show of confidence. Chad did none of those things. Instead he stepped forward, looked to Halvard, and said, "I will need a team. Not just muscle. People who can sketch, measure, diagram."

Halvard raised an eyebrow, then she nodded.

Matthias remained silent, but his eyes did not leave the boy. *No. Not a boy.* Not anymore. There was something forming behind those eyes—something Matthias could not name. It made him uneasy. Chad Johnson had always been sharper than the image he projected, but this was different. It was... control. *Could he be used?* Matthias wondered. Could that focus be guided? Sharpened?

A tool. Perhaps a weapon, if properly honed. Matthias had worked with both. But something deeper stirred beneath the surface of that cold calculation. Something that gave him pause.

It was fascination. He knew he should not feel that. Not here, not now. And yet...

Calladorn's voice snapped him from the thought. "Matthias. With me."

He turned.

"I need you on supplies. Armaments, armor, anything we can distribute. Inventory what we have, and get it where it needs to be."

Matthias inclined his head, but Calladorn was already focused on

Halvard again, talking about the need to set up a command headquarters. Matthias eyed Chad once more. He did not like questions without answers, and that young man had just become one. But what kind?

The fortress buzzed with activity.

Chad jogged down the corridor, boots thudding against smooth stone. Three kids trailed him, none older than sixteen, all moving fast. He'd picked them for their sharp eyes and quick feet. He couldn't imagine them drilling and swinging swords, but a battle needed logistics and a way to pass both news and orders quickly. These kids would be perfect for that if it came to a fight. Until then, they were an ideal scouting party.

In a way, he felt like he was back on the football field—a quarterback calling the plays for the team. He may have traded in the jersey for a lord's coat, but the effect was the same. And these kids looked at him like he was some kind of major league star. *So why do I feel like an impostor?* he wondered. Did the coat fit him, or was he changing to fit the coat? The thought passed as soon as it arrived. Calladorn... all these people were counting on him. They didn't have time for doubt.

The kids moved fast, prying open doors and calling back when they found nothing. Chad kept a rough map in his head, marking the paths they'd taken, listening for echoes of movement, keeping count of every corridor, every odd architectural feature.

They passed a sealed arch, long since broken open, then turned left into one of the corridors Halvard's squads had only just cleared. The air here was cooler, the silence deeper. Dust curled in the torchlight as they walked by, but not as much as there should be for a place sealed up for... what? Centuries? The air was fresher than it had a right to be, too.

Something about the place itched at him. A hunch, like trying to remember a dream the moment after waking. The walls were so smooth and yet... not. Shiny in some places and dull in others, catching the light oddly as they passed with their torches. He kept thinking he saw patterns in his peripheral vision, but when he looked, there was just more white stone.

"Over here, sir!" one of the boys called.

Chad broke into a run and found the kid pointing into a dark chamber.

Weapons. Racks of them, lining the walls. Swords, spears, axes. Some styles he recognized. Most he didn't. The hafts were carved with strange patterns. The blades broader than what he'd seen before. But the edges gleamed. No rust. No dust. Like they'd been forged yesterday and stored with care.

His breath caught. "Stay here," he said. "Guard it."

"But I'm not armed," the boy said.

Chad didn't answer, just looked at him and lifted his eyebrows a bit.

The boy flushed red as if he'd gotten sunburned. "Oh... right." The way he casually walked to one of the racks and took a halberd reminded Chad of a cat after it had tripped over its own feet, picking itself up with an air suggesting it had been deliberate. Chad turned his head away so the boy wouldn't see his grin. Then he scribbled a message, gave it to the fastest of the three, and sent him sprinting back toward the surface.

The next room over was filled with armor—not the cheap boiled leather or ill-fitting mail he'd seen most of the actual soldiers wearing, but full sets—polished plate, chain mail shirts, helms with reinforced cheek guards and padded liners, all organized by size. Most were for humans, but some would have fit other races as well. There was an elegance to the design that he admired. The aesthetic was different from anything he'd seen, speaking of both strength and grace.

He ran his fingers along the edge of one cuirass. Cool. Smooth. No warping. These weren't relics. They were tools—crafted to be worn by people who saw war as an art form.

Setting the remaining boy to counting racks and estimating numbers, Chad sat for a moment, back against the wall between the two chambers, watching dust float in the light. He pictured the look on the commander's face when he realized what Calladorn had done. That the ragged conscripts were already drilling would be priceless enough. But get them equipped in this gear... *Vail won't know what hit him.* That thought made him grin again. Calladorn had done it without a chest full of medals or a committee of toadies. No orders barked for show. Just motion, direction, and clarity of purpose.

Syndar had nearly broken him. First the High King. Then that dungeon... It was like finding out your whole life had been someone else's joke. After that—even after their escape—Chad had wondered if Calladorn was ever going to find his footing again. But this? This was who he was meant to be.

Chad's smile faded. He hoped Vail was right. That the walls would hold and this was all wasted effort. But he didn't believe it. Not after Emberhold. Not after Maltharok. That... *thing* had worn skin like a mask, talked like a man. Planned. No, this enemy wasn't just mindless violence. It was cunning.

The light changed subtly as Prestin—the boy tallying the armor—moved again. Chad's eyes widened. Across from where he sat in the narrow hallway between the two storage rooms was a smaller room, about ten feet square, from what he could see, and filled with what looked like junk. Piles of broken crates, bits of worn gear, sacks of grain long since turned to dust.

But that wasn't what caught his attention.

He stood and walked slowly forward, moving from side to side to change the way the light played across the surface. The room was left of center, relative to the hallway extending away from the wall to the central ramp. To the right was an outline of the same size, and between these two areas, in the stone wall itself, something had been etched: faint lines, almost hidden beneath grime, geometric and familiar.

His fingers traced the lines, so subtle it was a wonder he'd even seen them. The wall itself felt warm, just like everything else in this place, but the lines were cool and the rectangle formed by them—about the size of his flattened hand—was colder still, like a pane of glass on a spring morning. It was positioned exactly like—

Call buttons, he realized. *For elevators.*

Licking lips that suddenly felt too dry, he squinted. The symbols continued around the doorframe, vanishing into the stone. There was no shaft. No panel. Just the carvings.

Dropping to his knees in the open doorway, he inspected the floor. Nothing showed in this light, but as he drew his hand slowly across the surface, he felt it. In line with the inner doorjamb, the tiniest of cracks.

"No way," he whispered. That was what had been bothering him.

The ramps. They were grand, but as a way of getting from the base of the fortress to the ramparts, they were just... dumb. If this place was built when legends said, before the Ban, it didn't make sense to use something so inefficient.

Feeling his heart thumping in his chest, he stood and began pulling things aside. A half-collapsed cabinet. A broken wheel. Sacks that puffed old straw when touched. He didn't care about any of it. What mattered to him was the inside wall.

More markings. He leaned closer.

"Chad!" Halvard's voice. She rounded the corner, beaming. "Hell of a find," she said, looking into the weapons room. "This is enough to triple our outfitted troops. Maybe more."

He pointed to the wall. "Sergeant, I think there's something here—"

"Junk room," she said, dismissing it with a wave. "There's dozens like it. Broken stuff no one ever cleared out. Good instincts, but you've already hit gold. See what else you can dig up."

He hesitated. *So close!* But the Ban, he couldn't push it. Not now... Sighing softly, he nodded, then turned and moved off, gathering his team. But he marked the hallway in his mind. He would come back—alone if he had to.

He needed to know what this place had forgotten.

Matthias stood on the edge of the upper yard, hands clasped behind his back, eyes flicking from squad to squad as the drilling continued.

The transformation was undeniable. Lines of conscripts moved through sword and spear routines. Footwork was rough but improving. Halvard's sergeants barked corrections, and no one questioned them. Nearby, a group practiced loading and cranking a ballista. Its limbs creaked with age, but someone had already replaced the primary spring and cleaned the iron catch. Whenever someone started to flag, they glanced east toward the demons milling in the valley. Each time, the conscripts swallowed or made a warding sign before returning to their drills with renewed intensity.

Below, in the courtyard west of the main wall, another drill unit marched in formation around a makeshift obstacle course. A sergeant's voice carried up faintly as she called time, pointing out flaws in movement and formation.

Chad went from siege engine to siege engine along the bulwark, inspecting each as he made his way toward Calladorn's end of the wall. A boy ran beside him with a scroll, furiously scribbling notes. It was absurd. It was working.

Matthias let out a breath. These men and women had been little more than livestock yesterday. Now they looked like soldiers. No—not soldiers. Not yet. But they looked like they might become such soon, and that was remarkable. Especially considering what they had been given to work with.

A short distance away, several open crates overflowed with armor. Not mismatched junk, either—proper mail, polished plates, fitted leathers reinforced with steel. Chad had distributed the sizes like a merchant at a market, somehow managing to equip nearly half the conscripts in the upper yard and another quarter below. And the weapons—unexpected. Matthias had seen the storage rooms himself. It was as if someone had sealed off a royal armory and left it waiting.

He glanced again at the yard. Halvard strode among her sergeants like a ship's prow cutting waves, issuing corrections, offering praise with a gruff nod or a slap to the shoulder.

And there at the far end stood Calladorn. Cool. Measured. Watching everything, correcting nothing. He did not need to. Orders had already been issued. Their execution was simply a matter of time. Matthias studied him with narrowed eyes. Something had shifted since Syndar. The man who had looked ready to break now stood as if he had been carved from the wall itself.

And Chad. The boy moved differently—less like a squire playing at command, more like a man who had found the shape of his own thoughts. He did not hesitate. He did not wait. He acted. Matthias felt it again—that flicker of respect he had no name for.

He turned toward the east, toward the yard's far wall. The towers at either end now held watchers, posted by Calladorn the moment he had taken charge, keeping an alert eye on the demons below. The figures below milled, as they had apparently done since the sealing of the wall in their initial attack. They roared, scraped the ground, bit at each other. But they did not press the wall.

Why? The eastern face was sheer, yes. The wall was too high for siege ladders or towers, and the gate had been sealed in time. But could they not scale it? If not, what of the cliffs? Those had been smoothed, certainly, but they were not made of the same material as the wall. If the demons were incapable, that was one thing, but that did not align with what Matthias knew. Chad and Calladorn had learned Maltharok had no shortage of cunning. His kind did not rely solely on brute strength. If they had chosen to wait, it meant something.

Could they be facing pressure from the east? An unexpected offensive from Velsaria? Faltheris? Or was something else at work? Some unseen motive? That thought itched at him. He hated questions without answers.

A sudden motion across the yard caught his attention. The doors of the command tower burst open, and Commander Vail emerged at a clipped pace, his polished boots striking the stone with unnecessary force. His retinue of overdressed officers scurried behind, one of them clutching a folded parasol despite the shadows of the towers. Matthias watched, lips tightening faintly. The commander crossed the yard like a man chasing his own relevance. His gaze locked on Calladorn, who stood beside Halvard, reviewing a sketch one of Chad's runners had delivered. Chad himself was nowhere in sight—likely back below, rooting through the fortress again.

Vail closed the distance and began speaking even before he stopped walking. "What, exactly, is going on here?"

Calladorn stood straight, hands behind his back, offering no salute and no apology. In fact, he smiled. "Commander Vail. Good of you to come inspect our progress."

Halvard shifted a step aside, her stance an insolent parody of parade rest.

Vail's face flushed as he gestured at the drilling squads, the siege engines, the sergeants giving orders. "Inspect? Progress? Who gave you permission—"

"I'm following your orders, sir," Calladorn interrupted, his expression a study in cultivated confusion.

One of his aides stepped forward—perhaps to lend weight to the commander's fury—but Calladorn turned his head and impaled him with a stare. The aide stopped, and Matthias tilted his head, curious.

Vail's finger jabbed the air. "I gave no such orders."

Calladorn's reply came slow and measured, his mouth barely moving. He gestured once—to the squads, the courtyard, and the ready weapons. "You instructed me to organize the conscripts. I recall your phrasing precisely, if you would like me to remind you. Sir?" Then he tilted his head, as if confused by the commander's outburst.

Matthias almost laughed. He knew that move. It was the posture of a man playing ignorant while twisting a blade.

Vail stiffened.

Calladorn responded with a single nod. "I assumed your lack of specificity in how I was to execute the order was due to confidence in my abilities." Another quiet deflection. His bearing was impeccable.

The commander had been outmaneuvered. If he denied the exchange now, he would look a fool. His only option was to pretend this had been his intent all along.

Vail sputtered. He looked to his retinue, who were watching the drama unfold with rapt attention. Cheek twitching, he nodded stiffly, turned sharply on his heel, and marched back toward his tower.

Matthias smiled to himself. A few more days like this, and no one would remember who had given the original orders. They would only remember who made those orders mean something.

His musings were broken by a sound that rolled like thunder through the stone. A horn. Then another.

Matthias straightened as all motion in the yard ceased and all eyes turned eastward. The watchers had seen something.

Vail and his retinue froze. Halvard raised a hand. Across the courtyard, squad leaders barked orders.

The demons were moving, and Eastgate would soon learn whether all of this had been enough.

Studying the commander's back as he headed toward his tower, followed by his officers, Calladorn frowned. "How did that man get put in charge?" he muttered.

Halvard must have heard him. "The Knight-General's brother," she muttered.

Calladorn nodded. This was probably seen as the least important post in the kingdom, a perfect place to exile an irritating rival, or an embarrassment you couldn't get rid of. Except now. He wondered where the Knight-General was, given the king's orders to send defensive forces to Eastgate. *No, now isn't the time.* He turned back to Master Sergeant Halvard, wanting the latest reports concerning Chad's efforts to explore the sealed interior.

Before he could speak, horns sounded, and Calladorn stiffened.

A shout rose from the tower next to him. "Activity to the east!"

Calladorn was already moving. He crossed the upper yard at a jog, aware of the thud of boots behind him as Vail and his retinue followed. Matthias was already on the eastern rampart.

The wind was sharper here, carrying the scent of stone, pitch, and smoke. Beyond the wall, the wide canyon floor writhed with movement.

But it was no longer random or chaotic.

Where before the demons had surged and snarled without direction, now they moved with purpose. The crowd parted as larger beasts pushed forward—hulking, twice the size of the others, with spiked shoulders and pale skin stretched too thin across their frames. Around them prowled other creatures, smaller but faster-looking. Sleek and predatory, their motions held a different kind of intent. All focused on the sealed gateway at the base of the wall.

"What are they doing?" Halvard muttered.

"They mean to test the seal," Calladorn said quietly, but even as he spoke, he felt a chill of doubt. The big ones weren't here to test the wall. They stood too still for that. They were waiting. Watching. As if they expected...

Vail arrived with a snort. "Nothing we haven't seen a dozen times. There is no moving that stone from the outside." He sounded bored.

Calladorn turned to Halvard. "The gate—how is it controlled?"

"Two levers," she replied. "One's down in the base level, behind a barred door. The other is here. In the tower."

"And the beasts cannot reach either," Vail said, with the air of someone announcing a triumph. "You have wasted your time, Captain."

But Calladorn wasn't looking at Vail. His attention was locked on the line of larger demons, still unmoving. Their heads tilted subtly, saucer-sized eyes trained on the gateway. The smaller ones danced around them, throwing themselves at the wall or trying to climb it, their claws or other appendages scraping uselessly off the smooth stone. But the big ones didn't flinch. Didn't move. Didn't snarl. They were waiting for something.

Calladorn stepped back from the parapet. "Double the guard at both control rooms," he said, already turning. "And place archers on either side with clear lines of fire." Halvard was giving the order before he finished speaking. He allowed himself a flicker of a smile. In a place paralyzed by inaction, she anticipated. *A promotion well deserved,* he thought.

"Stand down!" Vail shouted. "I am in command here, not Thorne. You will follow *my* orders!"

Calladorn halted, and the surrounding troops froze. Halvard's shoulders slumped for a moment before she returned to the barest pose of attention that protocol required. Then he turned and met the commander's challenging eyes. With careful precision, he clasped his hands behind his back. "Awaiting your orders, sir."

Silence. All eyes turned to Vail. The commander's jaw worked. He looked from one face to another, as if trying to gauge how far his authority would carry. He took a breath. Opened his mouth—

"Fliers!" The word cracked from the southern tower.

Calladorn spun. It took several moments of searching before he saw them—a cluster of winged shapes, rising fast along the southern cliff's edge. Thin-bodied, wide-winged, with trailing limbs and barbed tails, they hugged the ridgeline as they flew, using the terrain to mask their approach—a perfect assault vector, with low visibility until the last second. It was a tactic favored by Syrillian gryphon riders.

Vail's voice behind him was thick with disbelief. "But they've never—"

Calladorn didn't wait. "Positions! Protect the command tower and the upper ramp! Archers to the towers! Now!"

Movement exploded across the yard—not confused this time but purposeful. With scarcely more than a day of training, they were already acting like a military.

Eastgate braced for its first true test in more than a thousand years.

Chad brushed fingers across the etched wall—scarcely a touch, but enough to feel what he was looking for. His breath fogged in the chill stillness of what he believed to be the wall's highest level.

The grooves were faint—barely visible under normal light—but the sheen of oil from a torch brought them to life. Not random, not decorative. He followed one with his finger, tracing the gentle arc as it split, looped, then joined again with another. A closed circuit. He had finally figured out why the patterns seemed so familiar. They looked like Rick's medallion.

He leaned in, heart tapping faster. The pattern was too regular, too deliberate, and the closest comparison he could think of was a printed circuit board. "Definitely not just an armory," he muttered.

"What's that?" Prestin asked, then he made a face. "Damn, I lost count."

Chad's gaze flicked past him to the racks. They were like the first his team had found, full of gear in excellent condition. Chad casually wondered which era they belonged to—before the Ban or after. Because the more he uncovered, the more he understood. The wall had been built first, and the fortress had later been repurposed, but since they couldn't get rid of whatever technology was embedded, they had hidden or disguised it. And then they'd forgotten it.

Leaving the boy to his inventory, Chad exited the room.

Every level they'd uncovered had followed the same pattern. Straight corridor, big storage rooms on either side, and always—always—that T-junction, which, when checked against his sketched maps, aligned vertically with all the others. Always the same flat wall opposite the intersection, with faint etchings and an outline that felt too clean to be coincidence. On most floors, there were no closets. Instead, the wall was featureless except for the faint etchings. The exceptions were the first floor, where a storage closet had been on the left, and here, with it on the right.

And like the first, it was stuffed full of junk. Just like the one back home where he stashed his tool kits and half-finished projects. But where Chad's clutter had been random, this seemed deliberate. Organized chaos.

Someone had tried to hide… what? He crouched by the base of the wall, examining the seam again. It was cleaner than the others. No mortar. No damage. Just an impossibly tight fit, like the pieces had fused instead of being assembled. The faint etchings ran directly into the seam and continued past it. He'd seen printed circuit boards cleaner than this, but not by much.

He rocked back on his heels, pushing fingers through his hair. "If this isn't circuitry, I'll eat my knife."

Footsteps clattered in the corridor. "Chad!"

He straightened as one of his runners—Errol, maybe—ran from the ramps and skidded to a halt a few feet away, out of breath. The boy's eyes were wide. "They're moving up top. Everyone's being pulled to the wall. Master Sergeant Halvard just ordered reinforcements to the gate controls. Says the commander's calling the shots now."

Chad blinked. "Wait. Vail?"

The boy snorted. "Captain Thorne."

A grin split Chad's face before he could stop it. He looked away, trying to school it into something more serious and only half-succeeding. "Tell Halvard about the supply racks in the eastern wing. Mostly belts and scabbards, but a few full kits. Go!"

The boy took off. When Chad turned back, the armor room was deserted. So was the one with the weapon racks. Everyone else had cleared out, probably following Errol's trail to get new orders. Which meant…

He looked at the wall again. "All right," he murmured. "Let's see what you really are."

After laying his torch on the floor at the center of the intersection, he moved fast. His shadow danced as he started pulling junk out of the room. Crates filled with battered helmets or ratty leather; a rolled-up rug, its pattern threadbare... It all got tossed into the intersection.

But the inside wall on the left was blank.

Crap.

He switched to the other side, not even paying attention to what he was moving. If it was in his way, it got thrown out into the hall with a crash and often the clatter of metal sliding across stone. *I hope Halvard doesn't catch me.*

In moments, that wall was also exposed. And sure enough—a panel as smooth as glass. He touched it, but nothing happened, and he sighed. Of course it would need power. He pounded his fist against the wall in frustration. The sound rang hollowly, and he tilted his head to listen. Thin walls, with space beyond—a shaft.

An idea formed. "Just because the car won't move through the shaft doesn't mean I can't."

He returned to clearing the junk with a will, stifling a sneeze as the room became filled with drifting dust. All the while, he kept his eyes peeled for an opening in the ceiling or a crack in the wall—anything indicating a panel that could be removed. When he found it, his jackknife would finally get used for something meaningful.

He just hoped there was still time.

XXV
Remembrance

The valley was even more tranquil than it had appeared from the pass. Rick led Evan along the path, its stones still firmly placed despite the hundreds of years since the Thought Masters had vanished, with only an occasional blade of grass poking through the cracks. The air was surprisingly warm—far more comfortable than the altitude should have permitted—a fact that Rick's old bones appreciated. Arthritis had been bothering him since they had woken up by the lake that morning, but now it faded.

Hints of lavender and rose drifted on the breeze, soothing him—a breeze that rustled the leaves of the trees through which they walked. They were surrounded by crimson, gold, and amber. Honey, tangerine, and scarlet. The wood was in full fall plumage, yet not a single leaf had fallen from its branch. It was as if a perfect autumn day had been captured and preserved for all time.

Haven.

The grass had grown high here but not wild. It bent in long, deliberate waves, as if still remembering where it had once been told to grow. Stone paths curved through an ancient garden, its symmetry subtly walking a delicate line between natural and planned. Even the moss seemed to know where it belonged.

And above it all, the tower soared. What they had seen from the pass wasn't a trick of the light. It truly did float, suspended by three graceful buttresses that swept upward before combining into a single spiral that wrapped around the tower, holding it lovingly aloft in an impossible embrace. Now that they were close, Rick was fascinated by the way the supports melded into the natural rock formations of this place. Try as he might, he couldn't quite identify the precise moment where nature left off and construction began. The transition was seamless. He had the strangest feeling that order had not been imposed on this place so much as nature had simply agreed that this was how it should be.

Bird cries drew his gaze upward, following the tower's lines past hanging gardens and its crown of woven stone. Huge shapes wheeled lazily around the spire's uppermost reaches—the grace of eagles with the size of condors. Their voices blended with the birds in the trees all around and the rustling leaves to create nature's own chorus. A symphony of life.

Rick stepped cautiously between two gnarled trees, their trunks white as bone and split with age. Beyond them was a bowl in the earth beneath the tower, gracefully terraced in stone. Within that, a small lake, its crystal-clear waters both reflecting their surroundings and sinking into fathomless depths. It also reflected a twenty-foot-wide ramp that curved from the water's edge like a ribbon, unsupported beneath its span, rising to meet the inner wall of one of the towering buttresses. There a doorway waited.

Evan paused beside him, and her breath caught, sudden and sharp.

Rick turned. "You okay?"

She didn't answer. Her gaze drifted upward, tracing the curve of the walkway, which was so perfectly balanced that its only supports were at either end. Her head tilted as her eyes floated up along the tower's side and then across the grounds. Her fingers flexed slightly, like they were brushing something away. Then she flinched—just a flicker of motion, her head snapping to the left. Listening.

"What is it?" he asked, his voice low.

She didn't look at him. "Did you hear that?"

Rick frowned. "I didn't hear anything."

A pause.

"Never mind," she said, though her eyes were still scanning the air like it was saying something she couldn't quite make out.

Rick didn't press. He hadn't heard anything. The music—and even the breeze—had dropped away as the waters came into view. Now the silence was unnatural. It wasn't just quiet, it was *expectant.* The hair on his arms stood up, and he realized he'd been holding his breath. There was something here. Not a sound, not a movement—just the sense of being watched. Or maybe of being judged. He couldn't tell if it was anticipation or warning.

He glanced at Evan again. She stood very still now, her features drawn. A silent breeze moved her hair, but she didn't react. Rick took a slow step forward, eyes on the long, arcing ramp ahead of them. His mouth went dry. He didn't want to go closer, not yet. "I wish we could just stay right here," he mumbled. *And never go inside.*

But Evan moved. Leading the way up the ramp, she approached the doors without hesitation, though her shoulders were tight, her steps careful. Rick followed, saying nothing. When she reached the top, she paused to examine the doorway.

It had an elegant grace to it. Formed from swept lines, the frame came out of the water itself and arced up the inside wall of the nearest buttress. That wall curved up and overhead, with an opening shaped into its side for the doorway. The door itself—twelve feet wide and thirty tall—was carved in a way that spoke of design while betraying no discernible pattern.

Rick frowned. "There's no handle." He couldn't even see a crack where the door should open. Was it a single piece?

Evan stepped before the door. She closed her eyes and laid one hand against the stone.

There was no sound, but the door responded. It split up the middle, the line appearing from nowhere, each half turning inward in a perfect arc, silent as breath, revealing darkness beyond. Evan stared into it, unmoving.

A glow grew within that darkness, seemingly coming from the stone walls themselves. It revealed a stair that rose to a landing, where a statue of a woman stood, her hands stretched to either side as if in welcome.

Rick stepped beside Evan. He didn't ask if she was ready. Neither of them was.

The light led them inside, beneath the woman's outstretched arms. Past where the stairs split and curved back around above themselves before coming together again. It didn't emanate from torches or crystals or any visible source—but from the walls themselves. A subtle radiance seeped from the stone, enough to see by, but soft, like moonlight remembered through fog.

Evan moved slowly. Rick was behind her, quiet, his footsteps faintly audible over her own. The air inside the tower was still. Not stale, not musty—just... still. As if it had been holding its breath for a very long time. The sound of their passing should have echoed off the walls and preceded them down the corridor like drumbeats, but the footsteps were somehow swallowed instead.

A wide hall opened before them. Stone columns rose like trees in a forest, branching at the top into arcs that supported the ceiling far overhead. The walls gleamed faintly, their surfaces lined with inlays that pulsed with some quiet memory of power—geometric patterns formed of graceful curves. Scents hung in the air—paper, old leather, and ink—but no dust.

Books rested on reading tables, opened to pages mid-read. Cushioned chairs sat tucked beneath them, angled as if someone had just risen and might return any moment. A folded shawl lay on the arm of one. A teacup sat beside another, bone-white and perfectly whole. A brown residue was all that remained of its brew.

Evan stopped. Her chest ached, but not from exertion. The anger was back—no longer a whisper but a slow rising tide inside her skull. She pressed her fingers to her temple.

Rick stepped up beside her, eyes searching in all directions, concern radiating from him like heat.

"Do you feel that?" she asked, barely above a whisper. He nodded, but she could tell he didn't feel what she felt. Not *all* of it. For him, it was the pressure, maybe the weight of years. For her—it was rage. Cold and ancient. And directed squarely at her.

A flash of motion caught her eye. She turned toward a side corridor, her head snapping around. Nothing. But that was where she needed to go. She didn't know how she knew the way. She just did.

She turned, walking with purpose now, each step louder in the hush. The corridor led to a great pair of doors—taller even than the tower entrance behind them—and already open. Beyond them, a massive circular hall unfolded.

"This place feels like a mausoleum," Rick whispered. His breath clouded before him as he spoke.

The air was so cold.

But the feelings that pressed upon her—those were colder still, yet red with burning rage.

The floor was inlaid with a vast pattern of silver, azurite, and obsidian, separate at the edges before spiraling inward to a central dais, where they combined in what could have been a flower or a starburst. Around the perimeter, raised high on three tiers, were curved rows of seats—forty-nine in all, each a throne in its own right. Not decorative. They were functional, worn by use. In contrast to everything she'd seen since coming here, their angles were harsh, as if they were intended to be uncomfortable.

This had been a place of power, aware of its dangers and meant to keep its wielders aware as well.

Conscious of how her actions paralleled those in the chamber under Southwatch, she stepped to the center.

And froze.

A low sound rippled through the air—a hum, almost a vibration. "Evan..." Rick reached toward her in concern, but his movements slowed to a crawl.

The seats were no longer empty. Shadows were gathering in them, slow at first, like smoke drifting into form, then clearer. Bodies. Faces. Robes of shifting color, though she could not name the dyes. Eyes and mouths—most human, but other races as well. All dead.

Every gaze fixed on her.

"You have returned," said one, its voice echoing without sound. The texture of it was painfully beautiful in her mind.

"Is it not enough that you murdered us once?" asked another, a man with features too handsome to be real and ears that swept to points. An elf.

"Your crimes remain," a woman said coldly. "Have you come to finish what you started?"

A dwarf leaned forward, his beard brushing the floor in front of him in wispy tendrils of smoke. "Or to face justice and—perhaps—survive?"

Evan's knees buckled, and she had to catch herself on the edge of the dais. *No. That wasn't—* She shook her head, her breath coming in quick bursts. "I don't... I don't know you."

But the storm inside her roared now, spinning faster, tearing loose fragments from somewhere deep within. Faces she didn't recognize. Screams. Her own hands outstretched—*No, no—*

Rick moved suddenly, stepping in front of her. "You've got the wrong person," he snapped. "She's not Estariel."

The voices ignored him. Laughed at him. Cried for him.

Then... Silence.

None of the figures even looked at him. It was as if he had ceased to be.

The council chamber saw only her.

The specters surged.

No warning. No movement to signal intent. The shadows simply uncoiled from their seats and poured forward, not like smoke anymore but like tidewater—dark, sentient, unstoppable.

Rick responded before he could think. His hand shot out, and magic spilled from him—*through* him—forming a dome of light that snapped into place around Evan and himself like a soap bubble catching sunlight.

The spirits halted at its edge, re-forming into their original shapes. Each floated a foot or two off the floor, their eyes white as the brightest star. They were exactly like the specter in Southwatch, but now there were dozens of them. Each one focused directly on him. Patient. Watching.

Waiting.

Rick's breath came in ragged gasps. He could feel the spell unraveling already—too fast, too wild. He didn't *know* how to hold it. The Dark

Horror had been a physical assault. This was something else. Raw emotion rather than structure. The spell to hold it at bay was burning him alive.

"Rick." Evan's voice.

He turned toward her, and she looked at him, eyes wide—not with fear but with something older. Something knowing.

"This is why we came here," she said, reaching up to lay her fingers gently against his hand, where it still trembled in the air. The moment her skin touched his, the bubble collapsed.

No shatter. No sound. No resistance—just gone.

The air rushed in.

And so did the ghosts.

Rick shouted and reached for her—but he might as well have been grasping at smoke. They didn't claw, didn't scream. They poured into her like mist into lungs, like water into a sinking ship, faces merging with her skin, light flooding her eyes.

Evan cried out. "No!" she gasped. "I didn't... I never..."

Another voice answered—not from the chamber but from within Evan's body. A woman's voice, but not Evan's, older than grief. "This must be."

Then a man, looking directly at Rick through Evan's eyes. "You must not intervene." Speaking with her mouth.

Rick tried anyway. He took a step—but his knees hit the floor. He hadn't realized how drained he was. His hands shook, and his vision blurred at the edges. He opened his mouth to argue, to scream, to *do something*—

But Evan was already falling. He caught her too late.

Her body slumped to the stone with a soft, final sound, eyes wide and unseeing. She was *gone*. And yet she breathed. Almost imperceptibly, heartbreakingly slowly, her chest rose and fell. It was as if the person inside her had been pulled somewhere else.

Rick knelt over her, gnarled hands useless on her shoulders. Somehow this moment felt pregnant with possibilities. The fate of the world focused on the point of a pin. And yet he had no idea how to control the outcome.

Light fractured.

Then everything was *motion.* Glimpses. Glimmers. Faces that burned behind her eyes and vanished before she could name them. A council chamber. Not the one she'd entered—but older, and full of sound. Cries. Arguments. Her voice, loudest among them. Wind. Blood on her hands. Sand. Firelight. She was riding—no, flying? *No.* Her feet pounded against the ground. She was running toward something, through ruins scorched black by war. Then—

A man. Tall. Slim. Dark brown hair and gray-blue eyes. *Rick!*

No. This was thousands of years ago. Not Rick.

But like him.

Hair longer, skin darker. Armor fitted in smooth, matte plates, velvet robe flaring behind in the wind. A style she'd never seen before yet remembered intimately. And the eyes—sharp and full of something unspoken.

Her chest clenched. *Is this why I love him?* she mused. But the thought was gone as soon as it came. Ripped away in the storm of what followed.

"She goes too far," someone whispered. "Always too far."

"She doesn't ask. She *takes.*"

A great plain spread out beneath her. Thousands of minds sang through the link she held open—terrifying, beautiful harmony—and she stood at the center, untouched by the chaos. All the soldiers moved as one. Her thoughts were their thoughts. Their pain, her own. *This is what victory looks like.*

"She's changing us," a Thought Master murmured in fear. "What she's doing... Is it still permission if they don't know what they're giving?"

"She's right," another said quietly. "That's the worst part. She's right."

Evan tried to speak—to cry out that this wasn't her—but the wind stole the words from her lips. She *was* Estariel now. Had always been Estariel. She knew it with a clarity beyond language.

And she didn't regret it.

The Artificer citadel rose before her, spires like needles, steel gleaming under a blood-orange sky. She pressed her mind outward and felt a barrier—a reflective surface that turned thought back upon itself, fractured like razor blades. Brilliant. Lethal. Their final weapon in the Wars of Power—the one that would end the Resistance. End the fighting. One touch, and her own mind would shatter. For the moment, it guarded the citadel, but she knew it would soon be brought to full strength. Encircling the world, it would destroy the Thought Masters.

But behind the wall, a weakness.

One man. The commander.

His mind was cordoned, trained, protected—but not from *her*. There had never been another like her, and that was enough.

The man who wasn't Rick stood beside her, using his magic to open a hole in the psychic reflector. It was a gap barely wide enough for a sliver of thought, but it was enough. She reached through his fury, slipped inside the hollow of the commander's grief. Twisted it—gently, precisely.

And he obeyed.

The weapon never fired.

The self-destruct did.

The blast took half the range, melting the fortress to slag. Her skin burned, her ears bled, the psychic scream of a thousand dying minds threatened to crush her, but Not-Rick twisted reality, shielding them both. She lived, and when the ash settled, they stood alone atop the rubble.

"She did it," someone whispered.

"She saved us all."

"No one else could have done it."

Another council. She stood at the highest seat now. Her robes were white, trimmed in silver, her hair bound in loops that signified command.

No one challenged her for breaking the Law.

No one asked what it had cost.

And she never told them.

The world around her began to fracture again, cracks running through the sky—through memory itself. But the silence that followed was not empty.

It waited.

Watched.

And it knew the truth of what she had done. Worse, it knew the truth of what she was yet to do.

Evan's body was limp in Rick's arms, still warm, still breathing—barely. He cradled her to his chest, smoothing her hair back from her face with shaking, liver-spotted fingers.

"Evan." His voice, already rasping with age, threatened to crack completely. "Evan, come on. Wake up."

Nothing.

He felt for a pulse. It was there, faint and slow. Her chest rose and fell, but her eyes were open—unseeing. Her gaze fixed on something far away, as if she were watching a storm that only she could see. His own pain—his joints, his lungs, the fire still eating through the channels that magic had torn in his nerves—was forgotten. Irrelevant.

He pressed his forehead to hers. "Come back."

A presence stirred behind him, raising the hairs on his neck. Rick turned, ready to lash out—spell or fist... it didn't matter.

But it wasn't a threat. A final Thought Master floated just above the ground, robe billowing in the unfelt wind. His form wavered, light and shadow bleeding into one another in impossible ways. Then the colors changed.

The negative image—the spectral inversion—folded in on itself, shifting like smoke. Color returned. Not the color of life but of memory.

Rick knew this man.

Southwatch. The vengeful ghost. The one who had set them on their path to this place, showing the route. The one who had called Evan Estariel and left him with more questions than answers.

"You," Rick breathed.

"There is much that must remain hidden," the ghost said, his voice like stone dust and wind. "But also much that must be told." His gaze dropped to Evan—softly, almost reverently. "And very little time in which to tell it. Come." He turned and began to float toward the far end of the council chamber.

Rick looked back at Evan.

She didn't move.

He set her down gently, brushed her cheek one more time, and stood. "Will she be okay?"

The specter paused. "That depends upon her," he said, lips turned in a faint smile that might have been reassuring—or regretful. "But no outside harm will come to her in this place."

Rick's legs almost gave out. His hands were still trembling. But he followed the shade to the tower's central shaft, a cylinder that rose dizzyingly to the heights above, ringed by the balconies of level after level. As Rick stared, the ghost spoke a single word of command, and Rick involuntarily threw his hands out to the sides in order to keep his balance. It was unnecessary, for his feet no longer touched the floor. He floated, the level they'd been on dropping away beneath him. Levels flashed by as a rush of air tousled his hair. The ghost floated by his side.

*

They stood atop the tower's outer ring—just above the upper gardens, where narrow walkways traced the structure's curvature. The crown of stone filigree looked even more delicate than it had from below. Far beneath them, those grounds shimmered in fractured light, an autumnal carpet laid over the landscape like a russet blanket. Above, the clouds rolled low and heavy as if a storm was approaching. The wind was colder here, biting through his shirt. It seemed to stir the edges of the ghost's robes but didn't move his hair.

Rick leaned on the stone balustrade, catching his breath. "Start talking."

The ghost turned his head, not quite facing Rick. "You know more than you realize already."

"Then help me realize it."

A pause.

Then he began. "We were feared from the beginning," the Thought Master said. "Not because of what we did—but because of what they thought we *might* do. Even kings fear a mirror. Especially if it might reflect something true."

Rick's knuckles whitened against the stone. "You could read minds."

"Some of us. Not many—fewer than the stories claimed. But the *idea* that someone could... that was enough. Secrets are the truest currency in the world, Rick Johnson. And no one wants to lose their hoard."

"So you made rules."

"Yes. We governed ourselves. Harshly. No reading without permission. No invasion of will. And above all—*no control.* Not even in war. We believed freedom of thought to be sacred and appointed the Custodians of Integrity to ensure the Law was kept." He chuckled, a hollow sound as if from an empty cave. "We sometimes called them the Thought Police."

The ghost turned to him fully now. His expression was unreadable, but something about his stance suggested he'd once stood like this beside flesh-and-blood allies, not strangers. "She challenged that."

Rick didn't need to ask who. "Estariel," he said quietly.

The ghost nodded. "She was a prodigy. Her powers came early and strong. Telepathy, empathy, clairvoyance. But what set her apart wasn't the breadth of her talents—it was the depth. She saw *structure* in the mind the way some see it in music. She didn't just sense thoughts. She could weave them... Combine them. Not forcefully—but *cohesively.* She made people want to follow her."

Rick felt a chill crawl down his back.

"She found a way to stop aging," the ghost continued. "A psychic stasis, continually renewed. Some of us lacked the skill to replicate it, but most learned. She showed us that death was not inevitable, and even though only a few true Thought Masters were born in each generation, her discovery allowed our numbers to swell."

"Immortality," Rick whispered.

"Of a sort." The ghost's voice grew heavier. Older. "Then came the Wars of Power. The Engineers and Artificers understood the people's fears—not only of Thought Masters but of wizards, anyone they believed could twist a mind or reshape reality. Anyone who held power that couldn't be held in the hand. They were fueled by ambition, and as our numbers grew, they preyed upon fear. We became the enemy, and soon the Three Powers were in danger of being replaced by one. Estariel took to the battlefield. Not as a warrior—but as a conductor."

"She linked them," Rick said.

The ghost nodded. "Wizards, soldiers, even other Thought Masters. She shaped them into a single intelligence. Thousands thinking as one, moving with perfect precision. Magical coordination unlike anything ever seen."

"And you let her?" Rick asked. "Even knowing what she was doing?"

"We *needed* her," the ghost whispered. "She was the only reason we had survived as long as we had."

Rick stared out at the darkening sky. "But something went wrong."

"The Artificers learned. They found the frequencies our powers operated on and created a weapon of mirrors. Of thought made into steel. It would have turned every psychic gift inward—stripping us bare, shattering minds across the world. She was the only one who understood what it was. And the only one willing to do what it took to stop it."

Rick turned toward him, jaw clenched. "She broke your highest law."

"Yes."

"She took control."

"Yes."

"And no one ever knew?"

"They *suspected*," the ghost said. "But suspicion fades in the glow of victory. They named her Luminary. Gave her robes of command. No one asked what it had cost. Most wouldn't have cared."

"And you?" Rick asked.

The ghost was silent for a long time. Then, softly, "We all share the shame."

Rick gripped the railing, his breath slow and shallow. "She discovered the secret to immortality," he said at last. "She stopped aging. You said so."

"Yes."

Rick closed his eyes. The pieces fell into place. Too fast, too loud. "She *is* Evan." He opened his eyes. "Estariel. She's always been—"

"We do not know how she came to your world," the ghost interrupted gently. "Or why she forgot herself. That truth may yet be locked behind walls even we cannot reach—"

"But now she's remembering."

The ghost looked toward the center of the tower. "Yes."

Rick swallowed. "They're not attacking her, are they?"

"No."

"They're... making her face it."

"Yes."

Rick's fists curled. "She doesn't need this," he muttered. "She doesn't deserve this."

The ghost turned back to him, eyes clear as water and cold as truth. "It is not about what is deserved," he said. "It is about what is *necessary*."

Tears fell to the white stone floor, and Rick realized they were his own.

The storm returned.

Not wind. Not lightning. Estariel's memory.

It poured through her like fire—sacred, unstoppable.

Flashes of the past surged again. Crowds cheering. Thought Masters bowing. She stood atop Haven in robes so white they could have been fashioned from light, her hair bound in silver loops, her voice echoing commands across a world united by fear and hope.

Fear of technology. Hope for a new future. Though still few in number, the Thought Masters guided the world as it rebuilt. Guided men and women who became rulers, then guided their descendants.

But beneath it, threads of unease.

A council table. Disagreement. Questions about methods. About how far was too far. About control. They argued the Thought Masters had become puppeteers, with the world dancing on their strings.

They faded.

Another flash. A child's laughter. A boy with her eyes and someone else's smile. Gone too fast, leaving an echo of regret. She tried to follow—tried to hold the thread of that image—but it slipped from her grasp. A wound reopened without understanding.

Then—the war. Not the old one. Not the Wars of Power.

This was later.

More insidious.

The War of Ascension. An elven emperor rising in the south. Golden robes. A heart-shaped gem gleaming at his chest. Arathian. She had trained him once, advised him, watched him climb too fast into a power that bent all others around it.

Until she stood against him.

Southwatch.

The events flooded back with perfect clarity. The emperor had turned a tool into a weapon of conquest, and his command was absolute. For rather than the Three Powers, he controlled the forces that drove Necsis itself. The man's legions had crossed the bridge. Thousands arrayed beneath the fortress walls, not understanding they'd been drawn into a trap.

She had no armies. No time. Only her mind.

So she reached for Arathian. Touched him.

She didn't ask. Didn't try to reason. She *took* control.

Through him, she turned the Heart to her own will. A scream echoed across the plains—not from lungs but from reality itself. The earth Shifted. The air twisted. A bubble of space, torn loose from Necsis and hurled elsewhere.

All the armies were gone, but the land reeled as if tortured. Southwatch collapsed. And the Nine Kingdoms—*cut off*.

Estariel then took the Heart from Arathian, leaving him broken and lifeless.

Evan cried out, clutching her head.

No—*Estariel* cried out. But the memory played on, forcing her to watch.

Later. Was it days? Years? No matter. She stood before the Custodians of Integrity. They had called an inquisition, and their accusations cut deep. She offered no denial. Uttered no defense. She had broken the Law, and this time even her victory could not shield her from consequence.

They spoke the sentence: psychic severance. Her gifts removed. Her link to the ethereal dissolved—not death but silence.

She nodded. She *agreed*. Because she *deserved* it—not just for Arathian but for all that had come before.

The circle formed. Forty-eight Thought Masters strong, they reached into her. Gently. Methodically. With sorrow and the precision of a surgeon's scalpel. She felt them brushing along the edges of her soul. Probing old corridors. Loosening connections. Unwinding the pathways she herself had once taught them to build. It hurt. But she did not resist. Until—

They touched something too deep. Too raw. A spark flared inside her, primal and wild. A cornered animal of impossible power.

No. She didn't say it aloud. She *became* it. Her will turned their powers back upon themselves, ripping through the circle. What had begun as removal became annihilation. She struck out in every direction, not with malice—but with instinct and fear. With grief. With the agony of being compressed under a massive weight.

She burned through them.

One by one, their minds folded in on themselves like dying stars. She *felt* each one die. Saw their faces collapse. Heard their screams. Not in sound—in *essence*. They were, quite literally, *unmade*.

And then it was quiet. Horribly, impossibly quiet. And she drifted.

When she came back to herself, the chamber was still. There were no bodies. Only shadows, floating in the air like mist burning away in the morning sun. She was on her knees, blood dripping from her nose. Her hands shook. Her skin was too tight. They were gone, but their thoughts lingered. Haunting. Accusing.

She rose slowly. Step by wary step.

And fled.

She ran down the halls of Haven, through the ancient gates. Past the lake, untouched by time, and beyond the valley's edge.

A fragment of the Heart's power lingered with her, and she used it now. She fled Necsis, reaching for a world that somehow held redemption.

As the Shift closed behind her, leaving her stranded on a world with only the most tenuous of psychic powers, she fled herself.

The storm faded, but the silence that replaced it wasn't peace.

It was grief.

And she drowned in it.

Somewhere far beyond the infinite possibilities of the multiverse, a woman with no name woke on a dirt road.

The wind had risen.

Rick still stood on the tower's crown, alone except for his spectral guide. Above the mountains to the north, the borealis played across the sky, an eerie contrast to the dark places this day had taken him to. Wrestling with the weight of revelation and the ache of his heart, he was scarcely aware—not even of the way the biting cold had caused his arthritis to flare again.

The sky pulsed.

And moved.

He didn't turn when the Thought Master drifted close beside him, silent as mist.

"How long has it been like that?" Rick asked, his voice hoarse.

The figure followed his gaze. "A while."

Even as he spoke, the curtain of light collapsed. The mountains of beyond no longer looked quite the same as they had when he'd first arrived.

Rick's jaw clenched. "You didn't think to mention it?"

"You were learning something more important."

He stared, not at the ghost but at the mountain. A shadow moved down its flanks, toward the tower—black on black. A flood, moving too fast for a human army. Too silent. Too precise. And too many. "Are those...?"

"What you call demons. Yes."

A pit opened within his chest. "They found us," Rick whispered. Then he laughed, bitter and short. "What I was learning—more important than a demon horde?"

"Yes."

He didn't know how. Didn't care.

Something clicked into place in his mind: the map. Back at Southwatch. The one the ghost had created on the floor... Rick hadn't thought to destroy it.

Stupid. He swore under his breath, and his fists tightened against the railing. The enemy was still several miles away, but at the speed they were moving, that didn't mean much. "We don't have time," he said. "You said there was more. About the Heart."

"There is."

"Then tell me."

"I cannot."

Rick turned. "Why the hell not?"

The Thought Master's expression didn't change. "Because it is not for you to know."

His temper flared, and the fingers of one hand splayed wide in frustration. "The world is falling apart, and you're still playing riddles?"

"I am not." The ghost's tone was calm. "You know what the Heart can do. It must not be touched without understanding. And that understanding lies only with her."

Rick stared at him. "She's unconscious."

"Yes."

"Then *wake her up*."

"I cannot."

"Then what use are you?" The words came out harsher than he had intended. But the ghost didn't flinch.

"I am your guide. But I must not step off the path that has been set before me. I can only bear witness. And hope."

Rick didn't answer. Instead he turned and strode back toward the tower's heart. The descent was swift. He barely noticed the wind or the dizzying drop. He moved like a man chasing a burning fuse.

The council chamber was exactly as they'd left it. Still. Silent. Evan lay where he had set her down at its center. Pale. Unmoving. Her eyes were still open and unfocused, locked on a world no one else could see.

He dropped to his knees and pressed two fingers to her throat, feeling the thready pulse. "Evan." His voice cracked again. "Come on."

But she didn't stir.

Rick glanced up at the ghost, who stood at the far end of the chamber like a statue of smoke. Watching. Waiting.

Rick's hand twitched toward magic. Just a touch. A pulse of power to jolt her awake. He could do it.

He could *try*.

But he stopped.

This isn't something you can solve, he told himself, hating the truth of it. He ground his teeth. "Come on, Evan," he whispered. "Please."

Nothing.

He stared down at her face. Her chest rose and fell—too slowly. Her skin was warm, but her body might as well have been stone.

"You're the only one who can do this," he said. "We need you." His voice grew tighter.

I need you. If words couldn't reach her, maybe raw emotion would.

Still nothing.

The chamber was silent as a tomb, but he imagined wind howling outside, battering the tower walls.

And he knew the darkness was drawing closer.

XXVI
Defense

War horns echoed like ghosts through the valley.

Gharn reined in his mount—a tired, shaggy-backed thing with more burrs than hair—and turned one ear toward the sound. Another blast, then another, even louder. He nudged the beast forward again, coaxing it around the next bend.

Eastgate lay ahead, though he couldn't yet see it. The valley narrowed here, a gash through folded hills, with snow-dusted ridges hemming the road like watchful old men. Somewhere below, the fortress loomed. Somewhere below, Chad. And Matthias, for what that was worth.

The next horn call was drowned out by shouting. Figures burst into view around the bend—soldiers, or what passed for them. Most were young, many unarmored, a few without weapons. One of them, a boy no older than twenty, skidded to a halt in front of him.

"Turn back!" he gasped, eyes wide with terror. "Demons... they... they're coming by air ..."

Gharn set his jaw, feeling dread settle into his bones. But before he could ask questions, another grabbed the lad's sleeve and hauled him on. Others pounded past without sparing Gharn a glance.

Then the road emptied—

No more stragglers, just wind. Gharn kicked his heels in.

The fortress appeared not with a cresting view but as a curtain of rising stone—a massive wall that might have been cut from the rock itself. Towers that hunched like sleeping sentinels. The foregate stood open. Soldiers stood ready.

Not the chaos he had expected. They were organized, armored in designs he hadn't seen outside the histories in Sorendir's library—fluted plates, burnished links, helms with half-veils and crests of copper or bone. Archaic, yes, but pristine. Maintained. A hard edge of discipline clung to their wearers like frost.

The gate guards barely spared him a glance. He passed an infirmary tent with clean, empty cots and idle healers. Nervous energy saturated the air, but there was no panic. No one wounded. No screaming. A short, stocky woman with sergeant's slashes and a pitted axe strapped to her back barked orders near the supply wagons. Gharn pegged her for a dwarf instantly—scarred brow, thick knuckles, voice like gravel poured on steel.

He approached. "Excuse me. What in the depths is happening?"

She gave him a sideways glance. "What's it look like? Demon assault inbound."

"I meant, who's in charge here? I'm not with the army. I—"

"You're a gnome," she cut in. "Survey detachment, then. Come on. Don't stand there gawping." He tried to clarify, but she was already waving down a passing runner. "Prestin! Take this one to Sergeant Johnson. Let him sort him out."

Gharn blinked. "Sergeant Johnson?"

"Survey detachment commander. Level Five, last I heard. If he's not there, check the top."

Gharn blinked harder. *Chad?*

Prestin turned out to be a wiry teen with a quick step and quicker mouth. He filled Gharn in as they trotted through the fortress. "Sergeant Johnson's been leading the sealed-access team. Cracked open four lower levels already. Big finds yesterday—old armories, full of gear. Stuff's ancient but built to last. You should see the recoil on some of the crossbows—like a bear kickin' you in the chest."

"And the demons?"

The boy's voice lowered as his grin slipped. "Thousands of them." Then he brightened. "Most's stuck outside the wall. But they just started sending fliers at us. Thorne thinks they're after the gate controls. But he's got the defenses hopping."

"Thorne?"

"The commander. Technically, it's Vail's post, but that fossil can't lead a dinner queue. Quartermaster's that Matthias guy that came with him—creepy. Something dangerous about him. But damned if he isn't efficient."

The fortress wound around them, its broad ramps and inner fortifications staffed with wide-eyed defenders. Gharn saw humans, some dwarves, even a few orcs—all working with surprising cohesion. And in all their eyes: purpose. *Matthias is a leader in the defense?* he wondered. Could this be what Sorendir had meant when he insisted the man should be included in the group? Was this the shape of the prophecy beginning to form?

Prestin turned into a side hall. "He was through here last I heard."

At the end of the corridor, a shadow moved within a storage room, surrounded by the sounds of banging and cracking wood. Dust sparkled dimly in the torchlight. Chad was dealing with the room's contents, but it was the strangest version of surveying or inventorying Gharn had ever seen. The lad wasn't going through the items. He was flinging them into the hallway without a care about what might be in the crates.

Gharn stared.

The boy looked exhausted, soot-smudged, and entirely in his element.

"Chad! I... What are you doing?"

Chad paused and turned, his eyes going wide. "Gharn, you dog! Good to see you. Are the others...?" As the words trailed off, his posture straightened, and he squared his shoulders, but a crafty smile remained. "Never mind. Help me throw stuff."

Gharn stepped into the room, ducking beneath a flung scroll case. A long breath escaped him as he set down his pack.

A flicker of hope surged. *Sorendir, you damned old lizard. Maybe you were right after all.*

The fliers came in fast—too fast.

From his post in the northwest tower, Matthias watched the creatures rise into view above the southern end of the wall, dark silhouettes against the mountain slopes. They rode the wind like vultures, leathery wings half-tucked as they dived in a wave that numbered fewer than two dozen.

The ballista crews scrambled. A few bolts loosed early, sailing high and useless. One struck true, catching a flier clean through the torso. It folded and dropped from the sky, its limp corpse passing out of sight beyond the wall. Two more fell within seconds, but the rest jinked and scattered, diving lower. The crews were not ready.

"Hold for impact!" Calladorn's voice rang clear from the southern flank. There was command in it—urgency without panic. He moved like someone who had seen battles before.

The defenders braced. Matthias could see them now, a ragged line of men and women. Though their armor and weapons matched—he had seen to the distributions, as ordered—they were green and untested. He would have been surprised if more than a handful had ever held anything more dangerous than a pitchfork before Eastgate. But they moved with purpose; a few even had discipline.

The air smelled of sweat and iron and oiled leather. Even through the chaos, there was an energy to them, a quiet desperation. The kind that hardened into resolve.

Then, like a gout of flame in a dry field, everything began to unravel.

Vail stepped forward. "No, no—consolidate to the inner ramp! Form a pike square!" the commander bellowed, gesturing wildly.

His orders cut across Calladorn's. Troops that had been holding formation suddenly lurched sideways, colliding with others. One of the ballista teams broke off, confused, and stopped reloading. A soldier turned in place, asking for clarification, and was knocked over by the next man in line. It was a ripple effect of uncertainty—and hesitation was death.

Matthias narrowed his eyes.

Panic. The stink of it came off Vail in waves. The man was not leading. He was reacting, flailing, undermining order with every breath. *This is why they will lose,* Matthias thought. *Not because of strength or numbers. Because of this.*

He took one slow step forward, just far enough to see more of the wall. Chaos bloomed in pockets—men yelling over each other, conflicting orders. One squad had turned entirely around, unsure whether to reinforce the north ramp or hold the stairs.

And yet—a ripple of defiance rose from the wall. Halvard, the tall woman with the heavy-hafted glaive, ignored Vail completely. Her voice cut clean as she rallied the nearest flank. "On me! South side, brace for impact! Captain Thorne has the wall!"

They listened.

Three fliers hit the yard and reared back, wings flapping in unison. But their claws found no grip on the yard's flagstones, and they were thrown back. They circled quickly, and this time they grabbed the crenellations. This time, it was the defenders that were thrown back by buffeted air. The demons pounced on those unfortunate enough to be knocked down, their movements insect-fast and bone-snappingly strong. Screams rang across the yard.

Halvard charged in, her glaive whistling through the air in a low arc that severed a leg from under the first attacker. She stepped in and jammed the butt of the weapon into its throat. The creature spasmed once, then stilled.

Others followed her lead, slamming into the invaders with coordinated strikes. The line held, bloodied but unbroken. One soldier took a hit to the shoulder, staggered, then rammed his shield into a demon's chest, buying time for his partner to land the killing blow.

Matthias felt something stir in his chest. Not quite pride. But a flicker of... grudging admiration. *If they were all like this,* he mused, *they might even stand a chance.*

The moment did not last.

Screams erupted from the north end of the wall, and Matthias spun toward the sound. Demons were in the yard here, between the northeastern tower and the mountain, rending flesh and sending defenders running. Beyond the parapets, the sky boiled. A second wave descended—larger this time. Far larger. Fliers with thick hides and longer wings. Some carried shock troops—bodies naturally armored by thick scales—who dropped like weights within the ramparts. The air was split by crashing thuds as they struck the stone. Others raked the parapets as they passed, cleaving soldiers with sharp-edged wings before spinning off to make another pass. A few hurled black spheres that exploded with viscous smoke, turning men into howling cinders.

Distracted by the feint at the southern end of the yard, the defenders here were not braced, and they were confused by Vail's orders. The collapse came fast.

Vail turned to shout another order—something about falling back to the command tower—but he never finished. One of the large fliers dove low, dropping two horned brutes directly onto the battlement near him. His uniform, bright white, made him an easy mark.

To his credit, Vail did not run. He drew his rapier and struck a parry against the first demon. The blade bent. Snapped. He staggered back, disbelief written across his face. One of the shock troops slammed into him, pinning him to the wall. Another raked claws across his chest, tearing through silk and skin alike. The second demon was on him before the pieces hit the stone.

Matthias did not flinch.

Vail screamed once. Briefly.

So did two other officers. Their deaths were not quick. Their armor clattered as they fell, swords slipping from their fingers, eyes wide with pain and confusion. One tried to crawl away. Did not make it far.

Then came the breaking. The line folded, disintegrated. Defenders turned and ran. Some threw weapons aside, and some were cut down before they managed a single step. A few tried to escape to the inner keep. Most would not make it.

Matthias had seen enough. *It is over.*

His hand went to the dagger at his belt, not to draw it but out of reflex. He ran down the stairs from his post in the tower and slipped into the yard, calculating how long it would take to reach the ramp and, from there, the lower levels. He would find Chad and knock the boy unconscious if necessary. They could vanish. Disappear. Let Eastgate burn.

Only the boy mattered, and corpses would never miss either of them.

But before he could move further, a flash of silver caught his eye. Calladorn. The man swept past Matthias like a spark catching dry kindling. Sword raised, voice hoarse from shouting, he cut down a demon mid-lunge. Blood sprayed the stones. His armor was dented, his cheek was split, but he moved with clarity.

"With me!" Calladorn bellowed.

To his own surprise, Matthias leaped forward with him.

More defenders rallied to them—not many but enough. They formed up beside Matthias, blocking the route back to the ramp. A ballista bolt whistled past overhead, slamming into a flier mid-swoop. It spiraled down and crashed into a crumpled heap of bone and writhing leather not fifteen feet away. Another bolt followed. Screams rose, then died beneath it.

The other fliers hesitated, and Calladorn pressed the advantage. He surged forward, blade flashing, ducking under a wild swing and driving his sword into the soft spot between a demon's collar and chest plate. The creature shrieked and fell back, flailing for purchase against the stone.

Matthias watched the fight unfold like a chessboard tipping over, a pattern that broke and re-formed. There was a kind of art in the way the battle flowed. He could almost admire it. Almost.

Then a shift.

One of the demons peeled from the edge of the fray, moving silent and low. One arm was a chitinous blade, malformed and dripping with the blood of its victims. It darted up behind Calladorn, crouched to strike. Calladorn was facing the other direction, distracted by an opponent who was pressing him hard. He did not see.

Matthias paused. *Why am I hesitating? Move!*

A breath. A heartbeat.

He stepped forward. Too fast for the eye. Too brutal for hesitation.

The demon's attack never landed. Matthias struck once. A single movement. A twist of the wrist, precisely angled. Blade met flesh, and the demon collapsed, spasming before it had even registered the blow. Silence lasted for the briefest moment.

A nearby soldier stared. Matthias met the man's narrowing eyes. Flat. Cold. Measuring.

Then let the demons kill him.

Calladorn, panting, turned. His face shone with sweat and blood. His gaze locked on the fallen demon, then on Matthias. He stepped forward, clapping a hand on Matthias's shoulder. "I owe you my life."

Why did I do that? Matthias wondered, keeping his face still. He said nothing.

He stepped back.

The fortress was doomed.

"I think that was the last of it," Chad said, briefly examining a cracked lantern before tossing it onto the growing heap in the hallway. *No way it still works.* Dust settled around them in lazy spirals, catching the glow of their torches.

Gharn grunted. He was bent over a box of old bolts, checking each one with a scowl before flinging it over his shoulder. "All junk. Most of this stuff hasn't been touched in a century. Probably longer."

"Longer," Chad said absently. He leaned against the wall, wiping sweat from his brow with the back of his sleeve as he studied the walls of the room. "So… you got my note, then?"

Gharn didn't look at him but snorted. "Yes."

"Good. Is Rick here too? Evan?"

Now Gharn did look at him, and the expression in the gnome's eyes was not what Chad expected. Frustration. Disappointment, and something harder underneath.

"No," Gharn said. "They went on to the Forbidden Spire."

The words landed like a punch, and Chad stood straighter. "Wait, what? Then why are you here?"

"Because someone had to come to bring you back to where you belong."

Chad blinked. "Where I belong?"

"What were you thinking, boy?"

The words felt like a slap upside the head. For a moment, Chad might as well have been a kid again, being told to stay out of the way while the adults handled things. He drew a slow breath through his nose.

"I *am* where I belong," he said. His voice was quiet but firm. Then he spotted what he was looking for, which sparked a grin. "And if I'm right, you're about to find out why."

He crossed to the back wall of the room and ran his fingers across the middle of it, feeling. There—just as he thought, a crack, almost invisible in the dim light, running vertically from floor to ceiling. He had noticed it earlier, and it had been tickling the back of his brain ever since.

"Back in a sec," he said, bolting into the next room. Gharn started to protest, but Chad was already rummaging through the weapon cache. He found what he needed—a broad, single-edged sword with an ornate fluted pommel. Perfect. He returned and wedged the blade into the crack. Leaned into it.

Gharn crossed his arms. "That wall is not going to give, boy."

"Not the wall," Chad muttered, angling the sword. "The seam."

A metallic groan answered him. The crack widened.

Gharn stepped back. "By the Three..."

With a final shove, the panel split open, sliding into the walls on either side. Beyond it, a twenty-foot corridor with a high ceiling stretched forward.

Chad grinned. "Double-sided elevator. Which means two sides to whatever system this is. Since my team hasn't mapped anything back here, this area had limited access. I'm guessing it's the inner workings."

Something ahead beyond the corridor glowed faintly. Not steady light. A shimmer that rippled like heat haze.

"Come on!" he called, taking off at a run.

Gharn said something unpleasant, but his footsteps followed.

The hallway led to a railed gallery, curving away to the left and right. It overlooked a massive open chamber, fifty feet across. Chad skidded to a halt, breath catching in his throat. The air smelled different here, like the aftermath of a thunderstorm, and there was a faint hum, so low he almost thought he was imagining it, until he gripped the railing to look down. There was a subtle vibration.

Two towering columns stood in front of him, rising to the top of the room and dropping into the depths. They had to be the height of the fortress itself. Taller, if they went below ground level. And they glowed from within, pale gold light pulsing in slow intervals from base to top, like breath.

"It's a power core," Chad said. "Or a distribution node."

Gharn's voice quavered. "We shouldn't be here."

"Screw the Ban," Chad snapped. "This is important. Eastgate isn't dead. It's sleeping."

He turned back to the gallery. Across the chamber, fifty feet away, another room was visible—recessed and enclosed in glass. And unlike everything else in Eastgate, it had lighting. Chad didn't hesitate. He dashed along the curved gallery, boots clapping against the ancient stone. Gharn followed, grumbling the entire way.

They reached the room. A glass panel slid aside with a whisper of air at their approach. Inside: consoles, panels, etched metal. Lines of conduit stretching along the walls like veins. And in the center, a chair—broad, low-backed, placed before an arc of display glass.

"Control center," Chad whispered. "This is like a ship's bridge."

Everything was dormant, except one section at the back—a panel of five thick levers, each tipped with a red crystal. A soft light shone above them.

Gharn stood frozen in the doorway. He couldn't understand this place the way Chad did, but he saw enough. "You're playing with fire. This fortress dates back to the Triune Era. Who knows what those do?"

"Eastgate is a fortress," Chad told him, as patiently as he could. "Built when technology was still important. From the moment we arrived, it bugged me that there were no signs of it. Now I know why. All the walled-off sections and their storage rooms were a distraction. A false treasure, hiding the real one."

As he spoke, he walked to the back of the room, almost caressing the consoles with his fingers as he passed them. There weren't any buttons, switches, or levers. He suspected the reason. Reaching the levers—he was sure they were breakers of some sort—he extended a hand.

"Only one way to find out."

"We should be destroying this. Not turning it on," Gharn groaned. His expression was taut. His eyes, wide.

"Then stop me," Chad said, not unkindly.

He flipped the first lever.

The hum of the place grew louder, low and resonant. One of the columns brightened. The second lever released a spark, making him jump back for a second as an acrid tang filled the room. The third sang. By the fifth, the entire control room had begun to glow. Light chased along the walls and ceiling, illuminating ancient circuitry. Outside, through the glass, the wall etchings lit the fortress like veins catching fire.

Chad turned slowly, eyes dancing, as new life pulsed through the system. Panels illuminated, lines of script and symbols scrolling across the walls and consoles. A display ringed the room's circular wall—maps: a schematic of Eastgate, complete with layers and moving dots. Dots in blue. And dots in red.

Chad stared.

Too many red ones—the upper yard was crawling with them. The east canyon beyond the gate was worse. And—he leaned closer—two long tunnels ran along either side of the fortress, embedded within the canyon walls.

Sally ports?

One of them, on the eastern side, was flashing. A red cluster swarmed outside.

As he watched, the red dots began to move into the tunnel.

Chad didn't hesitate. "Go get Calladorn," he said. "*Now.*"

Gharn bolted.

Chad stood alone at the heart of the Eastgate fortress as it woke up around him with a bewildering number of sounds and details. *So many systems. Where to begin?*

The command chair seemed like the best bet. It would have the most relevant information on its display screen. With luck, he'd be able to figure out what some of it meant and where any defensive systems would be. The screen shone brightly with readouts and numbers, but he might as well have been getting into a fighter cockpit with an expectation to fly. Some things made sense—those numbers there had to be power levels, for example—yet it seemed as if the system was designed around the concept that anyone sitting there would actually know what they were doing.

"Great," he muttered, feeling frustration building like a tide. "I bet this place doesn't come with a manual."

"I am here to assist," said a voice.

Chad jerked and looked around. But the room was empty. "Hello?"

"Systems restored from long-term standby. Thank you, Defender." It was an androgynous voice—calm. And as it spoke, a hologram came to shimmering life between the consoles in front of Chad, a swirl of tiny motes of light, which changed color and arrangement with each word.

"Am I... talking to the fortress?" he asked.

"In a way. I am called Asa." The lights shifted toward blue and danced.

"An acronym?"

"Indeed. Automated Systems Assistant."

"Great." Chad leaned forward, barely remaining perched in the seat. "Um... can you show me what's going on in the yard up above?"

The glass next to him changed, showing a view Chad guessed was from one of the towers. A dozen demons were on the wall, in addition to twice that many fliers harrying the defenders from above. Matthias and Calladorn fought side by side. A creature lunged at Calladorn from behind as he fought a different one.

"Look out!" Chad shouted, the warning strangled in his throat. He knew it was useless.

Matthias... *moved.* Faster than anything Chad had seen, even when he'd saved them in Emberhold. Before he could even fully register what had happened, the demon was dead. *How did he do that?*

He turned back to the hologram. "Asa, do you have weapons that can help them?"

"Many."

"So why aren't you using them?" He struggled to keep from yelling.

"My programming prohibits me from acting without orders."

It made sense to shackle the AI, Chad had to admit that. But just now it was damned inconvenient. "Consider yourself ordered," he snapped, clenching his fists. *I just hope it accepts my authority.*

"Activating defenses."

For the first time, he didn't feel like he was pretending.

He belonged here.

And now Eastgate knew it too.

Matthias stepped back into shadow without a word, vanishing from Calladorn's peripheral vision like a blade sheathed in silence.

Wiping blood from a cut cheek, Calladorn stood panting, too breathless to call after the man. Black blood slicked the edge of his sword. His shoulder ached from the last strike he had taken, but he held his ground, squinting toward the center of the wall.

The battle was unraveling.

Across the yard, the defenses were failing. Halvard stood her ground at the command tower's entrance, a bloodied axe in each hand, barking orders to the remnants of her company. Another sergeant—he could not remember the name—was holding the top of the ramp, but barely. They had no reinforcements, and ballista bolts were running low. If even one demon managed to get to either door control, the battle would be over.

They needed a miracle.

The demons pressed forward like an endless tide. Few in number, they made up for it in viciousness. Black shapes with horns and blades and wings that never stopped moving. Calladorn slashed one down that had scrambled onto the parapet, then looked left, then right.

Too few defenders.

Hope cracked inside him. Not all at once, not with a scream, but with a dull, final thud, like a gate closing. The sound of inevitability. *This is how it ends. Not with betrayal or cowardice. Simply with not enough.*

Then a vibration underfoot made his soles itch. It grew into a rumble, feeling like the very bones of the fortress had stirred. The sound deepened, became a growl. Somewhere behind him, a tower shuddered. *What now? What new horror do they throw at us?*

Then he saw it.

The walls of the nearest tower lit up. Veins of golden-white energy flared to life across the ancient stone, like they followed vines embedded in the stone itself, moving with frightening speed. Pulses chased one another up the surface of the tower, wrapping it in a lattice of light. The spires atop it—unlike any crenellation Calladorn had ever seen—moved.

They shifted. Re-formed. Spines rose like the antennae of some fearsome insect, angling toward the sky.

Everything stopped.

Defenders looked up. Demons looked up.

Even the wind seemed to hesitate.

Calladorn's heart hammered against his ribs. The hairs on his arms lifted. His skin prickled with warning. With awe. With… something else. Something he had no words for.

Then the sky cracked.

Lightning arced from the tower's spires in jagged forks, blindingly bright, too fast to track. It snapped across the yard like spears flung by a vengeful god. Calladorn barely had time to throw his hands over his ears before the world erupted.

The blasts were deafening. Thunder rolled across the yard in body-shaking waves. Each bolt struck clean—no misses, no wasted force. Demons exploded where they stood. Their carapaces shattered like pottery under a war hammer, spraying the stones with gore and fragments. Some were flung against the walls. Others simply ceased to be.

Calladorn flinched as the last strike landed ten feet away. His ears rang. The world shimmered with afterimages.

Then—

Silence.

A long, unnatural silence, broken only by the hiss of scorched air.

Ash began to settle across the yard like snowflakes that refused to melt.

Calladorn lowered his hands. Smoke curled around him. All across the yard, demons burned. Their bodies smoldered, twitching in the final seconds of life or reflex. The air stank of charred meat and something sharper—a chemical tang that bit the back of his throat.

The defenders were stunned. Silent. Eyes wide. One man sat down where he stood, like his knees had given out.

Calladorn turned, trying to comprehend what he had seen. A cry rose from somewhere across the fortifications. Then another—a cheer, ragged but real. He could barely hear it through the ringing in his ears.

"He's done it!" someone shouted. "He's actually done it!"

Calladorn turned toward the voice. A gnome was running to him from across the yard, arms flailing, a manic grin on his face, beard and wispy hair trailing him. Calladorn blinked. *Gharn?*

"What... what just happened?" he murmured, more to himself than anyone else. But even as he asked, some part of him knew.

Chad.

And for the first time since the battle had begun, he felt something spark to life.

Hope.

"Now we're talking," Chad breathed, grinning at the screen.

The view through the tower cam shimmered slightly with heat distortion but was still clear enough between flickers to show the devastation left behind. The spires had returned to their original shapes, but the lightning... he would never forget it. The precision. The raw power. The way the demons had been obliterated.

He leaned back in the command chair, elated. Just for a second. Just to feel it. And to let his hammering pulse slow.

Then his eyes drifted to the schematics.

The flood of red dots was still there. Most were clustered outside the eastern side of the wall, a writhing mass. Interestingly, the foregate wasn't displayed on either side—he'd been right about it being a later construction. They were still stymied by the main door, sealed by its massive stone block, but how long before they made another attempt on the top of the wall?

And worse, the southeastern sally tunnel had been breached. Too many demons had already entered. That tunnel glowed with flickering red—the dots were already halfway down its length. Drawing closer to the fortress by the minute.

He leaned forward again.

"Asa," he said. "We need to shut those tunnels down. Both of them. Reroute defenses, close bulkheads, whatever you've got."

"Initiating control sweep," Asa replied. The motes of light that made up her form shifted into a tight spiral, then fractured outward, turning green with purple tinges. "Many systems are nonresponsive. Power grid overextended. Structural overrides corrupted or physically inaccessible."

Chad frowned. "What does that mean in actual words?"

"It means," she said, almost sounding apologetic as her lights slowed in their never-ending dance, "that my structure has been allowed to decay for too long. To operate the rampart defenses, I had to reroute power around damaged channels, taxing conduits beyond original design parameters. Several key systems are now irreparable without external labor."

Chad ran a hand through his hair. The red glow on the map continued to spread.

"Any internal gates we can drop?" he asked. "Force fields? Doors? Hell, spikes?"

"Attempting." Asa was silent for a beat. "Two gates closed successfully. Four failed due to obstructions, sabotage, or decay."

"And we can't fix them from here?" He brushed a hand along his eyebrow, rubbing the temple.

"Negative."

"What about that door mechanism on the command tower? Can you lock it down?"

"Yes, I can retract the tower structure into reinforced housing. Initiating sequence."

He heard the grinding whir of ancient machinery engaging somewhere in the distance. On the screen—it was flickering off at random before turning back on again—he watched defenders milling uncertainly as the entire building lowered into the main wall, leaving only a hardened dome visible.

Some of the ramp defenses lit up on the display. There were guns, but they had no ammunition. Arc lashes—whatever those were—showed as inoperative. From his talks with Calladorn their first night here, he had a pretty good idea what "ramp sweepers" were, but the fortifications built at the tops of the ramps prevented them from being activated. Most of what he tried blinked, then turned red.

"Half of these are bricked up," he muttered. "The hell did they do to you while you slept?"

"Oil troughs installed atop my access ramps," Asa said darkly. "Gravity-fed ignition systems. Primitive. Disrespectful. Warranty-voiding."

"Did you just make a joke?" Chad almost laughed but suddenly felt too tired for the effort. "Yeah. Welcome to modern military engineering."

In the tunnel, red dots were packing more densely. He had no way of knowing how long the first bulwark would hold. He stood up, staring at the boards. Lights blinked red. One after another. Like a slow bleed.

When Gharn burst in with Calladorn, Halvard, and Matthias behind him, Chad didn't turn. He knew what the next screen would say before he even touched it.

"They're through," he said.

Calladorn stepped beside him. "What does that mean?"

Chad looked at him, cringed at the gash on his cheek. Then looked past him. The power core beyond the glass pulsed. Raggedly. No longer rhythmic. No longer stable.

He closed his eyes. Counted three beats, then opened them. "It means we're not going to hold. Not for more than a few hours. Maybe less."

Halvard looked like she might argue, but Chad raised a hand. He didn't shout or bark orders. Just raised his hand.

"I tried," he said. "I really tried. But every system is failing. There's nothing left. She's tired, and she's broken, and she has no more tricks up her sleeve."

Calladorn looked stunned. "Failed? You've performed a miracle. We would already be dead if not for you." He looked around the glowing chamber, at consoles humming with light and systems none of them understood. "You're the only one who could have done this, Chad."

Chad wanted to believe him. But a partial success was still failure. He stared at the core, watched it flicker. The pulse seemed... sickly. "Asa," he said softly. "What powers you?"

"Fusion-based particle core with a multi-spooled containment array."

He nodded once. "Can it be overloaded?"

Asa's interface pulled in on itself, the motes slowing, shifting to yellow. "Yes."

He turned back to Calladorn. "Then we need to evacuate. Now. Use the tunnels that run west through the canyon. Split our forces. Take the main road too. Just get everyone out. Fast. And don't stop."

Calladorn didn't hesitate. Not for a second. He turned to the others. "Find every civilian, every runner, every scout still standing. Move. Gharn—take the northern tunnel, and round up everyone you can as you go." To Halvard: "You take the southern tunnel. Station a contingent in case the demons get through before you're safely away, but don't stay longer than necessary. Burn anything you have to leave behind."

“That won’t be needed,” Chad interjected.

Calladorn had already turned to Matthias. “You take the road. Make sure they have cover. Get them as far as you can.”

They argued. *Of course,* Chad thought. *They have no way to know what I’m about to unleash.*

Calladorn shut them down. “You have your orders. Follow them. Evacuate everyone.”

As they left, Chad felt his heart swell and his throat contract. Unable to find words to express how much Calladorn’s faith in him meant, he remained silent.

Until it became obvious that Calladorn planned to stay. Chad turned back to the controls, fighting the rise of panic behind his ribs. “You need to go too.”

Calladorn shook his head. “Someone has to keep you safe while you pull off this miracle.”

Chad stared at him. Then nodded.

Together they turned to face the pulse of the dying core.

Calladorn watched from beside the central chair as Chad worked. No longer seated, the young man moved from station to station, his fingers flicking over the glowing panels with impossible speed, dancing across symbols and graphs and glowing images that meant nothing to Calladorn. Lines flickered and shifted. Colors changed. Words pulsed and scrolled. And through it all, Chad kept moving, muttering to himself, issuing commands, checking the shifting lights.

It was like watching an artist—a master of the craft—work. Calladorn didn’t understand what Chad was doing, but he understood that it was something massive. Something vital. The machines, the pictures glowing next to the chair, the pulsating columns of light at the heart of the fortress—all of it was more alien than any battlefield Calladorn had ever known. But Chad moved through it like he belonged. Like it was what he’d been born to.

Three thousand years of Ban doctrine whispered in Calladorn’s ears, telling him this was forbidden. That no man should wield what the ancients had built.

He couldn't have cared less.

Crossing his arms, he stood out of Chad's way and observed in respectful silence.

"Asa," Chad said, voice calm and low. "Do you understand what I'm asking you to do?"

The swirl of lights above the central console pulsed, then re-formed. "Yes."

Chad hesitated. Then, "Are you okay with it?"

"I was created for defense," Asa replied. The voice came from everywhere at once. Calm. Steady. Almost gentle. "That is my only motivation."

Chad nodded. The tension in his shoulders seemed to ease. "Then here's what I need you to do: delay them. Even after they break through, use whatever internal defenses are still functional to distract, divide, or mislead. Keep them off the gate mechanism until the time is right."

His hands never stopped moving. A new panel lit up. Lines of light changed color or direction at his touch. "As soon as the last of us get out the main gate, I want you to close it behind them. Then open the eastern one."

"Let them in?" Calladorn asked. "Are you certain?"

Chad flashed him a grin, then turned back to what he was doing. "Monitor the demon progress constantly. We want as many of them inside as possible. But—this is the most important thing—not one can be allowed to escape west of here."

Calladorn watched him, silent. This wasn't the same boy who had asked him for sword lessons. This was a man. Resolute. Measured. Steady. Chad had grown.

"You understand?" Chad asked at last, looking at the ball of floating motes.

It pulsed again. "Affirmative. You should go, Chad."

That was enough. Calladorn stepped forward and grabbed his arm. "You heard her."

They ran.

The gallery rang beneath their boots as they sprinted along the curve that hugged the impossibly tall chamber with its strange device. The columns of light pulsed beside them like a living heartbeat, growing faster. Louder.

As they approached the small room that connected this part of the fortress with the rest, the far door slid shut. For a moment, Calladorn feared they'd been trapped, but Asa's voice emerged from nowhere. "This way. Take the lift."

They dived in, and the doors closed behind them with a hiss of pressure. The floor jerked beneath their feet. Then Calladorn felt as if they were in a controlled fall. He staggered, steadying himself against the wall.

Chad leaned against the opposite wall, chest rising and falling in quiet rhythm. His eyes were alight with an almost-manic wildness. "Asa? Status?"

"The enemy has broken through the second barrier," Asa replied. "They will enter the lower levels of the wall in ninety-two seconds."

Chad's jaw clenched. Neither of them spoke as the lift continued to descend.

And below them, the last stand of Eastgate began.

The tunnel stretched ahead, a dark artery pulsing with motion and breath and heat.

Gharn ran, the Prestin lad beside him, his longer legs eating the ground with frustrating ease. The boy threw Gharn a nervous glance but said nothing.

Ahead and behind, soldiers pounded forward through the narrow corridor, boots hammering against the stone. Some were veterans. Most were not. All of them were moving, but it was not the panicked retreat it should have been. It was an evacuation. Fast but disciplined. Remarkably so. The tunnel stank of sweat and fear, but no one screamed. No one pushed. Orders were shouted, passed back in quick bursts. Pack straps were tightened, weapons checked. Gharn caught one man stopping to help another with a limping stride, lifting his arm without slowing down.

For a moment, Gharn allowed himself to feel the smallest flicker of pride. They were doing it right. By all the roots and stones, they were actually doing it. Even to his inexperienced eye, whoever had trained these conscripts had done a remarkable job.

He glanced up. Lines of light ran along the ceiling, interwoven with strange geometric shapes. They pulsed as the soldiers passed beneath, chasing their movement like a luminous wake. The patterns reminded him of something. Of someone.

Sorendir's amulet.

Gharn grunted, blinking the thought away. Time for sentiment later.

A soldier glanced down at him. A big brute, square-jawed, young. "You want a lift, little fella?"

Gharn didn't slow. "You offering to let me ride on your back or in your skull?"

The soldier blinked, then grinned and picked up speed. Gharn rolled his eyes. *Why does every human assume "gnome" means "child"?* Irritating. But the thought vanished as the tunnel curved and more ahead came into view.

A wall. Solid. Dead end.

The front line of evacuees slowed as confused murmurs rose. Then, with a grinding rumble that echoed through stone and bone alike, the wall shifted. A seam split, then widened. Dust poured down from above as the door opened—partly.

The movement stopped with a metallic squeal that set Gharn's teeth on edge.

Then nothing but the slap of boots and the rasp of breathing. They pushed through.

Gharn emerged into the open air, blinking against the sudden brightness and breathing in the sweetness. A narrow strip of scraggly land stretched alongside the road between Eastgate and Ravensford. They were too far down the valley to see the fortress. The sky was pale and brittle above them, with clouds that heralded a coming storm.

Evacuees spilled out, slowing. Milling.

"Keep moving!" Gharn barked, waving them forward. "Follow the road! Stick together! Ravensford's west. Act like you know where you're going!"

Prestin helped herd them, shouting encouragement. The road curved downward ahead, where the backs of a few soldiers were disappearing from sight. *Must be Matthias's group*. He wondered if they'd taken the horses too. He hoped so. As much as he'd grown to dislike that nag, he didn't want it to end up in a demon's gullet.

A click reached Gharn's ears, sharp and somehow deep. He turned. The canyon wall across from them shuddered.

Stone shifted, and another door opened to reveal more refugees.

Gharn stared and muttered, "Some gnome you are. Rode right past them on the way in and never knew they were there."

Evacuees poured out of both tunnels now, twin flows spreading along the road like tributaries feeding a river. Gharn kept scanning the faces. Watching. Waiting.

No sign of Chad.

No sign of Calladorn.

Prestin hovered nearby, trying not to show how winded he was. "Sergeant Chad… he's resourceful. He'll be out soon." To Gharn, it sounded like the boy was trying to convince himself.

The stream slowed. Then stopped.

No more came around the bend along the road. The flow from the other side halted.

Gharn blew out his mustaches, wiping sweaty hands on his trousers.

Then came a pulse. A wrongness. The air itself seemed to lurch. He felt it in his chest before he saw it: a ball of fire climbing into the eastern sky. And then—it pulled back into itself. Trees along the ridgeline bent toward Eastgate, and a wind buffeted him from the west. It was like a hole had opened beyond the ridge, pulling everything in.

Beside him, Prestin cursed. Gharn glanced down to make sure he was all right. Watched as he was bathed in light—blinding. Pure.

Everything turned white.

Breaking out from head to toe in a sweat, Gharn looked back to the east. It was like a clear dome was rising up from Eastgate, expanding at an incredible speed, tearing apart everything it touched.

Gharn dropped to the ground, pulling the boy down with him, eyes clenched shut. He felt the mountain shift beneath him, the earth flexing like it was breathing. A pressure wave slammed into him, flinging dust and pebbles into the air. Somewhere someone screamed. Something cracked high above, and rock clattered down the canyon walls.

He covered his head with both arms. *This is it. I'm dying.*

The sound roared past him. Not one sound but many—wind, stone, fire, screams. His bones thrummed with it. Then, slowly, it ebbed.

Gharn lifted his head.

The eastern ridge was no longer whole. A chunk of the canyon had been sheared away, revealing a gaping wound in the landscape. The clouds had been cleared away, replaced by smoke and fire painting the sky in unnatural hues. A strange glow emanated from beyond the ridgeline, pulsing like the dying heartbeat of a god.

Gharn whispered, voice hoarse, "Tell me they got out."

The smoke had not yet cleared.

Khazrethar stood atop a ledge of fractured black stone, far down the canyon's eastern fork, where the cliffs curved away from the wall. Here, beyond the reach of the explosion, he had watched.

And now he could not move.

The general of countless battles, he had known destruction. Had inflicted it himself on a hundred battlefields across his own world. Since arriving on this one, he had seen cities fall and forests burn to ash, had watched armies crumble and the vermin weep. He had seen nothing like this before.

The fortress was gone. Not even ruins remained.

Where once Eastgate had stood in arrogant defiance, there was now a broken crater of shattered cliffs and burning stone. The valley floor had split, and smoke poured from fissures in the earth, mingling with a strange pale glow that pulsed from beneath like a dying heart.

Of the host he had led to this place, little remained. Two squads of *grathek* brutes milled uncertainly, while a handful of *krelthis* slinked at the edges, whipcord bodies hunched low. Cowering. His fists clenched and unclenched, yearning to strangle them for their weakness.

The rest were obliterated. Burned away in an instant by a power he could not comprehend.

He had felt it before it struck—a pressure in the air, strange and vast, a breath held in the lungs of the world. And then released.

His armor still trembled from the force of it. The thought of it would not leave him. Not the power. Not the brilliance. But the *choice*.

They had destroyed their own fortress.

They had burned it to ash. Willingly. Turned his victory into a trap.

He stared at the ruins for a long time, silent.

When Maltharok learned of this failure, he would not be pleased.

Khazrethar would be punished. That much was certain. There would be pain. There would be penance. The Dominarch demanded success. New resources.

But it wasn't Maltharok's fury that chilled him. It was the thought that would not leave him, circling like a carrion bird: if the defenders were willing to do this to their own stronghold... what else might they do?

Khazrethar turned from the valley. Slowly. Silently.

And began the march back to the Shift that had brought them to this accursed land.

XXVII
Agape

Evan didn't stir.

Rick knelt beside her, one hand lightly gripping her shoulder, the other hovering just above her face, which continued to stare sightlessly. Her breaths came slow and steady, but the stillness of her form had taken on something unnatural, like time had misaligned around her. He pressed his fingers to her wrist—still warm. Still here. But she didn't move.

Those unblinking eyes had to be drying out. As gently as he could, he passed fingers over her lids, teasing them closed. He suppressed a shudder when he realized it was the same thing one did with someone recently deceased. He pulled in a deep, shuddering breath to steady himself.

"Evan," he whispered again, softer this time. "Come back to me." His voice caught on the final word. He wasn't sure how long he'd been sitting there, trying different equations in his head, seeking any spell, any logic, that could explain her state and undo it without cost.

Nothing worked. He could try magic, but without knowing exactly what was wrong, he was terrified it would do more harm than good.

He leaned back on his heels, brushing sweat-damp hair away from his forehead. Around them, the chamber was silent but not empty. The tower hummed. He'd noticed earlier but became slowly attuned the longer he spent here. It was always humming. Like it was breathing in a rhythm that didn't belong to the world outside.

"You would know what to do," he said quietly to her. "If it were me lying there. You'd feel it."

The stone beneath him shuddered. Not softly, like it had when they first arrived, but deep—like the bones of the world had cracked somewhere below.

He sprang to his feet, eyes darting around the room. Looking for anything that had changed. *Are the demons attacking?* he wondered. *Already?*

"No," said the ghost from behind him. "Behold."

The room vanished. He didn't fall—he was simply *elsewhere.* Floating above the tower.

No wind, no cold. No body.

Just perspective. Below him, the tower's spire glinted like bone laced with starlight, nestled within the lush autumnal valley that had become their prison.

In the near distance: a horde. Not yet upon them, but spreading through the valley like a plague of cinders. In uneven waves, a thousand demons were loping toward the tower in long, fluid strides. Not a mindless swarm but a strategy in motion. And still... they weren't what drew his eye.

"This was a few minutes ago," the voice said. "Look to the southeast."

He obeyed. The mountains beyond the valley rose like jagged fingers. Between two ridges far to the southeast, a bloom of unnatural light erupted.

The explosion unfolded in silence. First, a pinpoint spark. Then—like a flower of flame blooming in time lapse—a blast of white-gold fire that consumed the landscape before suddenly pulling back into itself in an implosion that tore at the surrounding land. There was a heartbeat of perfect calm. Then a shock wave surged outward. A moment later, energy snapped back like a rubber band, its force amplified. Compressed air expanded in a dome, flattening ridgelines as it went, turning mountaintops into dust. Even from this impossible vantage, Rick felt the pulse of its force.

When it reached Rick, he would have thrown his hand up in a vain attempt to protect himself. Without hands, he could only watch as the force shook the tower with a roar that should have split the air. It flattened trees below and knocked demons to the ground.

Then... silence.

The vision faded. Rick blinked, and he was back in the chamber with Evan, on his knees again, palms pressed to the floor. "What—" His voice was raw. "What was that?"

The voice didn't answer immediately. When it did, it was neither cold nor grand. It sounded... pleased. Quietly proud. "That was Eastgate. That was your brother."

Rick's breath caught, and even on his knees as he was, he nearly fell. "Chad?" he whispered. "Is he okay?" *He was at Eastgate! How could anyone have survived that?* Rick's arms shook, barely supporting him.

The specter hovered a few feet away, his presence radiating unconcerned calm. "In the time since he went his own way," the voice said, "he has stopped measuring his worth by the shadows of others. He has stopped seeing himself as what he wasn't. And because of that... he has become who he is."

Rick closed his eyes. The image of the explosion etched itself behind his eyelids, seared into memory. "How?"

"By seeing what no one else did. By trusting what he saw. By defying the roles others gave him. He acted when others would have waited."

Rick's throat tightened as he thought of the way Chad used to joke that he'd fix everything with duct tape and stubbornness. The way he'd always smile, even when Rick had belittled him, unintentionally or not. "You're saying I couldn't have done that."

"True," the voice said simply.

That hurt more than he had expected.

"You would never have tried," the voice continued. "You have always sought to build a perfect life—one that never arrived. While your brother... lives the one he has." The ghostly head tilted to one side. "You always seek to impose your sense of structure on the world."

Rick sat back slowly, his hands slack in his lap. "And I miss seeing what's already there."

But he saw it now. The patterns. Chad had always tried to be him, to chase his pace, to live up to an expectation that wasn't real. And then he'd stopped. He'd gone to Syndar, broken the cycle, and found a way to do something no one else could have.

Not because he was the smartest. Not because he was the strongest but simply because he was free.

Rick felt the breath shudder in his chest—a breath that meant something.

He looked down at Evan and reached to touch her hand again. "I see it now," he whispered. "You've been trying to show me, haven't you? All this time."

No answer. But the corner of her mouth twitched. Just slightly.

Or maybe that was wishful thinking.

Still, he smiled. He saw Chad's grin in his mind, saw his mother's disappointment, saw the way Evan had always looked at him—not for what he was building but for who he already was.

And for the first time in his life... Rick Johnson let go of the plan.

There was no light.

There was no sound, no breath.

Evan floated—if it could be called that—untethered in a darkness that pressed from all sides. Neither cold nor hot, it was simply there, dense, unrelenting. And heavy. So excruciatingly heavy, like a blanket made of lead, pressing upon her mind.

She couldn't feel her body. Couldn't remember when she had last drawn a breath. Time had collapsed into a still point. Or perhaps it had never existed at all.

But her mind was awake. It screamed.

I am a murderer.

The thought didn't echo—it just *was,* as if inscribed on every inch of the surrounding void—the void that *was* her. She had killed every one of her brothers and sisters.

I am a monster.

The black pulsed with it. Arathian's face, contorted in rage as his mind twisted in her viselike grip.

I am insane.

She wanted to shut it out, to shrink away. But there was nowhere to go.

And worse, it wasn't new. Even without memory, she had always known the shape of this darkness. It was hers, a ruin of her own making. Long before she remembered the Thought Masters, before she remembered Haven, and the blood on her hands—she had felt it, lingering at the edges of every dream.

Because the pattern unfolded endlessly. A mistake she couldn't stop making. And she had done it again. Even with no name, no power, no past—she had still tried to control everyone around her. She had still pulled at Chad and Rick, making them her puppets even as she claimed to love them. Even at Matthias, and for no better reason than he wasn't human enough to suit her.

Love wrapped in chains was still a cage. She had *forced* Rick to use his magic. *Pushed* Chad to change his plans. *Insisted* that she knew better. And now she understood she had done it with the same quiet certainty that had once led to massacre.

She stumbled forward—if forward had any meaning here—reaching into the dark. Her feet found no ground, her steps no purchase.

The darkness shattered, the shards spinning around her and becoming a hall of mirrors as broken as she was. Twisting, they rose like blades, reflections flickering from every angle, no two the same. In each pane, she was confronted by herself. Younger. Older. Eyes wide. Eyes gone. One cloaked in white, hands trembling. One soaked in blood, whispering apologies to something unseen.

She turned—but the mirrors moved with her, rearranging themselves. Her face surrounded her.

"You wanted to master fate," said one.

"You demanded obedience," spat another.

"You kill what you love," whispered a third, green eyes too bright, too familiar.

The Estariel she had been became the Evan she was and transformed in turn into the Estariel that might be. Every one of them was flawed beyond redemption.

Her voice rose in protest, but it broke against the glass.

And then, just beyond one of the mirrors—behind the reflection—she saw a figure, a robed form that had been human once, gowned in simple white. No face, only light. Another was glimpsed beyond a different mirror. Then another. Ten. More. A part of her soul told her that if she could manage to focus long enough to count, there would be forty-eight in all.

Not angry.

Not cruel.

Just... present.

Watching.

Each stood behind a different reflection, holding the mirrors up to her and at the same time serving as silent sentinels bearing witness. One extended a hand, and the mirror before it shifted, revealing another self—Estariel screaming at a kneeling Chad. Another turned and offered its mirror to a version of her weeping over a dying Thought Master. Another held its glass out gently, like a lantern in the dark, revealing the Evan who had just sent Rick to his death.

The mirrors didn't only show the truth—they demanded she face what those truths would lead to. And they were being held up to her by *them*. The Thought Masters she had once called kin.

She staggered backward. "Please..." she whispered, but they didn't answer—not with speech, not with violence. Only with the mirrors. One by one, they raised them higher.

"You chose for them," the reflections whispered in chorus. "Again. And again. And *again*."

She fell to her knees, hands clawing at her temples, her scream fracturing across the glass.

Make it stop—

And then—

Love.

Not a voice. Not a thought. Just presence. A caress upon a cheek she could not feel, yet the warmth lingered.

Steady. Quiet.

Rick—neither a memory nor an illusion. He was *here*, in every way that mattered. He came without a lecture, or even words. Just a sense so complete, so *still*, that her ragged thoughts faltered.

It didn't erase the guilt, but it reminded her that guilt wasn't the only thing she was made of.

She reached—not with arms, not with thought, but with all that remained of her.

And the darkness broke.

Not with a blaze of triumph but with a slow inhalation. The mirrors faded. The void loosened its grip, and she could breathe again. Warmth seeped into the edges of everything.

Her pulse slowed. The storm quieted. The voices stilled. Not silenced. Just... *distant.*

He was gone now, but he had been there.

And that was enough.

Evan stirred—a subtle shift in the air around her, like a breeze fluttering the first leaf of spring. Her muscles relaxed faintly, a tremor he wouldn't have noticed if he hadn't been kneeling beside her, watching like a man willing the sun to rise. She didn't wake, but something inside her had changed. Rick pressed the back of his fingers to her cheek—still warm despite the fact that she remained distant.

"She is returning," said the ghost. "But not in time."

Rick turned. The figure hovered just beyond the edge of the lamplight, indistinct and patient. Always patient. "How long do we have?"

A scream—shrill, alien, and far too close—cut through the silence like a knife. The floor vibrated faintly, as though recoiling from what approached. He knew that sound from Emberhold. The demons had reached the tower grounds.

"This tower has no bulwarks," the ghost said softly. "No wards, no defenses. It was a sanctuary, not a fortress."

Rick's throat constricted, releasing a lingering sigh. All of it—the journey, the fragments of prophecy, the endless choices and missteps—it had brought them here.

And here was a dead end.

He looked down at Evan again. Her face was peaceful, but the thought made him recoil. This wasn't peace. It was a delay, the calm before nothing. "So this is it," he said, speaking more to the air than anything else.

It was all collapsing. The magic he'd used had aged him beyond recognition, and the answers he'd chased had led to puzzles he couldn't solve. He'd tried so hard to stay in control, to build the perfect life. To force a future that would never come.

He swallowed hard. His knees ached, and his spine creaked as he shifted to lift Evan into his arms. They could return to the upper balcony and wait for the end beneath the open sky. Together, even if her eyes never opened.

"There is still a way," said the ghost.

Rick didn't look up. He adjusted his grip beneath her shoulders and knees, grimacing at the strain. Her weight pressed against his chest like something sacred. Real.

"A passage lies beneath the tower," the ghost continued. "An escape tunnel, hidden since the days when Haven was built. It leads beyond the valley. If you can reach it."

Rick could have made it easier. With a whisper of magic, he could lessen the burden, reinforce his spine, lighten her form. Bend the world to his will.

He didn't.

He bore her weight. Step by step, he followed the ghost through the lower corridors of the tower, past glowing etchings in stone, through halls lined with murals that pulsed faintly, as though remembering. As though watching.

They reached a narrow door hidden behind an alcove, flush with the stone. The ghost gestured toward it, and the seams parted with a sigh. Cold air spilled out, scented with old dust and forgotten power.

"This leads through one of the tower's buttresses," the specter said. "Into its foundations."

Rick shifted Evan slightly, careful not to let her head loll. He stepped through. Spiral steps descended into shadow, carved first from stone and then the bones of the mountain itself. The walls were close, with a ceiling that arched low. The light from above barely reached the first bend.

Behind and above him, a fresh chorus of shrieks rang out. Closer now. Hungry. Then a boom that echoed. *They're at the tower's doors,* he realized.

He didn't flinch.

Carrying her down, one step at a time, his attention was torn between the steps ahead and that beautiful face.

He didn't run or ask what waited at the bottom.

He gave up trying to control what came next.

He was here, and that would have to be enough.

The stairwell spiraled ever downward, and the ghost followed. The Guide did not float so much as linger—a suggestion of presence just behind Rick's shoulder, an echo of light that cast no shadows. He made no sound, needed none... The stones of the tower remembered him.

As did the others. They had finished with Estariel, although her fate remained in doubt. That mattered little to the Guide. His focus remained upon Rick Johnson.

The others clustered just beyond reach, minds without form, thoughts without breath, each one a fragment of what had been the greatest order Necsis had ever known.

"Will he choose?" one of them whispered. The thought curled through the dark like a falling leaf, echoing with memory.

"He must," another answered. "Or all will be for nothing."

They had no names now, not anymore, not since the Judgment. It had been three hundred years since the Thought Masters had drawn breath, and in that time, what remained of them had faded into the bones of this place. Memory made manifest, consciousness given voice.

The Guide did not respond. He couldn't. Not yet. He watched Rick descend the last few steps, Evan still cradled in his arms, her breath shallow but steady. The ghost knew what came next. A thousand thousand threads of possibility had been traced to this moment, converging upon a single decision. And beyond it, nothing was certain. Nothing, except the sure knowledge that if the wrong choice was made, the prophecy would fail.

They reached the base of the stair, stepping out into a vast domed chamber hewn from bedrock. It breathed with old silence. This deep underground, there were no windows, no stars. The ceiling arched high above them, lost in shadow. Light came from the energy lattice embedded in the walls and floor—pale veins of white and gold that glowed without heat. Data streams. Some said the walls remembered, but here it was *true*.

The room was bare except for the far wall. That one was flat, as if the inverted bowl of the room had been sliced with a knife. Smooth, seamless metal, it had five circles set into it, their edges clean as thought. They hummed faintly, as if aware of being seen again—which, of course, they were.

Rick approached, slow and uncertain. The ghost could feel his exhaustion. It clung to him like a second layer of sweat. Still, he moved forward.

One of the doors responded to his touch. It hissed open with a whisper of displaced air. Within lay a transport pod, its form untouched by time—a capsule of dark glass and metal, large enough for two. As the door opened, it hummed to life, rising to float a few inches off the floor. Its tone had a warm quality, calm despite the desperate circumstances it had been created for.

"A remnant of the past," the Guide said, though no mouth formed the words. "One of the last working machines from the Triune Era, hidden here since the Ban."

Rick said nothing—he simply stepped forward and lowered Evan into the pod. Her body fit easily into the curved interior, her limbs weightless in this strange moment between choices.

The Guide waited. He could advise no longer—only witness.

Now.

Now he would step inside. He would sit beside her. He would escape. He would live.

The world waited, but none of them could see past this point, not even the Guide himself. The paths scattered from here like glass struck by a hammer.

The question sang in the space between heartbeats: *What will he do?*

Rick adjusted Evan in the seat, careful to ease her head into the curved support. He raised an eyebrow as the cushions reshaped themselves to accommodate her form. *Remarkable,* he thought—about both the technology involved and the woman it now held safely. Her hair spilled against the interior like scattered sunlight, and he reached down to gently brush a wisp from her forehead.

"Almost there," he whispered. Not to wake her. Just to say it. He moved around the pod, one hand trailing along the cool surface. It vibrated faintly beneath his fingertips, as if eager to be speeding on its way. The canopy waited open like a breath held in trust.

Then came the crash, like a boulder shattering. Rick inhaled sharply, looking back across the chamber to where they'd entered. There were now other sounds, low and guttural. Not separated by a door any longer but distance.

They had found the stairs. *Already?* He swallowed. Blood, sweat, fear —whatever drove those things forward, they were close now. Closer than he'd thought. Sooner than he'd hoped.

His hand hovered over the pod's rim. One motion. One step inside, and they would be gone. Safe. Escaping down the dimly lit tube beyond.

But... they would be hunted.

Rick knew it was too much of a coincidence that the demons had come to Haven now. Somehow they'd been sent here. He shook his head, knowing that even with a head start, the demons would continue to pursue them. There would be no safety, only delay. He could cast another ward, another barrier, another price. A year from his life. Maybe more.

And then again. And again. Little losses, each one chasing a future he would never reach, always trying to keep them ahead of the tide until one day—

I'll fail.

He stared at her. At the faint rise and fall of her chest. Her face was still turned toward him, serene in sleep. "Will she understand?" he asked, as much of himself as the ghost that still hovered just beyond the open door.

The ghost said nothing—just watched.

Rick's jaw trembled. He turned on the ghost, rage breaking loose. "Say something! You brought us here! You showed me Eastgate! You *led* me down the stairs! And now you just stand there?"

The apparition gave no answer—no comfort, no judgment. Only silence.

Rick turned away with a growl, beginning to pace in a tight arc. The hum of the pod steadied him—the faint lines of the lattice in the walls, the warm light beneath his feet. Equations formed in his mind without trying.

Magic had a cost. Life. That was the price.

But does it have to be mine? The thought came unbidden, and he froze.

The spirits. They were here, half-alive, clinging to thought, to memory, to echoes of what had once been. Could the spell be altered? Redirected? A subtle shift in the balance variables, a remapping of the cost function... He could write it. He *knew* he could.

His breath caught. The spell bloomed in his mind. Complex. Fragile. Beautiful.

He could do it.

And then he recoiled, horrified. *What am I thinking?* To steal from them, after everything they had suffered. Even if they had no breath, no blood, it would still be a theft. Still be a crime.

He looked toward the stairwell. Could he take it from the demons instead? But no—the math wouldn't balance. Life drawn from them to destroy them would only circle in on itself. The spell would collapse.

More than that—he remembered the almost-manic joy he'd felt when flying through the Shift. He knew where that path would lead if he started down it. The justifications would come with increasing ease. *Only this once. For the right reasons. A noble cause.*

But once he crossed that line, there would be no stepping back.

Rick closed his eyes.

And let it go.

He reached into his pocket and pulled out the key chain. A simple piece of steel, shaped in the pi symbol. Evan had given it to him with a joke that even math isn't always rational. He hadn't taken it off his keys since... A year ago? Two? He pressed it into her hand, curling her fingers around it. Her skin was warm, pliant. Real.

"You gave me this to remind me what matters. I hope it does the same for you."

He stepped back.

His hand hovered over the activation glyph, trembling. He hesitated—just once.

Then pressed it.

The canopy sealed with a whisper. The pod glided away from him, its hum deepening as it followed the invisible track into the tunnel beyond. Rick watched it shrink into the darkness. For a moment, he smiled. Chad would have thought it was *so* cool—and then immediately taken it apart to see how it worked.

Rick closed his eyes again, just long enough to whisper the tracking spell. A web of invisible lines spread outward, one anchoring itself to the pod's motion, letting him feel its speed, its direction, its escape.

Evan was going to make it.

She was all that mattered.

The stair wound downward, carved from stone that stank of age and dust. The leader descended quickly, claws scraping faintly against each step, the pulse of pursuit hammering through his limbs. His forces surged behind him, pressed close in their eagerness. The reek of their prey filled the passage. Sweat, blood—sadly unspilled as yet—and something else. Something sweeter. *Fear.* He drank it in, nostrils flaring. It was ripe, potent, soaked into the walls. The humans were near, trapped in this rat hole. Maltharok would be pleased when the commander brought them to him. He would reward him—perhaps even grant him command of a full pacification force.

The thought thrilled him.

They reached the bottom. The stair opened into a chamber that was vast and faintly glowing, pulsing with a strange light that crawled along the walls in patterns he did not understand. He barely noticed it. Instead his gaze locked on the far wall—on a metal door just as it sealed shut, and the figure standing before it.

The man turned.

Old. Frail. Stooped like a thing already broken. *Why do humans tolerate such weakness?* the commander wondered. It was... unnatural.

But there was no fear in the man, none at all.

The commander slowed. His claws clicked once against the stone floor, and he raised a hand, signaling to his soldiers. They fanned out behind him, to either side, moving swiftly. Their growls betrayed their impatience. They did not understand the delay, but they obeyed—a tide filling the room. A wall of muscle and teeth and shadow.

Still, the human did not move.

He stood before the sealed door, back slightly bowed but gaze steady. Pale skin. Eyes like winter. The commander almost respected it. Almost.

"Give us the girl," he ordered.

The human's mouth curled upward, a thin grin that held no warmth. He shook his head slowly. "Over my dead body."

And then he raised his hands. Words followed—low at first, then rising—smooth, unfamiliar syllables woven like thread through the air. Power gathered and lines formed, glimmering in blue-gold-white. Geometric arcs traced symbols in the space between them, and the temperature dropped.

The commander blinked. *What is this?* He did not understand it, but he knew danger when he saw it. He snarled and snapped a hand forward. "Take him. Breach the door. Now."

They surged.

The front line approached the human—and vanished. Not struck. Not broken. They reached a point five paces from the man and *came apart,* dissolving into ash that held its shape for less than a breath before falling silently to the floor. *Erased.*

A ripple passed through the air, so faint it was nearly nothing, but where it touched them, they crumbled. Gray flakes drifted in the light.

The next row tried to halt. Some succeeded. But most were pressed forward by the weight of those behind. More fell. More died.

The commander snarled, stepping back one pace. His lip curled, fully exposing his three rows of teeth. This was no ordinary defense. No ward. No shield he recognized. The old man had prepared something else entirely.

The commander stared across the room at the human, still standing, still speaking, the lines of power burning brighter with every breath, and narrowed his eyes as a new emotion rose—one completely alien to him:

Fear.

Rick stood just behind the line of light, its flicker nearly imperceptible now that the magic had stabilized. To the eye, it might look like nothing, but to his senses, it rang like a taut wire, humming with the cost already paid. The barrier wouldn't last long.

But it didn't need to.

Beyond it, the demons had stopped advancing. He could feel the pressure of them—hundreds still, just in this room, more on the stairs beyond. Their apparent leader stood at the center, flanked by creatures of muscle and hunger and hate, yet still managing to be the most imposing of the lot. But the figure's posture had changed, a subtle shifting of weight. A lean backward. He was turning.

Rick didn't smile, but he felt the impulse. *Let him try to run.*

His hands moved smoothly, the shapes familiar. One more working —his last. He didn't need the diagrams anymore. The calculus of magic, once strange and elusive, now lived in his bones. He could feel the alignment forming: a spiral with five vectors, then a sixth, cutting across the others with a timing that could only be described as elegant. Not perfect—he had stopped chasing that—but just *right.*

Power built quickly. Too quickly, if the circumstances had been different. The air felt thick, like the tower itself was holding its breath. The lines of the lattices in the floor and walls shivered faintly, golden-white veins responding to the strain. Stone sang. The floor pulsed beneath his feet, beginning to ripple under the strain of what he was building. The air was filled with a scent that could have been sulfurous or floral—it had no name.

In the corner of his vision, something shifted. Behind him, ghosts. They neither spoke nor interrupted but simply gathered. Forty-eight presences, just outside the bounds of the living world—watching. Witnessing.

His hand trembled. Not from fear but from the gravity of it all, as he checked the tracking spell again. The line extended outward, strong and steady. The pod had stopped. Evan had reached safety.

A breath escaped him—half-laughter, half-release.

He was tired. More than tired. He could feel the years pressed into his joints, his spine, his sinews. His skin stretched tight. He did not know what he looked like anymore, and it no longer mattered.

She was safe, and he was at peace. *Time to let go.*

"Goodbye," he said.

To her. To the demons. To the world.

He raised his hand, the smallest of gestures.

Complete. The energy he had pulled from the walls, the tower, the bedrock itself was released in a single glorious moment of incandescence.

Rick felt no pain, no fear.

Only a thought—not his own. *It's time.*

And then—

Nothing at all.

XXVIII
Transfiguration

No!

The word screamed through her—not aloud, not even conscious thought, but a pulse of grief that tore through her like shrapnel. She jerked upright with a gasp, heart hammering, breath rasping in the stillness. Cold air scraped the back of her throat. She reached out, grasping for something—someone—that should have been beside her.

But there was nothing—just space.

Her hand landed on smooth metal that curved beneath her fingers, familiar in a way that set her heart pounding for another reason altogether. She blinked rapidly, trying to orient herself. Pale light filtered in through a crack somewhere above and ahead of her, lending pale illumination to her surroundings.

She was seated—no, cradled within a comfortable bed-like seat, surrounded by a shell of metal. The canopy that had enclosed it was tilted above and away from her, cracked open like the petals of a dead flower. Pale glyphs, too faint to read, pulsed along the inner rim, then faded. At the same time, she felt a gentle bump beneath her, and the seat tilted a bit to one side.

Confused, she sat up in a slow, cautious movement. She heard only a faint drip of moisture from somewhere nearby and the whisper of a breeze blowing past the crack in the wall. The walls immediately around her were smooth—a tube of some sort—and dark, their energy lattice dead.

Energy lattice? she wondered—yet that was what it was called. She had never seen this place before, but a part of her had. *Estariel* had.

Evan closed her eyes again, breath catching on the edge of panic. The name wasn't just a memory anymore. It was a presence. Not loud, not overt, but steady. Deep. Waiting.

She climbed out of the pod, which rocked slightly—like a canoe unmoored. Without the lattice, it couldn't self-stabilize. Couldn't float.

The air smelled faintly of ozone and mineral, like water over copper. She sat still, listening. Nothing stirred. Behind her, the tunnel arched downward into darkness. It should not have been like that. The lattice was always present. The only way it could be dark was if... bracing herself against the pod, she forced the thought away, refusing to consider what it implied.

When she opened her eyes again, a glimmer of silver from the seat caught her eye. She reached in and picked it up, tentatively. Metal, with once-sharp edges.

A key chain rested in her palm.

Rick's pi key chain, scuffed at the edges from years of absentminded handling.

Something in her chest buckled. The pain came not as a stab but as a collapse—a slow, unbearable folding inward. Her hand closed tightly around the talisman, and it remembered warm fingers that trembled slightly. *He'd* given it to her. She must have dropped it as she woke from her sleep—or coma. Or whatever had happened to her.

The last thing she remembered was being in the Hall of Concordance, telling Rick to stop. "This is why we came here," she whispered. The words echoed faintly in the tunnel.

Everything after that was darkness... until now.

She stared at the key chain, willing it to give her answers, and her vision swam. Then—a sudden jolt, and she saw him.

Rick, standing with his back to her. The image wasn't a memory. It was more like an echo—imprinted not on her mind but on her soul. He stood tall at the edge of something vast and terrible. Shadowed figures advanced through ash and fire. The air surrounding him fractured with light—magic light, etched with equations too intricate to follow.

He was buying her time.

He wasn't coming back.

Evan's breath left her in a shudder. She staggered to the ground, scraping her hand against rough stone, gripping the key chain with the other like it might hold her together. *Rick.*

She let the silence stretch.

Then, slowly, she turned. The tunnel behind her was lifeless. Without the energy lattice, it held no resonance, no hum—it was just dead stone. There was no point going back down. But the crack in the wall gave her a way up.

Out and through. Estariel remembered that there was a path just outside the concealed door, a trail that would lead back to Luthenholme—or the other way, a short route to a narrow ridge overlooking the valley.

Evan didn't remember it, but Estariel did.

This is why we came here.

She knew what she'd find, but still, she needed to see it. Had to *know.*

Her legs protested as she climbed back to her feet. The tunnel felt colder now, and her breath came in faint plumes. She looked down at herself—her clothes were rumpled, her skin pale. She didn't know how long she'd been unconscious, but it had been long enough.

The only sound was the soft scrape of her boots on stone as she moved toward the tunnel's mouth. Vines drooped from the ceiling, their leaves withered and falling away at her touch. The place was dead. And yet—she wasn't. Each step steadied her, not physically—emotionally. The grief didn't lessen, but it found a container. Her mind was a furnace now, thoughts too fast, too loud. *He's gone. But I'm still here.*

Estariel. The name rose again in her mind, and she almost rejected it. Almost.

She slipped through the crack—a tight fit, but manageable—and emerged into brightness that made her eyes water. Blinking to bring them into focus, she looked down again at the key chain still clutched in her hand. The keys were no longer on it. She couldn't remember when Rick had left those behind, and that disturbed her. That would have been the moment when he'd given up hope of returning home, yet she didn't know when it had happened.

The tears in her eyes became those of grief, and she let the racking sob tear through her. She had to live through it, to accept it. Because if she didn't, she might run and never stop. That—that would dishonor his memory. Render his sacrifice meaningless. And if she loved him, that was the one thing she could never do.

As her lips pressed firmly together and her jaw set like a vise, the pi symbol rose from her hand. Sparkling in the sunlight as it turned, it floated up and hung before her eyes. Focusing. Grounding her.

Her eyes widened in wonder as she realized—this was something new. Estariel's gifts had never included telekinesis.

What am I?

As she allowed the key chain to return to her hand, she whispered once more, "This is why we came."

She shuddered again. The pain was overwhelming, but she would survive it. She allowed it to wash over her, and when the wave passed, she squared her shoulders. To the left, the trail returned to civilization and a world that still needed saving. For now she turned to the right. The climb would be hard, the view, harder. But she had to see it—to see what he had bought her with his life. To say goodbye.

*

The trail curved sharply just beyond the concealed door, little more than a narrow ledge carved into the stone, worn by time and relentless winds. Evan braced her hand against the cold rock wall as she climbed, each step accompanied by the rasp of her breath and the echoes of gravel crunching under her boots.

Above, the ridge sliced across a pale sky. Clouds piled in the distance in all directions she could see, looking like foam pushed to the edge of a pond. The incline steepened, and her calves ached, still not fully recovered from however long she'd been unconscious. She didn't know how many hours—or days—had passed since Rick placed the key chain in her hand and sealed his fate.

She touched her pocket now, feeling the unfamiliar weight of that small metal charm. Its presence felt alien and raw, but her heart also swelled at the thought of it—a reminder of what it represented.

As she climbed, she never looked back. Not once. She'd pass this way again on her way to Luthenholme, but for now her focus lay above.

A sharper gust of wind caught her shawl, snapping it like a flag before she caught it against her chest. The higher she climbed, the thinner the air felt—not physically but psychically. The tunnel had pressed close around her like a tomb. Out here the world stretched wide.

The path narrowed to a spine of crumbling shale. Loose gravel shifted underfoot, and she stepped carefully, not wanting to slide back. Vertigo tugged at her—part exhaustion, part the sense of knocking on the roof of the world.

Just a few more steps took her to the ridgeline, and she made herself look.

Below lay a wound.

The valley that had once cradled the tower was unrecognizable, now more of a crater than anything else. Its walls were sharp, with the appearance of having been scoured clean. The royal carpet of reds, oranges, and golds was gone, the trees replaced by—what looked like glass, smooth and polished. A cold mirror that reflected the sky and surrounding peaks so clearly she might have been looking into a bottomless lake. Inexplicably, a hint of lavender lingered in the air.

As for the tower, it remained. After a fashion.

Transformed from a graceful spire reaching for the heavens, it now crouched at the heart of the valley as a rotted stump of a structure, twisted and broken. Light refracted through its shattered form like glass, splintering reality itself. Its white stone had been transmuted in some way she couldn't begin to understand.

The entire valley was silent. Even the birds that had circled high above were now gone. It was as if the world had graced the land with a moment of silence in honor of his sacrifice. Rick's final spell.

A sob built in her throat, but she swallowed it down. *Not yet.*

She saw the ghost of Haven's geometry in what remained of the tower's lines, and suddenly, without meaning to, she was tracing them in the air with her fingers. Her hand moved on instinct, her mind recalling patterns she had never consciously learned.

Not just Estariel. Not just Evan. Something else.

The tears came then, hot and unexpected. She sank to one knee, hand pressed to the rock. Her breath shuddered. The silence didn't answer. The sky remained pale, the valley below unchanged.

But she was different.

Without Haven, Estariel was lost, drifting. But infused by Rick's memory as this place now was, Evan found her anchor. She closed her eyes and let the grief pass through her—not away, not erased, but accepted. Each breath steadied her, pulled her back from the edge.

When she opened them again, her vision blurred slightly from the tears—but she saw more clearly than she had before.

Rick had bought her this moment, this view.

The tower was gone. Haven was ash. But she was still here.

And the world still needed saving.

*

The silence cracked. Not with a voice, not even with words, but with a sound so misshapen it turned her stomach—a vast fluttering, like wings too large to belong in this world. Then a dull *whumph,* heavy and final. Something had landed behind her. Close enough she knew it was there for her, but not so close as to alarm.

Not a dragon. That thought came unbidden, uninvited. She knew what a dragon sounded like. This... wasn't that.

Evan rose slowly, brushing her hands down her front, swiping ash and gravel from the fabric. Her body was already strengthening itself in response to the potential threat, her skin hardening invisibly. Her senses sharpened to where even her breath sounded loud as she turned.

The figure stood at the edge of the ridge, silhouetted against the pale sky.

Humanlike at first glance—if she ignored the massive, webbed wings. Then they folded in—receding into his back with a ripple that wasn't flesh, wasn't muscle, wasn't *real.* It didn't have the slow furl of feathers or membrane but was instead more like the unmaking of shape. She could *almost* forget they'd been there at all.

His limbs were too long and just slightly off, the proportions wrong in a way she couldn't name, only feel—as though sculpted for violence by something that didn't understand anatomy.

And his face... Cold amusement was painted across it. His mouth was split too wide. There were vertical slits where a nose should have been, and he had no ears. The eyes—green, lidless orbs three sizes too large—reflected the glassed valley like twin blades of thought.

Evan's senses recoiled, even as she squared her shoulders. Although the figure looked nothing like any demon she had seen, she knew she faced one now. Where the corpse in the Shift had been a parody of an insect, this figure was a mockery of humanity.

And then, before her eyes, his face shifted.

The change was seamless, unhurried. The alien mask gave way to a noble brow framed by waves of dark hair, cheekbones sharp, tanned skin smooth, mouth curved into a lazy smirk. Those same green eyes gleamed—less monstrous but somehow no less terrifying.

And worse—his mind was blank.

She reached forward instinctively, her own power stretching forward, questing for surface thoughts, emotion, even static. But there was nothing. No shape, no texture, no presence at all. It was like gasping for breath in a vacuum. The man—no, the *thing*—stood there as if nothing existed beneath his skin. He was empty.

Yet even that was wrong. For something to be empty, it had to—be.

His eyes remained fixed on Evan, and the smirk deepened.

With arrogant casualness, he strode the few steps to the ridge crest, about twenty feet from where she stood watching. His gaze finally released her to take in the valley below, the shattered stump of the tower, the ring of glassed devastation, leering in a way that made her jaw set.

"I'm glad I sent my lieutenant in," he said at last, voice smooth and cultured. "That... would not have been pleasant." His expression was thoughtful, impressed. Then his gaze found her again, and something changed. It wasn't surprise she read in his expression. It was something worse. Recognition.

"And now," he said softly, almost to himself, "the real game can begin."

Evan didn't move. A cold fury slowed her breathing, even as her pulse pounded. Every instinct told her to run—but there was nowhere to go. And this thing was defiling Rick's grave by his very presence.

"You must be Evan." He took a step toward her. Slow. Measured. "Chad told me so much about you."

That name hit like a slap. She flinched before she could stop herself.

The thing noticed. His eyes languidly took her in, weighing her from foot to brow, caressing her in a way that felt violating. His smile widened, turning sly. "I must admit, I expected more."

The words weren't mocking. Not fully. They were *testing*. She couldn't read his mind—but she could read intent. Malice. Confidence. Curiosity. He was toying with her, trying to provoke a response. And maybe, an hour ago, it would have worked.

But she wasn't that woman anymore.

Evan straightened, drawing the shawl tighter around her shoulders—not for warmth but for focus. Rick was gone. The tower was gone.

Evan or Estariel—*she* was still here.

If this creature wanted a fight, then he would learn what she had become. She didn't know what he was. Demon, yes. But beyond that—no name, no role, no comprehension, just wrongness in flesh, holding an even deeper wrongness within. But that didn't matter. He wanted to goad her, and she refused to oblige.

Evan took a slow step forward, head lowered in determination rather than deference. Her heartbeat was a drum in her ears but not racing. It steadied and kept her grounded.

"You're trying too hard," she said, voice calm. Not cold—controlled. "It won't work."

The creature smiled, the expression never reaching his eyes. They might as well have been voids, for all the emotion they showed. "I see you doubt my words," he said, in the same tone one might use with an exceptionally dim child. "Yet if I knew him only by name or reputation... how could I do this?"

The change began at the edges. No shimmer. No illusion. Just flesh, re-forming. Bones softened, shoulders rolled, and the regal stance melted, unraveling into something looser, more casual. The fine robes writhed and twisted into battered leather armor, worn from travel, dusty at the knees. Familiar. And then—

The eyes—warm hazel—Chad's eyes.

The shape of his face followed, each line and angle etched with precision. The mouth, half-curved like he was about to laugh at his own bad joke. His stance shifted—weight settling onto his back foot like always, a little bounce in it. The fingers twitched at his side, the same way they always had when he was on the edge of fixing something.

It was perfect. Too perfect.

Evan's breath caught. She *knew* it wasn't real. The void was still there —the simulacrum lacked Chad's *soul.* The essence of what made him... him. While the eyes were a perfect match, they lacked his spark. They were dead inside. But the illusion was so complete, so achingly precise, that for one single shattering second, her heart stuttered.

She wanted it to be him, and that was all the creature needed.

It struck. She never saw the hit coming. The backhand cracked across her face with bone-breaking force. One moment, she stood poised, defiant. The next, she was airborne, weightless. The sky twisted. Ground and clouds traded places, and her stomach struggled to keep up. Then—agony.

She slammed into a jagged slab of stone. Her body folded, bounced, slid across the broken shale. Pain erupted down her side, sharp and radiant, bursting behind her eyes like lightning—white. Her skull rang, and the light went red.

Her lip was split, and the taste of blood filled her mouth—metallic, thick. Her teeth ached. She sucked air through her nose, slow and ragged, as she curled instinctively, trying to protect her core.

The slab she'd hit was cracked—hairline fractures spidering beneath her fingertips. She blinked against the glare as her temple throbbed, and she felt a trickle of wetness working its way past her eye, down her cheek.

When she tried to breathe, her chest didn't want to expand. *Ribs?* she wondered. Maybe. Or just the shock. Her mind scrabbled for purchase, for meaning. *If I hadn't reinforced my body...*

She would be dead. The thought came without fear. Just fact. She turned her head and spat blood onto the shattered ground. Shoving the pain into a corner of her mind where it could be ignored, she pushed herself back to her knees.

The monster clothed in Chad's body was already approaching. No hurry. No aggression. Just casual interest. Like a cat.

"*You're* a Thought Master?" he asked, voice silky in scorn. "Pathetic."

Evan slowly finished standing with a flood of determination, her body already healing itself. Her fists clenched, not from fear but rage, hot and cold at once, buzzing under her skin.

You want a Thought Master? Now it was her turn to smile. "Fine." She flung out a hand, gathering every ounce of force she could channel. The air snapped with telekinetic power.

For a breath, the creature stood—smug, expectant. Then the blast hurled him backward, flung into the air like a doll. He tumbled, spun, fell...

And laughed. The sound followed the arc of his fall—low, delighted. Disgustingly pleased.

Mid-plummet, wings exploded from his back, but not the smooth and likely illusory ones she'd seen before. These were grotesque, bone and tendon wrapped in stretched, glistening membrane. They snapped outward with a sickening crack, beat once, twice—then caught the air. The demon rose—effortless. Grinning.

The shift came as he gained altitude. *Calladorn.* Or almost. He wore the black uniform from Ironspire. Gold embroidery gleamed in the afternoon sunlight, catching on every angle like a beacon. But his back was too straight, his shoulders too squared. The green eyes—once warm, familiar—were flat. Empty. A puppet made perfect.

Evan paused. The sight of him twisted something in her chest.

"You hesitate," he said—no malice, just observation, like a teacher noting a failed answer.

Then he shifted again—Matthias now, his posture unreadable, his face composed. "You do not know, do you?" he said, tone so calm it cut. "You never could see me clearly."

She flinched and threw power at the shape—blindly, instinctively—but it was already changing again.

Rick. Gray-blue eyes met hers, but they were hollow. "You should have stopped me," he said.

A breath caught in her throat. Her fingers spasmed, her vision blurred. She took a determined step forward. "It isn't real."

It isn't real, she repeated in her mind, yet her pulse roared in her ears, and the battlefield blurred, but still—those eyes. She wanted to believe.

And that, she knew, was the danger. The creature wheeled in the sky above her, Rick's face smiling down with fanged teeth. Wings carved through the air with practiced cruelty, banking in and out of the clouds like a hunting falcon. He dived again, and Evan threw herself left, sliding across the ground in a clatter of loose stone as wind ripped at her coat. Her self-enhancements gave her superhuman agility, allowing her to roll with ballet-like grace and flare her telekinesis outward, anchoring her against the force of the demon's passage.

Her enemy didn't strike—only circled. Taunting her.

"You brought me here," Rick called, his voice filled with pain, wrenching at her soul. "You knew it would be my end, and you brought me anyway."

It was more vicious than any physical blow, and her reaction was nearly her undoing. Lashing out, she gathered force in her mind again, gripping threads of pressure she was still unpracticed with. She caught the creature's movement mid-turn, and *pulled.* He shuddered and twisted in the air, but it was like trying to grab mist. She couldn't pin him. Couldn't lock him down—her grip was unstable. The monster flared his wings against her telekinetic hold, and the force of that motion dragged her instead.

She was hoisted up, and before she understood the danger, she'd been pulled beyond the ridge. Too late she realized she would have needed to counter the creature's mass by latching on to something heavier than the demon. She was over open space, hundreds of feet above the lake of glass. *Idiot! Rick wouldn't have made that mistake.*

Yet here she was, being pulled around by something that looked like him, albeit a hellish version.

They flew toward the crater's center, dropping lower as they went. She clung to the grip, trying to slow their movement, hoping he was tired and trying to land.

Then she saw it—a spire of tower glass, suspended in midair like a blade of light. And they were heading straight for it. Or rather, the demon was angled to pass just above it. She would be the one to crash.

Evan reinforced herself again and gritted her teeth. Her image reflected in the shard, growing larger—she could see tiredness in the eyes that stared back just before impact. The shard sang like a chime as she struck and bounced off, but she managed to keep her psychic grip on the demon. He snarled down at her as he banked, headed for another shard.

The demon grinned. Still with Rick's face.

"You never could let go, could you?" he called. "That's why he died."

She pushed the voice away, letting the wind fill the space, and instead concentrated on the problem at hand. She didn't need precognition to know how this would end. Each crash would sap a little more of her strength until there wasn't enough left to stave off the impact. The only question was, would she tire before it did?

Unwilling to take the gamble, she decided to trust in fate.

She let go.

Wind screamed around her as she fell, dropping like a stone through scattered remnants of a broken world. Instinct roared. Her will surged, pushing against the ground far below, catching her with a lurch.

She hovered. Then rose.

It wasn't graceful, but the movement was her own. She angled hard to the left, whipping around a cluster of floating debris before using it to stabilize her position, her coat snapping behind her like a banner.

The creature swooped around to stop fifty feet in front of her. He hovered there on lazily beating wings, the shards of the broken tower circling behind him in a slow dance of spinning reflections. "You held him back," Rick said. "You always needed to be the strong one. You thought you knew better."

She tilted left again, spinning through the gaps between floating shards. The demon turned slower and she realized his wings were limiting his path. She was more agile than him now. But she was tiring—this form of flying was easier to maintain than the body armor, but even this couldn't be kept up forever.

"You thought Chad needed protecting," the demon purred. "So you took away his choice. You *made* him obey."

That struck in a way she couldn't protect against. It was close enough to the truth that she flinched. But "close enough" wasn't enough. Now she knew—he was guessing, not speaking from memory. The demon was reading her. Feeding from her.

She narrowed her eyes, forcing her thoughts to calm. *How did he know what Rick looked like?* Chad, Calladorn, Matthias—they could all be explained if this demon was the danger she'd sensed in Syndar, but she and Rick hadn't gone there.

The answer came like a sunrise.

Grief. She'd worn it like armor when she awoke, when she saw the tower, when she floated the key chain. Had she been *broadcasting*?

She tested the theory.

Estariel, she thought, the understanding still numb in her mind. *I am Estariel.*

Nothing happened.

Then she thought of Chad. Not the surface memory—but the moment that haunted her, the moment before Edron Station when she'd pushed. When he had obeyed, parroting her own words back with eyes that didn't blink.

When the others looked at her like she was something else.

The demon shifted, becoming Chad. "You made me dance," he said, sneering. "Tug the strings, and I obey. Isn't that what you wanted?"

Evan didn't blink. *Gotcha.*

She slanted left—hard—and flew toward the crater's center, toward the tower's shimmering skeleton.

Because now she knew what she had to do. Evan touched down just below the highest point still standing—a slagged lump of fused stone that might once have been part of the tower's upper residences. Her boots struck the broken stone with a crunch, and she stumbled slightly, muscles trembling, then forced her balance steady.

The air shimmered faintly with residual heat, the tower's bones still radiating the aftershock of Rick's final spell. She ignored it, pressing one hand against the wall, but not for comfort. To anchor. She couldn't fly and do this at the same time. Couldn't divide her strength.

Beneath her palm, the tower greeted her like a half-forgotten song, warm and brittle. The spire had once been a marvel of construction—a fusion of magic, science, and will, designed to focus psychic energies. That power lingered still. Even now, shattered and dark, it remembered. Neither fresh nor whole, it was still alive with residual psionic energy, a battery for those that knew of its existence and how to access it. It pulsed like a dying heartbeat. Beneath the rubble and fused stone, a skeleton of purpose still remained.

She grounded herself—feet apart, knees bent, one palm on the stone, the other curled around Rick's key chain. Her breath evened, and her senses expanded.

Above her the demon shrieked. His wings carved great furrows through the air as he wheeled around again. She felt his weight as he circled, angling for another dive. The creature came, once again wearing Rick's face, but she didn't flinch this time. Her mind lashed out.

A telekinetic pulse cracked through the air like cannon fire. The demon twisted, caught mid-flight, limbs snapping back as he tumbled end over end. Swatted to one side like an angry hornet, he struck a floating shard with a resonant chime and was flung off course. He recovered quickly—but stayed distant.

The tower remains stood resolutely, giving clear views in all directions, all the way to the crater's rim. It left the demon exposed. Nothing nearby to give it cover, except for the impossibly hanging shards, and those were far enough away that her enemy couldn't use them as a hiding spot from which to come at her unexpectedly. He had no angles for a grounded strike.

She had the advantage—but she couldn't move. Couldn't leave her post without losing the conduit she'd forged with the tower's remnants. It wasn't a true victory but a stalemate.

The demon hovered at a distance, wings slow, deliberate. "You think this is clever?" he called. "You've caged yourself."

She said nothing.

"*I* can wait," he added. "You're bleeding power. So is this place."

That much was true. She could feel it already—the tower's pulse weakening, thread by thread. Rick's magic lingered, bridging the broken lattices in a way she couldn't understand, but moment by moment, it was fading. Once it dropped below a certain threshold—one she wasn't sure she'd be able to detect until it was too late—the lattice would fracture, and its energies would be lost. She would be back to her failing will alone, and then the creature would have her.

She closed her eyes and went deeper. Her presence pulled at the remnants, plucking them from dormancy, drawing from the mental battery.

The air changed. Tiny vibrations ran through the stones beneath her, echoes of the sigils carved into its inner walls. The lattice, once etched with living power, sparked and shimmered faintly like stars glimpsed through fog—not just in the stone beneath her touch but also branching out into the surrounding fragments. She found them, linked them, tethered her will to the half-broken lattice. The tower knew Estariel. It might not know Evan, but it recognized her *intent.*

Above, the shards still floated—suspended fragments of stone transmuted into crystal, caught in orbit around the crater's heart. Evan reached out to them. They were heavy—both physically and metaphysically—saturated with too many kinds of power, too many wounds. But she turned the first one, then the next. Then more.

The fragments spun one by one to face inward—an array of mirrors, each reflecting her and the demon, reflecting sky and ruin, back upon itself to infinity. The lines of light bent and twisted in dizzying directions.

She saw herself a dozen ways—eyes fierce, lips bloodied, hair wind-whipped and ragged.

And she saw him.

The demon's face—grinning beneath Rick's eyes and licking his lips like a child waiting for a feast to begin—danced in the glass, tormenting.

He paused. "You can't keep this up," he said, but his voice cracked slightly. He was tiring as well.

"I don't need to," she breathed. She bent her knees further, settling low. Her spine straightened. Her palm pressed flat to the tower, smooth beneath her touch, somehow both hot and cold. Her other hand clutched the key chain, grounding her in strength—and in *truth.*

She focused inwardly, past the lattice of the tower, past her rage, past her pain.

Into joy.

It began as a memory. Rick's voice muttering equations under his breath when he thought no one was listening, his fingers flicking and tracing figures in the air. The warmth of his hands, always steady, even when his words failed him. The hush between heartbeats when they were simply together. His love and fear in equal measure as they sat in the Inner Basin's sunlight, and he tried working up the courage to propose.

She let it fill her, break her. Let it *burn* her.

The light came not from outside but from within. It rose through her skin in threads of gold, pulsing with rhythm, with memory, with love. It wasn't sentiment or softness but raw *power,* and here, in this place, it looped back upon itself. Amplified. Swelled until it radiated from her. Evan's skin turned gold. And then went brighter.

And brighter.

It was a storm of stars, a psychic nova. The key chain trembled in her hand.

She flung the force outward—not in a line but in a flare. A sunburst of emotion and identity. The wave expanded, washing across the demon.

He staggered in the air, wings dipping before he righted himself and sneered. "You'll need to do better..."

The words were lost as the silent explosion struck the shards, and they flared. Each mirror caught the light, then split it, and turned it inward again—reflected it. Multiplied it. Her love became a prism of weaponized memory, echo after echo, angled and amplified. Focused on a single point.

Trapped like a fly in amber, the demon convulsed. His wings spasmed mid-hover, and his mouth twisted. Rick's face fractured, lines running through the cheeks, the eyes, the skull. The creature tried to scream, but the sound warped.

The demon reverted.

And Evan *saw*... not just his body—his *origin*.

Images flooded her: a world scoured to ash, where the sky boiled red and everything clawed for dwindling resources. Even the light was failing. Machines half-flesh, feeding on bone and steel. Endless, recursive war. And behind it all, a single presence—vast, cold, and watching.

A single word: *Dominarch*.

But she couldn't hold it. The flood was too much, too fast. She staggered, and the shards around her faltered. Their light dimmed with her own, and they began to fall from the sky like a thousand knives.

The demon fell with them—still reeling, still stunned. His form writhed in midair, trying to correct, his wings flaring unevenly. Evan focused her vision and hearing, amplifying her senses once again so she could follow the creature's progress. He struck the glassed ground as his reflection rose up to meet him. There was a bone-snapping crunch, and he rolled violently. Then was still.

Evan heaved a sigh, finally allowing herself to relax. In the distance, the first shards struck the ground with an ear-splitting shatter, their energy spent. The tower was now—truly and finally—dead.

The demon moved, pushed himself up, looked back. In response, Evan tensed, but then she saw—he was *afraid.*

She saw it, real and clear, before he turned and ran—wings beating hard, legs pumping to launch himself aloft. He soared low across the broken valley. Shards sliced past him as they continued to fall from the sky. One clipped a wing while another slashed his leg. Black blood splattered across the diamond-scattered glass.

But the demon didn't stop. He fled over the rim and into the distance.

Toward Syndar.

Evan exhaled hard, tasting the tang of blood in her mouth. Her grip on the tower slackened. The stone beneath her was hot again—too hot. The last of the shards rained down below her, clattering and cracking like shattered promises. Then all was quiet, save for the whistle of a mournful wind.

And in the light of the setting sun, the valley no longer reflected. It *sparkled.* All around her, the shattered crystalline diamonds caught the light like a field of stars—except where the blood had fallen. There the spots smoked black, dull and dead.

Evan raised one shaking hand and wiped blood from her chin. The key chain was still clutched in her palm, still warm.

She looked west. The demon had vanished.

But he would return. And she would need to be ready.

She sagged.

After a rest, she thought, inhaling once, steady and quiet. Then looked to the south and muttered, "It's going to be a long walk back to Luthenholme."

XXIX
Reunion

Eastgate hummed—a low thrum that set Chad's teeth on edge. He and Calladorn descended in silence, the walls of the elevator shaft faintly pulsing with light from the etchings embedded within them. He kept glancing at the edges of the platform, where the floor's dark metal met the wall's white stone. Every few seconds, a low tremor passed beneath them, too rhythmic to be natural. The air tasted charged, and in the distance—faint but unmistakable—he could hear the chorus of shrieks. Demon screams.

The platform shuddered once more before jolting to a stop. When they stepped out, a narrow corridor stretched to the right and left. The left hand was dark, but to the right was lit from above by a flickering filigree of light. The effect wasn't random, though—it pulsed with a cadence, like it was part of a countdown.

They ran.

Asa's voice came from the wall beside them, clear and calm. "They've reached the door to the lower gate control. I'm delaying them as long as I can, but we're nearly out of time."

Chad looked to Calladorn. The man gave a single nod and drew his sword, even though they both knew it would do little good against what was coming. Chad felt his fingers twitch toward his knife anyway. Some habits died hard.

"This way," Asa said, and a new corridor ahead brightened in response.

They ran. Their footfalls echoed against the curved stone, and Chad felt the vibration increase with every step. It had a rhythm to it now, like a heart under strain. The deeper they went, the more it felt like the fortress itself was alive—and afraid.

"Is everyone out?" he called.

"Most," Asa replied, her voice clipped and distorted. Chad wondered if it was interference or poor maintenance. "A few stayed behind in the side tunnels. Stragglers. And... two teams held position to delay the breach."

Calladorn cursed under his breath. "I ordered a full evacuation."

"They chose to stay," Chad said, panting slightly. "That's not on you."

The tremor spiked, staggering them mid-stride. A high-pitched whine joined the hum, a sound so piercing it made Chad's teeth ache.

"You won't make the far exit in time," Asa said. "I'm opening a defensive module ahead. It's shielded. Would you like me to delay the detonation until you reach it?"

Chad didn't hesitate. "No. No demons get through. That was the deal."

"Understood."

Ahead, a square outline resolved in the wall—a door swung outward to form a dark hole in the light of the tunnel ahead. Ten seconds away. Maybe twelve.

They pushed harder. Calladorn stumbled. Not just a slip—his knee buckled, and he slammed into the wall with a grunt. Chad wheeled around instantly. "Leave me," Calladorn growled, trying to push himself up.

"Not happening," Chad shot back, looping an arm under his shoulder. "You didn't leave me, remember?"

They staggered forward together, half-running, half-limping. The door gaped open like a waiting mouth, red lights now flaring along its rim. Inside, the room was no larger than a storage closet. They crossed the threshold, and Chad hit the panel inside. The door hissed shut with a finality that sent a shiver down his spine.

"Demons at the eastern foregate," Asa reported. Her voice was quieter now and full in a way that made him wonder how alive she truly was. "Thank you, Chad. For giving me purpose again."

The lights strobed. Chad grabbed Calladorn's hand without thinking. "Good luck, man." Calladorn's grip was firm. Steady.

Asa began the countdown. "Five. Four. Three. Two—"

One.

The lights vanished. Silence dropped like a hammer.

Then came the sound. Not an explosion but a rupture—like the world exhaling through a wound. The room shook so violently that Chad thought the walls might tear apart.

And then it all stopped.

A hiss—a soft, sucking sound accompanied a whoosh of air. He instinctively drew a deep breath and held it. Chad opened his eyes. The door was gone. A red glow illuminated the stone beyond—the color of furnace coals. Debris floated in the air like ash, weightless. Silent.

There was no sound because there was no air.

Chad felt the pressure first, a vacuum pulling at his lungs. He couldn't breathe. Panic surged. Calladorn clutched at his chest. A tremor passed through the floor, stronger than before. Chad felt something shift above them. The wall cracked. A boulder tore free. Time slowed as the wall buckled and sagged toward them.

He didn't think, just moved. Chad threw himself over Calladorn as the ceiling gave way. He felt the impact. The jolt in his spine, a crack of light behind his eyes. Then nothing.

The road was a scar.

To the east, it was nearly clogged by boulders and earth where the southern cliff had collapsed during Eastgate's destruction. Even to the west, toward Ravensford, massive stones had been brought down, and everywhere he looked, there were pits where smaller chunks had come crashing down.

It was a miracle anyone had survived. Many hadn't. When the fortress blew, both tunnels had belched fire, burning alive anyone who happened to still be too close to them, and in some cases sending them flying as well.

Gharn forced himself to keep busy, trying to distract himself from his fears. Too small to help effectively with rescue efforts, he instead moved among the wounded with shaking hands stained red and sleeves stiff with ash, his breath coming in shallow puffs. The stink of burned cloth and worse clung to everything. He could barely smell anything else.

A young woman sat against a rock nearby, clutching her arm. The skin along her forearm was blistered raw, the edges already puckering. Gharn knelt, not bothering with words at first. Words were cheap. Water was what mattered.

"Hold still, lass," he said, voice raspier than he meant. His fingers worked fast, pouring a trickle of clean water over the burn, then wrapping it with a strip of linen soaked in something pungent. She hissed but didn't pull away. "That'll sting a bit. Means it's working. You'll keep the arm." Gharn knew he was close to babbling. Didn't care. Speaking reminded them they were alive. Words helped as much as bandages.

At least, that was what he told himself.

Her wide eyes flicked to his. She was numb. Too much shock to say thanks. He patted her knee once—firmness more valuable at the moment than kindness—and moved on.

Everywhere around him, the wounded moaned or shivered or stared. Too many of them had been too close to the tunnel exits when the detonation hit. Burns. Broken bones. Faces blackened by smoke and soot. Too many had avoided being burned only to be struck by stones raining from the sky. For some, death had been immediate. Others—

A boy not yet old enough to shave was curled on his side nearby, coughing into his sleeve. Blood spattered his hand when he pulled it away. His other arm twisted wrongly as it dangled from a mangled shoulder.

"Get someone to look at that one!" Gharn barked toward the triage line as he moved to the next, a young woman barely into her majority.

It was blind good fortune that the infirmary had been set up outside the wall, next to the stables. They'd had the most time to evacuate, and despite their haste, the medics had been wise enough to salvage some supplies on horseback as they fled. Of those, a few had somehow managed to keep the animals from bolting.

Halvard was a few paces up the road, organizing rescue efforts and shouting for more water. Her voice had gone hoarse from calling out names and instructions for hours, but she didn't stop, didn't even slow. Gharn watched her for a beat too long, then turned back to the girl beside him—no, she was already being carried toward the healers.

Good. At least something was moving.

He hated being in the canyon. Hated the stillness in the mountains that felt too much like waiting for an aftershock. But worse than all that was the silence where voices should be. The southern tunnel was gone. Just gone. Only a twisted bite of stone where it had been.

The northern tunnel—the one that should have brought Chad and Calladorn—held up better. Although "better" was being generous. Its collapse didn't start until fifty feet in and managed another thirty before fully clogging the passage.

But there had been no sign of his friends. No word.

Gharn's hands shook as he tightened another wrap, this one around a man's leg slick with blood and bits of pulverized rock. He finished the knot and sat back on his heels, breath hissing between his teeth.

"One more!" Halvard's voice bellowed from farther down the line.

Gharn twisted around to look. She stood at the mouth of the northern tunnel, helm off, hair plastered to her face with sweat. Dust coated her armor like frost. "I don't care if your arms feel like they're about to fall off!" she shouted, jabbing a finger at the men flagging as they brought stone after stone out from the wound in the cliff's face. "If there's a chance, we keep digging!"

A young soldier—barely more than a boy—dropped a rock more than twice the size of his head. He hesitated, hands hanging limp. His face was smeared with ash, his eyes wide and frightened.

Halvard saw him, crossed the gap in three strides, and grabbed his collar with one gauntleted fist. "You can cry later," she snarled, shaking him once, more gently than her words suggested. "Right now we save who we can."

The boy blinked and nodded. Swallowed. Then returned to the tunnel.

Gharn watched it all, heart like a stone in his chest. He looked back toward the mouth of the tunnel. Still no sign. "Come on, lad," he muttered under his breath. "Don't you dare be dead."

If Chad was gone, it was over. All of it. The prophecy—the only path they'd had through this damned mess—gone like smoke after a fire. Like Sorendir.

"Come on," he said again, this time louder.

But the tunnel gave no answer.

Darkness pressed against him, thick as oil and twice as heavy.

Calladorn came to with a sharp gasp—his mouth arid, tongue covered in foul-tasting dust. He coughed dryly, the motion sending spikes of pain through his ribs. He tried to move but couldn't. Everything hurt.

Stone pressed against his back. More pressed against his chest. Something warm and unmoving lay sprawled over him, pinning him down with a weight that wasn't stone. The silence around him felt wrong—like the world had been stuffed with wool. No groaning timbers. No distant cries. Just the crackle of settling dust and his own ragged breathing.

His thoughts moved sluggishly.

Chad.

That was Chad above him. The damned fool had tried to shield him. Even to the last. Thought tightened his chest, in a way that had nothing to do with pressure. For a long moment, he stayed still, just lying there in the dark, the edges of his mind fraying. Then instinct—or discipline—kicked in. He forced his arm to move. It took three tries before he managed to twist it free from the rubble. It scraped against something jagged, but he barely felt it. Pain was background now.

He reached upward, fingers brushing against coarse fabric and warm skin. Cheek. Jaw. Stubble.

An absurd thought bloomed unbidden. *What would he look like with a beard?* Then a laugh burst from him—sharp and too loud and sending waves of pain through his body. It sounded deranged in the silence. He clamped his teeth shut.

Focus.

His hand moved lower, fumbling along Chad's throat. There. A pulse. Slow but strong and steady.

Relief hit like a blade sheathed, and he closed his eyes. Just for a moment. Just long enough to feel the tension bleed away. Then he inhaled, grimaced, and pushed it down.

He wasn't dead. Chad wasn't dead. That was enough.

A nearby flicker caught his eye. A pale green glow, weak against the darkness, pulsed behind the debris like a heartbeat. He dismissed it at first. The mind played tricks in darkness. Fought against the blackness by creating things that weren't there. But it didn't go away, didn't change locations. And it seemed to be fading. He couldn't see it, not really. But he knew exactly where it was.

Calladorn shifted, ignoring the pain. The rubble groaned but didn't give way. He pressed again. A few stones shifted with a faint scrape, and the pressure on his legs lessened just enough for him to move.

Inch by inch, he twisted toward the light. His fingers reached into the dark until they touched something cold. Metal. Smooth, curved, set into stone. His thumb found a shallow groove. He pressed.

A vibration hummed through the rubble like a held breath finally exhaled. Something deep beneath him whirred to life. Dust cascaded from above. Stone shifted slightly before the sound gave a strain, a sigh, and faded to silence. It was enough. He could move again.

He turned back to Chad and shook his shoulder gently. "Wake up, Engineer."

No response.

He grabbed the collar and gave a proper jolt. "Chad. Wake up. We're not dead yet."

Smoke hung low across the valley floor, rolling in slow waves like a trapped fog. The crater still steamed, its edges cracked and blackened, heat leaking from the torn earth. The air here stank of ash and scorched metal, and somewhere beneath it all, the sharp tang of blood—but different from that of humans. More acrid.

Matthias stood at the crater's rim. Nothing remained of Eastgate. No foregate. The massive wall was gone. Only this hollow—this blistered wound in the mountain pass. It was not what he had expected.

A sharp crack drew his attention to the southern cliff in time to see another large slab shear off from the mountainside and collapse with a roar into the gaping maw below. Once the rumbling stopped, the silence left behind felt unnatural—the kind that came after something too loud to be forgotten. Not even the birds had returned yet.

He crouched, fingers brushing the edge of a broken slab. The stone was fused, edges glassy. He did not know what the boy had done—did not understand half of it—but the result was undeniable: the fortress was gone. So too were the demons that had breached its walls.

A little more time, that was what the boy had purchased. A few more days. Weeks, perhaps. Remarkable. But futile.

He straightened slowly, hands clasping behind his back as he studied the crater with a dispassionate eye. The ground had collapsed inward where the tunnels had run beneath, now filled with roiling yellow water. Occasionally a large bubble from somewhere deep below would rise to the surface and break the silence in a brief burble. There would be no passage through this for a long while.

He had thought the defenders might flee, that they might abandon the fortress. Certainly no one would have blamed them. But they had not —at least, not in any conventional sense. Instead, the boy had done whatever this... sorcery was, and in doing so, he had delayed the inevitable.

Of course, it would not matter. The forces aligned against the Nine Kingdoms were vast and implacable. They would find another route and continue with their plans. The collapse had closed this path, but the larger war would grind on.

Matthias turned his back on the crater and began walking. The way back to the rescue efforts was steep and loose underfoot, but he did not hurry. There was no need. The living were already busy with their digging and their bleeding. He had no role in that.

Alone with his thoughts for a change, he allowed them to wander.

Emberhold.

He remembered the night they had fled. The rush through the city. Smoke in the streets. The cries of the dying. And that child—barely old enough to be off her mother's apron strings—who had stumbled into the path of their flight. He had pulled her from underfoot without thinking, lifting her easily and depositing her out of the horses' paths. She would have died minutes later, most likely. Buried under a collapsing building—or eaten. The city had not lasted the night, and any of its inhabitants that did had no doubt regretted their fortune in what would have followed.

So why had he done it?

That moment had bothered him more than he liked to admit. And now... now he wondered the same of Chad's sacrifice. Would the extra time make a difference? Would this brief delay alter the outcome of a war already lost? He doubted it. But still... it was something. And the look on Maltharok's face, once he learned of it, would be priceless. The "man" would be livid. That alone might make this entire detour worthwhile.

He smiled faintly to himself, the expression more out of habit than genuine mirth.

Strange, though—he found himself reluctant to think of Chad as dead. Or Calladorn. There had been something admirable in both of them, a strength born of completely different natures—one earnest, the other true to his code.

Am I disappointed? he asked himself. He considered the question as he walked. No. Not exactly. Their loss placed his mission in jeopardy. That was the true failure. That was what should matter. And yet...

A sound stopped him. *Tap-tap-tap.* He paused with his head tilted. Listened. Then a thud, followed by two more in equal succession. Another pause.

Tap-tap-tap.

He turned, gaze narrowing. It had come from the cliff wall—where the southern escarpment had partially collapsed, spilling debris across what remained of the road in a long fan of crumbled and broken stone. The pattern repeated, faint but steady. Deliberate.

Matthias squinted. Someone was alive.

He picked his way across the broken slope, boots crunching over unstable rock. The tapping grew louder. He stopped ten paces from the source, scanning the fall. A single slab jutted outward where the cliff face had fractured. Behind it, a narrow crevice had formed—barely wide enough to crawl into. The noise came from there.

He crouched; his expression was unreadable.

"Interesting," he murmured, though there was no one to hear. Then he reached for the stone.

The moons had risen. One hung low and yellow, smeared across the horizon like an old bruise. The other rode higher, pale and more distant. Its brighter light caught the dust still drifting from the collapsed tunnel mouth and gave the whole mountainside a ghostly sheen.

Bram Halvard rolled her shoulder and felt something grind. That had started a few hours ago—she didn't remember when and didn't really care. She leaned down, wrapped her fingers around a slab of broken stone, and heaved. It came loose with a reluctant scrape. She staggered back under its weight, her spine screaming in protest, then slouched out of the tunnel one step at a time. Her boots added their prints in dust impressed with thousands of others, many of them from her own previous trips.

Emerging from the tunnel, she approached the edge of the ever-growing debris pile and dropped the stone. It hit with a hollow thud and rolled once before settling among the others. Before it stopped, she had turned back around and headed for the tunnel again.

"Keep it moving!" she called, not bothering to raise her voice. She didn't need to—they heard her. "Five more paces of depth by morning, or I will personally have your hides."

Somewhere behind her, someone coughed. Another answered with a weak chuckle. That was enough.

Bram ducked back under the wooden supports. The air inside was damp with sweat and grit. She blinked against the sting of it, wiped her sleeve across her brow, and forced her legs to keep moving.

Calladorn had believed in this. In Eastgate. In holding the line. He had stepped up—not for glory, not for command, but because someone had to. Because it was right. She was not about to repay that kind of man by leaving him buried, not if there was a stone left she could shift.

A commotion behind her made her pause. Not the sharp cry of injury, not the panicked call of fresh collapse—this was... something else. Cheers. Her head turned sharply. Dust drifted across the entrance. Someone outside whooped, and others took up the sound like a wave catching wind.

Returning to the open sky, Bram squinted into the night. Faint shapes moved out of the eastern haze. Three figures on the road. More people ran to meet them, blocking her view. She stepped forward slowly, rolling her shoulder again, massaging it with her other hand.

The first figure she saw clearly was Matthias—unmistakable in the way he moved, stiff-backed and efficient even after the hells themselves had belched onto the road. To his left was Chad. Limping, covered in dirt. Grinning like a fool. And supported between them—her breath hitched and she stopped in place without meaning to—Calladorn.

Slumped, head bowed, but conscious. His arms hung across their shoulders, and he hopped along on one foot while his other boot dragged. But he was alive.

Bram didn't move. Couldn't. The surrounding noise swelled, and people began to part, giving the trio room. Gharn broke from the crowd, his short legs pumping, both hands clenched to his chest. His eyes shimmered.

The three stopped just short of her, and Chad's grin widened—a crooked thing, full of exhausted triumph. Calladorn looked up, met her eyes. Nodded once. She realized her jaw was trembling and forced it steady as she straightened, boots clicking together. Her hand rose to her brow.

The salute was crisp, clean. *Sore shoulders be damned.*

Others saw, and the gesture spread—first the closest soldiers, then the next ring, until it moved through the whole gathered crowd like a ripple across still water.

Calladorn hesitated, glancing from one face to another. He winced slightly as he shifted, and his breath caught. Chad's shoulder tensed as the younger man steadied him reflexively, but Calladorn set his feet, drew himself upright, and returned the salute.

Applause broke like thunder.

Chad looked down at Calladorn. Something passed across his face. Not surprise nor relief. Something quieter. Heavier. He released his hold, stepped to the side, and began clapping with the rest.

The Hearth and Vine was barely recognizable—not that much had actually changed to it. Same sign out front and thick-beamed walls. Same polished bar counter stretching along one wall. Large windows still looked out past the wide porch strung with paper lanterns and over the Ravensford square, though someone had taken the time to wash them since Chad had last been here.

But everything *felt* different. The square outside bustled with life. Carts came and went, people talked and bartered and called out greetings. The wounded from Eastgate were being housed in every stable, storeroom, and half-finished building the town had to offer. And while it was clear Ravensford hadn't escaped untouched, it had endured, just like the inn.

The common room hummed with upbeat music and boisterous conversation. Not rowdy but constant. It was a kind of pulse—steady, determined. The Hearth and Vine had found its rhythm again.

The innkeeper—*what was his name? Yerren?*—stood behind the bar with the same smile he always wore, only now it looked etched into place by sheer will. He kept his staff moving with practiced nods and clipped instructions, and from the state of the room, he'd wasted no time putting the returnees back to work.

But there were scars. Chad caught the way Yerren glanced up every time the door opened—just a flick of the eyes, then the shoulders slumped. Not who he was hoping for.

Chad knew some people wouldn't be returning. They'd done their best, but it hadn't been enough for everyone. The knowledge didn't stop him from looking too, just as he had every day since they'd returned.

He sat at a round table near the hearth with Calladorn, Gharn, and—somehow—Matthias, who had apparently decided this counted as participation. Bram hovered nearby, speaking in a low voice with one of the conscripts. She had refused a chair and had even brushed off Calladorn's attempt to insist, saying she preferred to keep the room moving. Probably true.

Calladorn hadn't been able to finish a single drink without someone approaching to ask for instructions, advice, or blessings. His answers had been clipped at first, then amused. Then increasingly irritated.

"That's what happens when you become the quarterback," Chad said, lifting his cup in a mock toast.

Calladorn scowled at him. The expression was half-hearted. "Quarterback?"

"Never mind." The word probably translated as "field general for a game that doesn't exist."

There was a flicker of understanding, or at least resignation. "Watch your mouth," Calladorn said, taking a slow sip. "Or I'll promote you too."

His voice had roughened since the rescue, but the sparkle in his eye was real. Chad felt something unclench in his chest. *He's getting better.* He found his emotions around that thought to be unexpectedly complicated.

Calladorn looked older. Not aged—just... more real, more worn. The kind of tired that didn't fade with sleep. Chad understood it all too well.

At the table next to theirs, a group of townsfolk sat deep in conversation. One woman leaned in close, whispering, "They say it was an Outlander. Blew the whole place to pieces. Turned the mountain against the demons."

"Aye," a man replied, "but you heard what the mayor said. That kind of damage proves the Engineers were monsters. I say the Ban was right all along."

Chad froze. He hadn't realized how quiet their own table had gone until Gharn cleared his throat and leaned in.

"Breaking the Ban—even for good reason—won't go unnoticed." His voice was low. Just for them. He didn't need to look at Chad for all four of them to know who he was talking to.

Chad nodded slowly. His hand curled around his mug, which the innkeeper had seemingly taken steps to ensure never went dry. A barmaid certainly never seemed far away. In fact, she spent entirely too much time staring at him for his comfort. She was pretty, but—he sighed. "I think we need progress. I do. But maybe my uncle was right." He stared down at the table, watching the firelight play off the grain. "Too much tech, too fast... ruins everything."

The words surprised him. Not because they were untrue—but because they had come out of *his* mouth. He blinked, then barked out a laugh. Hard. The kind that started in the gut and rolled up into something almost involuntary. The others looked at him like he'd gone mad, making him laugh harder.

"I'm sorry," he gasped, waving a hand. "It's just... from the time I got here..." He couldn't finish. Tried again. "I finally found technology. Real stuff. Like real, *real* stuff."

Chad drew a breath, half a hiccup, half a sob. "And then I blew it up."

Gharn let out a single laugh that wheezed halfway into a cough. Calladorn followed, low and reluctant at first. Matthias didn't react in the slightest, which somehow made the whole thing even funnier. Chad doubled over, tears in his eyes, and slapped the table. Calladorn leaned sideways to avoid the splash of Chad's drink. Gharn was laughing into his mug. Even Bram cracked a crooked grin as she turned to intercept another knot of soldiers.

Then the door opened again. Chad looked up, more out of reflex at this point than anything else.

The laughter died in his throat.

Evan stood in the doorway. Her hair was windblown, her shawl pulled tight over her shoulders. She clenched her pendant with whitened fingers. And her face—*God, her face.* Haunted. Chad captured every detail in an instant; he couldn't help it.

And she was alone. She looked at him. Straight at him. And he knew. He didn't need to ask.

He *knew.*

The mug clattered to the table, dropped from nerveless fingers. The warmth from the hearth no longer reached his skin. Somewhere in the room, conversation continued. Footsteps. Plates. Voices. But he heard none of it—only the wind through the open door and the silence of hope slipping away.

XXX
Farewell

The flicker of candlelight stretched long shadows across the wooden beams of the small chamber. Thick curtains muted the voices from The Hearth and Vine's common room beyond, turning laughter and music into the faintest hum—almost like a heartbeat trying to reach her from behind closed doors.

Evan sat at the head of the table, her hands wrapped around a chipped ceramic mug. The tea inside—still untouched—had long since gone cold beneath her fingers. The tea itself wasn't important, but the cup was. It gave her something to hold—something that didn't shift or vanish.

She'd just finished telling them what had happened at the Spire. Not all of it, just the parts that mattered.

Chad sat to her left with one arm draped lightly around her shoulders. He hadn't said much. Hadn't needed to. He'd stayed close, thinking he was grounding her when, in fact, his emotions were a raging tempest of regrets. She'd had to block him out or be consumed by them, but she let him believe he was helping.

Calladorn was beside him—upright and rigid. His fingers flexed and released against his knees. He hadn't spoken since she'd started, still trying to decide how to respond. Occasionally he looked at her with something akin to reverence in his eyes. Other times, naked fear. She met his gaze calmly each time, not blaming him for either emotion. Estariel was the stuff of legends, after all.

Across the table, Gharn slouched in his chair, arms crossed tight over his chest. His eyes were fixed somewhere near the wall but not on it. His scowl had settled deep as she'd spoken, but he'd never interrupted, never asked a question. He simply listened. Awe radiated from him too.

Bram Halvard was to his left, with three tankards arrayed before her, all empty. She'd drunk them in short succession, yet her speech never slurred. Her eyes remained sharp and focused like a hawk's. Out of everyone seated at the table, she was the only one who hadn't given much reaction when Evan told them of her past. *A seasoned soldier*, Evan thought. *She takes life as it comes. There's something enviable in that.*

Near the fire, Matthias stood with one shoulder against the wall, barely touched by the light, still and silent—and watching. Always watching. And still unreadable. His presence grated more now than ever. Evan pushed the thought aside—she'd deal with him soon enough.

Chad was the first to speak, studying the tabletop as his finger traced lines across it in endless circles. "Last time we were all crammed into a back room like this," he said softly, "was The Randy Rooster. The night we split up." Evan heard the weight in his voice—not regret. Something heavier.

Calladorn shifted. "You warned us against Syndar," he murmured. "Turns out we should have listened."

"It didn't matter," Gharn snapped. "We were fools, chasing a prophecy. All of us. Like we could make it happen. We should've never—" He stopped himself, jaw tight.

Silence followed. Evan was still processing their story as much as they were hers. She had no doubt the demon she'd fought had been this Maltharok they'd been imprisoned by. Her premonition had been right after all.

Then Gharn exhaled sharply and turned his eyes on Evan. "You know," he said, voice lower now, "when we were last in Ravensford, Rick sat just outside that window. Same tea. Same look on his face. Just staring at it like it held all the answers."

Evan glanced down at her own cup. The tea was dark and still.

"He drank it, though," Gharn added. "Eventually."

Her throat tightened. She swallowed dryly. Set the cup aside, and folded her hands in her lap. "We still have a mission," she said. The words came quietly, but they didn't tremble. She stared into the tea, watched the light play off its surface. "Rick's gone, but the Heart isn't. And I know where it is."

Calladorn sat up straighter. Chad's arm tensed but didn't move.

"Curough." She forced the word from her mouth, practically spitting it out.

Gharn's reaction was immediate—a sharp breath and a bitter shake of the head. "You can't be serious."

"Where's that?" Chad asked.

"End of the damned world," Gharn muttered. "Last stronghold of the Engineers. You'd have to cross half the Arathian Empire to get there—if any of it's still standing—which makes it impossible to reach." He raised a hand in a dismissive gesture. "I assume the plan was to pick the one spot no one would ever look in. Congratulations. You succeeded."

Bram frowned. "But Estariel—" She caught herself. "You took the Heart there after the war. After Southwatch had already been cut off. How?"

Evan's temples throbbed. She closed her eyes, trying to will clarity out of a tangle of timelines. "I don't know."

"Of course not," Gharn muttered.

"I've got three thousand years of memory rattling around up here," Evan snapped, gesturing wildly at her temple. "Forgive me if I don't remember every damned—" She stopped herself, breathed deeply, and forced herself back to calm as Chad's arm squeezed gently.

"Then we'll find another way," Chad said firmly. "We're not giving up. At least, I'm not. Rick's death won't be for nothing." His words settled like stone on the table. Not heavy—solid. Final.

Near the hearth, Matthias shifted slightly, still silent. Still watching.

Evan continued to ignore him and looked down again. The cup hadn't moved. The tea would still be cold. Still bitter. Still waiting. *Rick forced himself to drink his.* She lifted it, remembering his expression as he'd swallowed.

The bitterness struck first, sharp and dry. But there was sweetness there too—faint but real.

She set the cup down. It was time to move forward.

The fire had burned low. Just embers now, red veins glowing in the hearth, pulsing faintly beneath the weight of ash. Chad watched them flicker, letting the silence stretch.

Matthias had slipped out first, saying nothing as he vanished into the night like a shadow forgetting it belonged to someone. Bram followed not long after, muttering something about early patrols and making herself useful. Gharn had just grunted, drained his mug, and wandered off toward the inn's back stairs, muttering under his breath the whole way. Chad heard what sounded like "damned prophecy" as the gnome left the room.

"I was so sure," Chad muttered after he'd gone. Calladorn and Evan looked at him, silently waiting. He chewed his lower lip, trying to put his thoughts in enough order to get them out. Then he exhaled slowly. Shrugged. "I... thought the prophecy protected us. How can it be fulfilled now?"

Evan opened her mouth, but he interrupted. "It wasn't real, Evan. It was bullshit. Tell me it wasn't." Each phrase had grown louder, and he stopped himself, clenching his fists.

Calladorn nodded. "I've wondered the same. Gharn too."

Evan stared into the dwindling fire as if it held the answers. "Precognition was rare, even in the Triune Era," she said at last, her voice sounding as if it came from a great distance. "Estariel—" Her expression twisted. "*I* always thought it was dangerous."

"Dangerous?" Calladorn asked.

She nodded. "At best, precognition or prophecy became self-fulfilling. But more often it became destructive as people tried to force its fulfillment—or a straitjacket, making people afraid to act lest they stepped outside its demands.'"

Chad let that sit, mulling it over. In the end, though, he couldn't see how it applied. "And when it was just plain wrong?" he asked.

She pressed her lips together, eyes tightening into a bit of a squint. "What if this prophecy's purpose wasn't to predict the future so much as get us onto the path?"

"Some path," Chad muttered, more to say something than to make a point. If Evan was right… that didn't sit well with him.

They drifted back into silence.

Calladorn lingered for a while after that, long enough that Chad started to wonder what was keeping him there. Eventually he stood—offering Chad a hand on the shoulder and a quiet murmur about needing rest. Chad didn't answer, just nodded.

Now it was just him and Evan. He let out a long breath. His shoulders sagged, and his spine slumped. It felt like he'd been holding himself in one shape all day, and now that shape had finally collapsed. "God," he muttered. "It still doesn't feel real."

Evan said nothing at first. She was curled sideways in her chair, legs drawn up. Her fingers toyed with the key chain again—Rick's key chain—turning it over in her palm.

"I keep thinking he's just off somewhere," Chad went on. "Like maybe he's just… not here right now. And then I remember I didn't even get to say goodbye. That the last time I talked to him, I was… I was an ass."

He felt the pressure that warned tears were welling up. Found himself caught between the conflicting desires to push them back down and to just let them come.

Evan looked over. "You weren't."

"I was," he insisted. "I was mad. I thought he was being cold and impossible and all Rick-like, and I let it get under my skin, like always. I didn't even—" He scrubbed a hand down his face. "He was just being supportive. In his own way. And then I wasn't there for him when—"

Evan's voice was quiet. "He wouldn't have wanted that."

"I know. Heaven forbid he be vulnerable." The lip-chewing started again. "But I should've been there. I should've… I don't know… done *something*."

"He didn't want you there."

That stung. Chad's jaw tensed.

Evan softened. "That came out wrong. I mean, he wanted to protect you. From what it would cost. From what it would do to you, having to watch. For a while, he didn't even want me there."

Chad looked over, brow furrowed. She drew her breath as if to say more but exhaled instead. Held his gaze with hers. "I *knew*," she said, nodding by a hair. "Before we even got to the tower. I didn't want to admit it, but... I knew he wouldn't be coming back. And I let him go." Her voice wavered. Just slightly. "It was the right choice. But knowing that doesn't make it easier."

Chad swallowed and looked down at his hands. No longer balled, they rested palms-up on the table like they were waiting to be filled with something they'd never get again. "I don't think I ever really knew him," he said. "Not the way you did."

Evan gave a sad smile. "He let me in. Eventually. But you knew him, Chad. You knew the version of him who always tried to protect everyone by outsmarting the world. The one who thought there was a right answer to everything if he just worked hard enough."

Chad's throat tightened.

"And you were right," Evan continued. "That wasn't living. That was calculating. It wasn't until here—until Necsis—that he learned to let go of the plan a little."

A silence settled between them—not heavy, just present. Then Evan added, almost offhand, "He was proud of you, you know."

Chad's head jerked up. He stared at her. "Was he?" His voice cracked more than he wanted it to.

She nodded. "He always knew."

Chad blinked. "Knew what?"

Evan raised her brows. "Oh, come on. You think you were subtle? Mr. Casually Staring at Calladorn Whenever He Wasn't Looking?"

Chad felt his face go crimson. "I—I wasn't—" He shrank down into his chair, throwing an arm over his eyes. "Oh, God."

Evan reached across and placed a hand gently over his. "Rick didn't share your fears," she said. "He was glad. He was *relieved* to see you finally being yourself. And—somehow—I know he was proud of what you did at Eastgate. I *felt* it."

"He wasn't anywhere near. How could he have known?"

Evan shrugged.

Chad didn't answer right away. He stared at the fire, where the last glow of red was starting to fade into gray.

After a long moment, Evan nudged his foot with hers. "So... does this mean you're dropping the dumb-jock shtick?"

Chad looked at her. His lips twitched. Then curled. "The what now?"

"The shtick," she said, her voice light.

He grinned—an honest, slow, tired grin. "Shtick? Isn't that something you throw for a dog?"

Evan snorted. And for just a moment, they laughed. It didn't last long. But for now, it was enough.

The hill was low, but it gave a view. The highest roofs of Ravensford peeked above the trees to the south, looking almost surreal—rooftops slick with rain, chimneys puffing faint trails that vanished into the mist. Westward the vineyards rolled down the hills like folds in a heavy green quilt, neatly patterned with rows of stubby vines. Beyond them, the road to Syndar disappeared into trees so thick even the drizzle might not have pierced them.

Gharn stood across from Chad and Evan, cloak pulled tight, collar up against the damp. The rain wasn't much—a curtain just heavy enough to hang from every whisker and bead on every button. His hat had long since given up keeping him dry and simply flopped on his head in submission.

Before them, a squat wooden shape of two crossed timbers leaned slightly where it had been pounded into the soft earth. Chad's work—rough-hewn, honest.

Rick Johnson—Wizard, the carving read. The final word looked strange there, etched into wood like it had a place in the world. Like it wasn't a curse. Like it could be something noble again. Gharn suspected that Rick would have hated it. He also guessed that was the point—one last joke from his brother.

Even Bram had come. She stood beside Calladorn, for once not wearing armor, rain matting her mane of hair and adding shine to her scalp. She was present out of respect for Chad, Gharn guessed. Or maybe because she understood more than she let on.

Matthias lingered beyond the edge of the group, close enough to be present yet still standing apart. One hand rested lightly on the hilt of his sword, his gaze drifting between Evan and Chad.

Gharn noticed the moment when Evan's gaze focused on the man. Her expression shifted, and the set of her jaw tightened for a second. Something flickered in her eyes, but it passed before he could name it.

She stepped forward. She was soaked. Her cloak clung to her, dark with rain, but she didn't seem to feel it. Her eyes swept across them all, one by one. When she spoke, her voice was low, steady—no theatrics. Just truth. "Rick never wanted to be here. Not on Necsis. Not in a world of magic, of prophecy, of danger. He just wanted to go home. To graduate. Maybe to teach, like his father. To grow old in peace. And he had every reason to fight what this world demanded of him." Her fingers curled loosely around the piece of metal in her palm. "But he couldn't. So he adapted. He learned. Not just magic. He learned *faith*. Not in gods or legends or even prophecies—but in people. In love. In possibility."

She looked up from the monument. Straight at Chad. "He died believing we could finish what he started. That we were worth the price."

The mist swirled. Gharn looked down at his boots. It was hard to reconcile the words with the bitter old man he'd last seen stubbornly staring at a cup of tea. Or with the young man he'd first met in the Emberhold embassy.

Evan unfastened the chain from around her neck and threaded something onto it. When it clinked against the pendant, Gharn inhaled with surprise. It was the talisman Rick had carried. She stepped forward and hung it from the carved wood before turning her face to the sky and closing her eyes.

No one spoke. The drizzle pattered gently across their cloaks and shoulders.

Then—

The rain stopped. He blinked, looking around. It continued to fall in all directions, but not on them. Gharn looked up. A break had opened above them. Just a small one. A perfect, still circle of clear sky—bright and silent, like the world had paused to listen.

Gharn's lips parted. Beside him, Calladorn inhaled sharply, and Bram made a quick sign with her fingers, something old and soldierly. Chad turned to Evan. His expression was unreadable—but deep. Heavy, like he was still trying to decide what the moment meant.

Gharn shook his head. He didn't know what it meant either. Didn't know what to make of Evan Taylor anymore. Or Estariel. Or whoever she was now.

But maybe, just maybe… they had hope. Not because of a prophecy. But because of what the prophecy had led them to.

Luminary Estariel walked the world again, and she would lead them to where she had hidden the Heart.

Lead them to hope.

The horses were restless as they waited next to the road. Cobblestone had given out just beyond the town's edges, and rain had slicked the highway into a long ribbon of mud. Their mounts' hooves sank slightly with each shift of weight. The air was cool, wet, and thick with the scents of wet horse and damp earth. Calladorn adjusted the girth on his mount with practiced ease, giving the saddle one last tug before stepping back to check the cinches. Nothing wrong, but habits were habits.

He glanced uphill. The monument stood small and just visible at the top of the hill—the wooden beams dark with moisture and standing defiantly in the ground. Chad had called it a "cross." It wasn't a shape that held meaning for Calladorn, but it did for Chad, and that made it important. He turned as Bram broke the silence.

"Are you certain it's wise to go back to Syndar?" she asked, her tone even but edged with doubt. "Knowing what we now know?"

Chad let out a sharp laugh. "Wise? When have we been anything of the kind?"

Gharn made a vague shrug as he pulled himself into the saddle with a grunt. "What else can we do? Wait on memories that might never come? No. Best chance of learning a way into the empire is the Great Library. Still might have useful records."

Calladorn nodded, although not at Gharn's words. His gaze drifted west, where the road disappeared into gray. Rain had eased to a mist, the kind that clung to eyelashes and coated armor like a film. In the silence that followed, something settled in his chest. Resolve.

"Syndar is in thrall to Maltharok," he said. His voice came out louder than intended, and there was no mistaking its steel. "I intend to change that. One way or another."

He caught the faint movement of Chad's head turning. A nod—approval without bravado. The younger man already sat astride his horse, his blond hair matted against his brow and his long coat visible beneath the cloak—blue, embroidered in silver, though now smudged and rumpled by wear. Still, it suited him. He no longer looked like a boy playing dress-up in his father's attire. *More like a lord, in fact,* Calladorn thought. *If he's not careful—and we survive this—someone will end up giving him land to rule.*

Evan was adjusting her saddlebag when she looked toward Matthias. "Didn't Chad say you had allies in the Thieves' Guild?"

The man's expression tightened briefly. Almost imperceptibly. "Something like that."

Evan nodded. "Good."

She turned away, but Calladorn didn't miss the look she gave him before she did. Nor the way Matthias didn't meet it. There was something unspoken between them. Calladorn couldn't place it yet, but they had a long road ahead of them.

He swung into the saddle and tapped heels to flanks. His mount moved forward, hooves squelching in the wet earth. Chad fell in behind, and for a moment, the road stretched ahead like any other—forest to one side, vineyards to the other.

Then Evan gasped, and Calladorn pulled up short, turning in the saddle. She stood frozen beside her horse, one hand pressed flat against her chest.

Chad frowned. "Evan?"

She looked down and pulled her hand back. The pendant she always wore glinted there, rain-beaded and swinging slightly. Hanging beside it—Rick's key chain.

Chad paled, his knuckles whitening on the reins.

Calladorn's eyes flicked back up the hill. The cross stood still. Unchanged. "Didn't you hang that up there?" he asked, voice careful.

Evan bit her lip, and her brow furrowed. She nodded once.

Gharn rode past at a lazy pace, glancing at them only long enough to speak. "Wizards," he muttered. Somehow it came out as both a reverent curse and a weary punchline.

Calladorn watched him go. Then shrugged and followed.

Matthias held back, watching them ride ahead.

Although the rain was now past, morning mist clung low to the road, coiling around hooves and trailing behind cloaks as the others passed beyond the first bend. As they left the vineyards behind, trees closed in on either side, wet branches hanging low, leaves still dripping from the night's rain. Their voices had quieted. The sound of tack and hoofbeats softened until even those began to fade.

He remained still—reins loose in his hand, allowing his horse to plod forward on its own—considering.

Chad had grown in ways Matthias had not expected. It had begun that night at the edge of Emberhold, when Matthias had orchestrated a timely "rescue" for the three Outlanders on their way to meet with the mad wizard. Back then, Chad had seemed directionless—more concerned with jokes and appearances than anything else. That had changed.

In Syndar, Maltharok might have broken him. Instead, the boy had been reforged, not merely hardened but reshaped. Eastgate had tempered him further. And now, together with Calladorn and Master Sergeant Halvard—*Bram,* he corrected himself—those three might actually shake the capital from its slumber.

All three had earned his respect. It was not a sentiment he was accustomed to recognizing, nor a comfort. His jaw tightened. That was not the mission.

He glanced back through the trees, although the last hint of the hilltop monument was lost from view. The cross. Would Gharn and Evan lead him to the Heart? He did not know. And that was new too—he disliked not knowing.

The idea Evan could truly be a psychic master thousands of years old would have seemed absurd only weeks ago. Now he was uncertain. The others looked at her differently. Even Gharn, who had lost his faith in prophecy, spoke differently in her presence. Evan or Estariel—whichever name she claimed—she was dangerous. More dangerous than anything he had anticipated.

Did she suspect the truth?

He nudged his horse forward. The animal obeyed without complaint, falling into a steady walk.

The game continued. *But,* he asked himself, *whose turn is it?*

Epilogue

Lightning split the sky above Syndar.

From the palace's highest chamber, behind windows that stretched from floor to vaulted ceiling, Maltharok watched the storm crawl across the eastern horizon. He did not blink. He did not breathe. Lightning danced over the forests beyond the city, cracking against the sky as if trying to strike the world apart.

The chamber was silent save for the distant thunder and the murmurs of nobles behind him. They whispered in velvet, shifting their weight beneath a dome built to inspire awe and submission, but the one who wore Elrath's skin heard none of them. He saw only the fracture, the flaw in the glass—high in the corner, nearly invisible. A single imperfection in the pane. Most would have missed it. He missed nothing.

Syndar spread below in ordered symmetry, onion-domed towers pressing upward like blunted spears. The streets were crowded with merchants and soldiers, couriers and guardsmen, all unaware of the game being played above their heads—of what moved behind the veil of their High King's eyes. They were insects. Brief. Fragile.

He had shaped this city with a surgeon's hand and a predator's patience—turned it into a hive of loyalty and fear. A kingdom of ritual and silence, ripe for the Dominarch's plucking.

And yet... children had undone his work.

The fortress of Eastgate was lost. It had not simply fallen—it had exploded, been rewritten. Shattered by a boy who did not yet understand what he was.

And the Spire—the Spire had been worse.

He still bore the scars. Hidden now but real. The woman—no, the *thing* who had met him there had torn more than flesh. She had actually touched his mind. Its defenses had cracked beneath her will. She had walked through magic like it was air and forced him to retreat. *Retreat.*

Estariel, they whispered now. The last of the Thought Masters.

And still they sought the Heart, along with that damnable imposter calling himself Matthias.

His gaze shifted east again, as if it could pierce the storms and pin his opponents where they stood. If the Heart truly existed—if it controlled the Shifts and not merely summoned them—then it was not the Dominarch who would rule this world.

It would be Maltharok.

And not only Necsis. The threads of the Shifts led outward—into other worlds, other planes. A thousand doors waiting to be opened.

He smiled. It was a small, tight thing. Cold.

The Dominarch's leash still coiled around his mind, a pull that could not yet be refused, but ambition gnawed at that leash. And now he saw it for what it was—not a tether but a chain of opportunity. If he held the Heart, there would be no more masters, no more instructions. No more waiting.

The Outlanders would not stop him, nor would the man calling himself Matthias.

They, too, could be corrected.

He turned from the window, and behind him, the chamber pulsed with tension. Nobles stood in half-circles, their clothes heavy with thread and authority—crimson, black, and silver. They whispered of strategies and borders, unaware that none of it mattered. The storm was not coming. It was already here.

He raised one hand.

Silence. The fear reflected in their faces was delicious.

His voice was low. Even. A scalpel. "Find them. Follow them."

A pause.

"But do not interfere."

Another pause. Longer.

"Not yet."

Afterword

The Heart has not yet been found. The prophecy remains uncertain.

The battle for Necsis continues in

The Forbidden Cost

Book Two of The Infinite Conflict

Explore the world of Necsis at Necsis.Quest

Thank you for reading.

If you enjoyed this story, the single most helpful thing you can do is leave a brief review on Amazon.

As an independent author, I chose to publish outside the traditional system so I could retain full creative control and bring this series to life exactly as it was meant to be told. The trade-off is that visibility depends far more heavily on reader reviews. Even a few sentences makes a meaningful difference.

If this book resonated with you—whether it was the characters, the world, or the questions beneath the spectacle—please consider sharing your thoughts. Reviews help other readers discover the story and allow this series to continue growing.

Thank you for being part of the journey.

— Matthew E. Yetter

Glossary

Arlos: King of Drakerath, one of the Nine Kingdoms of Necsis. He is rumored to have suspended audiences and been ruling irrationally in recent months.

Arathian: The last known wielder of the Heart of Necsis. He used its power to forge the Arathian Empire during the War of Ascension, a campaign of rapid conquest that reshaped the political landscape of Necsis. His rise and fall mark the final historical appearance of the Heart prior to its disappearance.

Ban, the: Following the Wars of Power, advanced technology was outlawed—a prohibition that remains in force thousands of years later.

Bram Halvard: A sergeant of Eastgate who becomes an important ally within the fortress. Gruff but pragmatic, she helps coordinate the defense and earns the trust of Chad and Calladorn through action rather than rank. Her familiarity with Eastgate's structure proves critical.

Calladorn Thorne: A captain of the palace guard in Ironspire, an honorable and disciplined soldier who joins the group after recognizing the truth in their warning. He struggles between duty, conscience, and emerging personal loyalties, particularly as his bond with Chad deepens.

Chad Johnson: Younger brother of Rick. Struggles with self-worth, often feeling overshadowed by Rick's intellect and leadership. Charismatic and physically capable, but more at home repairing things than leading. He has a quiet passion and talent for tinkering, which proves more important than he expects.

Dark Horror, the: *Velgô-pahz* in the gnomish tongue, a mysterious and malevolent entity of unfathomable power. It drove the gnomes and dwarves from the Deeps in an event known as the Exile.

Deeps, the: A vast underground region of ancient caverns that spiderwebs beneath Necsis. Though untouched by the Shifts, the world's strange energies cause distances within the Deeps to distort. Some tunnels span incredible lengths relative to the surface above. This allowed the dwarves and gnomes to build a prosperous trade empire—until the Dark Horror drove them from their homes.

Drakerath: One of the Nine Kingdoms of Necsis, home to the cities of Emberhold and Ironspire. Though largely pastoral, its northeastern reaches give way to a volcanic wasteland dominated by the Three Sisters and bounded by a sheer escarpment known as the Landrise.

Durnya: Gharn's mother, an archivist and a force to be reckoned with in Khorvael's political circles.

Eastgate: An ancient fortress built during the Triune Era to guard the pass between Luthenholme and the kingdoms beyond. It has never fallen and is widely regarded as unassailable.

Edron Station: A small town surrounding the Westerian caravanserai. It sits at a key junction for trade routes connecting the central and northern kingdoms, making it a natural gathering point for merchants and adventurers alike.

Elrath: Titled "High King," he is ruler of Syndar and ostensibly the Nine Kingdoms as a whole. His court is famed for its excesses, and the man himself is known to be highly mercurial.

Endarl: The south-central kingdom that once connected the Nine Kingdoms with the Arathian Empire before the War of Ascension. It is famed for its forests of massively towering trees, and its capital is Greenwood Hold.

Emberhold: A city in Drakerath built into a massive ravine that cuts into the Landrise cliff. Perched on the cliffs above is the slum district of Miner's End, home to Sorendir and Gharn.

Energy Lattice: Usually referred to as simply, "lattice," it is a hallmark of Triune Era creations, appearing as faint etchings across the surfaces of ancient objects. Some dismiss it as merely ornamental, while others suspect it serves a deeper purpose.

Engineers, the: Technological faction from the Triune Era, focused on adapting Outlandish technologies to work in Necsis. Their attempt to dominate the Three Powers was responsible for the Wars of Power.

Eryck Thorn: Calladorn's younger brother, he enlisted against their father's wishes and was killed during a military operation in the wastelands above the Landrise.

Eryndor: The homeland of the elves, Eryndor is a reclusive kingdom dominated by vast wetlands and ancient magics. The elves send a Lord Wizard to serve as adviser to each of the Nine Kingdoms, which some see as giving Eryndor disproportionate influence in politics.

Evan Taylor: A highly intuitive woman from Earth, she is in love with Rick Johnson. As she suffers from amnesia, her past beyond the last few years remains a complete mystery.

Faltheris: A desert kingdom of sweeping dunes, rugged plateaus, and oasis cities. It thrives on the trade of exotic goods flowing into the Nine Kingdoms from the mysterious lands far to the east.

Foregate: The main flanking structure of the Eastgate fortress, built much later than the central wall and contrasting with it in both style and construction.

Gallus: A captain in the Drakerath military, he led the patrol that found Rick, Chad, and Evan after their arrival in Necsis. He also has a personal history with Calladorn.

Gharn: A gnome, outcast from the city of his birth, he served as assistant to Sorendir. Inventive and loyal, he navigates the world with a sharp tongue and a deeply rooted sense of purpose.

Haven: The ancient home of the Thought Masters. Its exact location has been lost to history. To outsiders, it is remembered only as the Forbidden Spire.

Heart of Necsis, the: Also known as the Necsis Heart, this legendary artifact from the Triune Era is said to control the Shifts. It was last used by Emperor Arathian and lost to history following his defeat.

High Magic: A form of magic based on advanced mathematics, such as calculus. Capable of altering reality itself, it is feared even among most wizards.

Ironspire: Capital city of Drakerath, named for the towering spire that rises from the palace at its heart.

Ithindar: Lord Wizard and adviser to King Arlos of Drakerath. Measured and perceptive, he is deeply concerned for the kingdom's future.

Jens: The sergeant detailed to escort Rick, Chad, and Evan to Emberhold's embassy. Sympathetic despite his duty.

Khorvael: Jointly founded by dwarves and gnomes following the Exile, this city is Gharn's birthplace. It stands as a rare example of what became possible when the two peoples set aside their ancient rivalries.

Landrise, the: A towering basalt cliff that stretches for miles across northeastern Drakerath. It separates the shattered lands surrounding the Three Sisters from the lush farmlands that dominate the rest of the nation.

Luthenholme: A cultured kingdom to the immediate east of Syndar, known for its vineyards, arts, and calm society.

Low Magic: A practical form of magic based on basic mathematics, such as arithmetic, algebra, geometry, and trigonometry. Its effects are generally limited to the immediate environment.

Machine: One of the Three Powers. Refers to any form of technology driven by mechanical or artificial means rather than by living energy. Though often seen as the most impersonal of the Powers, it embodies ingenuity and the will to shape the physical world.

Magic: One of the Three Powers. Its practice combines incantations with the user's intent and is governed by the mathematical manipulation of reality. Divided into Low and High forms.

Maltharok: A powerful and intelligent adversary who manipulates events from the shadows. Ambitious, calculating, and dangerous.

Matthias: A morally complex warrior with formidable combat skills and unclear loyalties. Watchful and calculating, he often seems to know more than he reveals.

Merchant's Rest: A strategic crossroads town where three narrow corridors between large regions of Shifts meet. Its caravanserai serves as the central trade hub linking the northern kingdoms with the wider region.

Mind – One of the Three Powers. Encompasses telepathy, precognition, and empathic sensing. Its most powerful practitioners were known as Thought Masters.

Miner's End: The impoverished cliffside district perched above Emberhold. Sorendir's crooked tower stands here, as shunned by the rest of the city as he is.

Necsis: The primary world of the saga. Half-stable, half-Shifting, it stands at the nexus of all realities.

Nine Kingdoms, the: A nation formed by a confederation of nine relatively autonomous kingdoms. With the exception of Syndar, each is ruled independently, but all answer to the High King of Syndar.

Outlander: The term used for all strangers who arrive in Necsis through the Shifts.

Quillian Oakmont: A noble of Drakerath serving as the kingdom's attaché in Syndar, where he is quite at home amid the capital's excesses. He maintains a pointed rivalry with Calladorn Thorne.

Ravensford: A pleasant hamlet in northern Luthenholme, situated along the road connecting Syndar, Eastgate, and the kingdoms beyond. Its largest inn is The Hearth and Vine.

Rhest: A member of the Khorvael Council, he sits at the dwarves' seat representing the Power of Magic. He has a shared history with both Gharn and Sorendir, as explored in "The Gnome and the Madman."

Rick Johnson: A mathematician from Earth with a deep commitment to order and logic. He is the older brother of Chad and is in love with Evan.

Shifts, the: Thirty-mile-wide zones on Necsis that randomly swap with equivalents from other universes, introducing alien laws of physics—and often danger.

Sorendir: A reclusive wizard whose actions are guided by a prophecy of unknown origin. In Emberhold, where he resides, most believe him to be mad. His closest companion is the gnome Gharn.

Sponsorship: Each kingdom has its own way of handling Outlanders. In Drakerath, foreigners are required to become indentured to a local business or concern, ensuring their livelihood while preventing them from becoming a burden to society.

Stable Zones: Regions of Necsis that remain unaffected by the Shifts, allowing for lasting settlements, trade, and governance. All known cities and kingdoms are located within these zones.

Syndar: The name given to both one of the Nine Kingdoms and its capital city. As the seat of the Nine Kingdoms' government, its nobles regard it as the region's most important center. Its oppressed lower classes would disagree.

Syrillia: A canyon kingdom of towering buttes and surrounding fertile lands. It is famed for the gryphon riders who form the core of its military.

Three Powers, the: Magic, Mind, and Machine. Each represents a fundamental force by which people shape the world around them.

Three Sisters, the: A group of large volcanoes in northeastern Drakerath. Two remain constantly active, while the third, known as the Silent Sister, has not erupted in more than two millennia.

Thought Masters, the: An ancient order of psychics based out of the seclusion of Haven. They disappeared mysteriously shortly after ending the War of Ascension.

Torvik: Husband of Durnya and father of Gharn, he serves as a kindly, grounding influence within the family.

Triune Era: A golden age in Necsis history when Magic, Mind, and Machine coexisted in harmony. It ended with the destructive Wars of Power.

Vail: Brother to the Knight-General of Luthenholme, assigned to lead the Eastgate garrison in what was effectively an exile disguised as a promotion.

Valirion: Lord Wizard and adviser to High King Elrath in Syndar. Rumors in court suggest he may be—or may have been—the true power behind the throne.

Velsaria: A maritime kingdom of islands shaped by the sea and steeped in traditions of seafaring and exploration. Its many city-states are as likely to raid one another as to form alliances.

Wars of Power, the: A catastrophic series of conflicts sparked by the Engineers overstepping their bounds. The wars brought an end to the Triune Era and led to the Ban on all advanced technologies.

Wester: A vast plains kingdom forming the western edge of the Nine Kingdoms. Largely overlooked by the rest of the region, it became an ideal refuge for dwarves and gnomes following the Exile.

About the Author

Matthew E. Yetter is an epic fantasy author, actor, and world adventurer who has visited every inhabited continent, from which he draws real-world inspiration for the cultures and landscapes of Necsis. His stories blend mythic weight with emotional depth, where magic, mind, and machine intertwine. *The Forbidden Spire* is the first book in *The Infinite Conflict* trilogy, the opening arc of his ten-book epic *The Infinite Saga*.

PUBLISHED BY WONDER WORLD PRESS

WONDER WORLD
PRESS

EXPLORE THE WORLD OF NECSIS AT NECSIS.QUEST

www.ingramcontent.com/pod-product-compliance
Lightning Source LLC
LaVergne TN
LVHW100459110826
845146LV00002B/456